Faith stood on Point Beach with Sir Michael and Captain Phillip gazing over the peaceful waters of the Solent. Close by was the Round Tower—the sturdy fifteenth-century fortification that guarded the entrance to Portsmouth Harbor—and immediately behind was the green-slimed seawall over which she could just see the convicts being herded along the road toward the wharf.

As Faith focused on the wharf, her eyes were drawn to a guard boat moving away from the wharf. Her eyes searched the grimy faces of the convict occupants until they came to rest on one at the rear. Her blood turned cold in her veins and in that split second, Faith's life altered immeasurably. She had glimpsed her destiny.

Gathering her skirts over one arm, she ran to the water's edge. Heedless of the shouts of the onlookers, she plunged into the water and began swimming frantically after the guard boat.

Lucy watched the distance between her and the country of her birth widen. She was relieved to have quit the hellish confines of Newgate, and was looking forward to the long sea voyage ahead.

As the guard boat chopped through the swell, Lucy pushed the hood back from her face and sniffed the salt air. It was wonderful to be at sea again. She swept the surface of the water with an expert eye; wind setting in from the north, tide on the turn . . .

Suddenly, a head bobbed up between two waves. Her senses reeled. The face was *hers*!

UNDER
SOUTHERN
STARS

Patricia Goldie

BANTAM BOOKS
NEW YORK • TORONTO • LONDON • SYDNEY • AUCKLAND

UNDER SOUTHERN STARS

A Bantam Book

PRINTING HISTORY
Published in Australia by Greenhouse Publications
Bantam edition / June 1989

ISBN 0-553-27725-1

Published simultaneously in the United States and Canada

Bantam Books are published by Bantam Books, a division of Bantam
Doubleday Dell Publishing Group, Inc. Its trademark, consisting of the
words "Bantam Books" and the portrayal of a rooster, is Registered in
U.S. Patent and Trademark Office and in other countries. Marca
Registrada. Bantam Books, 666 Fifth Avenue, New York, New York
10103.

PRINTED IN THE UNITED STATES OF AMERICA

O   0 9 8 7 6 5 4 3 2 1

With love, to my son, Andrew.

ACKNOWLEDGMENTS

To Jill Hickson, Caroline Serventy, Helen Waters and Belinda Byrne, whose hard work and unwavering support helped transform the dream of Hope's New Horizon into the reality of *Under Southern Stars*.

Thanks, you were magnificent.

CONTENTS

BOOK ONE

PART ONE
Journey into Darkness

1
Lucy Gamble

Monday, October 16, 1786

Lucy placed her father's fine leather pistol case on the bedside table and turned the key in the lock. The lid clicked open and there was the pistol: walnut butt inlaid with silver, breech and barrel filagreed in gold.

She took it from the case and sat on the bed recalling the exact words of the Admiralty official who had called at the house earlier in the day. "Madam," he had said, staring solemnly at her stepmother, Ruth, "it is my melancholy duty to inform you that your husband was lost in action on the seventeenth of July while his ship was engaged in battle with an American privateer."

His voice had rolled on like the monotonous tones of a bell and Captain James Gamble—husband, father, protector, provider, and anchor of their lives—was dead.

Lucy glanced at the weapon in her hand. How delighted he had been when she had presented it to him on his fiftieth birthday. Now, he would never hold it, never aim it, never fire it again.

On impulse she reached for the powder flask and loaded the pistol, step by step, as he had taught her, almost hearing his voice. *Pull back the trigger and that will draw the hammer, my darling. Then hold the stop spring down hard with your thumb and keep it there while you insert the powder.*

As she spread the powder in both chambers, pressed in the wadded balls and affixed the caps, noises from the square two stories below floated in through the windows: iron-shod carriage wheels rang on the cobblestones, mingling with the clatter of

3

hooves, the shrill cries of vendors, and the catcalls of revelers going about their nightly pursuit of pleasure. The incessant din of the city contrasted sharply with the deep silence in the house.

Lucy put down the pistol, crossed to the fireplace and stirred the embers with the poker until the flames sprang up with renewed life. Then she sat down at her dressing table. As she unpinned her hair and let it fall like a dark veil, curling and flowing over her shoulders, her thoughts returned to Ruth.

She had been eleven years old when her father had married Ruth and brought her to live at Grosvenor Square. In the ensuing nine years they had become friends but today, somehow, their grief had rendered them incapable of comforting each other.

"I must try harder," Lucy sighed. "Ruth will need my love and support in the weeks ahead. Perhaps, for her sake, I should call a truce with Richard."

But how could she—after what Ruth had said tonight? "No!" she exclaimed. "A truce is out of the question. This time Ruth's brother has gone too far."

"Please don't be cross with dearest Richard," Ruth had said as they had toyed with their supper. "I realize you wanted to wait until your father returned to make the announcement but, now he is gone, Richard thought it would comfort me to know that you and he are to marry. I beg you, don't delay the wedding because your father has died, he would not wish it, and my grief will be better borne knowing Richard will soon be the new head of our household."

Lucy flung the brush down on the glass top of the table. She had been struck speechless by Ruth's astounding statement.

"And now," Ruth had continued, pushing her plate aside and rising from the table, "you must excuse me, Lucy. Finding oneself a widow at twenty-nine is not pleasant, believe me." Pressing a handkerchief to her face, she had fled the room.

Lucy's green eyes flashed back at her from the mirror. How *dare* that tallowy reptile tell Ruth such a lie! Marry him? He was the most evil, loathsome, rake in London. Since arriving on her doorstep three months ago, he had pursued her relentlessly, pressing his suit in the most insolent, overbearing manner. Polite disinterest, cold disdain, open hostility—nothing had deterred him until she had threatened to report his conduct to her father. Since then, their relationship had deteriorated into exaggerated civility on his part and frigid silence on hers. She was amazed Ruth had not noticed. *Marry* him? What utter nonsense! She

4

would tell him exactly what she thought of that idea first thing in the morning.

"Then, perhaps he will leave," she murmured. "Even though he is Ruth's brother, he has certainly overstayed his welcome. In any case, when Father returns, he will send Richard on his way—just as he did last time."

Suddenly her heart twisted with pain. Oh dear God. Her beloved father would *never* return. He lay in a watery grave, deep in a distant sea, and was lost to her forever. Overwhelmed by the thought, she placed her head in her hands and wept brokenly until the chimes of the grandfather clock in the entrance hall roused her.

She climbed into bed and lay in the darkness listening to the faint moaning sound of the wind as it drew the smoke up the chimney and out over the rooftops of the city. At last sleep came, and with it, blessed release.

The Rose Tavern, Drury Lane

Acrid candle smoke hung over the crowded pump room like a dense fog. Coarse laughter and high-pitched squeals mingled with the oaths of the faro players studying their cards at the gaming tables, and an overpowering stench of unwashed bodies pervaded the air.

At a table in the midst of the melee sat a man with slick, black hair which formed a distinct widow's peak in the center of his brow. He was playing idly with the breasts of a young woman perched on his knee.

At first glance, Richard Newport's clean-shaven face appeared handsome but his eyes, devoid of warmth or pity, were the windows of a barren soul. His greatcoat, though fashionable, could not hide his bulk or the thickness of his neck.

Newport raised the wineglass to his thick lips and drank deeply. Tonight he was celebrating! That sanctimonious bore, Gamble, was dead—killed in the service of King and country. Now, nothing could prevent him from reaching his goal. He had put the first part of his plan in motion earlier this evening by telling Ruth he and Lucy were to marry.

With James out the way, Lucy would be no problem. He and Ruth were all she had now. James had been a solitary man and such friends as he did have were naval officers, pursuing careers at sea.

5

Richard's mind drifted back to the day he had received Ruth's invitation to join her in London. That letter had been timely, for he and his father had been quarreling bitterly over his lack of interest in the farm.

The instant he had seen Lucy, he'd wanted her. He sipped his wine, wondering what it would be like to hold her rounded breasts, to feel her hair brushing against his skin, to trap her lovely, lithe body beneath his, to see her emerald eyes begging him for mercy. . . . He frowned, and the yellow flecks in his eyes dilated. Initially, her cold rejection had infuriated him, but lately it had only strengthened his resolve to possess her *and* her fortune.

"The bitch will thwart me no more," he growled. Suddenly he was impatient to be gone. He lurched to his feet, cast the young whore aside, and jostled his way to the door.

His wet clothes discarded for a long woolen nightshirt, Richard sat slumped before the fire in his room, drinking brandy and thinking of Lucy. Thought followed thought, each more tantalizing than the last and soon he was gripped by an intense excitement. His thick body twisted convulsively in the chair. Then with a muttered oath, he leapt to his feet and moved swiftly along the corridor to Lucy's bedchamber.

The room was dark except for the pale moonlight filtering through the lace curtains at the windows, and the red embers glowing in the grate.

He strode to the bed. She lay with her hair spread around her like a dark halo, and through her gauzy nightgown he could see her breasts rising and falling gently with the rhythm of her breathing. With a low growl, he threw off the bedcovers, clamped a hand over her mouth and mounted her.

Lucy awoke instantly.

An immense weight bore down on her, crushing her in a viselike grip. She could not breathe. She could not move. Terror paralyzed her. He entered her, and the agonizing pain drove her to action.

She raked his face. Ripping. Scratching. Tearing. Her nails dug deep, drawing blood. He let go her mouth and forced her wrists back against the pillows. She gulped air into her suffocating lungs and screamed—a wild, strangled cry that echoed through the house. He knocked her senseless then savagely had his way with her.

"Lie still," he muttered when she recovered and started to struggle. "I've a mind to teach you how my wife will behave when I take my pleasure of her."

It was Richard!

Lucy lunged at him, sinking her teeth into his lower lip. He gave an agonized howl and released her. She flung herself to the edge of the bed but he yanked her back by the hair and grabbed her around the throat.

"Bitch! I'll kill you for that!"

He dug his thumbs into her larynx. The pain was excruciating. Lucy's temples throbbed and lights exploded inside her head. The lights turned crimson, then grew into a bloodred sea. The sea enveloped her, sucking her down into a black, airless pit. In her last dim moments, as her arms and legs flayed convulsively about, her hand connected with the pistol. She clawed at it. Then she had it . . . was drawing it down . . . squeezing the trigger.

The world erupted into flames and smoke, and she was free of him at last.

Ruth and the servants burst into the room, and in the blaze of their candles Lucy watched him sink slowly to his knees, an expression of profound surprise on his face. She dragged herself painfully to her feet, her eyes locking with his. When he saw their look, his surprise turned to terror.

"No, Lucy . . . please, I beg you."

The sound of her name on his foul, bloodied lips stung her into action. She raised the pistol, took careful aim and fired. The bullet plowed into his forehead, killing him instantly.

2

Captain Arthur Phillip R.N.

Midnight, Monday, October 16, 1786

Billingsley Hall, a two-story gray mansion flanked by tall elms, stood at the end of a long carriageway on the estate of Billingsley, not far from the village of Lyndhurst in West Hampshire.

This night, light streamed through the library's French windows sending bright shafts shooting over the wide, flat lawn at the front of the house, and the quiet was shattered by the hearty laughter of Sir Michael Billingsley, and his friend, Captain Arthur Phillip, who sat inside, by the fire.

The richly furnished library held many fine books and ornaments shipped to England from the four corners of the earth by vessels of the East India Company; above the marble chimneypiece hung a portrait of Sir Michael's father—a steely faced personage with dark piercing eyes, an aquiline nose and a no-nonsense mouth. In the flickering firelight, the likeness between father and son was striking.

After waiting many months, Captain Phillip had received his new Commission from George III and tonight the two men were celebrating.

Sir Michael carefully unrolled the Commission and read it aloud.

George Third & C., To our trusty and well-beloved Captain Arthur Phillip, Greetings. We, reposing especial trust and confidence in your loyalty, courage, and experience in military affairs, do, by these present, constitute and appoint you to be Governor of our Territory called New South Wales, extending from the Northern Cape, northern extremity—to the Southern Cape, southern extremity, and of all the country inland to the westward as far as 135th degree of longitude reckoning from the meridian of Greenwich, including all the islands adjacent to the Pacific Ocean, within the latitude of 10 degrees 37' south to 43 degrees 39' south, and of all towns, garrisons, castles, forts—and all other fortifications or other military works, which now are or may be hereafter erected upon this said territory.

"You are therefore carefully and diligently to discharge the duty of Governor in and over our said territory by doing and performing all and all manner of things thereunto belonging, and we do hereby strictly charge and command all our officers and soldiers who shall be employed within our said territory, and all others whom it may concern, to obey you as our Governor thereof; and you are to observe and follow such orders and directions from time to time as you shall receive from us, GIVEN AT OUR COURT AT ST. JAMES, THIS TWELFTH DAY OF OCTOBER 1786.

"Well, there it is, Arthur," said Sir Michael, placing the Commission on the table beside his chair. "Signed by Lord

Thomas Townshend Sydney, the Secretary of the Home Office, no less. I think New South Wales is a brilliant choice for the new convict colony. No need to build a prison when you arrive. The damn convicts cannot escape—they'll be surrounded by thousands of miles of uncharted ocean!''

Phillip's keen brown eyes sparkled with amusement. "I think you jump a little ahead of yourself, Michael. First I must assemble my convict Fleet at Portsmouth, then ready it to sail by year's end.''

Sir Michael chuckled. "The sailing date *is* a trifle ambitious. I know the government is anxious to rid our overcrowded prisons of troublesome inhabitants, but the Fleet ships have not even been chartered as yet. Who'll make the voyage with you?''

"I have received no official word. However, rumor has it that Captain John Hunter will be appointed my second in command and will take over the flagship when I assume governorship of the colony. The rest will be volunteers." He smiled widely. "Several men from my previous command have already signed on, including my friend Lieutenant Gidley King.''

"Would that I were twenty years younger." Sir Michael sighed, regretting his sixty-one years. "When will you meet Lord Sydney?''

"This week," said Phillip. He frowned, and his eyes grew vague. "If we are to reach New South Wales without sacrificing many lives, we must maintain the highest standard of health. When I meet Lord Sydney I will make that point most emphatically. Only the strongest, healthiest convicts must be selected for the voyage. . . . A doctor should be aboard every convict transporter—with perhaps an assistant on the larger ships—and it would be a good idea if the convicts were skilled in farming, carpentry, and—''

"Quite so," Sir Michael broke in hastily. "And have you charted a course yet?''

Phillip rose and, motioning for Sir Michael to join him, went to the desk where his charts lay. "Fifteen thousand miles of ocean lie between England and New South Wales," he said, jabbing his finger down on Portsmouth, "I count myself lucky to have John Hunter along. He is without peer as a navigator. . . .''

They bent over the chart, so engrossed that neither noticed the library door open and Sir Michael's granddaughter, Faith, step inside.

"Grandfather," she whispered.

Sir Michael looked up and saw her standing on the edge of the shadows, body trembling, face chalk white. "What is it, my dear?''

When Faith did not answer, he went to her and took her hand. "What is it, my dear?" he repeated, leading her to the wing-backed chair by the fire. "You look as though you've seen a ghost."

"Not a ghost, but something just as strange." She leant forward and clutched his sleeve. "You *must* help me find her, Grandfather. She is alone in a dark, horrible place and terribly afraid."

Sir Michael glanced over her head at Phillip. "*Who* is alone? *Who* is afraid? You are not making sense, Faith."

Faith stared at him with haunted eyes. "I don't know her name. Oh, this is so confusing!"

Sir Michael's austere countenance softened. "It's all right, my dear, you have had a nightmare." He proffered his glass. "Drink this brandy. In a few minutes the feeling will pass."

Faith pushed the glass away impatiently. "It was no nightmare, I assure you. When she first called to me, I thought it was the wind, but the sounds grew louder so I lit the lamp. Then I saw her, kneeling before a door, surrounded by darkness . . . 'Someone please help me, I am so afraid' she called over and over. Oh God, Grandfather, I thought my heart would break at the despair in her voice. I must find her, I must!"

Sir Michael shook her by the shoulders. "Wake up, Faith! It was just a dream. Do you hear?"

Faith brushed her dark hair away from her eyes, taking a deep breath to calm herself. Something in the movement of her hand caught Sir Michael's attention. He grabbed it and took a closer look. At the top of the right index finger, a faint scar ran downward in a straight line making a perfect cross with the first joint and finishing just above the second.

As he stared at it, his face now as ashen as Faith's, a drop of blood oozed from the scar and slid down her finger, like a tear, into her open palm. "My God, Oh, my God," he gasped.

Captain Phillip pried Faith's hand loose from Sir Michael's grasp. "It's nothing," he reassured them. "The merest scratch. Look, it has stopped bleeding already."

Recovering himself, Sir Michael helped Faith to her feet. "Come, my dear, I'll see you to your room and stay until you fall asleep. There is no need to be afraid."

Faith sighed. "I am not afraid *of* her, I'm afraid *for* her." She bid both men good night, brushed Sir Michael's cheek with her lips and left the room.

Seeing Sir Michael's troubled face, Phillip asked, "Can I do anything?"

"No thank you, Arthur. She will have forgotten it by the morning. Just a bad dream."

"But was it a dream, Michael? Faith may be a little willful at times, but she's a most intelligent young woman and not inclined to hysterics. She did say that she was not asleep—had lit the lamp, in fact. You don't suppose—"

"It was just a bad dream," Sir Michael insisted. "She will be quite herself by morning."

Phillip recognized *that* tone and knew it was pointless pursuing the matter further. "You're probably right," he murmured, walking to the desk and collecting his charts. "Well now, if you are sure there's nothing I can do, I shall take my leave. I will be returning to London at daybreak."

"Do not concern yourself about your farms, Arthur," said Sir Michael, accompanying him to the French windows. "I'll ride over once a week until Faith and I leave for Scotland."

He held out his hand. "If you have time, write to me at Carrigmoor. I am interested to hear how the outfitting of the Fleet progresses."

"Very well," Phillip rejoined, setting off toward the stables. "And when you return to Billingsley in the new year, come down to Portsmouth and I shall show you over the ships."

Sir Michael secured the windows and sat down again by the fire. Next month, when Faith turned twenty, he would give into her care the management of the Hall, three tenant farms, and all his East India holdings. He had been schooling her in their administration since she was fifteen and, although she was young to assume such responsibility, he was confident she could do it.

Everything he owned would one day belong to Faith. His sister, Lady Barbara Stewart, would make no claim. Her husband was Laird of Carrigmoor, a vast feudal estate in the Scottish Highlands of which Hugh, their son, was heir.

His thoughts returned to his immediate concern. Had the past come back to haunt him? "No," he muttered, "that is impossible. Faith had a nightmare. To believe otherwise is illogical."

He reached for his brandy glass with shaking hand, remembering how the blood had oozed from the center of the scar. Had his eyes deceived him? No, Phillip and Faith had seen it too. There *must* have been a wound. Old scars don't bleed.

Knowing he would not rest until he saw the scar again, he placed the guard before the fire, took up a lamp and ascended to the upper floor. He paused for a moment outside Faith's room to catch his breath before knocking.

"Come in."

She stood with her back to him, staring out the window.

"Let me see your finger again, my dear," he said, joining her and setting the lamp down on the wide ledge. He drew her hand close to the light and prodded at the scar but there was no fresh wound.

"Did I really cut my finger when I was a baby?" she asked.

Sir Michael pursed his mouth. "I've told you a dozen times, Faith. Your nurse carelessly left a glass within your reach when you were learning to walk, and she was dismissed without references because of it."

Faith sighed. "Why are there so many unanswered questions in my life, Grandfather? Why did my father leave my mother before I was born? Why did he never visit me? He must have known Mother died giving birth to me. What did he look like? How did he die? What was he—"

"I have ordered you never to mention that scoundrel in my presence!" Sir Michael shouted, his face working with emotion.

"Grandfather, please take me to London."

His eyes narrowed. "Whatever for? Much has to be done before we leave for Scotland."

Faith's chin came up. "Then you attend to matters here and I shall go to London alone. I am convinced she is there."

"She?"

"The woman in my vision."

"What utter nonsense!" Sir Michael exploded. "London is a great city, not a tiny village like Lyndhurst. How do you propose to find your phantom? If you told people you'd seen her in a dream they would think you mad—and they would be right! Put such foolish notions out of your head. After a good night's sleep everything will seem different."

Faith's green eyes glittered in the lamplight. Why was he so disturbed? "I do not understand why this has happened to me, Grandfather, but you must believe that the woman in my vision is alive, alone, and afraid. I beg you, please help us."

Deep foreboding swept through Sir Michael. *"Us?"* he gasped, stepping away from the intensity of her gaze. "Do you align yourself with this phantom against *me?*"

"No, of course not," she replied, exasperated. "I just want a few questions answered. Is that so unreasonable?"

He picked up the lamp and walked to the door. "It is a waste of time speaking to you while you are in this frame of mind, Faith. You have allowed a foolish dream to overtake your good sense. I bid you good night.''

Faith took her blue cashmere shawl from the chair and returned to the window. She shivered, remembering the terrible coldness that had woken her, and the soft moaning sound, like wind whistling down dark corridors on a winter's night. *Someone please help me, I am so afraid.* The words echoed through her mind and her heart thundered against her rib cage. ''Where are you?'' she whispered. ''Where *are* you?''

3

Newgate Prison

Midnight, Monday, October 16, 1786

The coach rolled to a halt at the entrance of Newgate Prison. With a loud grinding whirl the medieval gate built by Dick Whittington bared its wooden teeth, and the coach rumbled into the courtyard.

It drew up outside a grim three-story building and, as the gate descended with a heavy thud, two Bow-street Runners bundled Lucy inside and led her along a narrow passage to a room where four ruffians dressed in bits and pieces of uniforms sat at a table arguing. An oversize fire belched clouds of smoke into the small, stifling chamber but the turnkeys were too drunk to notice.

The head turnkey, a huge brute with a festering sore on his mouth, lurched to his feet. ''What you got there, lads?''

''A murderess,'' growled the Runner closest to Lucy.

The head turnkey ran a practiced eye over Lucy, taking in her fine floor-length cloak with its sable-lined hood, and her black leather, silver-buckled shoes. This was a proper lady—as fine a piece as he'd ever seen, even accounting for her injuries.

It had been a lean night; a couple of pickpockets, an old harlot far gone with pox, and a starving chimney sweep picked up breaking into a residence, but things were looking up. He leered at Lucy, displaying a mouth full of decaying teeth. "What you got to say for yourself, young mistress?"

Lucy stared at him wordlessly.

"You'll get no chitchat out of her," said the runner. "She's not spoke a word since we took her. Guilty as hell though. Still holding the murder weapon when we arrived, and the deceased's head blasted clean off his shoulders. She's the coolest piece I've ever seen—and that's in my report to the magistrates."

He took the irons from Lucy's wrists, nodded briefly to the turnkeys and left with his companion.

The turnkeys closed in around Lucy and the head one clamped a heavy hand on her shoulder. "What'll you give us for garnish, young mistress? You'd best show the color of your coin right quick if you be wantin' a few of our favors, eh, Jack?" He nudged his closest companion—an evil-looking youth with greasy hair that hung in strings over his eyes.

Jack pinched Lucy's cheek. "Aye. 'Tis dark in Condemned Hold with nought to light your way, and the rats there ain't been fed in a week."

Lucy looked at them with glazed, uncomprehending eyes.

The head turnkey signaled his companions. "Let's search her lads. By the looks of her, she'll make good sport."

Roaring with laughter, they forced her to lie back on the table. She screamed with terror as their hands moved in endless profane circles over her body, laying waste to all its secret places. The flames in the grate danced in and out of the smoke, forming a bloodred sea that rushed and roared around her. Then someone was shouting, and a moment later she was dragged to her feet.

A rotund man in a nightshirt stood at the doorway. "Shut that wench up!" he bellowed. "Her screams would wake Old Harry. Return her to the wards and find one who's willing!"

The head turnkey bobbed his head deferentially. "Yes, Your Honor, at once, Your Honor. But if Your Honor pleases, this one's a murderess come lately. Do you want for us to iron her?"

"No, man," cried the prison keeper, "just put her in the Condemned Hold until morning and be quick about it, or I'll have the lot of you manacled!" Cursing them roundly, he left.

"Put me in Keeper's bad books will you?" the head turnkey muttered, shoving Lucy against the wall. "Well, let's see how you like Condemned Hold. No one will hear you there, no matter how loud you scream."

He dragged her through a maze of corridors, up a flight of stairs and along a dark passageway to a large oaken door. "This be your quarters for the night, m'lady," he sneered. "I hope it's to your liking." He drew back the bolt, pushed her inside and slammed the door behind her.

Transfixed with terror, Lucy stood in the utter blackness of the Condemned Hold, retching as the foul stench overwhelmed her. She stepped backward and froze when a strange sound, like crackling eggshells came from underfoot. The hair on her neck rose and perspiration broke out over her face. For a moment she thought she would faint, but her courage returned and, trying to ignore the crackling, she retreated until she felt the door against her back.

With a sob of relief, she pressed herself hard against it and listened, her eyes and ears straining for any signs of movement. "Is anyone there?" she asked after an eternity of seconds. The towering silence continued.

She stretched her right arm tentatively along the door and recoiled. The wall was covered in slime. She shivered violently. God, it was cold.

She took four sliding steps to the right and came up against a raised wooden platform. Wrapping her cloak tightly around her, she sank exhausted to the boards. Gradually, the wild beating of her heart slowed and her breathing returned to normal.

"Father, where are you?" she whispered.

Fragmented thoughts formed a whole and with a stricken cry she remembered. Her father could not help her . . . Who, then? Ruth! Tomorrow, when Ruth recovered from the shock, she would surely come. Ruth *must* come.

A burning, itching sensation swept up her legs and spread in a fiery wave over her body. Lice—thousands of filthy, biting lice! Tearing at her clothes, she stumbled to the door and pounded on it, crying out for help, but no one came. Eventually, her legs buckled beneath her and she sank to the floor.

What had happened to her life? In a few short hours, her safe, comfortable world had become a grotesque nightmare. "Someone please help me, I am so afraid," she moaned, and gave in to utter despair.

4

Elizabeth Dudgeon

Tuesday, October 17, 1786

Outside Newgate's grim walls the fog lifted momentarily, revealing a hackney coach rolling along a road strewn with straw. Inside, the prison lamps were being lit as bleary-eyed officials prepared for the coming day. Upstairs in the Condemned Hold, Lucy awoke with a start and started into the darkness.

The nightmare was still with her—sleep had not borne it away—but the fear and panic of last night had changed into a calm emptiness. She was glad. Now she could concentrate on the task ahead—survival.

She thought hard. The turnkeys had demanded money. What did she have of value? She felt for her diamond earrings. Thank God! Still there. Her mouth twisted in a grim smile. The drunken men had been so intent on plundering her body they had neglected the treasures in her ears. She broke into a sweat, remembering the horror of their hands. Then thoughts of Richard came. With a supreme effort she forced them from her mind.

Where could she hide the earings? It was pointless to leave them where they were. She decided her hair was the safest place. "I'll braid it," she said aloud. "That will help keep out the filthy lice."

She took some red velvet ribbon from her petticoat, measured off a small piece and gnawed it through. She plaited her hair into a long braid, secured it with the ribbon, looped it onto her head, and knotted it around the hair on her crown. Then she pushed the earrings deep inside the plait, squeezed the clips together and twisted them in and out of several strands of hair as an added precaution.

Satisfied, she resumed her search, and by the time the bolt was thrown, she had a corded gold ring, the velvet ribbon, two silver shoe buckles and a dozen pearl buttons hidden in the hem of her cloak.

The door swung open and a lantern was thrust rudely into her face. Her pupils contracted painfully and she blinked several

16

times before she could see the two guards. They pulled her outside and one, struck by her beauty, grabbed her breasts.

Lucy kicked him viciously on the shin. "Keep your hands to yourself, you tallowy creature!"

He bellowed with pain and swung at her, but she nimbly dodged the blow and assailed him with a string of nautical oaths. The guard holding the lantern brayed like a donkey. "Lord! I'd give gold to see what the hellcats in Waterman's do with this one, Joe lad!" Laughing uproariously, they herded her along the passage and shoved her inside another oaken door.

Low muttering greeted Lucy's entrance to the Waterman's Ward and a multitude of formless swaying shapes rose from the floor.

"Who goes there?" demanded a coarse female voice.

"Name yourself," ordered another.

"Lucy—Lucy Gamble," said Lucy through parched lips.

Humming like hornets, the shapes swayed closer. Clawlike hands scratched at Lucy's skin and plucked at her garments. She tried to fend them off but there were too many. They were dragging her down . . .

"Stay the bloomin' garnish!" a young cockney voice beside her cried. "Otherwise there'll be nought left for any of us. Go back to sleep, it'll be light in an hour or so."

Muttering, the shapes melted back into the darkness. Lucy felt a hand tug at her cloak. She allowed herself to be led to the opposite side of the ward and pulled down against the wall.

"What'll you pay me to protect you?"

Lucy took a silver buckle from her cloak and pressed it into the other's palm. "Thank you for your assistance. What is your name?"

"Elizabeth Dudgeon. What's this you've given me?"

"A silver buckle from my shoe. Tell me, what is the garnish of which everyone speaks?"

"All who enter Newgate must pay garnish," the other said. "It's the rule. None escape it. Pay or be stripped—and better you pay else, with the stripping, the cold will get you if the jail fever don't."

"What garnish would satisfy them?"

"Lower your voice. Ears here are sharp and there's danger for me in this. If they thought I'd cut them out of a share, they'd tear me to pieces. Have you any valuables besides this buckle?"

Excluding the earrings, Lucy told her.

"Offer them the ring, and give the ribbon to Maria Hamilton.

17

She runs Waterman's. You'll know her from the clay pipe she smokes. Been in for a year this time—caught running a brothel. Stay out of her way if you know what's good for you. She's a mad dog when she's drinking, which is most of the time."

It was intensely cold. Lucy pulled her cloak down over her feet. "How did you come to be here, Elizabeth?" she asked politely.

The other gave a long sigh. "I got caught taking eight guineas off a client." She sniffed. "When I went for my trial in September eighty-three, the magistrate sent me up for seven years."

"Have you been in this awful place for three years?" Lucy gasped.

"Not on your life! Me and two hundred others were put on board the *Mercury*, bound for America. Lord, what a hell craft she was! The Captain was a scurvy bastard, and the crew not much better, the mangy dogs.

"But we did them in the end. As soon as the ship cleared the Channel two of our lads broke into the forward hold and stole some tools. They freed us from our irons and a bloody battle got going. The crew had the weapons but us convicts had the numbers and we soon got the upper hand."

"What happened then?" Lucy asked, her mind awhirl.

"Six days later, we made Torbay and I went ashore in the first longboat with John Best, the lad that led the mutiny," Elizabeth continued in a hoarse whisper. "John's a housebreaker by trade, so we didn't want for food or coin on the way back to London. We kept clear of the main roads and only brushed with the law once when John was spotted breaking into a grog shop in Amesbury."

A note of despondency crept into her voice. "I'd still be free today but I got pulled in by the runners six months ago when the chap I was with, Bill Narmo, got sprung picking the pocket of a worthy. So, here I am, sent up for seven years, and me not yet two and twenty."

The light had strengthend and Lucy could now see Elizabeth Dudgeon more clearly. She was dressed in rags and she was extremely dirty, but the grime could not hide her prettiness. Tight blond ringlets framed her heart-shaped face and her huge blue eyes gave her an air of innocence that her colorful language belied.

"But that's enough about me, girl," she said. "What's a fine looking piece like you doing in Waterman's?"

5

The Chapel

"Gave that man more than he bargained for didn't you?"
Elizabeth Dudgeon said with sympathy. "But, Lord, if I'd done
in every chap I'd taken a turn with, the streets of London would
run red with blood."

With the light growing stronger by the minute, Lucy was able
to see the Waterman's Ward at last. Perhaps the darkness was a
blessing she thought. The ward was about twenty feet square and
held, she estimated, some forty women. Many were covered in
crusty sores and weeping ulcers. Some lay moaning fitfully in
their own filth, while others growled and blasphemed at one
another, trampling lice and other vermin underfoot. Lucy shuddered, remembering the sound of crackling eggshells in the
Condemned Hold.

"Don't show them no fear or they'll have you for sure,"
Elizabeth muttered as a group of harridans approached. "On
your feet and brazen it out."

Lucy scrambled up.

"Show us your garnish and be quick about it or we'll strip you
to the bone!" shrieked a belligerent crone. Lucy recognized her
from Elizabeth's description as Maria Hamilton, the woman who
ran Waterman's.

Lucy proffered the gold corded ring. "I offer this as garnish,"
she said, trying to keep her voice steady.

Maria snatched the ring, bit down hard on it, then popped it
into a pouch at her waist. "Ain't enough," she said, her lined,
pockmarked face sullen.

Lucy handed her the red velvet ribbon. "Take this for yourself."

"I'll take your cloak too, you high and mighty whore," said
Maria.

Lucy longed to yield and walk away from the danger but the cloak
contained her valuables, and was also her warmth—the only thing
that separated her from the poor wretches lying on the boards.
Her mouth was dry when she finally spoke. "No, I don't think so."

An expectant hush settled over the ward as all eyes turned
toward the two women.

"Give me the cloak, you strumpet, or I'll slit you from ear to
ear!" screeched Maria.

19

Snakes of fear slithered in the pit of Lucy's stomach but she shook her head decisively. "No."

Maria sprang at her, fingers spread like talons. They fell to the floor in a confusion of arms and legs, rolling over and over. Maria was a seasoned streetfighter but the poor prison diet and the ravages of alcohol had taken their toll. Lucy was, quite simply, fighting for her life. She blazed with fury and strength. When next she found herself on top of Maria she jumped to her feet, yanked the brothel keeper up by the hair and flung her against the wall beneath the gratings. Maria slid to the floor, holding her head.

Gasping for breath, Lucy addressed the others. "I ask only to be left in peace—as I will leave you."

They stared at her for an eternity. Then, muttering among themselves, they slunk slowly back into the gloom.

Sickened by the debauchery of the women when they were released from the wards and allowed to mingle with the male inmates in the exercise quadrangle, and terrified of further violation by the turnkeys, Lucy retreated into a world of shadows.

Each morning she stayed in Waterman's until the passageway outside was clear of men, then she fled to the chapel and hid between the pews in the darkness of the upper gallery.

The chapel was a cold and dismal place, full of melancholy shadows, but at least it was usually deserted, so it became Lucy's refuge. There she meditated, prayed, and slept, for when she returned to Waterman's at night the moans of the sick and dying and the mindless ravings of the lunatics were so unnerving that sleep often eluded her.

When days, then weeks dragged by without word from Ruth, Lucy grew more and more despondent. Now her father was dead, Ruth was her legal guardian. Why was she withholding help? Lucy had nowhere else to turn.

Every day Lucy decided to go to the prison authorities, but her terror of violation always stopped her. "One more day," she would say, "I'll wait just one more day for Ruth."

When Elizabeth Dudgeon visited the chapel unexpectedly one afternoon, Lucy thought that day had come. "Is my stepmother here, Beth?" she asked as Beth slid into the pew beside her.

Beth, who spent her daylight hours employed in various survival activities around the prison, and generally gave the gloomy chapel a wide berth, shook her head. "No, Lucy. But I remember what you said about writing her another letter. I know someone who's getting out of here tomorrow. He'll deliver the letter to her in person if you pay his price.''

"Can we trust him?''

"Oh, yes!'' said Beth. "Bill's the one I got picked up with. He owes me a favor, does Bill, seeing as I'm back in here because of him.'' She produced a sheet of crumpled paper and a crayon from under her skirt.

"How did you come by these, you amazing creature?'' Lucy cried. "Paper is as scarce as soap in here.''

Beth smiled mischievously. "Bill took it from the Keeper's office while the clerk was occupied. There's none sharper than Bill at picking a lock.'' Her face became serious. "But here's the rub. Bill needs payment in advance. You'll have to give over the other silver buckle.''

Lucy hastened to reassure her. "Don't concern yourself about money, Beth. As soon as my stepmother comes it will be all right.''

"Well then, you'd best get on with it, girl. Lockup's in an hour and Bill needs the letter by then.''

6

The Mourning Woman

Friday, November 17, 1786

The courtyard of the George Inn resounded with clamor as the London coach disgorged its weary passengers. The driver, caked with red dust, shouted orders to the hostlers as they led away the horses; the guard, perched on the baggage basket, tossed trunks and portmanteaus into the arms of the servants; rosy-cheeked chambermaids rushed to and fro with refreshments; and curious guests hung out of upper-story windows shouting greetings and encouragement to those below.

Faith tied the ribbons of her green velvet bonnet tightly under her chin and stepped through the high-arched entrance. The wind often blew fiercely along the streets and squares of the ancient walled city, whipping the hats off the heads of the unwary.

She and Sir Michael had been in York for three days. The

coach trip from Billingsley had been intolerable. She did not know what was wrong with her grandfather. He refused to discuss the scar, the vision, or her father, and since arriving in York he had avoided her company at every turn.

She walked up Petergate Street and entered the Minster by the Great West Door. As she made her way slowly along the central aisle, afternoon sunlight streamed through stained-glass windows, painting the floor with rainbows.

She entered her favorite place, the Lady Chapel, and gazed in wonder at the East Window—a medieval masterpiece of mosaic glass. Her eyes traveled upward over bishops, kings, assemblies of saints, and armies of angels until they reached the uppermost tracery where God the Father—Alpha and Omega—presided over all.

She knelt and prayed.

Some thirty minutes later, Faith left the Minster and walked back through the crowded streets toward the George. The wind whipped the ornamental shop signs to and fro and, overhead, dark storm clouds gathered, but it was not until raindrops splashed onto the sidewalk that she ceased her idle browsing in a shop window and turned to go.

As she did she collided with a woman dressed in mourning who was hurrying in the opposite direction. When the woman saw Faith she gave a terrified cry and rushed away into the thundering rain as if all the devils in hell were pursuing her.

The eyes of every man followed Faith as she made her way through the dining room and joined Sir Michael at a table by the window.

She wore a taffeta dress of azure blue, trimmed with white fur. Her dark tresses were piled on top of her head in soft curls and secured with sparkling diamond and sapphire combs that matched the settings around her neck and in her ears. Her skin glowed and her eyes shone with excitement at being invited to eat with her grandfather. The two previous evenings, he had ordered that a tray be sent to her room.

Faith and her grandfather dined on thick tender slices of rare roast beef, with yorkshire pudding, asparagus, carrots, and golden roast potatoes, followed by strawberries, jellied tarts, and French champagne. The fine food and wine lightened their mood and soon they were on easier terms with each other.

"Today I spoke to an attorney who's just returned from Scotland," said Sir Michael. "Apparently, the snow has come early to the

Highlands this year and we'd be wise to leave York at our earliest convenience if we wish to get through to Inverness. Therefore, I've ordered that our coach be ready at first light tomorrow."

Faith's eyes lit up. "That *is* good news. I'm looking forward to seeing Aunt Barbara and Uncle Colin again. And I hope Hugh will return to Carrigmoor this Christmas. It has been four years since I saw him . . ."

"This was his last year of Law so he's bound to be there, my dear. Although why he went to Edinburgh in the first place I'll never know. As heir to Carrigmoor, his future is ordained."

He was definitely thawing. She reached for his hand. "The distance between us these last few weeks has greatly saddened me, Grandfather. Could we put our differences aside and be best friends again?"

Sir Michael's mouth set in a stern line. "That might be possible— if you have put that nonsense of a month ago from your mind."

Faith sighed. "Would that I could, but I keep hearing her voice and seeing her face . . ."

He knew he should let the matter rest there, but the compulsion was on him. He *had* to know. In a voice heavy with sarcasm, he asked the question that had hung on his lips for a month. "And what does she look like, this phantom of yours?"

Faith hesitated a moment. "You'll find this difficult to believe, Grandfather, but she looks exactly like me. Yet, I swear she is not me. Could she be a relative of my father's perhaps?"

Sir Michael's cheeks grew mottled with rage. "I shall not listen to this, Faith, nor will I speak of visions again *ever*. I advise you to put such thoughts from your mind—if you have the slightest value for your sanity!"

He bid her a terse good night then marched out of the dining room.

Faith turned from the frozen countryside flashing past the window and glanced at the grim-faced man opposite.

Was he right? Had she allowed an isolated incident to cloud her reason? Was her vision merely a symptom of an overactive imagination?

The coach jolted and lurched over the ruts in the road as it sped north toward Scotland. If the weather held, and they escaped the hazards that often plagued coach travelers, they should reach Carrigmoor in ten days. Tears pricked her eyes and a lump rose in her throat. How she longed to see Aunt Barbara. And Hugh. Had he changed?

She looked out at the desolate moors again and, for a moment, the face of the woman in mourning flashed before her eyes. The poor woman had clearly mistaken her for another. What was the name she had cried? Lucy? Yes, that was it. The woman in mourning had called her *Lucy*.

A few miles distant, on the banks of the Rye, close by the village of Pickering, Ruth Gamble sat sewing in the kitchen of her father's house. A large cheerful room with a high, black oak ceiling, the kitchen was the hub of the household. There were grander chambers in the old rambling house but, since her mother's death, her father spent his evenings sitting by the kitchen fire, smoking and reading until it was time to retire.

Ruth sighed and put down her sewing. Straight after the shooting, she had closed the London house and brought Richard's body home to Pickering. Her father had welcomed her, then left her in peace. He would not ask her to talk about Richard's death until she was ready.

She smoothed back her straight black hair that, like Richard's, had a prominent widow's peak, thinking of the strange incident in York the day before. She had been overwrought lately and that, together with the poor light and the heavy jolt, must have made her eyes play tricks. She could not possibly have seen Lucy.

A chill blast of wind swept into the room as John Newport came in from outside.

"Father, we must talk."

Newport listened intently as his weeping daughter related the events that had shattered her life. He went through a long ritual of lighting his pipe before making any comment. "James was an honorable man and I'm saddened by his passing; yet I'm convinced he died as he would have wished," he began. "I've no magical potion for your grief, Ruth. Time alone heals the wounds of the heart, and time will pass more quickly if you keep busy."

He paused to relight his pipe. "But now, I'm afraid I must cause you more grief by destroying the illusions you have about your brother. Perhaps it is better that he is dead."

"What do you mean?" Ruth gasped.

"Richard was not the man you imagined him to be, Ruth. Oh, I admit that, like you and your mother, I was bedazzled by Richard the child. I loved his boisterous, outspoken nature and his boundless energy. I laughed at his reckless ways and dismissed his misdeeds as mere childish pranks. But what is acceptable in a child cannot be tolerated in an adult. These last years, my blind love turned to bitter, bitter, disillusionment. The brilliant, heroic fellow I imagined my son to be simply did not exist. Richard the man was a ruthless, immoral scoundrel—completely preoccupied with self. Nothing mattered to him but what *he* wanted—what *he* needed. He used people up and when they had served their purpose, he tossed them aside without compunction.

"He was feared and detested in this county and his treatment of women was a scandal. Those he could not get by cunning, he took by force. There was even talk that he dabbled in the black arts—"

Ruth jumped up, tears streaming from her eyes. "How dare you say such terrible things about dear Richard, Father! You are bitter because he rejected your way of life. Well, I wholeheartedly agreed with his decision to leave Pickering. I could have opened many doors for him in London. James was a man of standing!"

John Newport looked at his daughter with distaste. She grew more like her dead mother every day: unintelligent of mind, uncontrollable of temper, and unforgiving of nature. Obviously, she mourned her worthless brother, not her noble husband.

"James was well acquainted with your brother's deficiencies, Ruth. The only door he would have opened to Richard was his front door, as he did on the previous occasion."

Ruth's eyes narrowed. "What are you saying?"

John Newport looked at Ruth with surprise. Was it possible she did not know? "The last time Richard stayed at Grosvenor Square he forged James's signature on some gambling IOUs. James discovered what he had done and had the servants throw him out."

"I don't believe you!" Ruth cried.

"James sent me the IOUs with a cover letter," John Newport replied grimly. "Shall I get it for you?"

Ruth wrung her hands. "Say what you will about Richard's gambling debts, Father. You weren't there the night he died. You didn't hear him beg Lucy for mercy. You did not see her calmly shoot him through the head as he knelt helpless before her. She murdered my brother and she shall pay for it with her life!"

John Newport rose and walked to the door. "You are unstrung, Ruth, it is pointless discussing this further. I've told you the truth about Richard. Whether you believe it or not is your own concern. I wipe my hands of the matter."

The snowcapped mountain peaks of the Great Glen glinted steely blue in the winter sunlight as the coach inched up the steep incline, and although it was only midafternoon, already the valleys were silent and deep in shadow. The coach reached the top of the rise and went careering down the other side into the Plain of Glenelgin.

The strain of the last two weeks showed on Faith's face as she anxiously scanned the frozen landscape. Then at last, above the sea of white, she saw the two stone bears that guarded the entrance.

"Look, Grandfather," she cried, her fatigue forgotten, "the gates. We're here at last."

They traveled along the tree-lined carriageway toward the castle that rose ghostlike from the mist, its battlements glowing pink in the dying rays of the sun. Then they were crossing the draw-bridge and rumbling into the courtyard where the family waited at the bottom of the steps.

Weeping unashamedly, Faith leapt from the coach and threw herself into Lady Barbara's outstretched arms. The ordeal was over. She had come home to Carrigmoor for Christmas.

7

Frances Hart

Tuesday, December 12, 1786

Lucy staggered along the passage toward the exercise quadrangle, her face hidden by the hood of her cloak. She would not usually venture into this part of the prison, but today she had to find Beth.

She was ill. Her head ached, her skin felt clammy and her legs could hardly hold her. The sickness had been with her for two days now and Lucy was afraid. Several women in Waterman's had died of putrid fevers during the last two months. At first Lucy had been appalled by the callousness of the other women, who hid the bodies and only gave them up for burial when the stench became unbearable. Now she turned a blind eye, for while the bodies remained, so did their food rations.

Drawing the cloak tighter around her, Lucy stepped into the exercise quadrangle. She felt as if she had passed through the portals of hell. Like hordes of chattering devils, the inmates of

Newgate trampled the frosty ground, battering and tearing at one another and mouthing obscenities. Heavily shackled men, their ribs jutting out from beneath filthy rags, crouched in groups throwing dice carved from soup bones. "What brings you out here, Gamble?"

Lucy glanced behind her and sighed with relief. It was only Frances, a woman from Waterman's. "I'm trying to find Beth Dudgeon. Have you seen her?"

Frances Hart was the finest needlewoman in Newgate and her garments, though threadbare, were exceptionally well kept. She was tall and large boned and wore her frizzy gray hair piled on top of her head in a raggedy bun. A perpetual frown creased her forehead and her thin mouth drooped alarmingly at the corners. Her shoulders sloped downward as if they bore the weight of the world's sins on them. "Not I!" she replied tersely. "That brazen doxy could be anywhere from Keeper's quarters to Jack Ketch's kitchen."

Lucy shuddered. Jack Ketch's kitchen was the room where the hangman dismembered the bodies of traitors and boiled them in pitch, tar, and oil. All who passed that place did so with eyes averted. As she thought of the sickening smell that came from there, Lucy heaved.

"You're as pale as a ghost, girl. And shivering and shaking like I don't know what. Are you ill?" said Frances Hart. "Here, lean on me. We'd best get you out of this cold."

"Thank you, Frances," Lucy murmured as the other woman placed a strong arm around her and led her along the passageway. "I felt faint but it seems to have passed now. If you do see Beth could you please tell her I'd like to speak to her? She knows where I will be."

By the time Lucy reached the upper gallery of the chapel, her legs would no longer hold her. She sank into her hiding place between the pews and as soon as the pounding in her head eased, fell into a deep sleep.

Beth's eyes filled with tears when she saw Lucy's pale, pinched face. She had never known anyone like Lucy before. Lucy shared everything she had—even the food from her mouth. Lucy always laughed at her silly stories, and sympathized when she complained. Lucy did not take like everyone else—she *gave*. Beth did not know what she would do if something happened to Lucy.

"You're a proper ninny, Beth," she muttered, spreading her shawl over Lucy's still form. "Weeping and wailing won't help.

What's needed now is for that stepmother to come. Even accounting for the delay, she must of got that bloomin' letter by now . . .''

A week after Bill had left Newgate, he had returned to the visitors' lodge with the news that the house in Grosvenor Square had been closed and Ruth Gamble had joined her father in Yorkshire. There had been nothing for it but to readdress the letter and give Bill a pearl button to put it on the York mail.

Ruth's mouth set in a hard line as she sat beside the kitchen fire, Lucy's letter in her hand. The writing was smudged and indistinct but still legible. She smoothed out the paper, held it closer to the light, and read aloud:

> "Dear Ruth,
> I know how much you loved your brother, and how shocked and grieved you will be by his death, but I beg you to believe that I had *no choice* other than to behave as I did. What happened cannot be told in a letter. Please come to the prison and give me a chance to explain. I have searched my soul and am convinced I acted in defence of my life that night.
> "It is difficult to survive in this monstrous place and I appeal to you, my legal guardian, to forward money so I can purchase food, clothing, bedding, and other necessities of life.
> "I desperately need legal assistance. Could you find it in your heart to contact Father's Bristol lawyers and send an attorney to me?
> "I appreciate how painful this is for you, my dear Ruth, but please do not let me down, I beg you. *You are my only hope*. Yours in love, Lucy."

Ruth gazed pensively into the fire. Her marriage to James had been a miserable sham. In fact, he had only married her to acquire a dependable live-in companion for his precious daughter. He had denied it, of course, but over the years the little things had given him away: he had always kissed Lucy first when he had come home from sea; his eyes had always rested on Lucy when the three of them had been together; it was Lucy he had sought out if he had any news.

Ruth glanced at the letter in her hand. Now James was dead

and Lucy, *her brother's murderer,* was asking for help. Well, well. She screwed the letter into a tight ball and tossed it into the fire. It flared brightly for a few seconds then crumpled into a heap of gray ashes in the fire's bed.

Beth didn't know what to do. Christmas had come and gone with no word from Lucy's stepmother and with every passing day Lucy grew sicker and more despondent. She no longer bothered going to the chapel, but stayed in Waterman's with the dying. It was no use taking Lucy to the infirmary. In that pesthole the sick were strung in hammocks and left to die unattended.

"What ails her then?"

Beth looked up startled to find Frances Hart standing over her. "If I knew that, I'd cure her," she snapped. Then, seeing the concern in the other's eyes, sighed, and softened her tone. "She can keep nought down but water soup and has grown so weak she sleeps all the time. Is it the jail fever?"

Frances Hart placed a hand on Lucy's brow. "Head's cool—that's a good sign. Weather's fine today. Why don't we take her to the exercise quadrangle? She'll be safe with us and the fresh air might do her good. The air in here's as foul as an offal yard." Frances gently shook Lucy's shoulder.

Lucy opened her eyes and sat up, but the dizziness came and she sank back to the boards. "I am unwell," she said dully and turned on her side.

Frances was not deterred. "Where's your pride, girl?" she asked, hauling Lucy to a sitting position. "Do you enjoy lying in this filthy hole with lice crawling over you?"

Lucy shook her aching head.

"Then, come with Dudgeon and me. We'll take you outside for a breath of fresh air. But you'll have to lend a hand, you're no feather, you know."

"Have you been in Newgate long, Frances?" Lucy asked a short time later as the three women trudged around the outer boundary of the muddy quadrangle.

"Since 1783—save for a spell on board the *Mercury,*" Frances told her, steering Lucy past a vacant-eyed lunatic who had wandered over to them.

Beth raised her eyebrows. "I don't remember seeing you aboard."

"I'm not surprised, Dudgeon. I stayed clear of the shameful goings on aboard that ship. But for the mutiny, I'd be seeing out my time in sunny Virginia instead of rotting in this filthy hole!"

"What are you here for?" Lucy asked hurriedly.

Frances's mouth turned down alarmingly at the corners. "For receiving two pairs of leather boots and a pair of red morocco pumps. Worth one shilling the lot! Seven years the magistrate gave me and, on my oath, it were my husband, Dave, as done it—and left me to stand the charge. Low, lying scum swore he'd get me out in a month if I kept my mouth shut. And here I am three years later." She cast baleful eyes around the quadrangle. "I come out here every morning hoping to catch a glimpse of him in this herd of swine. 'Tis all that keeps me going. If ever I find him, I'll kill him!"

Hearing the pain in her voice, Lucy squeezed her arm compassionately. "Oh, poor Frances. Has anyone helped you?"

Frances shook her head grimly. "Friends are hard to find when you need a helping hand, my girl. But you won't see me selling my soul for bread as them whores are doing. I'm a dressmaker by trade and I've built up a smart clientele among the well-to-do political prisoners over the years."

She smiled, and the cloud lifted from her face as her mouth curved up like a half-moon. "My, you *are* looking better. There's a lot to be said for a whiff of fresh air and a brisk morning walk in the country!"

"I feel much better," Lucy agreed, laughing. "My headache and nausea have gone. If my breasts would stop aching, I would be quite recovered."

Beth and Frances gawked at her. "How long since your last monthly?" asked Beth.

"Why?"

"Answer me, Lucy!"

"Last September. Yes . . . the end of September."

Beth and Frances exchanged knowing glances. "You're probably in the family way," Beth said glumly.

Lucy looked at her, horrified. "What are you saying? Oh, God! Not that brute's child! I could not *stand* it!"

"Be quiet, you're attracting attention," Frances cautioned fiercely.

But Lucy was beyond caring. "I'll not have it!" she cried.

Beth and Frances half dragged, half carried her to the nearest passageway, where she sank to her knees weeping wildly. Beth knelt and embraced her. "Surely, being pregnant is better than having the fatal fever, Lucy?"

"I would rather be dead than have that animal's child growing inside me!"

Beth began to cry as well. "D-don't take on so, Lucy. Frances and me'll look after you." She looked up at Frances. "Won't we, Frances?"

As Frances Hart stood in the dim passageway staring down at the two kneeling women, the ice that had long encased her stout heart began to thaw. Forcing a firm note into her voice, she said, "Now, listen here you two, what's done is done, and no amount of carrying-on will change it. God helps them as helps themselves. Up off that filthy floor, Lucy, and that goes for you too, Beth. We'll finish our walk and see this day out as best we can. Any more nonsense from either of you and I'll box your ears, you mark my words!"

8
Lady Barbara Stewart

Sunday, December 31, 1786

After another sleepless night, Faith left the castle at first light hoping a walk would ease her feelings of disquiet.

She was careful to keep to the path as she plodded across the silent, hummocky landscape. Once, when she had strayed, she had sunk to her armpits in snow. She passed the Clava Cairns—the mystical burial chambers of a warrior race that had roamed the land centuries before Christ—and plowed through the drifts until she reached the River Nairn.

She crossed the footbridge to the other side, climbed the steep bank and gazed over the slow-rising spur of land known as Culloden Moor. An almost tangible sadness hung over the famous battlefield, as if the earth still wept for the clansmen buried beneath it.

"I believe Grandfather is hiding something from me," She announced to the morning. She had obeyed him all her life, and in this matter of the vision she had felt duty bound to heed him, But it was no use. The harder she tried to quiet the voice inside her, the more persistent it became.

"She is more real to me than the air I breathe or the food I eat," she murmured. "I must find her. Until I do, nothing in my life will be right. When I return to the castle, I will speak to

Aunt Barbara. Perhaps she can shed some light on the mystery surrounding my father. If not, at least she may intercede with Grandfather.''

The decision made, she set off toward Carrigmoor with a new spring in her step.

Faith found her grandaunt in the drawing room, planning menus for Hogmanay.

Despite her fifty-two years, Barbara Stewart was still a beauty. She was tall, like her brother, and possessed the same high cheekbones and dark eyes, but there the resemblance ended. No harsh lines etched her countenance, rather, its soft contours expressed inner peace.

As she waved her grandniece into the chair opposite, Lady Barbara looked at her with concern. Faith had lost weight and there was a haunted expression in her eyes. "Good morning, my dear. I've been looking for you. I thought you might like to help me with the final arrangements for tonight's celebrations in the Great Hall.''

Faith smiled fondly at the woman who had been like a mother to her. "I'd be delighted to help, Aunt Barbara, but something has me perplexed. Could I talk to you about it first?''

Lady Barbara joined Faith on the longseat and reached for her hand. "Certainly, my dear. What worries you?''

With enormous relief, Faith began.

"Highland folk attach great credence to visions,'' Lady Barbara said after Faith had told her story. "They believe that those who 'see' such things possess the 'second sight.' Over the years I've heard stories similar to yours. Michael was wrong to treat your experience as he did, darling. Just because something can't be logically explained does not mean it should be discarded. Why, if we believed that, mankind would not have taken one step forward since the dawn of Creation.

"I don't know what possessed Michael to behave in such a way. All I can say in his defence is that he was distraught beyond measure when your mother died. Still, it is twenty years since then. I think it's high time Michael set aside his grief and attended to the needs of the living.

"You have every right to ask about your father, the scar on your finger, or anything else. And you deserve to be answered civilly and truthfully. What exactly would you like to know?''

"Everything you can tell me about Father,'' Faith replied.

Lady Barbara rose, and walked to the great gothic window. "The first Christmas, when Michael brought you to Carrigmoor, I asked about your father and Michael's answers were very vague. But he was so distressed about your mother's passing I did not press him. The little I know is this.

"After your grandmother passed away in sixty-three, Michael spent two years in Europe on East India Company business. Your mother was only sixteen then, so he sent her here to me. Margaret never settled to life in the Glen. She lived for the day when she could return to her beloved forests. I'll always remember her joy when she received Michael's letter bidding her to return home. . . ."

As her grandaunt spoke, Faith felt a sudden rush of yearning for the mother she had never known. If only she were alive—how different everything would be.

"I never saw Margaret again," Lady Barbara continued, looking down on the hustle and bustle of the courtyard, "but she wrote me two letters before she died. In the first, she spoke of her forthcoming marriage to your father, although there had been some difficulty obtaining Michael's consent. After they married, your parents moved to London and Margaret wrote again from there. She spoke most lovingly of your father and expressed her joy that she was expecting a child at the end of the year.

"You can imagine my shock when I heard your father had deserted Margaret and that she had died giving birth to you.

"Michael has never mentioned your father since, except once during your second Christmas at Carrigmoor. One evening, he told me he'd received word that your father had been an officer aboard an East India Company vessel which had sunk off the coast of Portugal with all hands on board."

Faith joined her at the window and held out her scarred finger. "Can you tell me anything about this, Aunt Barbara?"

"No more than you already know, my dear." She sighed. "Why did it bleed the night you had the vision? And why does the woman in your vision look exactly like you?"

Faith frowned, her green eyes troubled. "I'm convinced Grandfather is the only one who can shed any light on the mystery. Will you intercede with him on my behalf?"

"Of course. Tonight, after the banquet, I'll bring him in here and you shall join us. And now that's settled, would you do something for me?"

Faith's eyes twinkled. "Anything, Aunt Barbara."

"As this evening will be a grand and joyful occasion, it would

33

please me if you could set aside your troubles for a few hours and take special care with your appearance. It might help lighten your mood.''

''I promise to do you proud,'' Faith laughed. ''And as for my mood, it is already lighter than it's been for months.''

Hugh Stewart gazed at Faith with unconcealed admiration as she entered the Great Hall that evening wearing a rose pink velvet gown cut low at the neck. Draped over her shoulders was an exquisite shawl of Flanders lace that fell in elegant folds to the floor. Her dark hair hung in a mass of soft curls down her back, and diamonds sparkled at her throat and ears.

''Please forgive my lateness to table, Uncle,'' she murmured, curtsying respectfully to the Laird of Carrigmoor before sitting beside Hugh. ''I dawdled over my toilette and time slipped away.''

Sir Colin chuckled, his ruddy complexion heightened by liberal amounts of whiskey. ''Och, lass, a man would go without food for a week to behold the fruits of y'labors . . . aye, Hugh?''

Hugh appraised Faith with mock solemnity. ''In truth, she's a tolerably handsome wench, Father, but go without food for a week? That's too much to ask of even the most adoring swain.''

He is not getting away with that, Faith thought, settling her features into an expression of vast, unconcerned superiority. ''Four years in Edinburgh's hallowed halls of learning have not changed you, Hugh. Clearly, the way to your heart is, as ever, through your exceedingly avaricious stomach!''

Hugh raised an amused eyebrow. ''Nor have the last four years dulled *your* rapier tongue, Fae.''

It was a marvelous evening. Two hundred Stewarts, kilted and sashed, had gathered at the castle to welcome the New Year with as much revelry as possible. When the banquet was over, the tables were removed and the celebrations began in earnest. The younger guests danced the Highland reels and southern measures with wild abandon, while the clan elders sat about, clapping in time with the pipes and reminiscing on bygone days. Such a grand time was had by all that the new year was already two hours old before Lady Barbara enticed Sir Michael away from the festivities.

Faith found them a few minutes later, sitting by the fire, sipping brandy and laughing. ''Do join us, my dear,'' Lady Barbara invited. ''We were just discussing you. Isn't she breathtaking, Michael? You would be wise to prepare yourself for the suitors who are bound to come flocking to your door.''

Sir Michael refilled his glass. '' 'Tis no joking matter, Barbara. The young blades of West Hampshire have been at sixes and sevens over her for years. Still,'' he said complacently, ''she prefers the company of her old grandfather to a gaggle of posturing gallants. Eh, Faith?''

Faith bit back the retort on her tongue. ''I shall not deny that, Grandfather.''

Lady Barbara laughed. ''Now you are of marriageable age, your preferences will soon change, my dear. Why, in my day—''

''We need not rush things, Barbara. Faith is barely twenty.''

''May I remind you, Faith's mother was wed at eighteen,'' Lady Barbara rejoined.

''Yes, that is so,'' Sir Michael said carefully.

''And when the time comes for Faith to marry, you must promise I'll be there, Michael,'' Lady Barbara went on blithely. ''I greatly regret having missed Margaret's wedding.''

Sir Michael's eyes narrowed and a steely light came into them. ''Your request has been duly noted.''

Lady Barbara took a deep breath. ''By the way, why *did* James Gamble desert Margaret?''

An awful silence settled over the room and both women watched with alarm as Sir Michael's face turned scarlet. ''How dare you mention that infamous scoundrel in my presence, Barbara!''

''But *why* is he such an infamous scoundrel?''

He shook his fist in her face. ''I know what you're about, Barbara. You have listened to Faith's driveling nonsense and have decided to join forces with her against me!''

''Michael, my dear, Faith has a right to know,'' Lady Barbara tried to reason. ''I do not take her part against you, dear, I am acting on behalf of someone who is unable to speak—her mother.''

Sir Michael's eyes bulged. ''Silence!'' he roared. ''Silence, damn you!''

''I will *not* be silent!'' Lady Barbara cried. ''Faith has a right to the truth and neither she nor I will leave this room until the truth is told. Clearly, you are hiding something!''

His face suffused with rage, he lunged at her.

''Grandfather!'' Faith gasped, throwing herself between them. ''For pity's sake, what has come over you?''

35

"Get out my way!" he shouted. "No damned woman will tell me what to do!"

As he shoved her aside he seemed to lose his balance and suddenly he collapsed on the floor at her feet, his body twitching and a terrible gurgling sound coming from his throat.

9
The Commodore's Letter

Saturday, February 10, 1787

Faith stood at the top of the stairs bracing her body against the blinding snowstorm sweeping in on Carrigmoor.

Her grandfather had recovered from the apoplexy that had struck him down on New Year's Eve, except for a slight blurring of his vision and a weakness on his left side.

Faith rubbed her tired eyes. These last six weeks she had spent almost every waking hour with him. His constant demands trapped her; only when he slept was she able to slip away for a stroll in the grounds. That had been her intention when the storm had struck a few minutes ago. As she stared out at the savage, swirling fury a horse and rider materialized.

"Fool!" she cried a few minutes later, bustling Hugh into a downstairs drawing room where a fire was blazing brightly. "Fool!" she repeated, divesting him of his greatcoat and sending snowflakes flying everywhere. "What possessed you to be abroad in such weather? You might have frozen to death—or worse."

Hugh laughed as he brushed snow from his black, curly hair. "What could be worse than freezing to death? Except, perhaps, to be at the receiving end of your sharp tongue."

"Oh, do be quiet, Hugh," Faith said crossly, "you tease me to distraction. Admit it, you were foolish to take such a risk."

"Enough! No more!" he pleaded, raising his hands in supplication.

"Oh, very well," she relented, pouring him a measure of whiskey. "Come over here by the fire, you are blue with cold."

"How is Uncle today?"

36

Faith jostled the logs energetically with the poker. "Sleeping soundly when I left him."

Hugh stepped closer and took the poker away from her. "You look exhausted, Fae," he said softly, using his pet name for her. "Do take care, or we will have two English invalids at Carrigmoor."

Faith looked down at her hands. "It is difficult to rest, Hugh. Grandfather needs me. . . ."

Hugh placed his fingers under her chin and raised it until their eyes met. "The doctor says he is much improved. Come riding with me tomorrow, Fae. We'll visit the old fort at Davoit. Remember how we used to enjoy ourselves there?"

She gazed up at him. He was a wonderful looking man, tall and broad shouldered, with warm eyes and a wicked smile. His fortune was certainly not the sole reason he was pursued by women the length and breadth of the Great Glen. "I'd like to, Hugh, but you know how he frets when I am out of his sight."

Hugh frowned. "You must be firmer with him, Fae. The break will do you good. Besides, four years have passed since we spent time alone together. Would you like me to speak to Uncle?"

At that moment, Kenneth, Sir Michael's manservant, entered. "Master's awake and calling for you, Miss Faith."

As she turned to go, Hugh caught her around the waist and handed her a bulky letter. "This is for Uncle. As for the other, I will not take no for an answer. You're coming riding tomorrow."

"Look what I have for you," Faith said, waving the letter aloft as she entered Sir Michael's chamber. "A letter from Captain Phillip."

Sir Michael pulled himself up to a sitting position in the huge four-poster bed. "At last! I've wondered how he was faring. Take a seat, Faith, and tell me his news."

The letter had been written in London a month before and contained an extraordinarily detailed list of the eleven ships of the Fleet, their tonnage, masters' names, the number of convicts, crew, and military men each was contracted to carry, and a host of other details, all of which Sir Michael found fascinating. Faith turned to the next page.

The first convicts were embarked on the sixth of January at Woolwich: one hundred eighty-four males on board *Alexander,* and fifty-six females on board *Lady Penrhyn*. As Woolwich is close by to London, Gidley King and I decided to view proceedings. You will remember our last conversation, Michael, when I expressed concern that only the healthiest convicts should be chosen for so long and arduous a voyage (eight months is my most optimistic calculation). Well, the condition in which the poor wretches were sent down stamps the magistrates with infamy! It is impossible to describe the filthy appearance of the women, many of whom were mentally afflicted and sick with venereal diseases that must spread, in spite of every precaution taken. As they were near naked, I gave orders that they be clothed from *Lady Penrhyn*'s stores; but unfortunately, the day was extremely cold and I could not prevent a fever breaking out among them.

Faith shivered with sympathy.

"Read on, my dear," Sir Michael instructed gruffly. "Read on."

"The male convicts were hardly any better, most being so weak they were quite unable to help themselves. And, to make matters worse, no doctor's instruments could be found on board either ship.

"I have it on good report that the women are, on the whole, an assemblage of abandoned, shameless creatures who behave in a ferocious manner toward one another and the men who guard them . . ."

Phillip's letter outlined his views on the treatment of New South Wales natives and how the laws of the colony were to be administered, and concluded by inviting Sir Michael and Faith down to Portsmouth.

"What an enormous responsibility Captain Phillip has undertaken, Grandfather. Fourteen hundred people! It is more than the entire population of Lyndhurst and the surrounding countryside."

"Arthur is a man of great ability. If anyone can accomplish this voyage to the end of the earth, it is he." Sir Michael pushed back the bedcovers and eased himself to the side of the bed. "Tomorrow, you will write explaining why I am delayed at Carrigmoor." He swung his feet to the floor. "The sooner I am able to travel, the better. I do not want to miss visiting the Fleet."

"Nor I," Faith added emphatically.

Sir Michael beamed at her. "Ring for Kenneth, my dear. Tonight I shall join the family for the evening meal. It is high time I was up and about again."

Faith was delighted with the improvement in her grandfather that evening. The peevishness that had prevailed since his attack had disappeared and he spoke with all his old authority.

The subject of her father was one neither she nor Lady Barbara had dared broach with him again, but they had discussed the matter between themselves at length, and had decided to enlist the help of James Geldie on Faith's return to Billingsley. Geldie, a lawyer friend of Hugh's, could make some enquiries with the East India Company.

Hugh's voice broke in on Faith's thoughts. "Faith would certainly benefit from the outing, sir, she has been looking a little peaked lately."

Sir Michael frowned and folded his arms. "No, Hugh, I am afraid it is out of the question. A number of matters need to be attended to tomorrow—my reply to Phillip's letter for one . . ."

"Faith can write the letter when we return, sir. And I'll ride into Inverness with it the following day," Hugh rejoined cheerfully, then turned to Faith and winked. "Would you like to come with me to Davoit tomorrow, Fae?"

Faith took her cue. "Oh, very much! I have not ventured beyond the castle grounds in six weeks."

"Then it is settled," Lady Barbara said firmly. "Faith will go to Davoit and I'll place myself at your disposal tomorrow, Michael."

Faith and Hugh sat astride their horses on a hill overlooking the village of Davoit, which lay, half-buried by snow, beneath the ruins of an ancient fort.

Hugh turned and pointed to a rocky outcrop above. "There's the osprey's nest I was telling you about."

Faith squinted against the wind and stared. "Oh yes, I see it. But there is little left of it now."

"No, winter has wrought her usual carnage but, come spring, the ospreys will return to rebuild and produce another crop of young. Season by season, it never changes."

Faith sighed. "Would that my life could follow so simple a pattern."

He looked at her closely. "Oh, come now, Faith, if that were so you'd have died of boredom before you were four."

She smiled half-heartedly. "You still see me as the carefree child who helped you and Robert McBain explore those old ruins, Hugh, but I have changed."

Hugh leaned over and put his arm around her. "You will never change, Fae. You are as wild and free as the ospreys." He raised her hand to his lips and kissed her fingers one by one. "But you are troubled. Please, let me help."

Moved by his tender words and the gentleness in his voice, Faith turned away lest he see the tears in her eyes. "The sky is overcast, Hugh, perhaps we should be thinking of leaving."

He drew her closer. "Don't push me away. You know how much I love you."

Although Faith regretted her sharp reply, she was unwilling to discuss the vision with him lest he tease her. Forcing a smile, she brushed the snow off his shoulders. "I would never push you away, dearest. You and Aunt Barbara mean more to me than anyone else in the world . . ."

Hugh's eyes searched hers. "Not Uncle? Then there *is* trouble between you. I thought as much."

"A misunderstanding, that's all. Now, enough of this seriousness. I thought we came riding so I could forget my woes."

He kissed her cheek lightly, then let her go. "Very well, I will not press you further but, remember, if you want to confide in someone I am always available." He glanced at the sky. "I suppose we'd best be turning toward home."

Faith kicked her horse in the ribs and plunged down the embankment at reckless speed. "Och, no, Scotty lad!" she called over her shoulder. "I have changed my mind. I'm off to explore secret passages in old fort yonder. Catch me—if you can!"

Hugh swung his horse around and took off after her in a flurry of snow. This was more like the old Fae! "Scotty lad," indeed. She knew what happened when she called him that!

10
Stephen Porter, Attorney

Wednesday, February 14, 1787

Lucy pushed her hood away from her face and walked toward the man seated at a table in the corner of the visitors' lodge. When her name had been listed to appear at the Old Bailey Lent Assizes two weeks ago she had asked Bill Narmo to engage a cheap attorney on her behalf. Today, he had arrived.

A tall man of rather careless appearance with a sharp, almost hawkish face, he stared at her in a penetrating way. But his voice was surprisingly soft and had a faint Welsh burr. "Good afternoon, Mistress Gamble. I am Stephen Porter."

"Good afternoon, Mr. Porter," Lucy rejoined, sitting opposite him and looking at him gravely. "Thank you for coming at such short notice. Were you able to ascertain what evidence there is against me?"

Stephen Porter's blue eyes narrowed. How did this tattered waif with her educated voice come to call Narmo, one of London's most notorious pickpockets, "friend"? "Your position is extremely serious. The sworn statements of your stepmother and her manservant, and the reports of the Bow-street Runners who attended that night, are most damning."

Lucy was shocked. "What did the statements say?" she asked faintly.

" 'Premeditated' and 'cold-blooded' were the words most mentioned. Your stepmother swore that you had a loaded pistol in your possession, and that you fired a second shot at your fiancé while he knelt injured before you, begging for mercy. The Runners' reports stressed your calm demeanor after the shooting; and the manservant's statement substantiated both."

He leaned forward urgently, placing a hand on her arm. "Had your fiancé been unfaithful, perhaps?"

Lucy drew back from his suffocating closeness and, despite the chill in the room, beads of sweat formed on her forehead. "Richard Newport was *not* my fiancé," she said tersely, trying to fight her panic. "He came to my room by stealth that night, knocked me unconscious . . . and raped me. When I recovered my senses and struggled to free myself, he tried to strangle me.

41

It is ridiculous to say that my actions were premeditated. I had received news of my father's death that day, and I took his pistol to my room out of sentimentality as it was my last birthday gift to him. That I might need protection in my own home *never* occurred to me."

"And your calm demeanor after you shot Richard Newport?" the attorney prompted. Observing her pallor and the sweat on her brow, he wondered if she might be ill. Her manner was very stilted and withdrawn.

"My memory of what took place after I shot the beast is hazy, but I was greatly shocked, so perhaps I was more frozen than calm," Lucy said. "In any event, sir, by now Ruth will have recovered sufficiently to make an accurate statement. She knows Richard and I were never friends. The idea of a marriage between us was preposterous. Have you contacted her in Pickering?"

Thinking it unlikely that he would ever be paid for his services, Porter had taken little interest in Lucy's case. But moved by her plight, he decided to help her. "I'll write to your stepmother this very day urging her to rescind her statement. But I must warn you that, unless she does, you have little chance of being acquitted, Mistress Gamble. Her statement was most damning—most damning, indeed!"

"What of Julie Ryan, my abigail?" Lucy asked desperately. "She was there. She helped me dress before the runners took me away."

"Your stepmother dismissed her a day or so after the shooting and I've been unable to trace her. Shall I continue my search?"

Lucy nodded. "Yes, please. Julie will help me. You must find her, Mr. Porter."

"I'll do my best, Mistress Gamble, but if Julie cannot be located and your stepmother will not change her statement, you might be wise to plead guilty and throw yourself on the mercy of the court."

Lucy looked at him aghast. "But surely my case is one of self-defence, sir!" She drew back her cloak, revealing her thickened waistline. "See for yourself the fruits of Richard's attack. Is not my present condition proof that he raped me?"

Stephen Porter shook his head emphatically. "On the contrary. Indeed, the prosecution could argue that, finding yourself in the family way, you murdered Newport when he reneged on his promise to marry you."

"But how could I possibly have known I was pregnant? Even now I am barely showing."

"Can you *prove* you did not, Mistress Gamble? No, I believe such a disclosure would do your defence great harm." He flicked through his papers before continuing. "As the accused, you are forbidden to introduce new evidence at your trial. You must confine yourself strictly to answering the judges' questions. If you are clever, you can enlarge on your answers; but I warn you, do it carefully, so as not to offend the judges. They are invested with great powers and are at once your accusers, the chief witnesses against you, and the ultimate determiners of your fate."

He leaned closer. "I've done my best to acquaint you with your situation, Mistress Gamble, but, of course, it's for you to decide whether you will plead guilty or no. I can only add that, in my experience, an admission of guilt, heavily clothed in remorse and garnished with repentance, goes further toward softening a harsh sentence than a hundred unsubstantiated avowals of innocence. Will you keep that in mind when making your decision?"

"But, Mr. Porter, even if *I* cannot introduce new evidence at my trial, surely you can?"

"Attorneys have no powers in the high court. You need a barrister to act as your advocate there," he explained.

Lucy wrung her hands. "As my legal guardian, my stepmother controls my finances, sir. When you write to her, would you request that she forward money for my defence?"

"I shall. But, if the worst happens and you are found guilty of murder, here is what you must do. There is a medieval protection under law that is sometimes still employed by a condemned person. When asked by the Clerk of Arraigns if you have anything to urge why sentence of death should not be passed upon you, you must reply 'Your Honors, I plead benefit of the clergy.' Then recite in Latin, either a verse from the Lord's Prayer or a piece from the Scriptures. Do I make myself clear, Mistress Gamble?"

Lucy nodded.

"When that's done," he continued, "then, and only then, do you inform the court that you are with child. But be sure the prison matron already knows, so she can testify to that effect."

He looked at the pale young woman opposite. Her shabbiness could not mask her great beauty. It would be tragic if one so lovely were to die. "Conduct yourself in an orderly manner while the trial is in progress. But make sure to shed a discreet tear or two—that may help dispel the cold-blooded picture the prosecution will attempt to paint in the judges' minds. Now, have you any further instructions for me?''

Lucy shook her head. "I don't think so. Just write to my stepmother . . . and please try to find Julie Ryan.''

He rose. "That being the case, I'll take my leave of you.''

Lucy took a diamond earring from her pocket and held it out to him. "This is all I have, Mr. Porter, but it is quite valuable. I hope it will suffice.''

Stephen Porter looked wistfully at the lovely bauble and cursed himself for a sentimental Welsh fool. "Keep it, Mistress Gamble. Your need is greater than mine. I'll send my fee to your stepmother.'' He smiled and held out his hand. "Farewell for now, and every good luck.''

Lucy backed away. "Forgive me. I am grateful beyond expression for your help, sir, but the touch of a man is . . . difficult to endure. I hope you understand. Good-bye.''

After the interview, Lucy went immediately to the upper gallery of the chapel. Was it possible that she would hang? That thought had never crossed her mind. Until today, she had believed absolutely that Ruth would help her.

She glanced down at the symbolic coffin standing before the alter on the lower level. Only last week she had watched the condemned prisoners kneeling before it to receive the Last Sacrament. Would that be her fate also?

They had gone to their deaths in a variety of ways, those prisoners. Some, blaspheming and waving to the onlookers. Others, so intoxicated they had to be supported by the turnkeys until the hangman pulled the bolt on the trapdoor. A few had even managed an air of unconcern, but most were dragged to the scaffold screaming, or whimpering like dogs.

The baby stirred. She placed her hand on her abdomen and felt the miraculous movement within. Was this innocent child to relinquish its tenuous hold on life before it was even born?

She knelt and prayed that Ruth would rescue her from the darkness. "Please, Ruth, don't desert me,'' she whispered.

But it was no use, she could not go on. The first seeds of doubt were sown, and were blossoming into fears that sapped her faith.

11
Lieutenant Michael Perryman

Monday, March 5, 1787

The Surgeon General of the First Fleet, Dr. John White, glanced at the satchel containing the Admiralty dispatches to the Commander in Chief of Plymouth Port as he waited in the coach for his friend, Lieutenant Michael Perryman.

"Damn the weather," he muttered, listening to the rain thundering on the coach roof. It had been like this ever since he and Michael had left their homes in Worthing. The journey to Plymouth was tedious enough, with interminable delays at the turnpikes and the constant threat of highwaymen, but in bad weather it would be intolerable. Thank God he had Michael for company!

He peered out the window at his friend's tall athletic frame as he pounded on the front door of an elegant three-story Grosvenor Square residence. He had known Michael since childhood and was delighted to have talked him into coming on the expedition. But because Michael had applied so late, he had been unable to obtain a posting on either the flagship, *Sirius*, or its tender, *Supply*, although he was a naval officer. Eventually, after much string pulling he had been accepted as a Lieutenant of Marines on board *Friendship*.

"No luck?" he enquired as Michael leapt into the coach.

Michael thumped the roof to let the driver know that they were ready to leave. "I do not understand it, John. Every time I've called since returning to England, the place has been deserted. I will write to her as soon as I reach Plymouth. I must see her before I sail."

John grinned. "Another of your conquests, old chap?"

Michael laughed and set his shoulders more comfortably against the back of the seat as the coach lurched out of the square. "No, the lady and I have never met."

Lucy glanced apprehensively at the jury as they came back into the courtroom through a side door and resumed their seats. Three judges sat on a high bench directly opposite. Behind them, the paneling was draped in crimson cloth and above was a carved wooden canopy displaying the Royal Coat of Arms. Suspended from the canopy was a gold-handled "Sword of Justice" in an ornamental scabbard.

Behind Lucy three large windows overlooked the grim walls of Newgate, and beneath the windows sat members of the public. Mr. Porter stood at the rear of the room, but neither Ruth nor Julie Ryan were present.

The trial had gone badly. It was useless to pretend otherwise. The two Bow-street runners and Ruth's manservant had given verbal evidence against her, but Ruth's sworn statement, read by the Clerk of Arraigns, had done the most damage. In it, Richard had been depicted as a pillar of the community; a dutiful son, an affectionate brother, and a loving fiancé.

Lucy stared at the stony countenances of the judges. When she had tried to tell them that Richard had raped her, they had ordered her to be quiet. Shocked, she had lapsed into silence and withdrawn from the travesty taking place around her.

A hush fell over the shadowy courtroom. The Clerk of Arraigns collected the verdict sheet from the jury and handed it to the Chief Judge. The Chief Judge said in a voice that reached to every corner of the room, "Lucy Gamble, the jury finds that, on the night of Monday the sixteenth of October 1786, at eleven o'clock, you did, with malice and premeditation, murder Richard Newport. . . ."

Lucy's heart sank. Guilty. The last glimmer of hope gone. She had prayed and trusted that Ruth would help her and now, she was on the brink of death.

The Clerk of Arraigns rose from his seat beneath the bench. "Lucy Gamble, do you have anything to urge why sentence of death should not be passed upon you?"

I am glad I killed Richard, Lucy thought, *and I shall not be put to death because of it. Somehow, I must persuade these judges to let me live.*

She addressed them in a voice husky with emotion. "Your Honors, I wish to plead 'benefit of the clergy.' "

The Chief Judge stared at the beautiful young woman before him. "Can you recite a passage from the Scriptures, Lucy Gamble?"

"Yes, Your Honor."

"Proceed."

With tears streaming from her eyes, Lucy recited the passage she had memorized.

"Seeing the multitudes Jesus went up into the mountain

46

and when he was set his disciples came unto him and he opened his mouth and taught them saying—

Blessed are the poor in spirit: for theirs is the Kingdom of Heaven.

Blessed are they that mourn: for they shall be comforted.

Blessed are the meek: for they shall inherit the earth.

Blessed are they which do hunger and thirst after righteousness: for they shall be filled.

Blessed are the merciful: for they shall obtain mercy.

Blessed are the pure in heart: for they shall see God.

Blessed are the peacemakers: for they shall be called the children of God.

Blessed are they which are persecuted for righteousness' sake: for theirs is the kingdom of heaven.''

She looked beseechingly at the Chief Judge. "Please, your Honor, I humbly beg Your Honor, have mercy upon my unborn child. Do not deny it the right to life."

The Chief Judge looked toward the prison matron seated at the rear of the dock. "Is this woman in the family way, Matron?"

"Yes, Your Honor," the matron replied.

The Chief Judge conferred with his two learned colleagues, then called for order. "Lucy Gamble, the death penalty is waived. You are sentenced to transportation for life. May God have mercy on you."

"So, the bitch did not change her statement," Frances said sympathetically when Lucy returned to Waterman's.

Lucy's mouth set in a hard line. "Of course not. What a trusting fool I've been. Father would be ashamed of me." She turned to Beth. "Can you get an urgent message to Bill Narmo?"

Beth nodded eagerly. "What do you want him to do?"

Lucy worked two pearl buttons loose from the hem of her cloak. "Have him bring some paper and writing implements to the visitors' lodge as soon as he can. I have a relative who may yet be alive. I'll write to him. Perhaps *he* will help."

PART TWO
The Setting Forth

12
The Gathering Darkness

Saturday, April 28, 1787

The daffodils on the perimeter of the wide, flat lawn nodded to the jonquils growing in profusion on either side of the carriageway; waterfowl and deer drank from the clear waters of the Roman Lake on the edge of the lawn, and ducks glided to and fro between the water lilies. The air vibrated with the chirping of a thousand birds and the earth pulsated with new life, but the miracle of spring was lost on Sir Michael. He sat at his desk in the library clutching a letter to his breast.

Thank God, Faith had not seen it! Hearing her voice outside the door, he hurriedly shoved the letter into the desk.

"Good morning, Grandfather," Faith greeted him cheerfully. He looked a little flushed this morning, but since their return from Scotland his health had steadily improved. She hoped he would soon be well enough to resume some of his duties around the estate. At present, matters were entirely in her hands and the responsibility weighed heavily on her. She had woken up this morning with an uncanny feeling that she could not delay going to London any longer.

"Good morning, my dear," said Sir Michael. "What have you there?"

"A letter from Captain Phillip. Would you like me to read it?"

"Yes, indeed."

After the usual greetings, Phillip spoke glowingly of the Surgeon General, then he turned to the Fleet's impending departure.

"I am receiving daily orders to sail and that is my fervent desire, but I will not leave until I'm certain all the necessaries for the voyage have been supplied. As yet, none of the clothing I issued to the women on board *Lady Penrhyn* has been replaced, nor has any flour been received for the garrison, and there are other things too numerous to mention. If the authorities had their way, I am sure both the garrison and the convicts would be sent to the extremity of the globe in the same way as if they were going on a mere six weeks' passage to America.

"I have made myself unpopular with my constant complaints and never-ending requests, but unless I receive what I have asked for I fear I shall lose half the garrison and convicts on the voyage.

"I shall be arriving at Portsmouth on Monday the seventh of May to take command of the Fleet, and would be delighted to meet you and Faith at the George Hotel sometime before noon, if that is convenient. Afterward, we shall lunch on board the flagship, then tour the Fleet.

"I remain your most sincere well wisher, Arthur."

Faith's eyes danced with excitement. "The seventh is only nine days away, Grandfather. Oh, I am looking forward to it."

Sir Michael chuckled. "And I, my dear."

Hoping to take advantage of his good humor, Faith leaned forward. "When we return from Portsmouth, I would like to spend a few days in London on private business."

Sir Michael pursed his lips with displeasure. "Out of the question, Faith. The Fleet will be sailing soon. Surely you don't intend to miss that historic occasion because of some matter that could doubtless be handled by our London agents?"

"I said it was a personal matter," she replied softly.

Sir Michael raised his eyebrows. "What kind of personal matter, may I ask?"

She returned his stare unflinchingly. "I'd rather keep that to myself for the moment, Grandfather. I shall leave as soon as convenient to you, after we return from Portsmouth."

He drummed his fingers on the arms of the chair. "It will not be convenient to me *ever!* You will not desert me and run off to London on some foolish fancy!"

"I will only be away five days. Surely you can manage without me for so short a time. Kenneth will see to your personal needs, and the overseers and servants will look after the rest. Please understand . . . this is very important to me.''

He pummeled the chair with his fists, his face turning purple and his lips twitching alarmingly. ''I will not—I will not have it, I tell you! I will not tolerate such disloyalty!''

Shaken by the sight of him, Faith capitulated. ''Please, please do not upset yourself, Grandfather. It will be as you wish. Stay calm while I bring your medicine.''

As she sped from the room he took out the letter and tore it to shreds. So, she had not given the thing up yet. That was unfortunate. Still, he was certain he could handle her. He would continue to play the invalid, and keep her at his beck and call. With her mind thus occupied, she would have little time to think about the other.

Friday, May 4, 1787

Frances Hart elbowed her way through the crowd outside the Keeper's office and scanned the latest transportation notices. When she spied the names, she squinted, blinked, then whooped with joy, before racing away in search of Lucy and Beth.

She found them crouching in the passageway outside Waterman's examining a jar of colored threads. ''You'll never guess,'' she cried, dragging them to their feet. ''You'll never guess, not in a thousand years you won't!''

''We won't if you don't tell us—and that's a fact,'' Beth said cheekily.

''Lucy's name is on the transportation notice. She leaves for Portsmouth in the morning.''

Lucy and Beth looked at each other with dismay.

''But that's not the end of it,'' Frances gasped, ''not by any means. I'm down for the same ship . . . and so is Beth!''

Beth flung her arms around Lucy. Together! Was such a miracle possible? ''Are—are you sure, Frances?'' she asked. ''You wouldn't play a trick on me, would you? My name too?''

Frances swung her off her feet. ''I'm sure. Your name was first. Elizabeth Dudgeon, Lucy Gamble, and Frances Hart, all to be embarked on board the transporter *Friendship*.''

Lucy's spirits soared. ''*Friendship* is a fine name for a ship,'' she said. ''Perhaps our fortunes are changing.''

''Perhaps,'' Frances beamed. ''But enough standing around. There's work to be done—and precious little time to do it in. Where we're going, there'll be no turnkeys to bribe and no

50

friends like Bill Narmo to call on. We'd best scavenge all we can before getting out of this place!"

Monday, May 7, 1787

Faith stood on Point Beach with Sir Michael and Captain Phillip gazing over the peaceful waters of the Solent. Close by was the Round Tower—the sturdy fifteenth-century fortification guarded the entrance to Portsmouth Harbor—and immediately behind was the green-slimed seawall over which she could just see the convicts being herded along the road toward the wharf.

As Faith focused on the wharf, something strange happened to her perception of time, and in the vast space that opened between one second and another her eyes were drawn, like a magnet, to a guard boat moving with incredible slowness away from the wharf. With infinitesimal care, her eyes searched the grimy faces of the occupants until they came to rest on one at the rear. Faith's blood turned cold in her veins and in that split second, her life altered immeasurably. She had glimpsed her destiny.

Gathering her skirts over one arm, she ran to the water's edge, calling, calling. But the shrill cries of the gulls diving and swooping overhead drowned her voice. Heedless of the shouts of the onlookers, she plunged into the water and began swimming frantically after the guard boat.

Lucy watched the distance between her and the country of her birth widen with mixed feelings. Bitter beyond measure at Ruth's abandonment of her, she was, nevertheless, relieved to have quit the hellish confines of Newgate, and was looking forward to the long sea voyage ahead.

As the boat chopped through the swell, she pushed the hood back from her face and sniffed the salt air. It was wonderful to be at sea again. She swept the surface of the water with an expert eye; wind setting in from the north, tide on the turn . . .

Suddenly, a head bobbed up between two waves. Her senses reeled. The face was *hers!*

She leapt up and would have thrown herself over the side of the boat but two burly guards wrestled her roughly to the boards.

Faith floundered in the water trying desperately to keep afloat, but her garments kept drawing her under. Then, strong arms went around her and pulled her back to shore.

When the two officers dragged her from the water, Faith tore free and stumbled up the beach to Sir Michael. "I saw her, Grandfather," she gasped. "The woman of my vision. She's in that boat. Quickly, do something. We must go after her."

Sir Michael stared at her as if she was a stranger.

"Control yourself, Faith," he said harshly. "You are making a spectacle of yourself in front of Captain Phillip and his officers. Go to the coach this instant!"

"Grandfather," she sobbed brokenly, "oh, Grandfather, you *must* believe me. I saw her—the woman of my vision—she is in that boat. Please, please help us . . . I beg you!"

Sir Michael signaled the officers and Faith realized at last that he would do nothing. Panic-stricken, she ran along the beach toward the wharf but the officers soon overtook her and, as they bore her away, she saw the guard boat round Gilkicker Point and disappear into the gathering darkness.

13
The Friendship

Sunday, May 13, 1787

At three o'clock in the morning, Commodore Phillip gave the order for the ships of the Fleet to weigh anchor.

At four o'clock, as the first faint glimmers of light stole across the gray, misty waters of the Solent, the escort *Hyaena* came alongside the flagship.

At six o'clock, the signal cannon fired, and the First Fleet to New South Wales was underway.

Lieutenant Michael Perryman, standing on *Friendship*'s poop deck in company with Lieutenants Faddy and Clark, thought what a magnificent sight the tall ships made as they cut through the swell with bows dipping and sails billowing.

Lieutenant Ralph Clark clicked his tongue with disgust as he watched the crew going about their tasks. He was amazed they could work efficiently—most were still drunk from last night's excesses. "I am sure the crew have been with those whores below," he told the others. "The bulkhead between their quarters and the women's prison looks as if it's been tampered with. I told the sawyer to make it more secure but when he attempted it, some of the rascals actually threatened him. Mark my words, that lot will be as troublesome as the felons if we don't make a few examples."

"If you try to keep the crew and the women apart for the entire voyage, Ralph, you will grow old before your time," Michael said.

Faddy laughed. He liked Perryman's easy-going nature and ready wit, but found the deeply religious Ralph less amiable. "Yes, Ralph, if that's your tack, I suggest you also keep a sharp watch on the marines. Several privates were loitering around the women's hatchway last night."

Ralph glanced at the hatch six feet below him on the quarter-deck. It was left open during the day to allow fresh air into the women's prison, but at night the access ladder was removed and the hatch secured by crossbars. Well, the hatch might be impregnable, but there were other ways of getting at the whores. Their prison was directly above an aft storage hold, and adjoined a companionway that ran from stern to bow along the port side of the ship.

Dr. Thomas Arndell and the senior marine officer on board, Captain James Meredith, clambered out of the women's hatch and joined the other men on the poop deck.

"How are they below?" asked Michael.

"Quiet, at present," Tom Arndell replied, "but that won't last long. Before this day is out most will be suffering from seasickness. The stench is intolerable. I've suggested that we bring them up there in relays." He pointed to a small exercise enclosure that had been erected beside the women's hatch. Forward, directly behind the bow, a similar enclosure had been built for the male convicts.

Lucy, Beth, and Frances huddled together in a bunk at the rear of the women's prison. Because they had been last to come aboard they had been allotted the bunk farthest from the hatch—the only source of light.

Sixteen feet wide and eighteen feet long, the prison contained eight bunks (four on either side) that were separated from one another by wooden partitions. The prison was enclosed on all sides by bulkheads, and the bulkhead across the front had loopholes on either side of the door through which the guards could view the prison and fire their muskets if necessary.

Three children were crammed into the prison along with the twenty-one women, Edward Parkinson, aged three; Nancy Pugh, five; and Susannah Holmes's eight-month-old baby, Henry.

Lucy clambered out of the bunk and grasped the beam at the front of the dividing partition. The sea was smacking and thudding against *Friendship*'s hull and she could tell by the way the ship rolled and pitched that it was heavily laden and sitting low in the water. Her eyes were now accustomed to the gloom and she saw clearly the plight of her companions who clung to whatever they could, trying to avoid being thrown from their bunks.

Lucy remembered how she had been thrown to the deck of the guard boat six days earlier when she had tried to jump overboard. She had questioned Beth and Frances but they had seen nothing unusual in the water. Had her eyes deceived her? They must have! But the woman's face had been so clear, and the eyes—*her* eyes—seemed so desperate. She shook her head as she had done a hundred times since the incident.

"No, it is not possible," she murmured. Yet, the more she concentrated on that face, the clearer it became. She wanted to reach out beyond this realm, into another dimension and touch . . . what?

Friendship lunged forward, slid sideways down a wave, smacked hard on the bottom and shuddered violently before righting herself. Several women groaned and Sarah McCormick leant out of a front bunk and vomited into the slops bucket. Some of the women on board *Friendship* made Maria Hamilton seem like a vestal virgin by comparison, Lucy thought, casting an uneasy glance at the bulkhead behind her. The first night she had come on board, six crewmen had broken through that bulkhead and a huge brute named Tom Lewis had grabbed her in a slobbering embrace.

Lucy began to sweat and the bloodred sea rose before her as she thought of Lewis's loathsome hands moving over her body. But, thank God, a moment later Beth had come to her rescue.

"Well lad," she had cried, stepping between them. "It's come to a pretty pass that you choose to take your pleasure on some doxy far-gone with child when there are some of us here as have bags of tricks to show you!'' She had stood on tiptoe and whispered something in his ear. Roaring with laughter, Lewis had carried her through the bulkhead into the crew's quarters.

Lucy wiped the beads of sweat from her face. Every night since then, she had hidden at the back of the bunk while Beth went with Tom Lewis. Words could never express her gratitude to Beth. How could she ever repay her?

The ship plunged into another wave and Beth moaned pitifully. ''Come, Bethy,'' Lucy said gently, pulling her up and leaning against her in an effort to balance the ship's motion with her own body. ''Try to stand until you acquire your sea legs.''

''Oh, Lucy, I wish I was dead, I do,'' Beth wailed. ''This blasted ship keeps falling on its side. It'll sink, and . . . and we'll all be drowned. Oh, oh, my head's thumping so much I can't breathe proper. Oh, out my way, I'm going to be sick!''

Pandemonium broke out in the prison. All around her women screamed with terror but Lucy's spirits soared as *Friendship* shook free of a wave's grasp and leapt skyward like a wild, prancing steed.

How she longed to be up on deck watching the white foam breaking over the bow and feeling the sting of the salt spray in her eyes, but even down here in the darkness she could feel the awesome power of the sea. She and her father had been so happy when they had gone sailing together. *I am back,* she told herself, *back where I've longed to be, with the ship, and the sails, and the salt, and the spray, and the sea.*

14

Dr. Thomas Arndell

Wednesday, May 16, 1787

Dr. Arndell waited beside the hatch while the guards lowered the ladder into the prison.

The stench hit him as he climbed down the ladder into the darkness. It reminded him of an animal's lair. Motioning the guard to precede him with the lantern, Tom began his rounds.

Everyone was seasick and he could do little for them except

give water or wine to those who would take it. He moved along the bunks checking each woman in turn until he reached Jane Parkinson, Edward's mother.

She was extremely dehydrated and running a high fever. He had noticed her dry, racking cough and wasted body the moment she had come aboard and he was almost certain she had consumption. He raised her head and trickled a little wine down her throat. "Take your time . . .."

"Excuse me, Dr. Arndell," said a soft voice behind him.

He glanced over his shoulder and saw a young, pregnant woman balancing Parkinson's son on her hip. Despite the dim light, he could tell she was a real beauty. Even more surprisingly, she appeared completely unaffected by seasickness. The child lay against her, contentedly sucking his thumb.

"Forgive me for bothering you," Lucy continued politely, "but Edward is much improved and I thought, with your permission, I would take him up top and cook him buttered peas."

Flabbergasted, Tom could only stare. Her gentle manner and cultured tones were the last thing he had expected to find in this pesthole.

"Nancy Pugh is still too ill to eat," Lucy went on, "but the fresh air helps her so I thought, perhaps, I might take her up on deck also."

Recovering his composure, Tom hastened to reply. "Certainly you may take the children up, but the lad must begin with something lighter than peas. I'll give you some portable soup. Wait by the ladder and when I've finished here, I will carry the girl up top for you."

The rest of his round passed without incident but when Tom took little Nancy in his arms and passed Marg Hall's bunk, Marg gave a long obscene catcall. "Fancy your chances with the doctor do you, Gamble? You best mind your manners, girl, or you'll soon have another bastard in your belly!"

Ignoring the barrage of obscenities that followed, Lucy took a tighter hold on Edward and climbed the ladder to the deck. Every day she got stronger. The sea breeze and the hours of sunlight had worked wonders, as had the daily baths in the seawater barrel.

She followed Tom Arndell into the enclosure, set Edward down and reached for Nancy. As she did, her hand brushed against Tom's. She shuddered with revulsion and stepped back so quickly she almost tripped over Edward.

Tom could see her clearly now. What a beauty she was with

56

high cheekbones, lovely long lashes, and dark, arching brows. Her huge eyes gleamed green as emeralds. "Who are you?" he asked.

"My name is Lucy Gamble."

"Well then, Lucy Gamble, I'd best fetch that soup for the lad." He reached out and ran his hand down her cheek. "And while I am about it, I shall get you some salve. Washing in salt water soon dries the skin."

Lucy's cheek burned from his touch and snakes of nausea writhed in her stomach. "Take no notice of those women below, sir," she said icily, "I seek no favor from you. All I ask is your professional help with these poor children, the innocent victims of our magnificent judicial system. Do I make myself clear?"

"Perfectly," Tom replied stiffly. He turned on his heel, ascended the ladder to the poop and stomped across the deck to the officers' cuddy. Like a damned fool he had allowed a common felon to get the better of him!

He paused at the door and frowned. No, Lucy Gamble was a lady born, anyone could see that. He shook his head in puzzlement. How had she come to be on board a convict transporter?

He entered the cabin, greeted the other officers and rummaged through his medicine chest for a large jar of salve. Since his wife had died, grief had been his constant companion and work his only solace. With ninety-seven convicts, forty-five marines, nineteen crew, four marine wives, and five children to care for, his days were extremely busy, But Lucy Gamble was an enigma. "I shall find out all I can about her," he decided. "She seemed utterly terrified when I laid hands on her. God knows the horrors she has endured. . . ."

"What are you mumbling about, Tom?" asked Michael Perryman.

Tom grinned. "I have just discovered a divine goddess down in the women's prison."

The others roared with laughter.

15

May at Sea

May 28, 1787

"What can you tell me about the state of health aboard the other transporters, John?" Tom Arndell asked as the officers of *Friendship* entertained the Fleet's Agent, John Shortland.

Shortland was one of Phillip's most trusted officers, and had come on board earlier in the day to compile an inventory of convicts' trades and occupations. Because he was constantly going back and forth between the vessels he had become the eyes and ears of the Fleet.

"Our first official accident occurred when we were abreast of Falmouth," John Shortland replied with a grin. "A marine corporal on board *Charlotte* was wounded in the ankle while laying down a loaded musket. His bones turned the ball, which passed through a cask of beef and killed two geese mating on the other side! But how are things aboard *Friendship*? Are you all in good health?"

Tom nodded. "Yes, except for one or two chronically ill among the convicts." He chuckled. "Mind you, I was quite concerned about Lieutenant Clark for a time. I've never seen such a severe case of seasickness! But from the amount of pudding he's eaten tonight, he appears to be quite recovered."

Ignoring Tom's jest, Ralph fixed saucerlike eyes on Shortland. "I was taken aback by Commodore Phillip's order that the convicts be released from their irons and allowed the freedom of the decks during daylight hours. We have fifty-eight *Mercury* mutineers on board this vessel, sir, and most are complete scoundrels. Is it wise to allow such villains to roam free?"

The other officers shuffled with embarrassment at Ralph's indiscretion and Michael quickly changed the subject. "How is my friend the Surgeon General?"

"He sends you his compliments," Shortland answered. "And he bids me to tell you that although his health is good, his mood is melancholy."

"John, melancholy?" Michael raised surprised eyebrows.

Shortland's countenance split in a wide smile. "It appears he is wasting away for want of feminine companionship."

Michael's mouth twitched. "I commiserate with the poor chap. However, the doctor on this ship has had no such misfortune. Tom has found himself a dazzling goddess down in the women's prison."

"Really? From what I've seen of the damsels of the Fleet, he must have had the devil's own task locating her. Go on, old chap, I'm all ears!"

Michael's grin widened. "As my duties are taken up with supervising the male convicts I've not yet viewed this divine creature but Tom assures us she is the epitome of grace and beauty."

Tom laughed. "Pay him no need, John. As usual, he exaggerates. The woman in question was the only female aboard who did not succumb to seasickness and she has been of invaluable assistance to me in the management of the children. However, she *is* a great beauty."

"No doubt, Tom's tastes run to obscene language and pungent armpits," Captain Meredith joked as he refilled their glasses.

"As a matter of fact, she is very well spoken," said Tom. "And I vouch she has more intelligence in her little finger than you'd find in the entire collection of oafs here assembled." He rose, shouting to make himself heard above the laughter. "Now, if you gentlemen will excuse me, I've rounds to do. And Michael, as you are anxious to view the young woman, why not accompany me below? I could use some assistance with the wine cask and the lantern."

"It seems I am outmaneuvered," Michael said ruefully and followed Tom out of the cuddy.

As he watched Tom giving wine to Jane Parkinson, Michael heard a scraping noise at the rear of the prison. He swung the lantern around and saw the bulkhead boards move aside and a crewman's head appear. Then the man ducked back and the boards were quickly replaced.

Michael cursed loudly. "The damned crew have broken through the bulkhead. As soon as you are finished, we'll have to report it."

"What's a handsome sport like you doing that for, Lieutenant?" came a coarse voice from up front. "Here, hop in the bunk and I'll give you something that'll keep your cock limp for a week!"

Shrieks and catcalls rang out from all around.

"I have done what I can for Parkinson. Let's go," Tom muttered.

As the two men clambered up the ladder, Marg Hall fired a parting shot. "I didn't offer you my services, doctor. I hear Gamble's been doing plenty of that!"

"Be quiet, you disgusting woman, or I will have you stapled to the deck," Tom growled.

Later that evening, as Michael lay in his bunk listening to Faddy's snores harmonizing with the creaking of the ship's timbers, his mind drifted back over the events of the last few hours. Was Tom more involved with his convict than he cared to admit? He had certainly jumped to her defence in the cuddy. And later, in the prison, when one of the women had disparaged her, he had been most vocal.

"Gamble has been doing plenty of that!" the woman had said. *Gamble.* He had noted the name instantly. He called few men "friend." John White was one, and James Gamble, commander of his former ship, *Seahawk,* had been another.

Memories of the hellish night James Gamble lost his life crowded in on Michael and he twisted restlessly in the bunk. It was almost a year ago now. Why had the house in Grosvenor Square been deserted? Why hadn't she answered his letters? He reached over the side of his bunk, opened the sea chest and rifled through it until he found the small leather jewel box. Its contents were not something he could have left behind in England in the care of a servant. They were a sacred trust, to be given to her personally.

16

The Island of Tenerife

Thursday, June 7, 1787

Balancing his purchases precariously on one shoulder, Michael ascended from the shore boat to the deck of *Friendship*. Today, the day of Corpus Christi, he and John White had gone ashore to watch the religious celebrations.

He was thoroughly enjoying Tenerife, where the Fleet had been made most welcome. The town of Laguna, four miles inland, was the island's capital, but Governor Marquis de Branceforte lived in Santa Cruz so he could be close to shipping.

Michael stowed away his purchases and quickly returned to the deck. It was stifling below and stank of stale bilge water, rotting timbers and unwashed bodies. He found a shady area below the poop on the port side and leaned over the rail. The day was extraordinarily hot and the fierce sun burned his neck as he looked at the scene.

No fortifications were visible on the high ground above the town but forts guarded either end of the bay and, along the shoreline, several circular detached outworks connected by low parapet walls had been erected. He saw only a few cannons, but he had heard that more than a hundred could be mounted in the event of attack.

Hearing childish laughter, Michael glanced over his shoulder. A convict woman was dousing two small children with buckets of seawater. He smiled. The Commodore's decision to allow well-behaved convicts freedom of the decks while in port had been a humane one and, so far, only one convict had absconded.

He glanced longingly at the mysterious, cloud-shrouded peak of Mount Tenerife and moistened his lips. Yesterday, a profusion of delicious ices, obtained from its frozen caverns, had been served for dessert at the viceregal banquet. He could have done with one now.

Screams brought his pleasant reverie to an abrupt end. The convict woman was struggling with a crewman but her efforts to free herself were hampered by her being great with child.

Michael strode forward, grabbed the sailor's jerkin and pulled him off her. "Get back to your duties or I shall put you on report to the mate."

The sailor, a huge brute with a black beard and mad yellow eyes, charged at him, cursing. Michael fended him off and shoved him against the rail. The sailor grabbed a mallet and rushed toward him swinging but Michael ducked, drove his shoulder into the man's belly, and heaved him overboard. The sailor hit the water with a tremendous splash and started swimming toward the bow.

"Up you get," Michael said to Lucy, placing an arm around her and hoisting her to her feet.

"Let me go!" she cried, springing away for him.

Michael had seen some beauties in his time but none to

compare with this one. He glanced at the front of her dress which had been torn open in the struggle exposing the creamy swell of her breasts. Desire rose like a hot wave within him.

"Take those bawling children back to the enclosure," he muttered. "And do something about your bodice. No wonder you are molested when you parade about the deck in such a fashion."

Lucy's emerald eyes narrowed dangerously.

"How *dare* you speak to me like that, you insolent scara-mouch. Do you imply I would encourage such scum?"

She had to be Gamble, he decided. Her speech was educated and she *was* divinely beautiful. "I do beg your pardon, ma'am," he replied mockingly.

Lucy struck him with such force, he staggered.

"Allow me to compliment you on the power of your blow," Michael said. "Was your father a pugilist perhaps?"

"My father was a Captain in His Majesty's Navy, sir, and if he were alive, he would whip you soundly for your insulting treatment of his daughter!" She lifted the still screaming Edward onto her hip, took Nancy's hand and started toward the enclosure.

Michael reached her in two strides and grabbed her arm. "What is your name?"

Revolted by his touch, Lucy tried to pull free. "Lucy—Lucy Gamble. Take your hands off me!"

Michael let her go, a look of profound shock spreading over his face. "My God, are you James Gamble's daughter?"

Lucy froze. "Yes," she breathed, setting Edward beside Nancy, "yes, I-I am. Who are you?"

This tattered beauty, heavy with child, James Gamble's daughter? Michael could hardly believe it. "I am Michael Perryman from *Seahawk*," he replied with difficulty.

The name had a familiar ring to it. Lucy searched her mind. "Yes, of course, Lieutenant Perryman, my father often mentioned you before he . . . before he . . ." She bit her lip and tears rolled down her cheeks.

He reached out and squeezed her shoulders. "Lucy, please don't cry."

She stepped backward, her eyes imploring. "Don't touch me . . ."

"But what are you doing on this ship, Lucy?"

She shook her head. "I-I truly don't know. It has all been such a nightmare." The color drained from her face and she clutched her side. "I-I think I shall have to sit down. This has been rather . . . a . . . shock." Her legs buckled and she fell forward, striking her head on the deck.

He knelt beside her and caught her in his arms. "Fetch Dr. Arndell from the cuddy," he shouted to the poop guard. "and you," he said to Frances, who had rushed to Lucy's side, "take these children to the enclosure and quiet them."

Frances stood her ground. "She may need my help."

"Very well," Michael relented. "But you others get about your business . . . and someone take charge of these children."

Ralph jumped to his feet in horror as Michael and Tom trooped into the cuddy, followed by Frances carrying Lucy. "Have you taken leave of your senses, men?" he cried. "Get these baggages out of here at once!"

"This pregnant woman is injured," Tom said coldly. "Would you have me leave her out in the blazing sun? Or perhaps your Christianity dictates that I send her below where the air is so foul she's like to expire on the spot?"

Ralph glared at him. "Captain Meredith will hear of this. It is a fine circumstance when an officer of His Majesty's Marines must make way for common whores!" Snatching up his bible, he stormed from the cuddy.

"He'll be as good as his word, Tom," said Michael. "He is probably even now keeping vigil at the poop rail, anxiously awaiting Meredith's return."

Tom shrugged and turned to Frances. "You'd best be on your way now. Gamble will return to the prison when she is recovered."

Frances placed a protective arm around Lucy. "This girl needs me with her."

"It is all right, Frances," Lucy said. "I am feeling much better."

After Frances departed, Lucy looked out the porthole at the steep cliff guarding the entrance to the bay. "I'll warrant you, that is Pinta De Nago, Michael. Father always took his marking from it and steering close in with it when entering this port."

"As did Commodore Phillip," Michael said, joining her by the porthole.

"Did you buoy *Friendship*'s cables with empty casks to prevent them fouling?" she asked.

Michael gazed into her emerald eyes and felt as if he was drowning. "Yes. But when we examined the bowers, there was no reason to suppose we lay on foul ground."

Lucy turned to Tom. "My head has stopped aching Dr. Arndell. Shall I try to stand?"

"If you like," said Tom. "But keep a firm grip on the chair. We don't want any more accidents. . . ."

Refusing Michael's offer of help. Lucy swung her legs to the floor and stood up. She took two steps, clutched her side and doubled over.

"What is the matter?" Tom asked anxiously.

She grimaced. "I-I have a sharp pain on my right side . . . and another low down in my back. Have I done an injury to my baby?"

Tom could not possibly know the answer to that without a thorough examination but because she was terrified of being handled, he decided to leave her alone and hope that all would be well.

"You probably shook yourself up a little when you fainted," he said. "Try to stay calm. Everything will be all right in a—"

"She fell heavily a few minutes before she fainted," Michael broke in, and explained Lucy's struggle with the sailor.

"I see," Tom said carefully. "Well it would help to know how far along you are."

"I have been in this condition since the sixteenth of October," Lucy answered stiffly.

Tom did a quick calculation. That meant her baby was due toward the end of July.

"Are you sure my baby is all right?" she asked again.

Tom smiled. "Please don't worry. Rest here a while longer, then I shall take you back to the prison." He turned to Michael. "May I have a word with you outside?"

"What the devil did you mean by that last remark?" Michael asked as soon as they were out of earshot. "She can't go back to the prison. She is not one of them. Her father was my former commander. He died in action last year." Michael groaned and began pacing the deck. "I've never met Lucy before today, but James was always talking about her. He adored her. It was 'my Lucy did this' and 'if my Lucy saw that.' He was so proud of her. God, what am I to do, Tom? I can't send her back to that pesthole!"

"I know how you feel, old chap," Tom commiserated, "but we don't have any choice. Take my advice and resign yourself to it. It will go easier on her if you do. She is bound to suffer reprisals at the hands of those women if we single her out for special favor. You heard them the other night."

Michael watched the sun setting fire to the sea as it sank below the horizon. "There must be *something* I can do."

Tom patted his shoulder. "There is, I have tried to supplement her diet with nuts, fresh fruit, and milk, but she gives everything to the children. And I have told her repeatedly not to lift the young lad but she takes no notice of me. If she continues to do so, I'll not answer for the consequences. Will you speak to her?"

"Yes, of course," said Michael. "But couldn't we isolate her from the other women because of her present condition?"

Tom admired his persistence. "As a matter of fact, I have petitioned Francis Walton for a small area 'tween decks to use as an infirmary."

Michael's countenance brightened. "That is a good idea. When will you know?"

Tom sighed. "You can't hurry Walton. If I pushed him, the cantankerous old rumsot would back away from the whole idea. We must be patient, Michael."

Michael stared fixedly at the molten sun. *I have been in this condition since the sixteenth of October.* His soul cringed to think of the months of filth and degradation James Gamble's lovely daughter had endured. He turned to Tom. "What is this aversion she has to being touched by people?"

"Not 'people,' *men.* She was perfectly at ease with the convict woman who carried her into the cuddy. It may have something to do with the treatment she received in Newgate Prison. I looked through her papers, but learned little except that she was arrested last October and sentenced to life transportation for murder last March."

"Murder!" Michael groaned. "God, Tom, I feel as if I have stepped into a nightmare. Somehow I must get to the bottom of this. Can I count on your help?"

"Of course, Michael. It distresses me to see a woman of such character brought so low. But now we had best take her back to the prison. Sun's almost gone and Meredith and Faddy will be returning soon. It won't do our cause any good if they find her ensconced in their cuddy. You talk to her about her diet and I shall enlist the services of her friend to carry her below."

"How do you feel?" Michael asked as he entered the cuddy.

"Much improved, thank you," Lucy answered, turning away from the porthole.

He crossed to her side, folded his arms and looked down at her unsmilingly. "Tom tells me you will not accept food from him, Lucy. Is that true?"

She nodded and opened her mouth to explain. He motioned her to remain silent. "In the future, you'll eat and drink everything Tom and I give you. By supplementing your salt diet with fresh food, we'll be helping your baby. Do I have your word on it, Lucy?"

She looked down at her hands. "Yes."

"Tom also tells me that, despite his warnings, you continue to carry the convict children. Under no circumstances are you to do so again."

She pouted. "But little Edward will not understand."

"Little Edward will just have to make do until after your baby is born," he said firmly. "In the future you are to lift nothing heavier than a cup."

"I will do as you say," she sighed. "Thank you for your concern, Michael. But now I think I should go back to the prison, my friends will be worrying."

He crouched beside her and looked deeply into her eyes. "I hate the thought of returning you to that foul place, Lucy. But for the moment at least, we have no other option. However, you may be certain I'll not let the matter rest there. My God, if James saw you in this state he'd be insane with grief."

Lucy moaned softly and began to weep.

"Forgive me," Michael murmured, cursing himself for an insensitive fool. "I spoke too hastily and entirely without thought. Try to be strong. I shall think of something."

He patted her comfortingly on the shoulder but, feeling her flesh shrink beneath his touch, quickly withdrew his hand. "Enough of this gloom," he continued, forcing a cheerful note into his voice. "What an incredible piece of luck to have found ourselves on board the same ship. Such a miracle deserves a smile, surely."

She smiled through her tears. "Indeed it does! How did a Lieutenant of His Majesty's navy come to be a marine aboard a convict transporter?"

Michael entertained her with an account of his entry into the marine corps until Tom returned with Frances.

* * *

"What ails you?" Beth asked anxiously as Frances deposited Lucy on their bunk.

Lowering her voice to the Newgate whisper, Lucy explained what had happened.

"That's the greatest piece of good luck I've ever heard!" Beth exclaimed. "Now you'll have someone to protect you—and not before time. The bloomin' crew have been working on the bulkhead again and Marg Hall says they might break through tonight."

Lucy sprang up with alarm, screamed with pain and fell back in the bunk, clutching her side.

"Dear God, girl, have some sense!" Frances cried.

Lucy held her breath and prayed that the pain would stop. After what seemed like an eternity, it eased and she was able to straighten her legs and breathe normally again.

Susannah Holmes from the bunk opposite lent over Lucy, viewing her pale countenance with concern. "Anything I can do, Lucy?"

"No thank you, Susannah," Lucy sighed. "I brought this on myself. Dr. Arndell told me to rest, but when I heard that the crew intended coming through the bulkhead tonight I . . ."

Susannah flopped down on the bunk. "Don't worry about the crew, there are ways of dealing with them. Me and my bunkmate, Ann Baizley, don't want them bothering us either."

"Nor me," Frances said emphatically.

"Nor me," said Suzy Gought, a London crony of Beth's.

"Then, leave it to me," said Susannah. "I'll speak to my man, Henry, tomorrow. He'll make sure the crew get the message to leave us alone."

Beth shook her head doubtfully. "I don't think Tom Lewis will care what anyone says to him. He's a real bad one that . . . and he's got it on his mind to have Lucy."

Lucy shuddered and Frances hastily changed the subject. "Is Henry Cable the baby's father, Susannah?" She had noticed that the handsome, strapping convict enjoyed some influence with Lavell, Sidaway, and Best—the ringleaders of the *Mercury* mutiny.

Susannah smiled. " Yes. Henry and I met at Norwich Castle Prison in eighty-four, just after I got sent up. Henry and his dad were trounced by the magistrates the year before. Henry was lucky, he only got fourteen years, but his dad was strung up outside the castle the day I arrived. . . ."

*   *   *

It was almost midnight and *Friendship*'s decks were deserted except for the First Mate standing by the bower cable puffing his pipe, and six guards under arms at the fore and aft hatches.

Below, Lucy lay with her ear pressed against the bulkhead listening to the sound, like a dog gnawing a bone, the crew made as they worked on the boards. Keys rattled in the prison door and a few moments later a light floated through the darkness toward her.

Seeing her wet, strained face, Tom knelt beside her and motioned for Michael to hold the lantern closer. "What is it, my dear? Have the pains returned?"

Lucy placed a finger over her lips. "The crew are working on the bulkhead. I-I think they are nearly through. Don't let them take me, Dr. Arndell. I can't bear the thought of their hands on me. Oh, God, help me. If I lie here any longer listening . . ." Her voice trailed off.

"Damn them," Michael muttered, crouching beside Lucy. "Don't be afraid, Lucy. I will go to their quarters and stop this immediately. And I'll have a word with that scum who accosted you earlier today while I am about it. What is his name?"

Lucy stared up at him, her eyes glazed with terror. "No, don't single him out, please, you mustn't. Some of these women welcome the crew's attentions. They will know I told you." Her lips trembled. "But the thought of their hands moving over me . . . the thought of it." Her eyes were wide and staring, her voice rising. "I would go mad this time. I know it. I know it. I know it!"

"Hush, my dear," Tom soothed, "You have no need to worry. We will be discreet. We'll say we heard the crew when we came down on rounds—which is the truth."

Michael leant as close to her as he dared. "You are under our protection now, Lucy. Try to rest. We'll see you up on deck tomorrow as soon as we return from Santa Cruz."

A short time later, the scraping beside Lucy ceased abruptly. She sighed, closed her eyes and, as the last seconds of the day of Corpus Christi sped toward midnight, drifted into a deep, dreamless sleep.

Gigantic and majestic, like a beautiful multifaceted diamond, the mountain of ice rose glittering before her.

"Come," said the Guide, his deep voice rolling away in endless echoes, "we shall conquer it together."

Hand in hand they ascended the mountain, marveling at its great ice castles, the delicate beauty of its dawn-dipped snow-fields and the towering silence of its valleys.

"Prophecy!" cried a voice.

Standing on a hill beside a tall wooden cross was an old man clutching a broadsword. A thick mane of hair flew behind him in the wind, snakelike vines writhed around his body and his face, illuminated by the fiery glow of the craters, was fearful to behold.

"Who are you?" she asked.

"I am the Guardian," he answered and smote the snow at the foot of the cross. The snow melted and ran in steaming rivulets down the hill.

"What do you want of me?" she asked.

He pointed to the center of the cross that had her name carved on it.

"Prophecy!" cried the Guardian.

"Truth's word will stem the blood.
Strive then the tie to bind.
Duty the path to love—
Destiny, child, to find!"

Blood spurted from the center of the cross, mingled with the steaming rivulets of snow running down the hill and formed a river of blood that rushed along the floor of the valley.

"Time to move on," said the Guide.

"I'm afraid," she whispered, unable to tear her eyes away from the river.

"Do not be afraid," he answered, "I shall see you through."

He took her hand and led her past the river of blood, between the rotting carcasses, past the craters and pitfalls, beyond the Valley of Abaddon to a warm cave, wherein all was peace and tranquility.

"I have spent my life searching for you," the Guide murmured, taking her in his arms. "You are mine, and mine alone. Do you still deny it?"

"No . . ."

He kissed her and she moaned with pleasure. "Don't stop, go on . . . go on."

"Say it first," he whispered, "*Say* you love me."

The passion she had fought for so long to control, broke free. "I love you more than life itself," she cried.

He caught her fiercely against him but even as his mouth closed over hers, an intense pain tore through her and in its wake, rolling in from the furthermost reaches of her consciousness, came the faint, unmistakable cry of a baby.

She stiffened in his arms, sensing that the moment of their parting had arrived.

He crushed her more tightly against him. "You are not leaving me."

"From the beginning, we knew this moment would come," she wept. "I-I have my duty . . ."

The light left his eyes and he thrust her away. "Go, then," he said coldly, "and may your precious *duty* sustain us in the empty years ahead."

She ran to the rear of the cave, looking for the opening, but when she found it, she faltered. How could she leave him?

"Go!" cried a voice behind her.

She turned slowly but, even then, she turned before Time and there, in the space between one second and another, stood the Guardian.

"Where is the Guide?" she asked in despair.

"He is but a vision of another time," said the Guardian. "You have looked into the Mirror of Fate and seen reflections of the Future. Go! The Prophecy must be fulfilled!"

He smote the earth with his broadsword, Time moved forward, and she found herself running along a dark passageway that seemed to go on forever. . . .

Faith awoke with a start. A pain stabbed into her right side, and from somewhere close by came the cry of a baby.

She sat up. The baby cried again—a small, plaintive whimper. She blinked and stared around the shadowy room but there was no baby.

Perhaps the cry had come from outside?

She stumbled on leaden legs to the window. The world beyond trembled on the edge of dawn, glistening, gray, and deserted.

Confused, she returned to the bed and tried to collect her thoughts. Nothing came. Her mind was a drifting vacuum. Vague fragments continued to float in and out of her consciousness until, finally, a whole thought lodged in her mind.

She pulled the bell. After a while a key turned in a lock. Something jarred her memory—some question concerning the key—but the thought drifted away before she could grasp it.

"Margaret," she said to the maid, "pack some clothes for me, I am going to London."

"Yes, Miss Faith," said Margaret, and left, locking the door behind her.

Faith waited, breathing slow, deep, shivering breaths, in and out. "I shall get up soon," she decided. "When Margaret comes back, I'll do it."

Margaret returned with her grandfather and a great glass of honey brown laudanum.

"Back to bed with you," said her grandfather.

"No . . . I am going to London today." She rose with great effort and walked to the door.

Two servants barred her way, forced her back to the bed and held her down by her wrists and ankles. "Grandfather, please . . . this is not the way!" she screamed.

"Send for the doctor," she heard him say. "Send for the doctor, she is raving again."

Then came the laudanum and, after it, oblivion.

17

Lucy's Story

Friday, June 8, 1787

Michael and Tom returned to the ship early in the afternoon. They stowed their parcels below, then went back on deck with bags of figs and mulberries to distribute among the women and children. Afterward, they escorted Lucy to the shady section beneath the poop, seated her on a three-legged stool and ignoring the curious stares of those on deck, made themselves comfortable at her feet.

"Are you feeling better today, Lucy?"

"Very much better thank you, Dr. Arndell."

Tom smiled at her admiringly. She certainly did look better—splendid, in fact! Her luxurious hair hung down her back in glistening waves and her faultless complexion was beginning to tan. She returned his smile and and his heart missed a beat.

"By the looks of those sparkling eyes and winning smiles, Tom, I'd say Mistress Gamble is just fine." Michael took a tiny bottle of perfume from his pocket and dropped it in Lucy's lap.

With an exclamation of delight, Lucy snatched off the cap and passed the bottle under her nose. She dabbed a drop of the fragrant stuff behind each ear and gave Michael a melting smile. "I shall treasure it."

Not to be outdone, Tom handed her a tortoiseshell comb.

"Oh, Tom, how wonderful!"

Both men grinned from ear to ear. They had spent the greater part of the previous evening planning their method of approach. If they were to help her, it was imperative they gain her trust.

"Do you believe I was your father's friend?" Michael asked gently.

She stared back to him levelly. "Yes, Michael."

"And would you say that James trusted me?"

She nodded.

"Did you value your father's judgment?"

"Of course I did, Michael."

"Then will you trust me also, Lucy—and believe me when I tell you Tom and I intend to do all in our power to help you?"

"Yes," she murmured. "Thank you—thank you both, I am so grateful."

Michael gazed into her beautiful eyes. "It is not your gratitude we want, Lucy, it is information. To help you, we'll need to know how you came to be aboard this ship."

Lucy nodded but remained silent.

"What happened to your stepmother, Ruth?" he prompted.

The happiness faded from Lucy's eyes, but still she said nothing.

"Please tell us your story," he pleaded. "You are an intelligent girl. Surely you realize how important—"

"I do not know what I have become over the last eight months, Michael," she said coldly, "but, I assure you, I am no longer a 'girl.'"

She sighed. "Very well, I'll tell you how I came to be a convict aboard this ship." She began easily enough, but after a while her voice faltered.

"Last year, when Father went back to sea, Ruth invited Richard to stay with us at Grosvenor Square. He was a loathsome man—a besotted rake with bloodshot eyes and a horrible slobbering mouth." She shuddered violently as the memories came flooding back. "He made my life a misery. He would lie in wait for me: in the corridors, on the stairs, in the sitting room, in the drawing room, in the library. He'd press himself against me. And pinch me. And grab me. I hated him, but Ruth was so

72

happy to have him there, I did not know what to do . . ." She bit her lip and looked away.

"Go on," Michael said grimly, an intense rage at Richard Newport welling up within him.

"In the end, when I threatened to tell my father, Richard left me alone, but the day we received news of Father's death, he told Ruth that I had agreed to marry him. I was more than a little surprised that she accepted his lie so readily, for I had made no effort to disguise my dislike of him." She hung her head and fell silent.

"Go on, Lucy," Michael said gently.

She looked up at him and shook her head. "I can't."

His eyes held hers. "You must."

Lucy took a deep breath and the words tumbled out. "I decided to speak to him about it next morning but I never got the chance, because, you see, when he returned to the house that night, he came to my room and . . . and he raped me."

"Thank you for telling us, Lucy," Tom said gravely after she had finished. "I know how difficult this is for you, but take heart. Now we can set about returning you to your rightful place in society."

Lucy looked at Tom with hard eyes. "I have no illusions about returning to that world. There, I would be labeled 'murderess' and my baby 'bastard.' Better that I remain with my present company. These women do not care how my child was conceived, they have troubles enough of their own. And I have found good friends among them. But for Beth Dudgeon and Frances Hart, I'd not have survived my stay in Newgate. They kept me going when I had given up hope . . ."

Although Michael yearned to take her in his arms; reassure her, comfort her, carry her away to a safe harbor where he could keep her from harm he felt, instinctively, that if she was to be helped, a hard line must be taken.

He stood up and glared at her disapprovingly. "I can't believe my ears. Are these the words of James Gamble's daughter? Is this the spirit and courage of which he was so proud? If so, then I am glad he is dead!"

Stung to the core, Lucy bit back. "You could never understand how it felt to be left to rot in that unutterable prison by someone I had loved and trusted for nine years!"

"I can understand why Ruth behaved as she did, Lucy. She is a weak, stupid woman who has blinded herself to the fact that her brother was the scum of the earth, and she is probably sitting in your father's house right now, congratulating herself on how

73

easy it was to get rid of you. What I cannot understand is *your* spineless behavior. God, you are a disappointment!''

Lucy swung at him but he caught her fist in midflight.

"What would you have me do?"

"To begin with, I do not expect you to lie in that stinking prison meekly accepting your fate."

Tom slipped away unnoticed, immensely pleased with the way things were progressing. Lucy had plenty of fight left!

"Are you implying that I am weak and stupid like Ruth?" Lucy cried.

"What else can I think when you say it's 'better that I remain with my present company'? My God, I am surprised your father doesn't leap out of the ocean and strike you down where you stand. That you should condemn his grandchild to such a hellish life would be beyond his comprehension."

"How dare you bring my father into this! If you had an ounce of sense in that arrogant head of yours, you'd realize I have no intention of letting Ruth get away with what she has done."

The anger and anxiety flowed out of Michael. "That is what I've been waiting to hear, Lucy. Fight the whole damned world if you have to, but never give up." He lowered his voice. "Now, calm yourself. I have something very special to give you that, I hope, will help you remember who you are."

He took her hand and began leading her toward the hatch. Still angry, she tore her hand free. "Let me go. Where do you think you are taking me?"

He glanced around him. "Down to my cabin. I think we have provided these people on deck with enough sport for one day."

Lucy looked at the curious faces of the onlookers and blushed with embarrassment. "Oh God, what must they think?"

Michael shrugged. "We can't control the judgments they make so why concern ourselves." He placed a hand under her elbow. "May I help you down the ladder, or do you insist on managing alone?"

She stepped back from him quickly. "I can manage alone, thank you."

He gave an exaggerated sigh. "Very well, stubborn. But I'll go first, lest you fall."

"Make yourself comfortable on that bunk near the porthole," Michael said as they entered his cabin.

He opened his sea chest, took out the small leather jewel box and handed it to her. "The box is mine, but its contents belong to you."

Lucy opened the box and drew in a shuddering breath. Inside, was the gold charm her father had worn around his neck. She turned the disc over and read the inscription aloud.

"To my beloved Jamie—Margaret 11/4/66."

She looked up at Michael with misty eyes. "Mother gave it to him on their first wedding anniversary—one week before I was born. It was the last time he ever saw her alive. That night he received word of his father's death and traveled to Bristol. When he returned to London he learned she had come into early labor and died giving birth to me . . ."

Michael took the charm and fastened it around Lucy's neck. "Now it is where it belongs. Your father entrusted it to me the night he died, Lucy. To him, you were a jewel beyond price. Promise me you'll never forget who you are again."

"I promise," she said kissing the charm tenderly. "Father was the anchor of my life. When he died, I lost my way. But with the return of this precious talisman, I have found the right path again. How can I ever thank you, Michael?"

"By trusting me, and believing that I am your friend," Michael answered huskily.

She smiled, and his heart did a somersault as two irresistible dimples appeared in her cheeks. "I do trust you, Michael. And I *know* you are my friend."

He drew up a chair opposite the bunk. "Let us consider what's best to be done. I could write to my lawyers in Worthing—ask them to put your case in the hands of a competent London barrister."

Lucy nodded gravely. "And perhaps they could contact the attorney who spoke to me a few days before my trial."

"Didn't Ruth engage a barrister for you?" Michael asked incredulously.

"No, she did not. I wrote to her several times, and the attorney promised to contact her, but nothing came of it."

Michael's eyes grew hard. "What is the attorney's name?"

"Stephen Porter."

He wrote the name at the front of his journal and returned to the chair. "We were fortunate today, those in authority were either ashore or visiting the other Fleet ships. In the future, though, we will have to be careful. I don't give a damn what the others think, but Tom is adamant that your cause will not be furthered by throwing discretion to the winds. So I shall accompany him on his nightly rounds. That way, you and I can talk without causing gossip."

He paused and looked at her with the utmost gravity. "But, I want your assurance, Lucy, that should an emergency arise you will seek me out wherever I am."

She shook her head. "I can't do that, Michael. You would be disciplined."

"Unless you give me your assurance, I'll take you off this ship tonight."

He had said it softly but Lucy saw that he meant it.

She sighed. "You have my assurance."

He checked his timepiece and rose. "We had better return to the deck."

"Would you tell me what happened to Father?" she asked as she eased herself off the bunk. "The official from the Admiralty was very brief."

"Yes, of course. But may we leave it for another time? The other officers will be returning soon."

"Whenever you can. There is no hurry," she murmured, feeling the niggling pain in her right side again.

Michael handed her two parcels. "While ashore, I took the liberty of purchasing some Joppa soap and a few undergarments. We can't alter your appearance too drastically, but no one will notice these. They are plain, I'm afraid, but be assured, they are the best quality."

She smiled her dimple smile. "Thank you, Michael. We women are in dire need of such treasures."

"That is unfortunate, Lucy, but I will not take kindly to you handing these around. You are too generous with those people."

She laughed, a lilting sound that made his nerve ends tingle. "Don't be such a snob, Michael. There are some very fine women on board this ship. If you took the time to—"

"Spare me the details," he pleaded, "lest I beggar myself trying to feed and clothe them all!"

18

The Fleet Leaves Tenerife

Saturday, June 9, 1787

All day the red sun blazed down on the ships in Tenerife Harbor, turning their "below decks" into fiery hells, alive with rats and vermin.

"I won't see the light of another day if I don't catch a whiff of fresh air," Suzy Gought gasped. "I'm taking Nancy up front to sniff through the loopholes." Suzy caught the child to her breast and staggered toward the front, followed by Lucy and the others, but when they reached Marg Hall's bunk, she barred their way.

"Where do you think you're off to?"

"You'll have to share the loopholes with us, Marg. There's no air at the back," Beth panted.

"Too bad, Dudgeon. This part of the prison belongs to us."

"If you won't share the loopholes, we'll take the open space before the door," Frances persisted.

"Get back to your bunk you miserable old cow. You're well past a turn with the lads, as anyone can see. It were probably you as lammed!"

"Leave Frances alone," Lucy snapped. "I informed on the crew. And, every time I hear them at the bulkhead, I shall report them—unless they promise to stay away from those of us who don't relish being raped!"

"Our lads aren't good enough for you, are they Gamble?" Marg sneered. "Your tastes run more to doctors and lieutenants. Well, for all your airs, you're no better than the rest of us, you bloody murderess. God Almighty! If I'd a knife, I'd run you through!"

"What good would that do, Marg?" Lucy said calmly. "If you and these other women want to be with the crew, that is fine. But my friends and I also have rights. Tell the men to leave us alone and I'll be silent." She held out her hand. "Do we have a bargain?"

"I don't make bargains with bloody informers," Marg said, knocking Lucy's hand aside. "Get back to your bunk, Gamble, and here's something to help you on your way!"

She punched Lucy in the stomach.

Screaming, Beth sprang at her, and the prison erupted.

"What in blazes caused this?" Captain Meredith asked the guards who, a few minutes before, had summoned him from a card game in the cuddy.

"Dunno, sir," answered the sergeant. "One moment they was talking and the next—well, see for yourself. The place is a bloomin' battlefield!"

Meredith slid his musket through the loophole and fired over the women's heads. In such a confined space, the explosion was deafening. The women dropped to the boards like stones, their angry cries becoming frightened whimpers.

As soon as the smoke cleared, Meredith and the guards unlocked the prison door and stepped inside. Marg, Elizabeth Pully, Beth, and another woman were still locked in battle, but the others lay spread-eagled on the boards.

Meredith pointed to the four combatants. "Iron them, and confine them below on bread and water."

At daybreak *Friendship,* in company with the other ten ships of the Fleet, slipped out to sea with the aid of a slight land breeze, but by noon the weather had become so hot, conditions below decks were intolerable.

The women at the front of the prison could at least sniff the tepid air filtering through the loopholes, but those at the rear were in a terrible state. Beth, ironed and suffering from seasickness, was too weak to lift her head, Frances sat propped against the bulkhead moaning, and Lucy lay slumped across the front of the bunk, one arm around a fretful Edward.

"How are you women bearing up?" Tom asked gruffly, as he poured water into their mugs.

" 'Tis difficult to breathe, Dr. Arndell," gasped Frances, raising the mug to her parched lips.

Seeing Michael's stricken countenance, Lucy hastened to change the subject. "Will we be able to see Great Canary Island tomorrow, Michael?"

He nodded, not trusting himself to speak.

"Any more pains?" Tom asked, shocked by Lucy's appearance. Her face was swollen and her wrists and ankles were twice their normal size.

When Lucy remained silent, Frances clicked her tongue with annoyance. "Lucy was punched in the stomach last night, and she's been feeling poorly ever since."

Tom handed Michael the water cask and knelt beside Lucy. "I must examine you tomorrow, my dear. Why don't you bring Mrs. Hart along with you?" He looked at Frances. "You will make sure she comes to no harm, won't you, Mrs. Hart?"

"That I will," Frances replied emphatically, giving Lucy's shoulder a squeeze.

Lucy looked at Michael apprehensively.

"Think of your baby," he murmured.

She sighed. "Very well, if you think it necessary."

*　　*　　*

The next morning, after the examination she had dreaded was completed with a minimum of fuss, Lucy returned to the deck and stood at the quarter rail with the other women staring at Great Canary Island until a long, low whistle drew her attention. Gazing aloft, she spied Tom Lewis working on the shrouds. She walked quickly to the other side of the ship.

She heard another low whistle and saw Tom Lewis standing outside the enclosure beckoning to her.

"Why don't you give the great hairy brute a taste of your tongue, Lucy?" Suzy Gought suggested, making an obscene gesture at Lewis. "It does no good to show him a fearful face."

Lucy sighed. "You are right, Suzy." But it was already too late. Lewis had scented her fear and, like a predator, was stalking her. She waited with the others until he left, then she climbed awkwardly down the ladder to check on Beth, who was still very seasick.

"You can have this life at sea," Beth moaned. "I'll never get me insides used to it. Give me the streets of London any day. Oh, there it goes again, don't it ever stop?"

"If only I could take you up on deck, so you could look up at the sky," Lucy murmured. "Father said it helped if one could not see the roll and pitch of the ship . . ."

"Fat chance, Lucy! Lieutenant Clark swears that us four troublemakers will stay in irons for the whole voyage!"

"Don't take any notice of him. Dr. Arndell said this morning he will not rest until you and the others are released."

Beth struggled to a sitting position and looked at Lucy anxiously. "What did the doctor say about your baby?"

Lucy sighed. "To stay off my feet and to rest at every opportunity."

"Then what are you climbing down here for? I'm all right."

Lucy took her tortoiseshell comb from the hem of her skirt and began combing Beth's tousled curls. "Stop flying to my defence, Bethy. I am not your responsibility. In the future, look after yourself."

Beth's blue eyes filled with tears. "You're my only family, Lucy. I'd die if anything happened to you. I know how to deal with women like that lot up front—you don't. As for taking a turn with a chap every now and then, that means nought to me. It's my trade. I don't enjoy it, mind. But it's better than starving."

She inclined her head toward the bulkhead. "Them in there aren't no better or worse than any others. Except—" Her eyes widened, and she clutched Lucy's arm. "You keep away from Lewis. He's got his sights on you, he has!"

19

The Death of James Gamble

Tuesday, June 19, 1787

The officers of *Friendship* sat at the table in the cuddy, drinking and arguing. "If we don't release those four women soon, I'll not be responsible for the consequences!" Tom shouted. "They are alive with vermin and their wrists and ankles are covered with sores from the irons. Good God! They have been down there in the heat and darkness for ten days—isn't that punishment enough?"

Meredith leaned back in his chair and folded his arms. "Francis and I are loath to release them, Tom." He glanced toward the bushy-browed Shipmaster. "We believe those four are the ringleaders. If they are kept ironed the damned crew might be easier to handle."

"I wish all women were out of the ship," Ralph bleated. "And those four most of all. They are the greatest whores living. Craven, the carpenter, told me that they were the ones who first broke through the bulkhead to get at the crew."

"Perhaps you should tell Craven to fashion four coffins, Ralph," Michael said coldly, "since unless we release those women soon, I am convinced they will die."

Meredith sighed. "Oh, very well, you have my permission to release them."

Tom pressed home his advantage. "If the weather is fine tomorrow, James, could I have a detail of marines to explode gunpowder below? And perhaps the convicts could wash out their prisons in Oil of Tar and take their bedding up on deck to air. The rats, cockroaches, fleas, and lice have multiplied to plague proportions."

Meredith smiled broadly. "I'll say this for you, Tom, you are persistent. Michael, you are duty officer tomorrow. See to it, will you?"

"First thing in the morning," Michael said, rising to his feet. "Now, if you will excuse us, Tom and I are going below to release those four women."

"The humanity bug seems to have bitten Michael. He accompanies our good doctor on rounds every evening," Faddy commented after Michael and Tom had left the cuddy.

"His motives are hardly humane," Ralph said. "In my opinion, he is enamored of the convict, Gamble. He treated her most familiarly while we were in Tenerife. In fact, they caused quite a scene on the quarterdeck one day. Mark my words—"

"I spoke to Michael about that, Ralph," Meredith broke in, "and I am satisfied he is innocent of any impropriety. Gamble is the daughter of his former commanding officer, Captain James Gamble of H.M.S. *Seahawk.*"

Ralph's mouth gaped open. "Gamble's father a naval captain? How very odd. I've compiled a list of crimes from the convicts' papers, and Gamble is down for murder. In fact, she is the only one carrying that sentence."

"Gamble is not like the other convicts on board," said Meredith. "I would be interested to read her papers. Bring them to my cabin before you retire tonight, Ralph."

The next morning, as soon as Michael set the charges, he and Lucy slipped away to his cabin.

"We don't get many opportunities to speak in private," Lucy said as she eased her bulk through the narrow doorway.

"I hope we'll have more time together when we reach Rio de Janeiro," he said, making her comfortable on his bunk by propping pillows behind her back. "How do you feel today?" His heart contracted at the sight of her.

Since leaving Tenerife, Lucy had suffered considerably. The pains in her back and side never left her and she could no longer ascend the ladder to the deck without help.

"It is wonderful to stretch out and not bump into someone," she sighed, sliding down in the bunk so her head rested on the soft pillows.

"I wish I could bring you here more often, Lucy. But we must continue to be discreet. Captain Meredith could transfer me to another ship if he thought my conduct warranted it."

Noticing her alarmed look, he hastened to reassure her. "However, that is most unlikely. I told him about my friendship with your father, so that should forestall gossip."

The gunpowder exploded with a smacking thud that shook the ship.

"How good of Tom to cover for you this morning," Lucy said, when the sounds and vibrations had died away.

"He has great sympathy for your plight, Lucy. As a matter of fact, he's suggested that we petition the Commodore on your behalf."

He had drawn his chair close and, in the bright sunlight streaming through the porthole Lucy could see every detail of him—right down to the shiny metal buttons on his red uniform. His even features were clear and open: deep gray eyes with long lashes, dark blond hair, and a sensual mouth. She liked his mouth immensely. And she liked his self-assured ways.

"What good will that do?"

"It could take years to obtain your freedom through the English courts. So, Tom thought that, as Phillip will administer law in the new colony, he might also be empowered to reduce sentences and grant pardons. Therefore, I'll petition Phillip as soon as we reach Rio de Janeiro."

A smile played at the corners of Lucy's mouth. He was a supreme optimist!

He returned her smile. "Are you ready to hear about your father?"

"Yes. Please, tell me everything . . . leave nothing out."

"Well, the weather had turned foul and darkness was not far off when we finally engaged the *Jason*. Her commander was a cunning Yankee who had been the scourge of ships sailing that stretch of water for over two years. God, he led us the devil's own chase before we ran him down! When your father hailed him to strike his colors, he just laughed."

Michael frowned and his jaw set in a hard line. "After the battle began, I didn't see your father for some time, as I was stationed below by the guns. I'd not been at it long when blood flew from the arm of the man beside me. Lieutenant Bevaraine, my cabin mate, tied a handkerchief around the wound and sent the fellow along to the doctor, Booth. I could hear the cries of the wounded even above the sound of the guns. They were shrill, distorted—barely human. A midshipman close by had his leg shattered by a shot and, a few yards away, powder caught fire and burned the flesh from another's face. He raised his hands as if imploring God to do something about it then, mercifully, a passing shot cut him in two.

"When I went up top, the scene was the same—death and destruction everywhere. The ship's rigging lay strewn about the deck and both the main and the mizzen were shattered. There was such a pall of smoke, I couldn't see what condition *Jason* was in, so I ran aft to find your father . . ."

He drew Lucy's hands into his.

"As I reached him, he was struck in the chest by a piece of grapeshot. We looked at each other in disbelief—shocked, I suppose, that it had happened so . . . so casually. I can't explain it better than that, Lucy. There was no panic. 'Best take me below to Booth,' he said. So I did. Then I returned to the deck and took command of the poop.

"The men were magnificent. They fought like tigers while *Seahawk,* our gallant lady, shook from stem to stern. Suddenly, the call 'cease fire' rang out. A terrible silence settled over the ship and we all watched spellbound as the privateer struck her colors.

"As soon as I was able, I went below to see your father. But . . . nothing could be done, Lucy, his wounds were too severe. The doctor and I carried him to his cabin for his greater comfort and I stayed with him until the end.

"When he regained consciousness, he enquired about the men and the ship, then asked if he was done for. I shook my head, but he must have seen it in my eyes because he smiled and beckoned me closer.

" 'Give the charm I wear around my neck to my daughter, Lucy. Tell her she gave me enough happiness to fill a thousand lifetimes.' Then, he stiffened in my arms. 'But promise you will not take the charm while a breath of life remains in me, for I swore an oath to her who gave it that I would wear it always—my sweet, my dearest Margaret . . .' Then he closed his eyes and I watched helplessly as he slipped into eternity."

Michael bowed his head, and they sat in silence until he looked up at her saying, "I'm sorry . . ."

She gave his hands a little squeeze and, although her eyes shone with tears, her voice was steady. "Thank you for telling me, Michael. I think I know how difficult it was for you. But, in a way, you have set me free. There are no shadows or questions left. As you said, it just happened. After all the years, it just happened."

Michael gazed at her. She *was* everything her father had claimed: compassionate, intelligent, courageous, and beautiful. She also possessed James Gamble's strength of character and she had inherited his love for the sea. But, above all else, he sensed that she was passionate. *One day,* he thought, *I'll awaken your passion, Lucy. And it will be worth the wait. It will be worth it . . . for both of us.*

20

The Crew Break Through the Bulkhead

Sunday, June 24, 1787

Michael and James Meredith were compiling the new duty roster in the cuddy.

James cleared his throat discreetly. "Er . . . I read Gamble's papers. What's your attachment to this woman? She is a convicted murderess."

"She is not a murderess. She is in this intolerable situation because she shot a house guest after he had raped her."

"If she shot an assailant in self-defence, why is she here? Surely her father arranged legal representation for her?"

"Captain Gamble died in battle some months before Lucy was arrested. She received neither legal nor financial help from her stepmother, who was the rapist's sister."

"How close were you and Captain Gamble?"

"We were friends. I respected him more than any man I have ever known—and I am heartsick at what has happened to his beautiful daughter."

They were silent for a few moments.

"Can I do anything to help?" Meredith asked.

Surprised, Michael turned to him. "No, I don't think so, James. But thank you for offering. I have written to my lawyers, and when we reach Rio I will petition the Commodore. Until then, we must be patient. These things take time . . ."

Meredith liked Michael. He was a first-class officer, and a man one could depend on. "I believe you and Tom took Gamble up on deck the other night."

Michael looked at him levelly. "That's correct."

"As long as you are discreet, and take her up late at night, I've no objection. If questions are asked, you may refer the questioner to me."

Michael looked at his commanding officer with new respect.

"Thank you, James."

Lucy lay at the front of the bunk paralyzed with fear. The guards doing duty tonight were in the pay of the crew. Would they fetch

Michael if she asked them? She did not think so. But she could not just *lie* here, now the crew had broken through the bulkhead. Sooner or later, Lewis would come.

When he did, he was so quiet he almost caught her unaware. She heard the faintest creak at the bulkhead, then he was dragging her out of the bunk.

Michael and Faddy were awoken by banging on their cabin door and shouts of "Come quick. Crew's broke through the bulkhead!"

They threw on their uniforms and ran to the prison.

"Open the door," Meredith said, "Lieutenant Clark, come with me. Lieutenant Perryman, you and Faddy go to the crew's quarters." He stepped into the prison and shone the lantern toward the rear. Frances, Susannah, and Beth were struggling with Tom Lewis by the bulkhead, and Lucy was rolling about on the boards with her knees drawn into her stomach.

"Iron that sailor and get him out of here," Meredith ordered.

Lewis fought like a madman. It took six guards to subdue him, but eventually they got his arms behind his back, ironed him, and led him away.

Meredith signaled Ralph and pointed to Beth. "Get some clothes on this whore, then take her up top and iron her to the pump."

"She was only trying to help, Captain," said Susannah.

"Silence!" Meredith rasped. "You other women get back to your bunks or you'll be ironed also."

Ignoring him, Susannah knelt beside Lucy and stroked her head. "Don't be afraid Lucy, they have taken him away."

"Will it ever end?" Lucy moaned. "The pain . . . I cannot breathe . . ."

Tom crouched beside her. "Show me where the pain is."

"I think the baby's coming!" she sobbed.

Tom motioned to Frances. "Quickly, carry her around to the hospital."

21
The Flogging

The dawn sun daubed the decks and sails of *Friendship* in delicate pinks and golds but, to the west, storm clouds had gathered and these matched the look on Francis Walton's face as he stood, hands on hips, glowering at his crew.

Beside him, under heavy guard, stood Barnes, Hearn, Craven, and ordinary seaman Tom Lewis.

Ignoring the muffled screams floating up from the hospital, Walton addressed the men. "If it were up to me, these four blackguards'd be dancin' a hornpipe at the end of a rope as a lesson to you all that I'll tolerate it *no longer*. But Captain Meredith has requested that they be taken to the flagship and flogged to within an inch of their lives—within an inch—do you hear me? Well, I've said yea this time. . . . But if I catch any of you lying with those filthy pox-boxes below again, I'll strike your colors personally! I'll flay your backs to ribbons. Then, legal or not, I'll keelhaul the lot of you!"

He moved along the line and stared out each man in turn. "Now, get back about yer duties, you licentious, fornicating scum!"

As the sullen crew dispersed, a high, thin wail of a baby floated up from below.

Tom examined the baby and sighed. The poor little fellow had a webbed hand and foot.

He would long remember last night. No sooner had Lucy come into labor, than he had been summoned to Mrs. Russel's cabin where a quick examination had confirmed that she was also in labor.

He cut baby Russel's webbing and bound the wounds. Then, leaving him in Frances's care, he took a bottle of powdered poppy seeds and some cinnamon water from the shelf and mixed a potion for Lucy. "How are you feeling, my dear?" he asked, sitting down on the stool beside her.

"Recovering nicely," she said then cried out as another pain drove in on her.

"I commend your courage, Lucy, but think you're being a little foolish," he said severely. "I know you are suffering, why try to hide it? Really, we must work together if we're to do the best for your baby."

Lucy looked at him shamefaced. She had tried with all her strength to make the pains stop, it was too soon for the baby to be born. But the pains kept coming. "Forgive me, Tom. Of course I'll help you."

Tom lifted her into a sitting position and raised the draft to her lips. "That is the best news I've had since King George granted my Commission! Drink this, it will help loosen your muscles."

Dutifully, she did his bidding.

Tom eased her down onto the pillows and smoothed the damp hair away from her forehead. "Rest, my dear, and don't worry about anything . . . just let the draft take effect."

Lucy closed her eyes. She'd been so stricken with fear last night, she was incapable of defending herself against Lewis. Thank heavens Beth had arrived, for her screams had awoken everyone. Where was Bethy? She hoped things were not going badly for her . . .

"I know you are keeping something from me," Lucy persisted. "Is Beth in more trouble?"

"Yes," Frances admitted.

"Tell me what happened."

"Captain Meredith had her flogged today for fighting, insolence, and obscene language. Don't worry, she's all right. Dr. Arndell fixed her cuts as soon as they took her back to the prison, so don't you go thinking she's been hard done by. She brought it on herself. Cut the Captain's cheek with her irons. Lord! I don't know what's come over her lately—she's turned bad again, that's what! Once a whore—"

"What utter nonsense!" Lucy snapped. "What happened today is a mystery to me, but if Bethy hadn't given the alarm last night, I would be far worse off. Lewis had me down on the boards—" She stopped short, catching her breath in sharply.

"Another pain?" Frances enquired leaning over her anxiously.

Lucy sank back on the pillows gasping. "They certainly take the wind out of my sails. Where is Tom?"

"Him and Lieutenant Perryman are doing rounds in the men's prison. Do you want me to fetch him? He said I should if anything happened."

Lucy shook her head. "Leave him be, the pain is going. But, Frances, I would appreciate having a few words with Michael. . . ."

Francis smiled and patted her hand. "The doctor will call in here on his way to the women's prison. Why don't I go with him, and the Lieutenant can sit with you for a while?"

Soon afterward, Tom popped his head around the door. "Everything all right in here?"

Lucy smiled. "Yes, thank you Tom. But could Frances finish the rounds with you? I'd like to see Michael."

"I have missed you," Michael said as soon as they were alone.

Lucy looked at him closely. His face was gray with fatigue. She doubted he had slept a wink in the last twenty-four hours. "I've missed you too," she said cheerfully. "How goes it with the world outside?'' He brushed a stray strand of hair from her cheek. "At sunset, I saw a school of porpoises chasing shoal. They passed so close between the ships, only a miracle prevented them colliding with the hulls.''

"How is Beth?'' she asked softly.

His eyes met hers squarely. "I could do nothing to prevent the flogging, Lucy. Meredith had every right to punish her—she and another woman were locked in battle and when he tried to part them, she laid his cheek open to the bone. In my opinion, she got off lightly. She has a sore back and her deck privileges have been taken away, but at least she's under cover. The other three women found in the crew's quarters are still chained to the bilge pump.''

Lucy caught her breath and fell back against the pillows.

"Shall I fetch Tom?''

She shook her head. "No—and please don't worry, Michael. When this is over I shall have something wonderful to show for my pains. If the baby is a boy, I'm going to call him 'James.' ''

He smiled. "And if it's a girl?''

She thought for a moment, then her eyes sparkled. "I'll call her 'Margaret' after my mother. So, take that melancholy look off your face, this is a happy occasion.''

"You are an angel, Lucy,'' Michael murmured, raising her hand to his lips. "How delightful that we'll soon have a little replica of you.''

Lucy smiled her dimple smile. "You are most gallant, sir.''

The laughter left Michael's face. "Not gallant. I have been negligent in my care of you. When I think of that scum Lewis I— ''

"You were in no way responsible,'' she broke in. "How could you have prevented it? Please, Michael, let us talk of other things. Tell me about the Fleet.'' She gripped his hand tightly as another pain tore through her.

He half rose. "Shall I go for Tom?''

"No, stay,'' she pleaded. "I'll let you know when it is time. Could you describe Commodore Phillip? I've only seen him from a distance at Portsmouth.''

Michael gently wiped the beads of perspiration from her face. "He's not exactly handsome but has strong features and a nobleness of bearing. My friend John White thinks very highly of him. John says Phillip is the most humane man he has ever met—and a true pioneer. But you will see him soon enough. He is bound to inspect the Fleet when we reach Rio de Janeiro.''

"Let me go for Tom,'' he pleaded. "I feel so useless sitting here talking while you are in pain. . . .''

She squeezed his hand. "Tom will come back soon. Tell me about John White, it helps if you talk. . . ."

He looked at her apprehensively but obeyed. "Well, John and I saw little of each other over the last few years but we met again last Christmas. He spun me a glorious tale of carving a new civilization out of a mysterious virgin wilderness and, having nothing better to do, I decided to go along." Michael grinned. "John is an adventurous type who is always getting into scrapes. It's hard to believe he is a respected member of the medical profession. Yet Tom swears that he is absolutely brilliant with the knife. . . ."

He paused and looked over his shoulder as Tom and Frances entered the cabin.

"I am afraid neither of you will get much sleep tonight," Lucy said. "The baby is threatening to arrive any moment!"

Despite Lucy's optimistic prediction, the birth proved long and difficult. Aided by stimulants of savin juice, white wine, borax, and sugar, Lucy battled for another eight hours. Just before dawn, Tom thought he had lost her when her feverish restlessness gave way to a deep, trancelike languor. He snatched up a bottle of Burnt Shavings of Hartshorn and passed it under her nose, trying to revive her, but she did not respond.

He and Frances looked at each other desperately.

"Lucy!" he shouted hoarsely, willing her back. "Oh God, Lucy, don't give up now!"

A moment later, something inside her rallied and she opened her eyes. "It's all right, Tom," she said. "*She* is here. She has come to help me. . . ."

She gathered herself together, bore down with a supreme effort, and the baby, a tiny boy, was got away at last.

22

The Second Seed of Abaddon

The long, dark passage seemed to go on forever. On one side were rusty suits of armor clutching gigantic battle axs; on the other, huge oaken doors locked against her.

With every step she took, the pain in her side stabbed harder and the baby's cries grew weaker. A terrible sense of urgency overcame her and she began to run. "Hold on, hold on," she called, "I am coming!"

She came to a bend in the passage and passed into a vast field of green mist.

"Where are you?" cried a voice.

She turned slowly but, even then, she turned before Time, and standing in the space between one second and another was the woman of her vision, cradling a tiny baby.

Every feature of the woman's face was identical to her own, yet Faith knew this mirror image was not a reflection of herself but a separate entity. The baby's image, however, was indistinct. Its tiny chest was encased in darkness and its cries were very feeble.

"I have been calling you," said the woman of her vision. "Will you help me fight the Forces of Darkness?"

"Yes, my heart," Faith answered. As she took the woman's outstretched hand, long tentacles of darkness emerged from the green mist and wound themselves tightly around the baby. Faith pulled and strained with all her might and gradually drew the woman into the light. But the baby remained encased in darkness.

"We must bring the baby forth also," said the woman.

Together they grappled with the forces, but *they* would not yield the baby.

"You who have him, let him go!" cried the woman.

Out of the mist, broadsword in hand, stepped the Guardian.

"Woman, be gone!
This second seed of Abaddon,
This shadow on the sun
Must cease his earthly journey
Before it has begun.
His ill-begotten kinsman,
He, whom fate has sworn
Will wreak revenge on *Destiny*,
Already has been born.
He, who walks in darkness,
He, the nightmare's bane,
Crown princeling of the castle.
All hail, *Darian*!"

"I shall never give up my baby!" the woman cried defiantly, and renewed her efforts to free the baby.

"Heed my words, Mother of Destiny!" thundered the Guardian.
The woman turned to Faith. "Help me," she pleaded.

Together, they fought the Forces of Darkness until the green mist retreated and they pulled the baby free. But, even as the woman drew him to her breast, the Guardian raised the sword.

"Take care!" Faith cried. Her warning came too late. Down came the sword and she felt herself falling . . . falling . . .

"Wake up!" The voice summoned Faith from a dark maelstrom.

Faith opened her eyes to find her grandfather standing beside the bed, shaking her shoulder.

"Good morning, my dear," he said cheerfully. "My word, you *were* sleeping soundly. Normally, I would not have disturbed you, but it's time for your laudanum."

Faith sat up and looked around the room for the woman and baby, but they were nowhere to be seen. She shook her head, trying to clear it. "Grandfather, did you hear a baby crying?"

Sir Michael frowned. "Are you unwell again? You look flushed . . ."

"My head feels fuzzy and my throat is very dry," she answered vaguely. "Perhaps I have caught a chill. I-I think I shall ring for tea. Will you join me?"

He checked his timepiece. "Not this morning. I'm riding to the southern boundary farms. Stay abed. I will send your maid up with the tea."

She sighed and sank down against the pillows. "If you think bed is best."

"I do indeed," he said, setting the opium draft on the table and kissing her good-bye. "Rest well—and don't forget the laudanum."

She remained in bed until the clatter of his horse's hooves died away, then she rose and crossed to the window. Had the woman and the baby been another hallucination? They had seemed so real!

She looked at the golden day. Why couldn't she remember things clearly anymore? Perhaps her forgetfulness and confusion were manifestations of her madness? With a sense of shock, she realized that she did not know the day, or even the month. May? No—surely not. The world outside testified to high summer.

She rested her cheek against the cool window pane. Thinking made her head ache. *You were foolish to mention the baby to Grandfather,* she told herself. *Now he will probably increase the laudanum.*

She walked listlessly to the bedside table and picked up the glass. Time for the draft. She wanted no more burning, sweating flushes, or rats gnawing in her stomach. But as she raised the glass to her lips, something red caught her eye.

Blood was oozing from the center of the scar!

The glass slipped through her nerveless fingers, spilling its honeyed contents over the carpet while she stood, transfixed, watching the blood run down her finger into the palm of her hand—like a river of blood running along the floor of the Valley of Abaddon. "Oh, no, please God," she wept, "Don't let the nightmare of madness start again!"

When the maid came in with the tea a few minutes later, her mistress was standing by the bed staring fixedly at her hand.

"Good morning, Miss Faith," she said brightly, setting the tray down on the bedside table and retrieving the glass.

Faith looked up, startled.

"Will there be anything else, Miss Faith?" the maid asked, as she poured the tea. "Oh, you've cut your finger. Shall I bind it?"

"No, thank you," Faith answered vaguely.

The maid left, locking the door behind her.

Convinced that she was on the verge of an important discovery, Faith continued to stare at the scar. But confused images kept floating about in her mind and, no matter how hard she tried, she could not bring that for which she was searching into focus.

She returned to bed, drank the tea, carefully holding the cup in her left hand so as not to disturb the bloodstains; then, after a while, fell asleep.

The grandfather clock at the end of the corridor was striking midday when Faith next awoke. She looked at her hand. The bloodstains were still there!

The scar *had* bled! The blood *was* real! Wait. What if she was only imagining she could see the blood? But, hadn't the maid seen it too?

She tugged the bell cord and waited impatiently for Margaret to arrive.

"Would you bring some coffee and sandwiches, Margaret?"

The maid retrieved the tea tray from the table. "Yes, Miss Faith. Anything else?"

Faith held out her hand. "Do you think this cut needs attention?"

The maid peered at the scar. "No, Miss, not that tiny scratch."

As soon as she was alone, Faith opened the window and drew great gulps of fresh air into her lungs. Then, she examined her finger closely. There was no fresh wound. The mysterious blood had come from the scar.

Excitement welled up within her. If the blood was real, then it was her grandfather and the doctor who were mistaken, not she!

"Oh, Lord," she whispered. "If the blood is real, perhaps the woman of my visions is real? Perhaps I am not mad? Perhaps I possess 'the second sight' as Aunt Barbara suggested?"

Those questions created a premise of stupendous possibilities!

The maid arrived carrying the lunch tray and left, locking the door.

To allay suspicions, Faith devoured the food, then took up paper and pen. Initially, her mind refused to function, but gradually, clarity triumphed over confusion and she warmed to the task. Every time a new question came to mind, she wrote it on a separate piece of paper. Those questions were vital pieces of a puzzle she *must* solve.

She worked for three hours, then slept. When she awoke at six o'clock, she lit the lamp and continued writing until she heard the servants moving about in the next room, drawing her bath.

As she lay luxuriating in the tub a short time later, an uncanny yearning came over her. She sat bolt upright and looked at the clock on the tortoiseshell table in the corner.

She had gone twenty-four hours without the laudanum.

No need to panic, she told herself. *You do not have long to wait, the servants always bring it with the evening meal.*

However, her anxiety persisted. What if they forgot the draft tonight? She climbed out the tub. Best to be waiting when they arrived. Then, if the draft *were* missing, she could bring it to their attention. As she hurried from the anteroom the servants arrived with the trays. Relief flooded through her. The laudanum was there.

She dismissed the servants and reached for it. How she needed it tonight! Soon the tightness in her chest and the throbbing of blood in her head would go. Her confidence would return, the world would grow calm, and she would float into exquisite forgetfulness, whiling away the hours in exploration of vast, unknown regions of time and space.

Yet, as she raised the glass to her lips, she paused.

Why was she drinking this stuff?

She did not want to relinquish the small hold she had regained on her life, but what would happen if she did not drink the laudanum? Would she go raving mad, as she had in Portsmouth? Would she have to be tied down and watched night and day again?

Her stomach contracted, pains stabbed behind her eyes, her teeth started to ache. She had been a prisoner in this room for nearly two months and she longed to be free. If the blood and the visions were real, then she was sane. If she was sane, then she did not need the laudanum.

With shaking hands, she tossed the laudanum out the window. Then, lest she be tempted to drain the dregs, she rinsed the glass in the bath water. Panic swept through her. "Oh God," she whispered, "what have I done?"

Tears rolled down her cheeks. She felt so alone. The people she loved seemed so far away, almost as though they belonged to another lifetime. She knew she had only to reach for the bell cord and her grandfather would come. But he would call in the doctor, who would double the laudanum dose, and the nightmare would begin again.

Have courage, Faith, she told herself. *You can do it.*

She dried her eyes and gazed at the food on her plate. She had lost a great deal of weight. Perhaps she would feel better if she ate? She picked up the fork and began forcing food into her mouth.

When she finished eating, she read through her notes. After a while, her thoughts became more rational and she grew calm.

23

I Shall Endure

Tuesday, July 17, 1787

Michael and Tom stood at the taffrail discussing Lucy and the baby.

"Why is James so much smaller than the Russel child?" Michael asked.

"The months Lucy spent in Newgate and the fact that she did not carry him full-term have contributed to that. . . ."

"He's not in danger?"

Tom gazed aloft at the crew working on the shrouds. "His chances would be vastly improved if he put on weight. Unfortunately, Lucy's diet over the past nine months has left her with a deficiency of milk. I asked Mrs. Russel to supplement one of his feeds but she was most emphatic that she would not take a convict's child to breast. We'll just have to make do until we reach Rio. Then I will find him a wet nurse, build him up, and wean him."

Michael looked at the white, frothing wash trailing the ship. "How is Lucy?"

"I am not the least concerned about Lucy," Tom muttered, "She'll soon regain her strength. However, you may as well know, Lucy and the baby are moving back to the prison tonight."

Michael turned and stared at him with disbelief. "You can't be serious, Tom!"

"Nothing I can do about it. The women sharing Mrs. Russel's cabin could not sleep at night for her baby's crying, so they took their complaints to Walton. You can imagine how he carried on. If I don't move Lucy out of the hospital and Mrs. Russel in, he will turn it back into a grain storage."

He glanced at *Charlotte*, which had picked up a favorable tack and was closing fast. "The best we can hope for is a fair wind to Rio."

Michael searched *Charlotte*'s crowded decks as she flashed past. John White was nowhere in sight. "Even with fair winds, we won't make Rio in less than three weeks. Will that be soon enough for James?"

"I hope so," Tom said grimly.

That evening, when Lucy returned to the prison, Beth welcomed her with tears of joy.

"Thank God you have recovered, Bethy," Lucy exclaimed, passing the baby to Frances and hugging her friend. "And just as well, for I need your assistance with James."

Beth flushed pink with pleasure. "You'll have it, Lucy, I promise. But look at you, you're too pale by far. What do you think, Frances?"

Frances didn't know what to think. "Dr. Arndell says Lucy will soon improve when we get her up top in the sunlight and fresh air. But see you do your duty with this boy until she's got her strength back, you hear?" Frances gave the tiny bundle into Beth's care.

"Oh, Lucy," Beth whispered in rapture. "The beautiful little thing has got green eyes like you."

Sunday, July 22

Beth planted her feet on the deck, balanced herself against the quarter rail and gazed tenderly at the baby in her arms. James was such a good boy. He slept all the time and hardly ever cried.

She glanced toward the bow and saw John Best overseeing a gang of convicts by the forward hold. Best always had a smile and a wave for her these days and had offered her grog on several occasions but, because she was not sure Lucy would approve, she had declined.

Her mouth curled mischievously at the corners. Wait until Lucy saw the surprise! The other day she had asked Best if a crib could be made for Jamie and Moses Tucker, the convict carpenter, had agreed to do it.

She stared at the giant wrestling with a cask of beef by the hold. Moses Tucker was a mystery. Best claimed Moses had been huntsman for the Duke of Marlborough, Sidaway had it on good authority that Moses had been a smuggler down in Cornwell, Lavell swore that Moses had been a Devonshire forger; but nobody knew for sure, and Moses wasn't telling.

"Well, as long as he makes you a crib, Jamie, it don't matter where he sprung from. Ask no questions and you'll be told no lies, I say."

Lucy and Frances waved to Beth, as she crossed to the lee side. "Beth's turned into the world's best baby minder," said Frances.

Lucy smiled. "Yes, she loves Jamie dearly. . . ."

Frances patted her shoulder. "What you've done for that girl is a very fine thing, Lucy. It can't have been easy to hand him over."

"Is Jamie gaining enough weight?" Lucy asked anxiously. "He seems so small and quiet compared to the Russel baby."

Frances was acutely aware of the baby's frailty, but confirming Lucy's fears would do more harm than good. "Pish, girl! Jamie's just a slow starter. Don't you go comparing him to baby Russel—all babies are different you know."

"But I worry about him, Frances. The night he was born I saw tentacles of darkness growing out his chest. Then I called to *her* and together we pulled against the forces until they—"

"Really, Lucy," Frances interrupted. "If you don't stop taking on so, you'll lose what milk you do have. Then, where will you be?"

Lucy sighed. "You are right, I'm being foolish." She folded her sewing and put it away. "Time for lessons."

She left in search of the children and Frances rethreaded her needle. Thanks to Lieutenant Perryman and Dr. Arndell, Lucy had come a long way since her first terrible months in Newgate. She no longer cowered at the sight of a man and, although she still had nightmares, they were less frequent.

Frances glanced up at the poop deck and saw Lieutenant Perryman. She greatly admired the patience and restraint he had shown with Lucy. Particularly as it was plain he loved Lucy to distraction.

Frances shivered and her heart beat faster as she remembered the way she had seen him look at Lucy. If only a man would look at her like that. She glanced around the deck and noted with displeasure the performances of the other women who were trying to gain his attention. He could have his pick of any woman on board, including the marine wives, but he only saw Lucy.

She sighed. Perhaps when the Fleet reached New South Wales there might be a hard-working man who wanted a decent woman to share his bed. It would be good to wake up and know she did not have to battle through another day alone.

She glanced at the stitches in Lieutenant Clark's breeches and chuckled. She had gone right off her line. Ah, but Lieutenant Perryman's smoke gray eyes would set any woman to dreaming.

PART THREE
A Glimmer of Light

24
The Storm

Sunday, July 29, 1787

Faith put the pen down and flexed her fingers. At last, the letter to Aunt Barbara was finished. She glanced up at the Billingsley coat of arms on the ceiling: a rampant lion and roebuck holding a shield emblazoned with the letter *B*, beneath which was the Billingsley motto: I shall endure.

And, so she had.

Her retreat from the world of laudanum had only been accomplished because, by some miracle, her grandfather had been absent from the Hall on business.

The first day she had allayed the servants' suspicions by claiming a feverish distemper. The second and third days had passed in a daze of sweating, stomach cramps, running nose, and sneezing. By the fourth day the servants had not known what to do with her. The fifth day had been the worst: she had awoken in a ferment of agitation, with so much energy that she could not sit, stand or lie in one place for more than a minute. She had paced the floor from morning till night—backward and forward, round and round—ranting, defiant, trembling, timid, hating, bitter. On the sixth day she had sat by the window, as still and as motionless as a statue, gazing at the distant world and despairing at her isolation.

And always, there had been the laudanum. The laudanum that had to be disposed of, never drunk. The glasses that had to be rinsed, never licked. In the morning, out the window with the laudanum. In the evening, in the bath water with the laudanum.

Day after day the torment had continued until, on the fourth day, she had weakened—on the fourth day she had drunk the bathwater. Afterward, overcome with remorse, she had thrown the stuff out the window as soon as the maid left the room.

By the time her grandfather returned to Billingsley, she had regained sufficient control to continue her deception undetected.

Faith left her desk and walked to the window. It was time to put some of her plans into effect. Above all, she needed access to the world beyond this room. When the doctor came on his monthly visit tomorrow, she must convince him that she would benefit from a daily walk in the garden.

She went to her dressing room and selected a lilac taffeta dress that had always been especially flattering. The doctor was young, he would succumb to charm and pleading. Once she had gained the first small freedom she could find a way to send the letter to Aunt Barbara. She herself could not instigate an enquiry into her father's background, so Aunt Barbara would have to do it for her. Getting the letter away would require infinite care. She could not trust the servants with it—they thought she was mad. If it fell into her grandfather's hands, all she had gained in the past three weeks would be lost. . . .

When she had won back her freedom, she must regain control of her life. Her grandfather would not relinquish his hold over her willingly, but somehow she would manage it. Tomorrow she would ask a few questions about the estate—nothing too complicated, just a small show of interest.

Each day thereafter, she would ask something else, until they were communicating at their old level. And if she was patient, and if she persisted, then eventually she would escape the nightmare that her life had become.

25
Rio de Janeiro

Sunday, August 5, 1787

Commodore Phillip stood on the bridge of *Sirius* watching the Fleet ships threading their way around the fortified islands guarding the narrow entrance to Rio de Janeiro Harbor.

The Fleet had been standing off the coast of Brazil for two

days waiting for a favorable wind and, at four o'clock this afternoon, a gentle land breeze had sprung up.

As *Sirius* passed between the Island of Lage and the imposing cliff fortress of Santa Cruz, Phillip raised his arm and the ship's cannons roared out a thirteen gun salute that was immediately answered by those of Fort Santa Cruz. Phillip waited for the smoke to clear, then ordered the Master, Micah Morton, to point the bow at the Isle of Dos Cobres. By nightfall, the Fleet lay safely at anchor one mile northeast of the city.

"After weeks of ocean, Rio is a welcome sight," said Tom as he and Michael strolled the deck later that evening.

Surrounded by immense hills, Rio glittered on the western shore like a vast twinkling fairyland, its buildings lit in tribute to Commodore Phillip who had served in the Portuguese Navy for five years, and who was personally known to the Viceroy, Don Luis de Varconcellos.

Michael trained his spyglass on an English cutter standing at single anchor close by. "The sooner we get Lucy's petition to the Commodore, the better. I saw dispatches going aboard that cutter bound for Lisbon earlier this evening."

"I won't be attending the official welcome at the Palace tomorrow, since John White has called a doctor's meeting. If you like, I will deliver the petition to the flagship."

Michael shook his head. "No thanks, Tom. I'll hand it to Phillip at the reception. That way, I will be certain *he* gets it, not some minor official."

"Wise move," Tom agreed. "Only Phillip has the authority to help Lucy. And, speaking of Lucy, we must acquire a wet nurse for Jamie immediately."

Michael nodded gravely. "Of course, Tom. It's a miracle he's survived this long. I'll also buy a good milking cow. Better get it aboard before the other officers load up the pens."

The day was remarkably fine, and a wondrous fragrance drifted down from the surrounding mountains as Phillip and his officers ascended the jetty steps.

The Captain of the Palace Guard and a small rotund priest greeted them in the name of the Viceroy and conducted them under richly covered canopies through the cheering crowd to the Palace. The Palace Guard lay the Portuguese colors at Phillip's

100

feet as a mark of the high esteem in which he was held, then conducted their party to a large audience chamber. A few minutes later a rich, gold embroidered curtain at the end of the room swung aside and they were ushered into the Viceroy's drawing room.

Not until Phillip was on his way back to the jetty did Michael have a chance to give him Lucy's petition. Then, much relieved, he set off in search of a wet nurse for Jamie.

Thursday, August 9

Lucy peered at Rio through Michael's spyglass. How she longed to wander along those crowded thoroughfares looking for bargains!

She gave the glass to Beth and took Jamie in her arms. He had gained a miraculous amount of weight since Michael had brought the mulatto wet nurse on board. In just four days he looked a different baby.

Hearing someone clear his throat behind them, they turned. John Best nodded courteously to Lucy and gave Beth a conspiratorial wink. "Er . . . I have that article you ordered, Beth."

"Have you indeed, John Best? I was beginning to think Jamie'd be a grown man before I caught sight of it." She stamped her foot impatiently. "Well, man, what are you waiting for? Go on, fetch it!"

"What was that about?" Lucy asked, mystified.

"Oh, nothing much," Beth replied airily.

A few minutes later John Best arrived carrying Jamie's new crib.

"Oh, my God," Lucy gasped. "Oh, John, it's beautiful!"

Best set the crib on the deck and Lucy placed the baby in it. "Look, Beth, it has Jamie's name carved on the head board. And it rocks. Feel it!"

Beth rocked the crib. "Doesn't he look a proper little prince? And it's so deep and snug he could never fall out."

Lucy gave Best a dazzling smile. "Wherever did you get this, John?"

He was surprised by Lucy's friendliness. He had heard she considered herself a cut above the other women. "Beth told me the baby needed a crib so I got Moses Tucker to knock one out," he told her.

"Would you please, please, fetch Moses so I can thank him."

As Best departed, Lucy hugged Beth tightly. "You are so good and kind and thoughtful, Beth. If I searched the whole world over, I'd never find another friend like you."

Beth turned pink with pleasure. "Pish, Lucy! You're the one who's good and kind. Here comes John with Tucker in tow. You'll be lucky to get a word out of him—our Moses isn't much of a talker."

Lucy looked up at the giant standing before her. Moses Tucker had bushy hair and a black beard streaked with gray. His rough-hewn face bore the scars of a thousand confrontations with life. But life had not cowed Moses Tucker; the eyes staring back at her were intensely alive. She liked him instantly. And, liking him, she did something quite extraordinary—she offered him her hand.

When she spoke, her voice was as warm as her eyes. "This crib you've made for my son is the most beautiful I have ever seen, Moses."

" 'Twas nothing, Miss Lucy," he replied.

"No, Moses, it is *very* special. How can I ever thank you?"

Beth and John Best looked on with astonishment as a wide smile split Moses's grim countenance.

"If you're happy, Miss Lucy, that be thanks enough for me," he said.

26
The Christening

Friday, August 10, 1787

Major Robert Ross, Commandant of the Marine Corps, glared contemptuously at the women assembled below him on the quarterdeck of *Friendship*.

"Therefore, because of the continuing disgraceful, infamous conduct of the female felons on board this ship, Commodore Phillip has ordered six of the worst behaved from *Charlotte* to be exchanged for six of the best behaved from *Friendship*."

He cast a cursory glance at the list Captain Meredith had

handed him a few minutes earlier. "The following felons will depart the ship in the morning. Step forward when I call your name: Hannah Green, Mary Watkins, Ann Baizley, Susannah Gought, Elizabeth Hervy, Frances Hart."

Michael, standing behind Major Ross on the poop, cursed silently. The decision to remove good women from the company of bad was sound, but losing Frances Hart would be a blow for Lucy, and her departure from the ship could not have been more ill timed. On Sunday, the Fleet Chaplin, Reverend Johnson, was coming aboard to read the Sunday service and to baptize baby Russel. He had also agreed to baptize Jamie, and Frances Hart, bless her, deserved to be here to see it.

That evening, the six women for *Charlotte* packed their possessions and bid tearful farewells to those remaining. Frances was depressed. Although she was friendly with the women accompanying her aboard *Charlotte*, she could not envisage life without Lucy and Beth. Still, she told herself sternly, it would do them no good to see how miserable she was.

"Never mind, Frances, we shall be together again in New South Wales," Lucy said, taking her hand. "And meanwhile, a change of company and a change of ship might be interesting. *Charlotte* is larger than *Friendship*, so you will have more room to move around. . . ."

"And we'll look out for you every time *Charlotte* comes past," said Beth, capturing her other hand.

"Don't worry about me, my girl," Frances said sharply. "I'll be fine. Just be sure to look after yourselves. Lucy, you keep clear of those baggages at the front, and Beth, no more fooling with the crew, you hear?"

"You've no cause to worry about me, Frances. I've seen the error of my wicked ways, honest I have," Beth assured her. "But I'll bloomin' well miss you, you old grump!"

Frances glanced away quickly. "Now, don't go turning on the tears, miss—or I'll box your ears. Lucy's right, I'll be much better for the company of twenty good women. And I dare say it won't be long before I've plenty of washing and sewing to do for *Charlotte*'s officers. If truth be known, I was mighty tired of stitching Lieutenant Clark's baggy breeches!"

The following afternoon when Michael and Tom returned from

103

shore, they found Lucy in the women's enclosure. Tom handed toy horses to Edward and baby Cable, and a black rag doll to Nancy Pugh, who stared at it reverently. Then he clasped his hands behind his back and cleared his throat. "Everyone pay attention please. I have an important announcement to make."

The women stopped admiring the children's new toys and gathered round him expectantly.

"Tomorrow, after Reverend Johnson has read the Sunday service, he will baptize Jamie."

"And Beth shall be his godmother. He shall be christened 'James Michael Thomas Gamble.' "

"Lawks!" Beth exclaimed. "Never was a child better served by names!"

The warm sun shone down like a benevolent patriarch on those gathered on the quarterdeck.

Following Reverend Johnson's instructions, Lucy handed Jamie to Beth. She and Beth wore the white lace aprons Michael had bought in Rio, and they had adorned their hair with white frangipani from one of the native canoes that plied their trade throughout the Fleet.

She glanced at Michael standing beside her. He looked very handsome in his scarlet parade uniform and black boots—as did Tom, who was having a difficult time keeping young Edward quiet.

Jamie behaved very well until Reverend Johnson sprinkled water on his forehead. Outraged, he let out a lusty howl that drew an immediate sympathetic response from baby Cable.

Michael smiled and reached for Lucy's hand. Fingers entwined they listened to the rest of the ceremony, as the melodious bells of Rio rang incessantly and the lush green hills hummed with the songs of ten thousand birds.

Such was the day of Jamie's christening.

27

The Commodore Visits Friendship

Monday, August 13, 1787

Phillip fervently hoped that his words would reach the hearts and souls of the hundred convicts drawn up below him on *Friendship*'s quarterdeck.

"The conduct of most of the women aboard this ship is the most reprehensible in the entire Fleet, despite numerous attempts by the authorities to subdue it. In future, all promiscuous, drunken, and disorderly women will be punished in the same way as the men—by flogging.

"However, there may be some among you who wish to set aside the mistakes of the past, some who want to become the foundation stones of a new civilization—and it is to those men and women I address my next words.

"If you are clean in your habits, obedient to those in authority, and active in your work when we reach New South Wales, I give you my pledge that you will be rewarded with fair treatment, pardons, and land grants from Government.

"Although compelled by law to pay for your past crimes you are, nevertheless, free to choose your life's future direction. Will you reap the rewards of industrious labor or fall forgotten by the wayside? The decision is yours."

He dismissed them and led the officers into the cuddy.

"Those were eloquent words, Commodore," James Meredith said a few minutes later as everyone helped themselves to a cold collation, "but the fifty-seven *Mercury* mutineers aboard this ship have shown no inclination to mend their ways."

Phillip selected a bunch of grapes. "Perhaps you could demonstrate authority's good will by releasing the men and women chained to the pumps, Captain?"

Meredith's mouth tightened. "Very well, sir, if that is your command."

Phillip smiled. "Not a command, merely a suggestion. You are the disciplinarian here. However, while we are on the subject of your convicts, there is one I am most interested in—Lucy

Gamble. I received a petition about her earlier this week. Could I take her papers back to the flagship? I'd like to discuss her case with the Judge Advocate.''

Meredith glanced at Michael who was talking to Major Ross. "Of course, sir. Lieutenant Perryman, would you fetch Lucy Gamble's papers? The Commodore wants to look at them.''

"Lucy Gamble is a woman of breeding and character, sir," Meredith continued. "Her case is most puzzling.''

"I have no doubt that a serious miscarriage of justice has occurred in Lucy Gamble's case, sir," said Tom.

Phillip's eyes twinkled. "Your belief in this woman's innocence is noted, Dr. Arndell. Is she also virtuous and well behaved?''

"Indeed she is.''

"Then, why was she not transferred to *Charlotte?* My orders were specific, virtuous women were to be removed from the company of corrupt.''

"Her newborn son is extremely frail, so I decided to care for him myself rather than add to the Surgeon General's heavy workload, sir.''

"I see," said Phillip. He glanced over his shoulder as Michael reentered the cabin. "I understand from your petition, Lieutenant, that Lucy Gamble's father was your former commanding officer aboard H.M.S. *Seahawk.* Did he ever serve in the Portuguese Navy?" Phillip asked.

"No, sir.''

Phillip frowned slightly. "Strange, his name sounds familiar. Perhaps he did service with the fire ships around Elbe?''

Michael shook his head. "Captain Gamble was mainly employed on storeships, and later on frigates off the coast of America and Africa.''

Phillip looked at Lucy's papers. "Well, never mind, it will come to me. Perhaps something can be done from this end. The facts as you have presented them certainly warrant further inquiry.''

"Thank you for your interest, sir," Michael said with feeling. "I am most grateful.''

Phillip smiled, then turned to Meredith. "There are two other transporters and the storeships to visit, so I must leave shortly, Captain. But perhaps you and your officers would dine with me on board *Sirius* this evening?''

Meredith made no effort to hide his delight. "We would be honored, sir!''

Phillip led the way back to the deck and paused by the poop

rail for a moment, watching a gang of convicts erecting a new cooking caboose in the women's enclosure.

"Good God!" he gasped, the knuckles of his hands turning white as he gripped the rail. "Who is that woman . . . the one with the baby in her arms?"

Michael looked over the rail. "Lucy Gamble, sir, the woman we were discussing."

Phillip shook his head disbelievingly. "No, she cannot be. My God, I do not believe what I am seeing, there must be some mistake . . ."

"I assure you she *is* Lucy Gamble, sir." Michael replied, puzzled. The Commodore looked as if he had seen a ghost.

"I think we ought to be going, sir," Major Ross broke in.

Recovering his composure, Phillip turned to Meredith. "Thank you for the refreshments, Captain. I look forward to returning the compliment."

That evening, Phillip drew Michael apart from the group of officers gathered around the piano in the Great Cabin and asked him to take a turn around the deck.

"I have a list of questions for Lucy Gamble," he explained, handing Michael several sheets of paper. "Will you impress upon her that it is important she answer them as fully as possible?"

Hope stirred in Michael's heart. "Do you think you can help her, sir?"

In the pale light of the starlit deck, Phillip's face looked gray and stern. "I shall be honest with you, Lieutenant Perryman. These questions have nothing to do with her conviction. And, at the risk of sounding mysterious, I would prefer not to discuss the matter further until I have read her answers. So much depends on them . . ."

The men's eyes locked: Michael's challenging, questioning, Phillip's emphatic, firm.

Michael sighed. "Then I shall not press you, sir, but do you think you can reverse Lucy's sentence? It is the most blatant miscarriage of justice ever handed down by the English courts."

Struck by Michael's fervor, Phillip patted his shoulder. "When I assume Governorship of New South Wales, I shall be empowered to dismiss minor law infringements, pardon petty criminals, and reduce sentences at my discretion. But I doubt my authority extends to setting aside serious crimes, such as murder.

"However, do not be disheartened, I am sympathetic to Lucy Gamble's cause and will do whatever I can to assist. Let me warn you though, more may be at stake here than you could ever imagine."

28
The Discovery

The day of the Feast of Assumption festivities dawned hot and cloudless and all those in authority had left *Friendship* by mid-day, except Tom who was bleeding Sarah McCormick, and Michael who had taken Lucy to his cabin to complete Phillip's questionnaire.

"He expects your answers to be detailed, Lucy," he cautioned as he removed the bundle of papers from his sea chest. "Why don't you dictate them and I'll write?"

"All right," she replied, making herself comfortable on his bunk. "But why so many questions? What is it all about?"

He shrugged. "I'll learn more when I return your answers. First question: when and where were you born?"

"On the eleventh of November 1766, at my grandfather's house in Hartman Square, London."

"What was your mother's maiden name?"

"Margaret Joyce Billingsley."

"And her date and place of birth?"

"She was born—now, let me think—I know the month was December, but I am not sure of the year or date . . ." She thought hard. "1746, either the sixteenth or the eighteenth of December. But what has all this got to do with my trial and sentence?"

"I don't know. Where was your mother born?"

"I suppose, in her ancestral home—Billingsley Hall, West Hampshire."

"Next, he wants you to list every relative on your mother's side of the family."

Lucy frowned. "That will be difficult. Father was estranged from my mother's family. He and Sir Michael Billingsley had a falling out. The rift was never healed. I think Sir Michael Billingsley must be dead now. I wrote to him from Newgate but he did not reply. We had never met, but I thought he might be prepared to help."

Michael noted the information about Sir Michael. "Did your mother have any brothers or sisters?"

Lucy liked the way Michael smiled. Usually, his eyes, mouth, and face all joined in at once; but sometimes, like now, he smiled slowly and his eyes said something that made her nervous in the pit of her stomach. "No . . . she was an only child like me."

"Any other kin—uncles, aunts, cousins?"

"Sir Michael Billingsley had a sister who lived in Scotland, but Father never met her and I cannot remember her name. Sorry to be so vague. . . ."

They worked on for another hour until they were satisfied that Lucy had answered Phillip's questions to the best of her ability.

"Commodore Phillip has taken an uncommon interest in my case," Lucy remarked as Michael locked the papers in his sea chest for safekeeping. "Has he decided to help me?"

"He promised he'd do whatever he could within the framework of the law, Lucy."

Lucy rose and walked to the porthole. "The other day after his speech, you know, when he returned to the poop deck—he looked at me and, I swear, his face turned the color of chalk. He leaned over the rail and opened his mouth as if he were about to call to me. Then you spoke to him and he turned away. What do you make of that?"

"Perhaps he was struck dumb by your incredible beauty," he said as he joined her at the porthole. "Indeed, most men are. You obviously had no trouble charming that mammoth mute, Moses Tucker, into making Jamie's crib; whereas Lieutenant Clark has been waiting on his new desk for over a month. In fact, I would not be surprised if the wood used was from Ralph's stockpile."

She laughed and threw back her head with such a lovely easy motion that Michael ached to reach out and take her in his arms.

"Wrong on both counts," she said, eyes dancing. "Beth organized the crib as a surprise. She is the popular one, not I. And the men found the wood lying about in the hold."

He raised his eyebrows. "Really, Lucy, you are exceptionally naive if you believe convicts 'find' spare bits of mahogany lying about in holds—" He broke off and swore under his breath. "Damn! I have to go up top. *Sirius*'s cutter has just come alongside."

"Were you able to acquire the information I wanted." Phillip asked him as they finished their meal.

"Yes I was, sir," Michael replied, passing him a bundle of papers.

"Have a glass of brandy, Lieutenant, while I glance through these." Phillip sat down and read through the papers avidly. Then he rose and paced the cabin, his hands clasped behind his back. "We have a remarkable mystery on our hands, Lieutenant," he said at last. "Lucy Gamble's grandfather, Sir Michael Billingsley, is well known to me."

Michael raised surprised eyebrows. "He is alive?"

Phillip nodded, his countenance grave. "He most certainly is. Pour yourself another drink, you will need it when you hear my story. Remember how I told you I had heard the name James Gamble before? Well, some twenty years ago, when I settled in West Hampshire, I met James Gamble. In fact, I attended his wedding to Lucy's mother."

"Oh, I see."

Phillip moved his chair closer and sat down. "No, Lieutenant, I am afraid you do not see at all. Sir Michael Billingsley has a granddaughter, Faith, who is, I believe, Lucy Gamble's identical twin sister." Phillip related all he knew about the Billingsleys.

"This is incredible," Michael murmured when Phillip had finished. "Lucy has not the slightest idea of Faith's existence."

Phillip stared hard at Michael. "You knew James Gamble; why would he have instigated such a cruel separation of his daughters?"

Michael stiffened in his chair. "I cannot prove it, but I would swear on a stack of bibles that James knew nothing about Faith's existence. Moreover, Sir Michael Billingsley's assertion that James deserted his wife before Lucy—and Faith—were born is ludicrous. James was a man of honor. I was at his bedside the night he died. His last words were for Margaret and they were words of tenderness, not remorse!"

Phillip shook his head in perplexity. "My friend is also a man of honor. And he was most emphatic that James Gamble had deserted Margaret. I remember the bitter words he spoke the day he brought Margaret's body home from London. 'The infamous bounder deserted her. But he shall never see his daughter. I will raise her for my own, and may the devil take him!'—or words to that effect."

Michael's jaw set in grim line. "That statement cannot be true, sir. If James had deserted Margaret, how did he come to have custody of Lucy? I find some of Sir Michael's other actions questionable as well. Why didn't he reply to Lucy's letter? And why did he behave the way he did in Portsmouth when Faith saw Lucy in the longboat?"

Phillip refilled their glasses before answering. "You are assuming that Sir Michael knew of Lucy's existence. Perhaps he did not."

Michael walked to the porthole and looked out at the friendly lights of Rio. "None of this makes sense. If James had masterminded the thing, for God knows what reason, why did he tell Lucy where her grandfather lived? How stupid to run such a risk. No, it is Sir Michael's behavior that is open to question."

Phillip sighed. "The guilt or innocence of either party is pure supposition at this stage but the *facts* are these: Lucy and Faith share the same birthdate, the same parents, the same grandfather, and they are identical in every feature. There can be no doubt that they are identical twins."

"That being so, what is our next move?" Michael asked.

"I shall write to Sir Michael immediately, inform him of Lucy's existence, describe her present predicament and suggest that he puts his family affairs in order at the first possible opportunity. Also, we must lose no time in setting Lucy's appeal in motion. The Judge Advocate and I agree that it can only be done through the English Courts and Sir Michael, being a man of influence, is the best person to handle it.

"I shall also write to Faith who seems to have had an uncanny perception of what was happening to Lucy and has suffered greatly because of it. After the strange incident in Portsmouth, Sir Michael wrote me a letter of apology, mentioning that he had placed Faith under the care of an eminent London physician who was treating her for hallucinations.

"There are other things, strange things that I have not told you. . . . When I have had time to think them through, we shall talk again. In the meantime, would you prevail upon Lucy to write to her stepmother? The woman may be more reasonable now that ten months have passed since her brother died."

Michael returned to his chair. "I'll do that, sir. Perhaps when Ruth Gamble learns of Jamie's birth she will soften toward Lucy?"

Phillip nodded gravely. "I hope so. From your petition though, it appears she has behaved in a most vindictive manner."

Michael leaned forward in his chair. "What do I say to Lucy, sir?"

Phillip frowned thoughtfully. "I would tell her nothing."

"But she has a right to know about Faith!"

Phillip nodded. "Indeed, I do not dispute that. However, if we tell her now I think that, after her initial joy, she would become despondent at being unable to see Faith. The months, perhaps years of waiting, would be intolerable.

"On the other hand, if we wait until we reach New South Wales, she will then be able to look forward to a ship arriving with news."

The next day was the birthday of Joseph Francisco Xavier, Prince of Brazil. As it was another day of great celebration in Rio, all the officers of the Fleet had been invited to Court. Michael, who had volunteered to remain aboard *Friendship* as duty officer, breathed a sigh of relief as he watched the last shore boat depart. Except for a few unlucky marines who had drawn duty, authority had gone for the day, which meant he and Lucy could spend some time together. Just a few moments earlier she had slipped below, to await him in his cabin.

As he made his way along the dark companionway he wondered how long it would be before she was ready for romance. Well, romance might still be a long way off but, at least, she no longer shrank from his touch.

He found her sitting on his bunk, browsing through one of his books. He looked at her enraptured. Now she had regained her figure and was all soft curves. Around her trim ankles, he caught a glimpse of the white petticoat he had bought her in Tenerife. He thought of it next to her skin and the hot tenseness swept through his muscles. "Morning, Lucy," he said quickly. "I saw Jamie up on deck with Dudgeon. He looks marvelously robust."

She clambered to her feet and smoothed out her skirt, smiling. "Beth and I are finding him quite a handful these days . . ."

"Dudgeon is a strange one," he said as he closed the door. "She seems to have changed since Jamie came along."

Lucy frowned slightly. "Beth has always been the same sweet-natured person, Michael, you just have not noticed before."

He moved closer to her. "Come now, Lucy. We both know she has the morals of an alley cat."

Lucy's green eyes flashed. "Don't judge Beth by her behavior with the men. She comes from a different world to you and me. She was abandoned when she was six. Just think, Michael—six years old! Since then she has wandered the streets of London begging, stealing, and prostituting her body trying to stay alive. To a child, morality must have seemed a poor substitute for food—particularly as no one ever bothered to teach her 'right' from 'wrong' in the first damned place!"

"No need to swear," he muttered.

"I shall, if I feel like it," Lucy continued rebelliously. "I think it's time you knew she has used her body to protect mine several times. The first night we came aboard, for instance, when the crew broke through the bulkhead. Oh, pardon me—I see from the look on your face that you did not know they had broken through then. Now who is being naïve? Not only have the crew been with the women from the beginning, but those clove-hitched marines also!"

Michael frowned darkly. "By God! I will—"

"You will do absolutely nothing," she cut in. "I tell you this in strictest confidence. That first night, when Lewis grabbed me and would have forced me to go with him, Beth cajoled him into taking her instead. And she saved me last July—at great cost to herself—when she gave the alarm after discovering Lewis missing from his bunk. When you officers found her rolling naked on the boards with him, that was not from wantonness; in her haste to warn me, she simply neglected to dress."

Lucy tossed her dark hair away from her face and paced back and forth across the cabin. "Furthermore, when Meredith had her flogged for fighting he did not take into account that the poor lamb had been trying to protect herself from the fury of the three women she had betrayed in my interests."

Michael reached for her hand. "Forgive me, Lucy, I did not realize . . ."

Seeing his stricken countenance, Lucy's anger dissolved. "No," she sighed, "of course you didn't. It is really myself I am angry with, not you. From the beginning Beth was terrified of Lewis, but she continued to accommodate him because she was afraid of what he would do to me. And I, in my weak fear, allowed her to—" She broke off and hung her head. "I leave you to decide which of us behaved immorally."

"Lucy," he murmured huskily, "Lucy, dear . . ."

She raised glistening eyes to his. "Michael, can we *please* change the subject."

He had been profoundly moved by her words. She had taken his upper-class perceptions of courage and morality and flung them in his face. She had defended the virtue of a London prostitute and, in the process, shaken the self-assurance and superiority that were the foundations of Michael Perryman.

"Lucy, I . . ."

"Let's not talk about it any more," she said softly. "Tell me what the Commodore said when he read my answers."

He drew her down on the bunk. "Phillip sympathizes with your plight and has decided to ask an influential friend in England to seek justice for you through the courts."

Her hands flew to her face. "Oh, that *is* good news! Dare I hope that my freedom will be won?"

He captured her hands and squeezed them. "It will take time and patience but I am certain we shall win through in the end." Remembering Phillip's words, he went on. "But I am curious about something, Lucy, what caused the estrangement between your father and Sir Michael?"

Glad to leave the subject of convicts, Lucy launched into the explanation with fervor. "In the beginning, Sir Michael would not give his consent for my father and mother to marry. He considered Father too old, and he also accused him of wanting my mother's inheritance."

Michael repressed a smile. "That would not have gone down well with James."

"No, indeed! As Father was twelve years older than Mother, he understood Sir Michael's misgivings about his age, but he thought the accusation about the inheritance most unfair, as the least inquiry would have confirmed that he was well fixed.

"Eventually though, when Mother threatened to elope with father, Sir Michael gave his consent." She smiled ruefully. "Father said Mother was inclined to be a little headstrong and reckless at times. . . . Anyway, after their marriage they settled in London and Father did not see Sir Michael again until the night Mother died.

"You will remember I told you that, a week before I was born, Father traveled to Bristol for his father's funeral? When he returned to London, one of Sir Michael's lackeys was waiting on the doorstep with a message that my mother had come into labor and that Sir Michael had taken her to his house in Hartman Square.

"Father was surprised because I was not expected for another month, however, he hastened there and upbraided Sir Michael for taking Mother away from their home. Sir Michael then told Father that Mother had died giving birth to me, and accused him of bringing about her death by neglect.

"Father was so distraught and shocked by the news, he petitioned Sir Michael to bury my mother with her ancestors at Billingsley, then he took me up and left the house."

Michael pondered over this. That Margaret had died giving birth to identical twin daughters was beyond dispute; that James Gamble had removed Lucy from the house shortly thereafter,

114

was certain; but where did Faith fit into the puzzle? Even given James's distracted state, surely he would not have left her behind?

"How sad that they never resolved their quarrel," Lucy continued wistfully. "As a child, I fantasized about my grandfather. I imagined that he was a grand, gray-haired gentleman dressed in a golden cloak, who would one day ride up to my doorstep with armfuls of presents. But as the years passed and he never came, I accepted the truth—he did not care a whit about me. And now he is dead . . . and I shall never see him . . ."

Michael smiled at her tenderly. "Believe me, my love, that was *his* great loss."

Suddenly, his closeness was overpowering. Her skin grew hot where his fingers rested on her neck and her legs felt weak. Trembling, she turned toward him. But Michael's mind was elsewhere.

"I have to leave you, Lucy," he said reluctantly. "*Fishbourn* storeship is coming alongside with our salt pork."

He led her to the small table beside his bunk and pointed to the writing materials thereon. "This will not be easy, I know, but the Commodore and I both think you ought to write another letter to Ruth Gamble and tell her about Jamie."

"You cannot be serious!" Lucy exclaimed. "If she learns about Jamie she might try to take him away from me."

He placed his hands on her shoulders and drew her closer.

"Trust me, Lucy. I would never let that happen. If you tell her about Jamie, she might change her statement. Phillip is convinced that the more pressure we put on her, the better."

"Very well," Lucy said, taking up the pen reluctantly. "But only because you and the Commodore insist. Are you *sure* the letter is necessary?"

He walked to the door. "I am. You have a right to your freedom and Jamie has a right to his inheritance. Think of those things while you are writing."

30

The Fleet Leaves Rio

Tuesday, September 4, 1787

Accompanied by the incessant ringing of Rio's bells and a flotilla of native canoes, the Fleet set sail at dawn, steered up the southern arm of the harbor and, after exchanging a twenty-one gun salute with the cliff fortress of Santa Cruz, cleared the entrance and pointed east toward Africa.

Fair winds and blue skies followed the Fleet for five days, then the weather took a sudden turn for the worse, and the heavily laden vessels rolled and wallowed in the gigantic swell.

That evening, the atmosphere in the officers' cuddy on board *Friendship* was as foul as the weather. Ralph was suffering from a toothache, Faddy was drinking himself into oblivion, and Meredith and Tom, who had recently quarreled over the ownership of a piece of driftwood shaped like a ship, were barely speaking.

Michael was up on deck with Best and Cable, trying to place support slings around the terrified cow, which had twice broken down her pen.

"For God's sake you two, hold her!" Best yelled as he looped the strap around the spar for the tenth time. "If we don't get this done soon, us three and the bloody cow will all end up in the drink!"

In the women's prison, Lucy and Beth were leaning anxiously over Jamie's crib in which Moses Tucker had cut holes so that it could be strung between the beams like a hammock, thus decreasing the effects of the ship's violent motion.

Beth bit her lip to keep from crying out as *Friendship* lurched and plunged. She was afraid, but she did not make a sound, so as not to startle Jamie. Since leaving Rio he had kept nothing down. They did not know if it was seasickness he was suffering from, or an inability to drink the cow's milk.

She tried to think of something else. Dr. William Balmain had kept his promise and taught her how to milk. Although Tom had begun enthusiastically, he had soon become bored and disappeared below, so she and Will had been alone. She had taken Tom's place on the stool and Will had pressed her shoulder against the cow.

"That will prevent her kicking the bucket and save you much spillage, lass," he had explained.

The corners of Beth's mouth curled up mischievously. She had known how to handle that bloomin' cow in half an hour flat, but it had taken four whole days before Will was satisfied she could do it right!

Those four days had been the strangest and most wonderful days of her life. Strange, because Will had not put the word on her, and wonderful, because he had filled her head with tales of Balhepburn, Scotland, where he spent his childhood, and of all the other fascinating places he had been since joining the navy. He had even made Botany Bay, the fearful site of the new colony, sound exciting.

Jamie whimpered and Beth's thoughts returned to the present.

Lucy, who had been sponging his tiny limbs to get his fever down, looked up at her despairingly. "What more can I do?"

With a confidence she was far from feeling, Beth said, "Don't worry, Lucy, this old storm will blow itself out soon and Jamie will be as bonny as ever."

However, it was another week before the gale-force winds, driving rain and huge seas abated, and by then everyone was gravely concerned about Jamie.

As Lucy waited in the women's enclosure for Tom and Beth to arrive with the cow's milk, the first morning the convicts were allowed up on deck again, Susannah Holmes joined her.

"How is he, Lucy?" she enquired, glancing at Jamie's wasted body.

Lucy looked at her with haunted eyes. "He only managed a drop of water and orange juice. But here are Beth and Tom. Perhaps this time . . ."

"Would it help if I was to take Jamie to the breast, Dr. Arndell?" Susannah asked. "My son's as strong as an ox and would most likely take to cow's milk better than him."

They stared at her openmouthedly.

"Do you mean it, my dear?" Tom asked, as soon as he had recovered. "Much more work would be involved in feeding your Henry."

Susannah shrugged. "We all love little Jamie, sir. Besides, Lucy looked after my baby when I was sick."

"You are a very fine woman, Susannah," Tom murmured, "a very fine woman, indeed. Few would make such a sacrifice. Come, we'll go below to the hospital and see what can be done for Jamie."

Lucy's eyes glistened with tears. "Thank you, Susannah . . . thank you."

"No need for thanks, Lucy love," Susannah said gently. "What are friends for?"

31
Hugh Decides

Sunday, September 23, 1787

Carrigmoor Castle

My parents seem determined to marry me off to a chieftain's daughter, Hugh thought morosely as he sat fidgeting on the longseat beside the latest candidate, Fiona Stewart, listening to the nonsense his mother and Fiona's mother were uttering about the Autumn Ball.

On the opposite side of the room—broken arm in a sling, broken leg resting on a cushion—his father sat discussing clan matters with Fiona's father, Clarrie of Cantraydoun, a loud-mouthed braggart who was a member of the Inner Council.

Why do I allow this? Hugh asked himself for the hundredth time. *Fiona is passing fair, but I do not care for her in the least and, unless I put a stop to this madness, they will be posting the marriage banns.*

After glaring reproachfully at his mother, he joined the men. "How are the arm and leg tonight, Father?"

The Laird of Carrigmoor scowled darkly. Active by nature, he was finding the role of an invalid intolerable. "Pain's like to send me stark mad!"

Clarrie thumped his fist on the table. "Laird's not one to linger indoors with the women, aye, young Hugh? In the old days, we'd have got the gillies to take him about in a litter!"

Hugh ground his teeth. The Chieftain of Cantraydoun, who still ruled his tribe as his ancestors had done in the Dark Ages, always addressed him as "young Hugh," even at council meetings.

Sir Colin emptied a bottle of usquebaugh into a great pewter cup in the center of the table, then scoffed a great quantity of the fiery liquid before passing the pewter to his son. "The doctor says I'll not be on my feet until spring. Can you and Robert manage till then?"

Hugh drank dutifully from the cup and passed it to Clarrie. "Of course."

Sir Colin gave his son a petulant glare. "Robert's a good lad, he would ne'er let Carrigmoor go down. He was my right hand all the time *you* were away reading Law . . ."

Hugh grinned. "My foster brother does me credit."

Clarrie gulped down the usquebaugh, belched loudly and pushed the pewter toward his laird.

" 'Twas a rare stroke of good fortune that Robert found me the other day," muttered Sir Colin shifting about uncomfortably in his chair.

"Aye, laird!" Clarrie agreed. "A herdsman drowned in that self-same spot last year."

Sir Colin nodded grimly. "Robert reached me just in time. Another minute and I'd have been swept away by the current."

A pox on Robert McBain, thought Clarrie. *Had he tarried, young Hugh would be laird of the Stewarts, and my Fiona soon his lady.*

When Hugh came down for breakfast at dawn the next day, he found his mother already at the table.

"Good morning," he said, planting a kiss on her cheek and helping himself to a piece of her toast. "You are up and about early."

"I could say the same for you," she said, glancing at his riding outfit suspiciously. "Where are you off to at this ungodly hour, Hugh?"

He lifted the lid off the tureen and stared at the porridge with distaste. "I . . . er . . . have to ride into Fort Augustus. There is some farm machinery at Glendoebeg that I am interested in . . ."

Lady Barbara smiled knowingly. "So, it will not be the fair Fiona?"

A frown creased Hugh's handsome face. "No, Mother, it will not be Fiona."

"No one will do, except Faith, eh, Hugh?" she asked kindly.

"Am I so easy to read, Mother?"

"I have known forever, Hugh. Mothers sense these things. Have you spoken to Faith?"

A serious light came into his eyes. "I tried last Christmas, but she was troubled by something. The time was inappropriate . . ."

Lady Barbara nodded gravely. "Yes, she was deeply troubled. In fact, I am exceedingly worried about her." She put her teacup down and began weeping.

Hugh, who had never seen her cry before, was shocked. He went to her and took her in his arms. "Please let me help, Mother. I love her too."

"Oh, Hugh, I'm so worried," Lady Barbara sobbed, resting

her head on her son's broad shoulder. "I have heard nothing from Faith since last Christmas. Neither she nor your uncle have answered my letters. Something is terribly wrong—I know it! What am I to do?"

Hugh drew his distraught mother to her feet. "Why don't we go to the Blue Room? There, we will not be disturbed, and you can tell me everything."

"Perhaps Uncle was trying to prevent Faith from discovering some unpleasant aspect of her father's character?" Hugh suggested, after Lady Barbara had finished. "Maybe he was a drunkard or an adulterer . . ."

Lady Barbara shook her head emphatically. "Could anything be more unpleasant for Faith than to believe that her father had abandoned her mother a month before she was born? No, Hugh, there is more to this than my brother is willing to admit. He was definitely hiding something when I questioned him at Hogmanay. And when I persisted, he would have struck me down had Faith not stepped in . . ."

"So, you are saying he behaved that way because he was trying to protect himself—not Fae?"

"Yes, I suppose I am. He went to great lengths to avoid answering her questions. He even suggested that she was losing her mind!"

Hugh nodded thoughtfully. "I agree that was a bit extreme, but Fae is strong willed, such statements would not deter her for long."

"What do you think of the scar on her finger bleeding, Hugh?"

"I cannot imagine what caused such a remarkable occurrence, but if Faith said it happened, then it did."

"What will we do about this, Hugh?"

Hugh thought for some time before answering. "I would like to leave for Billingsley immediately but, with Father invalided, I cannot contemplate doing so, except in the direst emergency.

"However, your advice to Faith was sound, Mother. James Geldie would be an excellent person to enquire into her father's background. I shall write to him expressing my concern, and prevail upon him to deliver a letter to Uncle, in which I will state that if I don't receive satisfactory answers to my enquiries I shall go down to Billingsley."

Lady Barbara's eyes shone. "Oh, Hugh, what a grand idea. And, I shall write also."

Hugh was relieved that his mother's mood had brightened. "And, so we may be certain our letters reach James Geldie," he continued, "I shall ask Robert McBain to take them to London."

Lady Barbara saw the wisdom of her son's words. Robert McBain had been devoted to Faith since childhood. "When you write to my brother, Hugh, why don't you insist that Robert be permitted to speak to Faith in private? She might confide in him."

"An excellent idea," Hugh beamed. "Now, let's get on with our correspondences. The sooner they are written, the sooner Robert can leave."

Lady Barbara raised her eyebrows in mock surprise. "Does this mean you have decided to delay your trip to Fort Augustus, son?"

Hugh smiled sheepishly. "The farm equipment was unimportant, I just wanted to escape the hot-eyed Fiona and her churlish father. And I warn you, I will not tolerate any more matchmaking!"

Monday, September 24, 1787

Tom raised red-rimmed eyes and glanced at Michael, who was sitting on the other side of the crib with his head in his hands.

Jamie had pneumonia.

Tom had battled for five days to save him, but the disease had spread to every lobe of his lungs. Tom touched Michael on the shoulder. "Better fetch Lucy and Beth," he said in a low voice.

Michael looked at him blearily, not moving. Tom gave him a small shove. "Go quickly."

When Lucy entered the hospital she went to her son's crib and bent over him. His eyes were closed, and his hoarse, labored breathing filled the cabin. She touched his cheek. The heat of it seared her soul.

She knew, no one needed to tell her. She could see the tentacles of darkness growing out of his chest. She straightened, and looked at Tom. "Time to say good-bye, isn't it?"

Tom nodded, unable to speak.

Beth gave an anguished cry and buried her face in Michael's chest. "Oh, no! Blessed God in heaven, no . . . don't take him away!"

"May I hold him, Tom?" Lucy asked calmly.

"Yes, of course, my dear," Tom said.

Lucy cradled Jamie in her arms, rocked him back and forth and kissed his cheeks until Beth's wild sobbing broke into her consciousness.

"Don't cry, Bethy," she said softly. "Jamie has suffered enough—we must let him go. Come, give him one last kiss."

"I-I can't bear to think of him somewhere all alone," Beth cried, kissing the baby who had been the joy of her life. "He'll be afraid without us to watch over him . . . I know he will."

"Hush, darling," Lucy consoled. "You and I must be strong and help him see this through."

Beth looked into Lucy's eyes and understood. Choking back her sobs, she slid her finger into Jamie's fist in her usual way and felt a familiar pressure as his little fingers closed around it.

Minutes later, James Michael Thomas Gamble crossed the last plateau from life into death. They buried him at daybreak next morning.

They spoke no words over him, they were beyond that. For a few minutes, they stood silently around the coffin, which in life had been his crib, then Tom and Michael carried him to the rail and lowered him into the waiting arms of the sea.

A moment later, he disappeared beneath the white-tipped swell.

"Find your grandfather, Jamie. He will keep you company until I come," Lucy whispered. Then she placed an arm around Beth's shaking shoulders and gently led her below.

Sunday, September 30, 1787

Glimpsing lights in the distance, Hugh spurred on his horse. He was eager to exchange this chill, white world for the warmth and comfort of Carrigmoor; especially now that Fiona and her parents had returned to Cantraydoun.

No sooner was he inside the door than Lady Barbara rushed toward him, waving some sheets of paper aloft. "I have hardly been able to curb my impatience, Hugh. This letter from Faith arrived five minutes after you left for Davoit this morning."

Heaving a sigh of relief, Hugh snatched it from her. "Thank God, at last! What does she have to say?"

Lady Barbara's face became grave. "Her news is most disturbing."

"I do not find this letter disturbing," Hugh said when he finished reading. "In fact, I find it very heartening. The visions and the scar are a mystery to me, Mother, but Fae obviously has herself under control, and is determined to get to the bottom of this. Although, I disagree with her reasoning where my uncle is concerned.''

Lady Barbara sighed. "I confess, my brother has become an absolute stranger to me. Why he has kept Faith a prisoner in her room for two months is beyond my comprehension.''

Hugh frowned. "No, I don't mean that, I mean her decision not to question him. To my way of thinking, he must be forced to tell everything he knows.''

"But if she dares to ask questions, he will lock her up and force her to take the laudanum again.''

Hugh's eyes glinted. "Ah, but he can't lock me up, can he?''

Lady Barbara placed a hand on his arm. "Then you have decided to go to her, Hugh?''

He took her hand and led her closer to the fire.

"That I would go to her was never in doubt, Mother. The question was when. However, after receiving this letter I am convinced she can manage a while longer. I shall write to her tonight and tell her to expect me early in the New Year. Then, together, we shall solve this mystery.''

32
Capetown

Saturday, October 13, 1787

Phillip stood by the taffrail watching the approach of the shore boat containing Capetown's Harbormaster. The Fleet had completed the voyage from Rio to the Cape in thirty-nine days and, although a number of things needed to be attended to in Capetown, he hoped to be underway again in two weeks.

His first concern was the health of the people of the Fleet. Ninety-three convicts and twenty-three marines were ill. So as soon as he met Governor Van de Graaffe, he would petition him for fresh bread, meat, and vegetables.

Michael and Lucy leaned over the rail gazing at the lights of

Capetown. Although Michael had seen Lucy every day, this was his first opportunity to be alone with her since Jamie's death.

"I shall see Commodore Phillip in a few days," he murmured, placing an arm around her shoulders and drawing her closer.

"Yes . . . I expect you will," she said vaguely. "Doesn't Capetown look pretty at night? Father said the Palace Gardens are magnificent. Apparently, they contain many shady walkways and ostriches, tigers, zebras. . . . I expect you will see them tomorrow when you and the other officers attend the Governor."

Michael was very concerned about Lucy. Since Jamie's death, she had retreated into herself. "I am distressed to see you like this, Lucy. You make me feel so damned useless!"

Lucy looked up at him and he saw, sadly, that her eyes held no spark. "Oh Michael, I feel so *empty*. I am sorry." She made a visible effort. "Now, what were you saying? Oh, yes—the Commodore. I think we must be patient. Perhaps, when we reach Botany Bay, and other ships arrive from England, they will bring news from your lawyers and the Commodore's influential friend; maybe, even Ruth."

"You're right, the Commodore's letter may not even have reached England yet. . . . How is Beth? When Tom and I did rounds tonight, I thought she looked a little brighter."

Lucy kept her eyes on the lights of Capetown. "Jamie was the center of her life, Michael. She is lost without him. Sometimes she wakes up in the night thinking she can hear him crying . . ."

Michael's heart twisted painfully in his chest. "I am sorry, Lucy, for you, for her—and for me. I loved him too . . ."

"Yes, I know you did," Lucy said quickly. "B-but, can we please talk of other matters? It would be easier I think . . ."

Michael stroked her hair, twisting a dark lock through his fingers. "Well, I am still puzzled by that falling out between your father and Sir Michael Billingsley. Are you sure they never met again?"

"Reasonably so. When I was fifteen, I asked Father to take me to Billingsley Hall. Initially, he agreed, but afterward he decided against it."

"Why did he change his mind?"

"He thought Sir Michael might misconstrue our visit as an attempt to lay claim to my mother's inheritance. Father was very proud, as you know. . . ."

"Did your mother and father separate shortly before you were born, Lucy?"

She looked up at him startled. "Heavens, Michael, what a ridiculous question."

"That could account for Sir Michael never having contacted you. If he believed James had mistreated your mother . . ."

Lucy stepped out of his arms. "Father mistreat Mother? What utter nonsense, Michael!"

"How can you be so certain?"

"Really, Michael, you are being exasperating! Don't you think I would know? Father spoke of her often over the years, and although he had many opportunities to remarry, he chose not to. When I asked him why he didn't he said he had everything he needed—me, and his happy memories of Mother."

"But he did marry Ruth in the end."

Lucy considered his words and answered more calmly. "Yes, but I think he did it more for me, than for any personal needs of his own. The war with America was looming and, shortly before he met Ruth, he received word from the Admiralty that his next voyage would be an extended one.

"Theirs was an odd relationship. Ruth had no depth to her character and her lack of intellect often frustrated him. No, the more I think on it, the more I am convinced Father's one great love was Mother. Why do you think he wore her charm until the day he died? Mistreat her, indeed!"

Michael's mouth twitched. He could hardly expect Lucy to give an impartial opinion of Ruth. "Hush, Lucy, I meant no offence. It was just a thought, and a foolish one at that."

He took her hand and began pulling her along the deck. "Let's take another stroll. You were wrong when you said your mother was your father's one great love. He had two others that I know of."

"What are you implying?" Lucy asked in an affronted voice.

He chuckled. "Calm yourself, seadog. I was referring to you and the sea."

Two hours later, Michael and Ralph sprang to attention as Major Ross burst through the cuddy door. He returned their salute briskly and enquired as to Meredith's whereabouts.

"C-C-Captain Meredith's ashore, sir," Ralph stammered. "I-I am duty officer today."

Major Ross fixed him with a bristling stare. "When Captain

125

Meredith returns, inform him that all female felons are to make ready to depart the ship. Carpenters and sawyers will come aboard tomorrow to convert the aft prison into sheep pens. Naturally, those artificers are to receive *every* cooperation." He handed Ralph a written copy of his orders. "Is that clear, Lieutenant?"

"Yes, sir!" Ralph snapped out, clicking his heels and saluting.

Then Ross handed Michael a letter. "For you, Lieutenant Perryman. The Commodore requested that I deliver it."

As soon as Ross departed the ship, Ralph did a jig around the cuddy table. "That's the best news I've heard since coming on this accursed voyage! Those foul creatures to go, and well-behaved sheep to take their place. Whoopee! Oh, Betsy, dear, sweet wife, your Ralph is free of them at last!"

His mind in a turmoil, Michael left the cuddy and walked to the stern. Lucy, to be transferred? The orders were clear, there would be no circumventing them. His only course of action was to transfer to the same ship as her. . . .

He tore open the envelope. Inside was a brief note from Phillip inviting him to his lodgings in Capetown the following Saturday evening.

Saturday, October 27, 1787

Michael made his way despondently along the wooden quay. His interview with Major Ross had been unsuccessful. Ross had dismissed his request for a transfer saying curtly that, if he was to grant every fanciful request from his officers, he would be employed twenty-four hours a day and still not be able to arrange things to anyone's satisfaction.

Tomorrow, the women would depart the ship: Lucy, Beth, Susannah, baby Henry, Elizabeth Pugh, and her daughter Nancy to *Charlotte* and the other women to *Prince of Wales*. Jane Parkinson and little Edward would go on board *Lady Penrhyn*. Tom had told Lucy that Jane needed more specialized medical care than could be given aboard *Charlotte*, where the Surgeon General's time was limited, but in fact he feared Jane would not survive the voyage and had wanted to spare Lucy and Beth the trauma of another death.

During dinner, Phillip expressed bitter disappointment at the delays

126

he had experienced, and laid the blame squarely at the feet of the Governor, Monsieur Van de Graaffe, who had forced him to cool his heels for two weeks before granting him permission to purchase the much needed fresh food for the Fleet.

Once the meal was over, the conversation turned to Lucy.

"I was saddened to hear of Lucy's loss," said Phillip. "How is she bearing up?"

"The life has gone out of her, sir. She goes through the motions of living but nothing penetrates the barrier she has erected around herself. Even the news that she is to be transferred to another ship has left her unmoved," Michael replied disconsolately.

Phillip stroked his chin thoughtfully. "I am sorry to hear that, Michael. The poor girl has certainly had her fair share of misfortune. Did she tell you any more about the rift between her father and Sir Michael?"

"She told me a great deal, sir." Michael related what he had learned. "So, you see, your friend did lie about James deserting Margaret before the girls were born."

Phillip sighed. "I agree. I have thought long and hard on the matter and I am convinced that Sir Michael would have returned to Billingsley with both babies if James Gamble had, in fact, deserted Margaret. Therefore, Sir Michael must have concealed Faith from her father the night she was born—I can find no other explanation."

"Nor I," said Michael, "And your friend's crime—for that is what I consider it to be—has gone undetected for twenty years."

Phillip nodded gravely. "It seems so. Although, in my opinion, Sir Michael's success was due in no small part to James Gamble's unbending pride. Had he taken Lucy to Billingsley Hall at any time in those twenty years, Sir Michael would have been exposed."

Michael drummed his fingers on the table impatiently. "You probably have a point there, sir. But, all I can think of is the great harm Sir Michael has done Lucy and Faith."

Phillip rose and walked to the window. "Your concern matches mine, Michael. There are things I have not told you. It seems Faith had had an inner perception of Lucy's plight. Lucy's papers state that she was arrested on the sixteenth of October, 1786. I was at Billingsley Hall that night. I remember the date because I had received my Commission from the King . . ." He told Michael what had taken place in the library.

"What Faith saw does appear to go beyond the bounds of

coincidence, sir,'' Michael murmured. "But, to the best of my knowledge, Lucy hasn't experienced anything of like nature. What do you propose we do next?"

Phillip went to his desk. "We can do no more on the English front. But I think we can do something for Lucy. I have changed my mind, I think you should tell her about Faith. Perhaps the joy of finding a twin sister will ease the pain of losing a beloved son. What say you?"

Unable to contain his delight, Michael leapt up. "I like the idea! At the very least, the news will turn Lucy's mind away from her grief and set it on another course."

Smiling broadly, Phillip handed him the letter Sir Michael had sent him in Portsmouth. "Give her this. It will be something tangible for her to grasp. When do you propose to tell her?"

"Tonight, sir, as soon as I return to the ship. Lucy leaves for *Charlotte* in the morning . . ."

Although Michael was sorely tempted to ask Phillip to intervene in the matter of his transfer, he knew it would be unfair to ask Phillip to overrule Ross, so he held his peace.

33

A Question of Faith

"Why have you dragged me here in the dead of night?" Lucy asked sleepily as Michael pushed her into the cuddy and closed the door. "Couldn't whatever it is have waited until morning?"

"I apologize for the lateness of the hour, but what I have to tell you requires privacy and this is the only time the cuddy is available," he said.

"You are being very mysterious," she said, sitting opposite him at the table. "Has the Commodore come to a decision about me?"

"He has indeed. But his decision has nothing to do with your current circumstances. This is something else entirely—" He broke off, and ran his fingers through his hair with a frustrated gesture. "It's difficult to know where to begin!"

Lucy blinked, forcing her drooping eyelids to stay open. "Has it something to do with all those questions?"

He nodded. "Remember the day Phillip visited the ship and you thought he seemed shocked to see you? Well, you were right—he was flabbergasted! In fact, he mistook you for Sir Michael Billingsley's granddaughter."

"But I *am* Sir Michael's granddaughter," Lucy said. "Did the Commodore know my grandfather?"

"Yes, Phillip was—*is* an intimate of Sir Michael's. They have known each other for many years. Furthermore, your grandfather is still alive."

"Oh, is that all," Lucy murmured.

"No, not by a long shot. Phillip was shocked because he mistook you for Sir Michael's granddaughter, Faith."

Lucy's eyes opened wide. "Another granddaughter? Called Faith? But that's ridiculous. Mother was an only child."

"Yes, your mother was indeed an only child," Michael said slowly. "Now, I want you to listen very carefully, Lucy. Faith Billingsley is your sister—your identical twin sister."

Lucy's hands flew to her face. "What are you saying, Michael? I-I don't understand a word of it!"

Michael persevered. "You have an identical twin sister . . . and her name is Faith Billingsley. The night you were born, your grandfather took her without your father's knowledge and—"

Lucy jumped to her feet, her countenance distracted. "Took her? My grandfather? You mean Sir Michael Billingsley?"

"Yes," Michael replied. "Please sit down Lucy, and try to stay calm."

Lucy sank into the chair. "But you simply aren't making any sense, Michael."

He sighed. "Just listen . . . and concentrate. Apparently, almost twenty years ago, your grandfather returned to Billingsley Hall with your mother's body and a newborn baby girl. He told everyone that your father had abandoned your mother shortly before Faith's birth, but he made no mention of a second daughter—namely, you."

Lucy placed her hands over her eyes. "Michael, Michael, you *must* be mistaken, I have no sister. I-I am an only child . . ."

Michael captured her hands. "Believe me, Faith Billingsley *is* your twin. The Commodore has checked all the facts. Faith knows nothing about you either. Although, it appears that she saw you in Portsmouth . . ."

Portsmouth, the Solent, the woman with her face! Lucy's heart flopped over and, in the core of her, something infinitesimal that had always been out of place, righted itself.

129

"What about Portsmouth?" she asked softly.

"Phillip invited Sir Michael and Faith down to Portsmouth . . ."

His words rang in Lucy's ears: crystal clear, sharp, concise. ". . . and Faith must have seen you in the guard boat because she ran into the water . . ."

Tears rolled down Lucy's cheeks. "Yes, she swam after me . . ."

"You saw her then?"

"Yes," she breathed, "I saw her."

He squeezed her hands, emotion welling up within him. "That was your sister."

Lucy's lips trembled. "But, how could such a thing have happened?"

The despair and confusion in her voice tore at his heart. "Believe me, darling, it did. I know it sounds incredible, but every word I have spoken is true. The Commodore has farmed near Billingsley Hall for a quarter of a century. He attended your parents' wedding. He has confirmed that Faith was born on the eleventh of November 1766, that her parents are your parents, that you share the same grandfather, that you are identical in features . . ."

In a wondering voice, Lucy spoke her sister's name. "Faith, Faith." Then, as Michael watched, a change came over her. She stiffened in her chair and her eyes narrowed to green slits of fire. "Why were we separated? Who did this terrible thing?"

"We don't know why, but the Commodore and I are convinced that Sir Michael was responsible. In the beginning we also suspected your father but we are now satisfied he knew nothing."

Lucy closed her eyes and her face contracted with pain. "Oh, God, Father! He never knew Faith . . . nor she him. Now, it is too late!" She rested her head in her arms and wept brokenheartedly.

After a time, her sobs subsided and she raised her head. "Does Faith know about me?"

Michael nodded grimly. "She will soon, darling. Phillip has written to both her and Sir Michael. It appears that Faith has also suffered greatly, Lucy . . ."

Lucy nodded her head slowly. "Yes, she has suffered. But Faith is strong." She brushed the tears from her cheeks. "I believe that she has been with me almost from the moment Richard Newport died. As he faded away, she came. Like a beacon in the darkness, she was there for me . . ." She looked at Michael with shining eyes. "Oh, Michael, I sensed her presence, I swear!"

"I don't pretend to understand, Lucy, but I believe you," he murmured. "There seems to be a spiritual bond between you and Faith that transcends logic. Commodore Phillip was visiting Billingsley Hall the night you were arrested. At midnight, Faith came to Sir Michael and told him she'd had a vision of a woman calling out to her from a dark place—a woman alone and terribly afraid."

"I told you, I told you!" Lucy cried. "She has been the guardian of my sanity these last months!"

"But at a high cost to herself, I fear," Michael said sadly.

"What do you mean? Has something happened to her?" She sighed and sank back in her chair. "No, nothing has happened. I would have sensed it. For a while, after Portsmouth, she faded. But since the night Jamie was born she has been near. If I reached out, just beyond . . . just beyond." Her voice trailed off.

Michael handed her Phillip's letter. "The Commodore asked me to give you this. He thought it might help to establish things firmly in your mind."

Lucy opened the letter and read it aloud.

My dear friend,

I apologize for Faith's unseemly behavior the other day. Since that night at the Hall last October, she has suffered from an unsoundness of the mind. Regrettably, no amount of patient persuasion has convinced her that what she thought was a divine vision was, in fact, an hallucination.

These last few months, her condition has grown steadily worse until last Monday at Portsmouth when her madness finally took control of the little reason she had left.

I blame myself for not seeking medical advice sooner but, loving her as I do, I hoped some miracle would bring her to her senses. Yesterday, I placed her in the care of an eminent London physician, who has had a high degree of success treating disorders of the mind. He has prescribed isolation, rest, and liberal doses of laudanum.

Already the drafts have had a calming effect on her and I am encouraged to hope that, in time, she will be restored to me again.

Because her condition requires that she be watched day and night, I am unable to come to Portsmouth to view the departure of the Fleet as I had planned; however, I trust that the ensuing years will be kind to you, Arthur, and that your

expectations for the new colony will eventually be realized.
Until we meet again, my dear friend,
Michael B.

Her green eyes blazing, Lucy folded the letter. "The despicable, lying hypocrite. It is *he* who is mad. When he saw her suffering why did he withhold the truth?"

Michael shook his head perplexed. "I do not know. What could have been more important to him than Faith's sanity? Yet he loves her more than his own life, according to Phillip."

"Then may God protect her from such love," Lucy said bitterly.

Michael reached for her hand. "When did you write to him?"

"Early last year—April," she replied vaguely.

"He *must* have received the letter, Lucy. He was at Billingsley."

Lucy withdrew her hand. "Michael, would you do something for me?"

"Of course."

"Would you leave me alone for a while? I need time to think. Please, don't be offended, I am grateful beyond words for all you have done, but I . . ."

He rose. "No need to explain. I understand. Stay here as long as you like. I shall tell the guards to let you into the prison when you are ready."

She smiled her gratitude, and he left.

"Michael, wake up!"

He heard her call and awoke with a start. Except for a shaft of moonlight beaming through the porthole, the cabin was encased in darkness. For a moment he thought he must be dreaming, then he felt her warm breath on his face and her hands on his shoulders.

"Michael—wake up!"

She had come to him at last. He pulled her down and kissed her hungrily. But something was wrong. There was no answering passion, no spark, no glow. Her lips were tightly closed and her body unyielding.

"Lucy," he groaned.

"No Michael, please!" She pummeled his chest and he released her.

"What are you doing here? How did you get past the guards?"

"They were fast asleep, so I crept by them. Are you awake? We must talk."

"You took a great risk coming to my cabin," he muttered.

She leaned closer so she could see him more clearly. "My reputation you mean? Really, Michael, you've heard Lieutenant Clark, we convict women are all born whores."

He grabbed her and shook her. "Don't ever speak that way again, Lucy. I meant that you took a damned risk with me. Are you blind? Have you no idea how much I want you!"

She moved backward, as far away from him as she could. "I am neither blind nor stupid, Michael. I came here because you are my friend and I need your help. How are you fixed for money? I need some gold coin."

He released her. "Go back to the cuddy, I will join you in a few minutes. The walls of the cabins are thin."

She backed toward the door. "Please hurry. We have much to decide and very little time left."

"What is this about?" Michael asked tersely when he joined her in the cuddy.

"Don't be angry," she pleaded, "We will be parted soon. Let's not spend our last hours together fighting. I am sorry about the other, Michael, I am not without feelings for you. . . . But I am afraid, so afraid of it. Be patient with me."

The anger went out of him. "Lucy, darling," he said gently as he sat down opposite her, "I love you desperately. I think I shall go mad without you these next months. *There*, it is out in the open. I understand what you have been through. But you must not judge all men by Newport and Lewis. When a man and woman love each other, their lovemaking is a glorious experience, filled with excitement and passion. Many would say that love is the greatest of life's pleasures. What you suffered at Richard Newport's hands had nothing to do with love."

"Please, Michael. Don't make me think about the hands."

He saw the pupils in her eyes dilating and contracting, and his heart sank. "My hands are part of me, Lucy. I love you, and my hands express that love, darling."

She shuddered violently. "I am so afraid of the hands, Michael. Don't make me talk about the hands, I beg you!"

He sighed, defeated, and leaned back in his chair. "Will you try to come to terms with your fear, Lucy, for both our sakes?"

The pain in his voice was like a knife in Lucy's heart. She

wanted to make him happy, she wanted to bring him joy, but there was a sickness in her that she could not control. "I-I promise I shall try," she whispered. "You mean a great deal to me."

He looked at her steadily. "That's all I ask, darling. Now, what is it you wish to discuss?"

"I am worried about the letter Commodore Phillip wrote to Faith. If she doesn't receive it, I shall remain a phantom in her mind. What if my grandfather receives the letter meant for Faith? Would he pass it on to her? I think not."

"But why would he withhold it? Phillip has exposed him."

"Think carefully, Michael. The man has gone to extraordinary lengths to conceal his crime. I doubt he would perceive Phillip, who will be absent from England for years, as any threat."

Michael's handsome countenance creased in a thoughtful frown. "You know, Lucy, I think you have a point . . ."

Lucy sighed deeply. "When you went to your cabin, I sat here trying to contact Faith with my will, but I failed. Michael, I have so much love to give her, and many things to tell her. I-I long to hold her and never let her go. I cannot bear for her to be so far away!"

"Don't despair, darling, we shall find a way."

Lucy leaned forward urgently. "*I* must write to Faith. Phillip's reasoning was sound, but he did not allow for my grandfather's duplicity or his desire to keep Faith with him at any cost. There are a number of foreign ships at anchor here, and some, no doubt, are bound for England. Could we find a trustworthy seaman and pay him gold to deliver my letter to Faith?"

"But how could we be sure he *would* deliver it?"

"Or if you find the man, Michael, and arrange for me to meet him, I shall convince him to do it," she said confidently. "And I shall have no difficulty describing Faith's features. He need only look at me to see her in the flesh!"

Michael stared at her intently; it was as if a veil had lifted and she had come alive before his eyes. "Your plan is excellent, darling. I shall start searching for your mariner tomorrow, first thing."

Frances Hart could hardly contain her excitement when Lucy and the other women came aboard *Charlotte*.

"Ain't it grand to see you," she laughed, throwing her arms

134

around Lucy. "But where's my sweet boy? I've been saving my biggest kiss for him."

Lucy placed an arm around Beth's suddenly shaking shoulders and said haltingly. "I am sorry, Frances, but . . . but Jamie is dead, and there is nothing for it but to go on without him."

Frances gasped and turned white with shock.

Susannah handed baby Henry to Suzy Gought and took Frances's hand. "Come on, Frances, dear," she said kindly. "Show us our new quarters. They can't be worse than those on *Friendship*." She forced a cheerful note into her voice. "My, the news I've got to tell you! Guess who is pregnant?"

"Marg Hall?" Suzy Gought said, taking her lead.

"No, but you're close—Sarah McCormick! Sarah had Dr. Arndell going a treat. At one stage he thought she was dying of the pox when she came out in a rash and could keep nothing down, but, 'twas only the morning sickness. God, she's a devil, that one!"

"Guess which one of us has a sweetheart," said Suzy.

"Who?" Susannah asked gleefully.

"Frances Hart, that's who! His name's William Robertson and he follows her round like a faithful dog."

They giggled and the awkward moment passed. All chattering at once, they took up their possessions and clambered down the ladder.

When Michael arrived on board *Charlotte* next day, John White was not in his cabin, so he went looking for the marine Commandant, Captain Watkin Tench.

"What brings you to *Charlotte,* Lieutenant Perryman?" Tench asked, ushering Michael into his cabin.

"Could you tell me when John White is expected back on board, Captain? I have a private matter to discuss with him . . ."

"John has taken up lodgings in town," Tench told him. "Can I be of assistance?"

Michael looked at him levelly. "May I have permission to talk to a woman who came aboard from *Friendship* yesterday? I realize the request is unorthodox, but Lucy's father was my former commanding officer, and I am concerned about her."

"Permission granted. Why don't you take her to the stern? It's more private there," said Tench, who had already heard of Michael's connection with Lucy through James Meredith.

"Thank you, Captain. I will be visiting Lucy daily. Shall I report to you every time?"

Tench smiled. "That won't be necessary. I can rely on your discretion of course?"

Michael looked at him steadily. "You can, Captain."

"We had a fatality aboard *Friendship* this morning," Michael told Lucy as they made their way along the crowded deck to the stern, "Vallance, the Second Mate, fell overboard. Best and Sidaway jumped in after him but being exceedingly drunk, he sank like a stone." He handed her a parcel of writing paper. "I thought you might like to get started on that letter to Faith."

Lucy smiled so brightly he was dazzled. "Thank you, Michael. I am most eager to begin!"

"I seem to have found the way to your heart at last." He smiled in the slow way that Lucy found so disconcerting. "Tell me, how are you and Beth faring?"

She leaned against the rail and gazed aloft at the furled sails. "*Charlotte*'s prison is roomier than *Friendship*'s and not nearly as dark. Please don't worry about me, Michael, I will be fine. How goes your search for our good samaritan?"

He grinned. "All business today, aren't we? As a matter of fact, since you left the ship I have spent most of my time supervising the conversion of your old quarters into sheep pens. But I have been thinking hard.

"There are more than a hundred ships anchored in the bay and, as I can't possibly visit every one, I think the crew of *Friendship,* who meet other crews in the dockside taverns, are our best hope. We can expect to hear something toward the end of this week." He glanced over his shoulder. "I say, Lucy, isn't that Will Balmain down there on the quarterdeck with Beth?"

"The Thief of Death always catches us unaware, lass," William Balmain said sympathetically when a tearful Beth told him of Jamie's demise. "I have met him many times in my profession, yet I have never become reconciled to the swiftness with which he strikes." He gave her shoulder a comforting pat. "The final leg of this voyage will be long and difficult. At the end, no safe harbor like Capetown will await us—just a vast, wild land. Only the strong will survive the hard years ahead. Perhaps God, in His wisdom, spared your wee Jamie the struggle . . ."

136

Beth looked at William Balmain's striking, rough-hewn face. Beyond a doubt, he was a survivor. He reminded her more of a buccaneer than a doctor.

"Take my arm, lass," he invited, seemingly unconcerned by the attention they were attracting. "You and I shall stroll round the deck. Did you hear about the mutiny on board my ship, *Alexander?*"

Beth wiped the tears from her cheeks with the back of her hand and looked at him suspiciously. "Is this another one of your Scottish fairytales, Dr. Balmain?"

"Och no, lass," he said with mock horror. "The mutiny happened on the high seas a month ago, and the ringleader was none other than that daring scoundrel, Powers, who attempted to escape in Tenerife—remember I told you about him?"

Beth nodded, all attention.

"A rogue, a confidence man, and a blackguard of the highest order is Powers, although he has an air of innocence about him for all that! It happened when I was atop the mainmast—"

"Atop the mainmast! Ain't that dangerous?"

"No, once you get the hang of it, it is a bonny spot. I take myself up there whenever I need to escape from my fellow officers. Well, there I was, up the main, peacefully employed looking out for Spirma Castes—"

"What's a bloomin' Spirma Caste?"

"A whale, lass! As I said, there I was with little hope of spotting one in the thick conditions, when I heard shouts from below. When you look down at the deck from that height, people take on dwarflike proportions, and what with the wind wailing and the yards creaking, I could not tell what the commotion was about, although even from that height I could see something was amiss. I shimmied down the mast as fast as I was able, but I could not throw caution entirely to the wind as, with the heavy swell running, one false move would have left *Alexander* without a doctor."

"I would have been sick!"

"Seasickness is not a failing of mine, lass. I finally reached the deck but, by then, the mutiny was over, although it could hardly be called that. Not one blow had been struck. Apparently, it had been forestalled in the nick of time by a convict informer."

"Humph! It wasn't near as exciting as the mutiny I was in . . ."

He listened avidly while she spun him a fantastic tale about the goings-on aboard the *Mercury* and, by the time he took his leave, Beth was feeling much happier.

He's a wild lad, she thought as she watched him maneuvering his tiny craft through the choppy waters toward the quay. *He has the trappings of a gentleman, but he is reckless like John Best. I wonder what he wants with me. . . .*

She turned away from the rail and waved to Lucy and Michael. Well, no use her puzzling over him, he would let her know what he wanted when he was good and ready—and not a moment before!

PART FOUR
Aurora Australis!

34
Mr. Leslie Gellin

Friday, November 2, 1787

Mr. Leslie Gellin, First Mate of the schooner *Louise,* jingled the ten gold pieces in his pocket as he waited by the taffrail. Easy money this—money for nought!

As Lucy approached, she looked at Leslie Gellin closely. Perhaps fifty, he had a deeply furrowed brow and a tanned weather-beaten complexion but it was his eyes she focused on, and what she saw, she liked. They had no cringe or slide-away about them and she sensed that, if she could bring him round to her way of thinking, he was her man.

"Good evening, Mr. Gellin," she said, offering her hand.

Leslie Gellin blinked. *Jesus! What a beauty.* Even an old seadog like him could get his gander up for her! He snatched his battered three-cornered hat off his head.

"Evenin' ma'am. The Lieutenant tells me you have a letter you want delivered to a certain party in England?"

Lucy fought to repress a shudder as his hand claimed hers. She *must* establish a warm, open rapport with this man; the future—hers and Faith's—depended on it. The moment of panic passed and she smiled. "That is so, Mr. Gellin. The letter is to be delivered to my twin sister, Miss Faith Billingsley, who lives in West Hampshire."

"That will be no trouble, ma'am. *Louise* is bound for Plymouth and Hampshire is just a step from there."

Lucy handed him a bulky letter. "If you will look on the back of the envelope, Mr. Gellin, you will see that I have instructed my sister to pay you a further ten gold pieces upon delivery."

Leslie Gellin's eyes shone. Not ten, but twenty gold guineas. He was a wealthy man! "That's right generous of ye, ma'am."

Lucy looked at him piercingly. "Mr. Gellin, you have been recommended as a trustworthy man. Do you believe yourself so?"

Gellin stiffened his shoulders. *What was her tack?* "I am reputed to be a man of me word, ma'am" he replied slowly.

Lucy stepped closer. "Mr. Gellin, the letter means nothing to you, but it is imperative that my sister receives it. Therefore, the extra gold pieces are not so much generous as a fair squaring of our account. May I be absolutely frank?"

Gellin nodded solemnly. *Who was this Lucy Gamble?* He could see by the way she planted her feet on the deck that she was no lubber.

"If you are negligent of my instructions and deliver the letter to the master of Billingsley Hall instead of my sister, he will either give you ten times our agreed sum or send you direct to Davy Jones's locker."

"Jesus, ma'am!"

She had his attention now. His eyes were riveted on her.

"No need to worry, ma'am. Twenty guineas be more than enough. Your sister will get her letter, I'll stake my davy on it."

Lucy smiled at him warmly and steeled herself for the next part. "Glad to hear it, Mr. Gellin. Now, if you will give me your arm, we shall take a stroll. We have a great deal to discuss before we take our leave of each other . . ."

Leslie Gellin knew Lucy's life story by the time he left *Charlotte*, and she was certain that nothing short of death would prevent him delivering the letter.

Monday, November 12

Every inch of *Charlotte*'s decks was covered with provisions and stock and, with the people milling about, there was nowhere to be alone.

"I spoke to John White. If you need anything, go to him," Michael said as he led Lucy between two animal pens.

"Yes, Michael, I shall."

"Have you enough soap and sultanas?"

"Yes, Michael, I have."

"And blankets—I sent extra over with Tom. Did he give them to you?"

"Yes, Michael, he did."

"As we stretch farther south the weather will become colder, so don't give them away, Lucy."

"No, Michael, I won't."

Lucy had to change the subject. "Tom told me he received a letter from his sister in England. The ship that brought it only took eleven weeks to reach the Cape. If Mr. Gellin's ship is favored with good winds, perhaps Faith will receive my letter in February."

"Maybe sooner," Michael said tensely, pressing her down on some sacks. "Lucy, darling—I have to leave. They are calling from the longboat. I should have been back aboard *Friendship* an hour ago."

Lucy looked at him helplessly. "Oh, Michael . . ."

He gripped her shoulders and leant closer. "One kiss, Lucy—one kiss willingly given."

She nodded and closed her eyes. His hands came up under her arms, lifting her, and the next moment his mouth closed over hers. Michael's mouth—not Richard Newport's. The langour she had experienced that day in his cabin swept over her and she sought his lips with an answering response. His grip on her tightened and his mouth grew hard and demanding. Overcome with a need to touch him, she slid her hands up his back. Hard, warm skin . . . muscles moving under her fingers. Her pulse raced, and a feverish excitement welled up within her.

With a muttered oath, he pushed her away.

Startled, she opened her eyes. "Michael . . . Michael."

His eyes were glazed and the mouth that had kissed her so warmly was set in a hard line. She was confused. What had she done wrong?

"I must leave, Lucy," he said hoarsely, holding her at arm's length.

In a daze, she touched his cheek. "I don't understand. Why are you angry? What did I do?"

Some of the tautness left him and he smiled in his old way. "Hush, darling, you did nothing wrong. It is time to leave, that's all." He pulled her hard against him for a moment more, then released her, and was gone.

The Fleet dropped out into Table Bay and by midafternoon had picked up a favorable breeze from the south. The convicts crowded the decks. Some grew so melancholy they wept, but most stood in silence staring fixedly at the fast-diminishing African coastline.

As a crimson sunset highlighted their last tantalizing glimpse of civilization, Fate tossed a morsel of hope. The Fleet met up with the *Kent,* four months out from Portsmouth. Although she carried no letters, her news was good. Already ships were being taken up for Botany Bay. Then, even *Kent* was gone—the cheers of her crew fading as she crowded on sail for the Cape.

Soon afterward, the signal came for the ships to take up their stations and, with *Sirius* leading the way, they turned east toward the lonely, uncharted waters of the Indian Ocean and the wild, untamed land beyond. Their fate now lay in the hands of the navigators. The voyage into the unknown had begun.

35

Master Morton Arrives

Sunday, November 25, 1787

Sir Michael closed his eyes and settled back more comfortably in the chair. Outside it was bitterly cold, but here in the library, where the fire blazed brightly, it was peaceful and warm.

Six months had elapsed since the incident in Portsmouth and Faith had resumed many of her old duties, including the running of the household. As a sign of his trust and confidence, he had given her permission to travel unaccompanied within the borough this last week.

He and Faith were again on good terms, although the closeness they had once enjoyed was a thing of the past. He was willing to let bygones be bygones but still she held back—her former demonstrative affection replaced by studied politeness. But, despite her lack of warmth, he was satisfied with her progress. She never mentioned the visions and, except for one unpleasant incident recently, peace had returned to the Hall.

He frowned, remembering the arrival of James Geldie bearing letters from his sister and Hugh. He had been foolish to ignore those letters from Barbara. One or two carefully worded replies and the unpleasant interview with Geldie could have been avoided.

Hugh's letter had been particularly offensive but he had been forced to comply with its demands. Hugh enjoyed some influence with Faith and the last thing he wanted was Hugh on his doorstep asking difficult questions!

Sir Michael looked up to see his manservant, Kenneth, at the door.

"Begging your pardon, m'lord, Mr. Micah Morton awaits without and wishes to speak with you personally. He has recently returned from abroad and has letters to yourself and Miss Faith from Captain Phillip."

Sir Michael smiled, delighted. "Phillip! Gad, what a surprise. I did not expect a letter so soon. Show Morton in, Kenneth—and bring us hot rum!"

A few moments later when Micah Morton entered the library Sir Michael rushed forward eagerly. "Do come in, Morton," he said, pumping the mariner's hand. "You are most welcome, most welcome, indeed. Take a seat by the fire and warm yourself. I have ordered refreshments."

Micah Morton removed his thin gloves and tried to rub feeling into his frozen hands. "We have not met, Sir Michael, but I was aboard *Sirius* the day you and your granddaughter visited the Commodore in Portsmouth."

"Quite so, quite so, Morton. But, what brings you back to England prematurely?"

"I suffered a rupture in Tenerife, Sir Michael. So, the Commodore decided to send me home." Micah Morton removed two letters from his satchel and handed them to Sir Michael. "The Commodore asked me to deliver these personally."

Sir Michael took the letters and turned them over. "Letters from Arthur, eh? What an unexpected pleasure. Does everything go well with the Fleet?"

Needing no further encouragement, the mariner launched into a detailed account of the voyage. By the time he finished, long shadows were creeping across the library floor.

"I insist you dine at the Hall tonight," said Sir Michael. "My granddaughter will have a thousand questions to ask. Please, make yourself comfortable while I read the Commodore's letter. I confess, I am overcome with curiosity as to its contents. . . ."

Sir Michael folded the letter with trembling hands and glanced at the other letter in his lap. He had to destroy them before Faith arrived home. Otherwise, he was undone!

He jumped up, knocked over the table beside the chair and woke Micah Morton who had been dozing by the fire.

"What's that!" cried the startled mariner, crouching forward in his chair.

Sir Michael swore loudly. Morton! He had forgotten him. He must be got rid of. He flung open the library door, calling for Kenneth. "Forgive me, Morton, I just remembered a prior engagement which, in the excitement, entirely slipped my mind. My granddaughter will be distraught to have missed you, but there you are . . ."

"Never mind, Sir Michael," said the amiable mariner, "I'll stay at the Lyndhurst Inn tonight and return to the Hall in the morning before going on to London—"

"Absolutely not!" thundered Sir Michael, his face turning crimson. Then, recovering himself somewhat, "I mean . . . well, unfortunately we are leaving at daybreak on an extended tour of the Continent—" He broke off as Kenneth entered the room. "Kenneth, give Morton the bay gelding to take to London." He held up his hand as Morton protested. "No, indeed, Morton, I insist. The least I can do, under the circumstances. You have come far out of your way. Now, you really must excuse me, I-I am in a great hurry."

He snatched up the letters and, ignoring Morton's outstretched hand, rushed from the library. When he reached his room he read Faith's letter, then tossed it on the bed and paced the floor distractedly. What was he to do? How many other people had Phillip informed?

He cursed aloud and called himself a fool for not having had the presence of mind to ask Morton what other correspondence he carried. But he could not have risked Faith meeting him.

Perhaps he should go after Morton? He pressed his fists against his eye sockets, trying to think. His head throbbed and white spots danced before his eyes. How could he visit Morton at the inn? Hadn't he told him he was leaving for the Continent at daybreak? The white lines became white zigzags, distorting his vision.

Hearing Faith downstairs, he scooped up the letters, ran to his dressing room and stuffed the letters into the pocket of an old gray greatcoat he never wore. He only just made it back to his bedchamber before Faith knocked and poked her head around the door.

"Sorry I am late, but my horse threw a shoe and I had to visit the blacksmith's. I asked Cook to hold back the evening meal so I could bathe. You don't mind, do you?"

Noticing his high color and trembling lips, she stepped inside the room. "You look upset, Grandfather. Are you unwell?"

"Just a slight headache, my dear," he assured her. "Probably got it dozing in front of the fire all afternoon. Don't worry about the meal, I shall take the opportunity to rest."

"Please do," she said, and left.

He staggered to the other side of the room and collapsed on the bed. His mouth was dry and a million insects buzzed in his ears. When he closed his eyes, he felt as if he had dropped into an abyss. If Faith discovered the truth she would leave him—just as Margaret had left him after all the years he had devoted to her.

He breathed in deeply, trying to calm himself. Perhaps he was taking the letters too seriously? After all, Phillip would be away from England for years.

He sprang up in bed. Morton! Morton was the danger. Phillip, being a discreet man, would not have taken someone like Morton into his confidence, but Phillip may have disclosed what he knew to a mutual friend, say, Sir George Rose.

He fell back against the pillows and covered his face with his hands. No, even that was unlikely. Phillip would probably wait until he heard from him or Faith. Nevertheless, just to make sure he would have Morton set on on the way to London and any letters he carried stolen. And, first thing in the morning, he would issue orders to the servants that all visitors and letters arriving at the Hall be directed immediately to him. Nothing like this must happen again. Imagine if Faith, rather than himself, had welcomed Morton.

As Faith waited for Sir Michael in the dining room, she wondered what had upset him earlier. She knew her cold manner troubled him, but how could she pretend an affection she no longer felt? The road back to health and personal freedom had been too hard won.

Lately, her life had become a series of subterfuges. She had not been delayed at the blacksmith's today. By previous arrangement, she had met James Geldie at Southampton. Thus far, his enquiries about her father had been unsuccessful but she was confident something would eventually come to light.

Meanwhile, she had the support of Aunt Barbara and Hugh, which was very comforting. She smiled, remembering her discussion with Robert McBain. Seeing him, and hearing the news of Carrigmoor had been the real turning point in her recovery.

145

Hugh. She could hardly wait to see him! Her smile widened and her eyes sparkled. Today, James Geldie had given her a letter from Hugh saying to expect him early in the New Year.

"Excuse me, Miss Faith," said the maid, as she placed a tureen of turkey soup in the center of the table, "Kenneth said to tell you that the man will leave Dubrovnik at the King Henry Inn near the Richmond Turnpike."

"I am sorry, Margaret . . . what man?"

"The man as come to the Hall this afternoon, Miss Faith." The maid hurried out, almost colliding with Sir Michael.

"How is your headache, Grandfather?" Faith enquired, helping herself to some soup.

"Much better thank you, my dear."

"Would you care for some soup, Grandfather?"

"Yes, thank you, my dear."

How formal we are, Faith thought. "Who was the man that came to the Hall this afternoon?"

"W-what?"

"Who was the man, and why did you give him Dubrovnik?" she repeated.

"Oh, him," Sir Michael said offhandedly, "don't recall his name—some fellow from London with East India papers. His horse went lame so I offered him Dubrovnik."

"He said he would leave the horse for collection at the King Henry Inn. What were the papers about?"

"Oh, nothing important . . . just a letter of consignment and some bills of lading. I signed them and sent him on his way."

She looked at him closely. "Are you all right? You don't look well. . . ."

His hand trembled as he raised the spoon to his mouth and the boiling soup spilled down the front of his lace shirt.

"Damn it!" he shouted, jumping to his feet. His head was pounding and the room had become suffocatingly hot. "Please excuse me, my dear. My headache has returned. I think I shall retire . . ."

He turned and staggered toward the door but the room had become so dark, he could not find his way.

36
The Gulf Widens

Sunday, November 25, 1787

Five days since, when the Fleet had been becalmed eighty leagues east of the Cape, Phillip had ordered all convict black-smiths, carpenters, and gardeners aboard *Supply*. Frustrated at being constantly held back by the slower ships and convinced that those under his care would be better served if he went ahead to prepare a suitable site for them, he had split the Fleet into three convoys.

He would go in *Supply* with the convict artificers; John Short-land, the Agent, would command the second convoy comprising the speedier transporters, *Alexander, Scarborough*, and *Friend-ship*; and Captain John Hunter would command the third convoy comprising the three slower transporters and the three storeships.

"Let's hope *Supply* will get us to Botany Bay well ahead of the other convoys so we can clear ground and erect temporary shelters for the people and provisions," Phillip said as he clambered aboard *Supply* and shook hands with her commander, Lieutenant Ball.

"She will manage well enough if we keep in with fair weather, sir," Ball replied, nodding to Lieutenants King and Dawes, who had accompanied Phillip. "But she is sluggish in a squall. Would you and your officers care to see your quarters now?"

Phillip smiled. "Thank you, Lieutenant. Be sure to let me know the moment the Timekeeper comes aboard. A fine breeze is setting in from the nor'west, and I want to get underway as soon as possible."

He drew King aside. "After you have stowed your gear, Gidley, go across to *Alexander* and tell John Shortland I want him to keep company with us all the way, if possible. We will need the male convicts to labor."

"Yes, sir. And, have you any last word for Major Ross? He will probably ask . . ."

Phillip frowned. Ross was inclined to take offence where none was intended. When he had told Ross he had decided to split the Fleet, Ross had insinuated that *his* opinion should have been sought, even though the decision was strictly a naval one. Phillip

147

hoped he was wrong about Ross. The last person he needed on this expedition was a pompous narrow-minded obstructionist marine Major. "No, Gidley. Just wish him a Happy Christmas and say I shall see him at Botany Bay."

Christmas Eve, 1787

Sir Michael sat by the library window, staring at the desolate, white landscape. The second apoplexy attack had made a ruin of his formerly handsome features. His left eyelid was frozen in a perpetual wink, his mouth smiled on the right side and scowled on the left, and his once proud physique was twisted so grotesquely that he was only able to walk with Kenneth's help.

His mind, however, was unimpaired and he worried constantly about Faith discovering his secret. The servants now directed letters and visitors to him, and he was confident his investigators would soon establish Micah Morton's whereabouts, but he feared his influence over his granddaughter's life had ended.

Lately, she had been countermanding his orders to the household and outside staff; and she had also been traveling much farther afield than Lyndhurst without his permission. This last time she had been gone two days. When he had taken her to task about it, she had shrugged and said that she had ridden to Southampton on a matter that was no concern of his.

Faith's mind was in a turmoil as she dressed for dinner that evening. After two months of futile enquiry in the East India Company archives, James Geldie had turned in desperation to his Majesty's Admiralty and met with immediate success.

She flung the bulky report, which contained a detailed account of her father's long and distinguished naval career, on her desk and stalked to the window. "Liar!" she exclaimed. "Grandfather has lied to me all my life!"

Why hadn't her father bothered to visit her in twenty years? Tears rolled down her cheeks. She would have given anything to see her father—to just once have him hold her. . . .

She did not understand any of it. Hadn't he even been *curious* about her?

Perhaps her mother had been unfaithful and her father had had no choice but to leave her? "If I am a bastard, that would explain why he never visited me," she said aloud.

Was that why her grandfather had lied? Perhaps he had entered into a secret pact with her father to keep her from discovering that she was a bastard? If that was the case, who was her real father?

She picked up a brush and began drawing it through her tousled hair. If only she could confront her grandfather with the report. But that was impossible. The doctor had said he must have absolute peace and quiet, or else he was likely to suffer another attack.

Sighing, she put the brush down. "There is no need to torture myself this way," she murmured. "James Geldie has promised that he will seek an interview with Father's widow. She will surely be able to assist."

The scar on her finger began to throb. She looked at it, eyes widening. Thump, thump, it went, like a wildly pulsating heartbeat. A moment later, blind, unreasoning hatred surged through her.

"Don't trust Grandfather!" a voice within her warned.

She raised shaking hands to her temples and looked at her reflection in the mirror. How could she have such thoughts about the man who, until a year ago, had been the cornerstone of her life?

"I *want* to trust you, Grandfather," she whispered. "I *want* to close that ever-widening gulf between us. I *want* to believe you lied to protect me . . ." But the scar kept throbbing and the hateful thoughts persisted.

37

Sketches of Christmas

Christmas Day, 1787

Lucy stood at the quarter rail gazing at the calm and tranquil sea. The night was cold and clear, the sky a cluster of twinkling stars, and the ship's decks awash with silvery moonlight. Aft, music and laughter were coming from the officers' roundhouse, and from below came the voices of the women joined in song.

Silent night, Holy night,
All is calm, all is bright.

Her thoughts turned to *Friendship*, bobbing about somewhere on the limitless ocean. Michael was probably sitting in the cuddy with Tom and the other officers. How she missed him.

She shivered and wrapped the blanket he had given her more tightly around her shoulders. How warm his mouth had been the day they said good-bye. What could happen when they met again? Would he be content with kisses, or would he want more?

Yesterday, the women had made a Christmas pudding to which all had contributed. Last night they had taken turns to stir it and make wishes, then they had placed the pudding in a large cloth and sat up simmering it for hours. The result had been delicious. Now, everyone was toasting the season and singing carols as if they did not have a care in the world.

People are funny, Lucy thought with a wry smile. Here they were, thousands of miles from civilization, bound for an unknown land where the most they could hope for was years of heartbreaking toil and they acted as if they were sitting in some cozy tavern in the center of London. It made her feel positively optimistic.

She gazed out at the tranquil sea, her thoughts turning to Faith. Where was she on this Christmas night? She cleared her mind of all thought and focused on Faith, only her. . . .

Lately, every time she concentrated, she got closer. . . . The surface of the water blurred and a vaporous cloud enveloped her. She was in the dark passageway now . . . she could hear the wind . . . and see the light. She knew if she could just reach the light, she would be there. While her body remained by the rail, as still and as motionless as a statue, the wind lifted her spirit and swept it on . . .

Grosvenor Square, London

Ruth Gamble sat at the dining table admiring the large emerald ring on her finger. It had been in the safe until a month ago, when the mariner had delivered the letter from Lucy and she had suddenly been reminded of it.

She sipped her wine and glanced at the portrait of her husband on the wall opposite. The last time he had gone to sea he had left instructions that she was to give Lucy the ring on her twentieth birthday.

She clicked her tongue with annoyance as wine spilled down the bodice of her pink satin gown. Last month she had set aside her mourning weeds. Being young, and a woman of means, she doubted she would remain a widow long. Indeed, in the new year, she would go out into society again. A picture of Lucy, pistol in hand, standing over Richard, flashed into her mind, and she reached hastily for the wineglass.

Lucy had murdered Richard right before her eyes. Monstrous! Now Richard's son was on board a convict ship bound for Botany Bay. She gulped the wine and poured the remainder from the decanter into the glass.

Why was she alone on Christmas night? She had begged her father to come to London but he would not leave the farm—selfish, unreasonable man!

She glanced at the portrait of her dead husband with narrowed eyes. Lucy must have enticed Richard to her bed night after night, even the night they had learned about James. Disgusting, shameless Lucy!

She drained the wineglass and rang for Ned. When he appeared, she drew herself up in her chair. "Bring another decanter of wine, Ned," she commanded.

"Yes, madam. Would madam care for white or red?"

"I don't care what color, you fool, just bring more and be quick about it!"

Ned beat a hasty retreat.

Her father had condemned Richard. *I'm afraid I must cause you more grief by destroying the illusions you have about your brother.* Ruth clapped her hands over her ears, but fragments of his conversation pressed in on her. *Richard was not the man you imagined him to be . . .*

Ruth smote the table with her fists. "No, I will not believe ill of Richard! I—I know what I saw in Lucy's room that night!"

How could she know if Lucy had borne Richard a son? Was she to accept the word of a convicted murderess? The child could be anyone's.

Ned entered with a decanter of red wine. While he refilled her glass, her dead husband glared back at her accusingly from the portrait. His daughter! His grandson!

"Will there be anything further, madam?" asked Ned.

"Yes. Remove that painting this instant. I never want to see it again."

After Ned had departed with the painting, she glanced at the ring. *How beautiful it was!* She twisted it from side to side. The emerald caught in the light and sparkled like green fire—green, the color of Lucy's eyes!

Ruth lifted the glass to her lips and drained it.

Hearing a soft tapping on his door, Hugh stopped writing and glanced at the clock on the mantelpiece. Almost midnight. Who could it be?

"Come in."

His mother entered, wearing a floor-length sable coat over her night attire. Her hair hung loosely down her back and, for a fleeting moment, Hugh saw a striking resemblance to Faith.

"You are abroad late, Mother. Come to the fire and warm yourself."

"I could not sleep," Lady Barbara explained as she joined him. "You'll be leaving soon, won't you? You have been restless ever since Robert returned from the south."

"I shall leave at dawn. I was writing you a letter . . ."

"But you cannot leave tomorrow," she protested. "We are completely snowed in."

"I'll go on foot as far as Inverness, then take Wade's Road to Fort Augustus and the Corrieyairack Pass to Dalwhinnie. Once I reach Edinburgh, the traveling will be easier."

Lady Barbara's eyes were anxious. "Must you go on foot to Inverness? You will have to tramp fourteen miles over those hills and I have heard the wolves howling . . ."

Hugh laughed. "I come from a long line of Celtic warriors who have hunted in those hills since before the birth of Christ. I don't fear wolves, Mother." He grinned and patted the two claw-handled pistols hanging from his belt. "Besides, these dags you gave me for Christmas will protect me!"

She sighed resignedly. "I suppose it *is* time you left. Your father is almost recovered, so he and Robert ought to be able to manage."

"Yes, I am confident they can. They did splendidly while I was away at the University. I think now is the best time to go. . . . If I wait until the spring thaw, the streams will be raging torrents and the lambs—"

She pressed her fingers to his lips and smiled. "No need to justify your decision, Hugh. You have done your duty by your family. I am grateful for that. Go with my blessings—and take this."

She removed a finely filigreed gold ring set with three identical diamonds from her finger. "Give it to Faith with my love. It belonged to her grandmother."

"Are you sure?" Hugh asked gently. "I know how highly you prize this ring . . ."

Lady Barbara's eyes glistened. "It will comfort me to know that a part of me is with Faith. Now, I shall bid you farewell so you can get some rest." She kissed him and quickly left.

Hugh walked to the window. The night sky was clear and, if the snow held off until morning, the terrain would be rock hard and easy to traverse. Excitement surged through him. Thank God he was leaving at last! The waiting had been agony. If he had good luck with the weather, three weeks should see him at Billingsley.

"Fae . . ." he murmured.

Billingsley Hall

As the grandfather clock at the end of the corridor sounded the midnight hour in long, melancholy chimes, Faith put down her pen. This had been the longest, loneliest Christmas Day in memory.

On the surface, it had seemed normal enough. As usual, she and Sir Michael had attended the Christmas service in the village. As usual, friends and neighbors had called at the Hall to exchange gifts, drink toasts, and partake of the traditional Christmas turkey and pudding. Yet, beneath all the laughter, joviality and cheer had been the unusual, unbreakable silence between Sir Michael and herself.

The last chime rolled away in diminishing echoes. Christmas Day, 1787, was done.

Faith picked up the pen and began writing in her journal again. After a while, the fire in the grate caught her attention. How brightly it blazed, its warmth seemed to reach out and caress her face. Her heart swelled with joy. Alone? How could she ever have imagined herself so? She was *surrounded* by love. The room was filled with it! The flames in the grate danced higher and the wind rattled the window pane.

"Faith . . ."

Faith gasped with wonder. The woman of her visions stood between the fire and the writing table—like a puff of smoke . . . wispy and indistinct.

"Faith," she sang in unison with the wind. "Faith . . ." Then she was gone.

38

Land Ho!

At ten o'clock on the morning of the third of January 1788, as the battered *Supply* was making reasonable headway through the swell, a cry came from overhead, "Land ho!"

Gidley King dashed to the rail, pressed the spyglass to his eye and strained to catch his first glimpse of land in fifty-two days. Others were now taking up the cry. "Land ho! Land ho! There, on the starboard bow, land ho!" A moment later, the haze lifted and Gidley saw a long, low, dark line stretching across the horizon. Van Diemen's Land—the southernmost tip of Australia!

"Do you see it, sir?" he exclaimed as Phillip joined him.

"A welcome sight, eh, Gidley? Any chance of working in closer?"

King shook his head. "Sorry, sir. We've just taken a reading. The wind has shifted to the west."

The tender shuddered beneath them and her masts and rigging groaned. The little ship had been severely tested on this last stretch and life on board had been extremely tiresome.

"Not one of our speedier passages," Phillip commented.

"Indeed, sir, *Supply* is no *Europe* or *Ariadne*."

Phillip smiled. "True, but I would not wish those years or those ships back."

"Nor I, sir. I sense that dark shadow on the horizon is where our destinies lie."

Phillip raised his spyglass to his eye. "I confess, that thought had crossed my mind. But, being twenty years younger than I, you will make many more landfalls yet, Gidley."

"But never one as exciting or challenging as this, sir."

Phillip swept the horizon with the glass. " 'Never' is a word I have struck from my vocabulary. Three years ago, when you and I were retired from the navy on half-pay, we never imagined we would be standing here today. Yet, here we are."

The second convoy led by Shortland sighted Van Diemen's Land two days later.

That evening everyone aboard *Friendship* crowded on deck to witness the breathtaking spectacle of the aurora australis. Brilliant streamers of crimson, orange, yellow, white, and blue lights flashed across the horizon from cloud to cloud in a kaleidoscopic display. Later, Michael and Tom left the others and strolled to the bow.

"Francis Walton says Botany Bay is only eight hundred miles to the north," said Tom.

"If we are blessed with favorable winds, we should be there in two weeks," Michael said.

"It cannot be soon enough for me," Tom sighed. "After almost two months of salt meat and limited water, even the strongest among us are showing signs of scurvy."

Michael leaned against a spar and fixed his eyes on the western horizon. "I hope Lucy and the others are well, and that *Charlotte* has not become separated from her convoy. She is not a speedy ship."

Tom patted his shoulder. "I'll be greatly relieved to see the women also, Michael. And to set foot on dry land again—albeit an uncivilized wilderness. Oh, to sink my teeth into fresh roasted venison; to bathe in crystal-clear water; to stroll beneath shady trees . . ."

Michael gave a theatrical groan. "Stop it, Tom, you are driving me mad! But, if I were you, I would think twice about going in search of wild deer, you might meet something even wilder. The soldiers we evacuated from the American coast during the war told terrible tales of wild-eyed red men who roamed the woods with shrunken scalps hanging from their belts. . . ."

Amid much praise for Captain Hunter's navigational skills, the third convoy sighted Van Diemen's Land on seventh January.

Lucy, Beth, and Frances stayed up on deck all day taking turns to peer at the rugged landscape through the spyglass Michael had given Lucy. Surprisingly, even in the heat, the mountains appeared to have pockets of snow on them. For the most part, the coastline was uninviting, with avalanches of spray and spume shooting skyward as gigantic waves pounded against forbidding cliffs, but when darkness fell, a wondrous sight greeted them. Dotted across the dark hills were dozens of flickering lights.

"What a miracle," Frances said in awe. "To come all this way and find folk waiting . . ."

"The land must be habitable," Lucy breathed. "That is a good start . . ."

"But what sort of bloomin' creatures live here?" Beth asked apprehensively. "If I was to take notice of the tales I've heard, I'd not sleep a wink at night."

"You *do* go on, girl," Frances scoffed. "They're as like to be gentle, helpful folk, who'll pay us no mind, you'll see."

Beth sniffed. "Dr. Balmain told me they're as black as tar."

"Well, even if they are, we'll soon have them washing regular," Frances replied firmly.

"Sidaway told Suzy Gought they have red eyes that glow in the dark, and ten fingers on each hand," Beth added.

"Let's wait and see." Lucy laughed. "Besides, I won't be thinking of natives when I step ashore. I will be overjoyed to have space to move around in without bumping into someone else!"

A faraway look came into Frances's eyes. "When I step ashore, I will wash myself from head to foot, then find Jane and little Edward . . ."

"Think of having solid ground under foot again, instead of a rolling deck," Beth said longingly. "And to see fields of roses and daffodils—instead of blue sea, and green sea, and gray sea!"

39
Botany Bay

Friday, January 18, 1788

Phillip looked aloft at the billowing sails and sighed with relief. The wind had finally begun to blow in from the southwest and *Supply* had been making steady progress up the green, sloping coastline toward Botany Bay for the last few hours.

He trained his spyglass on a large hill shaped like the crown of a hat and his heart swelled with excitement. There was the hill, just as Cook had described. They were close, very close . . .

"Botany Bay! Botany Bay!" The cry went up.

At last, the harbor they had come fifteen thousand miles in search of, was in sight.

They came in around the headland Cook had called Cape Solander and stretched over to the north side of the bay. There, along the shore, brandishing immensely long spears, ran dozens of naked native men shouting something that sounded like, *"Warra! Warra!"* They were dark, with full-bellied bodies, narrow shoulders and thin, sinewy limbs.

After dropping anchor at a cove in plain sight of the entrance, so the other ships would see them, they hoisted out two longboats and rowed around the bay from north to south. The natives pursued them until they grew tired of the chase.

The land behind the arid, sandy shore had a sparse cover of spiky rushes, windblown shrubs, and stubby trees. Behind that was a dense forest of tall, thin-stemmed trees.

When their first cursory search revealed no fresh water inlets, Phillip decided to return to the natives who were waiting patiently, squatting on their haunches or leaning on their spears.

As they beached the longboats beside two canoes, the natives jumped up and shook their spears menacingly above their heads crying *"Warra, warra, warra!"*

Phillip asked Lieutenant Dawes to drape some colored beads over the stem of the nearest canoe. Dawes obliged and when he returned to the longboat, the natives stopped prancing and approached the beads, their warlike behavior forgotten as they gasped at the red, blue, and yellow glass glittering in the sunlight.

Smiling, Phillip stepped ashore and made signs of drinking. A bushy-haired native with a long beard indicated that Phillip should follow him.

"I am going," Phillip called over his shoulder to the others. "Wait here until I signal, and those of you who come ashore, remember—no firearms."

Armed with a smile and some beads, Phillip followed his guide to a clearing where he discovered a little stream. The water was warm and brackish, but quite drinkable.

Phillip indicated his pleasure and approval to the natives gathering in a clearing a small distance away, and beckoned them closer. They remained where they were, staring and silent.

He took another string of beads from his pocket and proffered it to his guide. But, although a look of intense longing came into the man's eyes, Phillip could not entice him closer.

He put the beads on the ground and stepped away. The man approached with much trembling, took up the beads with the tip of his spear and returned to the other natives, who gathered around him excitedly. Phillip raised his arm and signaled for his men to come ashore.

*   *   *

Next morning at daybreak, Phillip and his officers set out in the longboats and discovered several freshwater inlets but nothing that remotely resembled the rich green plains Cook had described. When the cool dawn gave way to an intensely hot day, they returned to *Supply* to breakfast on fresh fish.

An hour later, the cry of "Sail ho!" rang out. Everyone raced for the deck. Sails studded the eastern horizon and, by nine o'clock, they were close enough to be identified as *Alexander, Scarborough,* and *Friendship*.

"How long have you been here, sir?" Shortland inquired as Phillip and his officers clambered aboard *Alexander*.

"Only twenty-four hours," Phillip laughed.

"What do you think of Botany Bay, sir?" Major Ross exclaimed when he came aboard a few minutes later.

Phillip turned from Shortland and offered Ross his hand. "My observations don't match Cook's, Major Ross. But we are leaving on another excursion soon. Perhaps you and your officers would care to join us?"

"Indeed, we would, sir!" cried Ross.

Leaving Shortland to make an urgent perusal of the stock and provisions, they boarded the longboats and pulled toward the shore, the boredom and frustration of the last two months forgotten.

They followed a river on the southwestern corner of the bay inland for six miles. The countryside was low, boggy, and uninteresting and, finding no evidence of fresh water, they returned to the entrance and rowed to the southern extremity of the bay where they lunched on salt beef and some excellent port that the marine Quartermaster had thoughtfully brought along.

As he listened with half an ear to the other men discussing what they had seen, Phillip kicked the sandy soil with the heel of his boot. This section of the bay seemed the most suitable spot. The ground was reasonable and the water in the nearby rivulet was by far the best for drinking. But ships could not anchor here, for the harbor was too shallow.

Several freshwater streams trickled into the bay on the north side, but there the ground was swampy. And elsewhere, they had found only small brackish water drains.

He rose and, clasping his hands behind his back, strode to the water's edge. In his opinion, Botany Bay was unsuitable for a large seaport settlement.

Michael and Tom spent their first day ashore, bathing, fishing, and making friends with the natives. However, the green leafy glades and tall, shady trees Tom pined for were nowhere in sight, and it would have been impossible to slip away by himself, as the shores of Botany Bay teamed with sailors, marines, and natives.

That evening Michael and Ralph had the cuddy to themselves. After they had eaten, Michael left Ralph writing up his journal and took a stroll round the deck where, to his annoyance, he found Sidaway still chained to the pump. Cursing, he returned to the cuddy and snatched up his keys.

"What are you doing?" Ralph asked.

"Releasing Sidaway."

"You can't release that scoundrel, he is my pris—"

Michael strode out the cuddy, slamming the door.

"For God's sake, stay out of Lieutenant Clark's way," he muttered as he removed the convict's irons. "And make an effort to begin life here on a more positive note."

Massaging his swollen wrists, Sidaway walked to the rail and looked toward the shore. "I'd be obliged if you'd tell me what it's like, Lieutenant."

Michael joined him. "The natives are friendly, but it is no Garden of Eden."

"What about those flat grassy stretches back of the shore? Are they good for crops and cattle?"

"That's not grass, it is a type of spiky rush. The whole section puts me in mind of the English moors."

"Well, I ain't disheartened, Lieutenant. From my position here by the bloody pump, I've seen lots of land. We'll have plenty to choose from, for sure."

Michael left him and walked aft. Laughter drifted across the water from the other ships and, on shore the native fires flickered in the darkness. He turned his back on Botany Bay and gazed out to sea.

How much longer until she arrived?

40

A Question of Time

Sunday, January 20, 1788

Hearing a gentle snore Faith closed *Tom Jones* and tiptoed from the library leaving her grandfather sleeping soundly. She made her way toward the stairs but, just as she laid a hand on the bannister, a thunderous knock sounded on the front door. Who could be visiting at nine o'clock on a freezing Sunday night? she wondered.

The ancient Kenneth tottered to the door and drew the bolt and Hugh stepped inside, accompanied by a flurry of snowflakes.

"Hugh!" Faith cried joyfully, rushing toward him.

"Good evening!" he laughed, catching her in his arms and swinging her off her feet. "Will you give shelter to a weary Scot?"

"Whenever I see you, you are covered in snow and half-frozen!" she scolded. "Kenneth, please put Master Hugh's belongings in Grandfather's old room and bring hot refreshments to mine."

"I can't believe you are actually here," Faith exclaimed as she pushed Hugh into a chair by the fire and started tugging at his boots. "I did not expect you until March. How is Uncle Colin? Robert said his injuries were serious. And I know what the weather is like at Carrigmoor this time of year. How on earth did you manage to get through all the snow? And Aunt Barbara, how is she? I was shocked when Robert said Grandfather had not answered her letters. But, as I was confined to my room for months, he neglected to give me mine. In fact, I had no idea—"

"Whoa, one question at a time," Hugh laughed, holding up his hands. "Father is greatly improved in body, but his mind is not what it was. And Mother is fine now she knows you are all right." His eyes danced. "But that can wait—stand up so I can look at you."

She put his boots aside and rose.

"Ah," he murmured, pulling her down on his lap, "That is better. Suddenly, I feel *very* warm."

"Let go of me." She laughed. "The servants will be here any minute."

"A pox on the servants," he muttered. "I did not travel six hundred miles through driving snow to see *them*."

"Oh my, how times have changed. Once, you would not have traveled six inches out of your way to see me," she teased, curling her arms around his neck and pressing her nose against his.

"Nonsense," he retorted. "I have always been the happier for your company—even when you were a bothersome child. But what have you done to yourself? I like plump, voluptuous women, not skinny scarecrows."

"I am not too thin," she protested.

"I shall amend my statement," he grinned. "You are not skinny, you are positively nobbly. Be careful not to move too quickly, lest your bones spike my legs."

She jumped to her feet, but he caught her around the waist and pulled her back into his arms. They heard a loud knock on the door.

"Let me go," she pleaded, struggling to get free. "Kenneth will collapse from shock if he sees us like this—he thinks I am still a child."

"Only if you promise to share my supper," he answered. "We must begin fattening you up immediately."

"I promise, I promise," she whispered fiercely. "Only let me go."

He released her reluctantly.

"Come in, Kenneth!" she called, springing away from Hugh and adjusting her skirts.

As Faith and Hugh ate, they talked. Hugh told her how his mother had confided in him and of their decision to send Robert south, and Faith told him about Portsmouth and everything that had happened since.

"And now James Geldie has sent a report about my father's naval career."

He put his glass down and leaned forward eagerly. "Get it for me, Fae. I'd like to read it."

She got the report from her desk and handed it to him. "I am anxious to discuss it, but I shall let you read it first, so you can form your own opinions."

He rose from his chair. "Thanks, Fae. Now, if you will excuse me, I think I shall scrape some of this dirt off."

"Of course," she murmured, trying to hide her disappointment. "You must be tired, Hugh. I-I have been thoughtless keeping you so long, it's just that I have been lonely these last months . . ."

161

He smiled down at her. "I did not say I was tired, silly, just dirty. If you have a hot honeyed brandy waiting for me in half an hour, I could easily be enticed back."

Faith's emerald eyes sparkled. "The brandy will be waiting, but if you tarry a minute longer than the half hour, I shall come to your room and revile you for your tardiness! And don't forget to wrap yourself up after your bath, or you will catch a chill."

He raised despairing eyes to the ceiling. "You may look a trifle gaunt and wan but your sharp tongue is as healthy as ever."

When Hugh returned his high spirits had disappeared and his handsome face was serious. "Why did Uncle lie about your father being dead, Fae? And why didn't your father contact you?" He tossed the report onto the desk and joined her by the fire.

"I have asked myself those same questions a thousand times, Faith sighed, "and the only conclusion I can come to is that Mother must have cuckolded Father. That would account for his never having come to the Hall. You would hardly expect him to visit another man's child. And, that might also explain why Grandfather lied. Perhaps he was trying to keep me from discovering that I was a bastard . . ."

Hugh stared thoughtfully into the fire for some time before replying. "While that theory adequately explains your father's actions, Fae, it in no way explains your grandfather's. If it was just a matter of doubtful parentage, your grandfather would have taken my mother aside last year and told her the whole story. No, I believe he is trying to protect himself—not you. Your father is only part of it. Why has your grandfather refused to discuss the scar? What possible connection could it have to a man you have never met? And what about Portsmouth? One word from your grandfather that day, and Captain Phillip would have recalled the guard boat and the matter of your vision would have been settled once and for all."

Hugh frowned darkly and a dangerous light came into his eyes. "Instead, he locked you away from the world until you capitulated. God, I find it hard to contain myself when I think of what he put you through."

Faith's shoulders slumped. "If only I could confront him with the report."

Hugh's mouth hardened. "His latest attack is certainly a

setback. I wanted to confront him as soon as I arrived. Now, I think it best that I go to London and consult with James Geldie. Perhaps he has discovered something new. Your father's widow is bound to have information that will shed light on the mystery . . ."

The thought of him leaving dismayed Faith. "I will find it hard to let you go, Hugh."

He held out his hand and said softly, "Come, sit beside me, Fae." He put his arm around her and held her tightly. "Were it any other reason, I would not leave you, but I cannot allow you to suffer any longer. Because your grandfather's state of health is delicate, I shall make one last attempt to resolve this matter through James Geldie. But if he cannot help, then I shall return to Billingsley and we shall confront Sir Michael together."

Faith bit her lip. "Oh, Hugh, suppose he had another attack? I would never forgive myself."

Hugh frowned. "Nonsense, Fae. Suppose he had another attack and carried his secrets to the grave? Then, where would you be? As far as I'm concerned, if it becomes a choice between his well-being and yours, you have first priority. You have given him ample opportunity to disclose what he knows, yet despite your suffering he has remained silent."

Hugh was right. The matter had dragged on long enough. She sighed. "Let's go ahead with it then."

He placed a hand under her chin and looked deeply into her eyes. "Good. Now that's settled, let us put the morbid aside. I won't be leaving for twenty-four hours. We will spend the rest of the time discussing happy things. Mother has sent you a gift and I have an important question to ask you . . ."

She raised her eyebrows. "An important question, what could it be? You must tell me, else my curiosity will keep me awake all night."

He laughed. "It is far too late for important questions tonight. We'll have breakfast together in the morning and, if you eat six bowls of porridge, I shall ask you."

Faith pouted. "Very well, breakfast at nine. But don't expect me to meekly obey your every order, Hugh. Tonight, you have had your way—tomorrow is another day."

"Tomorrow is, indeed, another day, dearest," he said, drawing her to her feet. "And if I have anything to do with it, it will be a day we shall never forget."

He took her in his arms and kissed her passionately.

*　　*　　*

163

Faith and Hugh sat glaring at each other across the breakfast table.

"We are not leaving until you have eaten another plate of porridge, Fae."

Faith, a vision in lilac, shook her head emphatically. "I don't want porridge. I want my present and I want to hear your question."

Hugh leaned back in the chair and folded his arms. "You will get neither unless you eat more."

"But I've already had three helpings. Do you want me to be ill?"

He looked at the ceiling and whistled "John Peel."

"Why don't I drink another glass of milk?" she suggested.

"Be sure it is a large one," he said sternly. "And do hurry, Fae. The morning is a-wasting while you sit here bickering about porridge and milk."

Faith filled her glass brimful of milk, gulped it down and jumped to her feet. "Fast enough, O mighty suzerain?"

"Shall we?" he invited, walking to the French windows and pushing them open.

She took his hand and they stepped down onto the snow-encrusted lawn. "What shall we do first?" she asked breathlessly.

"Let's walk in the forest and look for wild ospreys."

"Fool!" she scoffed. "We aren't in Scotland now."

He squeezed her hand. "Maybe not, but think of the fun we can have trying to track them down. Where do you suggest we look first?"

"Africa?"

He swung her off her feet, twirled her around, then set her down and pulled the pins from her hair.

"You always do that," she exclaimed crossly as the dark locks cascaded around her. "Now, it will get wet."

He laughed. "I like it that way. Now, close your eyes and hold out your hand."

"No. If I do, you'll pelt me with snow!"

He grinned. "Not this time."

"Promise?"

"I promise," he said, placing a hand over his heart.

She closed her eyes and proffered her hand half-heartedly.

He dropped his mother's ring into it.

Faith gazed in wonder at the ring. "But Aunt Barbara treasures this . . ."

"It will comfort her to know a part of her is with you," he

said and slid the ring on her left ring finger. "Which brings me to my important question, Fae. Spending a few weeks with you every second year is no longer enough. I want you with me always. Will you marry me?"

Through all their childhood games, through all their reckless rides, through all their separations, Faith had known that one day Hugh would say those words to her. "So you have asked me at last, Hugh Stewart. What happened to those fine, fat lassies you have been pursuing from glen to glen all these years?"

He tried to grab her, but she eluded him.

"Have a heart, Fae," he groaned. "They never meant anything. No one has, since the moment I laid eyes on you, you know that. Be a good girl and put me out of my misery. Say yes."

Faith tossed her hair away from her face. "My first thought was to say no, Scotty, but I have changed my mind. If you catch me before I reach Roman Lake, why then, I shall marry you!" Laughing hilariously, she picked up her skirts and sped away across the lawn.

Sir Michael, who had woken to the sound of their laughter, reached the window in time to see Hugh tackle Faith to the ground. He watched them rolling in the snow for a few moments, then turned away—unable to endure the sight.

41
Phillip Decides

Sunday, January 20, 1788

With Michael's spyglass fastened to her eye, Lucy kept vigil on the deck, willing the dawn sun higher. The convoy had sighted Botany Bay at dusk last night, but Captain Hunter had prudently decided to stand off until morning before attempting to enter the harbor.

Conditions were overcast, but Lucy saw the break in the cliffs only moments after the lookout atop the main cried, "Botany Bay on the starboard bow!"

Time passed agonizingly slowly as her convoy crept in procession across Botany Bay toward the other Fleet ships but, at last *Charlotte*'s anchors went down and Lucy's spirits soared as a longboat put out from *Friendship*.

A short time later Michael clambered aboard and pushed his way through the excited crowd to her. Speechless with joy, she threw her arms around his neck and buried her face in his chest, relieved beyond measure that the weeks of waiting were over. Michael hugged her tightly against him, content just to have her in his arms.

He felt a tug on his sleeve and, looking down, saw Beth. He drew her into the circle of his embrace. "How is Beth?"

"Good, thanks. But we're bloomin' glad to see you, aren't we Lucy?"

Lucy looked up at Michael, her eyes shining with happiness. He was actually here! She caressed his chest and felt his heart throbbing beneath her fingers.

"I hope you women have followed my instructions and kept yourselves healthy," Tom said gruffly to those crowding around him.

"Yes, Dr. Arndell!" they cried in unison.

Dear Tom, Lucy thought, *he really cares about us.*

"How's Henry Cable?" Susannah enquired of Tom anxiously.

Tom handed her a parcel. "He's in good health and has sent these fish—My God! That can't be baby Henry? He has doubled in size since last I saw him!"

"He has that," Susannah affirmed proudly. "And he's walking. He looks so funny. He rolls from side to side like a drunken sailor!"

"How are Best and the other men?" Beth asked.

"All right, but Sidaway has been stapled to the deck," Tom told her.

"And how many fingers have the natives got?" she asked earnestly.

He laughed. "Five on each hand."

"I must say, you look to be in your element Lieutenant Perryman," cried John White, pushing his way into the group and pumping Michael's hand.

Michael laughed and slapped his friend on the back. "Well, Dr. White, you have certainly done it this time. Last Christmas, it was snowflakes and chestnuts around a roaring fire—this year, it's flies, heat, and natives!"

John looked over Michael's shoulder at the shimmering white sand. "What is it like ashore?"

Michael grinned. "Indescribable!"

John turned and shook Tom's hand. "Good to see you again, Dr. Arndell. How is everyone aboard *Friendship*?"

"In reasonable health, Dr. White. And so, I see, are my *Friendship* women."

A serious light came into John's eyes. "These women are the pick of the crop. Scurvy has begun to show itself in our convoy and many are extremely weak."

Tom nodded. "And on the other ships, also. Lieutenant Perryman and I are going aboard *Lady Penrhyn* shortly. Would you care to accompany us? We could do the rounds of the other ships after that, if you like . . ."

Seizing his opportunity, Michael drew Lucy aside. "I have to leave, Lucy. Are you all right, my darling? You look a little pale."

"I am fine," she replied softly.

"Do you need anything?" he asked, his eyes searching hers.

She shook her head, unable to speak.

He caressed her neck lightly. "Lucy . . ."

She sighed, feeling at once excited and afraid. "W-when will you return?"

He glanced at the uproar taking place aboard the other Fleet ships. "These next days will be difficult, darling. But once the people and provisions are got ashore, we shall have more time together. You understand, don't you?"

A storm of conflicting emotions welled up within Lucy. "It really doesn't matter," she answered huskily. "Nothing matters now you are here."

His hold on her tightened. "It's been hell without you, Lucy."

She stroked his face, feeling the slight stubbly growth on his cheeks and chin. "I missed you also . . ."

His eyes bored into her. "Do you mean that, darling?"

"I have spent sixty-nine days without you, Michael. Believe me, I know what I—"

"If you can possibly tear yourself away, we are ready to depart, Lieutenant Perryman," John White interposed.

Smiling resignedly, Michael joined him.

"And now, old chap," said the Surgeon General, as they moved toward the longboat, "tell me, what are the native women like?"

Michael grinned widely. "Indescribable, John—indescribable!"

* * *

167

The Great Cabin on board *Supply* was packed to capacity.

Phillip, flanked on either side by his naval and marine officers, rapped on the table with a mallet, and when the excited buzz of conversation ceased, he rose from his chair.

"Let me first congratulate every man for the part he played in bringing this expedition to a successful conclusion. Deducting days spent in the various ports, the 15,063 mile voyage from Portsmouth to Botany Bay was completed in one hundred and eighty-six days."

He waited for the polite applause to finish.

"That we arrived at all, is due to the magnificent skills of our navigators. That we arrived with the loss of only forty lives, is due to the devotion to duty of the Surgeon General, his able assistants, Arndell, Considen, and Balmain, and other ships' doctors. Three cheers, gentlemen, please!"

After the shouts of "Hurrah!" had abated, he went on.

"Now we have arrived, our first task is to select a suitable site on which to found our new colony. I and my officers have explored Botany Bay extensively. Not only is the soil poor and the land marshy for the most part, there is insufficient water to support a large settlement. Also, I believe the bay is too shallow and too exposed to be suitable for large ships. Therefore, I shall leave at daybreak with a small party and explore the coastline north of here as far as Broken Bay, which, as those of you who are familiar with Cook's charts will know, is not too far distant.

"Major Ross will supervise the clearing of ground on the southern extremity of Botany Bay as a precaution against our exploration being unsuccessful."

He stared at his rapt audience. "Once a suitable site is found, gentlemen, our next duty will be to establish a self-supporting colony that will provide relief for his Majesty's overcrowded prisons and a safe port for those of his ships that sail into these waters. The years ahead will be hard, but I have no doubt that we shall accomplish the task government has set us. Now our Judge Advocate, Captain Collins, will summarize my orders pertaining to your treatment of the local inhabitants. Thank you."

The young Collins, whose dark brows and eyes contrasted dramatically with his sandy hair, cleared his throat nervously before addressing his fellow officers.

"One. No member of His Majesty's forces, government official, seaman, or convict will be permitted to molest a native of this country.

"Two. Only in the most extreme circumstance—that is, when in actual fear of life—will a person be permitted to take up a firearm against a native. And you are to instruct those men under your command that, if such a need does arise, then the firearm is only to be discharged into the air as a warning.

"Three. Murder of a native will meet with the same punishment as murder of a white man. Death by hanging.

"Four. Care must be taken that no native weapon falls into the hands of a convict.

"Five. Our people are to treat the natives in a neighborly manner and, at all times, respect their property.

"Gentlemen, Governor Phillip desires that we cohabit with the natives in this country in peace and friendship. These orders are to be strictly adhered to, and any infringement thereof will be dealt with most harshly. Thank you."

Phillip rose again. "While the customs and appearance of natives may appear strange to you, gentlemen, think for a moment how odd we appear to them. Today, while Lieutenant Gidley King and a fellow officer were exploring, a party of natives approached and gave them to understand that they were confused as to our gender. It appears that they had perceived from our shaven countenances and odd attire that we were women.

"Lieutenant King, not wishing them to labor any longer under such a misapprehension, ordered a stout seaman (who happened to be very well endowed) to drop his breeches. The fellow obliged, the natives gave a great shout of admiration, and the matter was resolved."

He waited for the hearty laughter to subside, then smiled broadly. "Enough of rules, regulations, disciplines, and decisions. Let everybody come up to the deck where refreshments—and some champagne I have been saving for this occasion—await!"

"How is Lucy Gamble faring?" Phillip asked Michael when they met on deck a few minutes later.

"In good spirits, sir, and most grateful for your assistance. Learning of Faith Billingsley's existence has made an immense difference to her. She wrote to Faith from Capetown and is eagerly awaiting the arrival of a ship from England."

Phillip liked Michael Perryman. He was level-headed, intelligent and had never attempted to take advantage of the peculiar position they had found themselves in which Phillip knew the job of

Governor would leave him little time for personal relationships, but he hoped that he and Michael would be friends.

"The Surgeon General told me you were a First Lieutenant in the navy before this, Michael."

"Yes, sir. But when I applied to come on the voyage all the naval Commissions had been filled."

Phillip looked at him levelly. "Would you like to join my exploration party tomorrow?"

Michael was surprised and delighted. "Yes, sir, if my commanding officer will give his permission."

Phillip laughed. "That won't be difficult to arrange. Let's find Gidley King and ask him to add your name to those in my longboat."

Sir Michael had almost finished his meal when Faith and Hugh entered the dining room.

"Good evening, sir," said Hugh as he and Faith took their places at the table. "I apologize for our lateness, but we have been visiting the estate farms." He stared at his uncle's absurdly twisted features with sympathy. "How are you? I was sorry to learn of your recent illness . . ."

Sir Michael glared at him. "I find your expressions of concern hard to believe, Hugh. This is the first time in twenty-four hours that you have even bothered to make me aware of your presence in my house!"

Hugh inclined his head. "You are right, sir. Please accept my apologies. When I arrived last night you had already retired. And Faith and I left early this morning . . ."

Sir Michael's mouth twitched. "But not before you made a spectacle of yourselves on my lawn!"

Feeling Faith stiffen beside him, Hugh reached under the table and squeezed her knee. "I apologize again, sir—not for our little romp—but for any embarrassment we may have caused you." He filled Faith's glass and proffered the wine decanter to Sir Michael. "Care for some wine, sir?"

"Don't attempt to change the subject!" Sir Michael barked. "Why are you here? You received my answer to you letter via your lackeys, did you not?"

"I did, indeed," Hugh replied calmly. "But, to answer your first question, I came here expressly to ask Faith to marry me."

The nerves on the right side of Sir Michael's face jerked convulsively. "What damned impertinence, sir! I absolutely forbid it!"

"Please, don't upset yourself, Grandfather," Faith implored, reaching across the table and clasping his hand. "Hugh and I are so happy, and we want you to share our joy."

He snatched his hand away. "Be silent, Margaret! The bounder has swept you off your feet! What do you know of love? You are a child!"

"I am Faith," she cried in dismay.

"Faith . . . I meant Faith! Have you forgotten that this man is your cousin? If you marry him, your children will be monsters."

"What utter rubbish!" Hugh said. "We are cousins twice removed. And the Billingsleys have formed no prior union with the Stewart ancestry. Put aside your animosity and be happy for us."

"I'll say nothing more to you, sir," shouted Sir Michael, reaching for the bell. "Faith, I expect you in the library as soon as you have finished your meal. You shall read to me."

Faith shook her head. "Not tonight, Grandfather. Hugh is leaving for London in the morning and I want to spend the next hours with him."

Sir Michael's breathing grew labored. "Are you defying me, Faith?"

"Yes," she said, her chin coming up. "I am not a child to be ordered about. If you won't be reasonable to Hugh, then you can spend the evening alone. It is your decision . . ."

"I shall retire at once," he said frigidly, and signaled Kenneth to assist him from the room.

42
Sydney Cove

Wednesday, January 23, 1788

While the work parties ashore battled clouds of flies and mosquitoes, those on board the transporters huddled under canvas sails in an attempt to protect their fair skins from the sun's merciless rays. Botany Bay had entirely lost its appeal and everyone hoped Governor Phillip would soon return with news of a better place.

"Michael cannot be much longer," Lucy said as she anxiously scanned the entrance, "he has been gone almost three days."

"Looking for him won't make him come back any faster," said Frances, relieving her of the spyglass and training it on a group of native children splashing about in a stream on the north shore. "This heat is more than I can—" She broke off and groaned. "Here's the doctor with Edward. Good God, what have they done to the poor child since Jane died."

Edward was naked, filthy, and covered from head to foot in bites and blisters.

"Here, let me have him, doctor," Frances murmured, taking the listless child in her arms. "There, lad, everything's all right . . ."

"Let's get him out of the sun," Tom suggested as the women crowded around. He took a jar from his pocket and handed it to Lucy. "Edward is infested with vermin and severely sunburned. Wash him in fresh, lukewarm water, allow him to dry naturally, then smear him with salve."

"Our water allotment don't run to bathing, doctor," Frances said worriedly.

Tom pointed to a cask two sailors from *Friendship* were rolling along the deck. "I brought some with me—and an old shirt Edward can wear until I find something more suitable."

He drew Susannah aside and whispered, "Take that young rascal of yours for a stroll to *Friendship*'s longboat, someone manning the oars is anxious to see you."

Giving him a look of immense gratitude, Susannah picked up her son and sped away.

"Have you spoken to Dr. Balmain, Tom?" Beth asked with exaggerated casualness.

"I think he went with the Governor's party."

"Probably," she said offhandedly. "I wonder when he—they will get back?"

"I wonder," said Tom, giving Lucy a wink.

Aboard the *Supply* tender

Phillip hummed tunelessly as he stood before his mirror shaving next morning. The exploration party had returned to Botany Bay late the previous evening after the most amazing discovery. Port Jackson! Nowhere in the world was there a harbor to match it.

His light-hearted musing was interrupted by a strangled cry from above. "Sail ho, east of the entrance!"

Phillip stared incredulously into the mirror. Was the watch drunk? There were no ships within a thousand leagues of Botany Bay.

Lieutenant Dawes burst into the cabin. "Commander Ball sends his compliments, sir, and requests your presence on deck immediately. Two ships on the horizon. Can you believe it, sir?"

"What colors are they flying?" Phillip asked Ball on deck a few moments later.

"We can't tell, sir. They are still too far distant."

Phillip paced the deck thoughtfully. The two large ships standing off the entrance were having difficulty getting into the bay because of the adverse winds and currents.

"Weigh anchor, Lieutenant Ball. We shall bring about and creep a little closer to them."

"Do you think we may be under attack from the Dutch, sir?" asked Gidley King.

"That would not seem likely," Phillip replied vaguely, his mind on Port Jackson. No foreign power would cheat him out of that!

"Perhaps they are transporters from England," said Dawes.

"Too soon," Phillip replied, cursing himself for not having hoisted the flag over Port Jackson before.

"Could they be English loyalists from America, sir?" asked Ball.

Phillip addressed his officers. "I don't know who they are, gentlemen. Lieutenant King, hoist the English colors on Point Sutherland, then inform those in authority that when the ships arrive they will be out of bounds to visitors. I'll have no one but an Englishman taking possession of Port Jackson."

King nodded solemnly.

Phillip spent a frustrating day awaiting the arrival of the two strange ships. However, when evening came and they still had not reappeared, he decided that possession must take precedence over protocol. He would sail north to Port Jackson in *Supply* and Hunter could follow later with the rest of the Fleet.

Hunter, who had joined him shortly after the ships were sighted, agreed wholeheartedly. "Indeed, sir, it would be an exercise in stupidity to sit here politely while some foreign power hoisted its colors on the shores of *our* prize."

Although Phillip weighed anchor at first light next morning, the winds were so foul he could not work the tender clear of

173

Botany Bay until early afternoon. Without sighting the foreigners, he slipped up the coast to Port Jackson and, by nightfall, had dropped anchor at the entrance of the magnificent, sheltered cove he had chosen as the site of the new colony.

Saturday, January 26, 1788

At first light next morning, Phillip went ashore and took possession of the cove, which he had decided to call Sydney, after the Secretary of the English Home Office, Lord Thomas Townshend Sydney. It was the crowning moment of his life, for this beautiful little bay, with its fast-running freshwater stream was the culmination of two years' striving.

He placed his right hand on the flagpole. "I, Arthur Phillip, Governor of New South Wales, take possession of Sydney Cove, Port Jackson, in the name of my sovereign, King George the Third."

The simple words spoken, he turned and gave the signal for the honor guard to fire. A moment later, the red, white, and blue of England unfurled atop the makeshift flagpole and the tranquility of the morning was shattered by musket fire and the cries of ten thousand parakeets.

As Phillip watched their ascent, he was struck by how perfectly their pink and gray plumage blended with the dawn light of this new world.

43
"Truth's Word Will Stem the Blood"

Tuesday, February 5, 1788

Faith stopped beneath the brooding cedar at the side of the house and gazed apprehensively at the dark clouds gathering on the horizon. She expected Hugh to return from London this evening and she hoped he would arrive before the storm.

Sir Michael still refused to discuss the betrothal and, seeking some respite from his silence and disapproval, Faith had donned walking shoes and strolled down to Roman Lake.

As she stepped out from beneath the tree, a man passed through the portals at the end of the carriageway and walked purposefully toward her with a peculiar rolling gate. He wore a black coat that made a dark silhouette against the stark, white landscape and he carried an oversize canvas bag that bumped against his bandy knees.

He halted a few feet from her and removed a battered, square-fronted brown felt hat. "Ahoy there, Miss Faith Billingsley, I'd have known you anywhere!"

"How do you do," said Faith, puzzled. She had certainly never seen him before!

"I be mighty glad to make *your* acquaintance," he said, diving into the canvas bag and withdrawing a bulky envelope. "And I bring you greetings from Miss Lucy, far across the sea!"

"What is all this about?" Faith asked, taking the proffered envelope.

Leslie Gellin drew himself up to his full five feet, six inches and squared his shoulders. "Now then, Miss Faith Billingsley, that there letter has been brought to you by my hand all the way from Capetown, Africa. And, if you'll look on the back, you'll see how you are to square the account."

Faith turned the envelope over. "To be given into the hands of Miss Faith Billingsley who, upon receipt of same, will pay Mr. Leslie Gellin ten gold pieces, or the equivalent thereof. Lucy Gamble."

A great surge of excitement swept through Faith. *Lucy Gamble.* There, before her eyes, two separate pieces of the jigsaw puzzle were joined.

Lucy, the name of the woman she had been mistaken for in York, and *Gamble*, her dead father's family name. Lucy Gamble and Faith Gamble—Faith Gamble and Lucy Gamble. The pieces fitted perfectly!

Tears gushed from her eyes and she shook from head to foot as the world spun crazily around her. "Lucy and Faith Gamble," she sobbed. "Of course, that's it!"

She turned starry eyes to Leslie Gellin. "Wait here, Mr. Gellin, I shall fetch your money." But as she made to race away, he stepped nimbly in her path and snatched the letter.

"Hang in stays!" he cried. "I'll hold on to this if you don't mind. I've done a long, hard haul from the Cape and, my beauty, she promised me a reward."

"If this letter is what I think it is," Faith breathed, "You are deserving of far more than mere money, Mr. Gellin. Stay where you are, I won't be long."

Picking up her skirts, she sped across the lawn to the library and, ignoring Sir Michael's startled protests, took two handfuls of gold guineas from the safe.

"W-what is the matter, Miss Faith?" Kenneth quavered as Faith dragged him through the snow.

"Kenneth, this is Mr. Leslie Gellin," she said breathlessly. "You are to take him to Lyndhurst in the carriage and register him at the Inn. He is to be given the best accommodation and his account is to be sent to me."

She handed Leslie Gellin his money, and took possession of her letter. "I would be greatly obliged if you would bide at the Inn until morning, Mr. Gellin. I shall have countless questions to ask about Lucy Gamble."

Leslie Gellin agreed, they shook hands and, clutching Lucy's letter to her breast, Faith sped toward the Hall.

When she opened the envelope in her room a few minutes later, a tiny calico pouch dropped into her lap. She glanced at it curiously, then turned her attention to the great bundle of pages in her hand.

Tuesday, October 30, 1787
Capetown
My dearest, most beloved sister, Faith,

Words cannot express my emotions as I begin this, my first letter to you.

Let me introduce myself. I am Lucy Margaret Gamble, born at Hartman Square, London, on the eleventh of November, 1766; and my parents were James Donald Gamble and Margaret Joyce Billingsley.

Three days ago, I learned from the Commodore of the Fleet that you and I are identical twin sisters . . .

Word by word, sentence by sentence, the pieces that had been Faith's life snapped into place. By the time she came to the last page of Lucy's letter, only the parts pertaining to her scarred finger were missing.

Contempt is too inadequate a word to express my feeling for the selfish, lying hypocrite who robbed you, Father, and me of twenty years of love and companionship. I weep, as I know you weep, but tears will not bring back one moment

176

of these stolen years. Therefore, as restitution is impossible, you and I must settle for his confession. When you bring him to this accounting, spare him not, beloved. And know your sister Lucy will be there at your side. For, although physically we are independent; spiritually, we are one.

In the calico bag is Father's most treasured possession, the charm Mother gave him on their first wedding anniversary. He wore it until the moment he died as a symbol of their love. I send it to you as a symbol of mine.

I shall live for the day when we can be reunited and, until that day comes, Faith, *know* that I shall call to you on the wind and that my spirit will come to you in the stillness of the night.

Lucy.

Faith made her way quickly downstairs to the library. She found him sitting in the chair before the fire, just as he had been the first night she had gone to him for help.

He looked up expectantly as she entered but, when he saw the expression on her face, the words of welcome choked in his throat. "You look so strange. A-are you ill, my dear?"

She held out the charm. It spun before him, burnished gold in the fire's light.

"What is that?" he asked, reaching for it.

"Read the inscription on the back," she said softly.

He turned it over and read aloud. "To my beloved Jamie— Margaret eleven, four, sixty-six." He gasped and the charm slipped through his fingers to the floor.

She retrieved it and fastened the charm around her neck. "Notice the date? Mother gave it to Father one week before I was born—on their wedding anniversary."

"W-where did you get it?" he asked hoarsely.

Her eyes bored into him. "My sister, Lucy, sent it from Capetown."

"Your sister Lucy? You have no sister in Capetown. Have you taken leave of your senses again, Faith?"

She leaned over him. "By now, Lucy is on her way to Botany Bay, but you know that, Captain Phillip wrote to you."

He attempted to rise but she pushed him down. "Stay where you are. You are not leaving this room until you have told me everything, you despicable man."

His mouth twitched. "I can see by your eyes that you are ill.

If you don't control yourself, I shall summon the servants and have you removed to your room."

Faith's green eyes narrowed. "You have no power over me anymore, Grandfather. Confess!"

"Confess to what?" he blustered. "I don't know what you are raving about. You are deluded."

"Liar," she said dispassionately.

He fell back in the chair gasping. "I-I shall not tolerate you talking to me in such a manner, Faith. Have you forgotten that I am a sick man?"

"I have not forgotten. But I will not allow you to use your delicate state of health as a weapon. I have a right to the truth, you liar."

"Don't speak to me that way!"

"How would you have me speak to you?" she asked derisively. "You, who denied me the love and companionship of a father and sister for twenty years? Tell me, I would like to know."

"You will show me respect. I am your grandfather!"

Faith laughed contemptuously. "Respect! I wonder that you dare mention the word. People earn respect, they don't demand it as their right. I have trusted and respected you all my life and you have repaid me with lies and deceit. Tell me the truth!"

He pointed a shaking finger at the charm. "Foolish girl, you have allowed that thing to rob you of your faculties."

Faith clenched her fists to keep from striking him. "Your daughter gave this 'thing' to my father and it was his most precious possession. You will remember my father, I'm sure, he was the infamous bounder who deserted Mother some months before I was born—the same bounder who died in a shipwreck when I was two years old. Well, somehow, he managed to reincarnate himself and raise my twin sister in London."

She became aware that someone had entered the room and, glancing over her shoulder, saw Hugh.

"My God, Fae, what is happening? I could hear your voices from the carriageway."

Faith beckoned him to join her. "Look, Grandfather, your unacceptable nephew has returned from London in time to hear your confession. Tell him how you abducted me the night I was born—and how you have kept me apart from my father and my twin sister, all my life!"

Sir Michael tried to rise, but again Faith pushed him down.

"Don't listen to her, Hugh," he gasped. "She is deranged. Call the servants, she has been holding me here against my will!"

Faith laughed. "My mind has never been more clear. Tell Hugh how you managed to trick my father into leaving me behind the night Lucy and I were born."

Hugh grasped her arm and spun her around. "What are you saying, Fae? Who is Lucy?"

Faith understood the dismay and confusion in his eyes, but she did not have time to explain. "Lucy is my identical twin, Hugh. Try to be patient. Let this liar tell us how he abducted me the night I was born."

Sir Michael raised trembling hands to his temples and shook his head. "No, I did not abduct you—it was not like that. I did not do it intentionally, believe me. You just . . . happened to be out of the room when your father arrived . . ."

Faith bent over him. "That does not explain how Father left your house with Lucy but not me."

Sir Michael pressed his throbbing temples. "He and I had words. . . . He left in such a hurry, I did not have time to tell him."

"Really?" she scoffed. "Then, why didn't you send a servant after him to bid him to return?"

Beads of sweat formed above his lip. "I-I couldn't . . ."

"Why not? You knew where he lived."

He shook his head and Faith saw that there were tears in his eyes. "You must understand, Faith. Your mother was my life. I thought Fate had stepped in and given me a chance to retain a living part of her. Your father and I were bitter enemies, he would never have allowed me to keep you—and, he already had the other one didn't he? Why *should* I give you up? I had known Margaret all her life. He had only known her for two years!"

"Oh God," Hugh whispered hoarsely, "I cannot believe I am hearing this, Fae. You have a twin sister? Where is she? How did you discover her? James Geldie has no knowledge of her."

Faith looked at him with bitter eyes. "No, James Geldie could not possibly know. Grandfather concealed his crime from everyone. I received a letter from Lucy today. She is a convict aboard one of the ships bound for New South Wales. Be patient, Hugh, until I have finished here."

She turned back to Sir Michael. "Let us set aside the night of my birth for a moment and concentrate on the night Lucy was arrested—the night I had my first vision of her. When I came to you and asked for your help, did you seize upon it as an opportunity to right your wrongs? No, you insinuated that I was losing my mind and removed me to Carrigmoor."

179

So beset was she by emotion, that she began to shake. "Where was your compassion for my Lucy, locked away in that horrible prison? Even if you had said nothing to me, you could have established her whereabouts and helped her anonymously. Why did you choose to do nothing?"

"I was afraid, Faith. I-I didn't want to lose you."

"Was that also your reasoning when Lucy wrote from Newgate, asking for help, and when I saw her in Portsmouth?" Faith asked slowly.

He nodded.

"You preferred me to believe myself mad, and Lucy to suffer the horrors of transportation, rather than to confess what you had done?" she asked incredulously.

He looked at her with despairing eyes. "I hoped that, with her out of the way, you would become your old self again."

"What did you do with the letters Captain Phillip sent us from Rio?" Faith asked. "They contain Lucy's papers. We need them to fight her cause through the Courts."

"I think I burned them."

"What?"

"I cannot remember exactly because I received them the day of my last attack. But, yes, I think I would have burned them. With Phillip away from England for years, there was still a chance that I could keep you from learning about your sister . . ."

Faith drew herself up stiffly. "Well, you failed, Grandfather. You were doomed to fail from the beginning. You could not keep us apart. You see, the tie that binds Lucy and me is spirit, not flesh. Although, sometimes the flesh weeps, does it not?"

She held out her right hand and he saw the blood running from the center of the scar.

"Oh God, no!" he cried, covering his face and shrinking down in the chair. "Take it away, I cannot bear to look at it!"

Hugh put his arm around her and said gently, "We had best bind it, Fae."

She shook her head. "No, only truth's word will stem the blood. What else happened the night Lucy and I were born, Grandfather? There is more . . . and it has something to do with this scar. *Why* does it bleed?"

Sir Michael lowered his hands from his face and gave a long, drawn out sigh, filled with pain and remorse. "Sit down, both of you," he said wearily. "I shall tell you all . . ."

"After your grandmother died in 1763, Faith, I spent two years abroad. When I returned to the Hall, Margaret had changed. Oh, we were happy enough to begin with, then James Gamble appeared on the scene and had the effrontery to ask for her hand in marriage. As he was considerably older than she and, I suspected, a fortune hunter, I barred him from Billingsley and forbade her to see him. However, three weeks later, when she told me she was with child I had no choice but to let the marriage take place. Margaret was a rather headstrong girl and, before long, I realized that she had deceived me. We had a blazing argument and she and Gamble left for London.

"I did not hear from her again until the following September, when she wrote that she was expecting a child and invited me to call on her the next time I was in London. Accordingly, I paid her a visit and we spent a very pleasant afternoon together. But, when I was preparing to take my leave of her, she became ill. Although the baby was not due for another month, it soon became obvious that she was in labor. I overrode her objections and took her to Hartman Square where I could provide her with adequate care. The lodgings Gamble had acquired were primitive beyond description.

"I soon had her comfortably settled in her old room with a doctor and a midwife in attendance, and after dispatching a servant, at her insistence, to stand guard at Gamble's lodgings, I settled down to await the arrival of my grandchild.

"Just before dawn the midwife woke me and requested that I go immediately to Margaret's room. When I arrived, the doctor informed me that Margaret had just given birth to identical twin daughters, but that the ordeal had been too much for her and I must hasten to say farewell . . ."

He paused and passed a hand over his eyes.

"Go on, Grandfather," Faith prompted grimly.

"I-I went to the bed and took Margaret's hand . . . I begged her to stay with me, but she died a few minutes later without regaining consciousness.

"Then the doctor asked me to accompany him to the crib on a matter of the utmost urgency. I-I saw by his expression that something was amiss . . . so I set aside my grief and did as he told me.

"W-when I looked into the crib everything seemed normal. You were both well formed, and identical in features. But when the doctor tried to pull you apart he could not, because a pulsating cord of living tissue was looped around your bodies,

181

holding you in a tight embrace. And so you had been, according to the doctor, from the moment of your conception.

"The doctor asked if I knew of your father's whereabouts, and when I replied that I did not, he said I must allow him to sever the cord, for you and Lucy could not remain in that condition any longer.

"I gave my permission and he set to work. He experienced no great difficulty cutting the cord where it was attached to your lower bodies but, when he severed it at the point where it joined Lucy's hand to yours, you gave a plaintive cry and started bleeding profusely. At first, he could not stem the blood but, after working frantically for several minutes, he managed it.

"The midwife took you below stairs to a servant who had offered to act as a wet nurse until more suitable arrangements could be made, then she returned to the room and saw to Lucy's needs. Not long afterward, the doctor departed for a well-earned rest and the midwife departed in search of a wet nurse for Lucy. And that was the situation when Gamble burst into the room a few minutes later.

"As soon as he arrived he began upbraiding me for taking Margaret from his lodgings. I countered his accusations by demanding that he show some respect and lower his voice in the presence of the dead. The bounder stared at me in some consternation for a time—until Lucy's wailing roused him. Then he gave Margaret a fond kiss good-bye, took Lucy in his arms, and addressed me. 'Margaret would wish to be buried beside her mother at Billingsley, Sir Michael; therefore, I do earnestly charge you to see that done. But, for my part, I shall not be troubling you again in this life, and I ask that you have the decency to do likewise.'

"I assured the bounder that he could depend on it, and I am delighted to say that was the last time I ever saw him."

Faith looked at her hand. The scar had stopped bleeding. "Prophecy, prophecy," she said. "*Truth's word will stem the blood.*"

She murmured a vague excuse to Hugh, slipped out of the house and waded through the chill white world to the Billingsley burial ground.

Hugh found her weeping beside her mother's grave. "You will freeze if you stay here any longer, Fae," he said tenderly, drawing her to her feet and wrapping his arms protectively around her.

She rested her head on his shoulder and slipped her arms

beneath his greatcoat. "Forgive me, Hugh. I planned a happier homecoming for you. But now, all I can think of is my poor Lucy!"

Hugh clasped her tightly against him. "Don't apologize, dearest. Your sadness is my sadness."

She moaned in a low, tormented way that made Hugh's heart ache. "Oh, Hugh. What has he done to my Lucy? He could have helped her, Hugh, and he didn't. I want my Lucy. I *want* her!"

He raised her chin and kissed her wet cheeks. "You will be reunited with Lucy. I swear it on your mother's grave."

Her sobs subsided. "Do you mean it, Scotty?"

"Of course I mean it, silly," he murmured, brushing snow from her hair. "Why don't you and I go to your warm room? We have a host of plans to make."

They left the cemetery and set off across the sea of white, but had not gone far when Kenneth came stumbling toward them.

"Come quickly, Miss Faith. The Master has fallen down, and I cannot rouse him!"

Hugh placed Lucy's letter on the desk and joined Faith by the fire. "We will not find it easy to effect Lucy's release, Fae. James Geldie and I visited Ruth Gamble twice while I was in London but we got no farther than her front door. She is adamant that she will not discuss—"

"What reason did you give for seeking an interview?" Faith broke in, leaning forward urgently in her chair.

"That we were enquiring into her late husband's affairs on your behalf . . ."

Faith grasped his arm. "Did you mention my name, or did you just say you were enquiring on behalf of James Gamble's *daughter*?"

"The latter, I think . . ."

Faith expelled her breath and sank back. "Thank God for that!"

"What are you getting at?" he asked curiously.

"That's why you got such a cool reception. She probably thought you were lawyers acting on Lucy's behalf. She has no knowledge of me. I doubt that she has heard the name 'Billingsley.' And that is the way I want it to remain, at least until we have thought the matter through."

"But why?" Hugh asked. "Ruth Gamble's cooperation is vital."

Faith looked at him steadily. "I am aware of that, Hugh. Tell me, did you catch a glimpse of her?"

"Only briefly. The second time we went to the house, she left in the carriage."

"Did she have dark hair, a widow's peak and sallow cheeks?"

Hugh raised surprised eyebrows. "Yes, but how could you know that, Fae?"

Faith told him of her encounter with Ruth Gamble in York.

"What a remarkable coincidence."

"You may call it a coincidence," she said, "but I think a higher intelligence caused out paths to cross."

An urgent banging sounded on the door and a maid rushed in without waiting to be asked. "The doctor wants you and Master Hugh to come once, Miss Faith," she cried breathlessly. "Sir Michael is awake and calling for you."

When Faith arrived at her grandfather's bedside, she saw at a glance that he was very low. He had always been a robust man, but as he lay before her, propped up on pillows, his skin the color of parchment and his face enfolded in sagging flesh, he looked frail and shrunken. Mercifully though, the last attack had righted his facial features and the grotesque, clownish expression was gone.

His eyelids fluttered and his mouth worked soundlessly for a few moments before he managed a word. ". . . Lucy. Tell Lucy . . . sorry."

Faith stared at him steadily.

Tears oozed from beneath his wrinkled lids and rolled into the crevices of his sunken cheeks. "Forgive me, my dear."

Still, she gave no answer.

He raised his head and his nails clawed the starched sheets. "Forgive me, Faith . . . I beg you."

"Let God forgive you, Grandfather." Her voice sounded like ice on a winter's morn. "Lucy and I cannot."

He gazed at her with disbelief, his eyes wide and staring. Then the light left them and, weeping still, he fell back against the pillows, dead.

BOOK TWO

PART ONE
Striving for the Right Path

1
The Foundations Laid

Thursday, February 7, 1788

Perhaps I should set aside the past and begin rebuilding my life, Lucy thought as the crowded longboat wound in and out of the Fleet ships, heading for the west side of Sydney Cove. Faith will come to me as soon as she is able and, meanwhile, this brand new land holds promise of exciting days ahead.

Everywhere she looked there was movement, color and confusion. Sailors hung over the sides of ships waving and catcalling as the longboat skimmed past. Ashore, gangs of convicts, their pale skins blotched red from the sun, chopped trees, dragged logs and pitched tents. Women with distracted countenances chased children or walked slowly, balancing huge bundles on their heads. Scarlet-coated marines humped heavy equipment. Cattle lowed, pigs squealed, goats bleated, dogs barked, geese cackled, cocks crowed; and high in the treetops, myriads of brightly colored birds screeched displeasure at this invasion of their peaceful domain.

A few strokes of the oars and the moment Lucy longed for had arrived. As the boat came to the shore she scrambled to her feet, clasped Michael's outstretched hand, and for the first time in ten months stepped onto solid ground.

"Welcome to Sydney Cove." He gave her hand an affectionate squeeze and smiled widely. "What do you think of it?"

Lucy glanced around her. About fifty feet east of the fast-flowing stream that emptied into the southwestern corner of the cove, stood the partially completed canvas house of the Governor, surrounded by the tents of the colony officials. South of where she stood, the male and female camps were built on gentle wooded slopes and, beyond them, on some cleared ground close to the west bank of the stream, were the barracks. Here on the western headland the ground was level for about one hundred feet back from the shore, then rose sharply into a series of thickly wooded sandstone hills.

"I think it's grand," she said, scooping up a handful of white sand and letting it trickle through her fingers. "Oh, Michael, how wonderful to touch the earth again."

"How wonderful to touch you again," he murmured, glancing appreciatively at the high color in her cheeks and the way her glossy hair escaped in wisps from the thick coil on her head.

"Everything is in great confusion," she went on quickly, avoiding his eyes. "People are darting about as if they haven't the faintest notion of what they are doing . . ."

He smiled. "It's been that way since we came ashore."

Tom cleared his throat and said to the *Friendship* women gathered around him, "Would you like to see your new quarters?"

They nodded eagerly.

"Will we all be working at the hospital?" asked Beth.

Tom shook his head. "Only you, Mrs. Hart, Susannah Holmes, and Lucy. The others from *Friendship* will be employed by the colony officials on the east side of the cove. Collect your belongings from the boat and I'll take you across there now."

After Tom and the other women had departed, Michael led his four charges up the beach and along a bush track to the hospital.

"Have you seen Henry Cable, Lieutenant?" asked Susannah, as she struggled to contain her son and little Edward who were ecstatic at their changed conditions.

Michael took Edward's hand. "He is assigned to the timber-getters gang this morning. But everyone is ordered to assemble at ten o'clock for the reading of the Commissions and Letters Patent, so you will be able to talk to him then, Susannah."

"Lawks! I can't walk properly!" Beth exclaimed when her feet met the flat, unyielding earth with knee-jarring force.

"It will take some time to regain our land legs," Lucy laughed as they staggered into a large clearing surrounded by tents.

"This way," said Michael, leading them across the clearing, past four wooden huts belonging to the doctors and through the bush to a tent pitched beneath a huge native fig tree.

Lucy could not hide her disappointment as she stared at their new quarters. Although separated from the rest of the hospital by dense undergrowth, thus insuring privacy, the tent was so tiny she wondered how they could fit in.

"Tents are hard to come by at the moment, but as soon as more are unloaded I shall acquire another," Michael promised.

"Anywhere for a body to acquire a good scrub, Lieutenant?" panted Frances, her face flushed scarlet from the heat.

"Behind the hospital, a path leads through the hills to the other side of this headland where you'll find a small beach with a fresh water cascade. The walk is well worth the effort. Perhaps you could go there after the Surgeon General has spoken to you. But take a man from *Friendship* to stand watch, there are malingerers skulking in the woods."

"Are you sure we will be safe?" Lucy asked anxiously.

He brushed a strand of hair from her cheek. "This entire headland is out-of-bounds to convicts from the main camp, Lucy. Taking a man along is merely a precaution."

Michael returned with them to the clearing where John White and two of his assistants—Denis Considen from *Scarborough* and William Balmain from *Alexander*—were seeing to the patients, temporarily housed in tents until the portable hospital from England was completed.

Later, as the women splashed in the crystal-clear waters, they discussed their new duties. Lucy and Beth would care for the patients and Susannah and Frances would do general housekeeping for the doctors.

The distant beat of drums ended their frolic.

"Come on, everyone," Lucy called as she waded to the rock on which lay her new issue of clothing. "We cannot be late for our first official function."

As they fought their way through the noisy press of people gathered on the slope where the ceremony was to take place, the battalion was already on its way from the barracks.

"Here comes the band!" Beth cried, clapping in time with the music.

When the troops arrived, the colony officials and the marine wives assembled in the clearing at the bottom of the slope where a camp table and podium had been set up.

"I wonder what's in that?" Beth exclaimed, standing on her toes and pointing to a red box in the center of the table.

"The official documents, I expect," answered Lucy, casting a relieved look at Moses Tucker, Henry Cable, and John Best.

189

With so many rough-looking men present, it was reassuring to have them near.

Without warning, the troops encircling the convicts raised their muskets and fired three salvos in quick succession. The men jumped, the women screamed and the birds rose screeching into the air.

"Silence! Be seated!" the order rang out.

The Governor stepped ashore, the band struck up a rousing rendition of "God Save the King," the official party sat down, the troops fired another three salvos, and David Collins, the Judge Advocate, took up the red box and stepped onto the podium.

Listening to him read the documents, Lucy was struck by the extent of the Governor's powers. They must be almost as great as the King's, she thought. The government certainly has provided a stable foundation for this new colony.

When Collins finished reading, the troops fired three more salvos, the band played another verse of "God Save the King," and Phillip stepped onto the podium.

First, he praised the marines for their steady good conduct and the quality of their drill, then he addressed the convicts, who formed the majority of the thousand or so people gathered on the slope.

"All those prepared to play a worthwhile part in the founding of this, His Majesty's colony of New South Wales, have my promise that they will be treated justly."

During Collins's reading of the Commissions and Letters Patent the attention of the convicts had wandered, but now every eye was fastened upon the lean, gray-haired man who held such power over them. Phillip spoke of the natives.

"It is the government's wish that you treat the people of this country with benevolent, open-hearted friendship. If you treat them harshly, they will treat you harshly in return. If you treat them kindly, in time, they will come to trust you and all can live in peace and harmony."

Next, he spoke of law and order, and Michael, standing at the rear of the podium with the other officers, heard his tone sharpen. "During the voyage and since landing, leniency has been shown you; however, with the reading of the Letters Patent, the Civil and Criminal Courts of New South Wales are herewith established, and henceforth law and order will prevail. Wrong behavior will be dealt with swiftly, for not to punish the bad would do an injustice to the good. The industrious will not labor for the idlers. Those who will not work, will not eat.

"Furthermore, it has come to my notice that several of your number have made their way overland to Botany Bay thinking to seek passage aboard the two French discovery ships. Monsieur Comte de La Perouse has ordered his men to drive all who arrive into the woods. Those people now have two choices—to return to the settlement for trial and punishment, or to starve in the wilderness."

A low murmur ran through the crowd and people looked uneasily at their neighbors. The prospect of living in the wild, separated from even the meager comforts the settlement had to offer, held little appeal.

"Any person found loitering outside the perimeters of the settlement after Retreat has sounded will be arrested," the Governor went on firmly. "Any man found loitering in the women's camp after Retreat has sounded will be arrested. Any person found loitering in the out-of-bounds areas on the east and west headlands will be arrested. And any person found robbing the Government Provisions Store will be hung."

Phillip's grim words reverberated in the silence. But he was determined to conclude his speech on a lighter note. "Since arriving in this country, I have received many petitions requesting permission to marry. Those of you wishing to sanctify your relationships may submit your names to Reverend Johnson any evening after stop-work beats and he will make the appropriate arrangements. You are excused from work for the remainder of the day. Dismissed."

"Alas, gentlemen, you are eating all the remains of my stock," Major Ross told the officials and officers, who had gathered in a large marquee at the head of the barracks to enjoy a cold collation in honor of the occasion. "Last night, lightning shivered the tree under which the animals were tethered and killed six sheep, two lambs, and my prime pig."

Captain Campbell, Ross's second in command, pushed a piece of maggot-riddled mutton to one side of his plate. "Not only lightning but also spiders, flies, ants, and mosquitoes abound in this wretched country. Last night I was almost eaten alive. It is a disgrace that His Majesty's marine officers must sleep in the dirt. Where are our huts? Where are our comforts? Why hasn't the Governor rectified this appalling situation? No wonder our brave lads are dropping like deadwood."

"It is hardly the Governor's fault that several marines have contracted camp dysentery and scurvy," said John White as he and his assistants joined the table. "They are the result of spending many months on a salt diet, not of lying in the dirt."

"The Governor is empowered to control everything else that lives and breathes in this colony, why not the health of the battalion?" Campbell replied sarcastically.

"I am astounded at the power bestowed upon the Governor," Ross said in peeved tones. "He can even *pardon* the damned felons if he so desires."

"It is my understanding that Governor Phillip is not empowered to pardon traitors or murderers, sir," Michael said.

"He can grant stays of execution which amounts to the same thing," Ross blustered. "Today he showed remarkable leniency toward the scoundrels. Excused from their labors, indeed."

"I do advocate leniency, Major Ross, if it promotes harmony and industry," Phillip said good-naturedly as he, Hunter, and King joined the table. "I believe that hard work and fair treatment, not punishment and repression, will further this colony. Let's offer these people a way out of their degradation rather than driving them deeper into crime and despair."

"How could we do that, Your Excellency?" asked John.

"Well, we could educate them."

"*Educate* them!" Major Ross repeated incredulously. "Surely you jest, sir?"

Phillip chuckled. "Allow me to give you an analogy, Major Ross. A criminal is like a one-eyed man—his vision of the grand scheme is partially obscured by his ignorance. To continue punishing him is like putting out his other eye, thus ensuring that he becomes an even greater burden on society. Education may be the key that opens the door to enlightenment."

After the ceremony, Frances went walking with William, her beau; Susannah accompanied Henry Cable to a hut he had built from cabbage-tree stems; and Lucy returned to the hospital with Beth, Moses, and little Edward.

Along with the patients' tents, the hospital environs included a washhouse and well behind the portable building, a fire for cooking in the center of the clearing, and three marquees. The first was the dispensary and laboratory; the second, a provisions store; and the third—containing a long camp table, liquor cabinet, and other comforts—the doctors' mess.

"I suppose we should see to the needs of the patients," said Lucy as Moses led Edward away.

Beth nodded. "Here comes Irving, the convict doctor. Let's ask him what to do."

Irving set them innumberable tasks and soon they were dispensing tea mixed with tree sap to the dysentery patients, and gruel made from wild spinach to those with scurvy.

Unbeknown to Lucy, Michael had discussed this aspect of her duties with the doctors, and all had agreed it would benefit her to work among men who, because of their weakened condition, would offer her little threat.

The hours slipped by unnoticed and it did not seem long before the women heard the five o'clock drum beating. After washing at the well, they walked to Henry Cable's hut where the people from *Friendship* had gathered for the evening meal.

Everyone sat around the camp fire eating fish, salt beef, and biscuit and avidly discussing the happenings of the day. Most thought Phillip firm but fair, although Henry Lavell disagreed.

"The Governor's as soft as maggot stew and the damned military ain't no better. All them Privates think of is drinking themselves scraggers and pouncing on every nellie they comes across. And the colony officials aren't any smarter, neither. Surveyor Alt don't know how many chaps is working for him. The last two days I've shot off after the midday meal and he's been none the wiser, so tomorrow I'm going fishing all day."

Although some of the other men murmured agreement, Henry Cable shook his head. "Where's the sense in taking on the Governor and the military? Sooner or later you'll run foul of them, then where'd you be? There's no escape—unless you fancy your chances out there." He swung his arm in a wide circle, indicating the darkness beyond the camp. "We may as well get on with it and hope to get our pardon in the end."

"Jesus," Lavell sneered, his voice heavy with disgust. "I never thought I'd see the day *you* turned soft, Cable."

There was a long, uncomfortable silence.

"We'd best get back to the hospital, Lucy," muttered Beth and they left.

"Would you like to take a stroll along the beach?" Michael called to Lucy as they passed the mess tent.

With a mixture of delight and apprehension, she agreed.

"Michael, why is this headland out-of-bounds?" she asked as they made their way along the water's edge.

"Phillip plans to build on observatory and battery at the point," he replied absently, marveling at her grace as she stepped nimbly over the rocks, her skirt gathered to one side and her breasts thrust forward.

"Why an observatory?"

He dragged his eyes away from her. "To house the astronomical instruments. The Royal Astronomer believes a comet sighted in 1661 will reappear in the southern skies toward the year's end. William Dawes, whom you met tonight, is supposed to take charge of the observatory, but Major Ross is rather put out by the whole thing . . ."

"Why is that?"

"Because two officers are unfit for duty, and Ross thinks that Dawes, a marine officer, should be reassigned to garrison duty. But really this is very dull stuff." He took her hand. "I'm glad we came for a walk."

She smiled and the little dimples he loved appeared in her cheeks. "I'm glad, too. It is so beautiful here, and so peaceful." She stared at the lights twinkling in the darkness on the other side of the harbor. "The natives are very shy, aren't they, Michael? Have you seen many?"

He tightened his grip on her hand. "No, but they are certainly out there, Lucy. That's why you must not go anywhere unaccompanied. John has agreed that a man can go with you whenever you leave the environs of the hospital."

"Moses Tucker already does," she replied softly. "Since this morning he has hardly left my side. I'm glad he has been assigned to the hospital as a carpenter."

"That was no accident, Lucy. Unfortunately, I shall not always be on hand."

She turned to face him, her skin creamy smooth in the moonlight. "Will your garrison duties often keep us apart?"

"I am afraid so, my dear. With two officers sick, I am bound to have extra duty." He squeezed her hand. "Still, there will be many nights like this . . ."

After they had rounded the point, he led her to a secluded spot beneath an overhanging rock.

"Although I miss the freedom and privacy of my old life, if Faith were with me, I think I could be very happy living in New South Wales," she mused as they sat gazing across the water at the east headland. "It is the opposite of England's green and

194

ordered loveliness, yet it has a fragile beauty all its own. I love those tall, slender gum trees and the warm golden days.''

"The fragility is just on the surface," Michael murmured. "Underneath, this country is terrifyingly rugged. The roots of those slender gums are anchored so tenaciously in the ground it is almost impossible to extract them, and when we do, all we get for our trouble is timber riddled with termites. Even the damned birds mock us. Have you heard them laugh?''

"Oh, Michael, the birds are beautiful!" she protested.

He reached up and released the thick coil of her hair. "Everything seems dull beside you, Lucy. How I've wanted you!" He caught her in a passionate embrace and kissed her wildly, savagely, saying her name over and over.

For a while, Lucy clung to him, her lips seeking his, but when he forced her down on the sand she became afraid.

"Michael," she gasped, twisting her head away. "Please, Michael . . . don't.''

The panic in her voice brought him to his senses. Cursing himself inwardly, he released her and sat up. "Don't be afraid, darling, I would never hurt you.''

She knelt beside him and brushed her fingertips gently over his lips. "I am sorry, Michael. I love you, I love you . . . and yet, when you press close, the fear comes and I cannot control it.''

He got to his feet and drew her after him. "Don't worry, darling," he said with a calm he was far from feeling. "I know we can overcome it. Meanwhile, let's just be happy that we are together.''

Sunday, February 10

"On my way here, I saw two natives in the clearing behind the Governor's house," said Ralph Clark, glancing disapprovingly at Lucy and Beth, wondering why they were taking supper with the doctors. "The Governor presented them with red bunting and hatchets, but although he spoke to them at length, he could not induce them to venture closer to the main camps.''

"Have the natives caused any trouble to the pickets?" asked John.

Ralph scowled darkly. "Not yet, but I cannot say the same for those damned convict bitches. They have got our men into such trouble. Their camp is a huge brothel—no sooner does one man leave a woman, than another goes in with her.''

"Watch your tongue," Michael said coldly.

195

"No offence meant to present company," Ralph answered quickly. "I . . . er . . . it's just that today I attended the court martial of Private Bramwell. He was charged with striking a convict whore—woman named Needham, with whom he'd had connections on the outward voyage. The poor lad was given a hundred lashes. I think it is a disgrace."

It had been a joyful day for Lucy. Both Susannah and Frances had been married after the Sunday service; therefore she did not want to hear Ralph Clark's biased bleatings about convict women. She put her mug down firmly and rose to her feet. "I think his sentence was too light. We have Elizabeth Needham here in the hospital with a broken nose and wrist. Apparently, your brave Private beat her brutally when she refused to go into the woods with him, which, in my humble opinion, she was entitled to do as she is getting married in a few days." She turned to John. "If you will excuse me, Dr. White, I'll see to the patients' drafts."

"I'll come too," offered Beth, pushing her plate aside.

"Both of you sit down and finish your supper," ordered John. "The drafts aren't due for another hour." He fixed Ralph with a steady glare. "What do you want, Lieutenant Clark?"

"I came to tell Michael that Lieutenant Long, the Camp Adjutant, has just been arrested," he mumbled, removing his hat and sitting down.

"What brought that on?" asked Michael.

"Shortly after you took over the hospital guard this evening, Michael, the Commissions and Letters Patent were read again to us officers in the mess; after which, the Governor told Major Ross that in the future we were to supervise the convicts at work."

Michael raised his eyebrows. "Phillip gave Major Ross a direct order?"

"No, not exactly an order, I suppose it was more a request, but there was no mistaking his meaning, Michael. He said that with only convicts to supervise convicts, little labor was being done in a country that required the greatest exertion; therefore, if us officers saw convicts working diligently we could perhaps say a few words of encouragement to them, or if we saw them idling we could threaten them with punishment.

"Major Ross told him in no uncertain terms that we had been Commissioned to do garrison duty in this godforsaken country, not to interfere with convicts at their work. The Governor replied that any officer volunteering to do duty in a new colony must expect to do more than mere garrison duty; and Major Ross countered by saying that officers were already sitting as members of the criminal court and that, had we been informed by government prior to leaving England that we would be required to do such an irksome duty, most of us would not have volunteered. He said that the convicts ought to be erecting a fortress to keep the natives out and that it should take precedence over all other government works—''

"Surely Major Ross did not take the Governor to task in front of you officers?" Denis Considen cut in.

Ralph frowned. This was not the reaction he had been expecting. "I think Major Ross had every right to refuse the Governor's request, Denis. I also support his view that the Governor has been given too much power. Only two days ago, he overturned a unanimous verdict of the criminal court. We sentenced a convict to fifty lashes for stealing two planks from the rear of the Governor's house and Phillip pardoned the rogue and sent him back to work!"

John chuckled. "I can see the logic in that. Had the convict been whipped for such a trifle, he would have been unfit to work for a week. Do get on with it, old chap. Why was the Adjutant arrested?"

Ralph crammed his hat on his head and rose. "After the Governor left the mess, Captain Campbell congratulated Major Ross on the stand he had taken. The Adjutant, who was well into his cups, commented loudly that, unlike *some* pickthanking toadeaters, he had no objection to supervising convicts, or to sitting as a member of the criminal court. Captain Campbell demanded an immediate apology and when it was not forthcoming, he arrested the Adjutant for unofficerlike behavior."

Sunday, February 17

"My, you look suntanned," Beth told Michael admiringly, when he arrived at the hospital clearing to escort her and Lucy to service.

He grinned. "I should, after spending the last week idling in the sun. God! Five years of this will drive me mad. At least on His Majesty's ships men are gainfully employed. Where is the challenge in guarding work gangs from natives who never appear?" He glanced at the red shoes on Beth's feet. "Why, Bethy, what are those you have on?"

"Her new leather shoes," Lucy answered, slipping her arm through his and squeezing it against her side, the way she had seen Susannah do with Henry. "George Clayton made them for her."

Michael raised a quizzical eyebrow. "Who is George Clayton?"

"Who is *George Clayton*?" Lucy rolled her eyes dramatically. "The latest of Beth's adoring swains, that's who."

Beth giggled. "You're a fine one to talk, Lucy Gamble. We can hardly move around this place for all your lovesick admirers."

"Having Lucy and Beth on staff can be rather wearing at times," John said as he and the other doctors joined them.

"Some men even go so far as to injure themselves in the hope that these damsels will tend them. I tell you, business has never been better."

Everyone laughed except Balmain who was staring at Beth with fixed intensity. Plainly, John's wit did not amuse him at all.

Beth had not walked far along the path toward her tent after work that evening when she noticed Balmain leaning against a tree. "Will! You startled me. What are you doing standing there in the shadows?" She thought him the most exciting man in the world with his lean, sinewy body and heavy-lidded eyes that made her shiver every time he looked at her.

He ground out his cigar and stepped onto the path. "What's George Clayton to you?"

"N-nothing, Will."

Although his voice was icy, she could see that his eyes were blazing.

He grabbed her by the shoulders and shook her. "Damn it, Beth, you've been leading him on, haven't you?"

A thrill of excitement ran through her. There was no mistake, he was in a positive rage. "No, Will," she replied unsteadily. "Honest, I haven't."

The next moment his arms were around her and he was kissing her savagely.

"Oh, Will, why'd you wait so long?" she breathed, pressing herself against him and returning his kisses with wild abandon.

"Damned if I know," he muttered, scooping her up and carrying her into the woods.

Exhausted by their lovemaking, they slept in each other's arms until the first faint glimmers of dawn streaked the sky, then Balmain awoke. "Time to go," he said, reaching for his shirt. "Return the shoes to Clayton, Beth. If you need anything in the future, ask me."

"But I love them shoes," she protested sleepily. "Where's the harm in keeping them?"

Balmain grasped her short-cropped ringlets and yanked her up beside him so that her face was only inches from his. "Don't play the whore with me, Beth. Give them back."

Tears of pain and shock sprang into Beth's eyes. "I'm not playing the whore. I'm no harlot—leastwise, not anymore."

He tightened his grip on her hair. "I know exactly what you are, Beth. You will not defy me in this. Return the shoes to Clayton. By God, if I catch you with him or any other man I will— "

"I don't want no other man," she broke in. "It's you I love, Will. You've no need to worry. I'll keep the shoes so's not to hurt George's feelings, but I promise not to wear them again."

He shoved her away and stood up. "Give the shoes back today," he said, tight-lipped, "or it ends between us right now."

She scrambled to her feet and flung her arms round his neck. "Please don't say that, Will. If it's that important to you I'll— toss them into the bushes!"

As she bent to pick up the shoes, he caught her wrist in a viselike grip. "No, you will return them to Clayton tonight at Cable's. I want everyone to see you do it."

"Yes, yes, all right," she sobbed, burrowing her head into his chest. "I'll do whatever you want, Will."

A moment later, he was smiling in his old way. "There's my good lass," he said cheerfully, patting her bare behind. "Now, hurry up and get dressed. I'm on early call this morning."

2

Cross-purposes and Crooked Answers

Saturday, February 23

It had been a bad day for Lucy. John had told her at breakfast that little Nancy Pugh, who had been ill for some time, had died during the night; half an hour later Susannah had arrived for work with the news that Lavell and three associates had been arrested on suspicion of robbing the government store; and now, this evening, while doing rounds, she thought she could hear someone moving about the clearing.

However, when she went to investigate she found the clearing deserted. "Probably the wind," she said aloud, glancing up at the gathering storm clouds. It had been threatening to rain all day, and forked lightning danced continuously across the sky.

She returned to Baby Harmsworth's crib and continued gently sponging his wasted body. He was about eight months old and, like her own son, had been born on the voyage. As she patted him dry, memories of her loss overwhelmed her and the wretched emptiness came flooding back. After a while, she wiped her eyes and carried the bucket outside.

It was a fearsome night. A hot wind whistled through the trees, the sky to the south glowed red from bushfires and the air was thick with acrid smoke. Forcing Jamie from her mind, she emptied the water and walked to the fire. But as she bent over the caldron ladling hot water into the bucket, a heavy hand fell on her shoulder.

She jumped with fright and spun around.

Tom Lewis stood there staring down at her.

Her stomach gave a sickening lurch and she turned cold with dread. "Get away, Lewis. You have no right to be here. Sailors are forbidden to come ashore after taptoo."

His grip on her shoulder tightened. "I brung you a present, missy. Fished it out of the harbor today. It's prime . . . just like you."

The sound of his low, gutteral voice filled Lucy with revulsion. "If you don't let go, I shall strike you." She raised the ladle threateningly.

"No need for that, missy," he sneered, grabbing the ladle and tossing it into the bushes. "Here, take a look at this beauty."

With the fire at her back, Lucy had no choice but to open the oblong parcel he proferred. When she had freed the object from its sodden bindings she saw that it was a human arm, ghastly white and bloated, with long strands of sinew and skin trailing from the top. It rose up toward her, clammy fingers clutching at her throat. Lights exploded in her head and a terrible throbbing split her temples. Like molten lava, the bloodred sea descended upon her and sucked her down into the dark, airless pit.

"Lucy!"

A far away voice summoned her from the darkness. She opened her eyes and saw Tom, Beth, and Moses leaning over her.

She flung herself into Moses's arms and pointed to the grisly object lying beside the fire. "The hands . . . clawing at my throat!"

Tom picked the arm up gingerly. "Phew! Must have been in the water some time. Shark attack by the looks of those serrations round the shoulder. Where did you get it, Lucy?"

Lucy cowered close to Moses. "*He* said it was a present. Please Tom, make him go away!"

"No one here now, my dear," he said glancing around the clearing. "He must have taken off when you screamed. You know what these chaps are like, Lucy, they'll do anything to capture your attention." He replaced the arm in its wrappings. "Did you recognize the man who gave it to you?"

What should she say? If Michael discovered that Lewis had been near her, he'd probably kill him. But if she said nothing, *Friendship* would leave in a month or so and Lewis would be out of her life forever. "It was dark, Tom. Perhaps you're right, he just wanted to see how I would react." She gave him a strained smile. "Sorry, you must all think me an utter idiot. Go back to bed. I'll make myself a pot of tea and return to the ward."

Tom gave her hand a comforting pat. "We don't think anything of the sort, Lucy. Being shown a dismembered arm in the middle of the night would unnerve anyone. Take the rest of the night off, I'll do your duty. I can't sleep for the heat, anyway."

"Come on, Lucy, let's make that pot of tea," Beth urged as Tom departed across the clearing. "I need one as well. In all my life, I never heard such screams. They sent shivers up my spine, they did."

"You know who he is, don't you, Miss Lucy?" said Moses when he joined them outside their tent after making a thorough inspection of the grounds.

Lucy sighed. "Yes, Moses, but I don't want any trouble."

"Why would there be any trouble?" asked Beth. "The beast would just get the sound flogging he deserves."

"Flogging hasn't stopped him before, Beth. It was Tom Lewis."

Beth's hands flew to her face. "Oh no!"

"You'd best tell Lieutenant Perryman," Moses counseled gravely. "He'll take care of Lewis."

"No!" Lucy exclaimed. "Michael must not be told. Please, Moses, I don't want any trouble. In a few weeks Lewis will leave the colony and I'll be rid of him."

Moses smashed a fist into his palm. "I'll take care of the dog tonight."

Lucy's eyes widened with alarm. "No, they would hang you. Lewis isn't worth your life or Michael's career."

Moses looked at the beautiful girl sitting opposite. *Deep waters was Miss Lucy*—as deep and as pure as his clear-eyed Clair had been before some scum had raped and murdered her these four years past. "Tom Lewis is a bad man, Miss Lucy. Let me take care of him."

"You will do nothing," she said firmly.

"Then from now on I'll sleep outside your tent and keep company with you where ever you go," he countered.

"Moses, you already take care of me more than you ought . . ."

He folded his great arms across his chest and glowered at her. "I'll have your word on it, Miss Lucy, else I'm on my way to *Friendship* right now."

"Very well," she murmured, and bit her lip as emotion suddenly welled up within her. "If only Faith were here. God knows how much I miss her . . ." Her voice trailed off and tears rolled down her cheeks.

"Who's Faith?" asked Beth, placing a comforting arm around her friend's shoulders.

"My twin sister," Lucy answered slowly. Until now, she had preferred to keep Faith to herself. "My long lost, beloved twin sister."

Beth's eyes widened with shock. "Lucy! You never mentioned no sister. I-I thought you was all alone in the world, like me."

"I had no idea she existed until the Fleet anchored in Capetown." In a halting voice Lucy told them about Faith.

At the conclusion of the midday meal next day, the convicts were marshaled outside the marquee in which the criminal court was in session. Shortly afterward, David Collins emerged and handed down the verdict against Henry Lavell and his associates. All were found guilty of feloniously and fraudulently stealing beef and peas from the government store. Ryan, the receiver, got three hundred lashes and Barrett, Lavell, and Hall were sentenced to hang.

At sunset, the convicts assembled on the slopes between the convict camps where a makeshift gallows had been set up beneath a giant fig tree. They watched in silence as armed troops led the three unhappy men into the clearing.

"Hangings turn my stomach," Beth whimpered and hid her

face against Lucy's shoulder as the Provost Marshal led Barrett, the ringleader, to the foot of the ladder.

While mounting to the platform the convict displayed no fear, but as soon as the halter was placed around his neck he turned ashen, seeming to realize in that moment that his time on earth was done.

"I'll not do it!" came a hoarse cry from the foot of the gallows. The convict who had been given the odious task of hanging the men threw himself on the ground before Reverend Johnson with hands raised in supplication. When all argument failed to persuade him to do his duty, the Provost Marshal mounted the ladder, tied a handkerchief around Barrett's eyes and fixed the halter more securely around his neck.

"Take warning!" Barrett cried hoarsely as the drums began to roll. "I brung this on myself by keeping bad company. God have mercy . . . I've led a wicked life."

As Lucy watched in stunned disbelief, the Provost Marshal kicked the ladder from beneath Barrett's feet and launched him into the next world.

"Oh Lord," Beth wept as the drums rolled again. "Now they're taking Henry Lavell." But fortunately for the frozen-faced Lavell, as he placed his foot on the first rung of the ladder, David Collins arrived with a twenty-four hour stay of execution from the Governor.

"Sorry I could not spare you the ordeal of Barrett's hanging, Lucy, but everyone was ordered to attend," Michael explained as they walked along the beach toward the bend, later that evening.

Lucy glanced uneasily at *Friendship*, which was riding at anchor off the east point. Several men were moving about the deck; she wondered if one was Lewis. "We held a meeting at Cable's afterward and decided to petition the Governor for clemency. I hope he will be lenient, I haven't forgotten how helpful Lavell was in persuading the crew of *Friendship* to leave the women alone."

"I have not forgotten either," Michael murmured, taking her in his arms.

As his lips closed over hers, Lucy panicked. It was all she could do not to pull away.

"That kiss was decidedly unfriendly," he said, looking into her eyes. "Is anything troubling you, darling?"

She disengaged herself and turned away. "I suppose I'm tired."

In truth, she *was* tired. Despite the presence of Moses outside her tent last night she had not slept, and this evening every shadow seemed to move.

Michael placed his hands on her shoulders and turned her around to face him. "You're trembling, darling. Are you unwell?"

"It's nothing," she replied, then added, "No, Michael, that's not true. I feel quite out of sorts. If you don't mind, I'd like to retire early tonight." She broke free and started retracing her steps along the beach.

"Whoa there, not so fast," he laughed, catching her around the waist.

Don't be silly, she told herself, *Michael loves you, you have nothing to fear from him.* But the tightness around her chest increased and when he took her in his arms she felt herself sinking into that dark pit.

"Four days ago, Ross gave permission for a Private to marry a convict woman. It won't be as easy for an officer, but John, Tom, and Meredith have all agreed to support my application." His voice penetrated the darkness, and she felt his hands moving up and down her back like claws, tearing at the skin . . . exposing it.

"What did you say?" she asked in a daze.

He laughed and kissed her parched lips. "Surely you recognize a proposal when you hear one, darling. Will you marry me?"

"No!" she cried, struggling violently against him. "Let me go. I don't want to marry you, Michael. I can't stand the thought of such . . . such a debasement of my body. I'd rather die than go through that again."

He looked at her askance. "For God's sake, what has gotten into you, Lucy? When a man and woman feel the way we do about each other, the only sensible thing to do is marry. After a time, kissing isn't enough. I want you—I have wanted you from the first moment I saw you."

The threat of his words weighed Lucy down, and it came to her then that it was not Lewis, nor what Michael might do about Lewis, that terrified her, it was the physical act of love. And, although a part of her despaired at the revelation and at the hurt she was causing, nevertheless, the fear drove her on. "Well, I don't want you, Michael. Find someone else to accommodate your filthy desires."

Michael could not believe his ears. Lately, she had been so responsive. "There could never be anyone else for me, darling," he said gently, drawing her closer and kissing her cheeks. "Don't be afraid, I shall make you happy, I swear."

Suffocated by his presence, she pummeled his chest. "Only one person can ever make me happy. *She* fills my waking thoughts; *she* embellishes my dreams. Not you, Michael, or your vile needs. If you don't let me go this instant, I shall call Moses."

He stared at her with a mixture of anger and disbelief. "If you want me to leave you alone, just say so, Lucy. I've never begged for a woman's favors before—I'll be damned if I'll start now."

"I am saying it," she sobbed, "I *am* saying it!"

He dropped his hands and stepped away. "Are you sure this is what you want?"

"Yes," she sobbed, thankful to be free of him at last. "Leave me alone."

"Very well," he said remotely. "You have made your feelings perfectly clear. I shall see you safely to the hospital and that will be the end of it."

So bemused was Michael as he strode toward the barracks, he was almost on top of Cable and Sidaway before he noticed them.

"Who goes there?" he challenged, peering at the shadows in the bushes.

The two convicts stepped onto the path. "Only us, Lieutenant Perryman."

"What the hell are you doing here?" growled Michael. "I can arrest you for this. Taptoo blew ten minutes ago."

"We know, sir," said Sidaway, "but we've a petition for the Governor asking that he go easy on Lavell, Ryan, and Hall. You remember Lavell and Ryan, Lieutenant. They're both *Friendship* men."

Michael replaced the safety catch on his pistol and shoved it into his belt. "Of course I remember them. What's this got to do with me?"

"We want to take our petition to the Governor," said Henry. "Then, if he asks about Lavell and Ryan . . . er . . . Lavell meant no harm, he were just trying out the authorities—testing the wind, so to speak. After seeing Barrett swing, he's learned his lesson, and if the Governor'll give him another chance, Bob and me will see to it that he causes no more trouble. We give you our word on it, sir.''

Michael looked at them for a long moment, then held out his hand. "Give the damned thing here. I'll add my name to it and see that the Governor receives it personally. Now, you'd better come along with me and, if we're stopped, keep your mouths shut and let me do the talking.''

3

Plans and Plots

Friday, February 29, 1788

Billingsley Hall

Faith and Hugh sat opposite each other at the desk in the library. The pomp and ceremony of Sir Michael's funeral dispensed with, life was returning to normal.

Faith took Lucy's bulky letter from the top drawer and placed it between them. "How difficult will it be to obtain a pardon for Lucy?''

Hugh's handsome features were grave. "Extremely difficult, Fae. I'll need to confer with James Geldie.''

"Lucy's future depends on our choosing the right person to represent her interests, Hugh. Is James Geldie the one?''

"Most definitely, dearest. Not only does he have good family and professional connections, his legal qualifications are excellent. And remember, I shall be working with him every step of the way. Everything that can be done for Lucy *will* be done, I promise. Let's leave for London at the end of the week. I'll set up a meeting between James and the attorney who spoke to Lucy in Newgate. Then I think we should meet Ruth Gamble.''

"Ruth Gamble.'' Faith repeated the name thoughtfully. "I believe she is the key to Lucy's pardon. We must make her rescind her damning statement to the magistrates.''

Hugh flipped through Lucy's letter. "That will be difficult.

According to Lucy, the woman has behaved vindictively from the very beginning.''

"She certainly has. But I remember how unstrung she became when she saw me that day in York. Suppose we tricked her into believing that I was Lucy? That might prod her conscience and make her change the statement.''

"Surely you jest, Fae,'' he said sternly. "This is not one of our childhood schemes, this is a matter of law. Forcing someone to alter a legal statement by placing them under duress is both unethical and immoral. Neither James nor I would consider such a ploy.''

Faith's eyes narrowed. "Has Ruth Gamble behaved ethically or morally toward my Lucy?''

"Must we sink to her level?''

She stared at him, tight-lipped, for some time. "All right, Hugh, we will do it your way to begin with, but I warn you, where Lucy's freedom is concerned, I care nought for morality or ethics.''

"I understand your sense of urgency, Fae. But you are wrong to consider compromising your honor.''

"*Honor*? Damn it, Hugh, there are only two things I desire— Lucy's freedom, and to be reunited with her at the first opportunity. If honor gets in the way of that, honor can go to the devil.''

Hugh leaned back in the chair and folded his arms. Faith had changed since Sir Michael's death. With no one to repress her, all her old spirit had returned and, bursting with life and vitality, she was once more the wild, reckless Fae he and Robert McBain had chased through the glens of their childhood. He was at a loss to know how to handle her. "No need for profanities, madam. Just where do I fit into this grand scheme of yours? Has our betrothal slipped your mind, perchance?''

Faith looked at him closely. Although he was outwardly calm, color stained his cheeks.

"Oh, I love it when you are angry,'' she cooed, sliding into his lap and winding her arms around his neck. "Kiss me, Scotty.''

He pulled her tightly against him. "Sir Scotty to you, madam.'' His delight in her was endless. Her body's lithe, supple beauty ravished his senses. Sometimes, he felt he would drown in his warmth and fragrance. She was so open, so loving, so innocently seductive. She owned him body and soul.

"Forgive me,'' Faith whispered as they drew apart. "It's just that when I think of all Lucy has suffered I become quite distracted.''

He brushed her lustrous hair away from her face and set it behind her ears. "I know, dearest. But you must not let her become an obsession.''

Become an obsession? Lucy already was an obsession, and Faith gloried in her being so. She kissed his cheek and returned to her side of the desk. "All right, my lord and master, I'll abide by your rules, except that, for the time being, Ruth Gamble is not to be told of my existence. Agreed?''

He sighed resignedly. "Agreed.''

"And I want Bill Narmo, the pickpocket who helped Lucy in Newgate, to attend the meeting,'' she added as an afterthought.

"A pickpocket! What possible assistance can he be?''

"Probably none, but I want him there anyway.'' She raised her chin defiantly, but let her lower lip tremble a little.

Hugh, who knew that look of old, raised long-suffering eyes to the ceiling. "So be it. Now, what about us?''

"Us?''

"Yes, us! If we marry at once, the matter of our London lodgings will be vastly simplified.''

She smiled. "Oh, Hugh, your mother would be heartbroken if we just went and did it. And, in truth, I'd be disappointed also. Lucy and I have missed out on so much, I want her beside me when I marry. . . .''

Although her reasons were sound, Hugh was disgruntled. "Damn all mothers and sisters,'' he muttered.

"Now who's using profanities?'' She laughed. "Don't look so disheartened, Scotty. I may yet change my mind and demand that you wed and bed me. After all, it *is* leap year.''

"Bird! You must be jesting. The damned thing was seven feet tall!'' exclaimed James Meredith, before biting into a succulent piece of spit-roasted New Holland cassowary.

John White tossed the bone he had been gnawing onto his plate and licked his fingers. "Did it have wings?''

"Yes, but they were the size of a sparrow's and looked utterly incongruous on so large an *animal*.''

"Did it have feathers?''

"A few tufts of brownish gray fluff clung to its body, but its head, neck and legs were covered in hair,'' Meredith insisted stubbornly.

"Well, whatever it is, it certainly tastes delicious," said Tom. "Tell us more, James."

"It had a neck and head like an African ostrich, its skin had a purplish hue, its legs were long and tremendously strong and it could run as fast as a cheetah. The Governor's huntsman saw a flock . . . er . . . herd about six miles west of here so I'm going hunting again tomorrow. Would either of you care to join me?"

"Sorry," said John. "I'm sailing up the coast to Broken Bay with the Governor's exploration party. He's hoping to discover a river and some land suitable for cultivation."

"I'd like to come," said Tom. "The patients would benefit from some fresh meat."

Meredith slapped his back. "Glad to have you along, old chap. I spoke to Michael on my way over here and he will be joining us."

However, Michael was not destined to go on the cassowary hunt. Later that evening, he and Meredith were ordered to Major Ross's hut.

When they entered, Ross, who had been drinking tea with Captain Campbell, rose and puffed himself up importantly. "Lieutenant Perryman, I have summoned you and your company leader here on a most serious matter. Is it true that two evenings ago you delivered a petition to the Governor?"

"Yes, sir." Michael had thought the matter of the petition done with. Phillip had decided to spare the convicts and Lavell and Hall were now confined on an island in the harbor awaiting exile to a remote part of the coast.

"How dare you take it upon yourself to do so without first asking my permission, Lieutenant?"

"Permission?" repeated Michael, puzzled by Ross's vehemence. "As it was a civil matter, sir, I did not consider that I needed your permission!"

"A civil matter! How did you reach that conclusion, Lieutenant?"

"Because two men approached me privately and requested that I deliver the petition, sir."

"By men, I presume you mean convicts. Why did these villains single you out, Lieutenant?"

Michael looked at Ross with distaste. The man was so lacking in dignity it was impossible to respect him. "They were superintendents aboard *Friendship*. Therefore, I had been in close contact with them, sir."

"A close contact that you have since extended to the female

felons, eh Lieutenant?" said Captain Campbell, exchanging a snide look with Ross.

"While aboard *Friendship*, Lieutenant Perryman behaved impeccably toward the women," Meredith said stiffly. "One was known to him personally, however, as her father had been his former commanding officer."

"I am aware of that," Ross snapped. "Captain Campbell is referring to the disgraceful license shown the felon Gamble and another woman from *Friendship* since they were disembarked. On several occasions, both have been seen straggling about the hospital environs after taptoo, which is a direct contravention of curfew."

Michael was aware that his habit of spending off-duty hours at the hospital had not endeared him to his commanding officer but this was the first time Ross had challenged him on it.

"If you will pardon me for correcting you on that point, sir," he said politely. "The two women concerned attend to the needs of seriously ill patients at all hours of the day and night."

Campbell sniggered. "Just as they attend to the needs of doctors and certain officers at all hours of the day and night, eh?"

Meredith hastened to defuse the situation. "I have dined at the hospital often, Captain Campbell, and whenever those women have been present they have behaved with the utmost decorum."

Campbell raised haughty eyebrows. "That is not what I have heard. In fact, it is common knowledge that Gamble and Lieutenant Perryman hold moonlight trysts on the beach."

Michael took a step toward him. "How I spend my free time is no concern of yours, *sir*."

Ross's bulbous countenance turned scarlet. "It is certainly *my* concern, Lieutenant, when you bring dishonor upon this battalion. You showed utter contempt for my authority when you delivered that offensive petition to the Governor, and you show utter contempt for orders when you meet felons after curfew. Having set such a disgraceful example to the men of your company—indeed to the whole battalion—you are herewith confined to barracks until further notice. Dismissed!"

Faith stood in her grandfather's dressing room passing garments to Reverend Duckworth, the Vicar of Lyndhurst, who had called at the hall to collect clothing for the parish poor.

I still don't feel even a twinge of sorrow at Grandfather's death, she reflected as she sorted through Sir Michael's clothes. *I wonder what the venerable Vicar would say if he could read my mind? Probably, "Humph! Forgiveness is divine, young lady."*

"Humph!" The Vicar (or Humpty Duckworth, as he was affectionately called by his parishioners), uttered the sound that had made him famous throughout the district.

"What was that, Vicar?"

"There are some papers in the pockets of this greatcoat, Miss Faith."

"Papers, Vicar?"

"Documents, Miss Faith. And an envelope addressed to you."

4

March 1788

"Henry Dodd, my overseer, says that the natives often wander into the Government Farm to view the sheep. Apparently, they consider them a new variety of kangaroo. Though how they came by that assumption I'll never know," Phillip told Captain Hunter as the two men dined on board *Sirius*.

Hunter's grave countenance split in a smile. "I've never seen anything less like a kangaroo than a sheep. It's like comparing a coach and four to a man-of-war: both are built of wood, but there the similarity ends."

"Speaking of men-of-war, John, how are the repairs to *Sirius* progressing?"

Hunter's face settled back into its usual lines. "Slowly, I am afraid. With Gidley at Norfolk Island, Lieutenant Dawes inexperienced in naval procedure, and Lieutenant Maxwell behaving most oddly, I have few officers to supervise work. In fact, Maxwell's mental capacities have become so impaired, the men now call him Mad George behind his back. It's bad for discipline."

Phillip reached for his napkin. "Gidley's stay at Norfolk will be an extended one and young Dawes will soon be taking charge of the observatory so we do have a problem, John. However, we have a naval lieutenant attached to the garrison. Would you release a marine corporal and a few privates in exchange for him?"

"A naval lieutenant!" Hunter cried, delighted. "I'd release

them in a second. But Major Ross would never agree. He's been plaguing me for weeks to give him Dawes.''

Phillip smiled. ''Leave Major Ross to me.''

''Except for half a pint of Rio wine, which tastes and smells so offensive that nothing short of absolute necessity will induce my men to drink it, the provisions served to the battalion are the same as that served to the felons! I, myself, am reduced to six ounces of butter a week. Had I known such would be the case, I would never have left England,'' Major Ross declared hotly as he and Phillip discussed the marine detachment in Phillip's study two nights later.

''How is the hutting for the men coming along?'' Phillip asked, turning the conversation in the direction he wished it to go.

''Both my hut and Captain Campbell's are completed, but work on the barracks progresses slowly. We need more convict labor for that, and for the officers' private use. They cannot be expected to take up axes to clear land for their stock.''

Phillip baited the hook. ''I am afraid you will have to make do with the hundred convicts you have been allotted; other government works must be completed before winter sets in: stores for our provisions, a permanent brick hospital, an *observatory* . . .'' He paused hopefully, but Ross did not take the bait.

The major's mind was still on stock. ''In my opinion, *Sirius* should be sent to purchase more animals for the officers. As you know, mine were destroyed shortly after embarking.''

This man never thought anything through, Phillip reflected. ''Indeed, I intend sending *Sirius* to the Cape as soon as her crew has recovered from the rigors of the voyage and repairs are made to her hull, but as most of her carpenters are employed erecting colony buildings, it may be some time before she departs. By the way, Robert, have any of your officers expressed a desire to remain in this country once their tour of duty ends in 'ninety-three?''

''How can they make such a decision when they have not been informed how much land will be allotted to them as bounty?'' Ross asked testily.

''It could be many months before we receive further instructions from the government. In the meantime, I will allot your

212

officers two acres apiece to raise their crops and graze their stock.''

"That would ease matters somewhat," Ross conceded. "But they cannot clear the land without help.''

"Very well, each may choose a convict to cultivate and care for the land. As yet peas, beans, and cabbages do not thrive, but yams, turnips—''

"In my opinion, Governor, this barren country can never answer the intended purpose of the government. The soil is so arid it cannot possibly yield enough to sustain us.''

"Although the soil is light and sandy hereabouts, I believe it's as good as coastal soil in other parts of the world," Philip replied patiently. "Given time, we shall discover more fertile plots of land, but first we must house our provisions, our sick, our troops, our convicts . . . and build an observatory.''

This time Ross took the bait hook, line, and sinker.

"*Observatory!* I'd hardly call that a priority, sir. How much longer will Lieutenant Dawes be detained on the flagship? Collins has been unfit for duty since landing and now that two other officers are down with dysentery, I have been forced to disband the advance guard. With the natives threatening to attack at every turn, the situation could hardly be more serious.''

Phillip gave a delicate tug on the line.

"If Captain Hunter released Dawes for garrison duty, there'd be only one naval officer fit for duty on board *Sirius*. Would a corporal and a few privates suffice?''

"No, they would not! Surely the protection of this colony takes precedence over duty on board a ship lying idle in the cove?''

Phillip shook his head. "Sorry, Robert. You'll just have to hope that your officers make a speedy recovery. Another drop of port before you leave?''

Michael found Lucy in the marine ward nursing Henry Petrie, a young private in his company. As he stood in the doorway watching her tenderly bathing Petrie, who was good-looking in an insipid sort of way, anger began gnawing at his insides.

"Lucy!"

She jumped with fright and spun around.

Michael glared at her. "Come outside!"

Lucy's eyes flashed rebelliously, but she curbed the retort on her lips and followed him into the clearing. "What is it?" she asked sharply. "I'm busy.''

"Sorry to disturb you at work," he said tersely and told her he'd seen Beth crying.

"Where is she now?"

"At the well, washing her face."

Lucy knew she should go to Beth but suddenly she did not want to leave. *I must let him be,* she thought. *I love him but I am sick and I don't know how to get well. He is better off without me.*

After a strained silence, she said, "Please don't stay away from the hospital on my account, Michael, everyone misses you. Only last night Tom was saying—"

"I haven't stayed away because of you, Lucy," he replied coolly. "I have been confined to barracks for two weeks, that's all. Will you see to Beth? I am concerned about her. Good afternoon."

Four nights later, Michael went to the hospital for supper. "The detachment's in a complete uproar," he told his friends after they had welcomed him. "The trouble began when a private in Campbell's company struck a private in Meredith's company and called him a Portsmouth rascal. The court martial found the fellow guilty and gave him the choice of publically apologizing to the other man, or accepting one hundred lashes."

John looked up from the bandage he was rolling and fixed Michael with a choleric eye. "How could that throw it into uproar?"

Michael grinned. "When Major Ross read the verdict, he ordered the members of the court martial to sit a second time."

"Why?" Tom asked, mystified.

"Because he saw the verdict as an attempt to wrest authority away from him."

They all burst out laughing.

"After sitting a second time, the officers of the court martial informed Major Ross that they could not rescind their verdict, whereupon, Major Ross ordered them to sit a third time."

"A third time! This could continue *ad infinitum,*" said John, delving into the sack for another bandage.

"Not so," said Michael. "It ended rather abruptly half an hour ago when the officers of the court martial replied in writing to Major Ross that they had passed the sentence after strict deliberation and that they did not think themselves authorized to sit in judgment a third time. Whereupon, Major Ross arrested them."

With a gesture of disgust, Phillip tossed the letter on his desk, walked to the study window and glanced at the ships in the cove. After an absence of four weeks and six days, *Supply* had returned from Norfolk Island. He would rather have been discussing her voyage with her commander, Ball, than mediating in this noisome affair but with only sixteen officers in the battalion— and two unfit for duty—having five officers under arrest was ludicrous. A speedy solution to the problem must be found.

"Come in," he called, hearing a knock on the door, and smiled as David Collins entered. "Have you studied the correspondence I received from Major Ross and the members of the court martial?" he asked as he waved the Judge Advocate to a chair.

Collins nodded solemnly. "Yes, Your Excellency. How such a minor affair could have led to the arrest of five officers is beyond my comprehension. In truth, I wonder why the matter warranted a court martial in the first place."

"Have you any thoughts as to how we might resolve the problem amicably?"

"Perhaps you could suggest that the nine nonparticipating officers could vote on the matter, sir. Then it could be settled without official application to you and thus a general court martial would be avoided."

"Could it be avoided by claiming that, if it were assembled, insufficient officers would be available for garrison duty?" suggested Phillip.

David Collins's usually reserved features relaxed into a wide smile. "By George, I think you have hit upon it, sir!" He did a quick calculation. "If a general court martial was convened, only one officer would be available for garrison duty; the rest would be either members of the court, under arrest, or witnesses."

A smile played at the corners of Phillip's mouth. "And as there will never be a sufficient number, the convening of the general court martial must be postponed until the battalion returns to England. Draft a general order to that effect, David, then advise the five officers under arrest to return to their duties immediately."

"He did not even bother to inform me personally of his decision," Major Ross raged after reading Phillip's order.

"Had the government searched the world, they could not have chosen a man less suitable to govern this colony than that buffoon," Campbell rejoined in peeved tones. "Gad! When those five worms under arrest read this, harmony and order will be utterly destroyed."

Ross stared at him aghast. "My God, who can we trust, James?"

"Certainly not the Governor's aide-de-camp, George Johnston. Or the Judge Advocate. Or Captain Meredith. Or the five worms you arrested, or that upstart, Perryman."

"What about Lieutenant Dawes?"

"Oh, I should think so. But isn't the Governor adamant that he must remain on the flagship owing to the shortage of naval officers?"

Ross smiled triumphantly. "What if we exchanged Dawes for Lieutenant Perryman who, as you know, is actually a naval officer?"

"What an inspired thought, Robert," said Campbell, quite taken aback.

Ross rose and straightened his uniform. "I shall speak to the Governor immediately; and this time he will not deny me, for how can he object to exchanging a naval officer for a marine?"

Thus it was that, on the twenty-fourth of March, Lieutenant Dawes was transferred to garrison duty and a delighted Michael took up duty on board *Sirius*.

5

Bill Narmo

Faith gazed out the window at the horse guards parading below in St. James's Park. The week before, she and Hugh had secured separate lodgings in Downing Street, a genteel street close by the Thames and the Houses of Parliament. Although Hugh's rooms were dark and cold, she was well satisfied with hers, which comprised an airy bedchamber with a fire, two small rooms for her servants, a storage attic, and this rather elegant parlor.

"We must go," said Hugh, checking his timepiece. "I ordered a chair for ten."

They descended three flights of stairs to the street, boarded the chair, and before long arrived at James Geldie's chambers.

"So delightful to see you both again," said the barrister as he ushered them into his inner sanctum wherein sat two men: the first, a hefty middle-aged fellow with hawklike features; the second, an incredible lanky creature wearing a brown frock coat, diced stockings, and a round hat perched atop wiry red hair. *These two sharp-eyed soldiers of life must be Stephen Porter and Bill Narmo,* Faith decided.

As she entered, both men shot to their feet with exclamations of surprise.

"Miss Gamble!" Stephen Porter's soft Welsh burr rose to a shrill pitch. "How can this be? My information has you in New South Wales."

"Blimey, Miss Lucy!" Bill Narmo cried, clutching at his trousers, which were threatening to sink to his ankles. "What a turn you've give me! What's doing? Where's Bethy?"

"Gentlemen, allow me to introduce my clients, Miss Faith Billingsley and Sir Hugh Stewart," said James as he escorted Faith to a wing-backed chair by the window. "Miss Billingsley, Hugh, this is Stephen Porter, Attorney, and . . . er . . . Mr. Narmo."

Faith smiled at the two stunned men. "Please be seated, gentlemen. Let us dispense with formalities and proceed with the business at hand—that of procuring a pardon for my sister Lucy."

Stephen Porter produced a battered folder containing his correspondence with the firm of Worthing lawyers employed by Michael and explained that, although he had presented himself at Ruth Gamble's residence on numerous occasions, he had failed to gain an audience with her.

James Geldie was unimpressed with Stephen Porter's papers but delighted when Hugh handed over the documents discovered by the Vicar of Lyndhurst. "These will be most helpful, Hugh. I'll consult Lord Marsfield. He will advise us how best to proceed."

Faith leaned forward in her chair. "Has Lucy's abigail, Julie Ryan, been located yet?"

James shook his head. "My agents have made several enquiries but have not discovered her whereabouts. However, Julie Ryan originally came from Kinsale so she may have returned to Ireland."

"Then let us send someone to Ireland," said Hugh. "We must find her, James, she is the only person who can refute the statements of Ruth Gamble and her servant."

"Perhaps you could also send someone to Pickering where Ruth Gamble's family resides," suggested Stephen Porter. "Richard Newport may have behaved indiscreetly toward a local lass prior to attacking Miss Gamble."

"An excellent idea, Mr. Porter," cried Faith.

Shortly afterward, the clerk told them Lord Marsfield would be happy to meet his legal colleagues in his chambers at two o'clock.

When Faith took her leave, Hugh escorted her to the entrance of the Temple, secured a chair and bid her a fond good-bye. As soon as he was out of sight, however, she instructed the chairman to pursue the pickpocket, who had left at the same time.

She spotted him darting past a pie man and, waving her parasol wildly to and fro, cried, "Bill Narmo!"

The pickpocket stopped in his tracks, crouched low and shot a suspicious look over his shoulder. When he saw her, his comical features relaxed into a lopsided grin and, snatching off his hat, he elbowed his way through the roaring multitude to her side. "Cor! You didn't half give me a turn, miss. I thought it were the Runners."

"Quickly, Bill, into the chair or you will be trampled by the mob," she cried sweeping her voluminous skirts to make room for him.

He sprang nimbly up beside her.

"Where to, Bill?"

"Oh, never mind about that, miss. Just drop me at the end of the Strand. Where I'm going ain't no place for you."

"Fiddlesticks," she said firmly. "I want to speak to you about Lucy and we certainly can't converse in this din."

Bill gazed at the divine goddess beside him. Although she was the image of Miss Lucy, they were nothing alike. "I dunno, miss. The legal gents wouldn't approve of it, no, never."

"Nor would they approve of my plan, Bill. Nevertheless, I shall go ahead with it. And if you decide to throw in your lot with me, I promise you will be handsomely rewarded."

"Miss Lucy gave me pearl buttons and a silver buckle but I'd of helped her for nothing in the end, even sprung her if I could. She'd no business being in Newgate," he said sadly.

Faith's heart grew warm. Here at last was someone who had actually *known* Lucy. "It's because I want to spring Lucy from New South Wales that I have sought you out," she explained. "Will you help me to help her, Bill?"

218

Bill's face split into a smile. "Yes I will, miss—for Miss Lucy's sake, and for Bethy's."

"Thank you, Bill," she said solemnly. "Now, where is the best place for us to talk? I'm a stranger to London."

"Black Lion Inn, Water Lane," Bill called to the chairman, then settled back more comfortably in the seat. "Tell us the plan then, miss?"

"What are our chances of getting an 'ear' into the house in Grosvenor Square?" she asked, beginning to enjoy herself immensely.

6

As Motionless as a Statue

"Will, why do you treat me so badly?" Beth asked as she slid into bed beside him that evening.

"What do you mean?"

She hesitated. "Sometimes you treat me like a stranger."

He raised himself up on one elbow. "If we threw discretion to the wind we'd be the butt of every jokester in the colony, you little ninny."

"I-I don't mean we should be familiar with each other in public, but you could at least call me Beth when we're in the mess. Everyone else does."

"You ought to realize by now that I am not everyone else." He laughed, forcing her down on her back and climbing on top of her.

For a time their lovemaking drove all thought from Beth's mind, but later, as she walked to her tent, the depression returned. She loved William Balmain more than she had thought it possible to love a man, and when they were in bed together it was perfect, but she might as well be a block of wood for all the notice he took of her at other times.

She remembered George Clayton's loving words when she had given him back the shoes. "I'm a stupid fool," she whispered fiercely. "I won't marry a hard-working, decent man like George who loves me, yet I'll do anything to roll abed with William Balmain who treats me no better than a whore."

It had been a long hard day at the hospital and Lucy was looking forward to her break. "Come on, my dear," she coaxed, drawing into a sitting position an old woman who had attempted to hang herself the day before. "Drink this soup, it will make you feel much better."

As the old woman dutifully sipped the broth, Lucy's mind turned to Michael. Their estrangement was telling on everyone. This morning Tom had taken her aside and offered to mediate. She had thanked him politely and told him that there was nothing anyone could do. But was that true?

The old woman groaned and began to vomit.

"Damn! I should have been paying attention," Lucy said, surveying her ruined uniform with dismay.

"You go wash up. I'll take care of this," said Jane Creek, one of the trainees.

Lucy collected clean clothes from her tent and went looking for Moses but, when she heard that he was at the saw pits, decided to go to the bathing cove alone.

As she floated in the pool a short time later, allowing the cool water to cascade over her, she addressed herself once more to the problem of Michael. She loved him, but the thought of a closer bond with him was unbearable. Her fear of the physical was so strong it was like being caught in a steel web—the more she struggled against it, the more entangled she became.

She raised her face to the cascade, which, in the light of the setting sun, had turned into a golden fountain. *If only the sun's rays could endow these waters with magical qualities,* she thought, *then the water could flush away all my fears and Michael and I could be happy.*

As she pondered this thought, an idea came to her. Instead of locking the nightmares inside, perhaps she should tell them to Michael, tell them down to the tiniest detail—the flaming red sea, the cave of clawing hands, the dark pit.

She floated, musing, until the sun dipped behind the trees and her golden fountain turned blue with cold. Refreshed and uplifted, she dressed and set off along the track toward the hospital, feeling happier than she had in weeks.

"Michael will listen, I know he will," she said aloud. "And, once we have talked about it—" She broke off as a sharp crack, like someone treading on a twig, came from the bush directly behind.

"Anyone there?" she called, spinning around. Nothing stirred except the leaves on top of the trees. *Don't be silly*, she told herself, setting off at a brisker pace. *It was probably an animal scurrying into its burrow.*

The bushes rustled again, and onto the track sprang Tom Lewis.

When Lucy came to her senses, the day was gone and dark clouds were scudding across the moon. Rowlocks creaked and oars splashed in the water. She was lying on her back in a small rowing boat, and the only human sound was his breathing as he toiled at the oars. The boat was skimming swiftly through the water, which meant that they were heading upharbor for, had he been pulling against the ebb, their progress would have been less smooth.

When she tried to move, she discovered that her hands were bound behind her back. Angry tears scalded her eyes. Was her thoughtless action to cost her her life? Anger turned to rage. She *must* get away from him—she wanted to be with Faith!

Thinking of Faith calmed her.

Why was Lewis going to so much trouble when he could have had her by the waterfall? Before long, the chilling answer came. If her body was found close to the settlement he would be the first suspected. So, he would row to some godforsaken spot upharbor, rape her, murder her, then return to Sydney with no one the wiser. In a few weeks *Friendship* would leave the colony and, if her body were ever found, he would be far beyond reach.

Lucy ground her teeth. She had got herself into this mess, now she must get herself out. Surprise was her best weapon. She could not match his strength so she must outwit him. As a plan began to form in her mind, she flexed her muscles.

Flex, relax. Flex, relax. Over and over she did it. When the moment came for flight, she must be ready.

The boat scraped over sand and stopped. He jumped out and swore as he heaved it from the water. *Eyes closed, jaws relaxed, body limp*, she told herself. *Don't move, no matter what he does*.

He lifted her out the boat, slung her over his shoulder and plodded up the slope. From her upside down world Lucy glimpsed trees outlined against the sky, then she was on her back and he was tearing open her bodice. A scream rose in her throat. She fought it down and focused on Faith, thinking of all they would do, all they would say when they were together again. Father. She would tell Faith of his gentleness and compassion; how he

221

had encouraged her in all she did. Faith would share her inner-most secrets. She and Faith would hold fast to each other and they would have everything. Everything. *Everything.* A light crystallized in the center of the darkness. She passed through it into the midst. Faith was there, running toward her with arms outstretched . . .

"Senseless still, missy?" Lewis's guttural voice intruded and the image faded. "Rum will rouse ye."

His hands withdrew. Sand sprinkled on her face. Fresh air washed over her body.

From a distance now—"Screaming and writhing I likes 'em. Ho! Ho! Ho!"

She opened her eyes. The cove was washed in moonlight and he was moving down the slope to the boat. She rolled to one side and eased her arms from beneath her. *Wait, Lucy, wait,* she ordered, watching him with narrowed eyes. He was leaning over the boat, kneeling on one knee, leaning right into it with his back to her.

Now!

She scrambled to her feet, stumbled up the slope and ran into the bush, twisting and weaving, oblivious of the branches that scratched and tore at her. At first she kept to open ground, afraid of stumbling on her skirts, but then she hitched them up from behind and veered into denser bush. Her only chance was to hide; she could not outrun him.

Two minutes, she told herself as she forced her way deeper into the undergrowth. *Two minutes, then go to ground.* Counting the seconds, she ran, only vaguely aware of her surroundings.

A stream. Spray, moss, slippery stones, wet skirts impeding her progress. A high bank. Soft earth giving way beneath her, falling, clambering up, throat dry, heart thudding against her chest. She could hear him now. Quickly, somewhere to hide!

Moon shining on bramble bushes. Ten more strides. Then she threw herself on the ground and slithered like a snake through the brambles until their dark thorny foliage enclosed her on every side.

He seemed to be everywhere, charging through the bush like a deranged animal, blustering, bellowing, cursing, and shouting. And all the while, Lucy lay as motionless as a statue—listening, praying, and waiting.

"Where's Lucy?" asked Beth, sitting down beside Balmain and reaching for a soup plate.

"In the convict ward the last time I saw her," John replied vaguely.

"She's not there now," said Tom. "I thought you two were going to that meeting at Cable's tonight."

"We are, but she said we'd eat here first."

"Maybe she changed her mind and went on ahead," said Balmain. "Care for some bread, Dudgeon?"

When Beth arrived at Cable's, Moses was sitting by the fire with the others but there was no sign of Lucy.

"Isn't Lucy here?" she asked, surprised.

Moses shook his head. "She said you'd have a bite to eat at the hospital before coming here."

Beth's heart sank. "Anyone seen Lucy?"

"I did," answered John Best. "She came to the work gang looking for Moses. When I saw he was over at the saw pits, she took off."

Moses lumbered to his feet and started running toward the hospital.

"Wait for me!" Beth cried, picking up her skirts and racing racing after him.

The doctors looked up from their cards, startled, as Beth and Moses burst into the mess. "We can't find Lucy anywhere!" Beth sobbed, tears streaming down her cheeks.

John left his seat and walked quickly to her side. "Where have you looked?"

"In all the wards and everywhere!"

"She ain't at the hospital or Cable's, Dr. White," Moses said grimly.

"Perhaps she's with Michael," John suggested, smiling at Beth and patting her shoulder. "Yes, that's probably what happened. She and Michael have settled their differences."

"Oh, do you really think so?"

He nodded. "I think it's a distinct possibility. However, we'd best make sure, hadn't we? Will, row out to *Sirius;* and Tom, take a stroll along the shore to the west point, they often go there. Beth, could she be visiting someone in the women's camp?"

Beth shook her head. "No, everyone's at Cable's. Besides, Lucy wouldn't go off without telling anyone, would she, Moses?"

She glanced over her shoulder but Moses was gone.

After discovering Lucy's toiletries and a bundle of wet clothing close by the waterfall, Moses searched the cove and surrounding bush land for an hour but found nothing. His heart heavy with remorse and grief, he made his way to the east point where *Friendship* was anchored.

He waited until the moon disappeared behind a cloud then shimmied up the hawser line to the deck and searched the ship from top to bottom. Lewis wasn't aboard. He took cover under some canvas and thought furiously. Who among the crew was most likely to know Lewis's whereabouts? Craven! That weasel knew everything that went on aboard *Friendship*.

He dropped a rope over the side and slid down to the porthole affording the best view of the crew's quarters. Craven was there, drinking and playing cards with three of his mates.

Moses returned to the deck to wait until everyone retired. But, as luck would have it, shortly afterward Craven came up through the hatch and staggered toward the head. Moses crept after him, laid him out with a chop to the back of the neck and slipped over the side with him.

On reaching shore, he carried the groaning mariner into the bushes and slapped him about the face until he came around.

"What's up? W-where am I?"

Moses grabbed him by the jerkin and shook him until his teeth rattled. "Where's Lewis taken her, Craven?"

The moon came out and Craven, recognizing his attacker, struggled to sit up. "I'll have you flogged for this, Tucker."

Moses pressed his knife against Craven's jugular. "Tell me quickly where he's taken her or you'll never see another sunrise."

Although not the stuff of heroes, Craven held his peace for he was more afraid of Lewis than of any man alive.

Moses raised the knife in a stabbing gesture. "You've decided to die for him, have you? So be it, you dog, your blood's the same as any other's."

Seeing murder in the convict's eyes, Craven's courage deserted him. "Mercy, matey, mercy! He's been stalking her for weeks. Got a boat stowed at the cove where she bathes. Takes himself there every day to watch her. That's all I know, excepting I'm to cover for him if anyone comes sniffing around asking questions."

"Where's he taken her?"

"I dunno, matey. I swear it on me blessed mother's grave." He screamed as the knife cut into his throat.

"You never had a mother, Craven. Where's he taken her?"

"S-Sometimes, he rows to a cove upharbor to fish. Maybe there."

"Where abouts upharbor?"

"I dunno, matey, nobody does. Lewis don't talk much—excepting about her."

Moses thrust him aside. "You'd best pray that I find her alive, Craven. Otherwise, as God's my judge, I'm coming back to cut out your miserable heart."

With a stealth surprising in such a big man, Moses made his way through the sleeping settlement to Cable's hut and rapped softly on the door until Henry opened it.

"Any news?"

"Lewis from *Friendship* took her," Moses said briefly. "I need a boat."

Henry nodded. "Get your kit together and meet me at the west point in thirty minutes. Do you want me along?"

Moses shook his head. "The quieter we keep this the better."

"Has she been found?" Michael asked tersely as he joined the anxious group by the fire.

"We've looked everywhere," John answered. "She seems to have vanished without a trace."

"That's ridiculous, John, *someone* must know where she is. What's wrong with you people? Beth, stop that damned blubbering. Who saw her last?"

Beth tried to stifle her sobs. "John Best saw her at four."

"Four o'clock! Christ, that was six hours ago!" Michael glanced around the clearing. "Where is Moses? Isn't he supposed to be watching out for her?"

Beth started shaking and shivering as if she had a chill. "Moses is gone too."

He frowned at her darkly. "Pull yourself together, Beth. Lucy's life may depend on it. We must think. You know her habits better than anyone. Has she done anything unusual lately?"

Beth sobbed distractedly. "Sh-she made Moses and me promise not to tell you, Michael. Please God, don't let it be that!"

"You're making no sense," he muttered, giving her a little shake. "Not tell em what?"

"Tom Lewis has been menacing her again."

The spirit ebbed out of Michael and the world turned unutterably dim. His darling, all that he loved and cherished in life. "Tom Lewis?" he echoed as the darkness of despair rolled in.

She nodded. "I'm s-sorry, Michael."

He groaned and pushed her away. "Oh God, Beth, how could you be so stupid?"

Beth hung her head.

"This isn't Beth's fault, old man," John said gently.

Michael covered his face with his hands. He had been so blind. All the time he had been nursing his pride, she had been at risk. "There's only one thing left to do," he said, striding across the clearing toward town.

Phillip's aide-de-camp, George Johnston, tapped discreetly on the door of Phillip's study and poked his head inside. "Sorry to bother you, sir, but Lieutenant Perryman wishes to speak to you on a matter of the utmost urgency, so he says."

"Show him in," Phillip said, wondering what could bring Michael to Government House at so late an hour.

"You are the only one who can help me," Michael said as he entered the room.

"Sit down, man," said Phillip, alarmed by the raw desperation in the young lieutenant's voice. "What's the matter? You look like death."

After listening to Michael's story, Phillip sent for his huntsmen, then poured Michael and himself a drink.

"I'll not give you false hope, Michael. Finding Lucy will be very difficult. Every cove looks the same and every hill is more impenetrable than the one before."

Michael buried his face in his hands. "I know, sir, but I must try. I cannot sit around doing nothing, I would go mad. Oh God! She will suffer unspeakable horrors at the hands of that brute."

Phillip patted his shoulder. "My huntsmen, McIntire and Burn, have an excellent knowledge of the bush. If anyone can locate her, they can. Now, let us set aside despair and concentrate on clear thinking. Where might this Lewis have taken her?"

"Being a sailor, he would probably keep to the coast."

Phillip nodded thoughtfully. "Yes, that's as good a premise as any with which to begin. You, McIntire, and Burn check the coast as far south as Botany Bay. If you meet with no success, return to the settlement and we'll widen the search."

"How will you justify that, sir? Lucy is a convict . . ."

Phillip smiled. "I have been planning an extensive exploration of the lower and middle harbor. We can discreetly incorporate a search into that if needs be."

Michael grasped the older man's hand. "Thank you, sir. I'm eternally in your debt."

226

7

The Crescent-shaped Valley

When soft pink bands of light illuminated the eastern sky Lucy left her hiding place. Tiptoeing from shadow to shadow, and pausing every so often to listen, she followed the track of the sun until she came to a crescent-shaped valley with gentle green slopes that ran down to a curving stream.

Although she was extremely thirsty and her tightly bound wrists were swollen, her spirits soared. She was no longer the victim—she was the victor!

After drinking from the stream, she wedged a sharp stone between two rocks and worked her wrists back and forth until her hands were free. Then she ate her fill of wild celery and another plant that tasted like parsley, bathed her wounds, found a sheltered concave in an outcrop of rocks and fell asleep.

The next morning, she repaired her clothing as best she could then attempted unsuccessfully to catch the fat fish darting about the rock pools. It was as she sat beside the stream pondering how to accomplish this feat, that she heard noises in the underbrush some distance off. Was it Lewis? Heart sinking with dread, she fled up the slope to the rocks.

Shortly afterward, the bushes parted and a tribe of natives moved leisurely down the slope to the stream. Although the men looked frightening—their bodies were covered in scars and several wore bones through the gristle in their noses—the women were most pleasing, and the children, with their curly hair, luminous eyes, and little pot bellies, were adorable.

Despite their strangeness the natives were a welcome sight, and for the rest of the day Lucy enjoyed observing them. While the children frolicked about with several golden-coated wolflike creatures, the men, who were clearly the bosses, used immensely long spears to snare fish, which the women broiled on a large communal fire.

The following morning, when the natives left the crescent-shaped valley, Lucy followed at a discreet distance.

By dawn, Moses had reached the head of the harbor and was working his way back along the southern arm when he heard

227

something thrashing about in the undergrowth just beyond the next bend. He pulled quickly for the shore, hid the boat among some mangroves and proceeded the rest of the way on foot.

Five minutes later he stepped out of the bush on top of a small sloping cove and his heart leapt with joy. A small boat lay at the water's edge and he could hear Lewis cursing.

"Come out, missy, you're making it worse for yourself. God blast you, you bitch! Come on! There's no escape. I've got the boat."

With eyes turned cold and hard as flint, Moses strode down the slope to the boat, stove it in with a rock, then returned to the top of the rise. He did not have long to wait. Shortly afterward Lewis appeared, took one look at him and charged. Moses balanced on the balls of his feet and leapt. They met with a force that knocked both to the ground.

Lewis snatched up a rock and aimed at Moses's head. Moses twisted away and caught the blow on his windpipe. For a moment he could not breathe and this gave Lewis time to lock him in a bear hug. Moses grasped Lewis's throat but the sailor grabbed his wrist and, with disbelief, Moses heard his bones crack. Desperately he drove the heel of his hand up under Lewis's chin, trying to force back his head. The movement would have broken most men's necks, but Lewis only tightened his hold. Moses's face congested with blood as he gasped for air. The sky spun and the world turned gray. With a sense of fury, he realized he was losing consciousness. This knowledge gave him added strength and he forced the heel of his hand harder up under Lewis's chin. Lewis grunted and his grip around Moses's chest slackened. Moses gulped in air and forced his hand higher under Lewis's chin. The sailor's neck gave and Moses was free, but before he could gain an advantage Lewis kicked him away.

Moses hurled himself at Lewis again. They met with a clash of bone and muscle and rolled down the slope to the water's edge. Moses drove his knee hard into Lewis's groin then grabbed the sailor's throat and forced his head backward under the water. Lewis locked his legs around Moses trying to dislodge him but Moses held on grimly—driving that head farther under, inch by inch, until it was fully submerged.

Lewis's arms clawed the air and his body thrashed about wildly.

Moses increased the pressure.

A caldron of frothing bubbles rose to the surface then Lewis's arms and legs fell back limply into the water, his body jerked once, and he was still.

Lucy lay hidden in tall grass on top of a hill gazing down at a lush green valley. Almost clear of trees, the valley rolled westward in gentle undulations to the foot of a rugged blue mountain range that stretched across the horizon, north to south, as far as the eye could see. The scene was sublime: sky azure blue, grass waving gently in the breeze, and the waters of the small lake away to her right sparkling like diamonds in the sunlight.

The tribe she had followed for three days were nomads. They ate roots, berries, wild vegetables, fish, birds, and animals. They killed only for food and their possessions were few: crude weapons, lighted sticks to start fires, rush baskets, and a few fishing nets. They slept in caves or crude shelters fashioned from tree bark. Today, they had feasted on the ducks that dwelt in vast numbers on the shores of the lake, and now they were preparing to leave.

Each day when they had broken camp, Lucy had followed, but today memories bedeviled her. She thought of Michael, Beth, Moses, Frances (who had left the hospital to care for little Edward and the other Fleet Orphans), Susannah, and the doctors. By now, they would have given her up for lost. She missed them, yet she longed to stay in this place of peace and tranquility.

The natives were moving away toward the mountains; she must decide soon . . .

She thought of Faith and her eyes grew dim with tears. Some day, Faith would arrive in Sydney Cove looking for her. She could not disappoint Faith.

"Good-bye," she whispered to the departing natives, and descended the long grassy slope to rekindle their fire. Afterwards she took off her clothes and went swimming in the lake.

As she swam, she wondered if she could find her way back to Sydney Cove. Perhaps, but it would be extremely difficult without a boat. Thinking of a boat brought Lewis to mind. Would he still be at that cove? She thought it unlikely. If she traveled due east she must reach Sydney harbor sooner or later. Water was no problem, she had crossed seven streams in the last three days; as for food, she would survive off the land like the natives.

She returned to shore and donned her clothes. What about a boat? At the largest stream the natives had fashioned a crude craft by stripping a piece of bark off a tree and tying it at each end with vines. That was a possibility. Determined not to go anywhere near Lewis without a weapon, she found a smooth black stone and honed it on some rocks as the natives did. Then she selected a piece of forked wood and secured the stone in the fork with strips of stringy bark and sticky sap from a gum tree.

Hungry now, she sharpened the edge of a branch into a point and walked to the edge of the lake. She managed to spear a duck but it made such awful noises that she panicked and beat it to death with her hatchet.

At first, she was sickened, but later, as she sat by the fire eating her first hot food in six days, she felt rather pleased with herself.

"Faith would be proud of me." She laughed. And, with this happy thought in mind, she made a bed by the fire and settled down for the night. *Tomorrow,* she thought sleepily, *I shall begin my journey back to that other world.*

Three days later, Lucy reached the stream at the bottom of the crescent-shaped valley. She followed the stream to where it emptied into the harbor, then moved east from cove to cove. But the going was extremely arduous and, by sunset, she was near dropping from exhaustion.

Unable to find fresh water, she took shelter for the night beneath a large rock and was almost asleep when an unusual sound penetrated her consciousness.

Crack. Crack. Snap.

She crawled out from the rock, looked around her and saw a bright orange glow through the trees. *Fire.* But whose? Was Lewis still around? Although she told herself that she hoped it was he, for that meant a chance at the boat, when she tried to rise her fear was so great, her legs would not hold her.

For ages she sat there, tears rolling down her cheeks and fists pressed into her mouth, trying to will herself through the fear. Nothing worked until she thought of Faith. In the end it was the desire to see her sister that drove her into action. Clutching the hatchet and feeling every inch of ground with her toes before placing her full weight on it, she crept toward the glow.

When she reached the small sloping cove, she saw the boat at the bottom and, farther along at the edge of the bush, crouched over a fire, the dark shape of a man.

Lewis!

Lucy cowered behind a tree and tried to concentrate on the boat. Should she wait until Lewis fell asleep, then take it? She shivered violently despite the mildness of the night. No, that was too risky. The boat was beached high and it would require great effort to get it into the water. Her best hope was to sneak up on him while he slept and hit him with the hatchet. It would have to be an extremely hard blow—she would never get a second chance.

Could she do it? Could she go right up close and strike him? *If you want to see Faith, you must,* she told herself. *Just keep thinking of Faith and you* can *do it.* She eased herself down on her stomach and lay still, watching and waiting and listening.

Not long afterward, he wrapped himself in a blanket and settled down beside the fire. An hour passed. Then another. The fire dimmed to a dull red glow. Still, she dawdled. *Another half an hour, then I shall do it,* she promised herself and began counting out the minutes.

When the moment arrived, she crept along the sand until she was standing over him. *Do it!* she ordered. But as she raised the hatchet she hesitated. Something was wrong with Lewis's image. He had black hair, not gray . . .

She blinked several times, afraid her eyes were deceiving her. The image did not waver. Summoning up all her courage, she knelt beside him. Then she leaned so close her nose was almost touching his. There was no mistake, every feature of that face belonged to Moses!

Awoken by her cries, Moses sat up and wrapped her in his arms. "Miss Lucy, is it really you?"

"Oh Moses, where is Lewis?" she asked breathlessly.

He helped her up and led her to a mound some distance away. "There he is, Miss Lucy," he said solemnly. "He won't bother no one no more."

Beth sat toying with her food. "Ten days and still no word."

"Keep your spirits up," counseled Tom. "If she is lost on the north shore, the Governor's party will discover her."

"And don't underestimate our Lucy. She'll find her way back as soon as she is able," Denis added with false cheerfulness.

"Not after Lewis finishes with her, she won't," Beth replied tonelessly. "You don't know him, Denis. He's a vicious beast,

231

he is. Michael was right, it's all my fault. I should've told him no matter what Lucy said. Now, because of me, she's dead.''

Tom reached across the table and patted her hand. "Don't torture yourself this way, my dear. Try to eat your breakfast, you've lost too much—" He broke off with a hoarse exclamation, seeing Lucy and Moses at the entrance.

8

Marry in Haste . . .

Friday, April 18, 1788

When the Governor's party returned to Sydney Cove, George Johnston greeted them at the wharf with the news that Lucy had been found. Michael and John hastened to the hospital where she was taking the evening meal with the others.

"Lucy!" Michael cried clasping her in his arms and covering her face with kisses. "Lucy, Lucy, it's a miracle!" He pressed his face into her hair and hugged her tighter.

Although overjoyed to see him, Lucy was unnerved by the sheer physical force of his greeting. He felt her stiffen and hastily set her down. "Darling! Thank God you're safe."

She smiled, and the dimples he loved appeared in her cheeks. "Thank Moses, too. He was the one who found me."

John embraced her and led her to the table. "Sit down, madam, and don't dare move until you have told us all." He turned to Irving, the convict doctor. "Fetch a bottle of my best claret from the dispensary, old chap. No, fetch half a dozen. This is a celebration!"

When Lucy finally rose to go, Michael waylaid her. "I'd like a word with you, Lucy."

Lucy nodded and Beth, who had not left her side in twenty-four hours, reluctantly let go her hand.

"Why didn't you tell me about Lewis?" Michael asked gently as they walked along the shore toward the west point.

She sighed. "Because I didn't want you ruining your career over him."

"That would have been easier to endure than these last ten days," he said slowly. As soon as they reached the bend in the shoreline, he stopped. "Now we're alone, I want to hear the rest."

"The rest?"

"The parts you left out." With great tenderness, he clasped her hands in his. "You can tell me, darling. Did he rape you?"

"Are you sure you want to know, Michael?" she replied in a troubled voice.

"Remember how you felt about your father's death? You said that only by hearing everything would you be able to find peace of mind. It's the same with me."

"He didn't rape me. He ripped my bodice and fondled me. Then he went back to the boat for rum, and I ran away."

His eyes seemed to sink into their sockets and she saw the skin stretched taut over his cheekbones. "He can't live for that. When he returns to Sydney I'll kill him."

"He will never return," she said quickly, and told Michael what Moses had done.

"I owe Moses a great debt," Michael declared when she had finished. "He reminds me of a faithful old dog, the way he dotes on you. It's strange, because he has no time for anyone else."

She smiled, and his longing grew more intense. To have her so close, yet not to hold her was agony.

"I trust Moses the way I trusted my father," she went on. "I'm perfectly at ease in his company, he expects nothing from me."

"Not like I do, you mean?"

Lucy heard the raw pain in his voice and her heart went out to him. It was obvious that he had suffered greatly during her absence. Deep lines etched his forehead and his face wore a haunted expression. Her eyes filled with tears and when she spoke her voice shook with emotion. "Michael, darling, I love you but I am incapable of . . . of being with you. I have a loathing for things of the flesh that I can't control, even for your sake. Please, Michael, find someone else to share your life—someone who will lie with you and love you the way you deserve—I cannot bear seeing you suffer this way."

He looked at her, eyes glistening. "I could never love anyone else, Lucy. Let there be peace between us. Love me in spirit . . . and I give you my word, I'll make no physical demands upon you."

She took a deep breath. "I am sick, Michael."

He continued looking at her steadily. "I know, darling. We will just have to make you well. . . ."

"Did you see how Lucy pulled away from Michael tonight?" Beth asked Balmain as she prepared to leave his hut.

"Her recent experiences would account for that, lass. Did the scum have his way with her?"

"She says not."

"Superb woman, Lucy," he said admiringly. "Beautiful, compassionate, intelligent, and a born lady. The type every man dreams of marrying. Most of the men in the colony would give their right arm to be in Michael's shoes. Tom is in love with her, and Denis, and certainly Watkin Tench."

"What about John?"

Balmain smiled a little derisively. "I think our superior Surgeon General is rather partial to you."

"Oh, Will," she cried self-consciously. "A fine gentleman like John would never marry me."

He fell back in bed laughing. "*Marry* you? John! God you come out with some hilarious statements."

Early next morning, Beth dressed and took the path to the men's camp. It was raining, and by the time she reached George Clayton's tent she was soaked to the skin.

"George," she whispered, shaking him awake. "It's me, George."

He sat up, startled. "Beth! Something wrong, girl?"

She glanced uneasily at the other men in the tent. "I've something private to discuss with you."

Clayton tossed the blanket aside and reached for his boots. "You go ahead. I'll be out in a minute."

He joined her, and they walked down the slope to the flat ground near the mouth of the stream. The rain had eased to a slight drizzle, but Clayton seemed oblivious to it. "What's on your mind, girl?"

To Beth, gazing at the spars of the ships rising ghostlike out of the misty water, the whole world looked gray and dismal. "George . . ." She paused, trying to find the right words. "George, remember how you asked me to marry you?"

"Yes."

"Are you still of the same mind?"

"I am."

"I don't love you, George."

He swallowed hard. "I know."

"But I like you a lot . . . and I like the way you treat me. Maybe in time I could love you, George . . . but I'm not sure. You know there's been someone else?" She glanced at his impassive face but he said nothing, so she went on quickly. "If you take me on those terms, George, I promise not to go near him again and I'll try real hard to be a good wife."

He nodded. "That's honest enough for me, Beth. We'll see Reverend Johnson tonight after I finish work."

Lucy looked at Beth askance. "You can't be serious. Marry George Clayton?"

"We've already seen the Reverend and it's to be next Thursday," Beth replied firmly.

"But why, Bethy? You love Will."

Beth stamped her foot. "I'm nothing more to him than a whore to warm his bed. I've a right to more in life than that, don't I?"

"Of course," Lucy placated. "But what can George Clayton offer you?"

Tears of misery filled Beth's eyes. "A different name to Dudgeon, that's what! And I'd rather go through life as George's wife than be tossed out of William Balmain's bed when he tires of me. Will you be my wedding witness, or not?"

Lucy looked at her sternly. "Is this marriage truly what you want?"

"It truly is," Beth said dejectedly.

"Clayton is a damned lucky man," Michael said when Beth announced her intentions at suppertime.

"A damned insolent man more likely," growled John. "I hope the scoundrel realizes he won't have exclusive rights to your time, madam. Your place is here at the hospital. I can't do without you."

"Don't be talking rubbish, John," Beth said crossly. "Of course I'll stay on at the hospital. George understands that."

"Are you in the family way?" asked Balmain.

Her cheeks turned scarlet. "No, Dr. Balmain, I'm not!"

"Well, let's hope you soon will be, my dear," said Tom after a long and embarrassed silence. "And if you can tolerate another witness at the wedding, I'd be honored."

* * *

When Beth left the convict ward at midnight, Balmain was waiting for her in the clearing. "Damn you," he muttered as she came abreast of him. "Why are you doing this?"

"That should be obvious, even to you," she said stiffly. "Because George wants to marry me."

He glared at her, eyebrows bristling and mouth working with rage. "Very well, you win. In the future I'll be more open about things."

"I'm marrying George, and that's that," she snapped, trying to step around him.

He pulled her into his arms. "Don't be an idiot. Marrying Clayton won't change anything between us."

Beth hit him across the mouth and twisted out of his grasp. "We're finished, Will. I'm going to be faithful to George."

"You faithful?" he said fiercely. "Don't make me laugh. You're a born whore, Beth, the best I've ever had. Clayton won't satisfy you for long. You'll be back—and I'll be waiting."

9

The Portrait

Thursday, April 24, 1788

The day Beth married George Clayton, Faith met Bill Narmo for the second time at the Black Lion Inn.

"Ruth Gamble's manservant, Ned, is a fair butcher's cur," Bill told her as they entered what posed as the Black Lion's private parlor. "A right proper scrounger! The first time I chatted him up at the Red Boar he said he weren't in the habit of conversing with common shufflers like me. That's the tavern Ned takes himself to when he ain't bowing and scraping to his mistress." Bill selected a currant tart with a globule of yellow cream perched precariously on top. "It's been a slow business. No gabber, is Ned."

"Did you discover where Ruth Gamble goes and who she sees?"

"She don't go anywhere much—excepting St. James's Church on Sundays, sometimes to Douglas's for tea, and sometimes for a trot in the park."

Faith's perfect countenance expressed disappointment. "That's all?"

"Except, every Friday regular, she visits a cheese monger in Holborn. Ned says she loves her bit of Dorset and don't trust nobody to choose it."

"I see," said Faith, thinking the cheese might suffice if she needed to put her plan into effect. "Who are her friends?"

"As near as I can make out, she ain't got none. She's a bit of a tippler, you see. Likes her fair share of it, she does."

"Does she?" Faith said slowly. "Does she, indeed? That could prove most useful to our cause."

The pickpocket wiped cream from his nose with his cuff. "Begging your pardon, Miss Faith, but could you tip me to what you're on about?"

"I can't tell you much at the moment, Bill, just that I need to find out all I can about her. Do you suppose this Ned would spy on Ruth Gamble if we paid him a handsome bribe?"

Bill shook his head vigorously. "He'd more likely spill the whole jar of beans to her."

"Then you must become his closest friend, Bill."

Bill wolfed down another cake. "That's my plan. But, like I said, it'll be slow work. Master Ned fancies himself a step above the likes of me."

Faith took a wad of money from her purse. "Let's impress Master Ned. Buy yourself an outfit twice as fine as his then let slip that you have gone into service for a laird and lady from Scotland."

Bill's saucerlike eyes grew rounder. "That should do it, Miss Faith. He likes his lords and ladies, does Ned."

The following Friday, Faith and Bill Narmo met again at the Black Lion Inn.

"My goodness, you do look elegant," she exclaimed, eyeing his black wide-brimmed hat, black suit, black stockings, and silver-buckled shoes with approval. "I think you should come into service for me. It would be more convenient than meeting here."

Bill gave her a startled look. "Service? Me? Not bloomin' likely, Miss Faith. I'm a foggle and ticker man."

Faith gave his arm an imperious pat with her fan. "Nevertheless, Bill, I think you must accept my offer. We cannot have Ned discovering your true occupation, can we? How is your

237

friendship with Ned progressing? Did he warm to you after he saw your new outfit?''

"Warm to me?" cried Bill, as they made their way into the dingy parlor and sat down at a rickety table beside the dirt-encrusted window. "Me and Ned's as close as two warts on a witch's wiper. He's even asked me to the house."

"Oh, you have done well," she said delightedly.

Bill basked for a moment in the glory of her approval. "Ned says his mistress has been tippling something awful since the legal chaps called. He says the only other time she took to it so steady was last Christmas when she told him to take down the painting of the Captain. A proper turn she put on, screaming and crying, and spraying wine everywhere—"

"My God!" Faith cried. "Has Ned still got the painting? Captain Gamble was my father. Oh, Bill, I've never seen what my father looked like. I'd give anything to have his painting."

Bill drew himself up and squared his shoulders. "Don't worry, Miss Faith, if that noggin's still got the painting, he won't have it for long."

"Now the damned woman has retained Richard Erskine-Grey as her counsel," Hugh said crossly, as he and Faith dined that evening. "According to James, he is the world's greatest procrastinator so we are bound to experience interminable delays. God! Of all the rotten luck."

"Oh no," Faith groaned.

Hugh hastily curbed his outburst. "Oh, don't mind me, I'm just in a bad humor. Come, let's take a walk along the silver Thames, it's too fine an evening to languish indoors."

"Would you mind if I employed Bill Narmo as my man-servant?" Faith asked as they strolled arm in arm along the embankment.

Hugh stopped. "Good God, Fae, you cannot be serious! A damned pickpocket for a servant. What next? You'd be fleeced of everything you owned in a week."

Faith realized more drastic measures were needed. With a melancholy sigh, she turned away and gazed fixedly at the river.

She turned to him, eyes glistening with unshed tears. "I wanted to repay Bill Narmo for helping Lucy. He was the only one who did. And I thought it would be lovely having someone around who had actually known her. But you're right, I am just being foolish . . ." She allowed her bottom lip to quiver slightly.

Hugh felt like a mangy dog. "You're not being foolish at all, my darling. Of course you may have Narmo, if that is what you wish. I'll call upon Stephen Porter in the morning. He is bound to know where we can locate the fellow."

Faith threw her arms around his neck and kissed him wildly. "Oh, Scotty, will you really?"

Hugh's eyes twinkled. "You have my word on it. Now do control yourself, madam, else your reputation will be in shreds."

Monday, May 5

"Ned's still got that painting," Bill told Faith, after depositing his worldly possessions in her attic. "It's stashed in the cellar at Grosvenor Square. I'll swipe it next week if you like. I can pick a lock as good as I can pick a pocket."

"I couldn't possibly have you break the law on my account," Faith said blithely, her face flushed with excitement. "You can teach me to pick locks and I'll swipe the painting."

Bill's eyes nearly dropped out of his head. "*You*, Miss Faith? No, never!"

"Very well, Bill," she replied coolly, "I shall break into Grosvenor Square without your assistance. I mean to get that painting."

Bill's shoulders slumped and his trousers slid down round his hips. "All right . . . all right. But only on the condition you take me along."

"Good, I'm glad that's settled," she said cheerfully. "Shall we repair to the parlor door?"

Thursday, May 8

Faith folded Lady Barbara's letter and handed it back to Hugh. "What will you do?"

"I'll return to Carrigmoor at once. Mother is right. I have placed too much responsibility on Robert McBain; no wonder the chieftains are speaking out against me. And I have neglected Father. The burden of the last months has taken a further toll on his health."

Faith nodded gravely. "I shall miss you desperately, dearest. But I agree, you must go."

Hugh gripped her shoulders. "We will go together, Fae."

"But I can't leave London!"

In many respects the letter from his mother was a godsend, Hugh decided as he looked into the rebellious eyes of the woman in his arms. Faith became more willful with every passing day. She spent hours with that confounded pickpocket and she had no conception of the due processes of law. Her efforts to force Lucy's appeal along were frustrating for everyone, especially herself. Clearly, she needed to be taken in hand. His mother had always had a strong influence over her, perhaps she could persuade Faith to set a wedding date. Living with her like this was torture.

He ran his hands slowly down her back and squeezed her hips. "I'll have no more argument, Fae. We leave at the end of the week."

Faith knew she had little chance of winning this argument with coquetry, yet she felt she must try for she could not bear to forfeit her father's painting. She wound her arms around Hugh's neck and kissed him long and hard. Soon, the passion that always smouldered beneath the surface flamed into life. She loved this game they played. It was thrilling and dangerous. They played with the fire . . . and played with it . . . and always he drew back in time.

"Let's wait another week," she whispered. "I can have the coach sent up from Billingsley and we'll travel to Scotland in comfort."

Hugh took her face in his hands and kissed her again. "No, dearest. We leave Saturday."

In that case, Faith thought to herself, *Bill and I will have to get the painting tomorrow evening.*

Friday passed in a whirl of activity, as Faith packed for the journey and plotted for the robbery. Finally though, everything was ready, and late that evening, after kissing Hugh good night, Faith traded her billowing skirts for a footman's uniform, plaited her hair and crammed it under a gray felt cap.

By the time Bill tapped on her door she was quivering with excitement, for the prospect of seeing the inside of her father's house thrilled her beyond measure.

They tiptoed downstairs, let themselves out the house and were soon walking up Whitehall. The return journey had required careful planning, as two people hauling a painting through the streets of London in the dead of night would have undoubtedly drawn the attention of the traps. They had arranged to meet an associate of Bill's who owned a cart behind the house at two o'clock.

On arriving at the square, they scaled a wall at the rear of the house and crept through a shadowy garden to the back door. Faith set to work on the lock nervously, but thoughts of her father soon calmed her. This was *his* house; she was *his* daughter.

The door clicked open. They lit candles from the fire then headed for the cellar. As they descended the stone steps, Faith looked around her with dismay. The cellar was stacked to the ceiling with all sorts of odds and ends. "Oh Lord, Bill. How will we find anything in this jumble?"

Bill smiled cheerfully. "The sooner we start, the sooner we finish, Miss Faith. Be careful of the 'clangers.' "

Half an hour later, Faith found what she'd been searching for. "Bring your candle closer, Bill," she urged and with shaking hands drew away the sheet covering a large painting.

There stood her father, erect and handsome, his sword and the buttons on his naval uniform showing up splendidly in the candle-light. He had jet black hair, a wide friendly mouth, a determined jaw, and unwavering eyes that smiled at her approvingly.

"Come, darling," she said with a catch in her voice, "I'm taking you home with me."

10

A Complaint Against Captain Sinclair

"Why does the Governor want to see me?" Lucy asked as she and Michael crossed the footbridge to the east side of the settlement.

"Officially, he wants to ask you about the land to the west," said Michael, "but really, he is most curious to meet you."

They entered Phillip's canvas house and waited while George Johnston informed him of their arrival. A minute later, Phillip appeared at the door of his study. "Come in, my dear," he said, taking Lucy's hand and leading her inside to a chair by the fire. "How delightful to meet you at last. By God, you are the image of Faith! No one will ever tell you apart."

Lucy responded to his open-hearted greeting with a warm smile. "Am I really like her, Your Excellency?"

Phillip's weary countenance relaxed into a wide, beaming smile and his eyes crinkled at the corners. "Your beauty mirrors hers to the last strand of hair. And, no doubt, you have a thousand questions to ask, eh?"

Lucy clutched the arms of the chair and wriggled with anticipation. "Oh yes . . . yes!"

Phillip chuckled. "Better make yourself comfortable, Michael. This could take some time. Fire away, my dear."

"My other reason for inviting you here tonight, Lucy, was to tell you I have asked my friend George Rose, Undersecretary of the Treasury, to look into your case. Sir George is a personal friend of the Prime Minister, so be assured that his involvement will be most useful."

Lucy caught her breath. "Oh, Your Excellency, how can I ever thank you?"

Phillip smiled at her indulgently. "I am delighted to be of service, my dear. Faith is a particular favorite of mine. Now, let's turn to colony matters. Michael tells me that you fell in with a tribe of natives while at the head of the harbor."

"Yes, sir. I followed them west for three days before turning back."

Phillip rose and paced the floor with hands clasped behind his back. "The current hostility between our people and the natives puzzles me. Whenever I have encountered them, they have been most friendly."

"The tribe I followed were happy and peaceable," Lucy told him. "I can't imagine what provoked that brutal attack at Cockle Bay last week. When those two convicts were brought to the hospital, one had seven spears through him and the other's skull had been beaten to a pulp!"

"I know," said Phillip, shaking his head. "And there are rumors that the natives are cannibals. Did you see any evidence of this?"

"The chief wore a string of teeth around his neck but I saw nothing odd about that; every man in the tribe had a front tooth missing."

"Perhaps the cause of the trouble is our people stealing the natives' weapons?" suggested Phillip.

Lucy pondered on this. "Yes, those weapons are essential to their survival, sir. The natives would be incensed if they were stolen."

"Hmm . . ." said Phillip. "In that case, I'll issue an order that anyone caught stealing a native weapon will be severely punished."

"What would you like to do now that John has magnanimously given you the evening off?" Michael asked as he and Lucy walked across the bridge after taking their leave of Phillip.

She stopped and looked at him searchingly. "Michael, would you feel compromised if we visited Susannah Cable? She is always inviting me to supper."

He grinned. "I won't feel 'compromised.' I like Susannah."

They strolled along the new road as far as the storehouses then took the narrow winding track to Cable's and found Susannah and Henry sitting beside a roaring fire in their clearing.

"Evening you two," said Lucy smiling with pleasure at her friends. "Where's Beth? She said she'd be over after work."

"Liz Hervy from *Friendship* came by and she looked so sick Beth took her straight to the hospital," Susannah explained.

Henry rose and shook Michael's hand. "Hello, Lieutenant. Thanks for delivering the petition."

Michael sat down beside Lucy. "I saw Lavell today when I took provisions to the island. He seemed cheerful enough."

Henry tossed more wood on the fire. "Why didn't those ships that left last week take him and the others into exile?"

"The Governor has decided to put them ashore on the southern cape, and *Lady Penrhyn* and *Charlotte* were sailing for China."

"When will *Alexander* be leaving the colony?" asked Susannah.

"Probably some time in July."

Susannah bit her lip and cast a worried look at her husband. "That don't leave much time, Henry."

"Much time for what?" asked Lucy.

"Remember me telling you about the furniture and things those charitable folks back home shipped out for Henry and me aboard *Alexander*, Lucy? Well, the master won't hand them over. He's a nasty piece of work that Sinclair. The clothes would be mighty useful with winter almost here."

"That's scandalous!" Lucy exclaimed. "Swear out a summons against him."

"A convict summons a Ship master?" Henry scoffed. "Don't be daft, Lucy."

"The English laws apply to everyone, Henry."

"But even if we did summons him he'd just say the goods had been lost overboard."

"Then he'd have to reimburse you for what they were worth," said Michael.

"What use is money here?"

Lucy slipped her hand into Michael's. "It's not the money, it's the principle of the thing."

Michael nodded. "Exactly."

"Damn it, you're right!" said Henry. "How do I swear out a summons?"

"Meet me at the hospital wharf after work tomorrow and I'll take you along to the Judge Advocate," Michael replied, giving Lucy's hand a squeeze.

Beth made Liz Hervy comfortable and hurried to the mess in search of a doctor. To her dismay, Balmain was the only one there. "Where is everyone, Will?"

He left the table and walked toward her. "Tom and Irving are doing rounds at the barracks and the others are dining aboard *Sirius*. You look flushed, Beth. Anything wrong?"

Although Beth had been married to George Clayton for a month, her love for Balmain had not diminished. Consequently, she avoided him whenever possible. "I've just brought a sick friend in," she said stiffly. "Would you come and look at her? She has a high fever and can't see properly."

He took her arm. "Where did you put her?"

She snatched her arm away as if she'd been stung. "This way."

Liz Hervy was very ill indeed. They bathed her, bled her, and fed her a mixture of green rhubarb and yew juice, after which she lapsed into a fitful slumber.

"Sleep's the best thing for the poor soul," Beth sighed. "Oh dear, she does look frail."

He placed an arm around her crestfallen shoulders. "The scurvy weakens them to such an extent that they fall prey to every distemper. You look exhausted, lass. I think a nightcap is in order."

His touch was like a spark to dry kindling. Beth pulled away. "No, I'll stay here. Liz might need me."

"She'll sleep for hours," he said huskily and reached for her again. "I've some French brandy in my hut. We can—"

"No! I'm staying here."

He placed a hand under her chin. "Afraid to be alone with me?"

"Course not," she snapped. "I'm just thinking of your reputation, Dr. Balmain. It wouldn't do for you to be seen with a 'born whore' like me."

His hand dropped from her chin and he gave her a mocking salute. "Good night then, Mrs. Clayton."

On Saturday, the fifth of July, the colony's first civil court met to hear the Cables' complaint against Captain Sinclair of *Alexander*. As the case was a major event for the convicts, immediately after the stop-work beat they gathered outside the marquee serving as the colony's seat of justice.

Inside, David Collins swore in John White, Reverend Johnson, and himself, ordered those lucky enough to gain admission to be seated, and asked Henry to advance to the bench and be sworn.

After Henry had laid his complaint, *Alexander*'s mate, William Long, gave evidence that the Cables' parcel had come on board *Alexander* before the Fleet had left England and been stowed in the gun room, but that when the ship arrived in New South Wales the parcel had been missing. He said that during the voyage he had taken books that had fallen out the parcel to his cabin for safekeeping, but that when his cabin had become damp he had returned the books to the gun room.

Thomas Trimmings, the ship's steward, was then sworn. He stated that he had put the parcel in the afterhold with others belonging to the convicts, but that when the ship had arrived in New South Wales the parcel belonging to the Cables had been missing.

Next, *Alexander*'s master, Captain Duncan Sinclair, was led forward by the Provost Marshal. After confirming the evidence of his seamen, he stated that, since he had received no freightage for the Cables' parcel, he did not consider himself obliged to reimburse them for its loss.

All evidence being given, the tribunal went into a huddle and a few minutes later Collins rose and called for order.

"We, the members of this tribunal, disagree with the statement made by the master of *Alexander* that, having received no freightage for the missing parcel, he is not liable to reimburse for its loss. His ship was in the service of government, and paid to convey the convicts and the little property they possessed to this country; therefore we find in favor of the plaintiffs, Susannah and Henry Cable, and order the said Duncan Sinclair, master of the transport ship *Alexander,* to compensate them for the loss of their goods to the value of fifteen pounds sterling. Court adjourned.''

Wild cheering broke out in the courtroom and rose to a crescendo as the verdict was conveyed to those waiting outside. For civil jurisprudence in His Majesty's Colony of New South Wales it was, indeed, a brilliant beginning.

11

Duplicity and Duels

August 1788

Gales and torrential rain heralded in August, and all public labor was suspended. Many older buildings were damaged. Both the brick kiln and Major Ross's new house collapsed but the partially completed viceregal residence withstood the tempest, as did the brick hut Moses was building for Lucy.

At the hospital, relations between John White and William Balmain steadily deteriorated, and on the day of the Prince of Wales's birthday their rift came to a shocking head.

The celebrations began pleasantly enough. At dawn, the two King's ships fired several rousing salutes; at noon, the troops offered compliments to the Governor; and in the evening, the gentlemen of the colony attended a dinner at Government House, then adjourned to the barracks to toast the royal family and make merry.

In honor of the occasion, Phillip lifted the curfew so the convicts could participate in their own celebrations, and it was at Cable's bonfire jubilee that the trouble began.

"Time we left." George Clayton squeezed Beth's leg as they sat watching the revelers in the clearing. "I've gotta be at the Governor's Wharf by dawn. The timber-getters are going upharbor."

Beth, who had been enjoying the antics of the dancers, stopped laughing. "You'd best go on alone then, George. I have to return to the hospital. I-I just came over for a spell . . . didn't I, Lucy?"

Lucy looked at the unhappy couple on the log beside her. Since Michael was doing duty, she had volunteered to work the late shift so Beth was lying.

When Beth attempted to rise, George caught her around the waist. "No you don't! You're coming home with me. We ain't been together in weeks. Lucy'll work in your stead, won't you, Lucy?"

Embarrassed, Lucy shook her head. "I'm sorry, George. Dr. White is the only person with the authority to alter work rosters. You had better run along, Beth. Sarah Burdo will be eager to join the festivities."

When Irving relieved Beth at midnight, she crossed the clearing to the fire and made herself a pot of tea. From the barracks came the faint sound of cheering but here at the hospital, all was peace and tranquility. She carried the pot to the mess and sat down at the table.

What was she to do? George's clumsy attempts at lovemaking revolted her. No matter that he was her lawful husband, no matter that he was sober and hard working, no matter that he was kind and caring, she could not stand being around him. What was she to do?

"Aah, the elusive Mrs. Clayton."

Beth spun round. Balmain was standing at the entrance swaying slightly from side to side. "Go to bed, you're drunk," she said.

He approached her with slow, deliberate steps. "I'll go, if you come with me."

She leapt to her feet, shaking her fist at him. "Keep away, or I'll hit you!"

"I've kept away from you for months," he muttered, grabbing her and forcing her backward across the table. "For God's sake, Bethy, be reasonable."

"Let me go!" she panted, twisting her head from side to side, trying to elude his mouth.

"Unhand that woman, you rascal."

Balmain swore loudly and yanked Beth to her feet as John White came weaving toward them. "Stay out of this, White. It's between me and Beth."

John struck him across the face. "I said unhand that woman, you rascal."

Beth realized that John was as drunk as Balmain. "It's all right, John, me and Will were just funning . . ."

Balmain tightened his grip around her waist. "What Beth and I do is none of your business you infernal, interfering popinjay. And whosoever calls me a rascal is himself *thrice* so!" He shoved John in the chest and sent him flying back against the side of the tent.

John regained his balance with considerable difficulty, adjusted his jacket and advanced toward his attacker. "Unhand that woman, you rascal."

"Truly, John, I like Will's hands on me," Beth croaked.

"Retract those words you muckworm or, by God, you'll answer for them with your life," Balmain said icily.

John struck Balmain on both cheeks with the flat of his hand. "This is my answer, sir. Not only are you a rascal, but a rogue, a villain, and a blackguard."

Balmain released Beth and drew himself stiffly to attention. "Your servant, sir. I shall collect my weapons and meet you on the beach in ten minutes."

"They're going to kill each other. Do something! Do something!"

Lucy awoke from a deep sleep to discover Beth shaking her frantically. "For goodness s-sake . . . who?"

"John and Will! They're on their way to the beach!" She stopped and gave a little scream. "Look, there's John with his pistols! Stop him, Lucy!"

As John crossed the clearing, Lucy placed a restraining hand on him. "Have you taken leave of your senses, John? You and Will can't fight at duel."

"This has nothing to do with you, my dear," John said cheerfully. "The rascal has long been asking for it. Now, he shall have his wish." He disengaged himself and with a breezy salute set off along the beach path.

Lucy turned to Beth. "Have you seen Moses anywhere about?" Her voice faltered as Balmain came sauntering toward them.

"Will!" Beth screeched. "Please don't go!"

"What's this all about, Will?" asked Lucy, casting an apprehensive eye at the dueling case under his arm.

Balmain continued walking as if he had not heard them.

"What'll we *do?*" Beth sobbed.

Lucy bit her lip uncertainly. "We could run to Cable's. Henry might help. Or, failing that, we could alert the town guard."

Beth picked up her skirts and started to run. "There's no time. I'm going to to the beach!"

After a moment of indecision, Lucy followed. They arrived to find the two doctors standing about twenty feet apart, pointing pistols at each other. Two shots rang out simultaneously and echoed around the cove.

At the barracks, the celebrations continued unabated. However, Phillip, taking the night air on the Governor's Wharf, saw the fiery flashes and, thinking the hospital must be under native attack, began to run.

When the smoke cleared on the beach both men were still standing.

"Stop it! Stop it at once!" Lucy screamed.

"Time out to reload," Balmain called to John.

"Your servant," John replied, and reached for his other weapon.

Out of the corner of her eye Lucy saw a shadow sprinting along the beach toward them. Thank God someone was coming.

Shots rang out again, and this time Balmain staggered.

Beth rushed forward and flung her arms around his neck. "Will. Oh please stop, Will, please, please!"

"Get out the way," he rasped, pushing her roughly aside.

As Beth landed on her back in the sand, Phillip stepped into the men's sights.

"Desist this instant!"

"Stand aside, sir, this is a matter of honor," John informed him stiffly.

"No, sir, this is a matter of foolhardiness," Phillip replied severely. "If you wish to draw blood, I suggest you use lances on your patients. Return to your quarters at once, gentlemen. Otherwise I'll have you ironed and thrown into the guardhouse."

John and Will lowered their pistols and glanced at each other uncertainly.

"Your Excellency, I . . . er . . . we, that is, Dr. Balmain and I . . ." John's voice trailed off.

Phillip held up his hand. "No words could explain this shameful exhibition, sir. I shall expect you and your assistant at Government House at eleven o'clock sharp in the morning." Nodding curtly to Lucy he turned on his heel and strode along the beach, herding curious onlookers before him.

"Oh, John, how could you?" Lucy admonished, retrieving John's dueling case and leading him up the beach.

"The bastard got me in the thigh," Balmain muttered as soon as he and Beth were alone.

Beth scrambled to her feet. "How bad is it?"

He took a step and grimaced. "Not too bad. Help me to my hut, will you?"

She stared at the dark blotch spreading on the outside of his breeches. "You're bleeding, Will. Let me fetch help."

He shook his head. "No, the fewer people that know about this, the better. Just get me to my hut, Beth, please."

When they reached the hut she brushed aside his objections and, after helping him undress, inspected the long gash on his right outer thigh. Although the wound had almost stopped bleeding, the area around it was very bruised and swollen. She salved and bandaged it then helped him into bed.

He held out his hand. "Come here, Beth."

She pressed his hand to her heart and whispered, "Oh, Will, why'd you do it?"

"I've been going mad these last months, thinking of you with Clayton," he said hoarsely.

She saw his face working and realized that it had cost him dearly to utter those words. "I'm sorry for the mess I've made of everything, Will."

He gripped her hand tightly. "Beth, stay with me. Please."

"I-I can't, Will. I have to leave now."

He groaned. "Jesus! You're not going to him, are you?"

She knelt beside the bed and stroked his forehead. "No, it's over between George and me."

"You mean it?"

"Yes. I love you, Will. I've been such a fool."

He caught her against him. "Live with me, Beth. I'll treat you better, I swear it."

Shaking her had, she rose. "No, Will. I'll ask Lucy if I can move in with her. That way, I won't hurt George so bad."

"Damn Clayton. What about me? What about us?"

"We'll be together again, Will, but I can't just walk out on George and come to live with you. None of this is his fault, you know."

Balmain sank wearily onto the pillows and placed an arm over his eyes. "All right, lass. But promise you'll stay away from him."

Beth doused the lamp and walked to the door. "I promise. Now, go to sleep—and mind you're civil to John in the morning."

"Is Will all right?" Lucy asked as Beth entered the mess.

Beth sat down and placed her head in her hands. "Yes, the wound isn't much more than a graze." She looked up at her friend imploringly. "Lucy, can I move in with you? I made a big mistake marrying George. It won't do no good me staying with him."

Lucy poured tea into a mug and set it down beside Beth. "Of course you can move in with me, darling. We'll collect your belongings tomorrow while George is upharbor, if you like."

Beth twisted the mug around in her hands for a while, then asked, "Will you come with me when I tell him?"

"No, my dear," said Lucy, shaking her head, "that you must do yourself."

12

September 1788

"But I *cannot* remain at Carrigmoor, Aunt Barbara!"

"Then you and Hugh must marry immediately. It is most unseemly—indeed, it is untenable—that you and he are practically living together unchaperoned."

"But I want Lucy at my wedding," Faith cried. "She and I have missed out on so much, Aunt Barbara."

"My dearest girl, you are being most unreasonable. Many months will pass before you and Lucy can be reunited, surely you don't expect Hugh to wait that long?"

"Hugh has agreed to wait."

"Hugh would swim Loch Ness in the dead of winter with his arms and legs ironed if you asked him," said Lady Barbara wryly. "No, my mind is made up. If you won't marry, you must stay here under my protection when Hugh returns to London."

Knowing she could not sway her aunt with sighs or melting looks, Faith thought quickly. "If you let me return to London for

Lucy's appeal, Aunt Barbara, I promise to marry Hugh before we sail for New South Wales.''

A bright smile spread across Lady Barbara's face. "Oh, darling, you have made me so happy! My goodness, what a lot there is to do—your trousseau to be got ready, the clan summoned from England and Europe. Hmm . . . perhaps you ought to remain at the castle after all.''

Faith groaned inwardly. "Let's make the wedding a quiet affair, Aunt Barbara.''

"A quiet affair? Impossible! You are marrying the young laird of Clan Stewart. Your wedding will be a great occasion and the celebrations will last for weeks.''

"Then *you* must organize it, Aunt, for I will not miss my sister's appeal—and that's final,'' said Faith. Fighting back tears, she crossed to the large gothic window. Dark clouds brooded over the barren landscape and the light had almost fled the day. Suddenly, this romantic castle of her childhood seemed unbearably restrictive. She longed for the freedom of London where there were no rules or regulations.

Lady Barbara placed a gentle hand on her shoulder. "I do understand your concern for Lucy, my dear. But, try to be patient . . .''

Faith pressed her forehead against the windowpane. "How can I be patient when my Lucy is languishing in that godforsaken wilderness? Oh, I dread the endless days ahead!''

"Those endless days will pass more quickly if you have the loving companionship of a husband,'' her grandaunt insisted.

Faith turned away from the window and smiled wanly. "I shall speak to Hugh when he returns from Inverness this evening.''

However, all thoughts of marriage fled Faith's mind when Hugh strode in shortly afterward, waving a letter from James Geldie. "He wants us to return to London.''

Faith clasped her hands ecstatically. "Oh, Hugh, how soon can we leave?''

He walked to the opposite side of the room and held out his hands to the fire. "I have done all I can here until spring but I am reluctant to leave. Now that Father is permanently incapacitated, the chieftains of the Inner Council have been hinting that I should assume some of his clan duties . . .''

Faith went to him. "I know that your duty is here, Hugh. I shall return to London alone.''

He wrapped his arms around her and hugged her close. "My first duty is to you, my darling. Parents and clan come second. We'll set out at the end of the week.''

A great surge of joy swept through Faith. The end of the week, that was not so long. She kissed him enthusiastically. "Your mother has made me see how selfish I've been, dearest. As soon as we obtain Lucy's pardon, let's come back to Carrigmoor and marry before we sail for New South Wales."

He gasped. "Fae, darling, do you mean it?"

"Of course! But if you squeeze me to death, we will never be able to set the date. When do you think Lucy's appeal will be heard?"

"November at the latest."

"Then, let's marry in the spring."

He swept her off her feet and twirled her round and round. "Yes! Yes! As long as it's early spring!"

"Scotty!" she gurgled. "Scotty, put me down this instant!"

13

A New Beginning

Saturday, September 13, 1788

"To lose four men under such circumstances was deeply distressing, but the way the surf rages along that coast, I am grateful that more longboats have not capsized," the commander of *Supply*, Lieutenant Ball, told his fellow diners at Government House.

"Is there no safe harbor on Norfolk Island?" asked Hunter.

"None. Not even for so small a vessel as *Supply*."

"Nevertheless," said Phillip, "the Norfolk settlement must continue. Vegetables and grain grow luxuriantly there."

"I heard the wheat crop was a miserable failure," said Major Ross.

Phillip looked at him levelly. "Yes. But that is because the seed was injured by the weevil and heat on the voyage out, not from any deficiency in the island's soil." He selected a home-grown orange from the fruit bowl. "Which brings me to my reason for inviting you here tonight, gentlemen. As we cannot be certain that future vessels will preserve seed any better than we did, I propose that we transport thirty or so convicts to Norfolk to help cultivate the land."

"An excellent idea, Governor," said Ball. "Gidley King will welcome the extra labor."

Phillip smiled widely. "Yes, he has indicated as much. Second, I thought we could send a similar number to cultivate the arable land at the head of the harbor. And third, as we have only a year's supply of flour in the store, I propose we send *Sirius* to the Cape. Is she fit for such a voyage, John?''

Hunter smiled gravely. ''Yes, Governor, both ship and crew are ready. May I suggest that we land the guns so that the maximum quantity of flour can be taken aboard.''

''In my opinion, cattle, not flour, should be purchased at the Cape,'' Ross declared. ''The Government stock that was so carelessly lost last month must be replaced.''

''Quite so,'' Phillip agreed. ''But cattle take up a great deal of room, and those animals that managed to survive the voyage would have to be slaughtered the moment they were landed, so that our people could be fed. Furthermore, such food as they did provide would last only two weeks. Whereas the same quantity of flour would last six months. However, I have written to the Home Office requesting that all vessels sailing to the colony take aboard stock at the Cape, and there the matter must rest for now.''

Ross could not believe what he was hearing. ''But, Governor, there is only one cow left in the colony and she is so wild that none dare approach her. The officers of the battalion have been without fresh milk for a month.''

Hunter fixed him with a steely stare. ''We are discussing the needs of the whole community, sir. And if, in the interest of furnishing that community with the basic necessities of life, some of your officers have to forego fresh milk, then so be it, sir.''

''Come in, but mind you wipe your feet,'' Beth said importantly as Michael stepped into Lucy's parlor.

That the new hut had been a labor of love for Moses was evident in everything Michael saw as he gazed around him. Two bedchambers and a storeroom opened off the cheerful, high-ceilinged parlor, which contained a table, chairs, corner cupboard, and shelves built into the walls on either side of the fireplace. The fireplace itself was a work of art. Wide and deep, it had a beautifully drawing chimney and a circular domed brick oven.

''Hmmm . . . that smells delicious,'' Michael sighed as Lucy removed a large sugarloaf from the oven.

''Please be seated, everyone,'' she said, placing the loaf to one side and smiling. ''No, Moses, not there. I want my guest of honor at the head of the table.''

The giant mashed his cap in his hands. ''No, Miss Lucy, I can't.''

"Nonsense," she laughed, pushing him into the chair and sitting down beside him. "And in the future, you shall sleep in my old tent next door and eat breakfast here with me and Beth."

Moses slid lower in his chair and stared fixedly at his plate. "No need for that, Miss Lucy . . ."

"As *Sirius* is leaving for the Cape next week, I'd sleep easier, knowing you were close by these beauties," said Michael, deciding that this was as good a time as any to impart his news.

"Michael!" Lucy cried. "Oh, Michael, no!"

For the life of him, Michael could not help but be pleased by her dismay. "We received orders this morning," he said gently, his eyes locking with hers. "Apparently, there's only a year's supply of flour left in the store."

"B-but surely that will be enough, Michael. More ships are bound to arrive soon . . ."

"We can't pin our hopes on ships arriving from England, Lucy. As you know, any number of mishaps can delay them."

"But Michael—"

"Hunter has decided to circumnavigate the world. We'll go east, via the Horn, then across the Atlantic to the Cape, that way we should be back here in six months—"

"Six months! Oh Michael, six months is a lifetime!" Lucy stared at him, unable to go on. Beth bit her lip. Moses shuffled his feet.

Michael tore his eyes away from Lucy and focused on Moses. "So, will you watch over these two until I return?"

"Yes, Lieutenant," Moses replied gravely.

"Good!" Michael reached for a piece of sugarloaf. "Now, let's partake of this sumptuous feast before it gets cold."

Because Michael was caught up with the preparations for departure, Lucy saw little of him during the week. By the time the last day arrived, she was feeling very despondent.

Michael, on the other hand, was almost relieved to be going; being constantly in Lucy's company required great forbearance. However, it was infinitely preferable to the black hopelessness that had engulfed him when she had been missing. So he walked with her, talked with her, held her hand if she offered it, and prayed for a miracle. That she loved him, he was certain, and this was his only solace.

That evening, the doctors gave a farewell party for Michael. When the guests began arriving, Lucy and Beth retreated to the wards until Irving relieved them, then Beth slipped away to be with Balmain and Lucy returned to her hut.

She donned her nightgown and mechanically brushed her hair until it crackled and shone in the firelight. "How can I live without him for so long?" she asked in despair, jumping to her feet and flinging the brush across the parlor. She thought of the months they had spent apart during the voyage. How tedious those months had been, and how joyous their reunion at Botany Bay. She remembered the heady excitement she had felt when he had embraced her and looked deeply into her eyes. She wanted him to look at her that way again and she wanted to feel the breathless excitement, yet she dreaded what followed—the rasping breath, the hardening of his body, his hands tearing at her skin . . .

She curled her own hands into fists and squeezed them until the knuckles turned white and the nails bit into her palms. "I want to be well," she whispered. "I want to make you happy, Michael. I hate seeing the suffering in your eyes."

There was a knock on the door. Praying it was him, she rushed to open it.

Michael stood on the doorstep holding a bottle of Portuguese wine and two crystal glasses. "May I come in?"

She smiled and opened the door wide. "Of course. My goodness, it sounds as though everyone is having a good time."

"Yes they are, but I wanted to be with you," he said simply, uncorking the bottle and filling the glasses with wine.

She took a deep breath. "I'm glad you came, Michael, I've missed you."

"I've missed you too," he said, gazing at her across the distance that separated them. She wore the white nightgown he had bought her in Rio and her hair fell around her like dark mist. The firelight bathed her in a soft pink glow and her eyes were dark and mysterious. "You look very beautiful tonight."

"Thank you." She glanced away from him, unaccountably shy, and raised the glass to her lips. "This tastes good."

"Watkin Tench told me he intends to court you while I'm at sea."

"And what did you tell Watkin Tench?"

He looked at her in the way that both excited and disturbed her. "I told him that I had no claim on you but if he treated you with anything other than respect, I'd run him through when I returned."

She tensed and her eyes flashed. "You didn't tell Watkin the truth then, Michael. You do have a claim on me."

"Do I, Lucy?" he said softly.

Emotion welled up in her and her throat ached so much she could hardly speak. "Yes you *do,* darling, you own my heart. Please hold me, I can't bear the thought of you leaving."

When he took her in his arms she began to cry. "I-I am sorry for the pain I've caused you, Michael."

He sighed. "I'll not deny the pain."

"Please kiss me. I want you to, Michael, I really want it." She wound her arms around his neck and closed her eyes tightly.

He kissed her cheeks and eyelids, and after a time she relaxed. "I love you so much, Michael."

"I love you too," he murmured, placing his mouth over hers. Her lips were soft and they trembled beneath his. We are still a million miles apart, he thought with resignation, but at least she is trying.

"It's wonderful being together like this, isn't it?" she whispered.

"Wonderful . . ." He savored the warmth of her body and tried to draw her essence—the vibrant, radiant core that was Lucy—into himself.

She looked up at him, eyes glistening with tears. "I want to get well for us, Michael . . . I want to, but I don't know how . . ."

He smiled. "Tonight is a good start, darling. Keep trying, one little step at a time, and we'll get there."

"Yes," she sighed, resting her head on his chest, "one little step at a time . . ."

He moved his hands under the dark veil of her hair and stroked her neck. "We won't let this thing defeat us, will we?"

"No," she said with real determination in her voice.

At daybreak, Lucy left the hut and walked along the beach to the west point. The morning was remarkably still and the water, crystal clear, made hardly a sound as it gently lapped the shore.

"A golden day to sail away," she said, raising the spyglass to her eye and training it on *Sirius*. Captain Hunter and Michael were at the helm, Lieutenant Bradley was by the bow, Mad George Maxwell was circling the main, and the crew was scrambling over the rigging like a swarm of hornets.

Hunter gave the order, the anchor was raised, a rousing cheer went up from those lining the foreshores and the grand old lady of the sea shook out her sails and inched from the cove.

As the ship passed the west point, Michael waved.

Lucy waved back and watched him through the spyglass until he was no longer visible. For a long time she continued gazing out to sea. Then, brushing the tears from her cheeks with a determined gesture, she went home and carefully washed and stored the crystal glasses in readiness for his return.

PART TWO
Strands Intertwine

14
The Appeal

It was the final day of Lucy's appeal and Faith, dressed in a brown homespun dress with a brown felt hat perched on top of a bedraggled gray wig, sat with Bill at the rear of the public gallery.

King's Bench was a disappointment. She had expected Lucy's appeal to be heard by three learned judges in scarlet and ermine, ensconced on thrones in a great hall. Instead, the forum for Lucy's appeal was a gritty room crowded with attorneys, counselors, and the general public, and the chief judge, Lord Kenyon, was a heavy-jowled bulldog with coarse, contracted features, a purple nose, and an air of bristling superiority.

From the outset, Faith had been impressed by Erskine-Grey, Ruth Gamble's counsel, who was now delivering his final oration to a spellbound courtroom. The only time Kenyon had overruled the barrister he, Kenyon, had merely shaken his finger good-naturedly and said, "It won't do, Erskine-Grey, it won't do."

Ruth Gamble had been stony faced and unshakable, and James Geldie had been unable to throw doubt on anything she said. This had also been the case with Ned Robinson who, under Erskine-Grey's brilliant leading, had proved a valuable witness for the other side.

Erskine-Grey concluded and James Geldie rose to address the tribunal. "Lucy Gamble shot Richard Newport in defense of her person, yet because of the biased testimony of the two main witnesses for the crown she was found guilty of murder. Your Honors, justice must never be swayed by bias. This corrigendum *must* be corrected and this innocent woman pardoned.'' James continued making his points with calm, lucid reasoning so that, by the end of his speech, Faith felt quite confident.

The judges conferred and, after an interminable delay, Judge Kenyon called for order. "The rules of appeal pleading are specific: all allegations made by counsel for an appellant must be proven.

"In the first instance, this tribunal unanimously finds that counsel for Lucy Gamble has failed to prove that Richard Newport was a rake and a rapist.

"In the second instance, this tribunal unanimously finds that counsel for Lucy Gamble has failed to prove either Ruth Gamble or Ned Robinson biased.

"In the third instance—that Lucy Gamble had acted in defence of her person when she shot Richard Newport—counsel for Lucy Gamble has argued that Lucy Gamble loaded her father's pistol on a 'sentimental whim' and used it after being raped by her fiancé. Whereas both witnesses for the Crown, whom this tribunal has found to be competent, swore that they *saw* Richard Newport kneeling unarmed and wounded before Lucy Gamble when she fired the second and fatal shot. Therefore, this tribunal unanimously finds that counsel for Lucy Gamble has failed to prove that she acted in defence of her person when she shot Richard Newport.

"Appeal dismissed.''

"Don't despair, my dear, it is Judge Kenyon's interpretation of the law that is at fault, not the law itself,'' James Geldie consoled Faith that evening.

"As soon as we return from Scotland, James will lodge a Writ of Error before a superior court,'' Hugh said.

"A superior court!'' she said in an exasperated voice. "Are you saying we must go through this whole thing again?''

"I am afraid so,'' James replied gravely. "However, next time we'll argue before all twelve judges of the realm and I have no doubt that the original verdict against your sister will be set aside.''

"We will need to attack Ruth Gamble more forcefully next time, James, else the outcome will be the same,'' Hugh said gloomily. "The woman's resilience under questioning was amazing, Erskine-Grey must have coached her until she was word-perfect . . .''

As the two men rambled on, Faith looked disconsolately at the storm raging outside. Almost a year had passed and she was still no closer to obtaining Lucy's pardon. While she dallied in comfort, surrounded by the finest things life could offer, Lucy toiled in an unimaginable wilderness.

Why had she allowed these two men with their infuriating logic and pedantic obedience to the principles and precedents of law to influence her? She had always known Lucy's pardon would not be won with logical arguments and reasonable actions.

She made a silent vow to her sister. *Forgive me, beloved. From now on, we'll do it my way. Next Sunday, with the help of Bill and a broken carriage wheel, I shall give Ruth Gamble something other than victory to ponder over Christmas.*

Ruth Gamble applied more powder to her cheeks and smiled with satisfaction at her reflection in the mirror. The new blue outfit flattered both her figure and complexion, and although her eyes were still puffy from last night's indulgences, that would soon pass. In fact, she promised herself as she donned her bonnet, now Lucy's appeal was a thing of the past, there would be less solitary drinking and more socializing.

She descended the stairs and ordered the carriage to be brought around to the front entrance.

"I hope madam finds the sermon to her liking," Ned said as he bowed her out the door. Ruth shivered and drew her fur collar higher around her ears. Frost covered the steps and balustrades, and a chill, oppressive atmosphere hung over the day. A dense fog saturated the square and not the faintest glimmer of sunlight penetrated the gloom.

As Ruth listened for the rumble of carriage wheels, she heard footsteps approaching. Muffled and faint, they rang eerily on the cobblestones. She stared into the fog. How deep and dark it was, and how silent and somber the day. The footsteps were much closer, now. They could not be more than ten yards away . . .

Suddenly, like a curtain, the fog lifted and a woman stepped onto the footpath. She wore a long cloak that melted into the fog and a deep hood that hid her face.

"Are you lost?" Ruth enquired.

The woman stood there, not uttering a sound.

"Are you lost?" Ruth repeated uneasily.

With a swift movement, the woman threw back the hood.

Ruth froze with terror. It was Lucy, her face as white as

leprosy, her green eyes blazing with hatred. Ruth stumbled up the steps and pounded on the door. "Ned! For the love of God, let me in!"

Ned swung open the door and caught his swooning mistress. "What ails you, madam?"

"Look," Ruth whimpered. "Oh look, Ned, it's *her*!"

But though Ned peered long and hard into the fog, nothing moved in the murky gray.

15
A Highland Wedding

Saturday, February 28, 1789

Faith dismissed the chattering chambermaids and surveyed her reflection critically in the mirror. Her wedding dress with its long, ermine-trimmed sleeves and exquisite lace kirtle was of the whitest satin. Diamonds glittered at her throat, and a gossamer veil billowed from a garland of white rosebuds encircling her head. She wore her hair the way Hugh liked it, falling loosely down her back.

She walked to the window and stared out at the bonfires dotting the stark, white landscape. It was dusk, it was bitingly cold, it was her wedding day. Where was the joy? Where was the breathless excitement?

Her gloomy thoughts were interrupted by a loud rap on the door. Robert McBain had come in Uncle Colin's stead to escort her downstairs to the Great Hall. He looked extremely handsome in his kilt and clan regalia.

"Please come in, Robert," she invited with a friendly smile.

Robert remained where he was. "Will you gae alang wi' me now, my lady? We cannot tarry, the men are waiting without."

"Oh, very well then," she said crossly, scooping up her veil. "Lead on, lead on. Let's get it over with."

They descended the white marble staircase to the ground floor; Robert escorted her to a tiny room adjacent to the Great Hall and, with a curt nod, left.

Faith waited for the ceremony to begin, with a sense of

unreality. She did not belong with these strange, barbaric people, she belonged with Lucy—only her.

Inside the Great Hall the wedding guests were stamping their feet and chanting the ancient battle cry of the Stewarts. The din was deafening. Faith clamped her hands over her ears trying to block it out. *Oh Lord, Lucy, what* am *I doing here?*

A moment later, the outer door swung open and the Stewart Piper stepped into the vestibule. He filled his bag, fingered his chanter and, with drones spread and pipes screeching, strutted majestically toward the Great Hall.

Behind him, resplendent in regimental kilt, walked Hugh. His bonnet was trimmed with an eagle feather (the mark of his rank) and a heavy plaid fell from a silver and cairngorm brooch on the shoulder of his black velvet jacket. Lace decorated his throat and wrists and over his kilt hung a silver and leather sporran and a basket-hilted double edged broadsword. He looked like a magnificent savage from a bygone era; not at all like her adoring Scotty.

Robert McBain, bearing the ceremonial bull-hide target of the Stewarts mounted on a silver pike, followed immediately behind Hugh, then came the Bard, the Blaider, the swordsmen, the axemen, and the rest—all dressed in thigh-length kilts and wearing huge broadswords that scraped on the marble floor as they passed.

As the procession entered the Great Hall, the battle cry rang out again. Wild and pagan, it echoed along the ancient corridors of Carrigmoor making the whole world tremble. Faith pressed her hands together to her ears and remained so until Robert came to fetch her.

When she entered the hall the shouting ceased and a hush fell over the congregation. Hugh, waiting for her at the end of the aisle, caught his breath. Tall and elegant, like a dazzling white goddess, she floated toward him, her long veil billowing about her like a delicate mist. Despite the solemnity of the occasion, he smiled. The willful love of his childhood would soon be his.

Faith was startled by the hostility she saw in the sea of faces. It was etched into the withered cheeks of the old people, it was there, lurking behind the false smiles of the women dressed in sable and lace, and it was blazing in the eyes of the chieftains, arrayed like barbarous peacocks in colored feathers and furred cloaks.

Well, damn them, she thought, raising her chin defiantly. *I'll not let them see I care.* But Faith's disquiet increased as she took her marriage vows. *Why am I being plagued by these strange thoughts,* she wondered. *This is supposed to be the happiest day of my life.*

At the end of the long oration, the ceremonial dirk was brought forward. Faith kissed it, then she and Hugh exchanged rings and were pronounced man and wife.

The doors to the Great Hall were thrown open and the bagpipes screeched into life as Hugh led her outside to the courtyard and helped her into an open carriage. They drove across the drawbridge to where the humbler members of Clan Stewart waited to receive the traditional gold and silver pieces that the laird or his heir distributed the day he was wed.

While the bonfires blazed brilliantly against the velvety black sky, Faith looked on in stunned disbelief as men, women, and children punched, kicked, and trampled one another in their attempts to snatch the precious coins that Hugh cast about.

Mercifully though, the distribution of the coins was soon over and the newlyweds returned to the castle to join their guests in a sumptuous eight-course banquet.

Just before they entered the Great Hall, Hugh paused and asked, "How is my lady wife?"

"Hungry," Faith snapped.

He laughed and squeezed her hand. "Hungry for love, I hope. Tonight, you and I shall bathe in the fire."

"Hugh!" A flutter of excitement ran through Faith and she blushed. Ignoring the cheers issuing from the hall, he took her in his arms and kissed her passionately. Then, grinning from ear to ear, he led her to the table of honor and signaled for the feast to begin.

Course followed course, toast followed toast, and speech followed speech. It seemed that every chieftain must have his say about the young laird and his lady bride. Their accents were so thick, Faith could hardly understand a word they said and toward the end of a particularly tedious speech, she turned a bored gaze on the table opposite and saw a young woman in a bright green gown staring hungrily at Hugh.

Faith's eyes narrowed. Although the woman had a buxom build, a fine complexion and long hair of brilliant burnished copper, her eyes were colorless and set close together and her jaw was too square for her to be considered beautiful. The woman's eyes locked with Faith's and for a few moments they glared at each other in an ancient acknowledgment of rivalry.

You may think you have him, you insipid English cull, thought Fiona Stewart. *But you'll not hold him once he's grown tired of your looks. And you'll never be welcome in our glen.*

Before the dancing began, Lady Barbara led Faith away for a few minutes respite.

"I must be growing old, my darling," she laughed, as she removed Faith's veil in preparation for the dancing. "I doubt I'll survive one night of this—much less three weeks. How are you bearing up?"

"Well enough, Aunt Barbara, but why are the people so hostile?"

"The Carrigmoor Stewarts are the descendants of tribes which roamed these glens centuries before the Book of Genesis was written, Faith. They do not welcome outsiders—especially English ones."

Faith detached the gauzy veil from the rose garland and replaced the garland on her head. "Sounds as if they remained unchanged while the world has moved on."

"In many ways they have, but don't be too quick to judge them, Faith. They have great strength, these people, and their traditions have stood the test of time."

"Maybe so, Aunt Barbara. But Robert also seemed remote and he's a McBain, not a Stewart."

Lady Barbara's face took on an inscrutable expression and when she spoke, her voice was vague and melancholy. "You are incorrect, my dear. Although McBain is the name of the man thought to be Robert's father, his mother was the daughter of a Stewart chieftain . . ."

"Why is the bond between Hugh and Robert so strong?"

"Because they were wet-nursed by the same woman and under clan law, the milk they shared at birth imposes a lifelong obligation upon both. When they were younger they were extremely close, but lately . . ." Lady Barbara shrugged. "Your uncle Colin and Robert stand for the old ways, Faith. Whereas Hugh, with his university education and knowledge of the outside world, advocates sweeping changes to the farming methods. Colin's mind and body have deteriorated rapidly since his accident. Nowadays, he lives more and more in the past and has found a willing ally in Robert, who loves Carrigmoor as fiercely as he—" She broke off and smiled. "But enough of this gloomy talk. Now is the time for rejoicing. Let us return to the festivities."

As the hours dragged by, the celebrations grew more barbaric and the scene, with flaming pine knots and mock battles, resembled a viking's lair. For Hugh's sake, Faith bore the chieftains' kisses and pawings with good grace but when the time came for her and Hugh to leave, she almost wept with relief.

Later, in her chamber, as the giggling maids sponged her in scented water and clad her in a silky nightgown and a floor-length sable cloak, some of her tension abated, but when they led her through the labyrinth of dark passageways to Hugh's apartments in the east wing, the air of unreality returned.

What am I doing here? she asked herself, as the lamps illuminated the rows of gloomy portraits impaled on the walls. In truth, she had not given this marriage a moment's serious thought. Since Sir Michael's death, her whole being had been focused on Lucy. *It's too late to worry about it now,* she thought wryly as a manservant ushered her into Hugh's sitting room. *There stands my liege lord stripped of his regalia, and an expectant look on his face.*

"Thank God that's over," Hugh said, smiling and beckoning her to join him by the fire. "Care for some wine?"

Faith shook her head.

"Cat got your tongue?" he teased.

Her heart began hammering against her chest. "No . . . I just feel a bit strange, that's all."

"Then we'd best get you to bed," he whooped, sweeping her into his arms and charging into the next room. "There you are," he declared, dumping her unceremoniously on the bed and divesting her of the cloak.

"I didn't mean I was unwell," she protested. "It's just that this whole day has been strange. Those ferocious people in their furs and tartans, ranting and raving and stomping about. Even you looked like a wild barbarian . . ."

He pushed her down on the pillows and began tearing at the buttons of her nightgown. "I *am* a wild barbarian—and you are my captive slave. Grrhh . . . Arrghh!!"

She squealed, struggling violently. "No! No! Unhand me, you swine, or I shall call the guards and have you thrown into the dungeon with the rats."

"Your struggles are useless m'lady," he muttered, "my men have sealed off the passageways. This castle is mine!"

When Faith awoke, the sun was streaming through the windows, filling the room with brilliant light. Her despondency gone, she sat up and stretched luxuriously. In three weeks the celebrations would be over and she could return to London with Hugh; and while he and James labored over principles and precedents, she and Bill would employ other methods against the enemy.

16
Enter, an Old Knight

Wednesday, March 18, 1789

"Say yes, and on my honor, and on the honor of the battalion, my hand, heart, and blood will be yours for evermore," Watkin Tench avowed as he and Lucy crossed the hospital clearing, heading for the mess.

"For God's sake, Watkin, leave the poor girl alone," John White said as Lucy and Tench took their places at the table. "Can't you see she wants none of you."

"You may be right," Tench replied gloomily. "I just laid my life at her feet and she gave no reply."

Lucy reached for a muffin. "Dear Watkin, I was honored by your gallant words, but my heart is spoken for."

"Don't despair, old chap. Perhaps Lucy's twin sister will look upon you with favor when she arrives in the colony," Tom chuckled.

Tench's mouth gaped open. "Twin sister! Surely you are joking, Tom. There cannot be *two* such beauties walking the earth. Is this true, Lucy?"

At that moment Ralph ran into the tent looking like a shepherd whose flock had just been devoured by wolves. "Oh God, come quickly! We are undone. Oh God! This is the end!"

The doctors jumped to their feet and grabbed their medicine bags. "What's wrong?" Tom cried. "Has someone been killed?"

"Worse than that," bleated the wild-eyed Ralph. "Seven flowers of our battalion have been arrested for robbing the government store. Oh, the shame!"

"Don't be ridiculous," Tench rasped. "It must have been convicts."

"N-no, Watkin, they were marines all right! The commissary discovered a broken key in the door of the store when he arrived for work this morning. When it was identified as Private Hunt's, Hunt confessed and turned King's evidence. Over the past eight months, he and six others have been stealing regularly. The shame of it, that *marines* should do such a thing!''

Tench had paled visibly. ''Are any from my company?''

Ralph shook his head. ''They're all from Captain Campbell's. He is prostrate with grief.''

Following the arrest of the seven marines, speculation rose to fever pitch. Would the Governor keep to his word that anyone caught robbing the provisions stores would be executed, or would the men be spared because they were marines? Most convicts believed Phillip would find an excuse to spare them.

On the twenty-sixth of March, the criminal court sat and the Crown's chief witness, Private Hunt, testified that whenever he or his accomplices had been posted at the store, the others in the gang had robbed it while the man on duty kept watch for the patrol. Fortunately for the colony, Hunt had decided to rob the store alone one evening, but had panicked and turned his key the wrong way in the lock when the patrol had come by.

The jury pardoned Hunt but sentenced the six others to hang. Phillip refused clemency and at ten o'clock the next morning they were executed between the two storehouses they had so often plundered.

As the last drum roll faded, a dense silence settled over the scene. Many in the ranks of the dishonored battalion wept openly and the convicts, most of whom had arrived in a festive mood, stood with bowed heads. Although the six died bravely, Lucy saw nothing noble in their demise. Her heart went out to the Governor, who looked drawn and gray. Plainly, the burden of office hung heavily on him.

Faith gazed around her in wonder as she and Bill proceeded up the Strand. There were butchers, bakers, cabinetmakers, clockmakers, cobblers, chandlers, and countless others. The noise was deafening. People crammed the doorways and footpaths, pickpockets rubbed shoulders with lords, dockers mingled with magistrates, lackeys jostled ladies—and in the gutters muffin boys, shoeshiners, kidney-piemen, and oyster vendors fought over prime positions for their stands.

''We should of gone up Chancery Lane!'' shouted Bill.

"We have plenty of time," Faith assured him and returned to her delighted scrutiny of the passing parade.

Eventually, they arrived at Red Lion Square in Holborn and took cover in a lane directly opposite the entrance to Ruth Gamble's cheese monger. "You are *sure* she will come today?" Faith asked for the tenth time.

"She'll be here," Bill said cheerfully as he checked the square for Runners.

Soon afterward, a carriage rumbled into the square and drew up outside the cheese monger's.

"Watch for my signal," said Faith, removing her cloak and bonnet and handing them to Bill as Ruth alit and entered the shop.

"Coast's clear," said Bill. "Off you go."

She crossed the square to the cheese monger's window and saw Ruth at the rear of the shop. Faith spread out her arms and pressed her face against the glass, willing Ruth to look. A moment later she turned and glanced toward the window. She gave a bloodcurdling shriek, turned as white as snow, fell back against the shelves, then slid to the floor with cheese tumbling all about her.

Faith signaled Bill and they raced away. But they need not have hurried for the woman lying in a swoon on the cheese monger's floor was quite beyond pursuit. In fact, it took the nonplussed proprietor five minutes to rouse her.

Faith and Bill went to the nearest landing and hired a waterman to row them to Downing Street.

"What next?" Bill asked after helping the waterman shove off.

Faith donned her cloak and tightened the ribbons of her bonnet against the wind. "James Geldie's agents have failed to locate Lucy's former abigail, Julie Ryan, so your friend Ned is my last hope. Question him about her, Bill, but remember that we can't afford to arouse his suspicions, we need him for other things."

"Madam's been tippling something awful," Ned confided to Bill later that week as they sat drinking in a corner booth of the Red Boar. "Last night, she called me a shallow-brained churl and cuffed me in front of Elsie."

Bill pricked his ears. "Who's Elsie?"

"Madam's personal maid, and a more loose-mouthed tart you'd never find. She blabbed to the rest of the staff and I've had nothing but sly titters ever since. It's bad for me image, lad. I wish madam had let go of Elsie instead of Julie. Julie was a peach."

"Who's Julie?" Bill asked with studied casualness.

Ned slurped ale from his tankard. "Miss Lucy's maid."

"Were she a good 'un then, Neddy?"

"The bloomin' best, lad. Had a smart head on her shoulders and a tight mouth to boot. You wouldn't catch *her* blabbing, not Julie. I had plans for her, I did. Pretty as a petal she was."

"If she were such a good 'un, Neddy, why was she let go?"

"Madam an' Julie had a falling out." Ned's eyes narrowed. "Here, what's it to you, lad?"

Bill shrugged. "Nothing in particular, 'cepting my lady's on the lookout for an abigail, and if I found her a good 'un, she'd as like give me a handsome tip—which I'd be bound to split with my friend Ned." He gave Ned a conspiratorial wink.

Ned's melancholy features twitched into something resembling a smile. "Oh, I gets your drift, lad. Well, Julie's as prime as they come, but madam didn't want her around after Miss Lucy got took, so she sent her packing."

Bill nodded sagely. "That were the way of it, eh? Where'll I find her then, Ned?"

Ned scratched his head. "Couldn't rightly say, lad. But Mother Barret, the old-clothes woman might know—she and Julie was friends. Tell you what, next time the old bag comes by the house I'll ask her, if you like."

When Hugh awoke on Friday morning, Faith's side of the bed was empty. He found her in the parlor standing by the window. "You're up early, dearest."

She sighed. "I am unwell, my love."

He carried her into the next room and put her gently on the bed. "Lie there and rest. I shall have the doctor fetched."

Unable to look him in the eye, she turned her face to the pillow. "It's women's troubles, dearest. Doctors are useless at such times . . ."

A look of utter helplessness spread over Hugh's face. He sat down gingerly on the edge of the bed. "Would some smelling salts help, perhaps?"

Faith felt wretched for deceiving Hugh, but her determination did not falter. She needed time alone tomorrow night and this was the only way. "No thank you, dearest. I am afraid you'll have to go down to Billingsley alone, though. I could not abide all that bumping and jolting . . ."

"Of course not. We'll postpone our trip until next weekend."

Faith turned and gave him a tragic look. "But Hugh, we are expected."

"I will not leave you alone when you are unwell," he said firmly.

Wincing, Faith struggled to a sitting position. "Very well, dearest, I'll make the effort. There may be a letter from Lucy at the Hall . . ." She clutched her stomach and gasped. "Oh, I am so distraught. Here it is almost May and we are no closer to obtaining Lucy's pardon. What am I to do?" She held out her hand. "Help me up, dearest, I-I feel a little dizzy . . ."

He pressed her down on the pillows. "Stay there, darling, I'll go alone. You're right, a ship from New South Wales may have arrived in Portsmouth."

The following afternoon, while Faith was going over last minute plans with Bill, the landlord came to announce that Sir George Rose waited below. Bill slipped away to his attic room, and shortly afterward the landlord ushered the scarlet-faced Sir George into the parlor.

"Do sit down, Sir George," urged Faith, helping her grandfather's friend settle his ample person in a comfortable chair by the fire, and relieving him of his cane. "You look utterly done in. Those stairs are very steep."

Too out of breath to speak, Sir George mopped his brow with a huge red handkerchief and gazed at her fondly until he recovered. "Faith, m'dear—as lovely as ever. How delightful! Had the devil's own task tracking you down, the devil's own. Received a letter from Arthur the other day. Came by way of the Cape. *Sirius,* you know, sent there for provisions. Sink me if a damned Dutch merchantman didn't deliver it to our ambassador in The Hague. Arthur has explained everything, m'dear—*everything.* Damned shameful business. Don't know what got into your grandfather. Twin sister. By jove. All those years and not a word. Damned bounder!"

Faith's heart skipped a beat. "A letter from Captain Phillip? Oh, Sir George, did he mention Lucy?"

The Undersecretary of the Treasury withdrew a package from

his jacket pocket. "*Mention* her? My dear, he spoke of nothing else. Here you are, she's written a dozen letters."

Faith tore open the first letter and began reading it avidly, but after a while an empty, desperate feeling came over her and tears welled up in her eyes. "She sounds so happy and full of hope. Oh what am I to do? I'm having the greatest difficulty obtaining her pardon . . ." She shook her head unable to go on.

"There, there," he said, patting her hand consolingly. "Sir George is here now, and he will do all in his power to help you. First I must meet with your lawyers at their earliest convenience. Can you arrange it?"

"I no longer have any faith in the law," she sobbed, and told him about the appeal.

He squeezed her hand and looked thoughtful. "Tell you what, m'dear, I'm seeing the Prime Minister this afternoon. I'll speak to him about Lucy."

"Oh, Sir George, would you?" she gasped.

"You may count on it," he declared. "And there are others we can call on if need be. No reason to despair, m'dear." He glanced at his timepiece and struggled to his feet. "Must leave now. Expected at Westminster by two."

"Thank you for bringing me Lucy's letters." Faith handed over his cane and walked with him to the door. "I am so very grateful."

"No trouble at all, m'dear. Is there any other way I can be of service . . . ?"

"There *is* one thing, Sir George. Although Hugh and I have visited the Admiralty several times, no one there seems to know when the first ships are sailing for New South Wales."

Sir George chuckled. "Wish questions in the House were that easy to answer. Two vessels are presently being outfitted down at Woolwich—a transporter and a man-of-war. They leave for New South Wales some time in July."

"July!" Faith cried in dismay. "I'll never secure a pardon for Lucy by then."

"Nothing is impossible," said the portly keeper of the public purse, looking skeptically at the stairs. "I left my card on the table, m'dear. Send a message as soon as you make that appointment with your lawyer. And remember, chin up."

271

17
May 1789

"Land! Close under our lee!"

The officers on the bridge turned and saw a rocky headland with the sea smashing violently against it.

"Wear her round to westward and set the reefed mainsail!" Hunter shouted. He had no idea what dangerous ledges lay under the boiling sea. They'd not seen sun or stars in seven days and, consequently, no observations had been taken. With the sea running mountainously high and the prospect of another dark night ahead, their position was perilous.

He glanced at the strained faces of his officers. Like himself, they had not slept in twenty-four hours. "Nothing for it, gentlemen, but to crowd on every yard of canvas and order every spare hand to the pumps. . . ."

However, when another steep cliff loomed in the dying light, Hunter studied it intently then smiled for the first time in days. "It's Tasman's Head, gentlemen. I'd know it anywhere. We're on the eastern point of Storm Bay."

Michael joined in the cheering. The homeward stretch at last—not long now.

Lucy shivered and lowered the spyglass. Although the weather was fine, a bitter wind was sweeping the flat summit of the hill. Listlessly, she raised the glass again. A speck of white popped up on the horizon. She blinked, unable to believe she was seeing a ship, after all this time.

Was it Faith or Michael?

Trembling with excitement, she watched it move in through the heads and work up the harbor toward Sydney Cove. Low in the water, laboring, tattered and torn, the old lady came limping home.

With tears rolling down her cheeks, Lucy scrambled down from the tree and descended the hill on winged feet. "It's *Sirius*!" she cried, sprinting into the mess. "I saw her from the hill. Michael is home at last!"

The entire settlement gathered on the foreshores as the battered old ship slipped into the cove and dropped anchor beside

Supply. The longboat was lowered and as it began pulling toward the Governor's Wharf, Lucy caught up her skirts and ran.

Michael was so intent on Lucy's progress, he did not hear Captain Hunter addressing him until Bradley gave him a sharp nudge in the ribs.

"Keep the pumps going, Lieutenant Perryman. It would not do to leave them idle overnight. . . ."

"Yes, sir," he acknowledged, his eyes never leaving Lucy who had joined the crowd at the other end of the wharf. Then he was out of the boat and moving toward her. She was even lovelier than he remembered . . . tall and fine, with that dark hair whipping about her face.

Lucy could only stand and stare. He had lost weight and there was a look, almost of pain, in his eyes as they locked with hers. He smiled as he drew level, then he was gone, moving up the slope with the other *Sirius* men to where Phillip waited to greet them on the veranda of Government House.

"Oh, for heaven's sake, give it here." Beth snatched the comb and raked it through Lucy's wild locks as they put the finishing touches to their toilets. "Are you sure this apron looks all right? It's the only clean one I've got. Oh, I can't wait to hear the news. For all we know England could have sunk to the bottom of the sea."

"Calm yourself, Bethy, and give me back the comb, you're pulling the hair from my head," Lucy admonished smilingly.

Beth giggled. "Don't you play cool and collected with me, Lucy Gamble. Your cheeks are positively *glowing.*"

Unable to endure the waiting any longer, Lucy slipped across to the east side, walked along the road as far as the commissary's house and stood in the shadows by the garden wall watching the entrance to Government House.

Soon afterward, Michael appeared on the veranda and came walking along the path toward the bridge. She waited until he was abreast of her then stepped out in front of him.

"Hello, Michael."

He stopped in his tracks, his eyes devouring her.

"I wanted to see you first," she said softly.

He clasped her to him, covering her face, her shoulders, her throat with wild kisses. At first his need was so great he thought he would drown, but gradually the fever in his brain cleared and he drew back a little.

"Welcome home," she said breathlessly.

He groaned and buried his face in her hair.

Although Lucy submitted willingly, she was nevertheless relieved when the sound of laughter brought him to his senses. The other *Sirius* officers had gathered on Phillip's veranda and were bidding him good night.

"We'd better go," she whispered, her lips and face stinging from his kisses. "Everyone's waiting for you at the mess . . ."

"I can't see anyone tonight," he said fiercely, pressing her to him again.

"But you have to, Michael. Oh, my love, you must. They are all longing to hear your news. John has opened a cask of his finest mead and Beth is beside herself with excitement."

"Damn John, damn Beth. I want *you*!"

"I want you, too," she said quickly. "But the others would be hurt if we went off without a word. Please, Michael, please, darling . . ."

"All right, my love," he sighed. "I dare say John's mead must be tasted to be believed."

Lucy was taking a cinnamon loaf from the oven when Michael and some sailors from *Sirius* arrived the following evening with three heavy sea chests.

"What's in them?" she demanded as the men, puffing and heaving, deposited their load.

Smiling widely, Michael set about undoing the padlocks and chains. "Take a look, everything's yours."

Opening the chests was like exploring a treasure cave. There was a kettle fitted with an ingenious contrivance that allowed boiling water to be poured without removing the kettle from the fire; two ornate firedogs; a cast-iron backing plate for the fire; bolts of material; spices, perfume, soap, and other exotic toiletries; lace handkerchiefs, caps, aprons, shifts, petticoats, and nightgowns; books; a sewing box with dozens of colored threads; two wigs, curlers, combs; silk scarfs, bracelets, and earrings; a chess set, even silver candlesticks—but most exciting of all were the ready-made dresses.

She disappeared into her bedroom and slipped on a green velvet gown. "Oh, I love it!" she exclaimed, returning to the parlor and twirling around.

He surveyed the dress critically. "It's too big, but the color is perfect."

"Oh, Michael, I am so happy."

He took her in his arms. "Since making you happy is my main aim in life, I'm well satisfied. Now, darling, have you still got those crystal glasses? I purchased a case of fine French champagne in Capetown and I've brought a bottle for us to sample."

After eating, they sat on a blanket in front of the fire, sipping the champagne. "Beth will be overjoyed with her presents," Lucy said, spreading the green dress carefully around her so it would not crush.

He grinned. "I half expected her to be here tonight."

"She is at Cable's practicing for the play."

"Play?"

"We convicts have decided to perform *The Recruiting Officer* on His Majesty's birthday. Beth is Silvia, Bob Sidaway is magnificent as the rascally Sergeant Kite . . . and guess who I am?"

"I have no idea."

"Why, Lucy the maid, of course!" She gave an uncustomary giggle. "And Moses—oh Lord, Moses is the clown, Bullick."

Michael guffawed. "I don't believe it."

"It's true," she gurgled. "He was absolutely horrified when I suggested it, but after much persuasion he agreed. Now, he's the star of the show. Oh, Michael, he is so serious, he's funny." She burst into another fit of giggles.

She was so happy and lighthearted, she was positively radiant. It was heaven to be with her again after the long, dreary months at sea.

"John asked the Governor if we could use his old canvas house and Phillip not only agreed, but insisted on attending."

Michael put another log on the fire and filled their glasses once more. "Did you hear what happened to *Friendship,* darling?"

"No, but I hope she's in England by now, and that Faith has my letters."

"I'm afraid not. Shortland, the Agent, arrived at the Cape just as we were leaving. Apparently, *Friendship* and *Alexander* took seven months to reach Batavia and, by then, their crews were so reduced by scurvy only four men were capable of setting sails, so Shortland scuttled *Friendship.*"

Lucy burst into tears. "Oh no, how could he? The poor, brave little ship."

Taken aback by her reaction, Michael embraced her and tried to comfort her. "Shorthand had no choice, darling, there just weren't enough men to sail two ships. But you'll be pleased to hear he has undertaken to personally deliver your letters to Faith at Billingsley Hall."

This information produced a fresh spate of tears. "Oh no! I couldn't bear it if Faith was *still* in England."

The reason for her strange behavior suddenly came to Michael. His coolheaded, logical Lucy had absolutely no head for champagne. He lifted her to her feet and wrapped a shawl around her shoulders. "Let's take a stroll along the beach to our favorite spot, darling. It's a little stuffy in here, don't you think?"

She nodded tearfully. "Yes, my head does feel fuzzy. I hope I'm not sickening for something . . ."

18
Scotty Meets Lucy

Saturday, June 20, 1789

"Murder is killing with malice intent; manslaughter is killing in the course of a sudden affray," Lord Marsfield informed those gathered in James Geldie's chambers.

"Malice intent is not easy to define, sir, and even harder to prove," said Lord Worthington, eminent lawyer, member of the House of Lords and friend of Sir George Rose. "In fact, sir, malice intent can only be implied from the *exact* circumstances surrounding a killing. In Lucy Gamble's case, the facts point to malice intent because she loaded the pistol prior to the killing. Moreover, a sudden affray, if *unprovoked* by the deceased, can be murderous. In Lucy Gamble's case, both eye witnesses saw the deceased kneeling unarmed and wounded before Lucy Gamble immediately before she fired the fatal shot."

James Geldie nodded sagely. "While I agree that the borderline distinction between murder and manslaughter continues to give difficulty, my Lord, I believe there is insufficient proof of malice intent in Lucy Gamble's case. What was her motive? After all, she was betrothed to the deceased."

"Lucy was *not* betrothed to Richard Newport, gentlemen, nor did she lie in wait for him with a loaded pistol and malice intent. She shot him in defence of her person after he had raped her and tried to strangle her," said Faith coldly.

"Quite so, m'dear," said Sir George. "However, we are discussing the highest points of justice here, today—"

Faith rose. "To my way of thinking, *certainty* should be the highest point of justice. And as it is certain that Lucy is innocent, I have decided there will be no manslaughter appeal. Lucy deserves a full pardon and, by God, that is what she will have. Good day to you, gentlemen." She snatched up her parasol and swept from the room.

When Hugh returned to their lodgings, Faith saw immediately that he was very angry with her.

"Your childish outburst was most uncalled for, madam. Lucy's cause will not be furthered by offending such powerful men as Lord Marsfield and Lord Worthington. Their opinions are vitally important."

"What of my opinions, Hugh. Are they not important also?"

"Yes, of course," he began impatiently but she held up her hand for silence, then indicated the chair opposite.

"Excuse me, Hugh, but I think you had better sit down and listen to what I have to say."

He sat down and folded his arms. "Go ahead."

"Remember that day at the Hall, when I said that Ruth Gamble would not change her evidence unless we forced her to do so?"

"Yes."

"I warned you then that I was not interested in honor or ethics where Lucy's freedom was concerned; but when you insisted that the only way to acquire justice for Lucy was through the law, I acceded to your wishes. Now, a year and a half later, with the first ships about to leave for New South Wales, we are no closer to acquiring Lucy's pardon. And today, those honorable, ethical men as much as told me the best Lucy can expect from the law is a reduced sentence for manslaughter. Well, damn that! From now on, I revert to my original plan."

"And what is your original plan, pray?"

"To frighten that bitch and her slimy manservant out of their wits."

She held his gaze unflinchingly but swallowed hard. "I know this will come as a shock. The fact is, I have deceived you on a number of occasions lately . . ."

"What am I to do with you?" he asked helplessly when she had finished.

"You could give me your support."

"Support? So you intend to continue this vendetta?"

"I do, I must—until one or both of them break."

Remembering how resolute his wife had looked the day she had declared she desired only two things—Lucy's pardon and to be reunited with her as soon as possible—for the first time in his life, Hugh was afraid. She seemed to be moving beyond his reach. Devastated, he bowed his head. "I don't understand what you are doing, Fae, and I do not enjoy being deceived."

Faith sank to her knees before him. "I did not relish deceiving you, dearest, you must believe that. But Lucy is my heart, the core of my being. I will do anything to set her free—anything."

Still feeling the deadness of loss, he looked at her. "Will you promise to be honest with me in the future?"

She clasped her hands. "I promise, my darling. I'll even swear it on your sacred Stewart dirk if you wish."

A ghost of a smile played at the corners of Hugh's mouth. "No need for that, Fae, your promise is enough. Very well, I shall support you."

"Thank you, Hugh," she whispered and kissed him ardently.

He drew her onto his lap and held her to him, filled with relief that the danger was past. Although he would cede to no man, deep in his heart he knew that if he ever forced Faith to choose between him and Lucy, he would be the loser. He had no choice but to give in.

After a while he released her. "Now, perhaps you should tell me exactly what you have done to Ruth Gamble and her manservant. I want to be prepared if the Runners arrive on our doorstep with a warrant for your arrest."

Since circulating Julie Ryan's description throughout London, Faith had been inundated with callers but, so far, nothing substantial had come to light.

She tried to concentrate on the proposed visit to Grosvenor Square that evening but her eyes kept filling with tears, and in the end she rested her head in her arms and wept.

When Hugh returned to their lodgings and saw the six sea chests that Faith had been lovingly filling for months, he realized what was wrong. Tomorrow the sea chests would go aboard the convict transporter, *Lady Juliana*. "Don't cry, darling," he murmured. "You have done your best."

She looked up at him with agony in her eyes. "I should be on that ship, Hugh. You don't know, you just don't know what it's like for Lucy and me."

He took her face in his hands. "Tell me, Fae. Don't leave me dangling on the edge of your life, it is destroying me."

The tears rolled down her cheeks. "I cannot put it into words . . ."

"Try, Fae. *Please.*"

Faith's eyes took on a far away look and when she spoke her voice was soft and low. "She waits for me on a high place, Hugh. Sometimes it is green, sometimes gold, sometimes gray. And always, there is the wind. She sings to me on the wind, Hugh, such loving songs. And her eyes search the sea for me, back and forth, back and forth. While I strive, she waits. And her waiting is the harder."

At last Hugh felt that he understood the depth of her commitment. "I love you," he whispered, emotion making his voice hoarse. "And . . . I love your sweet Lucy."

Faith pressed his hand to her heart. "We love you, too, Scotty."

Thump. Thump. Thump!

The sound hovered on the edge of Ned's consciousness, persistent and relentless, until it finally roused him.

Muttering, he lit the candle, pulled on his gown and shuffled from the room. Things had gone from bad to worse in this house. The mistress was a raving tyrant; those tarts Elsie and Cook were smart mouthing him at every turn and now this—a bloomin' caller in the middle of the night.

"Quiet, you mongrel," he snarled at the grandfather clock as he passed. "Hold your horses!" he shouted, slipping the bolt and flinging open the door. "Who the—"

He got no further. Standing before him, face as white as death and hair blowing all about her, was Miss Lucy Gamble.

Ned slammed the door so hard the house shook on its foundations. Then, howling, he fled upstairs to his room, dived under the bedcovers and shook so violently that the bed rattled like a skeleton dancing a hornpipe.

"Open this door you jibbering jobbernowl!" Ruth Gamble's voice penetrated his hysteria.

Ned ducked his head out from beneath the blankets. "A-are you alone, madam?"

"No, Elsie and Cook are with me. Your screams would awaken the dead!"

"The *dead*! Oh, don't say it, madam. D-don't even think it!"

"Stop your blubbering and open up!" Ruth shrieked, attacking the door with her fists.

Reluctantly, he left the bed and sidled to the door.

"It were Miss Lucy, madam!"

"W-what did you say, Ned?"

"It were Miss Lucy," he repeated as he let her into the room.

Ruth sank into a chair. "Are you sure?"

He placed shaking hands to twitching face. "Yes, m-madam . . . and this is the second time I've seen her. She came at me in the park the other night. She means to do us in, madam." Ruth's fingers plucked nervously at her throat. "Go downstairs and see if she's still there, Ned. And on your way back fetch me a bottle of brandy."

"I ain't going near that door!" he shouted.

Ruth looked at him with hatred. She longed to dismiss him but she did not dare. "Oh, all right you craven coward. I'll send Elsie."

"Elsie won't see her—even if she is still there."

"What do you mean by that?" Ruth asked, puzzled.

"My friend Bill was standing next to her the other night and he couldn't see nothing!"

She looked at him suspiciously. "What *are* you babbling about, you fool?"

Ned rolled his eyes. "She's a specter, that one. She cursed me and threw witch's dust in my face."

"Had you and your friend been drinking?"

"Not so as *you* would notice," he muttered.

Ruth clicked her tongue with exasperation. "Ghosts don't appear in broad daylight, you idiot. I saw her in the middle of the day at the cheese monger's. No, she must have escaped from transportation, in which case, we have nothing to fear. In fact, the next time she pays us a visit I'll call down the Runners on her."

"That won't do no good," he said gloomily. "She's for us, that one. You mark my words, madam."

Two days later, Ruth came across an article in the "Home News" section of *The Lady's Magazine*. It was titled "The Biographical Memoirs of Lieutenant John Shortland, R.N.," and described that officer's perilous adventures in New South Wales. She read it several times, then rang for Ned. "Get your coat, you buffoon, we're going out."

Lieutenant Shortland looked up from his book as his manservant entered the room. "Yes, George?"

"Mistress Gamble, widow of the late Captain Gamble, former commander of *Seahawk*, is waiting without, sir."

"Gamble, you say? Now where have I heard that name before? Did she state her business, George?"

"No, sir, but she insists it is a matter of the utmost urgency."

"Then you had better show her in," declared Shortland and plagued his mind with the name, Gamble, until the bearer of the title entered, dragging Ned behind her.

"How do you do, Mistress Gamble," said Shortland. "I am afraid you have me at a disadvantage. I can't recall where we met . . ."

"We have never met, sir," she said sharply. "I have come about my stepdaughter who was transported to New South Wales two years ago."

"Oh, I see. How very unfortunate for you. Please accept my commiserations."

"Commiserations are not in order, sir, the creature murdered my brother. My great regret is that they did not hang her, and therefore, I want to know why the authorities allowed her to escape."

"Surely you are mistaken, madam?" said Shortland, somewhat taken aback by her belligerent manner.

"Indeed, I am not mistaken, sir! Both my servant and I have seen her on numerous occasions."

Shortland frowned. "To the best of my knowledge, madam, only one woman has ever absconded from Sydney Cove. A few days after we disembarked, she ran into the woods and was never sighted again. We thought she had perished, but I suppose she could have secured a passage on one of the French ships anchored in Botany Bay . . ."

Ruth leaned forward eagerly. "What was her name?"

"I cannot recall, madam."

"Well, you may not remember Lucy's name, sir, but you would certainly remember her. She is very comely with masses of dark hair and green eyes."

"Lucy Gamble!" Shortland exclaimed, connecting the name at last. "Why, of course . . . Lucy Gamble."

Ruth shot a triumphant look at Ned. "Then she *did* escape?"

Shortland laughed. "Good God, no! The escapee was an old offender—a Scot, I believe. Nurse Gamble works at the colony hospital. As a matter of fact I stopped at Lyndhurst on my way to London. Had some letters for her—" He broke off as Ned collapsed in a heap on the floor.

"Ned's wearing so many signals and amulets, he looks like a bloomin' gypsy," Bill informed Faith and Hugh on his return from the house at Grosvenor Square.

"Apparently, your plan is succeeding, Fae," said Hugh.

Faith, however, was disquietened by Bill's report. "Ruth's visit to Shortland could have been disastrous. I am sure he was the naval officer who called at the Hall last week with those letters from Lucy."

Hugh frowned. "Yes, I believe you are right. Though he obviously did not mention that or she would not be in her present frame of mind."

"Nevertheless, I think we should implement the next part of my plan immediately. With more ships due to arrive from the colony, who knows what other information may leak out." She turned to Bill. "Were you able to get the layout of the house?"

The pickpocket assured her he had, and after being furnished with pen and paper, drew a detailed sketch.

Faith studied the diagram intently. "Where is Ruth's bedchamber?"

"Why do you need to know that?" Hugh asked suspiciously.

"You're a hunter, Hugh, what do you do after you have cornered a fox?"

"I close in for the—Fae, just what are you planning?"

"Tonight, I shall close in for the kill," she answered softly.

"Oh Gord! You ain't gonna knock 'er off, are you, Miss Faith?" croaked Bill.

Faith patted his arm reassuringly. "Only in a manner of

speaking, Bill. However, by the time I have finished with Ruth Gamble tonight, she will realize she has no safe sanctuary."

Hugh was dismayed. "How do you expect to further Lucy's cause by frightening the woman to death?"

"I won't frighten her to death, Hugh. In fact, after I have laid the curse on her, I will offer her a way out of her predicament."

Hugh rose and began pacing the floor. "Curse her? Fae, what can you be thinking of? You may have fooled her half-witted servant with such twaddle but Ruth Gamble is an educated woman, she'd never taken in by it."

"I disagree," Faith said calmly. "Ruth Gamble grew up in North Yorkshire, a region steeped in medieval superstition."

"I think your plan is reckless in the extreme, Fae."

Faith sighed. "I agree the plan is reckless, Hugh, but, despite Ruth's performance in court, I believe she can be rattled—her reaction to me proves it. Also, she has been drinking heavily and that is bound to have muddled her mind. Please, you must let me try this . . ."

Hugh thought her plan absurd. However, even if he forbade her to go ahead with it he very much doubted she would comply. "Very well," he muttered. "But I shall accompany you."

Bill squared his shoulders. "Count me in too, Miss Faith."

"With two such able accomplices, how can I fail. Now, let's put our heads together and compose a suitable curse."

Hugh watched with trepidation as Faith worried the lock on the rear door of Grosvenor Square. A moment later, when a telltale click sounded, she planted a chalky kiss on his cheek and with a whispered, "Keep a sharp lookout, Scotty," followed Bill inside.

They crept to the front of the house then went their separate ways—Bill to lock Elsie and Cook in their rooms, and Faith, up the stairs to Ruth's chambers.

As she ascended, she looked about her with interest. How silent and sad was her father's house—as if all the love had drained out of it. "Don't fret, house," she whispered, patting the river sand and moss in her cloak pockets. "We Gambles will soon be back."

She slipped along the corridor and placed an ear against the third door in the right. Satisfied no one was moving about, she entered the room and crept to the bed.

Ruth Gamble lay on her back fast asleep, her mouth gaping open and a faint snore issuing from the depths of her throat.

Eyes narrowed, Faith stared at the woman responsible for Lucy's suffering. On the bedside table was an empty brandy bottle and a plate sporting a half-eaten sausage. Supper, no doubt.

She bent over Ruth and shook her shoulder. "Wake up."

Ruth turned her head from side to side and mumbled.

Faith shook her again. "Wake up!"

Ruth opened her eyes, saw the white-faced specter of Lucy swaying in front of her, and sprang up with a strangled scream.

Faith removed the moss from her pocket and said in a deep, singsong voice:

> Bullock blood,
> Hag-worm head,
> Graveyard moss
> To feed the dead.
> Cursed by ye
> Whose lying ways
> Have brought despair
> Upon my days!
> May doom, destruction
> Debasement and woe
> Dog your footsteps
> Wherever you go!

She tossed the moss into Ruth's lap. Ruth opened and closed her mouth like a fish with hiccups. Good, thought Faith, I have her attention. Now for the *pièce de résistance*. She took two handfuls of sand and raised her arms dramatically.

> Harken, Ruth Gamble
> Listen and learn
> Truth's word alone
> This curse will turn.
> Heed me, you harpy,
> Mark my words well,
> Confess your sins
> Or burn in hell!

She tossed the sand at Ruth who flailed her arms, gave a choking shriek and fell back against the pillows in a swoon.

After retrieving the moss, Faith made her way quickly downstairs to the first floor and joined Bill outside Ned's room. "Servants secured, Bill?"

He nodded. "Doubt they heard anything. Mistress Gamble hardly made a sound."

Faith slid her drag into the crack and sprung the lock. "I know, but there's no telling what this hero will do." She stepped inside, walked to the bed and shook Ned's shoulder. "Wake up, Ned."

The manservant awoke in an instant and was so overcome with terror at the sight of Faith, that he collapsed before she uttered a word of the curse.

"We'll give them a day or so, then if they don't come forward of their own volition, I'll go to Grosvenor Square and spout some intimidating legal jargon at them," Hugh promised Faith next morning at breakfast. "In the meantime, I'll set someone to watching the house. We can't have the woman running off to her father in Pickering."

They glanced up as the landlord's daughter arrived with the tea and a letter from Scotland, which Hugh opened straight away. "It's Father," he said grimly. "He has suffered a severe apoplexy attack and his condition is grave. Mother wants us to return to Carrigmoor immediately."

"Oh, how terrible," Faith groaned, her heart sinking with dismay. "Poor Uncle Colin."

Hugh drew her to her feet. "I'll leave for Scotland today, darling, but you must remain in London. Now you have run your fox to ground, you cannot allow her to burrow out of her hole."

"Hugh dearest, I am so sorry . . ."

He sighed. "Leaving you will be difficult, Fae, but I understand your bond with Lucy and I admire the single-minded way you have gone about securing her pardon. Perhaps if I'd listened to you in the beginning, we would be sailing to New South Wales with her pardon by now. Can you ever forgive me?"

"Forgive *you*?" She wound her arms around his neck and kissed him tenderly. "It is I who should ask your forgiveness. I have embarrassed you before your legal colleagues, and deceived you when you deserved honesty. I fear you have made a bad bargain in a wife."

He hugged her tightly. "Nonsense, my darling. You have made me happier than any man deserves to be. Just get the pardon, and come home to me posthaste."

19
Julie Ryan

Monday, September 7, 1789

"Miss Lucy!" The young woman let go her toddler's hand and flung her arms around Faith.

Noticing that the child was about to launch himself into eternity from the top of the stairs, Faith disengaged herself, yanked him inside and slammed the door. "May I have your name?" she enquired politely of the young woman.

"Miss Lucy," the young woman sobbed. "Oh, Miss Lucy, *dear,* I'd given you up for lost."

Faith led her distracted visitor to a chair and tried to explain. "Actually, I am Lucy's twin sister, Faith Stewart . . ."

With a look of bewilderment the young woman sank into the chair, whereupon the toddler, who had been demolishing the room, sprang onto her lap. Convinced that nothing would be accomplished until the child was removed, Faith summoned the landlord's daughter and paid her to take him walking in the park. Then she turned back to the young woman. "Let me explain," she said gently. "While I may look like Lucy, I assure you, I am not she. . . . But, tell me, are you Julie Ryan?"

Julie smiled. "It's me all right, Miss Lucy. A bit the worse for wear, but times have been hard since that terrible night."

"You are Julie!" Faith exclaimed. "Oh, Julie my dear, I have been searching for you forever."

Julie glanced at her anxiously. "What did they do to you in that prison, you poor lamb?"

Although Julie took some convincing, she finally accepted Faith. "It's a miracle," she said softly. "You're identical in every way, even your eyelashes curl up at the ends like Miss Lucy's. No one could ever tell you apart. I ought to know, I looked after Miss Lucy for years and I can't see even a strand of hair that's different."

"Tell me about Richard Newport," said Faith, reluctantly turning the conversation to more serious matters.

Julie set her teacup on the saucer with a clatter. "Do we have to talk about *him*?"

"I am afraid so. You want to help Lucy, don't you?"

"Oh yes, of course. It's just that thinking about him . . . well it brings back the bad memories like." Julie stiffened in the chair and wrung her hands nervously. "From the beginning, Richard was after Miss Lucy—ogling her and brushing against her. At first she were polite, seeing he was madam's brother, but when he started cornering her and laying his hands on her, she gave him a piece of her mind and said she'd have the Captain toss him out on his ear. After that, whenever Richard spoke to her, Miss Lucy just cut him dead."

"Did Ruth Gamble notice anything amiss between them?"

"She would have been blind not to. Just as she would have been blind not to notice what he did to me."

Faith raised her eyebrows. "To you, Julie?"

"One morning madam told me to take a clean shirt and a pitcher of water to his room. When I arrived he was standing by the water basin with nought to cover his nakedness but a shirt. He looked repulsive with his thick lips all slobbering wet and his eyes blood red from drink . . . ." She shuddered. "He ordered me to unbutton his shirt cuffs and pour water over his hands. I got the buttons undone, but when I tried to pour the water, I was shaking so much I spilled it down his shirt."

She paused and bit her lip. "He called me filthy names and cuffed me so hard my head almost fell off. Then he threw me on the bed and raped me most brutally. H-he was a cruel, vicious beast. That day I packed my belongings and went looking for Miss Lucy to tell her I was leaving. That's when the man from the Admiralty arrived with the news that the Captain was dead. So I decided to stay on a few days to help Miss Lucy through . . . ."

Julie's eyes filled with tears. "But that night I woke up and . . . oh Lord, Miss Lucy was screaming and Richard was roaring. Next there was a pistol shot and when we ran into Miss Lucy's room—oh, God almighty, what a terrible sight. Miss Lucy was crouching on the bed, her nightgown in tatters and Richard was kneeling at the foot of the bed clutching his side with blood oozing through his fingers." Her lips trembled and she shook her head.

"Go on," Faith prompted gently.

"Miss Lucy dragged herself off the bed and stood looking down at him as if she were in a trance. He called her name and reached out as if he wanted to touch her. She raised the pistol and shot him . . . ." Julie screwed her eyes tight and clenched her fists. "The bullet came out the back of Richard's head and then the room was covered in blood. He fell forward at Miss Lucy's feet and madam threw herself on top of him screaming his name over and over. Ned ran out. And then the people came . . .''

"What people?" asked Faith, now trapped in the horror with Lucy's maid.

"The people from the square. Sailors, harlots, hawkers, gentlemen singing at the tops of their voices—all of them pushing and shoving one another, trying to get a better look. A doctor pronounced Richard dead, but everyone could see that, for he had no head. The Runners arrived and asked questions. No, I think that was later, after I took Miss Lucy to her dressing room and put some clothes on her. Oh God, what a sight she was. Bite marks on her breasts. Throat bruised and bleeding where he must have dug in his nails. There was a lump on her temple and blood on her legs—''

"Please, no more!" Faith cried hoarsely.

As the seconds slipped by, and the world outside the window revolved, they stared at each other with haunted eyes.

John Newport was so deep in thought he hardly noticed the passing parade as the sedan chair moved through London's crowded streets. Five days ago he had received a letter from Ruth filled with references to curses and ghosts. Disturbed by what he had read, he had decided to find out exactly what was going on in Grosvenor Square.

"Here you are, Guv'nor, number twenty-six," said the chairman.

John Newport ascended the steps of James Gamble's elegant residence. When his polite knocks met with no response, he pounded on the door with his cane until a second story window flew open and a young woman stuck out her head.

"Git orf wi' yar. Mistress don't want no callers."

He shook his cane at her threateningly. "Open this door at once!"

The window slammed down and a moment later, another opened on the upper floor. "Is that you, Father?" Ruth cried.

"Yes, daughter."

Shortly afterward the front door opened and Ruth fell into her father's arms.

"Miss Lucy's lawyer and another gentleman are at the front door demanding to see you, madam," Ned exclaimed, bursting into the drawing room of Grosvenor Square later that day.

Ruth sprang from the chair in agitated violence. "Oh Father, Father, what will I do?"

"Stay calm and let me do the talking," John Newport said sternly, and ordered the quivering Ned to show the visitors in.

"Allow me to introduce myself, gentlemen," he said, striding forward with outstretched hand when James Geldie and Sir George Rose entered the room. "I am John Newport, Mistress Gamble's father. Your arrival is most timely; it saves me the trouble of calling on you. Please, be seated."

"We have come here on a most serious matter, sir," said James, disconcerted by the cordiality of their reception.

"Most serious indeed," John Newport responded. "May I speak candidly, gentlemen? I shall come directly to the point. If you assure me that no legal action will be taken against my daughter or her manservant, they will change their statements to the court."

James and Sir George were nonplussed. They had come here expecting to wage battle. "Are you aware of what you have just said, sir?" James asked incredulously.

"I am," John Newport answered solemnly.

"What considerations do you expect in return?" Sir George asked after a long silence.

"None, save the one I have requested—that no perjury charges be brought against them."

"And if we agree to that, they will support Lucy's appeal with affidavits?" asked James.

Newport nodded. "Not only that, *I* shall swear out an affidavit that my son was a liar, a cheat, a dabbler in black magic, and a brutalizer of women."

"Really, sir, I don't know what to say," gasped Sir George.

John Newport pointed to a pile of papers on the mantelpiece. "I have enough evidence of my son's dissolute life to persuade any judge in the realm to reverse the decision against Lucy. You may have it all if you agree to let my daughter go free."

James and Sir George held a hasty conference, then James addressed Newport again. "We will convey your offer to Lucy's representatives and we shall recommend that it be accepted."

"That is wonderful news, gentlemen," declared Newport, "and may I suggest that we exchange discussion or action so that Lucy and her son can be restored as soon as possible to their rightful place in society? She does have a child, my grandson, I believe?"

James cleared his throat. "Unfortunately, the child perished on the voyage to New South Wales."

"Dead." John Newport stared at the barrister with dismay. "That is tragic news, sir. The child would have been the one good legacy of an otherwise worthless life. Richard was the last of the Newport line."

"Then you are unaware that Lucy's abigail, Julie Ryan, also bore him a son?" said James.

Newport's countenance brightened. "Do you think Julie would allow us to see her son? I'd like to offer financial assistance."

James rose and walked toward the door. "She is outside in the carriage, I shall ask her."

When James returned with Julie and the toddler, Ruth rushed forward and knelt before the child. "Look, Father, he is the image of Richard!"

John Newport smiled at Julie. "What is his name?"

"Darian," she replied.

Faith breathed a sigh of relief when Sir George's carriage drew up outside her lodgings. "What happened?" she asked eagerly as everyone filed into the parlor.

"Brandy," gasped a purple-faced Sir George, staggering to the nearest chair. "Brandy, by God!"

"Did Ruth and Ned confess when they saw Julie?" she asked, hastily complying with Sir George's wish.

"Even before," said James and launched into a detailed account of what had occurred at Grosvenor Square.

"Are you certain they will support Lucy's appeal?" she asked apprehensively, hardly able to believe that the battle had been won.

He beamed. "Provided you, as Lucy's representative, promise that she will never bring perjury action against Ruth Gamble or her manservant."

Faith threw back her head and laughed. "What care Lucy or I for them. Let them have their miserable freedom. Oh, wait until Hugh hears this!"

James's smile widened. "John Newport has also agreed that Ruth Gamble will renounce all claims to your father's estate."

"And him and madam were so smitten with Darian, they want to adopt him," said Julie. "Darian took to madam like a bee to honey so I left him with her. It's best for everyone this way. He'll be loved and given all the advantages in life and I won't be reminded of his father every time I look into his eyes . . ."

"So, m'dear, Lucy will have her pardon after all," said Sir George, who had at last regained his breath.

"A *pardon* for Lucy?" she exclaimed. "Oh, how soon?"

The old knight chuckled. "Since time immemorial, kings have been empowered to grant charters of pardon."

"Then you had best seek an audience with His Majesty soon, Sir George," advised James. "For, in my opinion, the legal matters can be settled tomorrow."

20

Enter, the Guardian

Thursday, September 10, 1789

Faith sat in the Billingsley coach watching her father's house in Grosvenor Square. An hour earlier Ned had slunk away, and now John Newport, his daughter, and Darian descended the steps, climbed into a heavily laden carriage and rattled out of the square.

Faith let herself into the house and, ignoring the dust and disarray, ascended to Lucy's room. Like the rest of the house, it was much neglected. Faith drew back the curtains, opened the windows and walked to the dressing table.

As she gazed at her reflection in the mirror, everything blurred, and in the aftermath of the blurring, while the boundaries of her vision hung suspended in time, she penetrated her eyes and moved inward through the corridors of her mind to a misty place at the core of her being.

Suddenly, the mist lifted and she was in a valley filled with fiery craters that bubbled and boiled and rumbled and roared. The sky was black, and screeching carrion birds ripped and tore at the carcasses littering the valley floor. As the birds swooped about her, the sound of their great flapping wings was like the percussion of thunder.

"Prophecy!" cried a voice.

She turned, and standing on a hill beside a tall wooden cross was an old man clutching a broadsword. A thick mane of white hair flew behind him in the wind, snakelike vines writhed and swirled around his body, and his face, illuminated by the fiery glow of the craters, was fearful to behold.

"Who are you?" she asked.

"I am the Guardian," he answered and smote the snow at the foot of the cross. The snow melted and ran in steaming rivulets down the hill into the floor of the valley.

"What do you want of me?"

He pointed to the center of the cross and she saw her name carved on it.

"Prophecy!" cried the Guardian.

> Truth's word will stem the blood.
> Strive then the tie to bind.
> Duty the path to love
> Destiny, child, to find!

Blood spurted from the center of the cross, mingled with the steaming rivulets of snow running down the hill and formed a river of blood that rushed along the floor of the valley. Lying beside the river, face deathly pale, body grotesquely twisted, was a woman with *her* face.

As she turned away from the terrible sight, she realized that she had been in the Valley of Abaddon before—only then, there had been no woman lying beside the river.

A loud clanging sounded in her head, the valley wavered and grew dim and the next thing she knew, she was back in Lucy's room staring into the mirror with the grandfather clock downstairs in the hall chiming midday.

The following evening, after the army of cleaners had departed the house, Faith sat pondering the prophecy of the Guardian while she waited for James and Sir George to return from their audience with the King.

What had the words meant, she wondered. Fragments of former visions floated in and out of her mind: a beautiful conical mountain, the Guide, whose features were hazy like mist, and a baby crying. She was still musing on these things when Bill announced grandly, "Sir George Rose and Mr. James Geldie have come from the Palace to have a chat with you, Miss Faith."

"Please show them in, Bill," she replied.

"Faith, m'dear!" cried Sir George as the men joined her by the fire.

She stared at them anxiously. "Did His Majesty agree to grant Lucy a pardon?"

"Of course, m'dear. Scandalized by the whole business. Wants a thorough investigation—questions in the House, the lot. Utmost sympathy for your sister. Dictated her pardon on the spot. Called the Lord Chief Justice over from Westminster to sign it. Gad, Kenyon's face was the color of puce." Sir George handed her a nondescript piece of parchment containing the appropriate words of freedom and the seal of King George III.

Faith read it, then looked at the men with shining eyes. "This is the happiest hour of my life. My one regret is that Lucy must suffer imprisonment for at least another year." She looked at Sir George with questioning eyes. "Unless the Government intends sending other ships to the colony before the Second Fleet sails next January?"

A look of regret crossed his face. "Afraid not, m'dear. And it will be a miracle if the fleet leaves then. Pity Hugh ain't here, though. His Majesty mentioned tonight that the *Guardian* is still waylaid in Portsmouth."

Faith froze in her chair. The Guardian, giver of the prophecy, the fearful old man of her vision. "But, Sir George, you told me that ship left Woolwich weeks ago!"

"Just so. However, it's been held over while the King and cabinet sorted out land grants for the colony. Dispatches and seals left for Portsmouth today."

Faith jumped up. "Then, there is still a chance?"

"Chance, m'dear?"

"That I can reach the *Guardian* before it sails?"

"Depends when the dispatches get there and whatever the weather is like, I should think—"

"Julie! Bill!" Faith screamed, flinging open the door.

"Blimey! What's the matter?" Bill cried as he and Julie raced into the room.

Faith grasped Julie's arm. "Pack anything of Lucy's and mine that I can use on a long sea voyage. Don't go to any trouble, just pile everything into chests. Bill, hitch the fastest team of horses to the coach, and bring it around the front. Hurry! I want to leave in an hour."

She turned to the stunned men seated by the fire. "Gentlemen, I shall try to make that ship. Sir George, would you write a letter of introduction to the captain of the *Guardian*?"

"This is madness, m'dear," blustered Sir George. "You, a gentlewoman, sailing alone to an uncivilized land full of savages and felons. I will not allow it!"

"Lucy did it and so shall I!" she said rebelliously. "If you won't write the letter, Sir George, I shall do without it. I am going to my sister and no one can stop me.''

"What about Hugh?'' asked James.

Faith groaned. In the flurry, she had forgotten about her husband. She tried to marshal her tumultuous thoughts. "I-I don't expect either of you to understand this, but from the moment I learned about Lucy I have lived for our reunion. I *cannot* let this opportunity pass—even for Hugh.''

Sir George gazed at the portrait on the wall. Faith's determined expression and the angle at which she held her chin matched it exactly. This proud, willful beauty was indeed her father's daughter. Who was he to stand in the way of her heart's desire? he sighed. "Get me a pen and paper. You shall have your letter, m'dear.''

"For the last time, I beg you to reconsider. Hugh will be inconsolable.''

Faith turned away from the window and looked at James, who had insisted on accompanying her to Portsmouth.

"James, my need to be with Lucy is more than I can control. Hugh understands that. Be sure to tell him *not* to sail with the Second Fleet. Otherwise he will be on his way out to the colony while Lucy and I are sailing back to England.''

He sighed. "Yes, Faith.''

"And Bill and Julie?''

"Bill and Julie will run Grosvenor Square and I shall make sure they want for nothing . . .''

The coach passed Battery Point and drew up behind the sea wall not far from the old Round Tower and the wharf where Lucy had been loaded into the longboat two years before.

As Faith gazed out across the peaceful waters of the Solent the shrill cries of the gulls soaring overhead elicited a strange response in her and her eyes were drawn inexorably to a ship silhouetted against the golden orb of the setting sun. With a mixture of excitement and dread, she knew beyond doubt that ship was the *Guardian*.

"There it is,'' she murmured.

"How can you be sure?'' queried James as he helped her from the coach. "There are dozens of vessels anchored out there.''

"Come, James,'' she said, slipping her arm through his. "Let's find a boatman to row me out.''

Edward Riou, commander of the *Guardian*, looked at Faith warily. "You barely made it, Lady Stewart. We sail at first light."

Faith favored him with her most dazzling smile. "I consider myself most fortunate, Captain Riou."

Having a woman aboard a man-of-war, particularly such a stunning beauty, could be catastrophic, Riou reflected. "In my opinion, you would be better advised to return to shore immediately."

"Return to shore, Captain Riou? Whatever for?"

"We have no suitable accommodation, my dear lady. Every inch of space has been taken up with provisions for the colony and most cabins are divided into multiple berths. In fact, the only passenger not sharing is Captain Devereaux, who secured his passage eight months ago."

"I don't expect special favors," Faith said, trying the melting smile on him. "Any old thing will do. If need be, I'll sleep on the deck."

How understanding she was, and how unassuming, Riou thought, admiring her emerald eyes. "That won't be necessary, Lady Stewart. I am sure we can find something. But it will not be what you are used to, I'm afraid."

Hearing a knock, Peter Devereaux eased his tall frame out of the bunk, ducked his head under the lantern and reached for the door handle. Although he was only twenty-six, his dark, wavy hair was streaked with gray and his sinewy body bore the scars of many encounters with nature.

The son of a wealthy Virginian merchant, he had grown up with a lust for adventure and, on completing his education, had apprenticed himself to a Boston ship owner. Since then, he had spent his life whaling in the frozen oceans of the north and, for the last four years, had run a fleet of whalers in partnership with his father and brothers. Lately, however, the wanderlust had returned and he had decided to seek new fishing grounds in the oceans of the southern hemisphere.

He swung open the door and saw Riou. "Yes, Captain?"

Riou did not know what to make of Peter Devereaux. They were around the same age, and both were men of the sea, but so far, the American had resisted all his friendly overtures. "Er . . . I have a favor to ask, Mr. Devereaux. A woman passenger has just come aboard and . . . well, I was hoping . . ." His voice trailed off and there was a long silence.

"Hoping what?" Peter prompted.

Faith who had been standing behind Riou, stepped into the light, curious to see this person who could make the commander of the *Guardian* feel so ill at ease.

Peter looked at her appraisingly. Green eyes, sensuous mouth, stubborn child, spoilt, obstinate—trouble with a capital *T*.

Riou cleared his throat. "Hoping that you, being the only passenger on board with a cabin to yourself, would be willing to share, so Lady Stewart can be accommodated in comfort."

"I would be prepared to pay you handsomely for your inconvenience, Mr. Devereaux," Faith informed him in her most businesslike voice, annoyed by the insolent way his eyes were traveling over her body.

Peter opened the cabin door wider. "No need for that, Lady Stewart, I'll be happy to share with you."

Faith could hardly believe it. "I was told you were a gentleman," she said frigidly.

"What fool told you that?"

Faith tried another approach. "Although I am gratified by your offer, Mr. Devereaux, I am married so I must decline. What would you say to five hundred guineas?"

Peter shrugged. "Although I am gratified by your generosity, Lady Stewart, I must decline. However, my offer still stands—married or not."

She stepped closer and he saw the creamy color of her skin and smelled her fragrance.

"A thousand guineas, Mr. Devereaux."

"Not interested."

"Ten thousand guineas."

Ice-cold anger gnawed at Peter's insides. Ten thousand. That was more than one of his ships earned in an entire year. "My original offer still stands," he said softly. "Take it or leave it."

Faith was furious. How *dare* he refuse her! Only one course remained; she would have to shame the brute into it. An expression of helpless bewilderment spread across her face, her eyes grew misty and her bottom lip trembled. "I am afraid I must leave it, Mr. Devereaux . . ."

Peter gazed at her with admiration. Not only was she beautiful, she was a consummate actress to boot. "Then I shall bid you good night, Lady Stewart," he said, and closed the door.

PART THREE
Strains of the Guardian

21
Spring 1789

"Michael, here I am!" Lucy called from high up the fig tree. "I saw you rowing over from the north side."

"What *are* you doing?" he laughed as he joined her on the branch.

She handed him the spyglass. "Talking to Faith and watching for ships. Take a look, the view is marvelous."

"Hmm, it goes on forever," he murmured, sweeping the harbor and hinterland. "But why climb so high, darling. It could be dangerous."

"Dangerous," she scoffed. "This branch could withstand a hurricane; and it's only half as high as one of Father's mains."

He trained the spyglass on a longboat rounding Westpoint or Dawes Point, as it had come to be known. "Sorry, seadog, I forgot you climb masts. That looks like Tom and Watkin Tench."

"Oh, let's go down to the hospital wharf and meet them," she suggested. "I am eager to hear about that river they discovered. And perhaps they came across my valley on their travels."

He grabbed her around the waist. "You are going nowhere until you've kissed me, madam. I haven't seen you for twelve days."

"You set my head in such a spin, I need both feet firmly on the ground when I kiss you, sir," she bantered and caressed his lips with her fingertips.

Frustration nagged at Michael as he took her in his arms. Although she endured his embraces and kisses, her responses were merely tokens of feelings, not the feelings themselves. The spiritual love between them grew stronger every day, yet their physical lovemaking was a sham. It was spring—the time of nature's regeneration. Even this gnarled old tree was bursting with new life. He *had* to do something soon or he would go mad. Perhaps if they could get away, be alone together. . . .

The only exciting events in the colony over the last four months had been the discovery of two rivers. The first, at Broken Bay, had been discovered by Phillip; the second, fifteen miles west of the settlement at the head of the harbor, had been discovered by Tom and Watkin Tench. That evening, the second discovery was the main topic of conversation in the mess.

"The Governor thinks our river may be a tributary of his," Tench told John, who had been a member of Phillip's party. "He said you reached a point not far north of Tom and I, but that you were prevented from going farther by a waterfall."

John grinned. "Even if your river and the Governor's are one and the same, old chap, it's exceedingly good news for this colony." He raised his glass in salute. "A toast, ladies and gentlemen, to our two intrepid explorers, Tom and Watkin."

"Thank you for those kind sentiments, my friend," said Tench. "Tom may have been much taken with the solitude of the Rose Hill settlement but, after spending three months there, I am delighted to be back in the thick of things."

John's usually sunny countenance darkened. "I hope your homecoming was sweeter than mine, Watkin. No sooner had I stepped ashore than I found myself in court testifying against that ingrate, James Bird."

"Isn't he the chap you employ to catch fish for the patients?"

"That's the scoundrel," John muttered.

"It's your own fault, John. I warned you about Bird," said Ralph.

"For once you were right, Ralph," declared the Surgeon General darkly. "I did everything possible for Bird—excused him from other duties, even allowed him to keep part of every catch for his family. And instead of handing over the rest, he's been selling it around the settlement. God damn him."

"The more you give these felons, the more they expect," said Ralph. "And the women are worse. The only reason *Sirius* was sent across to the north shore to be overhauled was because the men work twice as hard when they are away from the whores."

Beth slammed her mug down. "I'm sick of the way you lump all us women in together, Lieutenant Clark. We're not all whores you know."

298

"You are a fine one to talk, Dudgeon," exclaimed Ralph, scandalized by her insolence. "You and those other harlots from *Friendship* are the worst offenders. Only last night I arrested that trollop, Sarah McCormick, for brutalizing a marine with a piece of wood and stealing his timepiece in the bargain."

"Because I came out on the same ship as Sarah don't mean we are boon companions," Beth retaliated hotly. "And, anyway, that was only one isolated incident."

"One isolated incident!" Ralph cried furiously. "I can name you a dozen. What about those lies Sarah Bellamy told the court about poor Meredith? Climbed in through her window and attempted to have connections with her, indeed."

"Here, what's this about?" Tench shouted gleefully. "James, you old rakehell."

Meredith shot a murderous look at Ralph. "I did not intend to have connections with her. I . . . er . . . only wanted to sleep on her hearth. It was uncommonly cold, you see . . ."

"Then there's Mason, another of your *Friendship* cronies, Dudgeon," Ralph went on. "She got twenty-five lashes for bringing a frivolous charge of assault against poor Private Pugh."

"Pish!" Beth thumped her fists on the table. "Us women are angels compared to you marines. Look at your court martials, and your hangings!"

Lucy rose and drew Beth after her. "Please excuse Beth's outspokenness, Lieutenant Clark. She has been nursing Elizabeth Chapman who was ravished by Private Wright and perhaps she has allowed that to warp her judgment. However, if convict women are the willing whores you say, one wonders why that 'flower' of your battalion needed to force himself on an eight-year-old child."

"Private Wright's behavior was inexcusable," Ralph acknowledged, his face flushed with rage and mortification. "But you aren't suggesting *all* marines are like him, are you?"

"Why not?" Lucy replied coldly. "You consider *all* convict women whores, don't you?"

Lucy had not long returned to her hut after ward rounds, when Michael arrived.

"If you've come about Ralph, I am not the least bit sorry," she said firmly. "Despite what he says, there are many fine people among the convicts."

He smiled. "I didn't come here to discuss Ralph, I came here to discuss us."

Lucy sighed and the tension went out of her.

Michael drew her to the table and they sat down. "I wanted to talk to you about the future, my darling."

"The future? I must confess I've thought no further than the day Faith arrives. What do you want to do, Michael? Pursue your naval career? I should think you have acquitted yourself well enough in New South Wales to be assured of promotion once you return to England."

He frowned slightly. "I did not ask you what the future holds for me, Lucy. I want to know if you think we have a future together."

Lucy's heart fluttered with panic. "What a thing to say, Michael. Of course, we have a future together. Things are getting better, aren't they?"

"Yes, darling. Slowly and surely we are making headway . . ."

She sighed with relief. "That's what I thought. Well, what about our future?"

"I have decided not to continue in the navy, or in any profession that would take me away from you for long."

She smiled her dimple smile and her eyes sparkled. "Then what is it to be?"

He clasped her hands tightly. "This country excites me, Lucy. I believe that with a little imagination and a lot of hard work, we could achieve great things here. Look at the potential market for growing crops and breeding cattle. If the estrangement between England and America continues, thousands of settlers will flock to these shores and they will need to eat."

"Oh, I agree, Michael."

"But I'd like us to go farther afield than Rose Hill," he continued, his eyes alight. "You know what I mean; you saw the hinterland today when we were sitting in the tree. The vastness of it sets my senses racing. What lies beyond that river Tom and Watkin discovered? What lies beyond the Blue Mountain range to the west? Endless rolling plains? Splendid forests? Rivers longer and wider than the Hawkesbury? When I think of it lying out there waiting to be discovered—"

"Oh Michael, it's a wonderful idea," she broke in eagerly. "We can begin by settling in my valley. When you see it, you'll understand why I am so anxious to go back. As for going farther afield, there's a gap in the mountain range not far to the west of my valley. Once we get established, we can try to find a way through there."

Michael was enthralled. The veil of reserve that always hung over her had lifted and revealed another Lucy—the one he had glimpsed when he had told her about Faith—an eager, alive, passionate, and determined woman. "Work on *Sirius* is almost finished, darling, so I shall soon have more free time. Think you can find that valley of yours again?"

"I am certain I could. I would simply follow the native path of the seven streams."

He grinned. "Then let's ask Phillip if we can go exploring."

She flung her arms around him and covered his face with kisses. "Oh, Michael that would be *marvelous*."

22

Chaumilley

Spring 1789

Not only did Phillip give Michael and Lucy his permission, he also donated hatchets, a fishing net, clasp knives, a compass, sugar, raisins, tea, rum, and shoe leather. Their friends contributed medicines, kangaroo-skin haversacks, a pair of riding breeches; and Moses, with the assistance of the *Friendship* shoemaker, fashioned Lucy a magnificent pair of knee boots.

Early on the morning of the thirteenth of October, Lucy and Michael boarded the flat-bottomed barge affectionately christened the Rose Hill Packet and set off on the three-hour trip upharbor.

The day was cloudless, the bush fresh and green, the blue water sparkled, and a heady fragrance of eucalyptus filled the air. When the harbor narrowed until it formed high banks no more than thirty feet apart, the barge tied up about half a mile below the Rose Hill settlement and Lucy and Michael continued the rest of the way on foot, following a well-worn path along the left bank.

Although Lucy thought she recognized the clusters of ferny trees, it was not until they reached the marine barracks on the outskirts of Rose Hill that she was certain she had been there before.

"This is definitely the crescent-shaped valley I came to after escaping from Tom Lewis," she announced, dumping her haversack beside a tree stump and pausing to catch her breath. She pointed to the outcrop of rocks on the rising ground beyond the barracks. "That's where I hid from the natives."

Michael swung her haversack over his shoulder. "That's good news, darling. Let's stow our gear in the hospital and take a look around."

They passed a provisions store and a little farther along came to a crude hut that they recognized from Tom's description as the hospital.

"Doesn't look much," Michael laughed, undoing the padlock and opening the misshapen door. The interior of the hut was as crude as the exterior. Destitute of all finery, it contained a table and chairs, a warped wooden workbench and an uncomfortable camp cot.

Lucy removed the chamois jacket he had bought her at the Cape and draped it over a chair. "The fireplace looks sound enough, I suppose it could be quite cosy on a cold night."

The sight of her made him ache inside. The riding breeches Tom had donated hugged her buttocks and fitted her long legs snugly, as did the boots Moses had made. Her hair hung in a thick plait down her back and formed damp curls around her forehead. Her shirt clung to her rounded breasts and he could see the hard points of her nipples through the thin white material.

Cursing under his breath he strode away from her. "I'll find Henry Dodd, and give him Phillip's letter."

Lucy ran after him and clasped his hand. "I'm coming, too."

At the end of the road, where the river swung round in a wide curve, was the crescent-shaped valley Lucy remembered, and a little farther on, just beyond where the natives had fished, was a bakery, a granary, and Henry Dodd's whitewashed hut.

The portly old overseer, who was responsible for supervising the convicts and cultivating the land, welcomed Lucy and Michael and invited them to share his evening meal. They accepted gladly and for three hours he kept Lucy spellbound with stories of Lyndhurst and amusing anecdotes about Faith, who had often visited Phillip's farm with Sir Michael.

Next morning, Lucy and Michael exchanged flour for bread at the bakery and climbed to a point that gave them a view of the entire valley. As neither had seen ground under cultivation in three years, they thought the fields of ripening corn, maize, and wheat beautiful, and equal to anything in England.

"Which way, my winsome guide?" asked Michael.

Lucy took careful note of the sun's position. "We'll travel due west until we reach the first stream. It's not far—three miles at the most."

He held out his hand. "I'll carry your haversack."

"No." She swung it over her shoulder. "If I'm to be a pioneer woman, I must get used to carrying heavy loads."

"Don't be like that," he laughed, tugging at the haversack.

She backed away. "No, Michael, I insist upon doing my share."

"Oh, very well, stubborn. You'll soon change your mind."

In the beginning, the country was gently undulating but it soon gave way to high, spiky grass and they almost stepped into the first stream before they noticed it.

"I told you it was here," Lucy cried, jumping up and down with excitement.

He swung her off her feet in a bone-crushing bear hug. "I never doubted you for a minute. Want to rest a while? You look flushed."

"No," she replied firmly. "I'd rather press on to the second stream if you don't mind."

As they trudged over the arid terrain, Lucy's feet, encased in the new boots, grew sorer with every step and by the time they reached the second stream she could hardly walk. So while they lunched on fresh bread and wine, she dangled her feet in the cool water and sighed ecstatically. Much refreshed, they trudged west for three hours until they met up with the third stream—a shallow, gently flowing brook with crystal-clear water and a pebbly bed.

As Lucy sank to her knees and scooped water into her mouth, Michael eyed her flushed countenance with concern. "We'll only continue on one condition, Lucy, that I carry your haversack."

She shrugged off the offending load and began tugging at her boots. "Agreed, darling. And I think I'll wade the rest of the way."

He joined her in the stream and they plodded along at a leisurely pace, laughing and splashing each other, until they reached the junction of the third and fourth streams. They soon got a fire going, and while they waited for the meal to cook, they sipped tea mixed with rum and sugar and gazed about them with interest.

"Night comes quickly in this part of the world," she murmured, looking at the purple sky. "One moment it's bright sunlight and the next, pitch dark. Not at all like England's gentle twilights."

Michael inhaled the woody, mossy scent of the bush and savored the silence, which was broken only by the crackle of the fire. "Have you noticed how quickly the temperature drops once the sun sets? You can be sweltering and then, as soon as night falls, you're chilled to the bone."

She shivered and moved closer. "What do you think of me finding the four streams?"

"I think you have inherited your father's uncanny sense of direction, along with another of his traits."

"What's that?" she asked curiously.

"His damned stubbornness! You were exhausted when we got to the third stream but you had to keep going, didn't you?"

She wound her arms around his neck and kissed him. "So, you *finally* admit that I have a fault."

He disengaged himself and scrambled to his feet. "It's not your faults that set my nerves on edge, madam, it's your damned attributes. Come on, let's take a look at that strange concoction you have on the fire. If I stay here billing and cooing with you much longer, I won't be responsible for my actions."

She laughed and held out her hand to him. "Your actions don't trouble me in the least, sir. You are always a perfect gentleman."

He yanked her up and caught her fiercely against him. "I warn you, Lucy. I won't go on living the life of a celibate much longer. One day, I shall treat you as any red-blooded man treats his woman."

They set off next morning and trekked for hours, following the fifth stream north until it merged with the sixth in a rugged ravine filled with deep shadows.

"*Yowi Yowi,*" Lucy said somberly. "That's what the natives called this place. They were so afraid of it, they camped in the next gully."

Michael took her hand and guided her away from the jagged rocks at the top of the dark precipice. "We'll do the same. I don't like the looks of it at all."

When the mist lifted the next morning they had no difficulty finding the seventh stream. "Nothing can stop us now!" Lucy cried jubilantly. "I could find the valley with my eyes closed."

"What are we waiting for?" Michael laughed. "Let's fly on winged feet through this enchanted wood to your paradise."

Oblivious of the spiders' webs and the thorny bushes they sped through the undergrowth until they reached a long tree-studded slope. "Here it is!" she cried joyfully, clasping his hand and clambering with him to the top.

The valley was exactly as Lucy remembered: lush, green, spare of trees, rolling away in gentle undulations to the foot of the formidable Blue Mountain range that lined the western horizon. "What do you think?" she asked breathlessly.

"It exceeds my wildest expectations," he said in awed tones. "No wonder you had to find it again. My God, Lucy, this *is* Paradise."

He pulled out a tuft of grass and examined the dark soil clinging to the roots. "The soil is so rich we can grow anything we want."

She tugged his sleeve and pointed. "See the lake and the stream? What do you think?"

"They're perfect. Look at the ducks—there must be hundreds."

She threw back her head and laughed. "Speaking of ducks, Michael Perryman, I think the least you can do is catch us a plump one for supper. The bird I caught I had to beat to death with a stone hatchet. It nearly ruined my appetite."

He leapt up and pulled her after him. "Your wish is my command. Shall we charge them like the cavalry, or sneak up on them like Indians?"

"Oh, let's sneak up on them."

Trying to stifle their laughter, they crept down the hill and took cover behind a copse of trees close to the lake. "Which one do you fancy?" Michael whispered, flattening himself on the ground and cocking his pistol.

Lucy took one look at the hundreds of ducks innocently paddling about on the lake and sank to the ground with her fists pressed tightly against her mouth.

"This is no joking matter," he said, straight-faced. "Show me which one."

As Lucy opened her mouth to speak, a peal of laughter ran out and the startled ducks rose in a cloud and flew away.

He tossed the pistol aside and lunged at her. "Damned inexcusable. Into the lake you go."

"Oh no I won't!" she gasped, scrambling to her feet.

"Oh yes you will!" He wrestled her to the ground and pinned her on her back.

"Sorry," she gurgled. "Really I am!"

As she tried to push him off her, he caught her wrists and flattened them against the grass. "Sorry's not good enough. Into the lake you go."

She smacked her lips together. "Let's kiss and make up!"

"You're not getting off that easily."

She raised her head and kissed him hard on the mouth. He groaned and then she felt his body hardening against her, heard his breathing grow ragged, and suddenly the laughter went out of the day. Alarm bells rang in her brain. Gasping, ragged breathing—a night long ago. The sun sank into a sea of blood and it was midnight. His hands moved in endless circles, ripping and tearing at her body, laying waste to its sacred places. She twisted from side to side, trying to break free but her movements only excited him more. A wild, strangled scream escaped her and she cringed, waiting for the blow . . .

From somewhere far away she heard Michael call her name. "Lucy . . . *Lucy!*"

The red mist cleared.

She looked up at him, saw the grief and despair in his eyes and knew she could not go on like this any longer. "Oh God, Michael . . . make it go," she sobbed.

He hung his head in such a defeated way, she was terrified.

"Michael, Michael, don't look like that. I want to love you. Show me, darling, show me *now*."

He raised his head and searched her eyes. "Will you promise to stay with me, Lucy? Stay with me and not let go?"

She nodded.

He gently loosened her clothes, all the while kissing her, whispering reassurances, surrounding her with love. He lightly stroked her neck, her breasts, her thighs, holding her with his eyes, telling her how beautiful she was . . . telling her.

A warm languor overcame Lucy and grew into an aching need. She moaned with pleasure, never wanting him to stop. A hard light came into Michael's eyes and his hands grew more demanding. Her body throbbed, swept by a wild excitement.

"Help me, Michael," she begged, arching upward toward him. "Please help me . . . help me."

He lowered his body onto hers and she received him rapturously, gripping his buttocks to drive him deep inside her.

The world spun.

He was movement and she was flame. Where he led she followed, and she stayed with him all the way until that moment of shattering ecstasy when he claimed her for his own.

They explored the valley, fished the river in the foothills of the Blue Mountains, swam in the lake, feasted on ducks and made marvelous plans for their future.

One morning, they drew the letters of their names in the sand beside the lake, mingled them into a word and carved the word *Chaumilley* on the tree under which they had consummated their love.

Every day they climbed the tree and surveyed their kingdom. Every night they lay beneath its sheltering branches and explored more heavenly kingdoms in each other's arms. And as the days and nights melted into one, life was such a boundless joy that they sometimes wept with the sheer wonder of it.

On the ninth day, as they sat on the hill at the spot they had selected for their house, Michael said, "We must think about returning to Sydney, my darling."

She turned away from the setting sun which was spinning golden webs across the valley and smiled tenderly at him. "I don't want to leave Chaumilley, ever."

"Neither do I, but our friends will be anxious by now. It would be selfish of us to remain . . ."

She sighed. "What will happen when we return?"

"It will be as before. You'll be at the hospital and I will resume my naval duties aboard *Sirius.*"

She sat up with a start. "Live apart?"

"For the moment . . ."

"But why?"

"If we were back in England, Lucy, would we live together before we married?"

"But Michael, we *are* married."

"In our eyes, my love, but not in the eyes of the law or the church."

"Then let's get married at once," she said impatiently. "It's not right for us to live apart."

He smiled. "I'll ask Major Ross as soon as we return."

Lucy looked at him with consternation. "Major Ross! That pompous fool will never give his consent. Can you not go over his head to the Governor?"

"I'll not compromise Phillip for our personal needs, Lucy. Although I have been transferred to *Sirius,* Major Ross is still my commanding officer. Protocol dictates that I ask his permission."

She pouted. "Well, you must do what you think is best,

Michael, but it will be torture living apart, loving you the way I do."

Remembering how torturously long his wait for her had been, Michael smiled. "No need to despair, darling. As soon as Faith arrives with your pardon, Major Ross's permission will be a formality."

"Surely Faith will come soon," Lucy sighed, her mind speeding to a far away place where the wind blew cold and everything was dim and gray. "Where are you?" she called. "Oh, where are you now, beloved?"

23
A Swishing Murmur Like Wind in the Treetops

Wednesday, December 23, 1789

Latitude 44 degrees south
Longitude 41 degrees east

Faith turned away from the shimmering gray swell and entered the plant house at the rear of the quarterdeck. It was her favorite place on the ship and over the last months she had spent many hours there caring for the plants destined for the colony.

She checked the freshly painted covering cloths on the roof to make sure no seawater was getting in, did a tour of inspection, then climbed the ladder to the poop deck and stood looking toward the bow until Peter Devereaux emerged from the forward companionway, whereupon she turned quickly away and stared at the sailors reefing the topsails high up the mizzen.

The problem of her accommodation had been solved by moving Superintendent Schaffer in with Reverend Crowther so that Faith could share with Schaffer's eleven-year-old daughter, Winifred. But Peter Devereaux's refusal to give up his cabin had earned him the condemnation of everyone on board.

He had kept to himself on the voyage, so she had seen little of him; but whenever they had spoken, although he had been scrupulously polite, he had looked at her with an arrogance that had set her nerves on edge.

She shivered, and wound the angora scarf tighter around her

face. The temperature had dropped steadily since they had left the Cape and today the wind was so cold it made her ears ache. Yesterday, they had sighted ice. It was beautiful—like loaves of white sugar floating on a navy blue sea.

"Good afternoon, Lady Stewart," said Captain Riou joining her at the rail. "If this wind keeps up we'll be in New South Wales in six weeks."

Faith gave the Captain a charming smile that she allowed to overflow to Lieutenant Quenton and the ship's portly doctor who had clambered up the ladder after Riou.

Peter stood at the bow with a set look on his face. The sky was dark and fog was falling from the rigging in large droplets. Since the ice had been sighted he had spent most of his waking hours on deck. Drift ice usually meant icebergs and although he had no quarrel with the way Riou ran the ship, he preferred to keep his own eye on proceedings.

Hearing laughter, he glanced over his shoulder and saw Lady Stewart surrounded by officers. Like bees to a honeypot, he thought wryly. But, to her credit, she treated them all with the same imperious charm and no unpleasantness had resulted from her being the only woman on board.

"Iceberg off the starboard bow!" The cry rang out from aloft.

Peter raised his spyglass and glimpsed the old enemy through clouds of rising mist. A huge brute with peaks at either end and a hollowed-out cove in the center. He gazed at it for some time until he heard Riou ordering out the cutter and jolly boat. Cursing, he strode toward the poop deck.

Faith stared at the gigantic mountain of ice through Lieutenant Quenton's spyglass. "Oh, those pinnacles on either end must be a hundred feet high. And look at that enormous cave in the center of the bay. I can see blues and greens, even violets in its depths. Oh, it's magical!" She plucked at Captain Riou's sleeve. "Please let me go in one of the boats, Captain. I must take a closer look at that fairy cavern."

"May I have a word, Captain Riou?"

Hearing Peter Devereaux's voice behind her, Faith spun around. He inclined his head slightly. "Afternoon, Lady Stewart."

"Good afternoon," she replied frigidly.

With a nod to Faith, Riou retired a short distance with Peter. "What is it, Devereaux?"

"I heard you order out the boats, Captain. May I ask why?"

Riou frowned. "What business is it of yours, Devereaux?"

Peter looked at him steadily. "I have hunted in the northern oceans for twelve years, Captain, and I have learned something about the unpredictability of icebergs. That brute looks dangerous. There seems to be an underwater ice shelf running between the bay in the center and the southern peak. See how the swell keeps flattening?''

Riou trained his glass on the spot Peter had indicated. "Yes, you are right . . ."

"And, high on the northern peak—see how the wind is forcing that crevice apart?" As Peter spoke a section of ice split from the peak and crashed into the sea sending a geyser of water shooting fifty feet in the air.

"I take your point, Captain Devereaux," said Riou, using Peter's title for the first time, "but we need water and this is a good opportunity to replenish our supplies. Men will be posted up the masts to keep a sharp eye on proceedings, and those in the boats have orders to stay well clear of the berg while they collect the loose ice."

"As long as the weather doesn't close in, that should be safe enough," Peter conceded. "But what about the woman? I heard her say she wanted to—"

"I am not a fool," Riou broke in coldly. "Lady Stewart remains on board."

Riou kept the *Guardian* tacking and laying well to windward of the iceberg while the boats collected the ice, and when they returned to the ship, he stayed at the helm for another half an hour before handing over to a midshipman and going below for his evening meal.

Peter, however, remained on deck. The weather had closed in and soon he could see no farther than a dozen feet in front of him. The old uneasiness began gnawing at his gut. Although the ship was making six knots to southward and they should be well clear by now, there was an icy sensation around his nostrils that he could only describe as the "smell" of icebergs.

Suddenly, the horizon ahead lightened as if the fog was lifting and he heard a swishing murmur, like wind in the treetops. The back of his neck began to prickle, his heart began to pound. He could not see it, but he *knew* it was there.

"Helm down!" he shouted, racing toward the stern. "Iceberg dead ahead!"

A moment later, the alabaster mountain of ice loomed out of the fog and hung suspended over the mast heads.

Riou reached the deck just as the bow of the ship ran under the iceberg. Men were dashing to and fro in panic as the ship plowed into the ice. He pushed the paralyzed Midshipman aside and put down the helm, holding his breath, expecting at any moment to see the ship dashed to pieces.

There was an ear-splitting crack and the deck shuddered beneath him.

The world stopped.

"She's struck the submerged shelf!" shouted Peter clambering up beside him.

Shaking from stem to stern, the ship bounced off the shelf. The wind rushed in taking the headsails aback and the bow swung around in the opposite direction.

"Yards!" Riou shouted. "Yards, damn you!" but the crew reacted slowly and before they could trace the yards round to fill on the other tack, the swell picked up the ship and smashed it against the submerged ice shelf again.

The aft sternpost and the taffrail disintegrated and the after beam on the upper gun deck split down the center like a twig. Peter flung Riou to the deck as splinters flew everywhere.

"Rudder? Tiller?" Riou questioned.

Peter shook his head. "Gone. Head her off with sail."

Calmly, and with great skill, Riou worked the crippled vessel out into the open sea while organizing the carpenters to sound the well and officers to check the damage.

"How high is the water in the holds?" Riou asked his carpenter.

"Two feet and gaining fast, sir. We canna' find the leak, sir. God, if we don't do somethin' we'll be feeding the fishes."

Riou stared steadily back at his officers. "Mr. Quenton, you and Mr. Harvey get the pumps working fore and aft. Mr. Brady, start hoisting everything from 'tween decks overboard. Mr. Sommerville, get those twenty-five convicts out of the forward prison and put them to work on the pumps. Mr. Sampson, find that leak. I want thirty-minute watches back to back on the pumps—the off watch to lighten the ship."

By nine o'clock the pumps were working so well, the hatches had to be battened down to prevent water running down 'tween decks again, for the scuppers could not vent it as fast as the pumps threw it up. But, as the hours dragged by, the water in the holds gained and an air of gloom settled over the ship.

At midnight, when Riou went below to assess the situation,

the water in the afterhold had risen to five feet and the men at the pumps were in despair.

"We're losing her, Capt'n," cried one poor devil, his face blue with cold.

"Rum, Capt'n. Give us rum to warm us!" begged another desperate-eyed mariner.

Riou made his way quickly through the ship to where Faith was comforting Schaffer's daughter, Winifred. "The men need refreshments, Lady Stewart, and I have no one I can spare. Would you and Winifred help?"

Faith jumped to her feet. "Of course, Captain. What shall we give them?"

"Those coming off the pumps can have cheese and biscuits and a dram of grog, but under no circumstances allow anyone near the spirits room. There's a cask of wine in the galley, mix water with it. And, Lady Stewart, you and Winifred should don your warmest garments." He left without further explanation.

At dawn, the *Guardian* was still afloat on the storm-tossed sea but she had seven feet of water in her holds. Faith, stationed in the dark hell of the afterhold, continued to feed the crew and convicts, who kept driving one another until they dropped with exhaustion and were dragged clear of the pumps so others could take their place.

During that day the winch broke and the water gained fast. "Where are the spare winches?" shouted Peter, who was taking a turn at the pumps.

The man beside him shook his head dazedly. "Don't think we have any, sir."

Peter eyed the water with disquiet. "Then we'll have to fix this one as best we can. Give me a hand, will you?"

The two men worked frantically, but by the time they got the pump working, the water had gained another six inches.

By the third dawn, Riou finally admitted to himself that the situation was desperate. During the last hour the pumps had choked several times and some of the men, sure their last moments on earth were at hand, had broached the spirits room.

He turned to Lieutenant Quenton. "Tell the Purser to put provisions and other necessaries aboard the boats, but make sure he's discreet. I don't want a panic on my hands."

However, there was no way to keep the provisioning of the boats a secret and before long a crowd converged on Riou demanding the boats he lowered.

"I cannot accommodate you all aboard the boats, gentlemen," the Captain told them calmly. "And with the sea running so high, I think your chances of survival will be better if you remain at the pumps."

"If'n we don't take to the boats soon, we'll be too bloody done in to man 'em!" shouted a bleary-eyed mariner.

Peter fought his way through the mob to Riou's side. He thought Riou had displayed admirable spirit throughout the ordeal but even he, for all his courage, could not hold this rabble much longer. They were either too drunk or too overcome with fear to hear the good advice he was giving them.

He cocked his pistol and fired it over their heads. As the sound echoed throughout the ship, everyone fell silent. "Captain Riou is right, men. You stand a better chance with the ship than rowing about in these seas."

"Return to the pumps," Riou urged. "If the situation does not improve in a few hours, I'll take a ballot for the boats."

"I am still of the opinion that your best chance lies in remaining on board, men," Riou announced to those gathered before him.

A drunken mariner dropped to his knees and raised his hands in supplication. "For the love of God, Capt'n, ye'll not deny us a chance to live."

"No, Mr. Glen, I'll not deny you that," said Riou. "Those who wish to take to the boats hand your names to Mr. Harvey. I will draw the ballot in ten minutes."

Has all my striving to find Lucy been in vain? Faith wondered as she stared at the crew's terrified faces. The wind was screeching through the rigging and hailstones pelted the decks. She doubted if these poor drunken wretches could get the boats into the water safely, much less steer them to a safe harbor hundreds of miles away. *I'll not go,* she decided. *I'm staying on board with Captain Riou.*

A drunken midshipman wearing Riou's gold-laced hat sprang onto the poop deck and waved a sword over his head. "*Damn* Riou's ballot. It's every man for himself. To the boats!"

Faith took cover as men stampeded in every direction. The large cutter, filled with drunken seamen, dropped onto the back of a wave and was propelled to safety by its cheering crew. The jolly boat was not so fortunate; it lost most of its occupants overboard before it hit the water. The longboat was stove in when the ship's hull crashed down on it. The largest boat, the launch, almost got drawn under the ship's counter and was cast adrift with only seven men aboard.

The cutter returned to the ship and its drunken occupants demanded a sail to replace the one they had lost overboard. While they hovered about, twenty men jumped into the water and tried to clamber aboard. The occupants of the cutter beat them off with oars and fists.

Sickened by the sight, Faith made her way toward the stern where Riou and Peter were watching the last boat—a longboat commissioned for *Sirius*—being hoisted out.

"Lady Stewart, thank God! I've been looking for you everywhere." The ship's doctor scooped Faith into his arms and jumped with her into the longboat.

Faith screamed and tried to break free but in the struggle her left foot became wedged under a thwart. Riou and Peter rushed to the rail but they were too late to save her. The longboat gave a sickening lurch and tipped its occupants into the sea as the hull of the *Guardian* came crashing down. Then, with Faith still trapped aboard, it slipped off the boom and fell bow first into the boiling water.

"Oh, my God!" Riou shouted hoarsely.

Peter launched himself over the side, stretching every inch of his body outward. He hit the water with a force that drove the air from his lungs and all feeling from his limbs.

As the shadow of the longboat passed over him, he shot to the surface, flung out his arm and grabbed hold of the side just as the swell picked the boat up and swept it away from the *Guardian*. He helped the wave all he could by flattening himself against the side and kicking furiously. Then, when its momentum slackened, he heaved himself aboard.

Amazingly, Lady Stewart was still there.

He freed her foot and dived for the tiller. "Down on your stomach and hold on!" he shouted as a mountain of water loomed on their starboard side. Muscles bunching under the strain, he swung the tiller round and held it rigid, dead into the wind, as the huge wall of ocean roared in. The bow turned agonizingly slowly. "Faster," he urged. "Faster, faster."

The boat kept lifting until it seemed to float on air, then it tipped over the precipice and careened down the slope of the wave. Peter clung desperately to the tiller as an avalanche of water poured in. Then, miraculously, the sky appeared and the boat was tossed onto the plateau of the next wave.

She was still there, her hair plastered against her face like sleek black snakes, her green eyes misty with terror. The boat was half-filled with water and he felt its dead weight as he brought it round into the wind. "Bail, damn you!" he shouted.

She came up on her knees like a sleepwalker and started scooping armfuls of water over the side.

"Faster!" he barked, taking the tiller in one hand and frenziedly shoveling with the other. "Faster or we're done for." They bailed like people possessed until the boat's buoyancy returned and he was able to steer it through the swell more easily.

With the immediate danger past, Peter's first thought was to step up the mast and try to find the *Guardian*. Leaving Faith stationed at the tiller with strict instructions to keep the bow into the wind, he moved forward to the locker beneath the bow. Inside was the standard survival equipment: an iron pot, mugs, plates, clasp knives; an oilskin pouch containing a compass, a quadrant and a tinderbox; another oilskin pouch containing a brace of pistols and shot; and a kit for repairing canvas. There were also two mutton hams and a four gallon cask of rum but no fresh water. It had either been forgotten in the panic or lost overboard.

He dragged the sails out of their haversacks and looked around for the mast. Then the exhilaration he had felt at besting the sea vanished and he shook his fist at the malevolent God who had set them adrift thirteen hundred miles from landfall with no water or mast. "Damn you," he cried. "Damn you and rot you to hell!"

"Mr. Devereaux, *please*," said Faith, her nerves stretched tight by his outburst.

He glared at the woman responsible for his predicament, he drew a mug of rum from the cask, sank it in a single toss, then drew another for her. "Drink this, it will help keep out the chill."

Faith followed his example and gasped, spluttered, coughed, and choked as the fiery rawness caught in her throat.

"Can you hold the boat into the wind?" he asked when she had recovered. "I must secure the weatherboards or the sea will pour in and we'll sink."

She gave him a slight smile. "Go ahead, Mr. Devereaux. And thank you for saving my life."

"Spare me your gratitude, Lady Stewart, your life is far from saved. Are you sure you can handle that tiller?"

"Quite sure," she snapped.

"Keep a sharp lookout for the *Guardian*. And, don't just sit there—bail!" he growled as he returned to the locker.

Faith steered, bailed, and scanned the ocean until she spied two objects bobbing about some distance to her left. "I can see something . . ."

Peter was beside her in an instant. "Point the bow at them and don't deviate, no matter what," he instructed, placing the oars in the rowlocks.

It took some maneuvering but they eventually got close enough to identify the objects.

"Two of the crew," said Peter. "Keep the bow steady while I bring them aboard."

"Aboard!" she gasped. "Whatever for? They're dead!"

"I know they're dead, Lady Stewart. It's their clothing I'm interested in, not their company."

Shocked, Faith slackened her hold on the tiller. The boat swung around broadside to the swell.

"Watch the bow, you fool!" Peter saw the consternation in her eyes turn to rage. *Good,* he thought. *She has to learn, and learn fast, otherwise we won't last the night.*

"Watch your tone, sir," Faith said, yanking the tiller back into position. "I am not a fo'c'sle hand."

"More's the pity, Lady Stewart. We'd stand a better chance if you were. In the future, don't pull the tiller around like that or you'll capsize us."

A few more strokes and they reached the first body. "Keep a sharp eye out," he ordered, heaving it aboard and setting about his grisly task.

"I can see oars floating over yonder," she said stiffly, still smarting from his disparaging remarks.

"Good! Keep watching, for other flotsam." Peter looked at her out of the corner of his eye. She was quite calm. Considering her situation, that was remarkable. Most females would be hysterical by now. "We're in luck," he told her. "This fellow's about your size. His oilskins will help keep out the weather and, with a bit of padding his boots ought to fit. Those leather things you have on are useless."

"If you think I'll wear dead men's clothes—" Faith broke off midsentence as he heaved the naked body overboard. It landed in the water with a feeble plop and floated past, face down.

"Where are the oars?" he enquired, joining her at the tiller.

She pointed. "And there's a cask a little farther on, but you can't see it just now. That big wave is hiding it."

316

"It's called a swell. Waves are things that ladies paddle their toes in when they spend a day at the seaside. We'll check it out once I've finished here. Don't forget, point the bow at—"

"You don't have to repeat yourself, Mr. Devereaux, I am not an idiot!"

"That remains to be seen, Lady Stewart."

"Stop calling me 'Lady Stewart' in that voice!"

"What do you want me to call you?"

"Nothing!"

He shrugged. "Okay let's call each other nothing. I was getting tired of 'Mr. Devereaux' anyway."

24
White Tombstones

They kept afloat that night by bailing and running out a sea anchor. When daylight crept in from the east, Faith crawled under the sails and fell into an exhausted sleep while Peter sat at the tiller taking stock of the situation.

Although the weather had cleared, it was too overcast to take a reading. The *Guardian*'s position had been 44 degrees south and 41 degrees east when it had struck the iceberg. Reaching the Cape in a craft this size without a mast seemed highly unlikely, but there were three uninhabited island groups in the vicinity— Prince Edward and Marion to the southwest and the Crozet group about five hundred miles to the east. These, he decided, were his best hope. The longboat had already been driven many miles south by the winds and currents, he had to get under sail as soon as possible. Even then, their chances of finding land were almost nonexistent. But he'd be damned if he'd sit back and let the sea have its way.

He woke Faith and, leaving her in charge of the tiller, set to work making a mast out of the spare oars.

They lunched on mutton and rum that did little to quench their thirst and returned to their tasks until sunset when, mercifully, some showers of rain swept in and they caught water in their mouths and handkerchiefs.

When it got too dark to work, Peter took over the tiller and Faith crept beneath the sails. But at midnight another gale came and he roused her to bail. She worked with grim determination, keeping her mind off their perilous predicament by thinking of Lucy and Hugh and the wonderful times they would share when they were together again.

Peter's thoughts, however, centered on their predicament. With careful management the mutton would last for some time but without water they had no chance. The current was carrying them south at a frightening speed and unless the adverse winds abated, the makeshift mast would snap like a twig the moment he stepped it.

On the plus side, the brand new longboat was extremely well designed and outfitted, but its sails, though excellent, were far too heavy for an oar mast. He'd have to make sails out of her dress and petticoats. The problem was getting her to part with them. . . .

By dawn, having not slept for three days, Peter was almost dead with fatigue. His eyes felt as if they were filled with stinging nettles and his body ached in every joint.

"Come here," he said to Faith. "You'll have to take over the tiller. I've put out the sea anchor. Keep the boat heading dead into the wind if I fall asleep . . ."

Glimpsing uncertainty in his bloodshot eyes as she eased herself down beside him, Faith realized he had no confidence in her capabilities. "Oh, for the love of God, stop your nonsense. I'm quite capable of holding a tiller for an hour or two."

"Wake me . . . anything . . . ice . . . rain." He stretched out his long legs, settled his shoulders more comfortably against the stern and fell instantly asleep.

"Wake up, damn you!"

Peter emerged from his black, deathlike slumber. "What is it?" he asked, voice slurred and hoarse.

"Over there—I think it's ice."

He stared where she was pointing. Gradually, his vision cleared. "God, you're right!"

"We don't have any water aboard, do we?"

He stared into the misty green depths of her eyes, losing himself.

"I asked you a question."

He noticed the blisters on her lips and realized with a sense of shock that this was the first time she had mentioned water.

"No," he said, taking up the oars. "No, there's no water, but if we can reach that drift ice . . ."

"Well, what are you waiting for?" she cried. "Row!"

Faith could hear the crunching, grinding sound of the blocks of ice rubbing against one another. Her parched mouth began to throb and as soon as the boat came abreast of one she let go the tiller and made a grab for it. The boat swung round and she plunged head first into the water.

"Stupid!" Peter shouted, yanking her back on board. "What do you think you're doing?"

"I want some!"

"Get back to the tiller. We'll have to harpoon a bit with the anchor and drag it clear of the rest, otherwise the boat might be damaged."

After they had chipped down enough ice to fill the two casks, Peter broached the subject of the sails. "We have enough food and water to last about two weeks, but unless we can make some sails we'll keep drifting south with the current."

"What's wrong with the sails we have?"

"They are too heavy for the mast I've made. I need your dress and petticoats to make lighter ones."

"You're just trying to trick me into wearing that dead man's clothes," she blazed. "Well, I won't, and that's final."

The next instant she was down on her back and he was tugging at her petticoats. "I do not intend to die because of your abysmal stupidity," he said.

She pummeled him with her fists. "Take your hands off me, you insufferable swine. I hate you!"

"You aren't my favorite person either," he muttered, ripping open her bodice. "In fact, I've never met a more spoilt and willful female."

Faith realized she had to capitulate or be stripped where she lay. "All right, you can have them, you cur. But get to the stern and turn your head while I change, or . . . or the next time you fall asleep I shall run you through with a knife."

"Spare me the shocking details," he said as he untied the tiller. "And get a move on, your modesty has wasted enough time. I can't work in the dark, you know."

As soon as Peter completed the mainmast and locking pin, he fashioned a yard and small topmast out of an oar hand. Then he set to work on the sails and by dusk Faith's flying petticoats had brought the boat round on a northerly tack.

319

They made good progress until sunset when the weather deteriorated once more. Many times during that terrible night, they came close to floundering. Only Peter's determination and seamanship saved them; but by dawn he was near dead with fatigue and when Faith took him a mug of rum and water she was shocked by his appearance.

"Get some sleep," she urged, trying to keep her voice calm. "I'll take over the tiller."

He tossed down the mixture and looked at her with tortured eyes. "You can't manage. The swell is twenty feet high."

"It doesn't look too bad," she replied with a confidence she was far from feeling. "At least the rain and sleet have stopped." She squeezed in beside him and wrenched the tiller from his hand.

"Are you sure?"

"Of course I'm sure!"

"Wake me if—" His head slumped to his chest and he slept.

After that, the days blurred into one another. The sails were too flimsy for the conditions, and the boat would make small gains to the north, only to be driven south by the adverse winds and currents. Then the weather grew so cold that frostbite became a problem and they huddled together under the canvas sails wearing every stitch of clothing on board.

With the arrival of the seventh or eighth dawn came a new menace. Icebergs. Ghostly white, they loomed silently out of the fog and, when the gray curtain lifted to reveal a cloudless day, Peter and Faith found themselves surrounded.

For Faith, caught in the grip of fever, the world had lost all sense of reality. The white monoliths floating before her eyes seemed bathed in an eerie light. Vaporous smoke rose from their valleys and delicate translucent blues, greens, and violets shone from the caverns studding their peaks.

"Beautiful, aren't they?" said Peter.

"Beautiful . . . and deadly . . . like white tombstones in a gigantic primal graveyard."

He stared at her, concerned. She had been at a low ebb for the last two days. Only her incredible stubbornness had kept her going. "Are you all right? Your voice sounds strange."

Faith stared past him at the bleak and bitter landscape. Nothing moved. Nothing breathed. Nothing lived. An aching loneliness took hold of her and her eyes filled with tears. Where was the color-drenched world of London? Where was her beloved Hugh? How she longed for him.

Before she could answer, the boat struck some submerged ice and heeled over. Peter shoved it clear with an oar and it righted itself but almost immediately came to a grinding halt between two blocks of ice. The air trembled and filled with ominous booms.

"Lend a hand!" he shouted over his shoulder.

Faith snatched up an oar and together they pushed and prodded the boat through the bucking, jostling drift ice until they got free. Shortly afterward a breeze sprang up and they ran for the open sea.

They made good progress north that day and Peter's hopes rose. Although they were unlikely to find a safe landfall, he had to try. The decision made, he turned to Faith. "From this moment there's no retreat. We sail north, or die in the attempt. Agreed?"

Her eyes locked with his. "Agreed."

The wind gradually strengthened until it was ripping the crests off the waves in sheets. The swell widened and steepened, snow and sleet fell and the world became a heaving, swirling hell. The sail ripped, the boat broached to under a bare mast and huge breakers roared in on it. Peter set a second sail and kept running before the wind, convinced it was their only chance.

Faith, crouching at the bow, expected every moment to be the last, but somehow the boat lived and by the next day, the wind had dropped and the sea had abated.

When she crawled to the stern with food, Peter was in agony. "Can't move my legs. Cramps."

She looked at him with a mixture of rage and despair. "Why didn't you call me? What good will it do us if I am safely tucked away at the bow and you are sitting dead at the tiller?"

She pummeled his legs until feeling returned to them; and after they'd eaten, Peter began repairing the damage to the masts and sails while she took over the tiller. The sea was shrouded in fog and it was difficult to see anything, but she caught a fleeting glimpse of something black.

"Look! There!"

Peter joined her and stared into the fog off the port bow. A moment later a long snow-clad, sloping headland appeared.

"Is it real?" she gasped.

He smiled, and to Faith it was like watching the sun emerge from behind a dark cloud. The harsh lines around his eyes vanished and he looked young, vital, and dazzlingly handsome.

"Yes. But God knows where it came from. My calculations put us at about 57 degrees south. No land has ever been sighted in these latitudes."

As he brought the boat about, the fog lifted and a forbidding island with sheer black cliffs that looked like the ramparts of an ancient fortress, rose out of the boiling sea.

"We'll never scale those," she said in awed tones.

"We'll circumnavigate. There's bound to be a cove somewhere . . ." He tacked and ran along the coast in a westerly direction until they came to a long, low reef that jutted out from the cliffs like a beckoning finger. "This looks promising!" he shouted above the roar of the surf. "Keep a sharp eye out!"

Faith craned her head around the sails. "I can see two little coves. Could we go ashore here?"

He glanced at her rosy cheeks and flashing eyes. "Yes. Ready?"

She nodded.

He tore down the sails and set the oars in the rowlocks. "If the boat founders, leave everything and stroke out for the shore."

He maneuvered the boat onto a wave and pulled toward the larger cove for all he was worth, praying they would not hit a submerged rock and capsize. His fears were groundless. As soon as they rounded the point, they entered a huge kelp field with long, winding fronds that completely flattened the surge.

"We're in luck!" he shouted as the wave caught the boat and hurled it at the shore. "When I give the signal, jump out and push!"

Faith crouched, waiting, as the shore rushed toward them.

"Now!"

Over the side they went and with strength born of joy, dragged the longboat clear. Then they flung themselves down on the pebbly beach, kissed those delivering stones, tossed them high in the air and whooped and catcalled until the forbidding black cliffs rang with laughter.

25
Ice Island

Directly behind the outcrop of boulders Peter had used as a marker when beaching the boat was a dank cavern. He built a rock fireplace in the lee of it, collected guano, kelp, and tussock grass from a hummocky hill on the west boundary of the cove and soon had a fire going.

Faith gazed about with interest. At the west end of the cove hundreds of black and white shadows moved backward and forward between the water and the tussocks. "What are they?"

"Penguins. Looks like we've put ashore at the entrance to their rookery."

Faith watched their antics, until the day dwindled into dusk and a full moon came out from behind the gigantic clouds above, bathing the mist-shrouded mountain in an eerie silver light.

"After all our weary wanderings, it's hard to believe we've come to rest in this strange, peaceful paradise, isn't it?" she said.

Peter pointed to the dark clouds scudding across the sky. "The peacefulness is a facade. Mother Nature has merely called a truce."

Not long afterward a bitter wind swept in from the south and turned their serene haven into a seething maelstrom of sleet and spume, so they retreated into the cave, climbed into their bedpiles and settled down to sleep.

Peter frowned as he surveyed the bleak cove. Facing due south, it was at the mercy of the elements and could not be considered a permanent shelter. However, their prospects for survival were good. Water could be obtained from the snowcapped heights and there was food here.

When he found more suitable accommodation he would go exploring. It was imperative that he find wood. With this thought in mind, he set off over the tussocks in search of breakfast.

Faith opened her eyes and stared at the glittering ice crystals on the roof for some time before remembering where she was. Seeing that Peter had gone, she donned her boots and scrambled outside. He was nowhere in sight but the fire was blazing and water was heating in the pot. While she crouched beside its cheering warmth, she gazed at the other creatures occupying the beach.

There were thousands of penguins. They skimmed through the water like skipping stones, propelled themselves onto the shingles then waddled up the slope into the tussocks. *Caaack! Squaarwwkk!* Their calls—something between goose cackles and canary trills—sounded so funny, Faith laughed for the first time in weeks.

"Deafening, aren't they?" said Peter, dropping a dozen eggs into the pot. "Their rookery is just over the hill. We'll never want for fresh eggs."

As soon as they finished the delicious red-yolked eggs, they scaled the rocky outcrop and set off along the other cove. It was much deeper than the first and had a narrow boulder-strewn valley running inland from the east corner.

At the entrance of the narrow valley was a cave about eight feet wide that sloped into the headland for about thirty feet. Free of kelp and with no watermarks, it faced west and was largely protected from wind and seaspray.

They left the cave and walked a short distance to the end of the narrow valley where they found a frozen waterfall.

"Tastes good," said Peter, chipping away a thick layer of ice until he reached water. "If we can find a suitable place to stow the longboat, this ought to do."

"I saw a place in the rocks between the cave and the reef," said Faith, splashing icy water on her cheeks.

They inspected it, decided it would suffice, then clambered out over the rocks to the end of the reef. As Faith gazed at the thick yellowish fronds of kelp writhing in rhythm with the swell, she was reminded of the trailing vines encircling the Guardian in her vision.

"Let's bring the boat around before the tide turns." Peter's voice vibrated in her ears, jolting her back to the present.

They spent the rest of the day moving what possessions they had into the cave, which proved much more comfortable than the first, once they got used to the deep boom of the surf.

When Peter decided to explore the coast to the west, Faith, eager to view the penguin rookery, asked if she could accompany him.

As soon as the tide turned they set off, following the penguin track over the tussocks, passing several sea elephants on the

324

way. The sight of the huge, belching beasts luxuriating in filthy communal wallows turned Faith's stomach. It was easy to understand how they had come by their name. The fully grown males weighed over two tons and were twenty feet long. When they were roused, their bulbous snouts stretched into trunklike protuberances.

At the crest of the next hill the terrain suddenly dropped into a saucer-shaped valley that was a living sea of black and white.

"My God," gasped Faith.

Half a million penguins rocked backward and forward on their nests, yapping, squawking, and keeping a watchful eye on the hawklike gulls perched on the cliffs. Faith could have stayed there for hours, but Peter wanted to explore the coastline before the tide turned, so they retraced their steps to the beach.

Later that day, Peter went fishing from the reef, and while he tempted Neptune's subjects with pieces of orange starfish, he planned his forthcoming exploration of the island.

Because the coastline to the east and west was a series of narrow beaches pressed against sheer cliffs, he'd have to go over the mountains. He stared at the mist-shrouded immensity above for a few minutes, then turned his attention on the western peaks. They looked less intimidating, he decided.

He saw Faith leave the cave and walk along the valley. He would leave her behind. She would be safer here than clambering over mountains. He would get in a stock of food, fuel, and furs and teach her to fend for herself before he left.

And he would make her a blubber lamp so she would have a light if it got too wet for a fire. The base was easy, that could be fashioned out of tin mugs. The wick was the problem. He searched his mind for a solution. He'd seen old timers wrap strips of raw blubber in strands of rope; but his rope was too precious. He'd have to improvise—dried elephant entrails would probably suffice . . .

After drinking from the pool, Faith climbed the rocky crag above their cave hoping to get a clearer glimpse of the mountain peak. It shimmered mysteriously, cloaked in cloud, and she had the strangest feeling that it was watching her as closely as she watched it.

She started as shrill screeches sounded from above. Perched on a ledge like medieval warlords sat two fierce-looking gulls. "Oh, very well, you nasty things, I'll go the other way," she declared and moved away to the right. But as soon as she started to climb again, they swooped on her with hooked beaks agape and talons spread. Thoroughly unnerved, she scrambled down the cliff.

"What happened to you?" Peter asked when he joined her at the entrance of the cave a short time later.

"Two gulls attacked me," she answered, dipping her handkerchief into the hot water in the pot and dabbing her bleeding head.

He inspected the wounds closely. "Hmm . . . these are quite deep. I'd best rub salt in them."

"I'm all right," she said stiffly.

"Don't be silly." He took the handkerchief from her and started to dab. *She was plucky,* he thought, and felt a grudging admiration for her.

"I'm not being silly," she snapped and tried to scramble to her feet.

Peter pushed her down and knelt behind her. "Sit still and listen. I have a favor to ask. Tomorrow I want to kill some sea elephants. Their blubber makes excellent fuel and we can put their skins to good use. We can't keep using our sails as blankets, they're too precious."

Faith tensed and her heart began to race as he gently brushed her hair aside and started bathing the wound. She hated him touching her. "What do you want me to do?"

"The bulls are too heavy to move when they're dead. Would you help me drive them out of their wallows and herd them down to the water's edge?"

He tipped her head back on his chest and reached for the sea salt. "Just wave a bit of oar above your head and scream as loud as you can. I'll do the rest."

She flinched as the salt stung her wounds.

His hands closed over her shoulders. "Did I hurt you?" he asked and his voice vibrated strangely in her ears.

Although it was freezing, sweat broke out over her body. She could feel it sliding down between her breasts. "Thank you, but, really, I can manage," she said quickly, pulling away from him and standing up.

Peter looked at her for a long moment, then shrugged and got to his feet. "See you later then."

"Where are you going?" she called after him.

"Over to the tussocks to kill some seal pups."

She jumped up. "Oh, no. Not the babies."

"To survive in this climate we'll need warmer clothing," he said dryly. "Boil down as much seawater as you can. In the absence of anything better, I'll treat the skins with salt."

"What next?" Faith asked as she and Peter dragged the boat ashore the next day.

He handed her an oar club. "Stay close and do exactly as I say."

They walked over the humpy mounds of tussocks behind the beach until they came on a huge sea elephant snoozing in a stinking wallow with his harem.

"He's almost finished moulting so he'll he ideal," Peter said softly and pointed to a mound halfway up the hill. "Stand there and wait for my signal."

As soon as Faith was in position, he walked up to the sleeping sea elephant, gave a bloodcurdling cry, and hit it on the head with his club. The startled beast reared up, its great tail spraying mud everywhere, sending the belles of the harem flying.

Faith could not believe the size of the bull. Peter seemed like a dwarf beside it. Moving surprisingly fast for an animal its size, it lunged at Peter. He leapt aside and struck it on the nose.

Bellowing and snorting, it retreated.

"Run for higher ground if it moves in your direction," Peter yelled over his shoulder, and clubbed the bull again. It came at him, trying to rake him with its great canine teeth.

Terrified Peter would be hurt, Faith charged down the slope screeching like a banshee and struck the bull with her oar.

"Get back you're too close!" Peter shouted and, as the bull rounded on her, hit it with tremendous force on the side of the head.

Bellowing and roaring, the elephant lumbered down the slope toward the sea.

"Keep turning it toward the boat!" Peter whooped. Yelling and catcalling, he and Faith herded the seal to the water's edge where he swiftly dispatched it.

Next, he taught her to fish.

At first, she found it a tame affair, until she got her first bite.

"There's something on the line!" she screeched. "Oh, I can feel it again! Quick, what will I do?"

"Keep a firm grip and draw the line in slowly and steadily—no, not like *that*!"

"Help me or it'll get away!"

"For God's sake, stay calm. This is how you do it . . . slowly and steadily."

Once they landed the six-inch monster, he tried to teach her how to remove the hook. This proved difficult as she was laughing so much the fish kept slipping through her fingers. But eventually she managed it and was so delighted with her accomplishment that Peter had the devil's task convincing her to return to the cave for breakfast.

As soon as the weather cleared Peter and Faith climbed the rocky crag above the cave. The gulls watched their ascent with indifference at first, then began to screech and flap their wings.

Faith halted in her tracks.

"You must not let them defeat you," Peter said firmly. "Climb around the other way and watch what I do."

When she reached the top he tightened his grip on the oar and kept climbing. Each time the birds swooped he fended them off until they retired to the ledge.

When he reached Faith, he lay on his stomach, hung his head over the cliff and pointed. "That's what all the fuss was about." At the back of the ledge was a nest with two babies. "Keep a sharp eye out in the future and if you see a nest, give it a wide berth," he advised.

They climbed a series of steplike terraces until they came to the sloping headland they had seen from the boat. Snow lay thick on the ground and the wind wailed and whistled through the crevices in the rocks.

"How beautiful it is," Faith sighed, cupping a hand over her eyes and gazing at the mysterious peak.

"No place to be caught in a blizzard." He pointed to a plump shag perched on a rock. "Feel like spit-roasted bird for dinner?"

"That was the most delicious meal I've ever eaten," said Faith, watching Peter light the blubber lamp.

"Think you could kill and dress a bird?" he asked as the lamp spluttered into life.

"I could if I had to, but I wouldn't like it."

"Could you fashion a fish hook?"

"From a hairpin? Oh yes, I could do that easily."

He snuffed the wicks out one by one. "Promise you'll never fish from the reef when the sea is breaking over the point."

"I promise," she said promptly.

"Here, you try to get it going." Peter lit a taper from the fire and supervised Faith's actions until she got the lamp going, then he took out the tinderbox. "Except for the boat, this is our most precious possession. Do you know how to refill it?"

"Of course," she replied looking at him with suspicion. "What is this all about?"

"I want to be sure you can survive without me," he said levelly. "I'll be leaving you in the morning."

Faith turned cold. "*Leaving* me?"

"I must explore the island. I'm unlikely to find other human inhabitants but—"

"I'm not staying here alone," she said. "I'm coming with you."

"No, I'll travel faster alone. And you will be safer here . . ."

She moved closer and smiled her most melting smile. "Please take me. I'll do everything you say."

He shook his head. "No."

"But you need me with you. What if you hurt yourself?"

"That's exactly why you must stay. If anything happened to me you'd be stranded up there in the mountains. I'm sorry, but that's my final word."

Dismayed, Faith lashed out. "You're just trying to get rid of me because you think I'm useless and stupid."

"That's not so."

"Don't lie. You've hated me from the beginning. And you blame me for getting you into this mess."

Peter frowned. "You're talking nonsense, I don't blame you for anything."

"Yes you do. Why else would you treat me so . . . so . . . *wretchedly*?"

He moved away. "If by wretchedly you mean I don't cater to your every whim, I've not had the time. I've been too busy keeping us alive."

"Cater to my every whim! The only thing I've ever asked you to do was give up your cabin, a sacrifice for which I was prepared to pay handsomely."

"I can't be bought for a handful of coins. Now, if you don't mind, I'd like to get some sleep. God, I'll be glad to get out of range of your shrewish tongue."

His words were like a blow. "Really? Well, there's no need to wait until morning for that. I'll remove my shrewish tongue from your swinish presence this instant."

329

"Where do you think you're going?" he asked as she stormed toward the entrance. "There are no inns around here."

"Where I go is no concern of yours."

He cursed. "Come back here this instant, you foolish woman. It's freezing outside."

She paused at the entrance. "You might be tired of my tongue, but I can't tell you how tired I am of your ridiculous, pompous orders."

By the time Faith reached the other cave she was shivering violently. She tucked her frozen fingers under her armpits as the coldness gradually worked up through the ground into her bones.

"Where are you?" Peter shouted.

"G-get back to your cave, you c-cur!"

He yanked her up and bundled her outside. "I didn't bring you this far just so you could freeze to death through your own stupidity."

"I'm not stupid, you odious tyrant. Let me go!" She pummeled him with her fists.

He grabbed her arm and dragged her along the beach until she wrenched free. "Where do you think you're taking me?"

"Back to the cave."

"Can I come with you tomorrow?"

"*No.*"

She folded her arms and flopped down on the shingles. "Then I won't come with you now."

"For the last time," he said in a deadly voice, "will you come back to the cave?"

"Not until you promise to take me with you."

He grabbed her by the hair, dragged her to the cave and tossed her unceremoniously onto her bed.

"I will *never* forgive you," she sobbed. "Not as long as I live."

Peter extinguished the lamp and returned to his bed. "Go to sleep."

Faith woke to find him shaking her shoulder. "I'm leaving now."

It was too dark to see his face but his voice was unusually soft. "Don't climb any higher than the gulls' nest or venture farther than the penguin rookery. And keep a fire going . . . it will help me find you again."

Faith knew then that no matter what she said or did he would not take her. "Please be careful . . ." she whispered.

His hand tightened on her shoulder for an instant, then he was gone.

330

If she were here, she would say something lyrical, Peter mused as he stared out at the dazzling white grandeur of the western summits. What a war she had waged. Yet, when he had left, she had been almost tender. . . . He did not understand her at all.

A chill blast of wind brought him back to the present. The light was fading fast and a mass of black cloud was converging on the island from the south. Cursing his luck, he looked around for cover. Although a crevasse barred his way on the right, there was a narrow ledge around its rim. He traversed it and descended into a ghostly white valley, hoping she had seen the approaching blizzard.

While the blizzard laid siege to the island, Faith spent the waking hours looking west and the nights huddled in her bed listening for his footsteps.

On the seventh day, when the sun rose half-drowned from the sea, she set to work restoring order: fishing, resalting furs, carting tussock, stacking guana, collecting eggs. Then she built a huge fire, wrapped herself in sealskins and settled down to wait.

At the end of the long twilight, he appeared. "I could see the flames from miles away," he said, smiling his wonderful smile. "They guided my steps all the way down the mountain."

26

The Mountain

"So we are alone on Ice Island without wood," said Faith.

He shook his head. "No, I'm not ready to give up yet. There's still the mountain and the east end of the island. As soon as I make warm clothing, I'll set out again. Such a trip can only be attempted in summer and time is running out."

"I suppose so," she said and lapsed into silence.

Peter grinned to himself. "Would you like to come with me?"

The transformation in her was remarkable. She spun around and grabbed his arm, her eyes flashing like emeralds in the sunlight. "Oh! Do you mean it?"

Peter was shocked by the wave of desire that swept over him at her touch. "Yes," he said slowly. "But you must do everything I say—not because I like ordering you around, but because it will be dangerous up there and I have more experience with these conditions than you."

Two wonderful dimples appeared in her cheeks and she looked so vibrantly lovely he caught his breath. "I promise to do everything you say and not argue about anything."

He gazed at her spellbound for a few more dangerous seconds, then ground down his desire to a more manageable level. "There's much to be done before we leave. We'll need fur bags to sleep in, hoods, ear protectors, gloves, vests—can you sew?"

She raised her chin in the old defiant way. "Not very well, but I am a fast learner. I may be a little stubborn at times . . . but I'm certainly not stupid."

He threw back his head and laughed. "I know."

Two weeks later, after transferring the longboat to the cave, Peter and Faith set out on their expedition. The seal-tooth spikes Peter had fastened to their boots made climbing relatively easy and before long they reached the snow-clad sloping headland. As if by magic, the dense fog lifted and the mountain of ice rose before them, glittering like a diamond.

Peter turned to her and held out his hand. "Come, let's conquer it together."

The fog clouding Faith's memory suddenly rolled away and she realized why he had always seemed so familiar. He was the Guide of her visions. Smiling, she placed her hand in his. "Yes, Peter, let's conquer it together."

They ascended the mountain, marveling at the delicate beauty of its snowfields and the intricacies of its ice castles. "It's like climbing the steps to heaven," she sighed, pausing beneath a cliff overhung with dazzling ice crystals. "Look, there are heaven's pearly gates—only, they are diamonds."

"So I see," said Peter, viewing the glittering edifice with less enthusiasm. It was thawing quickly and miniature avalanches were tumbling down one side.

They climbed the other side and found themselves on a long, narrow plateau covered with crevasses. Some were mere cracks, but others widened into yawning chasms.

Peter tied the anchor rope around their waists. "Place your

feet exactly where I place mine. Keep your knife handy and if I fall, cut the rope."

"No!" Faith cried in a horrified voice.

He gripped her shoulders and stared deeply into her eyes. "You promised you wouldn't argue."

"I won't cut the rope."

"You haven't the strength to haul me out. You'd come hurtling to the bottom with me."

"Better a quick death with you than to live alone on Ice Island," she said, and stared at him defiantly until he looked away.

They picked their way carefully over the plateau until they came to a seemingly bottomless crevasse that separated them from the next valley. There was no way across save a narrow finger of ice that bridged the void.

Peter studied it for some time then knelt and jabbed it with his knife. The ice was as hard as granite. "There's no sign of thaw in the ice so, in my opinion, it's safe."

"Then let's cross here," Faith said firmly.

He straddled the bridge and moved out along the ice stabbing as he went, until the rope grew taut. "All right . . . come across now."

Copying his movements, Faith slid out into the void. A freezing updraft caught her and for a moment she rocked dangerously. Then she leaned closer to the ice and fixed her eyes on his back.

Peter reached the other side and knelt there, gripping the rope, watching her come across. He was so proud of her, he thought he would burst. She never faltered. Slowly, calmly, she slid toward him, the rays of the evening sun bathing her in a golden glow. Then she was reaching for his hand, and he pulled her to safety.

"Well done," he said hoarsely and for the first time admitted to himself that he loved her.

Faith shielded her eyes from the blinding glare and pointed to a cloud of snow billowing upward. "Look at the way that snow is spinning. There must be a tremendous updraft . . ."

Peter studied the phenomenon with suspicion, then clasped her hand. "Let's take a closer look."

About twenty feet above the snow gave way to tiny claret-colored pebbles. Peter removed a glove and burrowed his hand into them. "These are warm. It appears that our mountain is an active volcano."

Faith stared at the ridge, terrified. Did the Valley of Abbadon with its fiery craters lie beyond? "Oh no," she whispered, falling to her knees. "The valley . . . the carrion birds." She raised shaking hands to her face and listened for the sound of their great flapping wings.

Peter knelt beside her and drew her hands away from her eyes. "What valley? What birds? What is happening to you, Faith?"

Roused by his use of her name, Faith searched his eyes. The Guide of her visions had led her to a safe place beyond the valley. "The birds tore at the carcasses . . . and then the Guardian came," she said vaguely.

Although Faith's words made no sense to Peter, he could almost taste her fear. "Don't be afraid," he said gently, drawing her to her feet. "I won't let any harm befall you. Let's see what lies beyond the ridge."

At times sinking to their knees in the crackling pebbles, they trod a tortuous path to the top where they discovered a large lake from which rose columns of steam. Faith was so relieved she staggered and would have fallen if Peter had not had his arm around her.

They circled the lake, pausing every now and then to dip their fingers in its warm waters and to gaze at the red and yellow pebbles lining its bed. After the frigid black and white world of the past month the warmth and color was a wonderful contrast.

They left the lake and walked across the plateau toward a raised circular rim in the center. The closer they got, the hotter the surface became.

Faith stopped. "I-I don't want to go any closer, Peter. What if *he* is there?"

Tightening his arm around her, he led her to the edge of the crater. "Look in, Faith. Face the fear."

The crater shelved into an inner rim then fell in a sheer drop to a dark hole fifty feet below.

"Where are you, Guardian!" Peter shouted.

Faith held her breath.

Nothing happened.

"You call," Peter insisted.

"Are you there, Guardian?" she cried, her voice echoing hollowly off the sides of the crater.

Again, there was no response.

"Ghosts gone?" he enquired as they walked toward the northern edge of the plateau.

"Thank you for everything, Peter," she said solemnly. "But most especially for that."

"Think nothing of it," he replied and pointed at the mountain's cone-shaped summit. "I see no reason to climb it, do you?"

She smiled. "No, I'd rather find wood, or eat a spit-roasted shag than waste another day up here."

The northeastern side of the island comprised wild snowcapped peaks, frozen plateaus, and endless descending ridges.

"No green valleys," she sighed.

"At least it's all downhill. And we won't give up hope on the green—" Peter broke off as the ground trembled. "The temperature seems to have risen," he said, placing a hand over a crack. "And the acrid smell is stronger."

A fierce gust of wind swept across the plateau and engulfed them in steam. "We'd best find cover," he said, tying the rope around their waists and clambering over the edge. "It wouldn't do to be caught up here in a storm." He cursed himself roundly as they scrambled down the slope toward the snowline. He'd been so bemused by her, he hadn't noticed the deterioration in the weather.

By the time they reached the bottom of the slope the steam and mist had turned into driving snow and the wind had increased to hurricane force. "We'll make for that ridge," he shouted, pointing to a long dark line about two hundred feet away. "Get behind me and hold on to my belt."

Head down he stumbled through the blizzard, praying his strength would get them through. A moment later when a tremendous gust of wind buffeted them, she let go, but the umbilical rope held and he stumbled on blind and half-suffocating with his arms stretched before him until his fingers came into contact with something hard.

He opened his eyes and ignoring the agony moved along the rock face until he found a gap three feet wide penetrating a short distance into the cliff. Not big enough for two, but it would have to do. He yanked the rope and she came half-frozen into his arms. Pushing her ahead of him, he stepped into the crevice.

Although only slightly less cold inside, the wind was gone. He helped her into one of their fur sleeping bags and squeezed in beside her. "Draw your knees into your chest and tuck your hands under your armpits," he told her and when she was settled, placed the second sleeping bag over their heads like a

335

roof and maneuvered his body down beside her so that his back was facing the opening in the rock.

Faith moaned. "I-I lost a glove . . . my hand feels as if the blood has frozen . . ."

Tentacles of fear clutched at Peter's heart. "Give it here," he said, trying to keep his voice calm. The hand was frosted with ice. He pummeled it, beat it, rubbed it, and raked it with his knuckles for an eternity, and when she finally cried out, his relief was so intense, tears scalded his eyes.

"Oh God, the pain!" she screamed.

"It will pass." He kept up the frantic rubbing. "It will pass—hold on."

He worked on the hand until he was certain every finger had returned, then he passed over one of his gloves. "Put that on."

"I can't take your glove," she whispered.

"You promised not to argue, Faith."

"Are you warm?" he asked after a while.

"On the inside. But the outside of me is still frozen."

"Cramped?"

"A bit, but at least we're alive, Peter."

"Try to sleep. I'm afraid there'll be no spit-roasted shag tonight."

Faith lifted a corner of the improvised canopy and blinked. Had the blizzard been a dream? The sky was a brilliant blue and the world was glistening, white, and silent. She shook Peter awake. "Good morning. We're still alive."

He groaned and flexed his cramped limbs. "Not so sure about that . . ."

After they had breakfasted on frozen seal meat, Peter took stock of their situation. Sheer cliffs overhung with ice blocked their way on either side, and directly ahead was a steep slope that dropped almost vertically into a valley thousands of feet below. "We can glissade this slope, or retrace our steps to the crater and try to find another way down tomorrow."

Faith searched his eyes. "What do you want to do?"

"The slope looks okay. However, it could open into another cliff and we'd go hurtling—"

"Spare me the details," she said. "Let's glissade."

"Throw your body backward, keep your legs stiff and your heels dug in," he advised as they exchanged haversacks to even the weight.

They linked arms and stepped to the edge.

"Ready?" He looked deeply into her eyes.

Faith raised her chin. "Ready."

He squeezed her arm tightly. "Bloodcurdling yells?"

She nodded and drew in her breath.

"Now!" he shouted and launched them into space.

Faith's stomach gave a tremendous lurch and for a few seconds her fear and excitement nearly strangled her. Then there was wind, space, her heels hit something solid, her knees ground into their sockets, and snow flew up in her face.

Although Peter tried to check their speed by stabbing his knife into the snow, it was useless. Faster they plummeted. Down. Down. Down. Hundreds of feet. Thousands. It seemed to go on forever. Then the slope leveled out and they came to a bone-jarring halt in a deep snow drift.

He pulled her to her feet and caught her to him in a wild embrace. "Next time we'll take the carriage. I promise."

"Next time I'll *insist* on it," she panted and clung to him for a few rapturous seconds before guiltily extricating herself. "Let me go," she laughed, pushing against his chest. "Did I survive the slope to be crushed to death by a bear?"

The remainder of their descent to Ice Island's northeastern shore was unspectacular. The following evening, when the daylight deepened into a twilight that never quite became night, the snowcapped ridges gave way to gray rubble and they found themselves at the foot of a tussock hill.

"Come on," Peter said. "I can smell the sea."

When they reached the crest they looked down on a steaming lake; and below the lake was a green valley. Not the green of moss, or the faded green of tussock, but something they had despaired of ever seeing again.

"Are they real?" he asked, voice hoarse with excitement.

"Yes," she said softly and squeezed his hand. "Leaves, beautiful leaves."

337

27
Erebus Speaks

The valley was deep and narrow with a stream rushing along its floor and a forest of woody plants. The plants grew so close together that Peter and Faith had enormous difficulty getting through their twisting vinelike branches.

"How can this miracle be?" Faith asked, dipping a hand in the warm waters of the stream. "Where did these come from?" She indicated the many plants and the clusters of yellow flowers sprouting from the center of enormous cabbage plants.

Peter pointed to the blue-eyed birds nesting in the rock crannies. "Perhaps their ancestors carried seeds here. I don't know. But thank God it happened."

They waded along the stream until it fell in a steaming cascade to a shingle beach forty feet below.

"We'll explore the beach tomorrow," Peter decided. "Let's find shelter. Then I'll catch us a bird for supper."

They were fortunate to find a cave that was as crisp and dry as the crust on freshly baked bread.

"A warm, dry place on this frigid island? I can't believe it," Faith sighed as she sank into the soft vegetation on the floor.

Peter felt the walls. "These are quite warm. The lake above must have something to do with it. Spread out our things to dry and I'll catch dinner."

As they sat by the fire enjoying their first hot meal in days Peter stared at the sky, fascinated. Red flames were shooting from the summit of the mountain; to the east, a red moon glowered, and to the west a golden sun dipped into a purple sea. "It's the strangest sight I've ever seen," he murmured. "It could be the canopy of Hades . . ."

Faith was more interested in the vegetation. "With so many flowers, there must be bees and bees mean honey."

"I'm too comfortable and well fed to go looking for bees," he said firmly. "Tell me something about yourself."

She raised her perfectly arched eyebrows. "Such as?"

"Such as why you made the voyage on the *Guardian*?"

"Oh that. It's a long and complicated story. You really want to hear it?"

He moved closer. "I want to hear everything about you, starting from the moment you were born . . ."

"Lucy couldn't possibly be as brave as you," he said after she had related the story of the pardon.

Faith was surprised by the compliment. "Praise, Peter? I thought you would berate me for my reckless ways. Everyone else does."

"I thoroughly approve of what you did—especially in relation to your grandfather. I would not have forgiven him either. In fact, I might've killed him."

"I think I could have killed him, Peter. But Lucy would not want that. You see, I know what Lucy thinks . . . and she knows what I think."

He captured her hands. "Tell me more."

Her eyes shone in the firelight. "Lucy lives in my heart. Oh Peter, I need her, I need her *so*. Will I ever see her?"

"You will see her," he said. "I promise."

She stared at him with a burning intensity. "I believe you, Peter. I believe you because you are the Guide." She told him then of the Valley and the Guardian, the prophecy, and every thought she had ever had about the visions.

"Can you hear that deep noise, like coaches rumbling toward us from a distance?" Faith asked Peter as they lay on top of their bedpiles in the cave.

"It isn't coaches, Faith, it's my heart. You're so close I have only to reach out and you'll be in my arms." He rolled over next to her and felt her chest. "Your heart's thumping too."

Faith jerked convulsively as his hands slid over her breasts.

"Your nipples are hard. Faith . . ."

"Don't," she moaned.

His mouth crushed hers in a wonderful passionate kiss and Faith's emotions collapsed in a tangled heap. She wanted him, how she wanted him. It had never been like this with Hugh. "No Peter, I can't do it," she gasped, wrenching her mouth free.

He kissed her neck and shoulders, his mouth bruising her skin. "I've got to have you, Faith."

She hit him, driving her knuckles into his cheek. "I belong to *Hugh*."

Without a word he got up and left the cave.

339

She found him next morning in the forest, hacking at the stem of a woody plant. "I'm sorry, Peter," she began. "It would have been wrong. Think of Hugh."

He stabbed the knife into the ground. "Our needs—yours and mine—are all I care about. I love you and whether you will admit it or not, I know you love me. We can't go back to our former lives, we can only go forward together. I love your spirit, Faith. It sets me on fire. You're brave, untamed, and indomitable. Every time I look at you I want you. I want you now. Can't you feel it?"

She bit her lip to keep from crying out. "Oh God, Peter, I don't know what to do. I am so confused. Hugh is a wonderful husband. I love him . . . I love him . . . and I won't do anything against him."

Peter's eyes hardened. "Stop lying to yourself, Faith." He brushed his hand lightly over her breasts and when she trembled, took her in his arms.

"Let me go," she sobbed.

He released her so quickly, she staggered. "Then go . . . and leave me alone, damn you!"

Faith fled to the waterfall and teetered on the edge, tempted to throw herself onto the shingles below. "Oh God, what am I going to do?" she wept. "How can I love Hugh, yet want Peter . . . and want him and *want* him?"

She scrambled down to the beach, tore off her clothes and stepped under the cascade. Gradually the warm water soothed her, and by the time she emerged and dressed again she felt much calmer.

She walked to a nearby rock and sat there trying to think it all through. The mountain was in a fearful mood. Tongues of flames danced around the cone-shaped summit. Above, the sky glowed pink and from all around came an ominous rumble like thunder.

A stupendous explosion—like the sound of a thousand cannons firing at once—shook the world. The air grew suffocating and the beach rose up and down in waves. The cliff split open and jets of steam shot high into the air. The waterfall turned into a river of boiling water and glowing pebbles fell out of the sky. "Peter!" she screamed as she began to scramble up the cliff. Peter appeared above, his face white and strained.

"Hurry, Faith, for God's sake!"

Faith glanced behind her and saw a huge wave rolling in.

Ignoring the scalding spray from the waterfall, she clambered to the top and grasped Peter's hand. He dragged her behind some rocks, pressed her to the ground and covered her with his body.

The wave hit the cliff with a tremendous smack and they were buried under an avalanche of water. They hung on grimly as the water fell back into the boiling sea.

Peter leapt up but as he reached for Faith the cliff split open and she fell in. She hung suspended in air for a moment, then clutched a little ledge. He threw himself down and reached for her but she was four feet below. He tore off his belt and wound it round his fist. "Get a foothold, then let go of the ledge and grab the belt."

Faith drove her foot into the cliff and let go of the ledge. The sudden weight almost pulled Peter's arms from their sockets. "Pull yourself up, hand over hand." He urged. "Hurry. the cliff's giving away."

Her eyes drew level with his and he yanked her over the top. They had only just made it. As they raced away the cliff collapsed into the sea. They ran for the cave, dodging flaming stones and hurdling fissures as scalding spray gushed from the cliffs above.

"I thought I'd lost you," he gasped after they had felt their way through the dust and darkness to the rear of the cave.

"Hold me," she wept.

He took her in his arms. "It's all right, it's all right. Don't cry."

She pressed harder against him, trying to get inside him where she could be safe. His arms tightened around her and they sank to the floor. "I've spent my life searching for you, Faith. You are mine." He kissed her and she moaned with pleasure.

"Don't stop, Peter . . . take me now."

"Say it first," he whispered. "Say you love me, Faith."

"I love you more than life itself," she sobbed and the passion she had fought to control broke free at last.

When Faith awoke the world was still and Peter was gone. Though her body still tingled, Faith's heart was heavy. What had she done? How could she have betrayed her beloved Hugh? Peter was a barbarian. There had been no delicacy to their lovemaking, no finesse, no lighthearted fun—just raw, savage excitement that had swept her beyond the bounds of reason.

She got dressed and went outside. The green valley was gone.

The woody plants were uprooted, the yellow flowers crushed beneath tons of boulders. There was no cliff above the beach, just a slope of jagged rocks covered with kelp and the broken bodies of penguins; and towering above it all was the mountain—a dark Erebus beneath a brimstone sky.

"Not much left," said Peter when she joined him on the slope.

"No," she answered stiffly.

He put his arms around her. "Don't worry, there's still plenty of wood for the boat. But, as soon as we've stacked it in the cave, we'll return to the other side of the island."

"Why?" she asked despondently.

"To see how the boat fared of course."

"Oh why bother?"

He scooped her into his arms and began walking toward the cave. "Remorseful and guilt-ridden, is it? Well, I've a sure cure for that."

"You're a savage!" she exclaimed.

He laughed. "So are you. If the boat is intact, we'll sail it around here and fit it out for sea. Then we'll get to hell off Ice Island before it blows itself to kingdom come."

PART FOUR
Strengthening the Tie

28
Chaos of Change

Table Bay, February 22, 1790

Sir,

I hope this letter will reach you before any account can be given of the loss of His Majesty's Ship *Guardian*. If it should, I am to beg you will make known to their Lordships that on the 23rd December, 1789, the ship struck on an island of ice, and that on the 26th all hope of her safety being banished, I consented to as many of the officers and people to take to the boats as thought proper. But it pleased the Almighty God to assist my endeavors with the remaining part of the crew to arrive with His Majesty's ship in this bay yesterday.

A Dutch packet is now under sail for Europe, which prevents me from giving you any further particulars, especially as at this instant I find it more necessary than ever to exert myself in order to prevent the ship from sinking at her anchors. I am, &c.,

Edward Riou signed the letter and put down his pen.

Once the boats had left the ship it had been relatively easy to convince the twenty-six crewmen, seven passengers and twenty-one convicts remaining that their only hope of survival lay in keeping the *Guardian* afloat.

The spirits room had been locked, the ship fothered again, and the pumping resumed. For six harrowing weeks, rudderless, and at times with sixteen feet of water in the holds, they had staggered across the Indian Ocean toward the Cape until they had met the Dutch ship that had delivered them to the Cape yesterday.

Those aboard the launch had also been spared. Its crew had been picked up by a French ship and brought here. But of the others who had taken to the boats, there was no word. They were missing, presumed drowned.

As he methodically listed the names of the dead passengers and crew who until nine weeks ago had been lively members of His Majesty's Ship *Guardian* bound for New South Wales, he wondered what would happen to the penal colony now the provisions were lost.

With hands tightly clasped behind his back and shoulders hunched forward, Phillip paced the veranda of Government House. Two days ago, the flag had flown from the newly erected lookout at South Head signaling the arrival of a ship. Thinking it was the long-awaited ship from England, the population of Sydney had dashed about in a state of wild excitement. However, it had only been *Supply* returning from Norfolk Island.

It was now two years and nine months since the First Fleet had left England, so Phillip was convinced that misfortune had befallen the provisions ships on their way out. With only enough food in the stores to last another twelve weeks, he had decided to transport two hundred convicts and two companies of marines to Norfolk Island where fish and vegetables were plentiful.

He smiled grimly, seeing Major Ross walking up the path toward Government House. He would put the noisome major in charge of Norfolk and send Gidley King back to England on the first available ship to report in person on the state of New South Wales.

Philip was confident that the colony would survive. Those who were industrious had thriving gardens, and the crop yields in Sydney and the settlement at the head of the harbor were slowly increasing despite the lack of fertilizer. But as the marines and the more indolent convicts depended entirely on the government stores for sustenance, he had decided that as soon as *Sirius* disembarked the new settlers at Norfolk, she would proceed to China for more provisions.

Lucy glanced sideways at Beth. "What did Sarah McCormick say to you earlier that made you so cross?"

Actually, Lucy had a good idea. It was common knowledge that William Balmain, who was doing a stint of duty at the head of the harbor settlement, was sharing his bed with Sarah's friend, Ann Fowles.

"She told me about Will and Ann Fowles," Beth said, her eyes filling with tears. "I've been faithful to him, why couldn't he be faithful to me?"

Lucy placed a consoling arm around her friend's drooping shoulders. "Ann is just a diversion, Bethy."

Beth sighed. "You're probably right. But that don't change my mind. I won't be going with Will when he gets back. He don't know the meaning of love, that one—it breaks my heart." She sniffed and angrily brushed away her tears.

"Oh Bethy," said Lucy tenderly. "I know how much you love him. Why not talk to him before you decide anything."

Beth stopped in her tracks. "You aren't sticking up for him, Lucy?"

"Of course not. But many men don't place too high a store on faithfulness . . ."

"Well, it's important to *me*. So William Balmain can sleep with whoever he likes, in the future, except me."

Tuesday, February 23

While Ralph was mounting the Governor's guard Major Ross paid him a visit.

"How would you like to go to Norfolk Island for a few years, Ralph?"

Ralph stared at him askance. "I'd hate it, sir. I couldn't leave my garden island, my cozy hut, or my dear friends Ross and Campbell."

"Never fear, Ralph. I shall be there beside you. Because of the Governor's gross mismanagement, we have only enough provisions for another twelve weeks. Therefore, as a matter of great urgency, two hundred felons and two companies of marines must be transferred to Norfolk. Naturally, with so great an increase in that island's population a more able officer than King will be needed to govern. I have offered myself."

"In that case, I shall gladly accompany you and Captain Campbell, sir," mumbled Ralph.

Ross clasped his hands behind his back and gazed at the distant hills. "Alas, Campbell must remain in Sydney. I need an officer of unquestioning loyalty to keep an eye on the Governor during my absence."

Ralph, who had no answer for that, nodded sagely. "Which companies do you plan to take, sir?"

"Meredith's and George Johnston's."

Ralph's countenance brightened. With Meredith and George along, it might not be so bad at Norfolk. "Then you have decided to dismiss the charges against Captain Meredith, sir?"

"That insolent degenerate, never! The personal honor of the detachment must sail with us on this historic voyage. All courtmartialed officers will remain in Sydney. I'm taking George Johnston, Kellow, Faddy, John-Ross, you, and Maitland-Sharp."

Maitland-Sharp! Ralph felt like weeping. Maitland-Sharp sniffed. Morning and night, sniff, sniff, sniff. And when Maitland-Sharp slept that sniff became a snore that could rock the foundations of Babylon. In the terrible two months Ralph had been billeted with Maitland-Sharp he had lost eighteen pounds and almost gone insane.

Lucy was taking inventory in the dispensary when Michael arrived that evening.

"The hospital seems to be in an uproar," he said after he had greeted her fondly. "What's the problem?"

"John just returned from the Governor's. Denis and Irving are sailing to Norfolk, Tom is to be appointed permanent doctor at the head of the harbor settlement and John and Balmain will administer Sydney hospital. Denis and Irving are dismayed, Tom's ecstatic, and John is most put out at the prospect of working full-time with Balmain. They've never been on good terms since the duel."

Michael sat on the stool beside her. "The settlement's in an uproar also. Transportation lists were posted outside the barracks an hour ago. You can't get near them for the crowd. And it's not much better aboard *Sirius;* we officers only learned about China an hour ago. Hunter's been closeted with the Governor all day."

Lucy's eyes filled with tears. "Then, it's true?"

"I'm afraid so, my darling. I will be gone at least four months."

Her features contracted with dismay. "Four months! Michael, I can't bear the thought of it. And you and Moses were to start work at Chaumilley next month."

He sighed and took her in his arms. "I'm rather concerned about Moses. When he saw his name on the Norfolk lists, he stole Ralph's boat and rowed out to *Sirius* to ask me if I could use my influence to get his name removed. I had the devil of a job convincing Bradley not to throw him in the guardhouse for theft.''

Tears rolled down Lucy's cheeks. "M-Moses is going to Norfolk?"

He brushed the tears away and kissed her lips. "With two hundred new inhabitants converging on the island, every available carpenter will be needed, darling. However, the mood Moses is in, there is no telling what he will do."

Lucy closed the inventory book and dowsed the lamp. "We had better find him. It seems that this latest decision of the Governor's has upset everyone in the colony."

Moses was seated in Lucy's parlor nursing a bottle of mead.

"Thank goodness you're here," cried Beth. "He's talking like a mad person."

Lucy tugged at the bottle. "That won't solve anything, Moses."

Moses held the bottle more tightly. "Leave me be, Miss Lucy. When I finish this, I'll be off. I'm going to Chaumilley. That wood we chopped at Christmas ought to be ready by now. I'll build the house so we can all live there like we planned."

"If you do that, Moses dear, you will break my heart," Lucy said softly.

The giant looked at her with consternation. "Break your heart, Miss Lucy?"

"If you run away, the soldiers will hunt you down."

"But if I go to Norfolk, I'll never see you again, Miss Lucy."

Lucy knelt before him and gripped his arms. "That's nonsense. I know this is a setback to our plans, Moses. But we must not let it defeat us. Michael will sail to China for provisions, you will build huts on Norfolk, and Beth and I will continue at the hospital. Let's do our best, and before we know it, the time will have passed and we'll all be together at Chaumilley."

On Sunday the twenty-eighth of February, the day John Irving the convict doctor received his pardon from Phillip, William Balmain returned to Sydney. He thought Beth's welcome rather subdued, but it was not until later when Lucy and Beth left the mess after supper that he realized something was wrong.

"See you in a few minutes, lass," he said, following them outside and turning in the direction of his hut.

"You go home," Beth said to Lucy. "I won't be long. Wait on a minute, Will."

Eager to kiss those cherubic lips and run his fingers through her blond ringlets, Balmain pulled Beth into the shadows beside the mess and took her in his arms. Although she had all the wicked wiles of a whore, there was an inner purity about her that he could never quite possess and it was that innocence that so excited him. But when he tried to kiss her, she twisted her head away.

"No, Will. I want to talk."

Her restraint aroused him more and when he spoke, his voice was slurred. "I've missed you, Beth . . ."

She pressed her hands against his chest and leaned backward. "That's enough, Will. Let me go."

"What's the matter with you?" he asked tersely. "You're as cold as a corpse. This is not the welcome I expected. Let's go to the hut, I want to kiss every inch of you."

"Fact is, Will, I won't be going to your hut tonight, or any other night for that matter. It's over between us."

He had half expected it. Gossip traveled fast between the settlements. He squeezed her rounded little buttocks. "No need to be jealous, lass. Fowles meant nothing to me. It's you I care about."

"Shame on you," she cried, twisting nimbly out of his grasp. "Fancy using poor Ann Fowles that way and not caring a fig for her feelings."

"What the devil are you talking about?" he muttered.

"You wouldn't understand if I stood here for an hour trying to explain it," she answered. "I'll not be wasting my time. Good night, Will. See you in the morning."

Balmain was not overly concerned. He knew she hadn't been with anyone else during his absence. *I'll give her a day or two to get over Fowles,* he decided. *Then I'll speak to her again. She'll come around.*

29
Adieu Dog Star

Friday, March 19, 1790

Michael stared at Norfolk Island's main settlement with disquiet as he watched the longboats being hoisted out. Huge waves were racing in procession to the shore and the water was swirling with vicious undercurrents. The wind howled and the surf broke with awesome force over a jagged reef running parallel to the west point.

Loading provisions into the pitching longboats proved a hazardous task and everyone on the bridge breathed a sigh of relief when the boats finally got away.

"*Supply* is signaling, sir," said Lieutenant Bradley.

Hunter saw the danger at once. The tremendous undertow had dragged both ships close to the reef. "Fore and main tacks!" he shouted as *Supply* tacked and came around on them.

"*Supply* won't weather the reef," Bradley cried hoarsely. "God, sir, she'll have to come right back on us!"

The officers on the bridge held their breaths as the *Supply* cut across the Flagship's bow. For a few heart-stopping moments it looked as if the ships would collide, then *Supply*'s sails filled and she raced away out of danger.

By this time, though, *Sirius* had lost the wind and was perilously close to the reef. "Put her in stays!" shouted Hunter.

The ship's head crept around into the wind agonizingly slowly. "Come on, old girl, you can do it," Hunter coaxed. But at the last moment the wind died and the ship wallowed, sails flapping.

"Wear her around, lads," Hunter cried despairingly. "Wear her and haul her in on the other tack. All sail! All sail!"

Sirius struck the reef stern first as she came about and her old hull bulged as if she was puffing herself up with indignation.

"Cut away anchors. Let go halyards. Sheets. Tacks." Hunter reeled off orders as the sea picked up *Sirius* and smashed her on the reef.

"Hold's filling!" came a desperate cry from below.

"Damage report?" Hunter turned to Hamly, the carpenter.

"She's a goner, sir."

It had happened so fast. The gray-faced officers looked at one another then back to Hunter.

"Masts away, lads!" he shouted. "If we can lighten her, the surge might throw her higher on the reef . . ."

Hunter's last order and his timely decision to let go the anchors brought the ship head on into the approaching sea and, consequently, saved the lives of the forty men on board, for had *Sirius* gone onto the reef broadside she would have been dashed to pieces.

To Ralph Clark and the two hundred spectators standing on the beach, it seemed like the end. The gallant *Sirius,* hope of the starving colony, *wrecked.*

"Gracious God," Ralph cried, sinking to his knees and clasping his hands. "Please spare those poor souls on board."

The *Sirius* men saw that they could expect no help from *Supply,* which was hovering helplessly some distance away, or from the longboats, which were unable to reach them through the seas. To further complicate matters, the wind had strengthened and the light was fading.

They attached a rope to a buoy and floated it ashore. Then they attached a hawser line to the rope and those ashore hauled it in and tied it around a pine tree. A grating seat was threaded through the hawser line and, two at a time, the men got away. The business of hauling them ashore was slow and dangerous as the surf kept breaking over them and some, including Captain Hunter, were exhausted and badly bruised by the time they reached the beach.

Michael and Moses were two of the last to leave.

"Can you swim?" Michael asked as they clambered into the wildly bucking seat.

Moses nodded. "Yes, Lieutenant."

Those on shore began hauling but the chair got only twenty yards before the sea caught it.

"Hold on!" Michael shouted as a gigantic wave knocked the chair sideways and sucked it under. He felt an excruciating pain in the center of his head and the world exploded.

"Thy . . . will . . . be . . . done."

The pain in Michael's head intensified as the incantation continued. He concentrated on the words and gradually the darkness melted into fuzzy gray.

"Forgive us our trespasses—Merciful God! You're alive!"

Michael opened his eyes and saw Ralph. "Where am I?"

"In the hospital hut. Don't move, old chap. You've lost a lot of blood."

"What happened?" Michael was surprised at the effort it took to speak. His jaws seemed heavy as lead.

"The felon you were with kept you from being swept out of the chair when it struck the reef. Lord, what a night! I almost met the Almighty myself. When I went out on the raft to assist those coming ashore, a convict fell overboard and took me with him. It was a miracle we—"

"Is Moses Tucker all right?" Michael interrupted weakly. "Moses Tucker, the man who rescued me."

"Oh . . . yes, I expect so."

"Could I speak to him?"

"Afraid not, old chap. Everyone's gone to Government House for the ceremony."

Michael was confused and disorientated. "Ceremony? Is Phillip here?"

"No. Governor Ross has put the colony of Norfolk under martial law."

Michael started up in bed. "My God! Has there been an uprising?"

"No, no this is merely a necessary precaution. Do lie still, Michael, or you'll start the wound bleeding again. After Governor Ross reads the proclamation, everyone will pass between the English flag and the colors of the battalion to signify that they will obey the laws Governor Ross deems."

"Enough of that nonsense," Michael broke in. "Did everyone get ashore safely?"

"Yes. We began bringing provisions from the wreck ashore yesterday. Much has been saved, but nothing of mine as yet. Last night the two scoundrels stationed on board to tend the stock set fire to the ship. Only through the swift actions of . . ."

Seeing that Michael had lapsed into unconsciousness, Ralph ceased his ramblings.

Monday, April 5

As Watkin Tench took the path toward the observatory, thinking to breakfast with Dawes, he spied a flag flying from the lookout.

"It can't be a ship from England," Dawes said a few minutes later as he trained the powerful astronomical telescope on South

Head. "The fellow standing beside the flagpole is hardly jumping with joy. *Supply* must have returned early from Norfolk Island."

"Looks as if Phillip is going downharbor to meet it," said Tench, noticing the activity on the Governor's Wharf. "Let's catch a lift in the cutter."

When the cutter rounded Ralph's island, Phillip, seated at the bow, trained his glass eagerly on the longboat forging through the choppy swell toward them. "There is Lieutenant King!" He waved to the friend he had not seen in over two years. "Why, that's strange. Lieutenant Waterhouse from *Sirius* is beside him . . ." Phillip's heart sank as King raised an arm over his head and gave the signal for disaster at sea.

"Gentlemen, prepare yourselves for the worst," Phillip said gravely. "I fear that an accident has befallen the Flagship."

"Everyone was saved," John told those gathered in the mess when he returned from Government House. "But, Lucy, I'm afraid Michael was injured . . ."

Lucy gripped the table and half rose from her chair. "Is he—"

John placed a comforting arm around her shoulders. "He is on the mend, my dear. And the good news is that Denis and Irving decided to send him back here where the facilities are less primitive."

At dawn next morning *Supply* anchored in Sydney Cove and soon afterward, Michael was carefully lifted out of a longboat onto the hospital wharf where Lucy, Beth, and John waited anxiously.

"Oh, Michael, look at you," said Lucy, clasping his hand and walking beside the stretcher.

He grinned. "I had to smash my head in, darling, otherwise I'd have been marooned on Norfolk for months with nothing to do but watch Major Ross play Governor."

Although Lucy was greatly relieved by Michael's cheery manner she could see that he had sustained a serious injury. He was extremely pale and heavy bandages swathed his head.

"Where are you taking me?" he asked as the stretcher bearers turned in the opposite direction from the wards.

Lucy squeezed his hand tightly. "To Denis's hut, my darling. Some members of the staff want access to you day and night."

Michael sighed contentedly. It was good to be home.

*　　*　　*

Lucy let herself quietly into Denis Considen's hut and crept to the chair beside the bed. She sat for a while stroking Michael's cheek with a feathery touch, then placed her mouth over his.

Michael stirred and opened his eyes. "Lucy," he murmured, his arms coming up around her.

"Oh, I've missed you *so* much," she sighed.

He held her closer. "Lock the door, darling."

"No," she said drawing away. "Not yet, you are still too weak. We'll wait a few days."

"I don't want to wait," he muttered. "Come here," But as he reached for her again, a discreet knock came at the door.

When Lucy opened it, Phillip was standing on the step. "Good evening, Your Excellency," she said, ushering him inside. "This is a pleasant surprise."

Phillip sat down beside Michael and patted his shoulder. "How is the patient?"

Michael grinned. "Definitely on the mend, sir. What brings you out so late?"

"I wanted to check your progress, and to have a private word with you. It concerns you too, Lucy."

Lucy sat on the end of the bed and squeezed Michael's foot.

Noticing her action, Phillip smiled. "Won't be long before you have him on his feet again, eh, Lucy?"

She smiled her dimple smile. "I certainly hope not, sir."

Phillip turned to Michael. "The loss of the *Sirius* was a bitter blow. She was such a grand old girl . . ."

"She was indeed, sir. However, we were lucky not to have lost *Supply*, also. It's a damned awful bay in which to land anything."

Phillip nodded gravely. "What was your opinion of the settlement?"

"Everyone was impressed by King's achievements. The crops and animals were thriving and the people were very healthy." Michael frowned slightly. "But I must say, sir, I think Major Ross's decision to place such a tiny village under martial law was extreme. The convicts behaved remarkably well through the ordeal. There was not the slightest hint of an uprising."

Phillip sighed. "Your opinions are shared by others, Michael. But, for the time being, Ross is removed to the place where he can do the least harm. Lieutenant King has laid solid foundations for that settlement, it will take Ross some time to turn it into chaos."

He leaned closer. "I came here tonight with a proposition. Do you intend to pursue your naval career once your tour of duty has expired.''

"No, sir, Lucy and I have decided to settle in New South Wales.''

Phillip was greatly heartened by Michael's reply. He and Lucy were exactly the settlers the colony needed. Young, energetic people with the foresight to look beyond the difficult years ahead. He was determined to use his position and influence to give them a helping hand.

"I share your vision. That's why I've come here tonight,'' he said after Michael had told him their plans. "In a few days the *Supply* will leave for Batavia to acquire provisions and as she already has a full ship's complement, the *Sirius* men must be otherwise employed until they can be returned to England and placed aboard other King's ships. Your position is somewhat more complex, Michael. Since you volunteered for the expedition as a marine, Captain Campbell could insist that you return to garrison duty when you recover from your injuries.''

"Yes, I expect so, sir.''

"Are you familiar with my experiment at the head of the harbor settlement last year?''

"You mean, giving the convict James Ruse thirty acres to cultivate, sir?''

Phillip smiled widely. "Yes, that's the chap. I know the project was frowned upon at the time, but it's beginning to work. Ruse now has three acres under cultivation and will soon be producing enough crops to support his family. Would you be willing to participate in a similar scheme? You could take up residence on that land you and Lucy favor and the government could provide the necessary tools and laborers.''

Michael struggled up in bed, eyes alight. "I'd like nothing better, but wouldn't Captain Campbell object?''

Philip laughed."Leave the cunning Campbell to me. Cultivating land is more important than standing guard over convicts who have nowhere to escape to, or watching out for natives who never attack.''

He smiled at Lucy. "As soon as Faith arrives with your pardon, my dear, I shall deed two hundred acres of Chaumilley to you as compensation for your wrongful imprisonment. And with the two hundred I give Michael, you should have a good start.''

Lucy's eyes shone. "It's a wonderful start, sir. Thank you for making us so happy; and thank you for your unwavering belief in my innocence.''

"One only has to look at you to be certain of your innocence, my dear." Phillip rose and walked to the door. "And don't you listen to that nonsense about the government abandoning us to our fate. I expect a ship daily . . ."

Lucy sighed as she opened the door. "I hope you are right, sir. I long to see Faith and—" Sudden tears filled her eyes and she could not go on.

Phillip, who was aware of her daily pilgrimages to the fig tree on top of the hill behind the hospital, took her in his arms. "Be patient a little longer, my dear. Faith will be watching that horizon as anxiously as you."

30
White Flashes

"Conditions seem perfect," said Peter.

Faith cupped her hands over her eyes and squinted at the clear, calm horizon. "I can hardly believe it."

After returning from the south side of the island, they had scraped the boat, caulked its seams, repaired its planking, erected the foremast and mainmast, built a cabin of sealskins, repaired canvas, prepared provisions, and carried out a thousand tasks but, although they had finished work two weeks ago, they had been unable to leave because of the weather. Now, at last, it was time.

Peter had planned the voyage down to the last detail. Once they were at sea he would teach Faith to work the sails, but her main duties would be to fish, bail, prepare their meals, and stand watch in fine weather so he could sleep.

Peter gazed at her fondly. Her hair was swept back from her face in a long plait and despite their odd diet, she looked remarkably healthy. Although she had taken some time to adapt to their new circumstances she now seemed perfectly content. These last weeks had been the happiest of his life and he could not envisage the future without her. He was almost certain she would stay with him if they made it back to civilization, but in a corner of his mind there remained a nagging doubt. "Like to take one last look at our cave?" he asked.

She shook her head. "Not unless you do."

He turned and stared at the sea. "The breeze is right and the swell's almost ideal."

"Then what are we waiting for?"

He took her in his arms. "For you to tell me you love me."

"I love you," Faith laughed and surrendered to his embrace. She had been happy with Peter. The overpowering physical attraction they felt for each other was only part of it. They liked the same things and they thought the same way. Although their marathon voyage had little chance of success, she was certain they would make it for she believed that Peter was the Guide, the one who would lead her to Lucy.

Beyond that, she did not dare think.

Thursday, April 29, 1790

Table Bay, Capetown

Captain Edward Riou, who had just returned from farewelling the Second Fleet to New South Wales, sat writing a report to Secretary Stephens of the Home Office.

> By the *Lady Juliana* transport, which sailed from this bay on the 30th March, I sent seventy-five barrels of flour and one pipe of Tenerife wine consigned to Governor Phillip. I had been so fortunate as to preserve the dispatches which I had received from the hands of Vice Admiral Roddam, for Governor Phillip, and I delivered them to the care of Lieutenant Thomas Edgar, superintendent of the *Lady Juliana*. In that ship I also sent the five surviving superintendents of convicts which were on board the *Guardian*.
>
> The *Neptune, Surprise,* and *Scarborough* arrived here on 14th April, and in them I sent under the care of Lieutenant John Shapcote, the Agent, twenty convicts which were all that survived of the twenty-five that were sent on board the *Guardian* at Spithead . . .

Riou paused, thinking with regret of the people who had taken to the boats. Nothing more had been heard of the vibrant Lady Stewart and so he had arranged for her effects to be sent back to England.

Faith sat at the tiller watching the sails billowing in the breeze. Last night yet another storm had hurled in on them but the boat had weathered it magnificently and they were now back on course. According to Peter's calculations they were at latitude forty-four degrees south—in approximately the same position as when they had gone overboard from the *Guardian*.

All morning she had been unable to shake the uncanny feeling that somehow they had sailed back into the real world after dropping out of it for seventeen weeks. Returning to the real world presented a number of problems. As soon as they reached New South Wales and secured Lucy's release, Peter wanted to return to Scotland and confront Hugh.

Faith fidgeted uneasily on the seat as she focused fully on her husband and family for the first time in weeks. How could she confront the family with her infidelity? The thought of what it would do to them horrified her. Aunt Barbara and Uncle Colin would be heartbroken and Hugh would be destroyed.

She murmured, "Some other way must be found. I can't shame Hugh and the family before the whole Stewart clan."

By now, Hugh would probably think that she had drowned. Why not stay dead—live in New South Wales with Lucy and Peter? Then Hugh need not be hurt. She pondered that thought for a while, then discarded it. If Lucy did not return to England, Hugh would come looking for her and discover his wife alive and living with another man.

She groaned. "What a mess."

Maybe, when she reached the Cape, she could give Peter the slip and return to Hugh. But how could she return to England without Lucy? And how could she leave Peter? But how could she hurt Hugh?

Something white flashed on the horizon. At first, she thought it was an iceberg but it was moving too fast. As if by magic, another piece of white popped up to the left of it. Then another. Faith rubbed her eyes and blinked. *Three* ships!

With shaking hands she tied the tiller to the thwart and crawled to the cabin. "Peter, for God's sake wake up. I can see three ships out there."

"Ships?" Peter echoed, still groggy with sleep.

She shook him. "Yes, three big white wonderful ships. And,

357

if you don't bestir yourself, they'll be past before we have time to hail them."

He scrambled outside and scanned the horizon. "My God, you're right. Quickly, try to attract their attention while I bring the boat round."

"Why can't they see us?" she cried, twirling an old blue petticoat over her head. "I can see them."

"We could be obscured by the glare or the troughs of the swell," he replied removing the pistols from the locker and loading them. "I hope they hear these, it's the last of the shot." He wrapped an arm around the mast to steady himself, aimed the pistols slightly to the fore of the lead ship, and squeezed the triggers.

Two cracks rang out simultaneously and sped across the surface of the water in diminishing echoes. But it was not the explosions that alerted the mariner stationed up *Neptune*'s main watching for icebergs, it was the puffs of smoke. "Sail on the starboard bow!"

William Ellington, the First Mate, cursed as he raised the spyglass to his disbelieving eye. "Jesus, there *is* a bloody boat out there! Look lively mates. Heave to . . . heave to!"

31

The Reflection of the Dirk

Wednesday, May 26, 1790

Carrigmoor Castle

The heat from the fire was so stifling, Hugh found it difficult to concentrate on the cards. His mother and father had retired an hour ago, and he, Robert McBain, and Clarrie Stewart, the chieftain from the northern glens of Cantraydoun, were playing Jacob.

Since Sir Colin's last stroke his mind had become as feeble as his body and these days he treated Robert, who now resided permanently in the south wing, more like a favorite son than a servant. This was puzzling enough, but Sir Colin's attitude to Robert's forthcoming marriage was the most perplexing of all. In three days, Robert would wed Fiona, Clarrie Stewart's daughter, and although Robert was extremely popular with the clanspeople and Fiona was a chieftain's daughter, their nuptials hardly warranted the pomp and ceremony Sir Colin had insisted on.

"Your play, Hugh." Robert's voice cut across his thoughts.

As Hugh perused his cards he wondered why he was participating in this charade. Lately, he and Robert hardly had a civil word for each other, and he could not stomach the loudmouthed insensate, Clarrie Stewart, who ruled his tribe as his ancestors had done in the dark ages.

"I've had my fill of cards this evening," he said, pushing his chair away from the table and getting to his feet. "I shall bid you good night, gentlemen."

Clarrie placed a restraining hand on Hugh's sleeve. "Bide a bit longer, young Hugh. I've a mind for a few more hands."

With an icy stare, Hugh removed the offending hand and quickly left the room. "Will this tedium never end?" he muttered as he strode through the dark passageways toward the east wing. "Must the entire castle be thrown into uproar because the son of a serving wench is to wed a local lass?"

Instantly, he regretted his harsh words. He had no real quarrel with Robert McBain who had given the family loyal service. It was the wedding that irked him, it brought back too many memories. When he reached his apartment, he poured himself a generous measure of whiskey and walked to the window. "God, Fae, how much longer?"

Surely she and Lucy would be on their way home by now. The *Guardian* had sailed from Portsmouth nine months ago. James Geldie had written that Fae and Lucy intended to travel to Scotland as soon as they reached England, but perhaps if he went down to Billingsley Hall some time would be saved. He was pondering this when a knock came at the door. Muttering under his breath, he flung it open.

There stood his mother, a worried expression on her face. "May I come in, Hugh? I know it's late but we must talk."

"I warn you, Mother, I am in a foul mood."

"And so you have been these last three days," said Lady Barbara, slipping her arm through his. "Is it Faith?"

"Her—and this blasted business of Robert's wedding. It makes no sense, Mother, and all I can get from Father is, 'Tis Robert's right.' "

"That's why I've come. Obviously, your father has no intention of enlightening you, therefore, I must."

Hugh looked at her closely. "So, there's more to this nonsense than meets the eye. I knew it."

Lady Barbara sat down and gazed into the fire. "Before your father and I were married, he had a mistress—a servant here in the castle . . ."

Seeing the pain in her eyes, Hugh said gently. "No need to go on, Mother, I know what he was like . . ."

Lady Barbara sighed. "No, Hugh, this must be said. I was ignorant of the affair for years, then one day I overheard two servants talking. When I spoke to your father about it, he not only admitted to it but also informed me that the relationship had continued after he and I had wed and that a child had been born of the union. That child was Robert McBain."

Her disclosure had no great effect on Hugh, who was aware of Sir Colin's philandering and knew of other children he had sired over the years. "Thank you for telling me, Mother," he said, clasping her hands and giving them an affectionate squeeze. "It certainly makes father's recent behavior easier to understand."

Lady Barbara looked at him with glistening eyes. "Since your father had his accident, Hugh, his mind has become increasingly disorganized. He lives more and more in the past and babbles that Robert McBain is the rightful heir to Carrigmoor—the 'savior' who will lead the clan back to the good *old* ways. Don't argue with him anymore, Hugh. Placate him and bide your time. One day, when you are the Laird of Carrigmoor, you will be able to make all the changes you want and no one will oppose you. Oh Hugh, I beg you!" The tears that had filled her eyes rolled down her cheeks.

Hugh took her face in his hands. "Mother dear, please don't distress yourself this way."

Lady Barbara's lips trembled with emotion. "I can't help it, Hugh. Your father keeps threatening to acknowledge Robert as his firstborn. What if he does so at the wedding?"

"Robert is a good man, Mother. It can do no harm if Father acknowledges him as his son."

"Oh Hugh, don't talk like that. Robert is loved and respected by the clanspeople. There would be trouble, I know it. You might even lose your inheritance."

"Mother, this is 1790, not the dark ages. Were Father to acknowledge Robert as firstborn a thousand times over it would not change the fact that he is a bastard. No one can take Carrigmoor away from me."

Lady Barbara looked at her son with fear in her eyes. "You have been absent from the Highlands too long Hugh, you have no comprehension of the feeling against you. Three months ago, on the night Robert and Fiona announced their betrothal, I could not sleep so I went for a stroll along the southern battlements. While there, I saw the fiery cross travel the length and breadth of the northern glens; since then I have seen it twice.''

"The fiery cross?'' Hugh's mouth twitched. "I thought that archaic call to arms ceased after the Battle of Culloden.''

Lady Barbara gripped her son's shoulders urgently. "Listen to me, Hugh. Soon it will be time for you to lead the Stewart clan forward in a new direction, but for a while, you must pay lip service to the *old* ways. Don the kilt, for the tartan weaves a magic of its own—and cater to your father's strange whims instead of estranging his affections with argument.''

Hugh smiled at her fondly. She was so loyal and so wise. "Set your mind at ease, Mother dear, I'll do as you suggest. Although I wish Robert no harm, Carrigmoor will be passed on to my sons, not his.''

Lady Barbara sank back in the chair with relief. "I knew you would see reason.''

The sun was bidding farewell to the purple hills by the time the lone horseman reached the portals of Carrigmoor. He paused for a moment to feast his tired eyes on the rugged beauty of the land of his forebears then, with a shake of his head, set off along the tree-lined carriageway toward the drawbridge.

The Stewart Piper, a man of ruddy complexion, who had inherited his post from his father and his father's father before him, stood at attention beside the fire in the drawing room, bone flute to mouth, waiting for the laird's signal.

Those gathered around the Piper had come to hear the ancient ceremonial song "The Craving of the Yoke" that was to be sung to Robert and Fiona by the Stewart Bard.

Hugh, standing behind his father's fur-lined litter, thought what a striking couple they made. Robert looked darkly handsome and Fiona's long russet hair glowed like burnished copper in the firelight. When he caught her eye, Hugh smiled, remembering the time his family had tried to maneuver him into marrying her. Although Fiona possessed the high color and robust build of the Highland lassies hereabouts, he had never been drawn to her, for she had a tribal nature and a narrow mind. Disconcerted by her scorching gaze, he turned away and winked at his beautiful English rose of a mother.

"Rout the tune!'' cried Sir Colin and signaled the Piper to begin. But as the Bard's rich baritone burst forth, the door opened and a servant announced that, "Mr. James Geldie from London wants words most urgent wi' Marrstar Hugh."

Hugh patted his father's shoulder. "You go ahead without me, Father. I'll see what James wants."

"*No!*" Fiona's voice was high and shrill. "No, Hugh, bid the man join us."

"Aye," cried Sir Colin. "A Geldie's always welcome in the glens of the Stewart."

The servant retired, and a minute later James Geldie entered the room. Hugh took one look at his friend's disheveled appearance and knew something was very wrong. "Good God, James, you look as if you haven't slept for days."

The barrister stared at him with haunted eyes. "I must speak to you in private, Hugh."

Hugh's heart turned cold. "Yes, of course." He took Geldie gently by the elbow and led him from the room.

Hands clasped behind his back, Hugh paced the floor of his sitting room. Although several hours had passed since James had told him about Faith, it seemed like a moment ago. He sat down, then jumped up and began to pace again.

"The *Guardian* struck an iceberg in the Indian Ocean and Faith was drowned," James had said.

Hugh pounded his forehead, but the words would not go away. He sat down again but it was no use sitting, he had tried that after his mother had left. He had tried to read too, concentrating on every word—driving the other words from his mind. But they hovered on the edge of his consciousness waiting to intrude the moment he let down his guard.

"*The* Guardian *struck an iceberg in the Indian Ocean and Faith was drowned.*"

Hugh clasped his hands so tightly the muscles in his arms and shoulders bunched. He had to find something to do, otherwise he would go mad. He would go riding. He hurried to his dressing room and changed. Then he remembered the last time he had gone riding with Faith and the words attacked.

"*. . . struck an iceberg in the Indian Ocean and Faith was drowned.*"

Hugh clasped his hands behind his back and strode to the window, feeling the strength right down to the tips of his toes. Outside, it was dark and still and starless; inside it was . . .

What would he do without her?

She was the reason he lived.

He squeezed the wooden window ledge, feeling the strength bursting out of his body.

Hearing a click, he spun around. Something had moved in the darkness near the door. Was it Fae?

I wouldn't be surprised, he thought. *It would be just like her to walk into the room and say "Hello, Scotty." Then I'd take her in my arms and we would laugh and this nightmare would be over.*

"Hugh." A breathless whisper came from the darkness. "Hughie, I *had* to come." Wearing the flimsiest of nightgowns, Fiona walked toward him.

Hugh stiffened with shock. "Fiona, what are you doing here?"

She took his hands and cupped them over her breasts. "Now that *she* is gone, Hugh, we can be together."

Hugh stepped back, almost gagging with disgust. "Go."

So blinded was Fiona by her need that she mistook the hoarseness in his voice for lust. "It's you I want," she said huskily, winding her arms around his neck and pressing her body against him. "I care naught for Robert. You are my own true love. Take me to bed, Hughie. I'll soon make you forget that English cull."

Hugh thrust her away then clenched his fist and shook it an inch from her face. "Get out of here, Fiona, or I will strike you down."

"Don't deny that you want me, lad. I've seen the lust in your eyes!"

Hugh laughed derisively. "Want you? I'd sooner mate with a cow." He turned his back on her and walked to the window.

"Liar!" Fiona cried, snatching up his dirk and advancing toward him. Hugh saw the flash of steel in the window and leapt aside as she brought down the blade in a lunging arc.

Panting, she came at him again. He caught her wrist and for a few moments they swayed like dancers. Then he forced the knife up her back until she cried out and let go the dirk.

"Bastard," she gasped, struggling to get free.

Hugh increased the pressure on her wrist, savoring the creaking sound of the bones as strength surged through the muscles and sinews of his hands.

Fiona stopped struggling and began to whimper. "Hugh . . . please. You're breaking my wrist."

He spun her around and sent her sprawling across the room. "Get out, quickly, before I kill you."

There was a sound of ripping as she tripped over the hem of her nightgown and fell to the floor. Then, she scrambled to her feet and ran from the room.

32
Laura Taura

Thursday, June 3, 1790

"Flag's up!" cried Tench, rushing into the mess. "The men are dancing around the flagpole at South Head. It's a ship from England at last! I can't believe it, after all this time."

When they ran outside, the settlement was in chaos. Women dashed up and down the High Street congratulating one another and embracing their children. The men from the work gangs had downed tools and were racing toward Dawes Point hoping to catch a glimpse of the ship. The parade ground at the barracks resembled a hornet's nest; and already, several small craft were moving out the cove into the harbor.

"I'm going with the Governor," cried John, taking off along the beach toward the bridge.

"Be back as soon as I can." Michael embraced Lucy and ran after John and Tench.

Lucy tugged Balmain's sleeve. "Can you and Beth manage for a while? I'd like to go up the hill for a bit . . ."

"Off you go, lass," laughed Balmain. "We'll be fine."

The day was dark and tempestuous and several times the large ship working in through the heads ran dangerously close to the rocks before dropping anchor in a small bay in the lee of North Head. Lucy watched it until darkness closed in, then descended the hill, sure that Faith was not on board.

Michael and the other men returned four hours later lugging sea chests between them. "Faith wasn't on board," he informed Lucy as they trooped into her parlor, "but there are six chests consigned to you. And don't despair, darling, other ships are on the way. There's so much to tell you. First, though, let's put these somewhere. They weigh a ton."

"The *Guardian* struck an iceberg on the way out and that's why no ships have arrived before this," John broke in.

"So, that's her name," said Lucy. "I couldn't make it out on her hull."

"No, the *Guardian*'s another ship. The one anchored in Spring

364

Cove is *Lady Juliana*," said Dawes. "She's got two hundred and twenty convicts aboard—all of them women. Ya hoo! That's probably why it took her eleven months to make the voyage."

"Any news of Faith?" asked Lucy.

Michael shook his head. "No one that I questioned had heard of a Miss Billingsley."

"Five *Guardian* survivors are on board," Michael added.

"Survivors?"

"From the *Guardian*, the ship that struck the iceberg. Somehow it managed to limp back to the Cape. But most of the provisions for the colony had to be heaved overboard."

"Sixteen chests of medicines, fifteen casks of wine, and all the bedding for the hospital," John lamented.

"Of all the rotten luck," cried Tench. "Had she reached us last January we'd all be in the peak of health by now."

"Lucy, let's see what's in the chests!" cried Beth excitedly. "Where are the keys, Michael?"

He fumbled in his pockets and handed them to her.

"Four other ships are due," he said, turning to Lucy. "So, you can stop worrying, darling. Faith is bound to be on one of them."

"Lucy, look at the lovely things Faith has sent you," said Beth. "Here are some diaries . . ."

Lucy snatched up the red leather volumes and retired thankfully to her chamber.

Sydney's ragged inhabitants lined the foreshores weeping and waving and the marine and convict bands played rousing renditions of "God Save the King" when the *Lady Juliana* anchored in the cove late the following afternoon.

Lucy felt lightheaded with happiness as she watched the scene from her parlor window. Although the sea chests from Faith contained many exquisite gifts—brocaded gowns, jeweled snuff boxes, trinkets, lace, and the like—her journals, with their wealth of information, were the treasures beyond price.

Lucy's throat ached and tears stung her eyes as the passengers from *Lady Juliana* stepped ashore and moved up the slope toward Government House. Soon it would be Faith stepping ashore. Lucy longed for that day, she lived for that day; and everything—even Michael and Chaumilley—paled into insignificance beside it.

"Beth and I were wondering what had happened to you,"

Lucy said when Michael, John, and Balmain walked into the mess. "The reception finished ages ago." She looked at Michael closely. "You are very pale, darling. Is your head bothering you again?"

Michael sat down beside her and clasped her hands. "Lucy, you must be strong. I have bitter news . . ."

"Oh God, Michael, you look awful. What's the matter?"

"This evening at the reception, we learned that Faith was on board the *Guardian*. One of the survivors mentioned her when he was describing what happened to the ship after it struck the iceberg. He knew her as Lady Stewart, not Faith Billingsley. The longboat she was in got caught under the *Guardian*'s stern. I'm afraid she was drowned, Lucy . . ."

Lucy smiled and squeezed his hands. "Oh, you poor darling. What a terrible thing to have heard. Don't worry, the person was mistaken. Faith is very much alive."

"Michael spoke the truth, my dear," said John. "The Governor questioned all the *Guardian* survivors. That's why we were so long. Phillip wanted to be certain of the facts before anything was said to you."

Observing the stricken faces of her friends, Lucy tried to think of some way to make them understand. "Listen carefully, all of you. Since the night I was arrested four years ago, Faith has always been with me, except for a short time before Jamie was born, and for a few days in the early months of this year." She placed Michael's hand over her heart. "She is with me now— very close. It's strange, I know, but nevertheless, true. You will just have to accept my word. She *is* alive. Now, how about a nice cup of tea?"

Monday, June 7

Michael, Beth, and Balmain met with John in his hut to discuss Lucy.

Michael slumped down on John's bed and shook his head. "This morning when I brought Schaffer and his daughter to speak to her, she was barely civil. 'Did you actually *see* my sister drown, sir?' she said. To begin with, Schaffer had the greatest difficulty answering her, as he was flabbergasted by her likeness to Faith. But when he recovered his wits and tried to describe what had happened, Lucy thanked him to keep his

366

opinions to himself, then turned on her heel and walked across the clearing to the wards."

"What am I to do?" asked Beth. "She insists upon keeping her appointment with the fortune-teller this afternoon just as if nothing's happened. It's a blooming nightmare. I feel like screaming."

"And I feel so damned useless," said Michael. "Every time I try to comfort her, she insists there's nothing to be sad about. But how can I pretend that Faith is alive?"

"Does the Governor still plan to call on her this evening," asked Balmain.

Michael nodded. "Yes, after supper."

"Thank God for that," said John. "I hope *he* can make her see reason. In the meantime, I think it's best for her to keep busy. By all means take her to the fortune-teller, Beth. It will give the rest of us some respite. The staff are creeping around the hospital as if the plague is upon them—even the patients are talking in whispers."

Laura Taura was the strangest person Lucy had ever seen. She had one blue eye and one green, and a streak of white running through the center parting of her jet black hair. She sat at a small square table in the center of her hut fingering a cube marked with strange symbols.

"What do you wish to know?" she asked in a deep, musical voice.

"Where is my sister, and when will she arrive in the colony?" said Lucy, seating herself on the chair opposite.

Laura Taura tossed the cube in the air. It landed in the center of the table displaying a symbol with a circle at the top and a cross at the bottom. "Your number is four." She tossed the cube again. It landed with the same symbol facing up. "Your sister's number is also four. Four paired equals eight. Eight is the number of fate. When were you born please?"

"On the eleventh of November, 1766."

"The eleventh of the eleventh, sixty-six," Laura Taura said slowly. "Aah . . . one doubled, plus six doubled equals eight—the number of fate."

She threw the cube again. It landed with the same symbol facing up. "The cycle will not break. When was your sister born please?"

"My sister and I are identical twins," Lucy replied.

367

Laura Taura stared at her fixedly, and Lucy felt that her soul had been touched by those eyes.

"Hence the doubled birthday," said Laura Taura. "Hence the perfect match. What is your name please?"

"Lucy Gamble."

"And your sister's?"

"Faith Stewart."

The fortune-teller shook her head. "No, her name is not Stewart. Stewart is wrong . . ."

"Perhaps you mean Billingsley," said Lucy. "That was her name before she married."

Laura Taura clasped Lucy's hands and stared at her fixedly. "Close your eyes. Picture your sister in your mind's eye. Move not a hair. Breathe not a word. And listen . . . listen carefully."

They sat for a long time in silence, then Laura Taura spoke.

> I see white-sailed ships—three.
> Many souls despair.
> There is weeping
> And gnashing of teeth.
> But your sister
> Approaches with joy.
> On the wings of the wind
> And on the waves, she comes.

"Laura Taura saw Faith approaching on the wings of the wind and waves," Lucy told Michael that evening as they took supper in her parlor.

Michael's face was set and grim. No matter what subject he introduced, Lucy always brought the conversation back to Faith. "Surely you don't believe such nonsense, darling."

"You should have seen her, Michael. Although she looked young she had a timeless quality about her. She gave the impression that she had access to a secret knowledge beyond the physical dimensions of this world. And when she looked at me, I felt that she could see into my soul . . ."

"Really, Lucy, what next!" Michael exclaimed irritably.

"She saw Faith approaching with joy," Lucy went on, smiling.

"Don't do this, Lucy. You are making everyone who loves you ill with worry. Faith is *dead*."

"No she isn't."

"Why? Because a damned fortune-teller says so?"

"No, because *I* say so."

Hearing their raised voices as he rapped on the door, Phillip was glad he had decided to approach the problem from another tack.

"Glad you dropped by, sir," said Michael, ushering him inside.

Phillip gazed around the parlor with pleasure. "What a cosy abode, Lucy. How did you come by that magnificent rug?"

"Faith sent it, sir," Lucy replied gravely. "I suppose you have come here to insist that she is dead, also."

"No, I've come here on another matter entirely, my dear. I have come about your pardon. Everyone seems to have forgotten why Faith was on board the *Guardian*."

Michael's despondency disappeared. "You're right, sir, the pardon had slipped my mind. Lucy, that night at the reception Schaffer told us Faith had obtained your pardon. Isn't that wonderful news?"

"Yes, it is," she replied vaguely.

Phillip patted her hand. "The *Guardian* survivors are willing to sign affidavits to that effect, and Schaffer's daughter can swear that Faith actually showed her the document."

"This means we can marry," said Michael.

Lucy shook her head. "Not until Faith arrives. We've waited this long. We can wait a few more weeks."

Michael looked at her with dismay. "And when the few weeks turn into forever? What then, Lucy?"

Her eyes narrowed dangerously. "Don't keep pushing me, Michael."

"Push you? My God, darling, you are driving me to despair."

"As Lucy's pardon will take some time to process," Phillip interposed quickly, "I think it best that she accompanies you into the hinterland, Michael. In a month you can return to Sydney and I will present her with the pardon and the land deeds to Chaumilley."

Lucy felt panic rising inside her. "But I can't leave Sydney," she protested. "I must be here when Faith arrives."

"That was not a request," Phillip said sternly. "It was an order."

Tears flooded Lucy's eyes. "Please don't make me go, sir. I have waited an eternity for Faith."

Phillip stood firm. "I have given the matter careful consideration, my dear, and I am certain that the trip to Chaumilley will

369

be of benefit to you. While you are there, you will have a chance to come to terms with Faith's death.''

"Believe me, sir, Faith lives. She *lives*."

"My heart wants to believe you, Lucy, but my head tells me she is dead.''

"Your Excellency, there is a bond between Faith and I that defies logic.''

"Yes, I am aware of that.''

"Then, against all logic, accept what I say. Don't send me away.''

"I must, Lucy. Not only for your own sake, but for the sake of the hospital staff. They have been working under a tremendous strain these last few days.''

Lucy stared at him through her tears. "There is nothing I can say to change your mind?''

He shook his head. "Nothing.''

"At least promise me that you will send Faith to Chaumilley the minute she arrives.''

Phillip's eyes blurred and he answered with difficulty. "I promise, my dear child . . . I promise.''

33
"Strive Then the Tie to Bind"

Tuesday, June 29, 1790

Peter gazed with pleasure at the tree-studded coves lining Port Jackson as the *Neptune* sailed upharbor toward Sydney Cove. "That's a sight to gladden any eye.''

"After seeing nothing but snow, ice, and sea for six months, I quite agree,'' Faith declared happily. "Even the air has a special fragrance—sort of earthy, dense, and spicy. It almost blots out the stench of the ship.'' She glanced toward the bow and shuddered, wondering what horrors would be revealed when the hatch of the men's prison was opened.

"Feeling unwell again?'' Peter asked, noticing her pallor.

"I was thinking of those poor men below. Oh, Peter, the thought of that prison turns my stomach.''

He caught her around the waist as she leaned over the rail and retched.

"Take your arm away," she whispered. "Someone might see."

Life on board the *Neptune* had been difficult. She had been sharing a tiny cabin with four wives of convicts, and since Captain Trail, the Master, had presented her with Hugh's letters, she had tried to keep her distance from Peter, who had been billeted with the officers of the New South Wales Corps, the volunteer regiment which was to take over from the marine corps. So far, he had gone along with her charade but she knew that he expected things to change as soon as they went ashore.

His eyes traveled over her hungrily. "Still playing your little games? I wonder why you bother, Faith. People already suspect that we are more than nodding acquaintances."

She pulled out of his grasp. "Please don't compromise me this way, Peter."

He smiled his wonderful smile. "I have more than *compromise* on my mind. I have been slowly going mad these last eight weeks."

"An honorable solution must be found to this mess," she sighed, trying to fight the nausea down to a manageable level.

The smile left Peter's face. "I don't consider our relationship a mess. We are alive, we are in love and we have our whole lives ahead of us. What could be more idyllic?"

"It's not that simple," she snapped.

"Why not?"

"You have forgotten my husband and family."

Again the doubt stirred in Peter's mind. "There is no point in dwelling on the dead past."

Faith's head began to throb as she remembered Hugh's loving letters. "Please, Peter, let's put it aside for the moment. I've waited a lifetime for today."

"Well, well, Lady Stewart. What do you think of Port Jackson Harbor?" Donald Trail the master of *Neptune* eased himself in beside her.

Faith looked at him with loathing. Beyond doubt he was the most cruel and evil man she had ever encountered. Several times he had stripped women and whipped them until their bodies were black with bruises. She could only guess at the atrocities he had perpetrated on the men. No one saw them, except when their bodies were tossed overboard. Suddenly, his noisome smell was more than she could bear. She leaned over the rail and retched again.

"Leave Lady Stewart alone, Trail, you are making her sick to her stomach," Peter said coldly.

Trail sneered. "Still acting as personal protector, eh Devereaux? No doubt the lady's husband has much to thank you for."

"Shouldn't you be getting back to torturing those poor wretches below?" Peter said contemptuously. "This will be your last opportunity. You may be interested to know that I have kept a written record of your doings. It should make fascinating reading for the authorities, don't you think?"

Trail spat on Peter's shoe. "You and your *lady* can stay on board until someone vouches for your passage, Devereaux. I'll not be put out of pocket for you."

"If that revolting man thinks I'll stay on board his stinking ship when it reaches Sydney, he has another think coming," Faith said as Trail moved away. "If he won't let me aboard a longboat I shall swim ashore to Lucy."

Peter raised an amused eyebrow. "That won't be necessary. I've arranged for us to go ashore with the officers of the New South Wales Corps. Fix your hair and try to put some color in your cheeks, or Lucy will faint with fright at the sight of you."

When *Neptune* and *Scarborough* sailed into Sydney Cove, three vessels were already riding at anchor. *Surprise,* which had parted company with the Fleet soon after Faith and Peter had been rescued, *Lady Juliana,* and the storeship *Justinian.*

"Not the thriving place I envisaged," said Peter, gazing through a borrowed spyglass at the crude huts dotting the western slopes. "How will they accommodate all these people?"

"Give me the glass," Faith demanded. "I might be able to catch a glimpse of Lucy."

Peter drew in his breath sharply and stared with disbelief at the four black slimy things scrambling out of the forward hatch. "God, Faith . . . don't look."

Alerted by the smell and the cries of the other passengers, Faith turned and beheld a sight she could not fully comprehend. "A-are they human?" she whispered.

For six months the male convicts had been left to rot in the dark, confined hell of the forward hold. They were naked, starving, crawling with lice, and smeared from head to foot in their own black, foul-smelling nastiness.

"Oh God, Peter, do something. Help them," Faith wept as she watched the stricken men rolling about the deck jerking with uncontrollable fevers and uttering the most bitter lamentations.

Peter ran forward to do what he could, but many were already beyond help. "Cover the dead with canvas," he shouted to the retching sailors. "Throw seawater over the rest. Don't stand about gaping—move!"

After the convicts who could walk were got up on deck, Peter and the sailors entered the prison. As they stumbled along the narrow aisle between the two rows of berths, they saw over two hundred men huddled together, too weak to stir themselves. Getting them into the shore boats proved a huge problem for most of the men were also blind. In the end they had to be slung over the side of the ship in cargo nets.

On shore, confusion and shock reigned supreme. Even the most hardened of Sydney's inhabitants were struck dumb by the enormity of suffering they witnessed. By midday three hundred sick and dying had been landed and the hospital grounds looked like the aftermath of a battle. Tents had been pitched on every available plot of ground and scores of white-faced volunteers wandered about not knowing what to do.

"Reverend Johnson, can I have a word!" John hurried toward the chaplin, who was standing beside a pile of dead bodies at the end of the hospital wharf.

"How can man behave this way to his brothers?" asked Johnson, tears streaming down his cheeks.

John patted his shoulder. "I don't know, old chap. But what's needed now is action, not tears. Run over and ask the Governor for more vinegar and blankets. And tell him to send someone upharbor to fetch Dr. Arndell and Nurse Gamble. Then you'd better bury the dead or we'll have a plague on our hands."

John walked along the rows of sick and dying and tried to take stock of the situation. Most of the men simply lay where they had been off-loaded. Those who could creep along on their hands and knees would have to be accommodated in the town, he decided, along with the elderly from *Lady Juliana,* who were taking up much needed space in the wards. The hundred from *Surprise* may as well stay in the wards. They were hardly any better off than these poor creatures. He hailed Balmain, who was about to enter a nearby tent. "Hold on, Will."

"Unless we get grass cut to lie them on, they'll freeze to death when the temperature drops tonight," said Balmain as they entered the tent. He placed a blanket over the nearest of the four men inside. "Look at this poor devil. He must have ten thousand lice crawling over him."

"Water, matey," whispered the man.

"We'll have to sponge them with vinegar before we do anything," said John, trickling water into the man's mouth.

"Beth and the nurses will have to attend to it, I'm too busy dressing sores," Balmain muttered. "The ulcers are the size of saucers. Where the hell is Beth?"

"Organizing groups of women to collect acid berries. They are the best antiscorbutic on hand."

Balmain knelt beside another man and peered at him closely. "This one's had it. We'll have to recruit people to remove the dead, we need the space for the living. Where are Tom and Lucy? There's so much to do!"

John patted his shoulder in an uncustomary show of friendship. "I've already attended to it, old chap. Just do the best you can . . ."

"I shall see to it at once," Phillip assured Reverend Johnson. "May I leave the burying of the dead in your capable hands? Take Cable's work gang out to *Neptune*. I've received word that there are several decomposing bodies on board. You had best bury them on the north shore well away from the settlement."

Faith was the first person Henry Cable saw when he clambered aboard *Neptune*. "Lucy! What are you doing here? Susannah said you'd gone upharbor with the Lieutenant."

Faith emerged from her stupor and stared at the young redheaded giant. "Where is Lucy?"

Henry scratched his head. "What's that, girl?"

"Nurse Gamble!" Reverend Johnson tugged Faith's sleeve. "You'd better contact the Governor immediately. He's about to send someone upharbor for you. Dr. White needs you at the hospital urgently."

"Very well," said Faith, deciding to play along. "Take me to the Governor."

Michael swung the axe over his head then brought it down in a blur of movement. It struck the trunk with tremendous force and the tree toppled to the ground. He wiped sweat from his brow and cursed. No matter how hard he worked, he could not drive out the frustration. Lucy stood firm against every argument. It was no use telling her to take a calm, rational look at the evidence. It was no use pointing out that her cherished convictions were wishful thinking. It was no use insisting that she stop living a lie. Nothing swayed her.

"Faith is alive," she would say, and that would be the end of it.

Bringing her to Chaumilley had been a waste of time. Every morning she took her journals and spyglass, climbed the hill and spent the day reading and scanning the horizon. The only alteration she made to the routine was at sunset when she went fishing down by the river.

"Someone coming, Lieutenant," called John Best from the crest of the hill.

Michael downed his axe and tramped up the slope. Natives often passed through Chaumilley on their way to the Blue Mountains and as long as you left them in peace, they caused no trouble.

Best pointed at a dust cloud a few hundred yards to the east. "They came out of the bush a minute ago. Looks like two people on horseback."

"Got a touch of the sun, John?" laughed Michael. "Governor Phillip's the only person in the colony with horses." He gave an exclamation of surprise as two riders emerged from the trees and halted at the beginning of the long stretch of open ground leading to Chaumilley. "It looks like Tom Arndell . . . and a woman."

The riders waved and the woman spurred on her horse and charged recklessly over the uneven ground toward him. On she came, her long hair flying behind her, until she reached the bottom of the hill. Then she sat up and waved wildly and Michael had no doubt who she was.

Faith drove her heels into the horse's flanks, lunged up the hill and flung herself out of the saddle into his arms.

His breath came out in great gulping sobs as he crushed her against him. "I thought you were dead!"

Because Lucy loved this man Faith endured his embrace for a few wasted moments, then gently but firmly extricated herself. "I must go to Lucy now."

Michael smiled. "She is down at the river. I'll take you to her."

Faith picked up her skirts and sped down the hill. "No need, my heart knows the way."

The mountains rode purple against the dusk sky and a silver mist clung to the riverbanks. Lucy wound in the line and waited, knowing it was time.

"Lucy . . ." The voice floated to her on the wind.

She rose and turned in the direction from whence it had come.

"Lucy, it's me. Where are you, my heart?"

"Keep coming, beloved, you are almost here."

Faith reached the top of the rise and saw Lucy only yards away. "Lucy," she sobbed.

Lucy moved toward her with open arms. It was such a short distance to travel after all the years. One moment they were still apart, and the next, they were one.

Faith felt Lucy's arms go around her and was at peace; Lucy felt Faith's heart against her, and was content.

BOOK THREE

PART ONE
Pilgrimage to the Past

1
Trail and Tribulation

Sunday, July 4, 1790

"Father said that, in the field of life, an enlightened man sows the seeds of modesty and reaps the love and devotion of others, whereas an arrogant man sows the seeds of resentment and reaps only humiliation and remorse," said Lucy as the Rose Hill packet rounded Dawes Point.

"What else did he say?" Faith asked eagerly.

"Let me think. . . . Oh, yes that the words of a slanderous man are always roundabout."

"And the words of a deceitful man are always confused," added Michael, smiling at them benevolently.

Lucy blew him a kiss. "And the words of a self-doubter are diverse—" She broke off as the slime-covered hulls of the Second Fleet rose around her like dung hills, their smell so revolting she was instantly reminded of the Waterman's Ward at Newgate. "Oh Lord," she murmured, staring at the multitude of tents pitched around the hospital. "Oh Lord, Tom . . ."

"I don't believe what I am seeing," said Tom. "John wrote that conditions were appalling but . . ." His voice trailed off and he shook his head.

"You would believe it if you had been on board *Neptune* when the convicts were brought up from the holds," Faith said, and covered her nose until the packet passed the ships and tied up at the Governor's Wharf.

"Would you like to go to Government House with Michael when he returns Phillip's horses?" Lucy asked Faith as they disembarked.

"No, my heart, I will come with you," Faith answered emphatically and linked arms with her.

Lucy gave her arm a little squeeze. "Very well, darling, but I warn you, it will be unpleasant." She looked about her, embarrassed by the attention they were attracting. "I think we should alter our appearance or the hospital staff won't be able to tell us apart. Perhaps you could wear your hair loose and I'll wear mine up in the usual way."

"Whatever you say," said Faith, keeping a sharp eye out for Peter as they made their way through the crowded streets to the west side of town.

The recent heavy rain had turned the hospital grounds into a quagmire and rivulets of water streamed into the tents where most of the patients lay on the bare ground beneath sodden blankets. They found John and Beth in the mess sorting through the medicine chests that had just come ashore from the storeship *Justinian*.

"John, Beth, I'd like you to meet my sister, Lady Faith Stewart," said Lucy proudly, leading Faith forward.

"Good God," gasped John, "which one is which?"

Beth ran to Lucy and hugged her tightly. "Oh, Lucy, can you ever forgive me for thinking she was drowned?"

"You couldn't possibly have known," Lucy soothed. "Say hello to Faith."

Beth extended her hand. "Hello," she said shyly. "Welcome to Sydney."

Faith gave Beth's hand a cursory shake. "Delighted to meet you, my dear. Your friend, Bill Narmo, said I must be sure to convey his best regards."

Beth's mouth dropped open. "*You* know Bill?"

"Indeed! He helped me acquire Lucy's pardon." Faith turned to John and held out her hand. "So pleased to make your acquaintance, John."

"The pleasure is all mine, Lady Stewart," said John, raising her hand to his lips.

"Call me Faith," she responded with a dazzling smile. "I feel as if we are already friends. Michael and Lucy have told me so much about you."

As John gazed into her emerald eyes, the misery of the past few days dimmed and the future seemed endowed once more with promise and hope. He gave her a crooked grin. "Honored . . . Faith."

"How many patients are there?"

Tom's question jolted him back to reality and he sighed. "About five hundred at the hospital and another hundred billeted in town. It's been an absolute nightmare, old chap. The staff have done their best but there haven't been enough hours in the day."

Tom patted his shoulder. "Where shall I begin?"

"If you take charge of the ulcer cases, I can concentrate on surgery."

"What shall I do?" asked Lucy.

"Transfer those patients needing surgery into the new portable, those with multiple complaints into the old portable, and the acute scurvies and dysenteries into the other wards. The less serious cases can stay in the tents."

"The poor things are their own worst enemies, Lucy," said Beth sadly. "The strong ones take the food and blankets off the weak ones, and . . . well . . . I haven't had enough nurses to watch them."

Lucy guided her gently toward the entrance. "Let's go to my hut. You can tell me all about it while I change."

Lucy pulled a shift over Faith's head and handed her a serge jacket. "Are you certain you want to do this? You look very pale, darling."

Faith smiled. "I am fine. But the smell . . ."

Lucy doused a scarf with perfume and tied it around her sister's neck. "This might help."

They left the hut and trudged through the mud to the clearing where they saw William Balmain crouching over a basin washing his hands.

"Lucy, thank the lord you're here, lass. There's a thousand things to—" Balmain broke off, shocked. "God Almighty, which one is Lucy?"

Lucy smiled. "I am Lucy. This is my sister, Lady Stewart."

Balmain searched Faith's features in vain, looking for a distinguishing feature. "Delighted, my dear Lady Stewart."

"Call me Faith. How can we stand on ceremony amidst such suffering?" responded Faith in husky tones that sent shivers up his spine.

"Your wish is my command, Faith." He gallantly captured her hand and raised it to his lips.

She may look like Lucy but she don't act like her, thought

Beth as she watched the little pantomime with narrowed eyes. *It's the first time I've seen Will behave like a mincing fop.*

Peter found Faith working with Lucy in the scurvy ward. He stood at the door observing them until Lucy looked up.

She knew at once who he was and smiled a greeting. "Good evening, Captain Devereaux. Thank you for bringing Faith safely to me."

Peter regarded her with a mixture of admiration and curiosity as he strolled along the aisle toward her. She was fire and she was ice—and something else, something indefinable.

"*Peter.*"

The way Faith uttered his name and moved toward him like a river rushing toward the sea, told Lucy everything.

"Are you ill?" Peter asked, gently drawing Faith closer to the lamp.

"No," she answered quickly. "But the stench of stale urine plays havoc with my stomach."

He proffered a bundle. "Your things from *Neptune*. I thought there might be something you needed."

"What she needs is fresh air," said Lucy, brushing a wisp of hair from her sister's pale cheek. "Perhaps you could take her for a walk along the beach, Peter."

Peter escorted Faith to the beach and drew her into the shadows beneath the hospital wharf. At first she returned his kisses ardently but as he began to unbutton her bodice she pulled away. "No, we can't—not here."

He groaned. "I am tired of playing games, Faith."

"This is not Ice Island, Peter. Here, I am expected to conform to certain standards of behavior. Please try to understand."

"I do understand. We must leave Sydney as soon as possible. *Lady Juliana* is departing in a few days. I can secure berths for us. The only honorable thing to do is return to Scotland and confront your husband. Procrastination serves no purpose."

Faith looked at him with dismay. "But that is impossible. Lucy is still officially a convict. Besides, she has no desire to leave New South Wales—" Faith broke off and pointed to a black bloated object caught between the wharf posts. "W-what's that?"

Peter went to investigate. "Another corpse. Several have washed up around the foreshores."

Waves of nausea enveloped Faith and she staggered.

He put an arm around her and led her away. "Let's find your sister. I think you've had enough fresh air for one day."

"What ails you, beloved? You look like death," Lucy cried when Faith and Peter entered the mess a few minutes later.

"We discovered a corpse wedged between the wharf pylons," Peter explained.

"Another of Trail's calling cards, no doubt," said Michael, extending his hand. "Pleased to meet you, Captain Devereaux. I am Michael Perryman." He introduced the others at the table.

"Do join us," John invited after he and Peter had shaken hands. "Sounds like you and Faith had yourselves quite an adventure when you went overboard from the *Guardian*. How did you stay alive in such seas?"

"Captain Devereaux is a master mariner," said Faith, squeezing in next to Lucy.

How rude! thought Beth. *She just shoved me aside as if I am of no account; and now Lucy is fussing over her like I don't know what.* She rose and picked up a bundle of bandages. "Well, Tom needs help in the ulcer ward. Coming, Lucy?"

Lucy set down a mug of sarsaparilla tea in front of Faith. "You'll have to manage alone, Bethy. As soon as Faith finishes her tea I'm putting her to bed. Wake me in three hours and I'll take over while you get some sleep."

"Wake me too," Faith called over her shoulder as Beth stomped from the tent.

"What's wrong with you, you silly tart?" laughed Sarah McCormick when she met Beth in the clearing.

"Nothing," Beth replied gloomily.

"A good tumble would put a smirk back on your face, my girl."

"Button your lip, Sarah. You know I don't turn tricks no more."

"Oh, la-di-da! Aren't we miss prim and proper these days? A tumble would do you the world of good—and if you've a mind to it, I know several lads as would oblige. I can name two, just like that." Sarah snapped her fingers.

"Oh, go on with you," scoffed Beth. "Who?"

"Doctor Balmain."

"Pish to him. Who's the other?"

Sarah rolled her eyes dolefully. "John Best—and more's the pity. I've had my eyes on him since the day I went aboard *Friendship*."

"Care to move in with me?" Michael invited as he and Peter walked Lucy and Faith home. "Denis Considen's hut is no palace but it's better than the barracks."

Peter smiled. "Thanks, I'd be most grateful."

"Don't be too grateful," said Lucy. "He will probably keep you awake all night talking about Chaumilley."

"I would rather listen to tales of Chaumilley than to Lieutenant Maitland-Sharp's snore," said Peter.

"Oh, you poor man," Lucy laughed as they entered her hut. "Maitland-Sharp's snores are legend in this land." She looked about her with pleasure. The fire was blazing and the parlor was cosy and warm. "Thank heavens, I didn't have the strength to carry wood in tonight. Who lit it, I wonder?"

Michael caught her in a bear hug. "Me, of course. I hope you appreciate what a wonderfully kind and considerate man you're marrying."

"Oh, I do." Her eyes danced. "How can I *ever* thank you?"

He smiled slowly. "I can think of several ways . . ."

"And I will thank you to keep them to yourself," she laughed, pulling away. "Now, off you go. If I don't put Faith to bed immediately she will faint at our feet."

Michael kissed her and walked to the door. "By the way, I am dining with the Governor tomorrow evening so I won't see you until suppertime."

An anxious light came into Lucy's eyes. "Will you speak to him about Moses?"

"We can't keep hounding him, darling."

She sighed. "I know, but please ask him once more . . ."

"Very well," he relented, "once more. But this is the last time, Lucy."

"Trail and the other Shipmasters have much to answer for, as do Calvert, Camden, and King, the contractors. As a result of the agreement they made with the Masters, the more convicts that died on the voyage, the more provisions the Masters had to sell at the end. I have written to the Minister recommending that such inhuman contracts be banned and that these Masters be prosecuted. However, by the time the ships return to England the scandal will be forgotten." Phillip frowned then sighed and shook his head. "But enough of that. How is Chaumilley progressing, Michael? Did you clod-mold the soil with grass and ashes?"

They discussed soil and crops for a while, then Phillip asked how Michael's laborers were behaving.

"Exceptionally well since I made John Best overseer, sir. However, if you could possibly see your way clear to transferring Moses Tucker back to the mainland I would be most grateful."

Phillip's eyes twinkled. "You can tell Lucy that he will return as soon as I can find a competent man to replace him." He glanced up as David Collins entered the study. "Yes, David?"

"The Second Fleet Masters have arrived, Your Excellency."

Phillip drained his glass and rose. "I'll bid you good evening then, Michael. Would you ask Lucy and Faith to dine with me on Friday evening? I am interested to hear their plans for the future."

Michael grinned. "I don't know about Faith's plans, sir, but as soon as Lucy receives her pardon, we will marry and settle at Chaumilley."

Phillip beamed. "That being the case, I shall push the pardon through with all speed."

Michael and Peter discovered not only the usual marine officers taking supper in the hospital mess that evening, but also Captains Nepean and Hill from the New South Wales Corps.

Lucy made room for Michael beside her. "You are back early."

"Phillip had a meeting with the masters of the Second Fleet," he answered, allowing his eyes to wander over her appreciatively. Several strands of hair had worked loose from the thick coil on top of her head and clung in little wisps around her neck, and her cheeks glowed pink in the candle light.

She noticed his look, and smiled in a way that set his heart pounding in his chest. "Does he intend to censure them?"

"He has recommended that they be prosecuted as soon as they return to England."

"In my opinion, Captain Trail should be tried for murder," said Faith.

Nepean nodded solemnly. "My sentiments exactly, Lady Stewart. Neither Trail nor his first mate, Ellington, had any interest in prolonging the lives of the convicts.''

Faith's emerald eyes blazed. "None whatsoever! How those two monsters can be permitted to sell their ill-gotten goods not five hundred yards from this hospital, where their victims lie dying *en masse*, is beyond my comprehension."

The officers chorused agreement.

"And their prices are outrageous!" Nepean added for good measure.

She is in her element with this fawning bunch of dandies, thought Peter, remembering the cluster of officers and male passengers who had paid court to Faith on board the *Guardian.*

"I think hanging is too good for that pair," Faith continued hotly. "They were always tossing men's bodies overboard, weren't they, Captain Nepean?"

Nepean nodded his head so vigorously, Beth thought he would do himself an injury. "Indeed, yes, Lady Stewart; and the men weren't the only ones to come in for their attention. Remember the time Trail stripped that convict woman before the entire ship's company and flogged her with a piece of knotted rope until she threw herself overboard?"

Beth shuddered, remembering her own experience with the cat-o'-nine-tails.

"Indeed I do," responded Faith.

"How ghastly!" cried Dawes. "Did Trail put about for her, Lady Stewart?"

Faith looked at him with despairing eyes. "Alas, no, he ordered Ellington to crowd on more sail!"

"The chap's an utter rotter," gasped Dawes. "Death is too good for such scum."

"Could you have Trail and his store removed from the vicinity of the hospital, John?" asked Lucy.

John reluctantly tore his eyes away from Faith. "I suppose I could swear out a complaint. However, by the time the matter went before the magistrates, the blackguard would be halfway to China."

"That is not good enough," said Captain Hill who, until now, had taken no part in the conversation. "Say the word, Lady Stewart, and I shall call the bounder out."

Fortunately, Faith's reply was forestalled by Captain Nepean who, being unable to see her, craned his head behind Dawes and tilted his chair back at such an angle that two of its legs broke and he crashed to the floor, seriously injuring his self-esteem.

"I know how we could make Trail move his store," Beth told Lucy when she, Lucy, and Faith returned to the wards a few minutes later. She related the plan that had been forming in her mind.

"I think it is a brilliant idea," Faith said enthusiastically. "How many women can you recruit, my dear?"

Beth counted on her fingers. "Ten nurses, and I could ask Sarah McCormick and her girls." She turned her back on Faith. "You know *them*, Lucy, anything for a lark."

Lucy looked at her uncertainly. "How can we expect them to take such a risk, Beth? If they were caught they would be flogged."

"We could tie handkerchiefs around our faces so we would not be recognized. That should—"

"Oh, Lucy, please let us do it," Faith interrupted. "I would adore to see Trail at the receiving end for a change."

Lucy smiled at her fondly. "I suppose I could ask Henry Cable to keep the watch on the other side of town. And provided we are quick about it, the risk would be small. All right, darling, we will do it."

As soon as Trail opened for business next morning, the hospital nurses and several "ladies" of the town converged on his store armed with brimming privy buckets.

"Get your arse outside, Trail!" screeched Sarah McCormick. "We women don't take too kindly to you and your rotten mate, Ellington, selling dead men's rations 'ere!"

Trail, with Ellington bringing up the rear, strode onto the porch. "Be off, you harlots, or I'll call the watch down upon you and have you flogged within an inch of your lives."

"You're the one as best be off you stinking, money-grubbing muckworm," cried Beth. "And here's something to help you on your way." With unerring aim she tossed the contents of her privy bucket in Trail's face.

Hooting and caterwauling, the other women followed suit and when Trail and Ellington retreated indoors, the bucket brigade emptied the remaining effluent over the porch and through the windows.

Later that day, on the advice of the Provost Marshal, who had conducted a half-hearted investigation into the affair, Trail and Ellington moved shop to the east side of town.

For the women, the victory, although small, was nevertheless glorious.

The following Friday evening, after she and Faith had dined with Phillip where it had been decided that she would receive her pardon at the end of the month, Lucy settled Faith in a hot tub then went looking for Michael to tell him the news.

Faith sat in the soapy water wiping tears from her cheeks and pondering her predicament. Although she had been happy with Peter on Ice Island and still felt an overpowering physical attraction for him, deep in her heart she was uncertain about spending the rest of her life with him.

She sighed, remembering Hugh and the colorful, exciting world of London. By comparison the thought of waiting for years while Peter went whaling hardly filled her with joy. But now she had found Lucy she would *never* leave her—even if it meant forgoing a life of wealth and happiness with Hugh or scandalizing society by living with Peter and giving birth to a bastard child. For, to further complicate matters, she was pregnant.

She gave a startled cry as a loud knock sounded on the door. "Who is it?"

"Me," called Peter.

Her knees felt suddenly weak as she stepped out of the tub and donned a white robe. She padded to the door and let him in. "I was having a bath."

"So I see," he said, noticing the dewy wetness of her skin and the way the robe clung to her body.

Faith blushed as his eyes devoured her and she began to shake. "I suppose you'd better come in."

"You're trembling," he said, drawing her closer to the fire. "Are you cold?"

His touch set her in such a spin she found it difficult to speak. "No, I am a little afraid . . ."

"Why?" he asked huskily, releasing her hair from its combs and watching it fall glistening and rippling around her.

When she did not answer, he stroked the silky skin of her cheek and drew her closer. "Why?"

"Because of what might happen," she whispered, and swayed against him.

"Let me set your mind at ease," he said, slipping the robe down over her shoulders. "We are going to make love." He lifted her into his arms and carried her into the bedchamber.

Neither noticed when Beth walked in some time later, nor did they hear when she ran out, slamming the door.

As Beth hurried along the path toward the clearing she ground her teeth with fury. After working for twelve hours without a break she sorely needed to sleep, but how could she with Faith and Captain Devereaux rolling about on her bed?

"Damn you, Lady Stewart," she growled, clenching her fists. "I don't care if you are Lucy's sister, I don't like your la-di-da voice or your high-handed ways. You think you're the only one with any rights to the hut, to the men . . . or . . . or . . . to *my* Lucy."

She searched the grounds and the wards for Lucy but when it started to rain she gave up, crept behind the bandage bags in the mess and cried herself to sleep.

2

The Queen of Hearts Departs

As the cold blustery days of July sped by on eagles' wings, Faith agonized over her predicament. Matters finally came to a head when Lucy returned to the hut to dress for the presentation of her pardon and found Faith sitting at the table weeping.

"Please tell me what is wrong, beloved," she pleaded, placing a comforting arm around Faith's shoulders.

Faith bowed her head. "I am with child, my heart."

Lucy was not surprised, in fact, she had been half-expecting it. "There is no doubt?"

"None whatsoever. I don't know exactly how far along I am, but I am beginning to show. Oh, Lucy dear, what will I do?"

"What does Peter want to do, Faith?"

Faith's face worked with emotion. "I-I haven't told him about the child. If he knew, it would give him more power over me."

"Power? I don't understand. He loves you, Faith, and you love him."

Tears spilled down Faith's cheeks. "Peter thinks everything is so simple, Lucy. We return to Scotland, tell Hugh to go to the devil, then sail away and live happily ever after. But Hugh is no ordinary man, he is the young laird of the Stewarts of Carrigmoor, an ancient tribe of Highlanders whose origins go back to Fergus the First. If I arrived at the castle with Peter and a bastard child, Hugh would be forever shamed before the clan. I cannot humiliate him or our family that way, Lucy—not for Peter, not for anyone.''

"Don't you want to stay with Peter?" Lucy asked softly.

Faith wrung her hands. "I owe Peter my life and he is wonderfully exciting to be with, but I have loved Hugh forever. He is the dearest, most understanding husband in the world. Then there's you, Lucy. I can't leave you. I can't, I can't.'' She covered her face with her hands and wept bitterly.

Faith's anguish overwhelmed Lucy and she burst into tears also. "I-I don't want to be separated from you either, beloved. Try not to worry, I shall think of something.''

Beth heard their sobs when she was still some distance from the hut. "What's the matter, Lucy dear?" she cried, bursting through the door and rushing to Lucy's side.

Lucy shook her head distractedly. "Faith and I must be alone for a while, Bethy. We have some urgent family matters to discuss.''

Blinking in shock at being thus rejected, Beth backed away. "Well Michael sent me to tell you that the Governor and everyone are waiting in the mess.''

Lucy jumped up. "Oh God, Faith, the pardon—I forgot all about it! Quickly, we can't keep the Governor waiting.''

"I, Arthur Phillip, Governor of the Territory of New South Wales and its dependencies, by virtue of the power and authority vested in me, do hereby pardon Lucy Margaret Gamble and do order that the term of life imprisonment for which she was banished to these shores be set aside . . .''

After reading the document, Philip took up a second. "Whereas full power and authority for granting lands in the Territory of New South Wales and its dependencies, has been vested in me, His Majesty's instructions under Royal Sign Manual bearing date respectively the Twenty-fifth day of April, One thousand seven hundred and eighty-seven, and the Twentieth day of August, One thousand seven hundred and eighty-nine, as compensation for wrongful imprisonment, I, Arthur Phillip, do by these Presents give and grant unto Lucy Margaret Gamble, her heirs, and assigns to have and to hold forever, Two hundred acres of land in one lot, to be known henceforth by the name of *Chaumilley* . . .''

He read that document through, and a third, deeding to Lucy the plot of ground on which her hut was built, then handed them into her care, grinning from ear to ear. "God bless you, my dear."

"Speech! Speech!" cried Susannah Cable.

Lucy addressed those gathered in the mess. "When I was arrested that October evening in 1786, I thought my life had ended, but it had only just begun . . ."

As Michael listened to her words he was filled with elation. Now that the number of patients was diminishing daily, she would soon be able to leave the hospital. Then they would marry and settle at Chaumilley. His pulse raced as he thought of what lay ahead. Days filled with work and laughter, and nights when he would hold her close and fan her desire until she begged for release. But most glorious of all, he decided, as Lucy finished her short speech and moved through the crowd toward him, will be to wake up every morning for the rest of my life and find her beside me.

"Well," she said, her lips parting in a radiant smile, "I am free at last."

"So you are," he murmured and took his free Lucy in his arms and kissed her long and hard.

When Lucy returned to the hut late that evening Faith was asleep, so she donned a warm jacket, ascended the hill behind the hospital and climbed to the top of her fig tree.

"One thing is certain," she said aloud as she gazed up at the starry heavens, "Faith must leave the colony at once or she will be ruined. Although we are separated from England by vast expanses of ocean, news of scandal is only ever one ship away."

She rested her head against the trunk and sighed. "Perhaps I should advise her to begin a new life in a foreign land with Peter and the child?" Lucy pondered the thought for some time then discarded it, sure in her heart that Faith would be unhappy living as an exile, cut off from the family and the life to which she had been accustomed. Nor was Peter Devereaux the type to slink away like a cowardly dog without confronting Hugh. Even if she, Lucy, managed to persuade Peter and Faith to head for foreign shores, Hugh Stewart, being a man of honor, would most probably track them down and demand satisfaction from Peter.

An hour later, still no closer to finding a solution to the problem, Lucy closed her eyes and cleared her mind of all thought.

She breathed in and out, and relaxed more and more until she saw herself, in her mind's eye, drifting across a snow-white plain toward a beautiful cone-shaped mountain. A full moon shone down the mountain, bathing it in brilliant light, and all was peace and tranquility.

"What is the solution to Faith's problem?" she asked. "I *order* you to tell me."

A wind sprang up; clouds formed above the mountain, blotting out the moon; rain fell from the heavens; lightning danced across the horizon; and thunder rumbled over the plain. A new thought germinated in the core of Lucy's mind. "Of course," she cried, her eyes flying open, "that is the only honorable way."

Early next morning Lucy gently shook her sleeping sister. "Wake up, darling, we must talk."

"I won't leave you, and that's final," Faith said defiantly, the rims of her eyes still red from the previous night's tears.

Lucy took her sister's pale face in her hands. "If you weren't carrying Peter's child, Faith, would you make a new life with him, or would you return to Hugh?"

"I would stay with you, my heart."

"That is not what I asked you," Lucy said sternly. "Think very carefully, then answer the absolute truth: Peter . . . or Hugh?"

Faith sighed. "Peter and I have had some wonderful moments together, but I would not like being married to a man who is always away at sea. I like being close to the people I love. I would return to Hugh. He understands me perfectly."

"Peter also understands you," Lucy reminded her softly.

Faith shook her head. "No, Lucy, he wants to dominate me and possess me body and soul, whereas Hugh—" She broke off, her eyes filling with tears. "What is the use of this discussion, Lucy? I can't return to Hugh because I am carrying Peter's child."

Lucy grasped her sister's shoulders tightly and gave her a little shake. "No, beloved. *I* am the twin who is with child."

Faith stared at her uncomprehendingly. "Are you pregnant also?"

"No, but if everyone thinks I am, then you and Hugh can be

reunited. For the next few months, you shall be Lucy Gamble, pregnant ex-convict, and I shall be Lady Faith Stewart, returning to her husband in Scotland.''

"But that's ridiculous. Michael would not enter into a bigamous marriage with me.''

"I agree the masquerade won't work if we remain in New South Wales, but if we were on our way back to Scotland it would be quite simple. Although a sea voyage is not ideal for you in your condition, we need travel only as far as China. Then, once you have had the child, we would resume our voyage.''

Faith began to see a glimmer of light at the end of the long, dark passageway. "I suppose it could work. . . . But would Michael agree to leave the colony? You know how keen he is to settle at Chaumilley.''

A shadow came into Lucy's eyes and she stared through Faith and past her. "Michael cannot leave the colony until the battalion is recalled. We must return to Scotland without him, Faith.''

The hope went out of Faith. "Leave Michael? No, Lucy!''

Lucy bit her lip to keep it from trembling. "When I tell him what has happened, he will insist that we go. We have no choice, Faith. We *must* leave the colony while there are still ships to take us. Years might pass before others arrive.''

"No!'' Faith cried. "I won't allow you to do this for me, I shall go away with Peter. Or return to England alone and find a reliable woman to care for the child.'' She buried her face in the pillow and the sound of her sobs sent fresh waves of desolation through Lucy. "Faith, beloved, this is the only honorable way. And it offers the best protection for your baby.''

Faith raised her head. "The baby?''

Lucy wiped the tears from her sister's cheeks and continued. "We will introduce the baby to the family as mine and when I return to New South Wales I shall suggest that it stays at Carrigmoor so it can have the advantages in life. Given the remoteness of the colony, surely the family won't object.''

Faith sat up. "No, in fact, Aunt Barbara would probably insist upon it.''

Lucy forced a smile. "So you see? All is not lost. You will be able to love and care for the child and yet still be with your husband.''

"Yes,'' Faith whispered. "That *is* something, but we would be deceiving them most shamefully.''

Lucy began pacing the floor in great agitation. "I know, I know, but the only alternative is for you to be separated from them for the rest of your life." She drew Faith gently to her feet. "Shall we go ahead with the plan?"

Faith nodded miserably. "Yes, but only if Michael agrees."

Lucy sighed. "He will. Let's get dressed and find him. Then we will make enquiries about our passage to China. Of the three transporters remaining in the cove, my choice is *Surprise*."

"Mine too," Faith agreed grimly. "I would not sail on either of those hell-ships *Scarborough* or *Neptune*." She removed her nightgown and selected a shift from the clothes racks. "What about Peter? He saved my life and I shall repay him with desertion."

Again, Lucy sighed. "While I am deeply indebted to him for bringing you safely to me, Faith, I can't allow you to ruin your life because of him. Had circumstances been different, I don't believe you would ever have been unfaithful to Hugh."

"But, the child, Lucy. It's his," Faith agonized.

"Peter cannot mourn a child he knows nothing about. Please get dressed, darling, it's late."

Faith pulled the shift over her head. "Oh God, how can I tell him I am returning to Hugh?"

Lucy turned away quickly lest Faith see the consternation in her eyes. "You will have to choose your words carefully. However, in fairness to Peter, I think you should leave him with no illusions. Otherwise he might sail with us in the hope of changing your mind and that would be disastrous. Now, do bestir yourself. Michael is going upharbor today and unless we hurry we shall miss him."

"Has anyone seen Michael?" Lucy asked as she and Faith joined the doctors in the mess for breakfast.

"He left on the packet with Devereaux and the timber-getters ten minutes ago," said Tom. "They'll probably camp overnight and return tomorrow evening."

Lucy, who had been dreading breaking the news to Michael, did not know whether to be alarmed or relieved. "Did he leave a message for me?"

Tom shook his head. "No, but he seemed rather excited about the bags of seaweed Henry Cable brought him."

Lucy smiled. "He hopes to use it as an alternative to compost."

"How does it feel to be a *free* woman, Nurse Gamble?" John asked with a twinkle in his eye.

Lucy selected a muffin from the platter. "Delightful, thank

you, Dr. White. In fact, if you can find someone to replace me this afternoon, I'd like some *free* time."

John smiled widely. "I can find someone to work in your place, Nurse Gamble, but I could never find anyone to replace you."

Nicholas Anstis, a grim, gray man with a permanently furrowed forehead and bushy brows that hung over his eyes, glared suspiciously at Lucy. Women—especially beautiful ones—were nothing but trouble on long sea voyages. "*Surprise* is a rough-and-ready craft, Nurse Gamble. We've no facilities for the fairer sex."

"Captain Anstis, I came to this country as a guest of His Majesty. I am no stranger to hardship."

Anstis glared balefully at Faith. "Maybe so. But that don't apply to Lady Stewart here."

What an insufferable old grump, Faith thought, matching his stare icily. "Sir, I spent the earlier part of this year in a disabled longboat dodging icebergs. Compared to that, your craft will be a pleasure palace."

"Who's to pay?" Anstis asked brusquely.

"You will be fully reimbursed upon your arrival in England," Faith informed him in frigid tones.

"Not good enough!" Anstis shouted. "I need someone in authority at this end to guarantee it."

"I am sure we can arrange something to your satisfaction, Captain," Lucy said. "Please say you will take us, otherwise we must seek passage on *Scarborough* or *Neptune,* and their facilities are more primitive than yours. . . ."

Anstis remembered Lucy Gamble well. In 1788, when he had been first mate on board *Lady Penrhyn,* his nephew, John, a fo'c'sle hand, had fallen ill and Lucy had nursed him with the utmost tenderness until he died. It would be a poor thing to repay her kindness by refusing her passage on *Surprise.*

"Oh, all right," he muttered. "If you can find someone reliable to vouch for your passage money, I'll take ye."

"Would Governor Phillip do?" Faith asked haughtily.

Anstis's eyebrows met in the center of her forehead. "He'll do nicely, ma'am."

"Oh, I *am* relieved," said Faith.

"When will we sail, Captain?" Lucy asked quickly.

"If the weather holds—daybreak Monday."

Lucy and Faith looked at each other with dismay. Monday was only two days away.

"This is a pleasant surprise," Phillip declared when Lucy and Faith were ushered into his study.

Lucy came straight to the point. "Faith and I have a favor to ask, sir."

Phillip beamed. "Ask away."

"We want to return to England, sir, and Captain Anstis of *Surprise* has agreed to take us provided someone of good character vouches for our passage money. Will you do it?"

Phillip stiffened in his chair. "Leave the colony? I don't understand, Lucy. Aren't you and Michael planning to marry soon?"

Lucy twisted her handkerchief nervously around her fingers. "Unless Faith returns to England immediately, her husband will make a needless voyage to the colony."

"As well as that," Faith interposed breathlessly, "there are a number of business matters which require my urgent attention. Grandfather's interests, the Hall, the estate farms. I-I left in such a hurry, I had no chance to organize anything."

Something is very wrong, Phillip thought. *Why are they both so ill at ease?* "What does Michael think of all this?" he asked sternly.

Lucy bit her lip. "He does not know yet, sir. I only decided this morning . . ." Her voice trailed off and she looked away from his penetrating gaze.

After a long, uncomfortable pause, Phillip said, "Why doesn't Faith return to England alone, Lucy? You and Michael can join her when he resigns his Commission next year."

"No, sir, I will not be separated from Faith."

Noting her distress, Phillip decided against pressing the matter further. Obviously, she had private reasons for leaving the colony and it would be indiscreet of him to plague her. "Very well, my dears. Tell me your plans and I shall do what I can to assist you."

When Lucy arrived at the wards that evening, she led Beth into the dispensary. "I have something to tell you before you leave . . ." She paused, not knowing how to say the words.

Beth looked at her with dismay. "What's wrong, Lucy? You look so sad."

396

As gently as possible, and leaving out Faith's pregnancy, Lucy explained what she planned to do.

"I suppose your trollop of a sister talked you into this," Beth choked.

Lucy was taken aback by the vehemence in Beth's voice. "No, it was entirely my decision and I'll thank you not to speak about Faith in that way," she said coldly.

"Why not? When she isn't flaunting herself at the doctors and officers, she's rolling naked on *my* bed with that Captain Devereaux. Face it, Lucy. Your precious sister's no better than a common whore.'

Before Lucy realized what she was doing, she struck Beth across the face. "Oh God," she gasped, "please forgive me, Bethy I didn't mean it."

Beth burst into tears. "Y-yes you did. From the moment she arrived you haven't spared a thought for me. Y-you are leaving, abandoning me, just like my mother. If you love me so much, how can you go away?"

Lucy embraced her. "I won't be gone forever, Bethy, and you aren't being abandoned—Michael will be here for you. Believe me, I hate the thought of leaving but I have no choice. There are urgent family reasons . . ."

Beth wrenched out of her embrace. "Family reasons, eh? Well, that puts me in my place. I ain't family, I'm just the nobody you met in Newgate."

Although Lucy longed to tell Beth the whole truth she did not dare. "You *are* family, Bethy, but this is something I must do for Faith. Trust me. And please try to understand . . ."

"I don't understand, Lucy, I-I don't understand at all. Why can't that trollop go back to England and leave us be? You and I were happy before she came here and turned our lives upside down."

Lucy's eyes narrowed. "I know you are hurt, Beth, but I won't have you speaking about Faith like that."

Her face contracting with bitterness, Beth marched to the door. "Good-bye then, Lucy. I'll stay with my *friend*, Susannah, until you have gone."

Beth did not return to the hut that night, nor was she in the mess the following morning when Lucy and Faith arrived for breakfast wearing identical hairstyles.

John looked up and laughed. "Which one is which?"

"Can't you tell?" Lucy asked in Faith's most imperious tones.

John's eyes twinkled. "You're Faith."

Lucy sat down opposite Tom "Who do you think I am, Tom?"

Tom scratched his head. "Damned if I know."

Lucy was relieved. If the doctors could not tell her and Faith apart, how could a casual acquaintance on board ship?

She reached across the table and clasped John's hand. "Tomorrow, Faith and I will be leaving for England aboard the *Surprise*. I am sorry to give you so little notice, John, but we only decided yesterday—"

"I beg your pardon?" John's face was a mask of shock.

"I am sorry to give you so little warning, but we decided only yesterday . . ."

"What *are* you talking about?" Tom gasped. "Michael made no mention of this."

A band of tension tightened around Lucy's chest. "Michael doesn't know yet." The silence grew until she felt like screaming. "I will speak to him as soon as he—"

"By God, you *are* serious!" John exploded.

"Why are you leaving so suddenly?" Tom asked suspiciously.

"There are family reasons."

"What family reasons?"

Although Lucy trusted the two men seated opposite, she kept her peace. An idle word, or slip of the tongue—no matter how unintentional—could ruin Faith. Michael was the only one she could risk telling. "I am sorry," she said, looking pleadingly from Tom to John, "my reasons are personal."

"So, it's good-bye," Tom said slowly, his face pinched and gray. "No by your leaves, beg your pardons, or explanations. Just good-bye Tom and John, and off you go . . ."

Tears flooded Lucy's eyes. "Don't speak that way, Tom. I am not deserting you. In a year or two I will return to New South Wales and Michael and I will marry as we planned."

"How can you be so selfish!" John shouted. "Michael wants to marry you *now*, not in ten years' time."

Lucy stared at him hopelessly. "Michael will understand."

"No, he won't—any more than Tom or I do."

Unable to quell the snakes of nausea writhing in her stomach, Faith clamped her hands over her mouth.

"All this shouting in making Faith ill," Lucy said, rising to her feet. "There is no point to this discussion, my mind is made up. We leave tomorrow."

By the time the Rose Hill Packet returned to Sydney that evening, Lucy was panicking.

"Peter has just gone into Denis Considen's hut but Michael isn't with him," said Faith who was keeping watch at the window.

Lucy snatched up her wrap. "He's probably still at the boat; I'll run over to the east side and meet him while you speak to Peter. Hurry, there isn't much time." She paused at the door. "Be firm with Peter, darling. Everything depends on it."

Faith nodded grimly. "Don't worry, I won't weaken. Please tell Michael . . . tell him I'm sorry." She shook her head in a lost way. "Oh, Lucy, are you sure we are doing the right thing? Michael will get such a shock. Can't we wait?"

"The longer we delay, the more intolerable it will be for everyone." Lucy opened the door. "I must go, Faith. See you at the hospital wharf when Retreat beats. Don't be late, Anstis would love an excuse to leave us behind."

The Governor's Wharf was a hive of activity when Lucy arrived a few minutes later. Spying John Best clambering ashore, she pushed her way through the crowd to his side. "Good evening, John. Where is Lieutenant Perryman?"

"Hello, Lucy. The Lieutenant got a lend of a horse and took the bags of seaweed to Chaumilley," Best said cheerfully. "He'll be back at the end of the week."

Drawing in a shuddering breath, Faith knocked on the door of Denis Considen's hut.

"Glad you could come," said Peter as he ushered her inside. "Why so solemn?"

She stared at him. "Peter, I must tell you—"

"Later," he said firmly, taking her in his arms. She clung to him, drawing in his strength, knowing this was the last time he would ever hold her. "You are mine and mine alone," he murmured. "Say it, *say* you love me, Faith."

As the words jangled like a discordant bell in her brain, Faith wondered where she had heard them before. Then she remembered —in the cave on Ice Island, the first time they had made love.

The bell kept ringing, shrill and jarring. There had been another time, another place, when she had heard those words. With dread, she remembered that the Guide had spoken them after leading her beyond the Valley of Abaddon. Then, she had answered, "I love you more than life itself."

Did she love Peter Devereaux more than Hugh, more than honor, more than life itself?

Forcing down the panic, she looked him straight in the eye. "I don't love you, Peter. I am returning to my husband. Lucy and I will leave at daybreak aboard the *Surprise*."

He crushed her tightly against him. "You are not leaving me," he said, his voice thick with pain and despair.

"From the beginning, we knew this moment would come," she wept."I-I have my duty . . ."

The light left his eyes and he thrust her from him. "Go, then," he said coldly, "and may your precious *duty* sustain us in the empty years ahead."

She stumbled outside into the night, her mind in turmoil. What was she doing? How could she leave him, the Guide of her life? Only he could lead her to safety.

She turned back toward the hut, but even though she turned slowly, she turned before Time and there, in the space between one second and another, stood the Guardian, barring her way with his broadsword.

> Your fate is sealed
> Seed of Fallacy.
> In the world of the *fixed*
> There is no free choice.
> Go! The prophecy
> Must be fulfilled.

He smote the ground with his sword, Time moved forward, and Faith found herself in a dark passageway that seemed to go on forever.

"Where are you?" cried a voice.

"Hold on," she called. "Hold on, my heart, I am coming." A moment later, the dark veil lifted and she saw Lucy standing at the end of the hospital wharf.

Peter heaved himself the last few feet to the top of North Head and strode across the desolate plateau to the edge. Opposite, the Union Flag fluttered on South Head. Below, gigantic waves smashed against the cliff. To the east, the first glimmer of dawn lit the sea.

He turned his back on the sunrise and searched the gray waters of the harbor for *Surprise*. Aided by a howling gale she came toward him, bucking and rearing, her sails silhouetted against the windswept sky.

"She has left me," he muttered with a mixture of rage and disbelief as the ship hit the swell at the entrance. "Faith has left me. She is gone."

There was an aching hollow in the pit of his stomach and suddenly he wanted to vomit. "Jesus," he groaned, "Jesus . . . I'm *afraid*."

As the ship passed out into the open sea the words of a long forgotten poem echoed, like a distant bell, across the bitter valley of his thoughts. He whispered.

> Oh, Muse,
> White Goddess of the moon,
> Queen of grace and beauty,
> Ninefold nymph divine,
> Huntress of my heart,
> Siren of my soul,
> Mistress of my mind;
> Why did you
> Lift me to the stars,
> Lead me with yourself,
> Love me for your own;
> Then leave me here to die
> Upon this unknown shore
> *Empty*, and alone?

3

The Brothel on the Hill

"Hello!" Michael dumped the haversack inside Denis Considen's hut and grinned at Peter. "Won't be long. Just going over to Lucy's."

Peter saluted him with a half empty brandy glass. "Join me?"

Michael's grin widened. "It's a bit early in the day for me."

"It won't be when you hear my news." Peter kicked a chair out from the table. "Sit down."

"Have a heart, Peter. It's been a week since I saw Lucy."

"My news concerns her." He uncorked the bottle and filled a glass. "Sit down and drink that."

Michael eyed the brandy dubiously. "All of it?"

"Believe me, Michael, you're going to need it."

Might as well humor him, Michael decided, tossing back the fiery liquid. "Right then, Peter, I'm braced. What's this all about?"

Peter looked at him bleakly. "Lucy and Faith left last Monday aboard *Surprise*."

"*What?*" Michael's face turned ashen. "Why?"

"Faith decided to return to her husband and, apparently, Lucy could not bear to be parted from her."

Michael shook his head. "No, it doesn't make sense. Lucy wouldn't leave the colony without telling me."

"Did you and she have an argument before you went upharbor?" Peter asked; but Michael ignored him and sat hunched over the table still shaking his head. Suddenly he got up and walked to the door.

"Where are you going?"

"To her hut. You're lying drunk."

Peter reached for his jacket. "I'll come with you."

Michael wandered around Sydney making arrangements to return to Chaumilley. Nothing made sense. Lucy had never hinted that she wanted to return to England. What had happened while he was upharbor?

Beth was convinced that Faith had forced Lucy to leave but he didn't believe that for a moment. From the beginning, Lucy had made the decisions and an adoring Faith had willingly complied. The Governor believed it had been Lucy's decision to leave the colony; John and Tom could shed no light on the mystery; and neither did the note.

Michael unfolded the scrap of paper John Best had given him and read the hastily scribbled message for the umpteenth time.

Michael, I know how confused and angry you will be when you read this, darling, but *I had no choice.* I love you; that will never change, but Faith needs me and I am unable to break the tie that binds us. When *Surprise* reaches

402

Norfolk Island I will tell Moses what cannot be committed to paper—he can pass it on to you when he returns. Look after Bethy; she thinks I have abandoned her, but I am not abandoning anyone. Please go on with our plans for Chaumilley, darling. And trust me, I know what I am doing. Forgive me, I can't bear the thought of hurting you. I will write as soon as I can. All my love, Lucy.

Michael screwed up the note and tossed it away. How long was he supposed to wait this time? Two years? Five? Ten? And what could she tell Moses that she couldn't have told *him* two weeks ago? Anger gnawed at his insides all day and by the time he walked into the hospital mess that evening he was in a towering rage.

Peter was desperate to get away and had signed on as a fo'c'sle hand aboard the *Scarborough,* which was leaving in the morning. A few acquaintances had gathered to give him a send-off.

It's like a damned wake, Michael thought, as he gazed at the gloomy faces around the table. Beth sat huddled against him, red-eyed and brimful of tears; John slouched in his chair, surly and silent; Tom barely spoke; Balmain left with a muttered excuse; Tench and Meredith bickered over trifles; and Peter looked like someone who had just discovered his illness was terminal.

Finally, Michael could stand it no longer. "Come on, old chap," he said, jumping up and pulling Peter after him. "Let's go to Cable's. I'll cadge some grog and we can drown our sorrows."

"Can I come, too?" Beth asked, looking at him with tragic eyes.

He patted her cheek. "Only if you put a smile on your face."

"Henry won't have any grog," she said as they crossed the clearing. "Now he's Chief Constable of the nightwatch, he don't keep contraband goods on the premises. But I know where we can get some." She pointed to the sandstone hills lining the western promontory of the cove. "Up at Sarah McCormick's tavern."

"I've just lost my taste for spirits," Peter muttered after they had climbed the narrow, twisting lanes to Sarah's door. He had frequented many such seedy taverns and knew what to expect. Trouble, always trouble. He was not in the mood tonight. "Let's go back to Denis's and finish that bottle of brandy," he urged.

Michael laughed. "Sounds like they are enjoying themselves. *I'm* going in."

Beth clasped his hand. "Me too."

Resignedly, Peter shouldered aside a drunk, opened the door and stepped down into a large, low-ceilinged, smoke-filled room packed to the rafters with people. He eyed the blackened walls and the grimy faces of the patrons with distaste. "What a filthy den."

However, the atmosphere had the opposite effect on Michael. Placing an arm around Beth, he pushed his way through the roaring throng to the bar.

"Sarah! Over here, Sarah!" Beth screeched. "Got any Honeysuckle Heaven for my friends?"

Peter stared at Beth with surprise. She looked as innocent as a newborn lamb but she obviously counted the blousy harlot behind the bar as an intimate.

Sarah McCormick, an old hand at sniffing out trouble, took one look at Peter and Michael and decided to get rid of them quick smart. "Sure thing, Bethy. I'll pop out back and get it, then you and the gents can be on your way."

Michael paid for the liquor and turned to Peter. "See Beth back to the hospital, old chap. I fancy a few hands of Brag." Without waiting for an answer, he picked up his cask of wine and shouldered his way to the card tables.

Peter shrugged and looked at Beth. "Go home."

Beth glared at him rebelliously. "No. I want to stay with Michael."

He bundled her outside into the alley. "There's nothing you can do. Go home."

"Want to join the game?" Michael invited as Peter drew up a chair next to him.

Peter shook his head. "No thanks, Poque's my game."

Michael went back to studying the six sailors at the table. One of the men from *Neptune* was particularly obnoxious—a redheaded, foul-mouthed giant who was not only a big drinker and a bad loser, but crowed like a rooster every time he won.

Though he continued to down glass after glass of wine, Michael played his hands unemotionally, biding his time, watching his mark and waiting for the right opportunity. Just after eleven, it came. The dealer asked redheaded Neptune for discards.

"I'll hang on to these five beauties, matey!" Neptune whooped.

Michael studied his cards. A pair of deuces. Perfect. The betting lasted three rounds, then the others dropped out.

"You quitting, too, Lieutenant?" Neptune chortled.

Michael pushed ten coins into the center. "Your ten, and I shall raise you ten."

"Ya-hoo!" crowed Neptune. "Your ten, and another ten!"

Michael felt a pleasurable tightening in his gut. "Your ten . . . and another twenty."

Neptune picked up his cards and fanned them. Four knaves, the best hand he'd had all month. He counted out his money and slammed it down. "Twenty, and another forty, matey!"

Like lightning, Michael retaliated. "Your forty and another eighty, friend."

Neptune glared at Michael's impassive face. The bloody dandy was bragging every round. He fanned his cards and shuffled his feet. Eighty to look. How had the betting got so high? He'd be a pauper if he lost. A terrible thought assailed him. What if the bastard also had four of a kind? He stared at his four knaves. Suddenly, they did not look so good. Sweat broke out on his brow.

Michael saw it and smiled. "Your bid . . . friend."

Peter saw it and flexed his fingers under the table.

Neptune fidgeted in his chair.

"I said, your bid."

"I'm out," Neptune muttered, tossing in his cards. "What did you have?"

Michael smiled at him derisively. "Cost you eighty to look, friend."

"You'll get no more out of me!" shouted Neptune, and flipped over Michael's cards. "A pair of deuces! By God! I had four knaves!" Neptune turned to his three shipmates. "Bloody dandy thinks he can play us all for oafs!"

Michael rose, reached across the table and grabbed his jerkin. "That will cost you eighty, welsher."

Neptune jumped up wildly. Michael blocked and brought up a left swinging under Neptune's jaw which sent him reeling backward. Drinks and cards went flying everywhere. Peter kicked the nearest of Neptune's mates in the groin. The man crumpled to the floor with a thin scream. The other two men lunged at him. Peter drove a shoulder into one and kicked the other in the knee as they fell on him.

Roaring like an enraged bull, Neptune scrambled to his feet and pulled out a long-bladed knife. Michael crouched and beckoned. "Come on, you gutless welsher. What's keeping you?"

Neptune spun the knife in his hand, drew it back over his shoulder and lunged. As the knife flashed down, Michael grasped

405

Neptune's wrist in an iron grip. He yanked the sailor round and wrenched the knife up his back.

Neptune fell on his face and Michael came down knees first. *"Aagh!"* Neptune grunted and let go of the knife. Michael reefed him up by the jerkin and flung him into the crowd.

Arms flaying, Neptune charged again, catching Michael under the eye and across the mouth. Michael tasted blood and his head hummed. Neptune brought up his knee aiming for Michael's crotch, but Michael turned in time and took the blow on the thigh. Panting now, Neptune jabbed at Michael's ribs. Michael punched him in the stomach, on the bridge of the nose and followed through with an uppercut that almost took off the sailor's head.

Neptune's legs buckled under him and he sank to the floor, blood streaming from his face. "Enough matey," he groaned, throwing up his hands. "I've had enough."

Blind rage encompassing him, Michael dragged Neptune to his knees, held him with one hand, and lay into him with the other. Neptune's head snapped to one side and he collapsed on the floor, out cold. Michael kicked him viciously. "Get up, you coward!"

"Someone stop him!" Sarah screamed.

Two men grabbed Michael from behind. He shook them off like flies and turned on the crowd. "Come on, you bastards. Who's next?"

Peter pushed an assailant out the way and laid a hand on Michael's shoulder. "Enough, Michael," he said calmly. "Let's go."

Michael swung round. "Back off, Peter, I've no quarrel with you."

Peter stared at him steadily. "Nor any man here. She's gone, and there is nothing you can do."

"Gone?" Michael clenched and unclenched his fists, his dazed mind struggling to comprehend. "Gone?"

Peter nodded, his mouth twisted. "And not a damn thing we can do," he said bitterly. Then he shrugged and held out his arm as Michael staggered. "Come on, man. Let's get out of this rat hole. I have to be on board in another hour."

"What will you do?" Michael asked Peter as they stumbled back to Denis's hut.

"Oh, I don't know. Probably work my way back to Boston and go on with my plans to establish a fishery in the Southern Ocean. What will *you* do?"

Michael shook his head. "What can I do? She was my life."

"Well, I hope you find a more useful occupation than beating up every dumb bastard who looks at you sideways. You could come back to America with me. Extra hands are always welcome aboard ship—and no questions asked."

Michael shook his head. "No, I am done with the sea. I'll work the land Phillip gave me." His eyes grew bleak. "But I'm not setting foot on Chaumilley again. I have wasted enough of my life on her. God, I hate her, Peter."

The bitterness leapt again in Peter's heart but when he spoke his voice was gentle. "No you don't, Michael. You're angry. Hang on to that—it will help you get through the next few months." He held out his hand. "Good-bye, Michael. Good luck."

Michael gripped his hand tightly. "Good-bye, Peter—and thanks."

"Mama, where are you? Don't leave me all alone, Mama!" Beth started up in bed, her body clammy with sweat. The fear was back, clutching at her heart.

Beth had been six when her mother had left their Bloomsbury lodgings and never returned. Soon after, the landlord had thrown Beth out on the street and she had learned to fend for herself, begging and stealing in the company of other abandoned urchins. "Home" had been any hovel that provided a share-bed for a farthing a night.

She lit the candle with shaking fingers and glanced at Lucy's empty bed. Now that Lucy had abandoned her, who would protect her? "Only Michael," she sobbed, dressing with shivering haste and rushing out into the night. "He's the only one who cares what happens to me now."

When she reached Denis Considen's hut it was in darkness and her heart sank. Was Michael still at the tavern? Tentatively, she opened the door and sighed with relief when she saw him sprawled naked across the bed, one arm over his face and the other dangling on the floor, still clutching a glass.

She removed the glass and shook him. "Michael, wake up, it's me." He muttered something incoherent and rolled toward her.

"Oh, Michael," she whispered, noticing the cuts on his face. "What have you done to yourself?"

"Lucy, that you?" he slurred. "Lucy darling . . . don't go away."

"I won't," Beth whispered, climbing into bed beside him and stroking his chest. "Please hold me, Michael. Now she's gone, you're all I've got."

His arms went around her and she cuddled into him feeling warm and safe. "Hold me tighter, Michael." She kissed him with open mouth and probing tongue, using all her skill to arouse him. Being far gone with liquor, he reacted slowly, but she drew him along, fanning his desire until he responded and his savage caresses set her on fire.

"Now, Michael, now, quickly . . . quickly," she begged. He bore down and she clung to him as the world erupted around her.

Michael opened his eyes and winced as needlepoints of light stabbed into them. His body felt as if it had been bombarded by tons of rocks. Beth stirred and pressed her face into his shoulder. He looked down at her uncomprehendingly? Beth? What was she doing here?

He sat up and ran his hands through his hair, trying to remember. Fragments of a nightmare came back to him. "What have you done, you stupid bastard?" he said, scrambling out of bed and reaching for his breeches.

He staggered outside, was sick, then plunged his head several times into a pail of cold water, trying to block out the memories of the previous night.

"Lieutenant Perryman!" John Best came walking toward him along the path. "God Almighty, what happened to you?"

"I got into a fight," Michael muttered. "What do you want, John?"

"You told me to let you know when the packet was leaving for Rose Hill," Best began, then his face stiffened.

Glancing over his shoulder, Michael saw Beth standing in the doorway of the hut wrapped in a crumpled sheet. "Go back inside," he said brusquely.

Beth smiled. "Morning, John," and retreated into the hut.

"When does the packet leave?" Michael asked, anguish clutching at his heart.

"In an hour," Best muttered.

The tension drained out of Michael and he sighed with relief. "Thank God. I can't wait to get out of Sydney. You and the men start loading, John. I'll be there in a few minutes."

Best turned and strode quickly away, thinking that if he didn't get out of range fast, he would blacken the Lieutenant's other eye.

Michael returned to the hut and began stuffing clothes into his haversack. "I am sorry about last night, Beth. I have no excuse. Please forgive me."

Her eyes widened. "Forgive you for what, Michael?"

"For using you. I must have been mad with drink. I wouldn't hurt you for the world, Beth."

She giggled, a silly tinkling sound that set his nerves on edge. "You didn't hurt me. Oh, Michael, you were so *wild*."

She reached up and touched the cut under his eye. "Let me put some salve on that, then we'll go to the mess for breakfast. A strong cup of tea is what you need."

He captured her hands. "There's no time for that, Beth. I'm leaving in an hour. I've decided to work the land Phillip gave me, Worthing."

"Well, then, I'll come with you. I don't like it here, now Lucy's gone."

He felt like striking her. "Don't speak about Lucy."

"All right, Michael, whatever you say. But don't you think I should come to Worthing? You'll need looking after . . ."

"No, Beth."

"Please, Michael, I-I don't want to be alone. You're the only one here who cares a fig about me."

He took her face in his hands. "Bethy, I have to be alone for a while . . . to think things through."

She could see it was pointless pressing him further. "I'll walk to the Governor's Wharf with you then, will I?"

He slung the haversack over his shoulder and strode to the door. "I'd prefer that you didn't. Good-bye, Beth."

4

Norfolk Island

"Take tiny sips," Lucy urged, as *Surprise* dived to the bottom of another deep trough.

"Why am I so seasick?" Faith moaned, raising the water bottle to her mouth. "I had no trouble on board the *Guardian,* or in the longboat with Peter." She took a few sips then recorked the bottle. "Oh, Lucy, what have we done to Peter and Michael?"

Lucy turned away quickly lest Faith see the anguish in her eyes. "Please, Faith. We cannot change anything . . . and talking about it makes us more miserable."

"We should have waited until Michael returned to Sydney. We could have left on board the *Scarborough* a week or so later."

"No, we couldn't. The *Scarborough* was Peter's only way out of the colony. I am certain he would not wish to stay after you—" She broke off, hearing a cry from aloft.

"Land ho—bearing east by south."

Thank God, Norfolk Island at last. Lucy felt almost weak with relief. As soon as they went ashore, she would ask Denis Considen to examine Faith, whose ill health was causing her much concern. Then she would speak to Moses. He was the only person, besides Michael, she dared trust with Faith's secret.

"Come on," she said, helping Faith up. "Let's go up on deck and see the view."

A short time later, *Surprise* dropped anchor a mile off the eastern point of Norfolk Island's main settlement, Sydney Bay, which nestled on the edge of a huge pine forest.

"What monsters they are," said Lucy, eyeing the two hundred-foot trees with awe.

"This is one variety you could not climb," Faith said, reading her mind.

"Don't be so sure," Lucy replied and they smiled at each other for the first time in a week.

Sydney Bay was about a mile wide between its two headlands and had a coral reef running parallel to it. Although the reef looked impenetrable, soon afterward, a small craft put out from shore and headed toward what appeared to be a narrow channel.

As Lucy and Faith watched the boat battling through the surge, Captain Anstis stomped past on his way to the stern.

"How soon may Nurse Gamble and I go ashore?" Lucy enquired in Faith's haughtiest voice.

The look Anstis gave her would have shattered granite. "Madam, landing in Sydney Bay is an extremely perilous procedure. The tide can shift as much as six points in half an hour and is often so strong, boats can scarcely pull ahead." He pointed to the shore boat which was making little headway through the channel. "Note the difficulty that craft is experiencing. Take my advice, stay on board."

Lucy and Faith exchanged pained glances. Anstis was impossible. During the heavy weather of the last few days he had ordered them below, but had permitted male passengers to remain on deck. "I am sure your advice is sound, Captain," said

Lucy, "however, my sister wishes to say farewell to Dr. Considen, who is doing a tour of duty here."

"I will see about your little pleasure trip after I land the two hundred convicts and provisions," Anstis growled and stomped off.

"Anyone would think we had ordered him to hand over the ship," Faith said hotly.

"He thinks women are simpering creatures who sit around sewing doillies all day and never say 'boo' to a goose."

Faith's chin came up at a dangerous angle. "Well, we'll show him."

Lucy shook her head. "No, darling, we'll suffer his rudeness until we reach Canton, then we will dance a hornpipe on his poop deck and tell him to go to Davy Jones."

As the shore boat drew closer Lucy recognized the two occupants. "Why, it's George Johnston and Ralph," she cried in a delighted voice. "Ralph Clark is the sandy-haired one, and George has his back to us. When they come aboard, give them a reserved hug and say as little as possible. If things become too difficult, plead a headache and go below."

Faith smiled confidently. "Don't concern yourself, my heart. When I focus on your mind, I almost become you." She leaned over the quarter rail and waved. "Hello, George. Hello, Ralph."

George and Ralph were so confused by the sight of Lucy and Faith together that neither paid much attention to which woman was which.

"God! It *is* good to see you again, Lucy," laughed George, swinging Faith off her feet. "Would you have our letters, my dear? And perhaps a spot of liquor? There's not been a drop on the island in over two months."

Faith laughed. "I can quench your immediate thirst, George, but you must row over to the *Justinian* for your letters. She left Sydney a few days before *Surprise*."

"However, we have a private letter from Governor Phillip for you," Lucy added.

"I had forgotten that," said Faith. "I'll go below and fetch it—and some wine."

"Lucy looks ill, Lady Stewart," said George as soon as Faith had left.

"She has been very seasick, Captain Johnston. I want Dr. Considen to see her but Captain Anstis insists that we remain on board until the convicts and provisions are landed . . ."

"Would you like me to speak to him?"

Lucy shook her head. "He would consider it interference—and it's a long way to China, Captain Johnston."

Faith returned with the letter and two bottles of port and soon afterward the officers rowed over to *Justinian* in search of letters from home.

Tuesday, August 17

Finally Anstis agreed that Lucy and Faith could go ashore after the last boatload of convicts.

The weather continued fine most of the day, but toward midafternoon when the wind strengthened, Lucy anxiously eyed the dark clouds lining the horizon. "If he doesn't let us leave soon, it will be too late."

"Oh, he is an impossible man," said Faith, pointing to the convict women clambering into the cutter. "Only six women and a baby are aboard that boat. We could have fitted in easily."

As the cutter cast off and headed toward the channel, a monstrous shark rose from the inky darkness beneath *Surprise*'s hull, knifed silently through the water toward the boat and attacked the oars.

"What is it doing?" Lucy asked Anstis who had come to tell them they could go ashore.

"Looking for a feed, madam," he said glumly. "Sharks are the carrion of the sea. They follow ships like vultures follow dying animals. Be ready to embark the minute the cutter returns and make sure you're back on board by midday tomorrow. We sail for China on the evening tide."

The shark rolled over, exposing its white belly. "Lucy, something horrible is going to happen." Faith drew in her breath sharply and clutched Lucy's arm. "I can hear the baby crying. It cries and cries." She cupped her hands around her mouth and called. "Come back! Come back!"

As the cutter turned into a channel a wave rose from nowhere and struck it broadside. The boat slewed sideways onto the reef, filled with water, and all on board disappeared beneath the surging surface of the sea. The surge sucked back and the channel was filled with struggling people and pieces of boat.

Outside the reef, the shark circled.

Some people on shore waded into the water but the waves drove them back. Eventually, a convict got out past the breakers but as he reached one of the women a wave picked him up and smashed him against the reef. He went under and never came up.

The shark thrashed about outside the reef and the water turned red.

"Avast!!" shouted Anstis.

Startled, Lucy spun around and saw that *Surprise* had fallen fast to leeward.

"Make sail, you clove-hitched idiots!" Anstis shouted to the crew.

They scrambled back to their posts and set the sails with lightning speed. As the sails filled, the wind shifted to the south and the ship ran in dangerously close to the reef.

"Oh, Lord," Lucy murmured, remembering what had befallen *Sirius.*

"Throw her in stays, you dogs!" cried Anstis.

The ship wore slowly around to the other tack.

Lucy gripped the rail. There was so little space to maneuver . . .

A moment later, the sails filled and the ship sped away out of danger.

"I suppose that is the end of our going ashore today, Captain," sighed Lucy.

Anstis gnashed his teeth. "It's the end of you going ashore at all, madam!" He kicked the mate, who was slinking past. "Henceforth, we'll stay under sail while off-loading cargo. Then, if the weather blows up sudden, we'll be in proper trim for working. Aye, Mr. Harvey?"

"Aye, Capt'n!" said Harvey, scampering out of range.

"But I have a friend on the island I must visit," Lucy protested.

Anstis turned scarlet with rage. "You'll visit the undertaker if you try to go ashore in these conditions."

"You are being utterly unreasonable," Faith snapped. "Many people have gone ashore without mishap during the past few days."

"Unreasonable, is it? Then go ashore, blast you, but if the weather blows bad don't expect me to risk men's lives coming after you. We leave for China on the evening tide whether you're back or not. Now, be off with you. I've just lost a cutter and four of my crew and I've more to do than stand around passing the time of day with shallow-brained simpletons."

Faith placed a comforting arm around Lucy. "Don't take any notice of him, my heart. He would not dare leave us behind."

"Yes, he would—you know he would. He'd leave us marooned

413

on that island for months if we gave him half a chance. We'll have to stay on board!'' Tears rolled down Lucy's cheeks. ''I longed to see Moses again. I could have told him about the baby.''

''Write him a letter,'' Faith said gently. ''We can pay one of the crew to deliver it . . .''

''It's too risky. Moses cannot read or write. He might show the letter to someone.''

Faith gazed disconsolately at the waters around the reef. With the shark and the debris gone she could hardly believe that the tragedy of the cutter had even occurred. However, the pain in her abdomen stabbed harder and she could still hear the baby crying. ''Do you trust this man, Moses, with your life, Lucy?''

Lucy wiped the tears from her cheeks and took a shuddering breath. ''Yes.''

''Then I shall trust him with my secret. This is what we will do . . .''

''Come in,'' Denis Considen called as a thunderous knock sounded on the door of his cabin.

When Moses entered, Denis waved him to a chair and placed two letters before him on the table. ''These were delivered from the *Surprise* an hour ago, Tucker. They are from Lucy Gamble. One is for you; the other for Lieutenant Perryman. Shall I read yours?''

Moses nodded, and Denis began:

Dear Moses,
By now, you will know that my sister, Faith, and I are returning to England. You must understand that I have a family matter to take care of which *cannot* be set aside. If I had been able to come ashore I could have explained everything but Captain Anstis has made this impossible.

Rest assured, Moses, that I have not forgotten our plans for the future. Although this latest turn of events is a further setback, do not despair. Governor Phillip has promised you will return to the mainland as soon as he finds a competent man to replace you. This will probably be early next year, when *Supply* returns from Batavia.

Only Michael must read the other letter I have sent you, Moses. If, for whatever reason, you are unable to deliver it to him, I charge you to destroy the letter without opening it.

Your love and loyalty mean the world to me. Even though we shall be far apart, you will be ever in my heart. Thank you for everything, my dear friend, and please keep on the right path until we meet again in 1793. Lucy.

Moses snatched up the two letters and lumbered out of the hut. When he got to the beach the wind was tearing through the treetops, storm clouds were rushing in from the south and the flagpole was bare. *Lucky Miss Lucy had not come ashore.*
"1790, 1791, 1792, and some of 1793." He crouched in the sand and slowly and deliberately stroked the months of four years. With infinite care, he placed four strokes beneath every month for the weeks. More than one hundred and fifty weeks—all with seven days apiece. . . . With painstaking thoroughness, he began to stroke out the days. By the time he finished it was too dark to count the strokes, but their legions marched relentlessly across his soul.

The waves roared over the reef, thundered into shore and swept up the beach. When they retreated, his strokes were gone.

The sky was black. The sea was black. The world was black. Only the lights of *Surprise* offered a glimmer of hope.

He took off his boots, waded into the water up to his waist then plunged in. For almost a minute, he managed to stay beneath the seething caldron of foam then, lungs exploding, he shot to the surface. He caught a brief glimpse of *Surprise*'s lights before an avalanche of water descended on him and the current sucked him under.

Anstis stood by the bow cursing roundly. When the safe landing flag had been lowered an hour ago, only one boatload of cargo had remained on board. Now he was stuck here with the wind gusting to gale force and the sea mounting a full scale assault on his hull.

He jumped as a furled topsail tore loose with a tremendous *c-r-ack*.

"That's it," he shouted. "I'll not stand around like a landlubbered duffer while my sails are shredded—not for a boatload of salt pork, I won't. Aft on the double, you sons of bitches! Raise the anchor! Spring to it, I say!"

Hearing the commotion above, Lucy swung her feet off the bunk and reached for her all-weather jacket. "I think I'll go up top. Sounds as if we are about to get underway."

"I'll come too," Faith volunteered.

They ascended the companionway to the deck and watched the crew scurrying over the ship, like agitated beetles, preparing it for sea. Before long, the sails were set, the anchor was up and everything was at the ready, but just as Anstis gave the order to heave about a cry rang out form aloft.

"Man overboard—on the windward side!"

"There he is!" cried a fo'c'sle hand as everyone rushed to the rail.

"Hold her steady into the wind!" Anstis ordered, grabbing a rope, looping it like a lasso and hurling it at the man thrashing about in the water. On the third attempt, he caught hold of it and was hauled aboard.

"It's one of them convicts from the island," said the mate. "Shall we lie to and set him ashore, Capt'n?"

Anstis staggered backward as a fierce gust of wind bore down on him. "Not on your bloody life. Let's run for the open sea while we still—" He broke off and stared in stunned disbelief as Lady Stewart flung herself to the deck and clasped the convict in her arms.

PART TWO

Dark Days of Dust and Ashes

5

The Magic Tortoise

Sydney's gardens drooped under the noonday sun and the normally fast-flowing stream was no more than a trickle when Michael disembarked on a blistering summer's day in January 1791.

Two ships were anchored in the cove: the *Supply,* and a warped, weed-hung hulk named *Waaksamheyd,* which had been hired to transport provisions from Batavia. With the arrival of the two vessels, several comforts had been reintroduced to the colony and Michael look forward to collecting the supplies he had ordered.

When he entered the hospital mess a few minutes later, Beth and Balmain were sitting at the table talking to John and Rachel Turner, the Second Fleeter John had engaged as his housekeeper. Obviously, John and Balmain had had other things besides medicine on their minds these last months—both Beth and Rachel Turner were pregnant.

"Michael!" Beth squealed, flinging her arms around his neck. "Michael, Michael, you're back!"

News of Michael's return spread quickly and before long several of his friends had gathered in the mess.

"It went right through the Governor, entering his shoulder just above the collarbone, piercing the fleshy part of the chest wall and penetrating five inches out his back." Balmain described to Michael in gruesome detail the near fatal spearing of Phillip a few months earlier. "I had the devil's own job extracting it."

"How could such a thing have happened?" Michael asked. "The natives dote on the Governor."

417

"It was entirely the Governor's fault," Dawes said peevishly. "He has an unshakable belief in the goodness of those people and refuses to go among them armed."

"Do you remember Bennalong and Colbee, the two natives who lived with the Governor for a while last year?" David Collins asked. "Well, last September, when the Governor learned that they were camped at Manly Cove with fifty of their tribe, he paid them a visit. Bennalong introduced us to many of the elders and we were just about to leave when he pointed to a man standing at the edge of the woods. As the Governor stepped toward him, hands held out in greeting, the fellow lifted a spear from the grass with his foot and flung it clean through the Governor. The Governor took hold of the spear and moved toward the boat, but the spear was twelve feet long and kept sticking in the sand, so he told Waterhouse to break it. Whilst Waterhouse was doing that, several other spears were thrown. The crew came ashore from the longboat and while they helped the Governor, Bennalong, Waterhouse, and I kept the natives at bay . . ."

"The whole incident could have been avoided if His Excellency had armed himself before going among the natives," Dawes muttered. "I hope he has finally learned his lesson."

Meredith looked at him with disgust. "Why do you always disparage him, Dawes?"

"I still have the highest regard for him, Meredith, but unlike you I do not worship the ground he walks on," Dawes answered stiffly.

Not long afterward, the officers of *Supply*, who were leaving for Norfolk Island the following day, came by for a farewell drink, and Michael took the opportunity to enquire whether they had any orders concerning Moses.

"All *Sirius* survivors will return to the mainland," said David Blackburn, the Master.

Michael chuckled. "I dare say Captain Hunter will be pleased about that. He is not a great admirer of Major Ross."

Blackburn shook his head doubtfully. "When Hunter hears that the Governor plans to send him and his men back to England on the *Waaksamheyd*, he may wish he'd stayed on Norfolk."

"What's wrong with the *Waaksamheyd*?"

"She smells as sweet as a corpse in a heat wave, and her Master is a sordid, unprincipled Dutchman who makes the Angel of Death seem friendly by comparison. Can you imagine sharing a mess with *him* for eight months?"

"I'd bunk with the devil himself if it meant getting out of here," Tench retorted morosely. "However, with the trouble brewing in Europe there's no telling when our battalion will be relieved."

Later that evening, Beth visited Michael in Denis Considen's hut. She wore a blue dress that matched her eyes and looked rather like a roly-poly with her protruding abdomen and rounded breasts.

"Being pregnant definitely agrees with you, Beth. You are positively blooming," he said as he showed her to a chair.

She laughed and fluttered her long eyelashes. "I *feel* positively blooming. I've not had one sick day. Balmain and John think I'm a wonder." Her eyes searched his apprehensively. "Are you pleased I am pregnant, Michael?"

His mouth twitched. "Couldn't be happier. I see Rachel Turner is also pregnant. It must have been a particularly pleasant spring at the hospital."

Beth giggled. "Not only at the hospital—Government House is on the stork's list, too. David Collins has got Ann Yeats in the family way and there's talk that the Governor is often abed with Elizabeth Evans, a maid in his household. Wouldn't Ralph Clark be scandalized?"

Michael uncorked a bottle of Batavian wine. "Indeed he would. Shall we toast your approaching motherhood?"

"You look very handsome and tanned, Michael," she said, peeping at him from beneath her eyelashes. "I like your beard. It makes you seem so . . . so distinguished."

He grinned. "Distinguished or not, it comes off in the morning. Care to look through these crates of goods I ordered from Batavia? You're welcome to anything, except the brass bed."

She fidgeted in the chair. "The thing I'd like best in the world is to live at Worthing with you."

Michael raised surprised eyebrows. "Wouldn't Will object to that?"

"Oh, him and John won't mind, as long as you take me into Tom when my time is near. What do you say, Michael—can I?"

He stared at her huge doll-like eyes. They weren't anything like Lucy's, which slanted upward at the corners with heart-stopping sensuality. "Sorry, Beth, it's out of the question."

"Oh, please, Michael. It's what we planned. Remember what

Lucy said before you left for Norfolk Island? One day you and her and me and Moses would all live together at—''

"Leave Lucy out of this," he said sharply then cursed himself as he saw her hurt expression. "I know how lonely you must be without her," he went on more gently, "but returning to Worthing with me is not the answer. Anyway, in your present condition, you should stay here at the hospital where Balmain and John can look after you."

"How can you say that?" she whimpered, and burst into tears.

Seeing her eyes awash somehow exasperated Michael. "Because it's true, damn it! Look, Beth, you and I are friends, and I'd like to stay that way, but if you keep on with this nonsense, our friendship will be over. Do I make myself clear?"

"P-perfectly clear," she sobbed, jumping up and rushing from the hut.

As Balmain was cutting across the clearing, he met Beth. "Evening," he said cheerfully. "Want to walk down to the wharf and watch *Supply* get underway?"

"No thanks, Will," she mumbled, dropping her head and hurrying past.

"Whoa!" he laughed, catching hold of her arm. "What's the matter with you?"

She raised her head and he saw her eyes were red and swollen. "Come on, lass," he said, bustling her toward his hut. "I think you need someone to talk to."

At midnight, Michael was woken by a furious banging on the door. When he opened it, Balmain stood there glaring at him with fists clenched and a face like thunder. "I've come about Beth," he rasped.

Michael glanced pointedly at the clock in the corner. "Couldn't it wait until morning? You may have just come off duty but—"

"No, it can't wait!" Balmain exploded, pushing past him and striding into the parlor. "Where's your sense of decency, man? Why won't you take Beth to Worthing?"

Michael was nonplussed. "I should think that's fairly obvious. She happens to be pregnant and Worthing is hardly a holiday cottage in Cricklade."

"She's a strong, healthy woman, used to the hard side of life. You have a duty to take her."

"How the hell do you work that out? If anyone has a duty to her, it's you. You're the baby's father."

Balmain let go a string of obscenities. "*You're* the baby's father, you ass!"

"Are you mad?" Michael gasped. "I was only with her once. You're not telling me she got herself pregnant from *that*?"

"Woman don't get *themselves* pregnant. Beth says you are the father, and I've watched her like a hawk since we parted—she's not been near another man."

Heart-sinking consternation swept over Michael. "God," he groaned. "Of all the accursed ill-luck."

"My sentiments exactly," Balmain muttered. "The poor girl won't find any happiness with you, you unfeeling bastard. You haven't the faintest conception of what you and Lucy have done to her. Lucy picked her out of the gutter, showed her a better way of life, then promptly dumped her, and you gallantly got her pregnant then took off for Worthing, or wherever it is you hide out these days feeling sorry for yourself. When Beth was a whore at least she fitted into a certain level of society. Now, she belongs nowhere."

Michael's eyes glittered dangerously. "Thank you for those pearls of wisdom, Balmain. Coming from you, they're a revelation. Get out and leave me alone. I've got a lot of thinking to do."

Balmain strode to the door. "Think about it all you like, you bastard, but if you sneak off without her, I'll come after you!"

Michael dressed hurriedly and climbed the hill behind the hospital to Lucy's fig tree. The sky was black and spectacular flashes of lightning danced across the horizon. It reminded him of a night aboard *Friendship* when he and Tom had taken Lucy up on deck to give her some respite from the heat of the woman's prison.

Why had she left him? After six months of soul searching he was no closer to an answer. In that last scrawled note she had promised Moses would be able to explain everything. Michael frowned darkly. Despite his avowals that he had finished with Lucy, in truth he was living for the day Moses would return.

Lately, however, another unanswerable question had assailed him. If Lucy had given him up for Faith last July, would she ever put him first? He doubted it. Time would strengthen the tie that bound them, not diminish it. But he must not think of Lucy, he must concentrate on Beth. Was he honor bound to offer her his protection?

What is *honor,* anyway? he asked himself. A sense of propriety? A code of behavior? A self-imposed concept of right and wrong?

"To hell with honor," he growled, slamming a fist into his palm. "I don't want to be lumbered with Beth and a baby. I want to be left alone."

"May I come in?" Michael asked tersely when Beth opened the door to his knock the following morning.

"I-I suppose so," she murmured.

After casting a cursory glance around the spic-and-span parlor, he looked through the doorway into the other room. Lucy's bed was unmade. Seeing it in disarray sent waves of pain through him. He tore his eyes away and stared at Beth unsmilingly. "I have an appointment with the Governor later today. If he gives his permission, you can come to Worthing as my housekeeper. But I don't want you to think that I—" He got no further. With a long, high-pitched wail, Beth flung herself into his arms.

"You look ill, sir. Is your wound still bothering you?" Michael asked as he joined Phillip on the veranda of Government House.

Phillip smiled wryly. "So, you heard about my escapade at Manly? I know that most of the officers think I am foolish to go unarmed among the natives but, in my opinion, anyone who attempts to win people's confidence by force is the fool." He pointed to a hut on East Point, outside of which squatted several natives. "I have won their confidence. Now my friend, Bennalong, and his family live permanently among us. I hope that soon others of his race will follow."

They discussed colony affairs for a while, then Michael reluctantly raised the reason for his visit. "I shall be leaving Sydney tomorrow, sir. Would you permit Elizabeth Clayton, a nurse at the hospital, to be my housekeeper at Worthing?" He paused, trying to find the right words. "As a matter of fact, sir, she is carrying my child."

Phillip pursed his lips. He had heard gossip about Michael and Beth and had hoped it was untrue. "Is this what you really want, Michael?"

"My wishes are not the only consideration, sir."

"Very well," Phillip replied gruffly. "But, for God's sake, man, don't throw your life away. Hold fast. This time of misfortune will pass."

Michael smiled bitterly. "Hold fast. Strange you should mention that phrase, sir. Lucy's father often said that in times of adversity, one should *hold fast* to the magic tortoise. Whenever I asked him to explain he just looked mysterious. It was his way of inducing me to think deeply about what he had said, I suppose . . ."

"I love a good riddle," said Phillip. "Any other clues?"

"Only that the 'magic tortoise' needs no earthly food because it nourishes itself in air."

Phillip pondered at length. "Hmmm . . . if 'magic tortoise' is the symbol of truth, and the nourishment is *spiritual* succor, then it might follow that the man who holds fast to the truth will make no mistake whatever the adversity of the time. Michael, do you trust Lucy?"

"I did once, sir, but now, I'm not sure I even knew her."

Phillip leaned over and gripped Michael's shoulder. "Lucy loves you, Michael. That is the truth. Hold fast to it."

6

The Homecoming

Friday, February 25, 1791

Lucy paused on top of the rise to admire the spectacular scenery. All around her rose the snowcapped mountains of the Great Glen, and on her right, an awesome avalanche of water cascaded into a river that roared down a narrow gorge into a rugged valley.

She straightened in the saddle and massaged her aching back. Yesterday the road had become impassable south of Dalwhinnie so they had abandoned the coach and traveled across the Corrieyairck Pass to Fort Augustus by packhorse. They had set out today as soon as the snow had stopped, and now, at last, she could see the lights of Inverness twinkling in the distance.

"Another hour should see us there," Moses said as he brought his team of horses to a halt beside her.

Lucy smiled at him fondly. He had been a tower of strength the last seven months. After reaching China, they had boarded a Dutch ship bound for England and, on arriving in Portsmouth three weeks ago, had collected the coach from Billingsley Hall and traveled posthaste to London. There they had been welcomed joyously by Julie Ryan and Bill Narmo, who had proved to be excellent custodians of her father's house in Grosvenor Square. The following morning, after a hurried conference with James Geldie, they had delivered Phillip's letters to Sir George Rose, who had promised to keep her informed of shipping movements between England and the colony. The next day they had left for Scotland; and now, their journey was almost over. Tomorrow evening should see them safely at Carrigmoor Castle.

"What *can* you find to smile about?" Faith asked peevishly as she reined in her horse. "I am so cold the blood has frozen in my veins. What a dreary, desolate country this is."

Lucy pulled Faith's fur-lined hood closer around her face. "How differently we look upon the same scene, beloved. I see magic mountains and mysterious glens. You see tortured peaks and savage passes. I see rainbow cascades and misty streams. You see morasses and desolate moors."

Faith threw back her head and laughed. "Oh, Lucy, you do exaggerate sometimes."

As Lucy listened to that heart-warming sound, glad relief flowed through her. Faith had not laughed in months. Since losing the baby on a wild winter's night two weeks out of Norfolk, she had been deeply depressed.

No more gloom and despondency, Faith told herself firmly as she passed between the portals of Carrigmoor. You have traveled the world for this moment, so be happy. Thoughts of the baby she had lost crowded her mind and tears pricked her eyes. Stop it, she ordered. The last link with Peter is severed and you are once more the loving wife returning to your husband. But as her horse clattered over the drawbridge into the vast cobbled courtyard all she felt was an aching emptiness.

"What a magical place," Lucy breathed. "I wouldn't be surprised if Merlin and Morgan Le Faye appeared with a fanfare of trumpets." She pointed to a square white tower soaring high about the battlements. "What is that?"

Faith took her hand and they ascended the steps to the entrance. "The original castle keep. No one goes there any more."

As they were ushered inside by a gape-mouthed servant, struck dumb by their amazing likeness, Lucy gazed about her in awe. The vestibule was all marble; white marble floors, white marble pillars, white marble busts in white marble niches and a magnificent white marble staircase that curved round the walls to an upper gallery hung with paintings.

As the servant led them upstairs, Faith's stomach fluttered nervously at the thought of seeing Hugh again. Could a husband tell if his wife had been unfaithful?

The Grand Dining Room of Carrigmoor was vast, with a beamed ceiling, polished wooden floors, and rectangular bay windows. In front of the windows was a raised wooden dais and running lengthwise along the dais was a planked table at which forty people could comfortably dine. Magnificent tapestries covered a side wall, and set into the other was an immense fireplace before which slept two wolfhounds.

In the corner of the room, between the fireplace and the dais, a stairwell led down to the kitchens and, although the heat of the fire was intense, the people at the table were shivering from the chill blasts of wind that roared up the stairwell—all, that is, except Sir Colin Stewart, Laird of Carrigmoor, who sat at the head of the table in a high, thronelike chair with its back to the stairwell.

Also at the table were Lady Barbara, Hugh, Robert McBain, and his wife, Fiona.

"I'll no hae my seed smothered in thistle and marigold!" shouted Sir Colin, smashing down a hammer on the marble block beside his plate with such violence that Lady Barbara jumped. "You will sow it when the leaves cover the pyot's nest and not a day before."

"If we sow the seed in April, Father, the seed will not mature until the autumn gales set in and we will lose half the crop." Hugh spoke slowly and distinctly, enunciating every word with care.

"The *old* ways are the best!" cried Sir Colin.

Hugh exchanged a frustrated glance with Robert and lapsed into silence. The day Robert had married Fiona, Sir Colin had acknowledged him as his son before the entire clan. Now, Robert answered to no man except Sir Colin. Initially, Hugh had been irked by Robert's elevated status. Lately, however, they had been united in a common cause—that of preserving Carrigmoor which was fast falling into ruin under Sir Colin's mindless mismanagement.

Hugh glanced up as two cloaked figures glided through the gloom to the table. They halted at the edge of the dais and one threw back her hood and said, "Hello, Scotty."

Hugh went rigid with shock. Faith, dead these last nine months, stood there smiling at him with a hand on her hip and her breasts thrust proudly forward. There was no mistaking those green emerald eyes, or the wisps of dark hair clinging to her face and neck. She laughed in a long-remembered way that wrenched his heart. "Cat got your tongue, Scotty?"

Hugh came slowly to his feet and moved toward her like a sleepwalker. For a few moments, he stared down at her, nonplussed, then he crushed her against him, and felt not the gray phantom of his dreams but warm, living flesh. "Fae . . . is it really you?"

"Yes, Scotty," she murmured, covering his face with kisses, "And this is my Lucy." She reached out and drew Lucy into the light.

"Hello, Hugh," said Lucy, tears spilling from her eyes.

Lady Barbara came to them then, her face working with emotion. "Faith, my dear—and Lucy." They drew her into the circle and all four stood entwined, laughing, talking, and weeping.

"This is a miracle," Hugh gasped.

"A blessed, blessed miracle," Lady Barbara echoed. "Hugh was about to depart for New South Wales . . ."

"Now he has no need," Faith cried gaily.

He looked deeply into her eyes. "It really *is* you, Fae? I'm not dreaming?"

Faith felt a rush of tenderness for this dear companion of her youth. "Of course it's me, but what have you done to yourself, Scotty? You look so gaunt. A fine welcome home this is."

Sir Colin beat a wild tattoo on the marble block with the hammer. "Ow! Ow! Cease I say!"

Lady Barbara led Faith and Lucy forward. "Colin dear, Faith has come home. And here is her sister, Lucy."

Faith was shocked at Sir Colin's appearance. He had gained a vast amount of weight, and his once handsome countenance was crisscrossed with grotesque purple veins. "Hello, Uncle Colin."

He glared at her without recognition then addressed his wife, "Woman of the house, get y'self to table and see to the guests."

Lucy examined Sir Colin carefully as she sat down. She had seen that same expression on the face of Mad George Maxwell. "How do you feel, sir?" she asked gently.

The belligerence in Sir Colin's eyes gave way to a look of utter bewilderment. "I am well, lass, but I do not know why I am here."

She patted his hand. "It's mealtime. Eat up, before your food gets cold." To everyone's amazement Sir Colin picked up his fork and shoveled food into his mouth.

As soon as Lady Barbara recovered from the shock of her husband's meek compliance with Lucy's request, she introduced Robert McBain.

"Hello, Robert," said Lucy, wondering why the man Faith had described as a loyal servant was dining in grand style with the laird's family.

Robert was hard eyed and strong looking with a square granite jaw, surly mouth, and dour expression. Yet when he spoke, his voice was soft and mellow. "Welcome to Carrigmoor, Lucy. May I present my wife, Fiona?"

Although Fiona had a fine complexion and beautiful long russet hair, her eyes were the ugliest Lucy had ever seen. "Welcome," said Fiona, smiling, but no warmth shone from those eyes which glittered venomously from beneath meager eyelashes.

Something *very* strange is afoot, thought Faith, astonished to find Robert eating with the family. "So, you are married, Robert McBain."

"These nine months past," Robert replied. "You'll remember Fiona—Clarrie of Cantraydoun's daughter?"

Faith acknowledged Fiona with slight nod, then turned back to Robert. "Would you excuse us, Robert? We have family matters to discuss . . ."

Deciding that tonight was not the time to assert his rights, Robert addressed Lady Barbara. "With your permission, dear Lady, Fiona and I will escort the laird to the drawing room for his nightly noggin."

"Ow! The noggin!" cried Sir Colin as the servants transferred him from the throne to his fur-lined litter. "Up Cun! Up Con! Heel lads!" With much excited barking from the wolfhounds, the group left the room.

"Is Uncle Colin drunk?" Faith asked when they were alone. "And why were Robert and that red-headed creature here? In fact, why are you dining in this freezing cavern, Scotty?"

Hugh jumped to his feet and pulled her after him. "Same old Fae. Home five minutes and brimful of questions. Well, I have other matters on my mind. Mother, Lucy, will you excuse us?"

Lady Barbara laughed merrily. "Off you go! Lucy and I have twenty years of catching up to do."

Faith and Hugh ascended the stairs to the second floor and entered the labyrinth of dark passageways. Passageways that forked to the right. Passageways that wound to the left. Wide passageways, narrow passageways, short passageways, long passageways. Eerie, echoing passageways and dank, dark passageways lined with dusty portraits of Hugh's ancestors.

Faith shuddered, remembering the oath of fidelity she had sworn when she had kissed the Stewart dirk on her wedding day. Was it her imagination, or did the eyes of the ancients glare back at her malevolently?

When they reached Hugh's apartment, he led her into the bedchamber and stood clasping her hands and gazing at her with shadowy, pain-filled eyes. "After so long I hardly dare touch you, Fae. Help me . . ."

"My darling," she whispered, drawing him down on the bed and twining her arms around him. "It's all over now. Try to forget, Scotty." She caressed him and spoke to him lovingly until his nightmare faded and he was consumed with fever and urgency.

"How will I find my way downstairs in the morning?" Lucy asked apprehensively when Lady Barbara ushered her into the King's bedchamber.

"No cause for alarm. You are next door to Faith and Hugh." Lady Barbara took Lucy's face in her hands and kissed her with the utmost tenderness. "Good night, my dearest. It was more wonderful than I can say having you here at last."

After Lady Barbara left, Lucy dismissed the two sleepy maids and surveyed her sumptuous apartment. The furniture was ebony, inlaid with mother of pearl, and the carpet and curtains were of the deepest blue velvet. A portrait of Mary, Queen of Scots, hung in the place of honor above the chimneypiece and gold and porcelain ornaments were scattered everywhere; but most impressive of all was the huge four-poster bed. Six blue satin curtains striped with lace hung around the bedposts, and spread across the bed proper was a deep blue satin quilt embroidered in silver thread. Emblazoned on the headboard was the Stewart arms depicting two rampant bears with hammers crossed over a shield.

Lucy bathed in a tub of warm, scented water and climbed wearily into bed. "What a loving homecoming," she sighed as she sank into the exquisite softness and closed her eyes.

Aunt Barbara was so motherly, she thought sleepily. Hugh adored Faith. Uncle Colin was a problem. Robert, a hard, proud man. Fiona's eyes . . . malice festering. The old White Tower, high above everything, like her fig tree on the hill.

Michael . . . where was he? Reach out . . . hold his hand. Feel him rub his thumb over her knuckles. Gently, back and forth, back and . . . forth. Back . . . and . . . forth.

7

The White Tower

Lucy swung open the door of the uninhabited north wing and stepped tentatively inside. Sundays at Carrigmoor were interminable: family devotions until noon, a meal of cold beef and hard-boiled eggs, more family devotions until four, then everyone returned to their suites for private prayer.

To escape the suffocating confinement she had decided to explore the White Tower, which, according to Hugh, had been built in the latter part of the thirteenth century on the site of a ruined Roman bastion.

Before her stretched a dark, musty passageway guarded on one side by legions of rusty suits of armor and on the other by innumerable doors leading into empty apartments.

She bit her lip uncertainly, wondering whether to venture farther. "Don't be foolish," she told herself and waded through the deep shadows until she came to the door of the spiral staircase that led up to the White Tower.

The heels of her shoes echoed eerily on the bleached stone steps as she ascended to the top and stepped through a narrow doorway into an octagonally shaped chapel.

Built of the same bleached stone blocks as the staircase, the chapel had immensely thick walls and an inner ring of eight white pillars supporting a high, cone-shaped roof, under which stood a rectangular altar set on a circular dais.

Pale light filtered in through the narrow slit windows and bathed the altar in a milky whiteness that contrasted starkly with the circle of sable darkness behind the pillars.

Lucy shuddered and cast a nervous glance over her shoulder. The wind whistled through the wall slits with a weird, unearthly sound and conjured up visions of pagan gods and ancient rituals.

She moved into the blackness behind the pillars and felt her way gingerly along the wall until she discovered the door Hugh had mentioned. After much effort, the threw the bolts and stepped out on to the battlements.

The view was magnificent: to the west lay a barren, trackless waste surrounded by snowcapped mountains; to the east, black tumbled hills; to the north, Nairn and the Firth; and below, a sheer giddying drop into a wooded ravine.

Lucy mounted the steps and strolled along the walkway to a section where stones had been removed from the wall and thick oak beams extended beyond it at intervals. Planks had been laid over the beams to form a platform, and suspended above the platform, between scaffold posts, was an iron bell.

Lucy climbed over the wall and jumped down onto the platform. "It's like stepping off the world," she sighed, grasping the bell post as the wind swirled around her.

"Lucy, for God's sake, what are you doing?" Lucy turned and saw Hugh was leaning over the wall with a strained expression on his face.

"Why is this platform here?" she asked curiously.

"In medieval times, the castle occupants used such extensions to drop boulders on their enemies while they remained protected. Come inside, Lucy."

"And the bell?" Lucy patted its pitted exterior.

"In the past it called the Stewart clan to arms. Nowadays, it is only rung when the laird dies, or his heir is born. Lucy, please. I can see the damned planks swaying in the wind."

She gave him her hand and allowed him to draw her inside the wall. "What brings you up here, brother dear?"

"Fae thought you might be exploring the White Tower, so I volunteered to come looking for you."

Lucy raised an eyebrow. "You could have sent a servant to fetch me. What is the real reason?"

He led her into the chapel and bolted the door. "In truth, I am worried about Fae. She is so distant these days . . ."

"You cannot expect her to be the same Fae who left two years ago, Hugh. A lot has happened to her since then. Just be thankful that her life was spared—and that she loves you."

"Does she, Lucy? She calls to him in her sleep."

Lucy's throat contracted. "Who?"

"Peter, the Guide. Who is he, Lucy?"

Lucy sighed. "If I explain a little of what happened will you promise to let her be, Hugh?"

He nodded grimly, and as they made their way back to the inhabited part of the castle, Lucy told him all she dared.

"Must I be content with that?" he muttered. "You have said virtually nothing about Devereaux."

"You will have to wait until Faith is ready to tell you the rest, Hugh. Now, do I have your word that you will let her be?"

He looked at her long and hard. "Yes, Lucy, but it's difficult watching someone you love slipping away."

She reached out and squeezed his hand. "I know, dearest. Be patient. Soon she will move toward you again."

When they entered the Grand Dining Room it was in complete uproar. The family were protesting loudly, Sir Colin, tossing bits of bannock cake over his shoulder, was beseeching the Almighty to keep foxes and eagles away from his flocks and the wolf-hounds were snapping and snarling at each other, vying for the bounties of his hand.

Lucy stared at Sir Colin with concern. The buttons of his shirt were fastened too tightly around his throat and his face was suffused with blood. "Please quiet the dogs, sir," she said, snapping open the buttons at his neck and seating herself on his immediate right.

He stopped tossing the cake and beamed at her. "Certainly, my child. Con! Cun! Away lads!"

The dogs lumbered back to the fire and soon afterward a servant entered carrying a beautiful silver teapot on a silver tray.

"Tea, laird?"

"Tea!" cried Sir Colin. "That vile foreign evil! That damned pernicious beverage! The President's denounced it, Bumper John's denounced it and, by God, I denounce it! Take it away and bring my claret."

Hugh groaned inwardly. Although tea drinking had been introduced to Carrigmoor a quarter of a century ago, last week, for some unaccountable reason, his father had taken a violent set against it.

"Come, come, Father," he laughed. "You've said many times what a great stimulant the importation of tea has been to the commerce and industry of Scotland."

"Commerce and industry be damned! Tea drinking's an evil,

431

effeminate practice that has corrupted the morals of our nation. I'll not have it served at my table!''

"Uncle Colin, why are there two bears with crossed hammers on the Stewart arms?'' Lucy shouted above the crashing of the hammer and the howling of the dogs.

Sir Colin's tirade ceased and he exploded into delighted laughter. "Ha, ha! Now . . . the hammers are the standard of our glorious forebear, Donald the Hammerer.''

"Tell us about Donald,'' Lucy coaxed.

Everyone breathed a sigh of relief as Sir Colin set aside the hammer and launched into a story they had heard countless times during the last month. "Now, in 1310, Donald's father, Duncan, the second son of the chief of the Appin Stewarts, traveled north to Inverness after a falling out wi' his father.

"Now, one dark night, Duncan's neighbor, Green Colin Campbell razed Duncan's keep and slew all within except Duncan's wee son, Donald, who was suckling at the breast of his foster mother in the blacksmith's hut in the woods . . .''

The Laird of Carrigmoor continued this rigmarole until his head dropped to his chest and, mercifully, he slept.

"What's to be done with him?'' Lady Barbara asked with tears in her eyes.

Hugh placed a comforting arm around her shoulders. "Please don't distress yourself, Mother, one day he'll recover his faculties.''

"I doubt it,'' sighed Faith. "What do you think, my heart?''

Lucy stared sadly at the old knight asleep in the chair. "All you can do is keep him as active as possible, be firm with him within the limits of his understanding and try to curtail his intake of alcohol. Drinking only befuddles him more.''

"How can we stop him drinking when he won't listen to anything we say?'' Hugh wanted to know.

"Perhaps we could add a wee drop of water to the wine,'' suggested Robert.

Or a wee drop of belladonna and bat's blood, Fiona thought to herself. *Then Robert would be Laird, I would be Lady, and* our *sons would inherit the castle.*

Lady Barbara reached for a green decanter. "What a good idea, Robert. We can do that easily. Colin always drinks from this.'' She turned and beckoned to a manservant. "Hugo, fetch a jug of water . . . and a fresh pot of tea.''

* * *

432

The following morning Faith arrived in Lucy's bedchamber waving a letter from Sir George Rose. "News from London, my heart."

Lucy eagerly tore open the envelope and scanned the pages. "Damn, damn, damn! Ten ships are departing for New South Wales—all within the next twelve days. My letter to Michael will never reach Portsmouth in time."

Faith thought quickly. "We'll send a relay of couriers direct from Inverness to Portsmouth. Give me the letter and I shall set things in motion immediately."

If only I could be on board one of those ships, Lucy thought as she took the letter from the desk. But neither Faith nor the family were ready for such a separation and, in truth, as much as she missed Michael, neither was she.

"Have you told Michael why we left the colony?"

"I could not commit such matters to paper, Faith. Letters often go astray. It was one thing trusting Moses, but—"

Faith stared at her intently. "If you don't tell him, Lucy, I will." She walked to the desk with deliberate steps and sat down. "Write," she said, dipping the quill into the ink and holding it out.

Lucy shook her head. "No, Faith. If the letter fell into the wrong hands, not only would you be ruined, but our family would be forever shamed. After living at Carrigmoor, I realize how right you were about that."

"Dear Michael," said Faith, beginning to write. "The reason Lucy and I left the colony—"

"All right, you win," Lucy sighed, drawing a chair up beside her. "We shall write it together."

"You should know that Hugh spoke to me yesterday about Peter Devereaux," Lucy told Faith as they stood at the entrance steps waving farewell to Hugh, who had volunteered to ride into Inverness with the letter.

A look of shock spread across Faith's face. "Peter! But I have never mentioned him to Hugh."

"You have been calling to him in your sleep. Please, Faith, you must try to forget him—for Hugh's sake."

When Faith spoke, her voice was hoarse with emotion. "Believe me, Lucy I *am* trying."

Lucy clasped her tightly. "Oh, darling, I'm sorry you are so unhappy. Hugh loves you desperately."

Tears spilled from Faith's eyes. "I know I have hurt him, Lucy. But now I have something wonderful to share with him—

something which I hope will ease his pain." She paused, and a flicker of joy crept over her drawn, pinched face. "I am pregnant, my heart. Perhaps this child will help us find each other again. I hope so . . . I hope so, because I *do* love him, Lucy."

8

Enter, Benjamin

Sunday, May 1, 1791

Beth counted the roof planks, there were twenty-four. She considered herself a good counter, reader, writer, and cook. "And soon, I will be a good mother," she murmured. "Just like Elizabeth."

She smiled, hearing Elizabeth Burleigh, Tom's mistress, moving about in the parlor, talking to baby William. This room was William's, but it was hers for the duration of her lying in.

Swiftly the pain came, stabbing into her belly. She held her breath and kept counting the planks until it subsided. The contractions were coming closer together now. Soon it would be time to call Elizabeth.

The pains came again. Beth drew in her breath and slid down farther in the bed. Would the baby be a boy or girl? she wondered.

When the pains went away, she opened her eyes. She had hoped Michael would stay with her for the birth but he had been anxious to return to Worthing and she had not insisted. Although Michael treated her kindly, there was not a hint of the lover about him. He had not even bothered to kiss her good-bye when he brought her into Parramatta.

She drew up her knees as another contraction came—really severe. "Elizabeth!" she called, scared now. "Elizabeth, you'd better fetch Tom. I think it's time."

Elizabeth stuck her head around the door. "I'm on my way," she said calmly.

Saber-sharp, the pains came again, jabbing and twisting. "Lucy," she cried. "Oh, Lord . . . I want Lucy!"

"What's all this weeping and wailing about?" Tom asked,

entering the room with Elizabeth. "I can't give you Lucy, but would a brand-new baby suffice?"

"I-I think I'm a bit afraid," she stammered, wiping tears from her cheeks with the back of her hand.

Tom raised an eyebrow. "Whatever for? You and I have delivered dozens of these little blighters."

"I know, but this time it's *me* who's the mother, Tom."

His eyes twinkled. "And what a wonderful mother you will be, my dear. Now lie back, relax, and leave the rest to me."

Soon afterward, Beth was delivered of a fine baby boy whom she named Benjamin in honor of Michael's father.

9

The Hovel in the Heath

Thursday, September 15, 1791

Why am I always so melancholy? Lucy wondered, as she knelt in her herb garden weeding. *I live in a splendid castle, I have plenty to keep me occupied and I am surrounded by a loving family.*

Nevertheless, she *was* miserable because, every day, she missed Michael more. News from the colony had been scant: one letter from Sir George Rose containing a newspaper clipping about Gidley King's marriage to a Cornish girl and his subsequent promotion to permanent Lieutenant Governor of Norfolk Island; and another letter from James Geldie, informing her that the Master of the transporter *Mary Ann* had agreed to purchase farm stock for Michael at St. Jago.

Have I the strength to leave Faith after the baby is born? she wondered. *Can Faith survive here alone when she is so out of harmony with the hierarchy of the clan?* Lucy had been mystified when Laura Taura had said that Stewart was the wrong name for Faith but, seeing Faith and Hugh together, she thought she understood. Hugh was too lenient with Faith. She needed someone firmer, someone like Peter Devereaux who had known when to let her have her head and when to reel her in . . . Lucy gave a startled cry as a coach thundered past along the carriageway.

"Ah, the lovely Lucy, giving succor to her trees." Fiona

laughed when she saw Lucy's fright. "How caring she is. What an absolute angel she is. What an utter whiggamore she is!" At least it was easy to tell the abominable twosome apart nowadays—Lucy was the one without the hump.

How that hump *haunted* Fiona.

She smote her abdomen with clenched fists. *I'll not let Faith beat me to the cradle. No mewing brat of hers will be heir to Carrigmoor.*

She glanced covertly at the box beside her on the seat. Her father had devised a plan to rid them of the hump without any suspicion falling on her or Robert.

Thinking of Robert made her head ache again. The clan wanted Robert, not Hugh, to be laird for, although baseborn, Robert was Laird Colin's firstborn and a true Scot. No limpid English blood flowed in Robert's veins, *his* mother had been the daughter of a Stewart chieftain. Robert had only to say the word and the clan would stand behind him to a man. Yet he seemed perfectly content with his lot and whenever she spoke of his rights, he reprimanded her severely. She ground her teeth. His infernal English family had turned him against her—she had seen them telling him lies. "Every day, whispering, behind their hands," she panted, fury mottling her complexion.

"Steady!" she stopped herself just in time. *Don't think of them,* she told herself, settling back in the seat and staring out the window. *Think of Jonet.*

When the coach stopped to let a herd of cattle pass, Fiona noticed one of Lucy's silly saplings beside the ditch. What a boon to her father's cause they had been. The tenant farmers hereabouts believed trees sucked the nourishment from the soil and sheltered pestilent seed-eating birds. They bitterly resented the English bitch planting trees along their boundaries. She burst into laughter at the thought, but stopped when her head began to pound again.

"Sit quietly and think about trees and the pain will go away," she counseled herself. "There are acorns, birches, rowans, firs, mazes of yews, and gardens of elders. Witches use elder sticks as magic horses. Put a baby in an elder cradle and it will pine and die . . . ."

When the coach reached the outskirts of Craggie, Fiona ordered the driver to wait for her at the inn and went the rest of the way on foot, following a path that twisted through a dense wood then opened into a clearing encircled by dark hills. In the clearing stood a hovel of unmortared stones with a turf roof held down by rocks.

Fiona approached with trepidation and knocked. The door

opened to reveal a hag with a face of withered skin that sagged from her cheeks and hung from her chin.

"Yes?" asked Jonet Addie.

"I am Fiona Stewart. My father, Clarrie of Cantraydoun, spoke to you a month ago," Fiona answered with quavering voice.

Jonet stared fixedly at her for a minute then motioned her inside.

A peat fire blazed in the center of the one-room hovel and the smoke, having no means of escape except through a small hole in the roof, clung to the rafters. A cot covered in animal skins occupied one corner and shelves stacked with blackened receptacles lined the walls. In front of the fire stood a stone slab table, on either side of which was a three-legged stool.

"Did you bring the items and the gold?" asked Jonet, waving Fiona to a stool.

"Yes," said Fiona, placing the box on the table and sitting down. She handed over four gold guineas.

Jonet pocketed the money, hovered around the shelves then returned to the table with a knife, scissors, hammer, nails, needle and thread, two earthenware bowls—one containing laurel leaves and the other, a sticky substance that looked like glue—and an eight-inch wooden cross.

She took the objects from Fiona's box and examined them carefully. There was a ball of Faith's hair, slithers of her fingernails, a white silk scarf, a ball of lint painstakingly collected from her undergarments, and a lace handkerchief spattered with her blood. Jonet stared hard at Fiona. "This will succeed only if *She,* who presides over the Fates, desires it. What is the name of the prey?"

"Faith Stewart."

Jonet took up the knife, placed laurel leaves in her mouth and, chanting a strange incantation, carved Faith's name in the center of the cross.

> Cardea—
> Queen of the Universe,
> Mother Eternal,
> Mistress of the Elements,
> Empress of the Gods,
> Goddess of Life-in-Death
> And Death-in-Life,
> Guide thy servant's hand
> To form this effigy.

She affixed Faith's hair to the top of the cross, the fingernails on either side of the crossbeam, and stuck the lint to the cross in the shape of a pregnant torso. Then she fashioned a garment from the white silk scarf, dressed the effigy, took Faith's blood-stained handkerchief and began knotting it.

> Cardea—
> Goddess of the Earth,
> Goddess of the Moon,
> Goddess of the Seas,
> Goddess of the Underworld,
> Put a knot in
> Faith Stewart's head
> And a dagger in
> Faith Stewart's belly
> So she will lose
> The child she doth carry.
> By Puziel,
> By Guziel,
> By Psdiel,
> By Prziel,
> I ask it!

She tied the handkerchief around the effigy, frenziedly hammered a nail into the effigy's protruding abdomen and chanted ever faster the words of her spell. The words grew into a piercing whistle and a fearful wind rushed in through the roof and roared around the hut until she cried, "Amen. Amen. Selah!" and slumped over the table.

When she had recovered she handed the hammer and eight nails to Fiona. "On the night of the next full moon, when Faith Stewart's soul leaves her body in sleep, climb to the temple of Light and Darkness, and this is what you must do . . ."

Fiona listened intently as Jonet Addie of Craggie instructed her in the ways of the dark side of the moon.

10

Arrival of Admiral Barrington

Michael paused on top of the slope and gazed about him. The sun had not long risen over Chaumilley and in the half-light of dawn the foggy valley looked as if it was covered in snow.

He descended to the flat and waded through the long grass to the lake. The name was still visible on the tree trunk and, as he traced the letters with his fingertips, memories of that glorious spring evening when he and Lucy had first made love flooded his mind. "Lucy," he whispered, "where are you, darling?"

When no answering echo of her sweet, low voice drifted to him through the mist, he climbed the tree and surveyed their erstwhile kingdom. They had made such plans. Did she still remember? Was that why she had sent the horses?

Yesterday, when Captain Nepean of the New South Wales Corps had ridden out to Worthing to warn him that natives had been attacking settlers in the new settlement of Prospect Hill, he had delivered a letter from John.

On the ninth of July, the transporter *Mary Ann* had arrived in the colony bringing female convicts, flour, meat, and two farm horses from Lucy. As other ships were soon to follow, John requested that Beth return to Sydney Hospital immediately. Already there were almost three hundred patients and he desperately needed her services.

Michael was only too happy for Beth to return. Although she was sweet-tempered and obliging, just having her around irritated him. After learning of Moses Tucker's tragic drowning at Norfolk Island, he had driven himself to despair wondering *why* Lucy had left him. Now, with the arrival of the horses and with the prospect of letters, he had reason to hope again.

"Despite everything that has happened, I know she still loves me," he said aloud as he descended from the tree. "She must have had another reason to leave, apart from a desire to be with Faith. The problem is, I am too far away. I'll speak to Phillip when I go back to Sydney, and if he will allow John Best to manage Worthing, I'll return to England with the battalion and work things out with her."

Four days later, after settling Beth and the baby into Lucy's hut, Michael accompanied John to the hospital enclosure to inspect Lucy's horses. They were plain beasts but sturdy of bone and in reasonable condition considering the long sea voyage they had endured.

When John returned to the wards, Michael rowed out to *Mary Ann* and spoke to Captain Munro, the Master. Munro, however, had no information about Lucy as all his dealings had been with her agent, James Geldie, who had paid him a princely sum to purchase a dozen farm animals at St. Jago. He apologized for the loss of the other animals, a loss that he attributed to them being unused to dry feed, and soon afterward the two men parted.

Michael then proceeded to Government House, hoping to make an appointment with Phillip. "George, what are you doing back in Sydney?" he exclaimed when George Johnston greeted him in the main foyer. "Your tour of duty at Norfolk was supposed to end next year."

"I returned in May," George informed him jovially as they shook hands.

The corners of Michael's mouth twitched. "How did you manage to coerce Major Ross into releasing you?"

"Officially, my war wounds were acting up, but just between you and me, old chap, I'd had a gut full of Ross."

"Come, come," said John. "Surely life at Norfolk wasn't that bad, George?"

"It was worse than you could possibly imagine. Ross issued so many orders, counterorders, passwords, and counterpasswords, the inner and outer guards didn't know whether they were coming or going."

"Did Ross order a search for Moses Tucker?" asked Michael. "He was such a strong swimmer. It's hard to believe that he drowned."

"Although we searched thoroughly, we found nothing," George replied. "Denis Considen thought Moses might have taken his own life. The day Lucy left Norfolk, she wrote Moses a letter saying that the Master of *Surprise* would not allow her to come ashore and say good-bye to him. But I think the Master was wise to disallow it considering the tragedy that had occurred the previous day, and the fact that Lucy was pregnant."

Michael regarded him with a mixture of affront and disbelief. "Lucy was not pregnant, George."

"Didn't you know?" John asked, placing a companionable arm around Michael's shoulder and taking him aside.

"No, I didn't," Michael said slowly, "and I don't believe you. It's was a mistake."

"There's no mistake, Michael. I received a letter from Denis. Although he didn't let on to Faith or Lucy, he was very concerned about Lucy's condition and doubted she would carry the child full term. I . . . er . . . still have the letter. Would you care to read it?"

Beth lay in bed anxiously waiting for Michael to return from the barracks. Tonight they would share the same room and she was hoping for something more between them. "Hello," she said brightly, when he opened the door. "I've been waiting for you."

He stared at her with exasperation. Why did she have to be so damned obvious? She had on a sheer nightgown and reeked of Lucy's French perfume. "No need to," he said tersely.

She wriggled suggestively and the nightgown slipped off one shoulder exposing a pink-nippled breast. "You're late. The celebrations finished an hour ago. Where have you been?"

"I've been having a private celebration. Were you aware that Lucy was pregnant when she left the colony?"

Beth's eyes widened. "Pregnant!"

He sat down on his bed and tugged savagely at his boots. "Then you didn't know either?"

"Well, Michael, that's hardly surprising. Lucy stopped telling me things the moment Faith arrived. Fancy her going on a long sea voyage in that condition—after all the trouble she had with Jamie."

"My sentiments exactly," said Michael as he stripped and climbed into bed. "Well, I don't give a damn about her any more. As soon as I return to Worthing tomorrow, I'll set about putting my life in order."

She slipped out of her bed and climbed in beside him. "Please don't run away again, Michael. Stay another day or two.".

He swore under his breath and turned his back. "I'm not running away. Now, if you don't mind, I'd like to get some sleep."

She stroked his buttocks. "Michael, please make love to me. It's been a year since either of us—"

"I don't want to make love. I want to go to sleep."

"Damn you," she cried. "You don't give a fig about me. The only person you ever think of is Lucy, Lucy, Lucy." She burst into tears and Michael hated himself all over again.

Oh, God, he thought. *What am I doing to this woman?* He

turned back to face her. "Don't cry, my dear. You are right. I have been bemused with Lucy. The moment I heard about the horses I wanted to toss everything in and go chasing off to England after her. Now I don't know what to think."

"Return to England!" Beth looked at him with terrified eyes. "Oh Michael, are you abandoning me too?"

He gnashed his teeth with frustration. "I will never abandon you, Beth. Whatever paths our lives take, I will look after you and Ben. But it's time you started thinking about a new life for yourself. When your pardon comes through you will be free to go wherever you please. If you wish to live in Sydney, I shall build you a house. Or, if you would rather live at Parramatta, I can—"

"I don't want a house in Sydney or Parramatta. I want to be with you and Ben at Worthing."

"Well, there's no need to decide right this minute. Think about what I have said and when I return to Sydney we will discuss it again."

She looked at him, her eyes brimful of tears. "Promise?"

He nodded. "I promise."

"A-and you won't abandon me?"

"Never. Now, go back to your bed and let's get some sleep. I want to leave early in the morning."

On the evening of the sixteenth of October, shortly after the last Third Fleet transporter, *Admiral Barrington,* anchored in Sydney Cove, Watkin Tench arrived at Lucy's hut with a bundle of letters for Michael.

He's lucky to have so many friends who can write, Beth thought, as she sorted through the pile. Then she noticed the handwriting on one of the envelopes and the happiness disappeared from her day. She removed the envelope from the bundle with a sinking heart. There was no doubt, the writing was Lucy's. The fear engulfed her and the world of the past year shattered into a thousand pieces. "Why did you have to write to him, Lucy?" she wept, turning the letter over and over with agitated violence. "Why couldn't you just *leave us alone*? You've got everything. Ben and me have only got him."

On the evening of the twenty-fifth of October, Governor Phillip held a public dinner and a ball at Government House to commemorate the anniversary of His Majesty's accession to the throne and to farewell his friend, Commander Gidley King, who had arrived aboard the man-of-war *Gorgon* and who was leaving the next morning to take up his commission as permanent Lieutenant Governor of Norfolk Island.

After a leisurely supper with Susannah, Beth returned to the hut and settled Ben down for the night. It was no easy task as the continuous firing of ships' cannons throughout the day had made him irritable. Thus, she was furious when a thunderous knock sounded on the door.

When she wrenched it open she was surprised to find William Balmain, who was leaving for Norfolk in the morning to relieve Denis Considen as that island's chief doctor.

"Shssh," she cautioned crossly, placing a finger over her lips. "I've just got Benjamin to sleep. Why aren't you at the ball?"

"I want a word with you, lass," he whispered, creeping into the parlor after her.

"A word about what?" She carefully drew out a chair from the table and motioned for him to do the same.

After he had followed her example, he sat down and tugged nervously at his cravat. "Would you and the laddie care to come to Norfolk with me?"

"No thanks, Will."

"Why not?" he demanded, raising his voice an octave.

"Hush up. Because I don't love you, that's why."

"You did once, lass."

"Yes. But everything's changed . . ."

He swallowed loudly. "No promises, mind you, but I . . . er . . . might consider marriage . . . at some future date."

Beth smiled mischievously. "I'm already married to George Clayton. You *know* that, Will."

"Well, married or not, I think you and the laddie should come. Sydney can be a wild old town at times. Who will protect you once I leave?"

Beth was touched by Balmain's concern. Despite their past differences he had been a good friend and she would miss him. "Please don't worry yourself, Will. Me and Ben have Michael."

Balmain's countenance darkened. "A lot of help *he* is, living out there in the wilderness."

"Now, Will, if you start in on him again, you'll have to leave."

Balmain gave an exasperated groan. "Michael Perryman loves Lucy. Stop chasing rainbows, Beth, and come to Norfolk with me."

"You're wrong. Michael has definitely finished with Lucy."

Balmain reached across the table and captured her hands. "Are you certain this is what you want?"

"Absolutely certain."

"There's nothing I can say to dissuade you?"

"No, and now that's settled, perhaps you will wipe that gloomy look off your face so we can have some fun."

Will brightened. "I'd like nothing better than a bit of fun with you, lass. It would be a bonny send off."

"Not that kind of fun, Will, my whoring days are over. You'll have to settle for a cup of tea and a chat."

Did Michael still love Lucy? And if Lucy returned to the colony what would happen to Ben and her? These questions haunted Beth as she lay tossing and turning in bed after Balmain left. She swung her feet to the floor, padded into the parlor and removed Lucy's letter from Michael's bundle.

What *had* she written?

Beth turned the letter over and over until she could endure the uncertainty no longer. "Sorry, Lucy," she whispered as she tore open the envelope with trembling hands. "Sorry, sorry, sorry, but I have to know."

The letter confirmed her worst fears. Filled with love and tenderness, it lamented the events that had caused Lucy to leave the colony and revealed her reasons for doing so.

After Beth finished it she sat hunched over the table with her head in her hands. Why had Faith come to the colony and ruined their lives? If she hadn't got pregnant to Captain Devereaux, they'd all be living happily at Chaumilley by now . . .

Beth carried the letter to the fire, covered it with embers and prodded it with the poker until only ashes remained. Then, weeping with guilt and remorse, she swept the ashes into the cinders box, carried them outside to Lucy's garden and buried them deep in the earth.

11

Night of the First Full Moon

The trouble with Fiona began on the evening of November fourth, not long after Sir Colin had retired and the family had sought the warmth of the drawing room.

The conversation was general until Lucy mentioned that she had seen a group of people dunking a fully clothed child in an icy pond earlier that day.

"What you witnessed was probably the 'sprinkling' of a cripple," Lady Barbara told her. "The local people believe that the waters of certain ponds and streams can cure all manner of ailments. In fact, every aspect of their lives—be it baptism, death, or setting out on a journey—is preceded by some mysterious sign or ceremony."

Hugh laughed. "Really, Mother. Next you will be telling us that they still score witches."

"Although the kirk has outlawed the practice of witchcraft, the people still believe in witches," Lady Barbara said firmly.

"How did one 'score' a witch?" Lucy asked curiously.

Lady Barbara laid aside the baby jacket she had been embroidering. "At Hallowmas, when witches met in the ruins of deserted monasteries for midnight revels with the devil, townsfolk often descended upon them and cut crosses over their eyebrows so the evil powers would be bled from them. Even though Hugh scoffs at such things happening in these enlightened times, I often see folk place thumb to palm and make the sign of the cross when they pass the hovel of a hag reputed to possess the 'evil eye.' "

"Oh, show us how it's done," Faith pleaded.

As Lady Barbara placed a thumb in her palm, Fiona leapt from the longseat and advanced toward her threateningly. "You'll not mock the old ways you insipid old cull!"

Hugh jumped to his feet and stepped in front of her. "How dare you speak to my mother that way."

"That's enough, Fiona!" shouted Robert, jumping to his feet also.

Fiona rounded on him, eyes ablaze. "This ignorant old Englishwoman has no right to ridicule us, Robbie!"

"The Lady Stewart may do and say whatever she pleases in her own home, Fiona," said Robert. "It is not for you to tell her nae."

"Carrigmoor's not hers, it's yours and mine. The Laird Stewart said as much the day we were wed—he named you firstborn."

Robert clamped a heavy hand on her shoulder. "Hold your tongue, woman!"

Fiona tore free and backed toward the door. "I won't hold my tongue, and if you've an ounce of sense in your head, you'll not listen to the lies these English dogs whisper behind my back." With a wild shriek, she ran from the room.

"Please pardon her, lady, she's not been herself lately," Robert mumbled and hurried after her.

445

"It is my fault," sighed Lady Barbara. "I know how sensitive Fiona is about clannish customs."

"Nonsense, Aunt Barbara," said Faith. "The creature is definitely not right in the head."

"Mad or not," Hugh said grimly, "she will never speak to you like that again, Mother."

"Why does she hate us so passionately?" asked Lucy.

"Because we are English, my heart."

"Fiona's hatred for our family goes deeper than that," Hugh said. "She has grown up under the sway of a tyrant who is utterly resistant to change. We'd best watch her closely after her performance tonight—*and* her scheming snake of a father. Obviously, they aspire to the lairdship."

"And Robert?" asked Lady Barbara. "Is he to be trusted?"

Hugh frowned. "Robert is an enigma. I am unable to ascertain where his loyalties lie."

"I think Robert should definitely be watched," said Faith. "And the Brieve, and the Blaider—in fact, every member of the Inner Council."

After the family had retired, Lucy visited the library in search of a book on clan history. She scoured the dusty shelves without finding anything of interest and was about to give up when she discovered a crumbling manuscript titled *Liber Mysteriorum* (or *Book of Mysteries*). It had been written by Dr. John Dee who, more than a century before, had been imprisoned in the Tower of London for casting horoscopes and practicing enchantments.

So engrossed did she become in this work that she lost all sense of time and only when the ebony clock on the wall began chiming midnight did she reluctantly lay aside the manuscript.

She left the room and began climbing the marble staircase to the first floor, but had not gone far when a gust of wind gutted her candle. As she paused, undecided whether to retrace her steps or go on, she beheld a sight that froze the blood in her veins. Directly above, a hooded phantom with a ghastly white face glided along the gallery and disappeared into a dark passageway beyond.

Clutching the bannister for support, Lucy ascended to the landing and stumbled into the drawing room.

As she poured a glass of brandy with shaking hands, she almost laughed at the absurdity of it. *Really*, Lucy, she admonished. *You cannot be serious—a dark specter haunting the hallways of Carrigmoor in the dead of night? Reading the manu-*

script has played havoc with your imagination! But, the gallery had not been shadowy, in fact, it had been *flooded* in moonlight.

From somewhere deep within her, a primal instinct stirred. She sensed danger all about her; she could smell it in the air. With a determined look in her eyes, she picked up the poker, let herself out of the room and tiptoed along the gallery.

When Lucy entered the uninhabited north wing, she heard a distant banging, like steel striking against stone. She hid her shoes and sped past the army of armored sentinels to the entrance of the White Tower.

As she stepped through the doorway into the stairwell, the hammering ceased abruptly and, for one heart-stopping second, she thought she had been heard. A moment later, however, the hammering resumed—this time accompanied by a strange wailing chant. Gripping the poker tightly and pressing her back against the wall, Lucy ascended the stairs.

> Blood to blood,
> Bone to bone,
> Dust to dust,
> Goddess of the Underworld,
> Queen of the caverns of Hell . . .

Higher and higher Lucy crept as the words resounded hollowly around her.

> Send thy son, Hermes,
> To conduct its soul
> To everlasting death
> In the furthermost
> Silt of the Universe . . .

Lucy inched her head around the doorway and peered into the chapel.

Spangled moonbeams shone through the slits in the walls, bathing the altar in dazzling white, and standing before it, hammering frenziedly, was the phantom. Lucy slid into the darkness behind the pillars and watched in horror.

The chanting grew ever faster, until the words ran into one another and became a shrill whistle that pierced the core of Lucy's being. Clamping hands to ears, she retreated farther behind the pillars and prayed that the ungodly sound would end.

"Amen. Amen. Selah! It is done. I have won!" cried the

phantom and, snatching up a spiked object from the altar, glided toward the door.

The fear left Lucy as she glimpsed the venomous glitter in the depths of those awful eyes. Her suspicions had been correct. The phantom with the chalk white face was Fiona.

Gigantic and majestic, its glassy spirals sparkling brilliantly in the moonlight, the cone-shaped pinnacle rose before her. For a time she circled its icy surrounds filled with peace and tranquility, then a change set in and from somewhere deep within the white fortress she heard the faint, unmistakable cry of a baby.

Overcome with a terrible sense of urgency, she beat on the rock. It parted, and she found herself in a long, dark passageway that seemed to go on forever. "Hold on," she called as the baby's cries grew louder. "Hold on . . . hold on . . . I am coming." She rounded a bend in the passageway and discovered a huge oaken door. With frantic fingers she threw the bolts and heaved it open.

Inside was a vast moonlit pavilion with a white marble floor and lofty walls covered in tapestries of gruesome battle scenes. In the center of the pavilion, holding a silver bell, stood a divinely beautiful woman. There was about her a strange, meaningful aura of secret knowledge, hidden wisdom and absolute power. Entwined in her blond flowing tresses were garlands of white elder flowers and in the center of her forehead, just above her brows, a small moonshaped mirror pulsated light. Her snow-white garments clung to her slender body in elegant folds; around her waist, rotating in clockwise and counterclockwise directions, spun six silver rings; and draped over her shoulders was a cloak as dark as midnight. Standing at the right of the goddess, clutching a broadsword in one hand and five dice in the other, was the Guardian. To her left, the masked corpse of a man lay on an altar and prostrated over him—its features obscured by a blood-spattered cowl—was a weeping specter with a knife protruding from its back.

The goddess rang the silver bell.

"Warning!" cried the Guardian and cast two dice to the floor. Sounding like hollow thunder, the dice rolled the length of the pavilion and came to rest at Faith's feet with the word *OF* uppermost.

The goddess rang the silver bell a second time.

"Warning!" cried the Guardian and cast another two dice to the floor. Again, they rolled the length of the pavilion and came to rest at Faith's feet, this time with the word *AN* uppermost.

The goddess rang the silver bell a third time.

"Warning!" cried the Guardian and cast the last die to the floor. It rolled the length of the pavilion and came to rest at Faith's feet with the letter *I* uppermost.

"Behold!" cried the Guardian and pointed to the altar. The legs of the corpse parted and a baby emerged. The goddess pulled it free and offered it to Faith, but when Faith tried to enter the pavilion an invisible barrier barred her way. The goddess slapped the baby's buttocks. It cried and cried.

Faith pummeled the barrier. "Let me in!"

The goddess raised the bell above her head and rang it a fourth time.

"Warning!" cried the Guardian and struck the white marble floor with his broadsword. The pavilion disappeared, Time moved forward, and Faith found herself in the long, dark passageway that seemed to go on forever. With every step she took, the baby's cries grew louder and shafts of pain stabbed into her belly.

Lucy had just climbed into bed after returning from the White Tower when she heard Faith scream. She rushed next door and found Faith and Hugh struggling on the bed.

"She awoke screaming," gasped Hugh, his face as white as Faith's.

Lucy climbed onto the bed and took Faith in her arms. "Try to stay calm, beloved. Are you in pain? Tell me what ails you."

In hoarse, choking whispers, Faith told them what she had glimpsed in the Mirror of Fate.

12

The Sage of Ardclach

During the month of November, Faith often woke at midnight plagued by pains and nightmares. Lucy suspected that the strange rite Fiona had performed on the night of the full moon was somehow responsible, but how could she prove it? She kept her peace until one morning toward the end of the month when she decided it was time to confide in Lady Barbara and Hugh. She found them in the drawing room discussing the forthcoming chieftains' banquet.

"Come, sit by the fire with me," Lady Barbara invited, giving her a welcoming smile. "Where is Faith?"

"She is unwell," Lucy answered gravely. "I am extremely worried about her, Aunt Barbara."

Hugh's handsome face settled into grim lines. "Such pain is not normal, Lucy. I have sent to Davoit for the doctor."

Lady Barbara set down the banquet menus. "Oh, dear, with Faith ill and Colin behaving atrociously, I wonder at the wisdom of holding the chieftains' banquet next Saturday."

Hugh rose and walked to the fireplace. "The chieftains' banquet is a tradition, Mother. Considering the unrest in the clan, I think we would be unwise not to hold it. No matter how grossly Father behaves, the chieftains will obey him implicitly."

Lady Barbara's shoulders slumped. "But Hugh, I am so humiliated by the way he treats me. This morning he threatened to imprison Hugo and me in that dreadful dungeon beneath the White Tower because Hugo brought tea to my bedchamber."

Hugh smiled. "Try to keep your sense of humor about such things, Mother. Everyone knows that cavern of darkness was sealed a century ago."

Lucy drew in a deep breath. "Speaking of the White Tower," she began and launched into a detailed description of what she had seen.

"How utterly ludicrous," Hugh scoffed.

"Normally, I would agree with you, Hugh," Lucy went on gravely, "but because Fiona performed her ritual only minutes before Faith had that vision, and because Faith has been ill ever since, I cannot simply dismiss it."

"Fiona makes me uneasy," said Lady Barbara. "Sometimes I think her mind is quite unhinged. I agree with Lucy that the matter ought to be taken seriously."

"Very well," sighed Hugh. "I'll have a lock fitted to the door of the spiral staircase, and then we shall haul that stupid woman in here to have an accounting of herself."

Lucy clutched his sleeve urgently. "By all means, lock the tower door, but please don't breathe a word of this to Fiona, or we will never discover what is going on in her sick mind."

"Is there a local person who is able to interpret dreams?"

Hugh looked at her askance. "God, Lucy, you're not suggesting we call in some ignorant old hag with a sack of hemlock under one arm and a bag of bones under the other?''

"Not someone on the dark side, Hugh," said Lady Barbara in exasperation. "Someone on the light side. In the village of Ardclach lives a learned sage who is said to be schooled in the old ways. Let's take our problem to him."

The dark cloud of worry lifted from Lucy's mind and suddenly she felt like singing. "Yes," she breathed, "he is the one. Moses and I shall leave for Ardclach in the morning."

The road to Ardclach was a precipitous track of mires and gorges. Lucy and Moses traversed its icy wastes and waded through its raging streams until a fierce snowstorm forced them to take shelter for the night in a disgusting hovel, posing as the Ardclach Inn. "The Waterman's Ward was a palace compared to this," Lucy complained, as she tried to make herself comfortable on the lumpy lice-infested straw in the corner of the pump room.

"Aye," Moses muttered, glaring balefully at two ragged ruffians eyeing her lasciviously.

"The Highland people are so hostile," she sighed as the ruffians quickly averted their eyes. "I'll be glad to return to my friends in Sydney."

Moses placed his pistol in his lap, "Me too, Miss Lucy."

She looked at him with dismay. "But you cannot return to the colony, Moses. You would be arrested for absconding."

"Where you go, so go I."

"But, Moses—"

"Where you go, so go *I*, Miss Lucy," said the giant with absolute finality, and although Lucy debated the issue at length with him, he would not be swayed.

Ignoring the Gaelic mutterings of the sleepy innkeeper, they settled their bill at dawn next morning and set out in search of the sage. Soon afterward they came to a gentle valley at the foot of which was a trickling stream and on its banks, half-hidden by the vitrified ruins of an old Iron Age fort, stood a chapel.

As Lucy dismounted and handed the reins to Moses, sunlight broke through the clouds and lit the scene with such a delicate glow that she sighed at the pure romance of it and thought wistfully of Michael.

Gathering up her skirts she descended the hill and entered the chapel through a low-arched doorway. A monk knelt at the altar singing, and the sound of his voice was so pleasing she listened for some time before discreetly clearing her throat.

The slight middle-aged man who rose and walked toward her looked as if a breeze would blow him away but his gaze was compelling and his smile was the warmest Lucy had ever encountered. "Why have you come, my child?"

"I am deeply troubled, sir," she said, and unburdened herself.

"The rite you witnessed was an invocation of the malevolent beldame 'Cardea,' one of the crueler aspects of the Ninefold Goddess who, before the birth of Christ, was worshipped as the Queen of the Universe," he told her. "The words the woman Fiona used, and the fact that she was hammering at something on the altar, leads me to suppose that she was 'nailing' an effigy of your sister. My child, you must find that effigy, dismantle it piece by piece, cast every piece into a fire built of birch branches, then bury what remains after the burning—ashes, nails, scorched twigs, everything. Being a Christian priest, I make no comment on the ritual of 'cleansing an effigy,' I simply relate the method by which such evils are rendered harmless."

He fell silent and pondered with frowning intensity for a great length of time before continuing. "The goddess who appeared to your sister was not Cardea, but the celestial Dame Ceres, Queen of the Universe. What is the message on the dice and what are the four warnings of the bell? The fact that the sacrifice on the altar had already occurred when your sister arrived at the pavilion, leads me to suppose that the death depicted is almost inevitable. However, the battle scenes in the tapestries may hold the key to prevention. If your sister has the vision again, she must pay particular attention to the tapestries.

"I think that the *second* warning—that of the dice—directly concerns your sister because they roll to rest at her feet. The phrase 'of an *I*,' warns not only of the evil *eye* of witchcraft but also identifies the person seeking to do her harm as 'Fiona.'

"The *third* warning revolves around the birth in the aftermath of the sacrifice upon the altar. Here, in an astounding act of goodwill, the Queen of the Universe personally intervenes in your sister's fate and delivers the baby. However, your sister is prevented from claiming the baby by an invisible barrier. Therefore, despite the divine intervention of the goddess, your sister may yet lose her baby if she is not vigilant."

The sage clasped his hands and lowered his head in a prayerful pose. "I think that the goddess rings the bell a *fourth* time to warn you personally of danger, my child."

A numbing coldness came over Lucy. "Me?"

"In nature, nothing is closer than identical twins. They develop from the same seed, are of the same sex and genetic construction and share the same sac in their mother's womb. Although you are separate souls, your hearts, minds, and bodies are tightly interwined. Indeed, it is possible that you were not meant to be separate entities and perhaps that is why the gods have taken such an interest in your destiny."

He shook his head perplexed. "I am unable to interpret the fourth warning, but if your sister has the vision again, tell her to pay particular attention to the markings on the bell. I repeat, the fourth ring of the bell is *extremely* significant for you."

He rose and led her to the door. "Your sister can 'see' beyond tomorrow with her inner eye and you can 'hear' the sound of silence with your inner ear. Use these God-given gifts to protect yourselves from the danger ahead. I shall pray for you."

13
Laying of the Laird

The usually empty passageways of Carrigmoor were crowded with barbarically dressed clanspeople when Lucy returned from Ardclach on the evening of the chieftains' banquet; and there was such an air of turmoil about the place that she found the prospect of her first major social gathering in six years, quite daunting. After a hurried conference with the family, she sped to her apartments, bathed, and donned a beautiful blue velvet gown trimmed lavishly with white fox fur.

When she arrived at the Grand Dining Room the guests were seated, and the banquet was about to begin. Sir Colin's throne had been moved to the center of the table on the dais and there he sat—resplendent in tartan and furs—presiding grandly over his rowdy clan. The chieftains of the Inner Council and their wives had joined the family at the long table, while the lesser kith and kin occupied the tables in the main body of the room.

As Lucy slid in beside Faith, Sir Colin hammered on the block and signaled the Piper. "Let the banquet begin!"

The strains of "Robin Adair" rang out round the room, and an army of servants circulated around the tables laden with platters of venison, pigs' hearts, goats' livers, calves' heads stewed in wine, neats' tongues, turkeys, geese, small fowls, all manner of vegetables, loaves of hot bread, bannocks dripping in butter, capons, oysters, mince pies, gravies, garnishes, plus a superior selection of liquor.

With clamorous cries of "Long live our laird!" the guests tucked into the succulent fare, and soon the room was assailed by such an uproar of sound that even the unhappy baying wolf-hounds, being chased by a pack of ferocious children, could not be heard.

Faith cast a disapproving eye at Fiona's father, Clarrie of Cantraydoun, who sat opposite. The man's rough dress and crude speech were surpassed only by his atrocious table manners. "Bloody trees!" he bellowed, conveying a slice of meat to his mouth with his dirk—an evil-looking weapon with an eighteen-inch blade and a cairngorm-studded handle—"Their bloody roots suck the goodness from our soil; their bloody shade withers our grain; and their bloody birds peck the heart out of our seed." As gravy mixed with saliva oozed from the corners of his mouth, Faith's stomach churned.

"Sir," she said, fixing him with a steely stare, "it is indecent to fill your mouth so. And pray, sir, do not toss your bones on the floor or blow your nose on your table napkin; it is a discourtesy to your hostess."

Clarrie poured usquebaugh into the great pewter cup standing in the center of the table. "Can't you keep this prattling woman quiet, laird? In the old days, lassies were taught in the nursery to hold their tongues in the company of men—aye, daughter?"

Fiona lowered her vulture's eyes. "Yes, father mine."

"Fortunately sir, the old days are gone," said Lucy. "In these enlightened times we use knives and forks at table, not dirks."

Sir Colin belched loudly and reached for the pewter. "Henceforth," he cried, "women will be seen and not heard in the house of the Hammerer!" His edict elicited rousing cheers from the male company and thereafter, as toast followed toast, the pewter passed rapidly round the table.

Spurred on by Clarrie, Sir Colin ranted and raved with the rest until Lady Barbara, terrified of the consequences if he continued drinking usquebaugh at such a rate, ordered a servant to bring the green decanter to the table.

"Here is your special claret, laird," she murmured, setting it before him.

Clarrie gave an almighty belch. "Pah! Claret's only fit for women and swine—aye, laird?"

Sir Colin farted explosively and pointed to the decanter. "Take it away and bring more usquebaugh, woman of the house!"

Lady Barbara blushed crimson. "Please don't drink any more, Colin. It's not good for you . . ."

"You'll not let a whingeing woman dictate to ye—aye, laird?" shouted Clarrie.

"Nae! Get to your chamber, woman of the house!"

"You cannot speak to Mother in such a way," said Hugh, placing a protective arm around Lady Barbara.

Sir Colin stared at him without recognition. "Who are you to question the Steward Laird, you loitering knave?"

"Your son and heir, Father."

"Son, maybe, but *not* heir—aye, laird?" shouted Clarrie of Cantraydoun, triumphantly.

As everyone turned toward the dais, hopeful that the Stewart laird would settle the matter of his lineage once and for all, Lady Barbara leaned forward urgently in her chair and gripped Hugh's arm.

Sir Colin smashed down the hammer on the block. "Whosoever brings me the head of Green Colin Campbell on a platter will be heir to four thousand!" His head dropped to his chest and he gave a long, snuffling snore.

"Quickly, lay him out flat or he will suffocate where he sits," Lucy cried, rushing to him and ripping open his shirt. Hugh and Robert did her bidding but it was no use, Sir Colin died before they got him to the floor.

With the pipes playing a slow, ranting dirge, the men of the Clan Stewart carried their dead laird downstairs to the Laying Chamber, a gloomy apartment with gray marble walls hung with rusty military equipment and clan regalia. Only two pieces of furniture relieved the room's austerity—a gigantic four-poster bed of polished yew and a high-backed chair with carved claw arms and a peculiar triangular seat.

The men lay the dead laird on the bed, Lady Barbara took her place in the vigil chair, the women set to work with frankincense and myrrh, and the great iron bell atop the battlements began to toll.

455

"I have never been so cold," Faith said crossly, as she and Lucy donned mourning dresses and veils on the day of Sir Colin's funeral. "Even Ice Island was not as cold as this." Her voice faltered and tears flooded her eyes. "Peter always made sure I was warm . . ."

"No one expects you to go trudging three miles through the snow to Craggie churchyard when you are so close to your time," said Lucy quickly. "Stay home, as Hugh suggested."

Faith raised her chin proudly. "My place is beside Hugh, not lying abed in a doze."

"But you look so pale and drawn, Faith."

"Is it any wonder? I cannot sleep at night for the pains in my belly and that accursed bell bong, bonging in my brain."

"Well, if you must attend the funeral, then at least ride in the carriage, darling."

Faith's eyes flashed. "I'll not have that vulture, Fiona, or her reptilian father calling me a weak-willed Englishwoman. Today, I shall show Clan Stewart what James Gamble's daughter is made of."

At noon, the funeral cortege assembled in the courtyard and, with torches flaring and pipes ranting, set out across the desolate landscape toward Craggie. As Lady Barbara stumbled through the snow at the head of the mile-long procession, she was grateful for Hugh's strong arm. She was bone-weary from her almost sleepless vigil of the last four days, but she consoled herself with the knowledge that the ordeal was almost over and that, so far, there had been no trouble. However, as she stepped inside the gate at Craggie churchyard, Clarrie of Cantraydoun and several chieftains broke ranks and barred her way.

"Only the men of Clan Stewart may view the dead laird at his grave," Clarrie said.

Hugh stared at him contemptuously. "The Lady Barbara has more right to be at the laird's graveside than any man present. Let her pass."

"Do you scorn the old ways?" Clarrie cried righteously.

Hugh unsheathed his broadsword. "I'll not debate the matter further, you churl. Step aside or it will be the worse for you."

Robert pushed his way through the crowd. "If the lady wants to be with her laird till the end, I say, let her. Is that your wish, dear lady?"

Lady Barbara, who would have gladly bowed to tradition and

stayed outside the gate, nodded mutely. Hugh had taken a stand and she had to support him.

"So be it," said Robert, unsheathing his broadsword. "Who challenges?"

Nonplussed by Robert's action, the chieftains resumed their places and Clarrie, finding himself the lone dissenter, also retreated.

The danger is past, thought Lady Barbara as the last clods of earth were thrown on the coffin at the conclusion of the ceremony. *With Colin safely buried, Hugh can claim his rightful inheritance.*

14
The Fellowship of War

When Lucy, Faith, and Lady Barbara descended the white marble staircase to the ground floor the next morning, the vestibule was humming with excitment. Hugh's induction ceremony was about to begin and the clansmen, dressed in black and white mourning tartans, were jostling into the Great Hall, while the women hovered outside in whispering clusters.

"With the door closed, we will miss everything," Faith said querulously.

Lady Barbara removed three cassocks from the cupboard. "Put these on, my dears, they will keep the dust off your dresses."

"But there isn't any dust," said a puzzled Lucy as she slipped a cassock over Faith's bulging torso.

Lady Barbara smiled mysteriously. "Where we are going, there will be. Women are forbidden to witness the induction of a laird, but High has decided to create a precedent." She walked to the cupboard. "Above is an old minstrel's gallery overlooking the Great Hall. It was boarded up years ago but Hugh inspected it last night and found it to be quite safe." She stepped into the cupboard, ran her fingers along the top shelf and released the catch. The back swung open with a faint click. "It will be dark and dusty up there, but don't worry about spiders, Hugh cleared away the webs last night."

Hugh glanced up at the minstrel's gallery and smiled. No

doubt his three loyal women would be in position by now, which was probably just as well for he had few friends in the main body of the hall. In fact, the air bristled with hostility.

Robert entered at that moment and, accompanied by thunderous applause, walked down the aisle to the dais. He nodded gravely to Hugh then sat in an ornate chair that formerly had been occupied by Sir Colin's foster brother.

May as well get the thing over, Hugh thought and signaled the Brieve to begin.

The Brieve thumped his broadsword on the floor and shouted, "The laird's son will speak!"

Ignoring the veiled insult of "laird's son," not "young laird" or "Stewart heir," Hugh walked to the front of the dais and stared at the sullen gathering until the last rebellious murmur died away. "From this day forward, the annual 'laird's duties' will be abolished and tenant farmers will no longer be required to till my infields, collect peat for my fires, or repair my roofing.

"From this day forward the old runrig system will be abolished and tenant farmers will be granted twenty-year leases, provided they agree to drain away their wastelands and enclose their fields . . ."

As Hugh outlined the changes he planned to make, Clarrie, seated in the front row with the chieftains of the Inner Council, glanced at the bare crest on Robert's bonnet. Fiona had followed his instructions and removed its strap and buckle. No ordinary member of the clan was permitted to wear the crest so—only the laird and his heir had that privilege. Clarrie was certain every man in the hall had noticed the missing strap and would understand the significance of it. How long will Robert wait before mounting the challenge? Clarrie wondered, staring fixedly at his son-in-law, hoping to catch his eye. But Robert sat with arms folded, looking straight ahead.

"For too long, our roads have been rutted tracks in summer and hopeless quagmires in winter," Hugh went on. "Next spring we shall widen and seal them, then we will be able to deliver our produce to market in one fifth the time. And, as a further sign of goodwill, I shall supply a farm cart with spoked wheels and revolving axel to every tenant farmer who agrees to implement the changes I have outlined."

A murmur of excitement ran through the hall.

"I'll have no gravel roads that wear down my horses' hooves!" Clarrie cried, jumping to his feet.

"Before another year is done, every treacherous pack track on

Stewart land will be a thing of the past, Clarrie of Cantraydoun,'' Hugh replied coldly. "If you are concerned about your horses' hooves, I suggest you shoe them. At the conclusion of my induction, any man wishing to avail himself of my offer can—''

"Imposter!" cried Clarrie. "Robert McBain is first-born of the Stewart, not you!"

As pandemonium broke out, Hugh signaled the Brieve to call for order, but the Brieve stared stolidly ahead. Not until Robert joined Hugh at the front of the dais, did the outcry subside.

"I make no challenge to the lairdship of this clan," Robert said in ringing tones, grasping Hugh's shoulder. "Although I am firstborn of the Stewart, I am his baseborn son. My foster brother Hugh is the rightful heir and has my loyalty and allegiance until death.'' He smiled at Hugh and extended his hand. Hugh grasped it and looked deeply into his brother's eyes. Then Robert turned and glared at the Brieve with icy ferocity. "Let the laird's induction begin."

The Brieve exhorted the assembly to silence; Robert escorted Hugh to the laird's throne and the Bard came forward bearing the insignia of office: a gold amulet, a horned helmet, a sable cape, and a ring of great antiquity.

After recounting Hugh's lineage from Fergus the First to Sir Colin, the Bard urged Hugh to follow his forebears' noble example, clothed him in the raiment and led him to a stone block at the center of the dais. Hugh mounted it, then the Bard gave into his hand a white wand. When Hugh had taken the laird's oath, the chieftains encircled him and took their oath of allegiance.

Hugh then addressed them, saying, "I hereby acknowledge Robert the McBain my flesh and blood, and order that, henceforth, he be known as Robert the Stewart, brother of Hugh.'' He removed the amulet and passed to the Bard. "I name my brother, Robert the Stewart, *Tanist* of this clan."

Robert's induction to the second most powerful office was similar to Hugh's, except he placed only one foot on the stone block when taking the oath.

Lady Barbara, watching from the minstrel's gallery, wiped tears from her eyes. "How could I have so misjudged Robert? He really loves Hugh."

"Yes," whispered Faith, deeply moved by what she had witnessed. "He has adored Hugh from the time they were children. I hate myself for doubting his loyalty."

"There, there, darling," Lady Barbara soothed. "Don't upset yourself. We shall make it up to him."

Fiona found Robert in his bedchamber removing his regalia. "Why did you do it?" she screeched, running to him and pummeling his chest. "We could have had it all!"

He stared at her with distaste. An opaque film covered her eyes and froth spattered her lips. "Control yourself."

"I hate you!" she screamed. "I've always hated you. I only married you to be near Hugh. He and I cuckolded you countless times before that English bitch returned from the colonies."

Robert laughed contemptuously. "Nonsense, Fiona. Hugh has never given you a second glance. It's Fae he loves—always has, and always will."

"You spineless muckworm!" she screamed. "My father is right! You'll never be anything but Hugh's cringing lapdog."

"If your father had bothered to consult me about his aspirations to power, I could have saved him the humiliation of today."

Fiona's face contorted with fury. "Don't belittle *my* father, you piece of dog mire. I hope your bastard's blood boils in your veins and a thousand lamias suck it dry. Die! Die! So I can dance on your grave." She flung open the door connecting their bedchambers and called to her maid. "Pack some clothes!"

"Off to Cantraydoun?" he enquired sarcastically.

"Yes, you low dolt! Now there is no hope of you becoming laird, the farther I am away from you, the better."

He gave her a cheerful salute and strode from the room. "My sentiments exactly. Farewell, my *sweeting*."

After methodically ransacking the outer rooms of Fiona's apartment, Lucy turned her attention to the bedchamber but found nothing. Perhaps Fiona took it to Cantraydoun, she thought, opening the door of the dressing closet. Although the clothes racks were bare, the upper shelves were stacked with bits and pieces of frippery.

Lucy climbed up on a chair and rummaged through the piles until her fingers came into contact with something hard at the back. However, the shelf was so deep she could not quite get her hand around the object. "Damn," she said, standing on tiptoe and straining her fingers further.

"What *are* you doing?"

Startled, Lucy let go the shelf, missed her footing on the chair and crashed to the floor.

"What are you doing?" Robert repeated, as he helped her up. "Why are you ransacking my wife's closet in the dead of night, Lucy?"

She bit her lip. "If I told you, Robert, I doubt you'd believe it . . ."

"Try me."

"I was looking for an effigy of Faith." She told him the entire story.

"Fiona certainly dislikes Fae, but witchcraft, rites, and effigies . . . it makes no sense, Lucy."

"We aren't dealing with sense. We are dealing with medieval magic. When you surprised me in the closet I thought I had discovered something. Will you get it for me?"

Robert frowned darkly. "I think you are being foolish."

"Nevertheless, humor me." She took up the lamp and returned to the closet. "Reach right to the back in the corner," she instructed as he extended his arm along the shelf. "Feel it? Something hard."

He withdrew a canvas bag and handed it down to her.

Conscious of his disapproving look, Lucy returned to the bedchamber and undid the bag's fastenings. "I think Fiona wore this to the White Tower the night of the full moon," she said, removing a dark cowl.

"That's hardly damning evidence," he answered tersely.

She delved into the bag and pulled out a heavy object wrapped in the tatters of a white shawl. Goose bumps rose all over her body. "Oh God, Robert, look!"

Robert stared at the grotesque spiked pregnant doll with stunned disbelief. "Give the abominable thing here," he rasped, "I'll toss it into the fire."

Lucy drew away from him. "No, it must be dismantled piece by piece and burned in a birchwood fire."

"Surely *you* don't believe in such things, Lucy?"

Lucy rose. "I know nothing about magic, Robert, but the sage of Ardclach is an expert. I shall follow his instructions to the letter."

Robert sighed deeply. "Whatever you think is best. I shall escort you to your apartment."

"You must do something about Fiona," she said as they walked along the icy passageways toward the east wing. "I will not tolerate her threatening my sister again, Robert."

In the flickering lamplight, he saw the determination in her

461

eyes. "No need to concern yourself. In the future, I shall keep Fiona under tight control. However, with Hugh ensconced as laird, her vile, silly practices should cease. She is not an evil person, Lucy—just misguided, and greatly swayed by her father."

"I hope you are right," Lucy said as they stopped outside her door. "Thank you for seeing me to my room, Robert. I am sorry to have placed this burden on you."

In a most uncustomary gesture, the dour Scot raised her hand to his lips. "Nothing you say or do could be a burden to me, lovely Lucy. If Fiona causes you or Fae any further problems, seek me out immediately. Good night."

15

Hogmanay

The house of Clarrie of Cantraydoun, a thatched two-story abode with ancient walls, narrow windows, and a door of hoary oak, stood in the midst of a barren, treeless waste.

Seated at the table in the low-ceilinged living room were Clarrie, his wife, Fiona, and the dozen ill-kept villains who comprised the elite of his tribe.

"My friend, Jock, from the castle has heard no plan to drive us off our land, chief," said a scruffy ruffian, picking his teeth with a serrated fingernail.

"Does a wolf forewarn its prey?" snarled Clarrie. "I've told ye, there's none to be trusted but our aen."

Fiona's eyes glittered. "My spineless husband is to blame for this. I pray to Queen Cardea for his death a dozen times a day."

"And your prayers will be answered, daughter. He'll die by the dirk—along with Laird Hugh."

His words exploded in Fiona's brain like musket fire. "No, Father, never say it, not Hugh. Do what you like with Robert but Hugh is my aen true love."

"M-murder the laird," stammered his terrified wife. "No, husband. We'd all end up gallow's meat."

The veins on Clarrie's temples pulsated. "Don't tell *me* nae, woman. We'll be in no danger if we do it right."

"But we'd be the first suspected," she bleated.

"Not if Fiona returns to the castle and makes peace with Robert and Laird Hugh."

Fiona gave a high-pitched scream. "No, Father, please don't make me. Those English culls are always watching me and whispering behind my back."

Clarrie shook her by the throat. "Back you go, Fiona, to reconcile with Robert and beg forgiveness of Laird Hugh and the ladies. I need you at Carrigmoor, not here in your attic room." He thrust her aside. "Listen carefully, all of you. This year, with the castle in mourning, the feast of Hogmanay will be held at the meeting hall in Davoit . . ."

When Fiona returned to Carrigmoor on Hogmanay Eve, the first thing she saw on entering her bedchamber was the empty canvas bag on her bed. A low growl rose from the depths of her throat. "How dare they plunder my room. How *dare* they."

"Ah, the loving wife returning to the arms of her husband," said Robert, entering the room through his connecting door. "Or have you come to collect that filthy thing you had hidden in your closet?"

Fiona moved toward him, intending to rake out his eyes, but Queen Cardea waylaid her.

"Where are your wits, Fiona? Kiss his lips so I can pass the poison into him."

"Yes," said Fiona, pressing her arms tightly against her sides to keep her hands from flying up and tearing Robert's face to shreds.

He raised his eyebrows. "Yes, what?"

"Yes, I repent, I repent, I repent."

"Tell him the lying tale," ordered the Queen.

Fiona locked her arms around Robert's neck. "God has punished me for my manifold sins, Robbie. On Christ's birthday, I miscarried our child. Forgive me, Robbie." She pressed her lips hard against his.

"Thrust your tongue to the back of his throat so the poison will pass more quickly into his body," commanded the Queen.

Dutifully, Fiona complied.

Revolted by her hot, dry tongue, Robert quickly stepped away. "What did you say, Fiona?"

How Fiona exalted in her victory! Soon his blood would turn to mud in his veins, his teeth would rot in his gums and his skin would become a morass of weeping sores. "Tis true enough,

463

Robbie," she said contritely. "Oh, the poor wee bairn. Forgive your Fiona and she will swear before every archangel in heaven to be evermore your obedient, loving wife."

He eyed her skeptically. "How so in the family way? We've not been together in months."

Her answer was ready before his mouth closed over the last word. "Not *so* many months, Robbie." She swayed weakly against him. "Help me to bed, husband, the ride from Cantraydoun sapped my strength."

Fiona kept to her apartment all day and joined the family after dinner. "Good evening," she said brightly as she entered the drawing room. Ignoring their frigid looks, she opened her novel and methodically turned the pages until the Queen ordered her to ask the question.

"What's to do for Hogmanay, dear lady?"

For Robert's sake, Lady Barbara answered the question civilly. "Because we are in mourning and Faith is almost at her time, we women have decided to remain at the castle. However, Hugh has to ride into Davoit later this evening to deliver the laird's address so, if you want to attend the festivities, you could accompany him and Robert. But you must make up your mind soon, Fiona. The house servants are leaving in half an hour and if the carriage is to be got ready for you—"

"Please don't trouble yourself, dear lady," Fiona interposed breathlessly, as Lady Barbara reached for the bell cord. "I am happy to spend Hogmanay here with you." She returned to her book for a while, then cast a covert glance at Hugh.

"Don't do that!" snapped the Queen.

"But I should have lain with him all these years," Fiona protested.

"You shall have him at the end," promised the Queen. "Sip your wine, they are watching."

Fiona dutifully raised the goblet to her lips then returned to the novel and counted exactly two hundred seconds before turning the page.

When the clock on the mantelpiece chimed ten Hugh sighed. "Time to go. God! What a foul night to be abroad. Listen to the wind roaring round the battlements."

"Now!" commanded the Queen.

Fiona scrambled to her feet with such violence the book

crashed to the floor. "I shall see you downstairs to the door, Robbie."

"Don't trouble yourself," said Robert, viewing her deathly pallor with disquiet. "You look unwell."

"Oh, it's *no* trouble," she replied sweetly. "I must fetch a shawl from my apartment, in any case." She accompanied them downstairs, hovered about the entrance steps until they were out of sight, then collected a lighted torch and ascended to the southern battlements to give the signal.

"I distrust this new Fiona even more than the old," said Faith as soon as Fiona had left the room.

"I also," Lady Barbara said grimly. "I wonder if she actually was with child."

"She certainly looks ill," murmured Lucy, "but sick or not, I don't want her near Faith."

Lady Barbara sighed. "My feelings exactly, Lucy, but how can we ask her to leave? She *is* Robert's wife."

When Fiona returned a few minutes later, Lucy stared at her with alarm. "Where have you been, Fiona? You are blue with cold."

"How dare—" Fiona abruptly broke off and smiled at Lucy with feverish, glittering eyes. "Oh dear, how foolish of me, I have forgotten my shawl. Well, never mind . . ." She retrieved her novel from the floor and resumed her methodical turning of the pages.

The old Fiona is still there, Lucy thought uneasily as an uncomfortable silence settled over the room. But she has an added dimension of cunning this evening.

Faith dropped her needlework and clutched her abdomen. "Lucy! Oh Lucy!"

"Pains, beloved?" Lucy joined her on the longseat.

Faith grimaced. "That one was definitely the real thing."

Lady Barbara clasped her hands excitedly. "Oh, heaven be praised. My first grandchild. You had better ride to Davoit and fetch Hugh and the doctor, Moses."

"Dog fly!" Fiona screeched, leaping to her feet and flinging the novel at Moses. The giant grunted as its metal edge struck him on the side of the head.

Lucy rushed forward and shoved Fiona in the chest. "How dare you hit Moses!"

465

With a high, uncontrolled titter, Fiona backed toward the door. "Don't think to match *me*, Lucy. You've no idea how strong I am."

"Get out!" cried Lady Barbara. "Don't you come *near* my girls!"

"You'll spurn me no more in life, you silly old cull," Fiona screeched and ran from the room.

"She is mad," said Lucy, examining Moses's injury. "Aunt Barbara, would you ring for some salve? This cut is quite deep."

"I'll have to fetch it myself," said her aunt. "The servants left hours ago."

"No, no, *no*!" Faith gasped, shaking her head distractedly from side to side. "Ride as if your life depends on it, Moses! Find Master Hugh. The tapestries are awash with blood and the men are wearing mourning tartans."

Robert glanced apprehensively at the riverbank on his left. "Keep away from the edge, Hugh. This is where our father met with his accident . . ."

Hugh checked his horse and moved to the right, but the road was no better on that side; boulders and bushes, borne down the mountain by the recent torrential rain, lay strewn all about. "The servants will have to return to the castle by way of Craggie. I could wish Hogmanay to the devil this year, Robbie. Only wolves and Highlanders would be fool enough to venture out in such weather."

"At least there's a full moon to light our way, and it isn't snowing."

"Not yet," Hugh growled, easing his horse around the bend. He cursed and pulled on the reins as a man in Stewart mourning tartan sprang out in front of him. "Idiot! Have you no sense? You could have killed us both—" Hugh broke off as several men scrambled up the ditch and tried to drag him out of the saddle.

"Ambush!" Robert shouted hoarsely. "Into the river, Hugh!"

Hugh drove his heels into the horse's flanks. The terrified beast lunged forward, scattering men in every direction, and galloped along the road until a bullet plowed into its rump. Hugh kicked free of the stirrups and dived into a dense thicket. Snorting and squealing, the horse bolted along the ditch until it was cut down by a hail of bullets.

Hugh raised his head and looked around. The ambushers had chosen well. He was cut off by a barren, treeless hill with sheer rock faces on either side. His only chance was the river. He ducked as the ambushers ran past, making for the horse. There was not much time. Being careful not to dislodge the snow on the branches above, he slithered on his belly like a snake, searching for a safe place to cross the road.

The current swept Robert some distance downstream before he realized Hugh was not with him. He edged through the flow, grasped a branch jutting out from the bank and heaved himself out of the water. Gulping air into his lungs, he scoured the moonlit crests of the water. Hugh was nowhere in sight. Beset by a nameless dread, he clawed his way up the steep bank to the road. He could hear distant shots above the roar of the river. "Low cowards," he cried, leaping into the underbrush and taking off in a crouching run toward the sounds of battle.

The ambushers were almost on Hugh, closing in on every side, beating the underbrush and firing at random. He had to move soon or it would be too late. A bullet whistled past his cheek and hissed into the snow a yard away. Another shot rang out and a burning pain engulfed his left arm just above the elbow. His insides contracted with shock. *Don't look at it,* he told himself. *Go now, while you still can.* He leapt to the top of the ditch in two scrambling strides. Two more, and he was halfway across the road heading for a clump of bushes. Shots exploded in his ears like thunder. His body tore apart as bullets thudded into it.

"No!" he gasped, his momentum carrying him into the covering bushes. "No! I'm not ready yet." He tried to rise but his limbs had no power. The strength was seeping out of them, like a wave retreating from the shore. "I won't—not like this," he raged. "The river must be close."

He blinked several times, trying to focus but his sight was gone. He stretched his arms in front of him, feeling for the edge of the bank. "Thank God," he sobbed as his clawing fingers dislodged an avalanche of pebbles. "Pull yourself over, Hugh, not much farther now . . ."

* * *

"He's down!" Clarrie shouted triumphantly. "Got you, Laird Hugh! Got you, you English dog!" But as he placed his pistol against Hugh's temple, a shrill whistle rang out from halfway up the hill.

"Riders coming, chief!"

Clarrie cast a hurried glance over his shoulder. A horseman had just thundered around the bend and a tremendous commotion was coming from the underbrush. "Away, men!" he shouted, dashing to the other side of the road. "We canna be caught here!"

"Run as far as you like, Clarrie of Cantraydoun," Robert called hoarsely. "There's no place on earth you'll escape me." He knelt beside Hugh and took him in his arms. "Oh, God, Hugh, what have those bastards done to you?"

Moses halted the horse and leapt down beside them. "Blessed Mother," he gasped when he saw Hugh's injuries. "We'd best get him home." He held out his arms. "Here, let me have him, Master Robert."

Robert clasped his brother tighter. "No," he sobbed. "I'll take him. Help me get him into the saddle."

Lady Barbara left her post by the window and ran to Faith's bed. "They've just ridden into the courtyard. One appears to be injured . . ." She clutched Lucy's arm. "Lucy, I *know* it's Hugh. I feel it in my heart."

Supporting Faith between them, Lucy and Lady Barbara hurried through the dark passageways and reached the first floor as Robert, soaked with blood, appeared at the top of the marble staircase carrying Hugh.

"My God," whispered Lucy. "Take him into the drawing room and put him on the longseat." She drew Moses aside. "Go to Faith's bedchamber and collect implements, sheets, binders, potions—everything. Hurry, Moses!"

As the giant sped away, Fiona sprang out of the shadows. "Poultices and potions are useless, cull. The matter is gone beyond *your* sway."

Brushing her aside, Lucy ran into the drawing room after the others. "Sit in the wing-backed chair and try to hold on," she told Faith, who was kneeling at the end of the longseat, supporting Hugh's head.

"Don't worry about me. Help Scotty . . . please."

With horror, Lucy examined Hugh's wounds. His arms, legs, chest and neck were riddled with bullets. There was nothing she could do. She battled ineffectively to stem the bleeding then looked at Faith and shook her head.

Faith bent lower over Hugh. "Your child is on the way, Scotty. Can you hold on?"

"Sorry, Fae," he sighed. "No regrets?"

Her tears splashed on his face. "No regrets, dearest."

He turned blind eyes toward Lady Barbara, who was kneeling beside him clasping his hand. "Mother? Where are you?"

Lady Barbara raised his hand to her lips and covered it with kisses. "Here, darling."

"It's dark, Mother . . ."

"Don't be afraid; Mother has you."

"My beautiful English rose," he whispered, and died.

The enormity of his passing held them spellbound until Faith sank to the floor groaning. Lucy came out of her stupor and beckoned urgently to Moses. "Kneel behind Faith and support her. Robert, bring the lamp closer."

Five minutes later, Duncan Hugh Stewart, the new laird of Carrigmoor, entered the world with a lusty howl.

"Are you coming upstairs, Aunt Barbara?" asked Faith as Moses lifted her gently in his arms.

Lady Barbara drew up a stool beside the longseat. "No, I shall bide awhile with Hugh." She raised stricken eyes to Lucy. "Can you manage without me, my dear?"

With tears in her eyes, Lucy picked up the baby and followed the others to the door. "Yes, Aunt Barbara. Join us as soon as you are able."

"When I have lit you to the east wing, I will ride into Davoit to consult with the chieftains," Robert told Lucy as they ascended to the floor above.

"The chieftains!" Faith's mouth twisted with bitterness. "What use are they?"

"They must be told, Fae . . . it is the way."

"The way! I am tired of 'the way.' Most of those men will rejoice at Hugh's passing."

"You do them an injustice, Fae. They will not rest until Clarrie of Cantraydoun is hung."

Faith turned her face into Moses' shoulder. "Oh, settle it however you please. I wash my hands of the entire Stewart clan."

Robert glanced down at his blood-caked hands and shuddered. "I wish it were that easy . . ."

"Robert needs your help, Moses. Go with him and keep him from harm," Lucy whispered as Moses laid Faith on the bed.

"But who will help you, Miss Lucy?" he protested.

"Lady Barbara and I can manage, Moses. Go along now."

Shoulders drooping, Moses followed Robert from the room.

With infinite care, Fiona inched her head round the doorway. Although the room was blanketed in shadows, Hugh saw her and acknowledged her presence with his eyes. *Patience, my love,* she said soundlessly. *Soon, the old one weeping beside you will depart and we shall be together.*

"Don't waste time!" snapped the Queen.

"But you *promised* I could have him for my aen."

"Pah!" scoffed the Queen. "What care I for promises? Death, blood, and vengeance are all *I* desire. Find the dirk. There's work to be done while yet the moon waxes."

Fiona descended to the ground floor and ransacked the rooms with frenzied stealth until she found the Stewart ceremonial dirk.

"Indeed, a comely weapon," the Queen said approvingly as Fiona slid the eighteen-inch shaft from its jeweled scabbard and raised it aloft. "You know what to do, Fiona—first, the sacrament of steel, then the baptism by fire. Go!"

Like a pale ghost, Fiona sped up the white marble staircase.

Lady Barbara gazed at Hugh with concern. "I cannot bear the thought of you being so cold, my darling. It will do no harm to cover you. I shall fetch a rug from my room—the sable one, with the Stewart crest—that is fitting."

As Lady Barbara rose, Fiona brought the dirk down in a lunging arc and buried it up to the hilt in her back. The blade broke the bone, passed through her heart and protruded two inches out her chest.

Fiona withdrew the dirk and bent over Hugh. "Oh, best beloved of my heart, be alive with love for your Fiona." She placed her mouth over his and kissed him long and passionately, but his lips gave no response. "What's this, love?" she wept. "Do you scorn me even in death?"

Hugh's only reply was an icy stare. Her sobs becoming frenzied screams, Fiona drove the dirk into his chest, again and again.

He did not struggle. He did not fight.

Lucy looked at Faith and the baby who were sleeping soundly. At least something had gone well on this terrible night. Despite everything it had been a remarkably easy birth and, although mother and child were exhausted, both were doing fine.

Sighing, Lucy lit a lamp and made her way back through the labyrinths of darkness toward the drawing room. Only hours ago, Hugh had been sitting at the card table laughing; now he was dead. She shook her head. The violence and suddenness of his passing was impossible to comprehend. "Michael, darling," she whispered, "when we are together again, let's make every moment count. One never knows . . ."

When Lucy entered the drawing room a cold, clammy feeling crept up her spine. Was it her imagination or did the room reek of blood? She set down the lamp and walked to the longseat. "Please don't sit alone in the dark, Aunt Barbara. Come upstairs to Faith's apartment where it is warm. I have made us a pot of tea." When Lady Barbara didn't answer, Lucy embraced her. "Oh, Aunt Barbara, how can I help?" She drew back as a warm wet substance soaked into her dress. When she looked down, she was saturated in blood. She sprang to her feet and watched with frozen horror as her aunt crumpled to the floor. Then she saw the dirk protruding from Hugh's chest and the ghastly carnage that had been wrought on him.

"What madman, what insane, frenzied—"

The answer came in a rush. *Fiona!*

From far away came a muffled bang, like the sound of a door slamming with tremendous force, followed by a high, drawn out scream.

"Oh God," she sobbed, "Fiona is up there with Faith and the baby."

Arming herself with a poker, she ran through the chasms of darkness toward the east wing. When she burst into Hugh's sitting room, Faith was struggling violently with Fiona who was trying to hurl the baby into the fire.

Lucy rushed forward and struck Fiona a vicious blow across the back. Fiona dropped the baby on the hearthstone a foot from the flames. Faith pounced on him and, having ascertained he was not injured, sat him in the wing-backed chair, snatched up a poker and went to Lucy's aid. Desperately, the rained blows on Fiona.

"Retreat, Fiona!" commanded the Queen. "You are strong but you cannot defeat the entire army."

With a low sobbing moan, Fiona fled the room.

Lucy ran to the door and locked it with trembling hands.

"She would have thrown him into the fire," Faith sobbed, clasping her howling son to her breast. "My precious, precious boy. I heard him crying. When I opened my eyes, she was standing over his crib covered in blood. Oh, Lucy, I've never seen so much blood. And you—look at the front of your gown."

Lucy examined Duncan carefully from head to foot. "Thank God he is a sturdy little fellow." She led Faith into the bed-chamber and in hushed tones told her what had taken place downstairs.

"Poor Aunt Barbara," sobbed Faith. "This is a nightmare, Lucy. Everything I saw in the vision has come to pass."

Lucy gripped her shoulders. "Tell me exactly what happened when the goddess rang the bell the fourth time."

Faith concentrated with all her might. "She raised it above her head. It had numbers carved on it—fours and fives—and some-thing else. . . . Yes, now I remember, as the bell spun in her hand I saw gallows posts." Tears rolled down her cheeks. "Oh, Lucy, poor Aunt Barbara. What will we do?"

Lucy walked to the window. The wind was not a howling gale and snow was falling in blinding sheets. "We must get help. But we can't take a newborn baby out in this blizzard."

"The carriage?" Faith suggested. "I am weak but I know I could help harness the horses."

Lucy shook her head. "We would be in tremendous danger all the while we were fiddling with the carriage and if, by some miracle, we did get away without being bludgeoned to death by Fiona, if we lost control of the carriage in these conditions we'd freeze to death before anyone found us."

"Leave Duncan and me here and ride into Davoit alone."

"Out of the question; I would be gone for hours."

"Then, let's stay here. The servants will probably return at first light . . ."

Lucy paced the floor. "Daylight is still six hours away. Fiona could raze the castle by then. The fourth ring of the bell haunts me, Faith. The markings on it—fours and fives, you say? And gallows posts? Of what further danger does the goddess warn?" She drew in her breath sharply. "Of course! Four and five add up to nine. The *Ninefold* Goddess rings the bell a fourth time alerting us to salvation, not danger. If we ring the bell atop the White Tower everyone from miles around will converge on Carrigmoor.''

''But how will we reach the White Tower with that madwoman stalking the passageways?''

Lucy hugged her. ''I can do it.''

Faith recoiled. ''No, Lucy, I won't allow you to go out there alone.''

Lucy drew her down on the bed. ''We cannot leave Duncan unprotected. Therefore, only one of us can go. I am stronger.''

Faith leaned against the bedpost and closed her eyes. *''No.''*

''Would Peter Devereaux sit here and wait meekly for death?'' Lucy asked softly.

Tears slid down Faith's cheeks. ''No, he would discover the enemy's weaknesses and exploit them.''

''What are Fiona's weaknesses, beloved?''

''She had no mind, so we can out-think her.''

''True . . . and she cannot be in two places at once. Therefore, while you remain here protecting Duncan, I shall draw her to the White Tower.'' Lucy reached out and brushed the tears from her sister's cheeks. ''Don't be afraid, darling, I will use the same tactics on Fiona that I used on Tom Lewis—take her by surprise, then outrun her. Once I reach the White Tower I can lock myself in and I will be perfectly safe. Where does Hugh keep the key to the spiral staircase?''

Faith leaned forward urgently. ''You are determined to go through with this?''

Lucy looked away quickly so Faith would not see her lips trembling. ''We have no choice.''

Faith sighed forlornly. ''Very well, my heart. I accept that only one of us can go and, as you are the stronger, it must be you.'' She walked to Hugh's dressing room. ''Hugh kept some personal keys in an old dispatch box but most of the household one hang in the kitchen.''

''Oh God,'' gasped Lucy, ''I don't relish the thought of rummaging around down there.''

However, a shiny new key labeled tower was in the dispatch box.

While Faith set about extinguishing the lamps, Lucy donned two pairs of woollen stockings and exchanged her bloody garments for riding breeches and hunting jacket. She embraced Faith, unlocked the door, and slammed it behind her.

"Fiona!" she screeched, flying toward the north wing. "Here I am, Fiona!"

Her eyes wide and staring, her heart pounding against her ribs, Lucy ran the gauntlet of that dreadful castle. Within every shadow lurked a new menace, around every corner waited a new terror and by the time she reached the north wing, only her instinct for survival kept her going. *Not much farther,* she told herself as she sped past the silent sentinels guarding that last long passageway. *Not much farther, Lucy. Run. Run. Run!*

She reached the door of the spiral staircase and felt with fumbling fingers for the lock, but as she did so she heard a high wailing sound that made the hairs on the back of her neck stand erect. Flying along the passageway toward her was a ghastly white specter.

Frantically, she fitted the key into the lock. The door swung open. She stumbled inside, locked it behind her and sank sobbing to the floor. A moment later the door shuddered and shook and wild unearthly screams filled the air.

Completely unnerved, Lucy crawled under the stairwell and cowered against the wall. "Oh God, help me," she wept. "Please God, help me." A moment later, the furious assault on the door ceased, but the following silence was even more terrifying. Had Fiona gone after Faith and the baby?

Fear added strength to her limbs, Lucy ascended the spiral staircase to the chapel. No milky moonlight greeted her tonight. She felt her way around the outer wall to the battlements door and drew the bolt. The door flew open with tremendous force and the North Wind rushed in, whirling and shrieking like a thousand banshees.

Bending almost double Lucy stepped into the swirling maelstrom of snow and clawed her way along the battlements to where the great iron bell hung between its gallows posts.

She jumped down and grasped a post as the wind whipped around her, tearing her hair from its bindings. "Imagine you are up a main," she told herself, looping a leg around the post and reaching for the chain.

Up, up, went her arms, stretching hands . . . straining fingers. Then she had it and was yanking it down as hard as she could.

"Bong!"

Deep, hollow, rich, and vibrant tolled the bell, rolling over mountain and glen to Davoit, Craggie, Inverness, and Nairn. How she exalted in its solemn sound!

With renewed strength Lucy rang out their salvation a second time and a third. But as she reached for the chain a fourth time, she hesitated. The sage of Ardclach had warned her that the fourth ring of the bell was significant to her safety. But what further danger could there be?

"The fourth ring of the bell is *extremely* significant, Mother of Destiny," whispered the Ninefold Goddess from behind the North Wind as Lucy tugged at the bell chain.

Lucy glanced behind her and there on the wall stood Fiona, gigantic battle-ax poised to strike.

As the bell tolled a fourth time, Fiona brought the ax down. The bell's retracting chain swung Lucy high in the air. The ax buried itself in the bell post. The North Wind spun Lucy round and round. Fiona let go the ax and grabbed Lucy's legs. Lucy kicked her in the chest.

Fiona staggered backward across the platform, teetered on the edge with arms spread and eyes blazing, then, with a high wailing scream dropped into the void below.

Sobbing with relief, Lucy sank to the platform and gave thanks for her salvation. Then, when she recovered her strength, she descended the spiral staircase, stepped through the remains of the door, which Fiona had pulverized with the battle-ax, and returned through the valley of darkness to where Faith waited with the baby.

PART THREE
Return to the Future

16
April 1792

As the farm cart rolled into a deep rut, Beth glanced through slanted eyes at John Best. What's wrong with him? she wondered. He hasn't spoken a word since we left Parramatta. "Will Michael be surprised to see me, John?"

Best gave a noncommittal grunt and stared straight ahead.

She brushed a fly off Ben's cheek and licked her lips nervously. *Would* Michael be pleased to see her? Except for a note last December, explaining that he could not spare the time to come to Sydney, she'd heard nothing from him in six months. Last February, the transporter *Pitt* had arrived with more letters from Lucy: three for Michael, one for her. She had destroyed them also. Tears stung her eyes. She hated herself. But now she had begun there was no turning back. Two weeks ago, when she had received her pardon, she had decided that, for Ben's sake, she must go back to Worthing and try to work things out with Michael before Lucy returned to the colony.

She thumped him on the shoulder. "What's wrong with you, John Best? We've been on the road four hours and you haven't said a civil word."

He halted the cart and spun round to face her. "I don't feel civil toward you, Bethy. Why are you chasing after the Lieutenant? He's Lucy Gamble's man."

"He is not!"

He leaned toward her, face flushed with anger. "If you leave him alone he'll straighten things out with her and you know it."

"No, he won't! He told me he was *finished* with her forever."

"A likely bloody story. The Lieutenant's for her and she's for

476

him—and that's that. So let's turn the cart around and I'll take you and your boy back to Parramatta.''

Beth grabbed his arm as he jerked the reins. "No! I've got important letters for Michael from the Governor and the Surgeon General, and some from England.''

"*I* can deliver the letters.''

"You can't! They were given to me in trust.''

"Have it your way,'' he growled, urging the horses forward, "but you're making a bigger mistake with the Lieutenant than you ever did with Balmain or George Clayton.''

"Don't you dare talk about Will or George to me, you—you *insufferable* man.''

"Don't you dare use stupid fancy words on me,'' he retaliated and kept his silence for the rest of the journey.

They passed through the gates and rolled along the track toward the house. Beth's heart fluttered when she saw Michael open the door and step out onto the wide veranda.

"Brought you a couple of visitors, Lieutenant.'' Best jerked the cart to a halt at the bottom of the steps and jumped out. "I'll get the men to help me unload.'' He nodded briefly to Beth and strode toward the outbuildings on the far side of the yard.

Michael stared unsmilingly at her. "Hello, Beth. What brings you and Ben to Worthington?''

He was more handsome than ever, Beth decided: tall and tanned, with a hard, muscular body and smoky gray eyes that set her pulse racing. "I-I thought you might like to see how much your son's grown.'' She handed Ben down to him.

Michael bounced the wriggling infant in his arms. "My God, he is heavy. What have you been feeding him—bricks?''

Beth giggled and the tension between them eased. "Don't do that!'' she shrieked as she set Ben on the ground. "He'll get filthy. Put him on the veranda. Show Daddy how well you can crawl, Benjamin.''

After Beth fed Ben and put him to bed, she joined Michael in the parlor and related the latest news from Sydney—Denis Considen's return to the hospital, the departure of Major Ross and the battalion, the arrival of the *Pitt,* and Phillip's continuing ill health.

"Anyone heard from Peter Devereaux?'' he asked when she paused for breath.

"No.'' She launched into an amusing story about an Irish convict who had lost his way while searching for the road to China.

After six months of solitude Michael wondered how he would cope with her prattle. If the amount of baggage she had brought was any indication, she planned to stay for some time. Still, Ben was delightful. Michael smiled, remembering his son's crablike movements across the veranda. It would be a joy having him at Worthing. He listened to Beth for a while longer then escaped to his bedchamber.

17

The Britannia *Plot*

Wednesday, September 26, 1792

Beth glanced nervously at Michael from beneath lowered lids. He preferred his own bed to hers but he adored Ben so they had been reasonably happy until John Best had returned from Parramatta last week with the monthly provisions and a letter from Governor Phillip requesting that Michael come to Sydney.

The cart rolled down the hill on the outskirts of Sydney, passed by the burial grounds and entered an avenue of red gums. Had Governor Phillip received a letter from Lucy? "Why does the Governor want to see you?" she asked, as they emerged from the wood into the hustle and bustle of the High Street.

"I don't know," Michael replied vaguely, gazing about him with interest. In the year since he'd been to Sydney it had changed remarkably. The ramshackle hovels of the First Fleeters had been replaced by neat mudbrick cottages, set six feet above the road on grassy banks.

"You must have *some* idea," Beth said peevishly as they passed by the dilapidated marine barracks and entered The Rocks, the home of Sydney's less savory citizens.

"There's Bob Sidaway." Michael saluted the convict, who

looked more like a country squire than a reject of Mother England's prisons. "He must be doing well these days."

"Michael! What about the Governor?"

Michael frowned. Why did she have such an infuriating curiosity about matters that did not concern her? "I've told you a dozen times, I have no idea what he wants. I shall go to Government House and make an appointment to see him as soon as I unload."

The following evening, Michael dined with John White and George Johnston at the new barracks, an imposing structure of mudbricks and mortar, built on the site of the old burial grounds on top of The Rocks.

After toasting absent friends and dispensing with other social pleasantries, they turned their minds to more serious matters. "Your return to Sydney is most timely, old chap," said John. "I have an exciting business proposition for you—the opportunity of your lifetime. According to Major Grose and Lieutenant Macarthur, all that's needed to get this colony on its feet is a spot of free trade. The officers of the corps have decided to charter the *Britannia* and send it to the Cape to purchase goods, livestock, and rum."

"Rum is more negotiable than gold in Sydney," George declared enthusiastically. "At the moment, the asking price for it is three shillings a gallon. Just think of the profit to be made on a hundred-gallon cask."

Michael's mouth twitched. "I take it you're also in favor of this little venture, George?"

"Up to the hilt!" George executed an imaginary sword thrust. "Grose and Macarthur have spoken to the master of *Britannia*, and Captain Raven has agreed to place his vessel at the cartel's disposal for a fee of twenty-two hundred pounds."

"Which brings me to my proposition," John continued. "Originally, the charter was to be divided into eleven shares—ten to the corps officers and one to me—but as I plan to return to England when I can wangle a leave of absence, I thought you might be interested in my share."

"What does Phillip think of all this?" asked Michael.

George shrugged. "Officially, he is bound to uphold the Government's charter with the East India Company, which prohibits free trade, but his private opinions are more flexible."

"A month at sea to get this damned land dust out of my lungs and I shall be as spry as ever," Phillip answered in reply to Michael's concerned enquiry about his health. "Tell me, how's the *Britannia* plot coming along?"

Michael looked at Phillip levelly. "They have invited me to join the cartel. Frankly, I'd be interested to hear what you think, sir."

"I cannot, with propriety, take any position other than the official one, Michael; otherwise it would appear that I was condoning contraband trade. However, I believe free trade must be introduced if this colony is to progress."

"Then you will not obstruct the charter?"

Phillip shrugged. "When Grose requests permission to purchase the Corps's extras, I shall advance the official reasons why he and his officers should not go ahead with the venture, but it would be humbug of me to actually forbid it when, in a few months' time, Grose, as Governor, will ring in a new era for this colony."

Michael looked at Phillip with concern. "I have heard rumors about your impending return to England, sir, but I hoped they were just that."

Phillip put down his knife and fork and reached for his glass. "I find myself drained of energy, Michael. The greatest service I can render this country is to transfer the reins of office to a more active man, return to England and plead the colony's cause in the halls of power."

"Was that why you invited me to Sydney, sir?"

"No, it's this damned business about Moses Tucker. I notified the authorities in England that he drowned."

Michael smiled widely. "You have me at a disadvantage, sir. What the devil are you talking about?"

"Tucker is returning to the colony with Lucy."

A dull, leaden feeling descended on Michael. "Moses is alive?"

"Surely Lucy wrote to you about him?"

"I had no idea he was alive, or that Lucy planned to return to New South Wales," Michael said slowly and with supreme effort. "Except for the two farm horses, I have not heard from her since July 1790."

Phillip took a letter from his jacket and passed it across the table. "You had better read this, it arrived on board the *Britannia* six weeks ago."

The letter, written at Carrigmoor Castle the previous December, explained about Moses and informed Phillip that as soon as Faith, who was expecting a child in the new year, had recovered from the birth, Lucy and Moses would return to the colony.

As Michael read the letter, the numbness inside him gave way to blinding rage. "You'd think she could have had the decency to let me know about Moses; and whether our child survived the voyage back to England," he rasped, dropping the letter on the table.

"I am sorry, Michael, it was not my intention to cause you pain. The tone of her letter was so friendly, I assumed she had been in contact with you."

Michael tossed down his drink. "What will you do about Moses?"

Phillip rubbed his chin thoughtfully. "If I am still in charge when she returns, I shall send him to Chaumilley in her care, but if Grose is Governor then he must decide."

"For God's sake, sir, she is a sea captain's daughter, not a farmer. How can she expect to run a property the size of Chaumilley single-handedly?"

Phillip framed his reply carefully. "Er . . . it seems that she does not expect to run Chaumilley alone. In the letter, she says, 'Sir, could you find it in your heart to allow Moses to work out the remainder of his sentence with us at Chaumilley?' Whom does she mean by *us*?"

"She certainly does not mean me," Michael said bitterly. "Perhaps she has married. That would explain why I have not heard from her."

When Michael strode into the hut Beth saw the fury in his eyes and her heart sank. "What did the Governor want with you, Michael?"

"Lucy wrote him a letter. Did she write to you also, Beth?"

The suddenness of his inquiry caught her completely off guard. "I-I . . . yes, but I didn't tell you because . . . well, I-I thought it would upset you."

He gripped her shoulders. "Did Lucy mention the baby?"

"What baby?"

"What baby do you think? *Her* baby!"

"Not her baby, Faith's baby—" Beth broke off with a strangled cry. "Oh no, Michael, I didn't mean that. I-I am so confused I don't know what I am saying."

"I know about Faith's baby," he muttered impatiently. "Lucy mentioned it in her letter to Phillip. She said that she and Moses would return to the colony as soon as Faith had the baby."

"Oh, *that* baby." Beth sighed with relief. "B-but if Moses returns to the colony he will be arrested."

Michael's eyes narrowed. "Are you telling me you knew Moses was alive?"

Beth's hands flew to her face. "No! Oh, I don't know . . . I don't know. Please stop shouting, Michael, or you will wake Benjamin."

He smashed his fist on the table. "You are hiding something from me. Get the letters, Beth. I want to read them."

"No Michael, I can't." She looked guiltily toward the fireplace. "You see . . . I burned them."

He glared at her for a moment then strode out from the hut, slamming the door behind him.

18
Expectations and Realizations

Sunday, October 7, 1792

"I'm sure it's a flag," Lucy cried excitedly, passing the spyglass to Moses who had been pacing the decks of the *Royal Admiral* with her since dawn.

He examined the white dot on the western horizon. "It's South Head all right. I'd stake my life on it, Miss Lucy."

Lucy picked up her skirts and did a wild jig around a rope pile. "We made it, Moses. Oh, what a day it will be."

Moses's grim features split into an uncustomary smile. "The Lieutenant's not far afield now."

Lucy's eyes sparkled with joy and happiness. "No, indeed, Moses. If Governor Phillip releases you into my custody, we can be at Chaumilley by tomorrow."

Lucy placed the spyglass to her eye and sighed with pleasure, "Sydney."

The dismal little village of the Second Fleet days was gone. In its place stood a good-size town, alive with activity. But she was glad to see her hut and the hospital still there—*and* the fig tree on the hill. She trained the glass on the spot near Dawes Point where she and Michael had often gone. "Not long now, darling," she whispered. "One more day . . . and one more lonely night."

Accompanied by a colorful flotilla of shore boats, the *Royal Admiral* worked into Sydney Cove and dropped anchor beside the *Atlantic*. An hour later Faith, Lucy, and Moses were seated in the main foyer of Government House waiting impatiently for Phillip to dispense with the protocol of the vessel's arrival.

"Welcome! Welcome!" Phillip's lined, pinched face was wreathed in smiles as he ushered them into his study. "Captain Bond told me you were on board." He embraced Faith joyfully. "Faith, my dear, this *is* a surprise. I thought you had settled for life in the Scottish Highlands."

Briefly, Faith related the tragic circumstances that had prompted her return to the colony.

After Phillip had offered his heartfelt condolences he accepted Moses' surrender. "Because you have given yourself up voluntarily, Tucker, and because your previous conduct has been exemplary, I have decided to grant Mistress Gamble's request. You may serve out the remainder of your sentence at Chaumilley." He scribbled a note to David Collins and told Moses to present himself at Judge Advocate's office posthaste.

"I shall be forever in your debt, sir," said Lucy after Moses had shuffled from the study.

"I, also, Captain Phillip," added Faith. "Moses is devoted to Lucy. How he managed to reach the *Surprise* that night is a mystery to us all. The seas were mountainous."

"Is Michael well?" Lucy broke in eagerly.

Phillip's brow furrowed. "Michael is in excellent health, my dear. He and your friend, Elizabeth Dudgeon, live on a property not far from Chaumilley."

"Why aren't they living at Chaumilley?"

The furrows in Phillip's brow deepened. "Michael wanted nothing to do with Chaumilley after you left, Lucy. These last two years, he has worked his own land. He has a fine house, fourteen acres under cultivation . . . and he and Elizabeth Dudgeon have a child."

"Whose child?"

"Their child, Lucy."

Her face turned the color of yellow parchment and a vein started throbbing on one side of her throat. "*Their* child? Are they living together as husband and wife?"

"Yes," said Phillip. "Yes, they—"

Faith burst into tears. "Oh no! How could Michael do such a thing?"

Lucy sat very still, looking straight ahead, her fingers clenching and unclenching, her lips slightly parted.

Phillip went to her, clasped her icy hands, and tried to rub some warmth back into them. "Lucy, I am sorry. I see that you had expectations . . ."

"Expectations?" she said hollowly. "Yes, I suppose I did have . . . expectations."

Faith knelt beside the chair and embraced her. "Oh Lucy, my heart, my dearest darling. What will we do?"

Lucy's lips trembled. "Take me away from here, Faith."

Faith helped her up. "Please excuse us, Captain Phillip."

Phillip pulled the bell cord. "You and Lucy shall stay with me at Government House. The servants will show you upstairs to your rooms and when Tucker returns, I'll have him bring your belongings ashore." He patted Lucy's shoulder consolingly. "Michael is in Sydney at present. Do you wish to speak to him, my dear?"

Lucy recoiled. "No!"

Phillip nodded gravely. "I understand. But, I must warn you that tomorrow evening I am holding a reception to welcome the *Royal Admiral*. Michael will be invited."

Faith's sobs grew louder. "I shall *never* forgive Michael for this."

"The fault is not his," Phillip said reprovingly. "When Lucy left the colony, Michael believed that she had abandoned him for another life."

Faith stamped her foot. "I won't accept that. He should have known Lucy had a good reason to leave."

"He seemed to be coming to terms with his disappointment, Faith, but then he learned that Lucy was pregnant." Phillip turned to Lucy. "I take it the child did not survive?"

Lucy stared back at him fixedly. "No, the child did not survive."

"Lucy, we cannot go on like this. Tell Captain Phillip the truth," Faith urged as the servants entered.

"Be quiet," Lucy said sharply, and drew her quickly from the room.

Understanding at last why they had left the colony, Phillip

484

watched them ascend to the upper floor. "Yes," he sighed. "Lucy would have done that. It was the only thing she *could* do . . ."

Faith walked to the window of Lucy's bedchamber and unlatched it. "What a stuffy room. Mine is much cooler. Would you like to change with me, Lucy?"

"No, this is fine." Lucy joined her at the window, which overlooked picturesque Sydney Cove. "I used to lie awake at night imagining this scene." Her eyes traveled to the hut on the western shore.

Faith red her mind. "I can't believe he has done this."

"I-I find it difficult to accept also. Although, I suppose it's logical. Two years is a long time. No, I don't really mean that. It doesn't make any sense at all . . ." Her voice trailed off.

"And . . . and why would he choose *her*, Lucy?"

An icy anguish clutched at Lucy's heart. "I can't bear to think of him and Beth together—having a child." She gripped the windowsill so tightly, her knuckles turned white. "That child should have been mine."

Faith hugged her but Lucy thrust her away. "Don't touch me. I don't want to be touched." Seeing the shock and grief in Faith's eyes, she tried to explain her rebuff. "I'm sorry, beloved. I feel as if I've been violated. I reacted the same way after being raped by Richard. I could not bear anyone touching me and so I went inside myself where no one could reach me. I must not let that happen again. Will you help me overcome it, darling?"

Faith stopped crying. "You are my life, Lucy. I will help you all I can. Do you want to return to England?"

In her mind's eye, Lucy saw a lush green valley rolling away to the foot of a rugged blue mountain range and a tree with spreading branches. *Their* tree. The tears came, like a river breaking its banks. "I want to go home to Chaumilley," she sobbed. "Far away from everything that hurts."

Faith clasped her weeping sister tightly. "Then that's exactly what we'll do, my heart."

After Lucy's sobs subsided, she paced the floor with great agitation. "If I am to remain in New South Wales, I must somehow come to terms with *them* being together. Otherwise, I will live in fear of meeting them." She swung around and faced Faith. "However, I'd appreciate it if you could coerce Captain

485

Bond into unloading our cargo at the first opportunity, Faith. I want to get out of Sydney as soon as possible."

Faith adjusted her taffeta skirts in a businesslike manner. "Consider it done, my heart. I'll speak to the old tartar at the reception tomorrow evening. Do you plan to attend?"

Lucy bit her lip. "I don't want to, but I think I must. If Michael happens to be there and we meet, well, at least it will be over." She wrung her hands. "Faith, I don't know if I have the strength to face him."

"You have more courage than anyone, Lucy. And I'll be there beside you every step of the way."

"Perhaps he won't come . . ."

Faith's emerald eyes narrowed dangerously. "Oh, he'll be there . . . and we shall greet him with such charm and sweetness, the tongues of the gossipmongers won't know which way to wag."

19

The Reception

Michael learned of Lucy's return from John White. He received the news with no outward show of emotion, accompanied John to Government House where they left messages of condolence for Faith, then he made his way up the hill to the barracks and sat through the meeting of the cartel in a daze.

Beth learned that Lucy was back when she called at Susannah Cable's for afternoon tea. Greatly shaken by the news, she spent the next few hours anxiously awaiting Michael.

He returned to the hut at dusk and, except for announcing that they would move in with John the following morning, refused to discuss the matter. Then the invitation to the reception arrived.

"Surely you won't be going" Beth exclaimed, her heart sinking.

He shrugged. "Why not?"

"You can't *wait* to see her, can you?" Beth blazed.

"I don't particularly want to see her, but Sydney's a small place and we are bound to meet sooner or later. It may as well be tomorrow evening."

"Please take me home to Worthing, Michael. I-I hate it here."

"Beth, you know I can't leave yet. We are still arranging the chartering of the *Britannia*."

"Don't give me that. It's not the bloomin' *Britannia* that's keeping you here. And, anyway, why was I left off it?"

"I beg your pardon?"

"Don't raise your eyebrows and 'beg my pardon' in that tone. You know what I mean. Why isn't *my* name on the invitation?"

"Don't be ridiculous," Michael said wearily. "Protocol dictates that wives, not housekeepers, be invited to official functions. John won't be taking Rachel Turner and, if Tom were here, Elizabeth Burleigh would not be accompanying him."

Tears began streaming down Beth's cheeks. "Then why will Lucy and that stuck-up sister of hers be at the reception? They aren't anyone's wives."

Michael cursed under his breath. He loathed emotional, unstrung women. One of Lucy's most endearing qualities was her composure under stress. "You are deliberately misunderstanding the situation, Beth. Governor Phillip has known Faith since she was a child. Naturally, he would invite her and Lucy to stay with him and, as his guests, they are bound to attend the reception." He opened the door. "Don't make supper for me, I shall be late."

"Are you going to see *her*?" she cried shrilly.

"No, I'm going up to the barracks to get some peace."

Lucy and Faith avoided several callers the next morning but when John White was announced, they welcomed him and led him to Phillip's sitting room where John handed Lucy the keys to the hut.

"How is Michael?" Lucy asked. "Are he and Beth happy together?"

"Really, I have seen little of them,," he said gently, observing her red-rimmed eyes. "However, they both dote on their son, Ben."

"Oh," said Lucy, and hung her head.

John raised her chin so that their eyes met. "Michael was angry and bitter after you left, Lucy. Then, just as he was coming out of that, he learned of your pregnancy. That really shattered him."

"Surely he received Lucy's letters?" Faith exclaimed, ignoring Lucy's warning frown.

"Letters?" John looked from one to the other. "To the best of my knowledge, Michael never received any letters."

"B-but he must have received my *first* letter," Lucy exclaimed. "I sent it early in ninety-one. It explained about the baby and why I left Sydney so suddenly."

John shook his head. "I am certain he didn't. In fact, when I told him you had arrived he asked if you had the baby with you." He paused and looked at her questioningly. "I assume . . ."

"The baby died two weeks after we left Norfolk Island." Lucy suddenly felt very afraid. If Michael had not received that letter, where was it? After all they had been through, was Faith still at risk?

The night was oppressively hot and the scent of charred gum leaves wafted through the air. In the main reception room of Government House the elegantly attired guests converged like a hive of excited bees. The men's eyes constantly strayed to the doorway and the women cast covert glances at Lieutenant Perryman who stood talking to the Governor, the Surgeon General and Captain Bond of the *Royal Admiral*, in a group near the door.

Sensing a lull in the conversation, Michael glanced toward the door and saw her. She was so divinely lovely, he could hardly believe she was real. She wore a pale green dress of the most delicate, diaphanous material, which floated around her as she moved. Her long, lustrous hair hung loose about her shoulders and she had caught it back from her temples with satin ribbons. A diamond and emerald pendant sparkled just above the creamy swell of her breasts. Faith, dazzling in diamonds and gold taffeta was only a pale replica of the whole that was Lucy.

Lucy moved through the crowd to his side and said in her low, sweet voice, "Hello, Michael."

He smelled the fragrance of her—the long remembered, hauntingly familiar fragrance of her—and looked into her eyes. She was very nervous; her irises flickered back and forth and she was worrying her lower lip, biting it the way she did when she was uncertain. He glanced at the pendant, longing to drop his eyes lower to those lovely breasts, study their movement, count their rise and fall, but he knew if he did he'd be lost. He took her hand and unconsciously began to rub her knuckles with his thumb in the old, familiar way. "Hello, Lucy."

Lucy could neither move nor speak. *If I stay exactly as I am,* she thought, *I might survive.* But a tight band enclosed her chest and the room was spinning. She felt trapped, with no way of retreat . . .

"Hello, Michael," said Faith, stepping forward and linking her arm through Lucy's. "*So* grand to see you again." Her smile was warm but her eyes told Michael to let Lucy go.

Reluctantly he complied. "Hello, Faith. Please accept my condolences. I never knew Hugh or your aunt, of course, but . . ."

"Thank you, Michael. Everyone has been most kind, haven't they, my heart?"

"Yes," Lucy murmured.

"And none more so than *dear* Captain Bond." Faith turned Lucy so her back was to Michael. "This marvelous man was so moved by our plight, Captain Phillip, that he gave up his own magnificent cabin and bunked with the first mate so we could weep in peace."

Phillip's spirits lifted. This Faith was vastly different from the young beauty Sir Michael Billingsley had kept so tightly in check. This Faith held everyone under her sway, even old Bond who was puffing and preening like a peacock. He entered into the game with gusto. "You have my eternal gratitude, sir."

Several officers of the New South Wales Corps, led by Captain Hill, pushed their way into the group. "Good evening Lady Stewart, Miss Gamble."

"Captain Hill!" cried Faith. "Oh, this *is* a surprise."

Hill bowed over her hand. "I am overjoyed you remember me, Lady Stewart."

"How could I forget the gallant officer who offered to dispatch that detestable Captain Trail?" Faith dazzled him with a smile.

"Care to dance, Lady Stewart?" he asked as the band struck up a rousing march.

Charmed by Hill's audacity, Faith decided that she would, indeed, take a turn around the floor with him. But first, she had some unfinished business with the Master of the *Royal Admiral*. "Thank you, Captain Hill. However, I rather hoped that dear Captain Bond . . ." She gave Bond a helpless, melting look and fluttered her eyelashes.

Needing no further encouragement, Bond whisked her away.

As several officers converged on Lucy, Phillip laughed and held up his hand. "Stand aside, gentlemen. As Governor of this colony, I claim the right." He bowed to Lucy. "My dear, may I have the pleasure?"

Longing to escape the intensity of Michael's gaze, Lucy gratefully accepted Phillip's arm.

20

Encounters and Accusations

The next day, after Faith had selected a home site on the east side of town, she went picnicking at Manly Cove with the officers and ladies of the corps.

Lucy and Moses spent the morning on board *Royal Admiral* arranging for their cargo to be unloaded then, after purchasing a sow and an English dunghill cock from the market, they made their way to Lucy's hut. While Moses puttered about outside repairing animal pens and fences, Lucy rummaged through her sea chests setting aside things for Chaumilley.

Toward dusk, they walked up the hill behind the hospital to see whether Faith was returning downharbor. Lucy climbed to the top of the tree with the spyglass and Moses sat on a nearby rock diligently whittling a wooden soldier for Duncan until he noticed Michael ascending the hill with a small child on his shoulders. Thinking a meeting had been arranged, he scrambled to his feet, saluted Michael solemnly and retreated a discreet distance down the hill.

When Lucy saw Michael walking across the plateau, her first reaction was to jump from the tree and run away, but realizing how foolish that would appear, she climbed down with as much dignity as she could muster and waited for him to join her.

"Still climbing trees, I see." He lifted his son off his shoulders and set him down on the grass.

Lucy knelt beside Ben and studied him with a mixture of wonder and despair. A perfect mingling of his parents, he possessed Beth's blond ringlets and Michael's smoky gray eyes. "My goodness, you are a beautiful boy. What is your name?"

Bitter thoughts stirred in Michael's mind. By rights, Ben should have been their child. They had wanted children, lots of children. . . . He crouched beside Ben. "This is Lucy. Say hello the way Father taught you."

"Hello, Lucy." Ben extended his hand then changed his mind and reached for the spyglass.

She passed it over. "It's Daddy's; he sees big ships through it. Want to look at the big ships, Ben?" She scooped him up, swung him around until he was laughing joyfully, then carried him to the edge of the plateau, where she tried, unsuccessfully, to coax him to look at the ships in the cove. "Whew! He's heavy," she said, setting him down and massaging her aching arms. "How old is he?"

"Almost eighteen months." Michael observed her closely. She was pale and there were dark smudges under her eyes. He wondered if last night had been sleepless for her also. Growing uneasy under his gaze, Lucy bit her lower lip. The action elicited an immediate response from Michael. His heart started pounding, his body quickened with intense physical desire and blinding rage overtook him. "Why did you leave me, Lucy?"

"I-I told you why in my letters—because of Faith. You didn't expect me to let her go back alone?"

"What letters?"

"Didn't you receive *any* letters, Michael?" Lucy had never seen him so angry. His nostrils were white and flaring and his eyes were pools of fury.

"You sent Beth and Phillip the letters. I got the damned farm horses. Answer me, Lucy. Why did you leave me?"

But something else plagued Lucy's mind—something beyond the missing letters, something beyond Michael's rage. Suddenly, it clicked. Ben was *eighteen* months old. She stared at him with anguish, remembering his pledges of undying love and unending faithfulness. And the first time his love had been tested he had taken her best friend, Beth, to his bed. "I never left you," she said slowly. "You left me."

"What the hell sort of answer is that?"

"Take it however you like." As she turned to go, he grabbed her arm and spun her around. "I asked you a question, Lucy."

"Take your hands off me, Michael."

Rage erupted like a volcano inside him. "Certainly, Lucy. I have no desire to detain you." He dropped her arm and took a step backward. "John mentioned that you lost our child. Should I offer consolation, or congratulations?"

Lucy recoiled as if he had struck her. "Oh, Michael, how *could* you?"

Distraught by the pain and bewilderment in her eyes, he reached for her. "Lucy, darling, I didn't mean it. Please forgive me . . ."

"No," she whispered, her face working with emotion, "No, Michael, I won't forgive you for that." Before he could stop her, she leapt over the edge and plunged headlong down the hill.

Moses sprang to his feet and clambered toward her. "Miss

Lucy, not so fast, you'll fall.'' His warning came too late. Lucy tripped on the hem of her skirt and slid down the slope on her stomach, arms outstretched before her.

"Lucy, for God's sake!'' Michael tucked Ben under his arm and scrambled over the edge. "Stay where you are.''

When Lucy saw him careering toward her, she jumped up and continued her reckless descent until she reached Moses. "I hate him . . . I hate him,'' she sobbed, twisting her head wildly from side to side. "Get me away from him, Moses.''

Moses shook his fist furiously at Michael then guided her gently the rest of the way down the hill.

As Michael watched them go, the anger he had nurtured in his heart for two long years withered and died. Lucy was neither cold nor uncaring; Lucy was deeply hurt. Although he still did not understand what had gone wrong between them, he sensed that she had been absolutely steadfast and that he was the one who had failed them.

Lucy stormed back and forth in her room, weeping and raging until her insides and throat were raw. "I won't be rational, logical, composed, and understanding,'' she sobbed. "I won't forgive him for what he said—nor for taking Beth to his bed. How dare he do that? How *dare* he!''

She walked to the writing desk. If Ben was eighteen months old, he must have been born in April 1791. She deducted two hundred and sixty-seven days from April. The answer made her even more furious. Ben had been conceived either the last week of July, or *very* early in the August of 1790. Therefore, Michael and Beth had been together from the beginning. She called him every nautical obscenity she could lay her tongue around and when that did not help, kicked the furniture until a servant arrived with a note and informed her that Lieutenant Perryman was waiting below for her answer.

"Is he?'' she blazed, ripping open the note.

It was brief. "Lucy, come downstairs. We must talk. M.'' Lucy's mouth worked as she tried to compose an answer that would adequately express her feelings. In the end, she retrieved the crumpled page of calculations from the wastebasket and thrust it at the startled servant. "Give him that. And tell him to go away.''

Wednesday, October 10, 1792

Susannah Cable gave an exclamation of joy when she opened her

492

front door to Lucy and Faith. "Come in, come in," she invited after they had embraced, then added, as she bustled them into her parlor, "Beth and Ben are here."

"L-Lucy!" Beth cried and, unable to tell the twins apart, stared from one to the other like a terrified bird until Lucy said stiffly, "Hello, Beth."

"Lucy, dear . . . h-how are you?" Beth's voice trailed off and she gazed at her former friend with a mixture of guilt and despair.

"I am well, thank you." Lucy retreated to a chair on the opposite side of the room and busied herself in settling her skirts.

"Delightful to see you again, Beth." Faith gave Beth and her curly headed tot a long, appraising look. The child was adorable.

Beth's eyes narrowed. There she was, the sister trollop, cause of all the trouble. "Hello, *Lady* Stewart."

Faith raised perfectly arched eyebrows. "Really, my dear, I think we know each other well enough to dispense with such formalities."

Ben slipped off the seat, toddled across the room and stuck out his hand. "Hello, Lucy."

Beth's mouth gaped open and Faith's eyebrows rose higher as Lucy shook his paw vigorously and said, "Hello, Ben, want to play 'giddyup'?" She set him on her knee and jogged him up and down until Susannah arrived with cordials.

"Will you and Faith live in Sydney, Lucy?" Beth asked quickly.

"No, as soon as our goods are off-loaded, we shall leave for Chaumilley. How are you finding farm life, Beth?"

Beth was dismayed by Lucy's disclosure. Only thirty acres separated the boundaries of Worthing and Chaumilley. "Michael has built us a lovely house at Worthing and imported all manner of comforts from the Cape, even a big brass bed. But I suppose you'd find life here a bit primitive after that castle in Scotland, Lucy."

"That is quite enough!" Lucy snapped. "You know perfectly well what kind of accommodation I have been accustomed to, Beth." But it wasn't the accommodation that had set Lucy's nerves on edge. It was Beth's mention of the big brass bed.

Scarlet with mortification, Beth scrambled to her feet. "Benjamin and me had best be on our way. M-Michael likes us to be home before dark."

"Off you go then, dear," said Faith "and do take care of Michael. He looked as miserable as a moor mouse at the reception. If you can't keep him happier than that, he's *bound* to stray.''

When Michael returned to John's house later that day, Beth was waiting for him on the veranda.

"How come Ben knows Lucy?"

Noticing Rachel Turner hovering at the sitting room window, he turned on his heel and retreated along the path.

"Answer me, Michael!" Beth picked up her skirts and hurried after him.

"They met yesterday on top of Observatory Hill," he muttered, striding toward the beach.

"Why didn't you tell me?"

"Because I thought it would upset you. Obviously I was right."

"I'd rather hear it from you than find out like I did. When Lucy came to Susannah's this afternoon, Ben jumped on her knee and said 'Hello, Lucy' as clear as can be."

Michael grinned. "What a marvelous memory. He was with her only a few minutes."

"Don't give me that! He must've been with her for hours. He don't go to folk straight off."

He shrugged and kicked the sand with his boot. "You know how good Lucy is with children. She made a fuss of him, that's all."

"A-and did she make a fuss of you?" Tears gushed from Beth's eyes and coursed down her cheeks.

"Oh, for God's sake, show some restraint," he muttered. "You are being ridiculous."

"I'm not being ridiculous! Ben is my baby and I won't have you taking him and sneaking off to meet people behind my back."

"I am not in the habit of 'sneaking off' anywhere. Lucy and I met quite by chance yesterday. However, let me make one thing quite clear. I shall meet whomever I please without asking your permission to do so."

"B-but I have a right to know!"

"What makes you think that?"

"Because we . . . well we . . . .''

"Because we slept together once and never will again?" he prompted.

She covered her face with her hands. "Oh, Michael, I-I am

494

sorry. It's been a bloomin' terrible day. It broke my heart seeing Lucy again. I-I swear I won't set foot outside the door until she and her horrible sister have gone.''

A coldness, like death, clutched at Michael's heart. "Gone?''

"Lucy said she was leaving for Chaumilley as soon as her goods came ashore.''

Michael felt lightheaded with relief.

"I don't know what she's thinking of,'' Beth went on. "Can you imagine anything more foolish than two white women living out there in the wilderness alone?''

"They won't be alone. Moses will be with them and he is as good as ten ordinary men.'' Michael escorted Beth as far as the hospital and continued into town. Lucy would need strong, trustworthy laborers. Henry Cable was the best person to organize that. He'd have a few words with Henry then return to John's and pack. With the *Britannia* now officially under charter to the cartel, there was no reason for him to linger in Sydney. If he left early tomorrow, he could spend some time at Chaumilley repairing the well and putting things in order. *But I'd better be careful about it*, he thought, *or Lucy will think I am interfering and retreat even further*.

21

A Godfather for Duncan

Lucy sat in the lead cart watching Moses and the laborers spreading branches across the dry, rock-strewn riverbed. Although the trek to the Worthing turnoff had been relatively straightforward, since striking out in a northwesterly direction through virgin bush land, their progress had been slow and arduous. She was glad she had persuaded Faith to remain in Sydney with Duncan.

Lucy removed her wide-brimmed hat and mopped her brow. The horses and carts donated by Phillip, and the ten able-bodied men Henry Cable had hired, had been a tremendous help. And now, if Surveyor Alt's directions were correct, there was only this last rivulet to cross, a hill or two to climb and she would be in the magic world of Chaumilley.

In procession, the four heavily laden carts lumbered over the

495

riverbed into more open ground and soon Lucy spied familiar territory.

"We're here!" she cried, jumping from the cart and flying up the long, tree-studded slope to feast her eyes on the valley rolling away to the foot of the Blue Mountains. Chaumilley! A little less lush, perhaps, but the lake was there, and the ducks. She raced down the hill to the hut Michael had built and was delighted to find it still intact. A few loose floorboards lay about, but the shingled roof had stood the test of time and she was sure Moses could make it habitable.

Her excitement mounting, she ran out back to her garden. It was a sad ruin. The beds of herbs and vegetables she had painstakingly planted two years ago were a jungle of weeds. "Never mind," she said, yanking out clover by the handful, "I shall soon get you shipshape again, garden. But first I had better check the well. God knows what condition it will be in after two years . . ."

She ran to the well, rolled back the rocks, tossed aside the planks and peered into the darkness. It smelled moist, mellow, and earthy. She dropped in a pebble and, a moment later, heard a lovely plunky splash.

"Moses!" she screeched, dashing to the lead cart, which had just appeared on top of the rise. "Moses, come quickly. The hut is all right—and so is the well."

She waited impatiently while he confirmed her findings then, leaving the men to set up camp, sped through the long grass to the lake. Although she crept as soundlessly as a cat over the last twenty yards, the ducks took flight, winging away toward the Blue Mountains as they had done the first day.

"Damned inexcusable" he had said, "into the lake you go." She walked to the Chaumilley tree and rested her cheek against the trunk. "Close your eyes and just let it happen," he had said. How rapturously she had received him. And afterward they had lain together beneath the stars, hearts and souls united, making plans . . .

Lucy parted the long green fronds hanging from the tree and stepped through the leafy bower to the edge of the lake. "Let him and Beth lie in their big brass bed," she said, splashing cool water on her face. "You have more to do than think of them, Lucy Gamble. There's the house to build, the animal enclosures to erect, the land to be plowed, and a hundred different things." She jumped up and twirled around. "Oh God, it's good to be home."

*   *   *

Ten days later, Faith descended on Chaumilley with Duncan, Hester, a cook, two housemaids, a cartload of plants, Captain William Hill, and an escort of foot soldiers.

Although she preferred the hustle and bustle of Sydney to the peace and tranquility of Chaumilley, Faith made the most of her new life, dividing her time between managing the domestics and taking long rides in the country, plotting a reconciliation between Lucy and Michael, planning to increase her fortune—and dreaming about Peter Devereaux.

Realizing that to profit from the introduction of free trade into the colony she must wangle her way into the cartel, she had offered Captain Hill five hundred guineas for a silent partnership in his share of that elite little band. Hill, financially stretched because of gambling losses, had accepted her proposition and gallantly returned half the money. More fool him! Considering the future profits to be made, her offer had not been overgenerous.

Reconciling Lucy and Michael was a far more complex problem—particularly as Lucy had threatened her with dire consequences if she interfered. However, when the cook mentioned that settlers of outlying farms attended an open air church service at Prospect Hill every second Sunday, Faith devised a plan which she hoped would bring them together for a few hours at least.

She bided her time until, one evening at supper, Lucy mentioned how much Duncan had grown.

"Hmmm," Faith agreed vaguely and, after a long pause, added, "I suppose we ought to think about having him christened. Would the Governor agree to be his godfather, my heart?"

"We could certainly ask him, darling."

Here goes, thought Faith. "Then perhaps we ought to make some definite arrangements, my heart. Captain Phillip will be quitting the colony in a month or two."

Lucy agreed wholeheartedly, and suggested that they go to Prospect the following Sunday and speak to Reverend Johnson after the service.

Sunday service at Prospect proved to be more a social gathering than a muster of worshipping souls and although Faith enjoyed the outing, her plan to reunite Lucy and Michael failed. They never went within fifty yards of each other.

She nursed her disappointment for a week and was on the

verge of defying Lucy and riding to Worthing when Michael arrived at Chaumilley with two enormous farm horses. Faith greeted him ecstatically and directed him to the lake.

Michael discovered Lucy planting spinach. He paused, heart thumping, then dismounted and led the animals forward. "I thought you could use these." He took in every inch of her. She wore a faded sun-bleached blouse and an old pair of riding breeches which hugged her buttocks and accentuated her long legs. Her arms and neck were tanned and she smelled deliciously of damp earth and moss.

"Returning my gift?" Her voice was remote, and resentment smoldered in her eyes.

He patted the neck of the nearest beast. "Certainly not. But as my crops are in, and I won't be plowing for some time, I thought you might like to swap these for two of Phillip's horses. You will need to work very hard to get the ground fit for planting."

She sighed with relief and some of the hostility left her. "Thank you. Perhaps you could show me how to work the plow? I need to know the correct way before I can I instruct the men."

"Have you cleared any ground?"

She reached up and patted the other horse. "Only one acre. That declivity down by the river that you decided was—" She stopped and bit her lip.

"That's a good place to begin," he said quickly. "Shall we take a look?"

Not trusting himself to help her mount, he climbed into the saddle and waited while she clambered onto the other beast. "What crop will you plant?"

She looked at him questioningly. "Maize?"

He considered for a long moment, then shook his head. "No, it's too late for maize. Try turnips, they'll help meliorate the soil for next year. Another thing, Lucy, have the men scrape moss off the trees. In the absence of manure, it aids the soil."

"How long does it take to clear an acre?" she asked, coming abreast of him.

He saw the tiny beads of sweat under her eyes—eyes cool, and deep, and green. "Four good workers can do it in ten days; but don't let them just scratch over the surface; the soil must be pulverized . . ."

"I have ten good men," she said, soft lips curving. "Henry hired them. Some are old *Friendship* hands." Then she was away, firing questions at him like bullets. They didn't get around to harnessing the horses to the plow until dusk, when Faith joined them and invited him to stay for dinner.

Seeing Lucy's hesitance, he declined and, soon afterward, left. They had not spoken one personal word all day, but once, when she had laughed at something he'd said, that light had come into her eyes and, for a moment, the old spark had blazed between them. He nurtured that spark all the way home and by the time he reached Worthing it was glowing so brightly in his heart that the aching emptiness of the last two years had vanished.

Every morning Michael awoke determined to ride to Chaumilley, and every morning he decided against it, knowing that if he forced things, Lucy would retreat into herself and he would lose the ground he had gained. He had no illusions—they were in deep trouble, particularly in the matter of Beth—but as long as that spark flickered, he believed there was hope. So he stayed away, and counted the days until the next Sunday service at Prospect.

Lucy stood on the hill behind the hut surveying Chaumilley at sunset. The mountaintops glowed, the river was veiled in a blue mist, and the valley was deep green and quiet. This last week had been very productive. Not only had Moses and the men laid the foundations for the house, but they had also pulverized the soil on the cleared section of land the way Michael had instructed.

Lucy ran her hands up the back of her neck and pinned the stray strands of hair on top of her head. If she went to Prospect tomorrow, Michael would be there with Beth. Although she had felt quite comfortable with him at Chaumilley, she did not want to see he and Beth together. Why had he lied about the letters that day on the hill? No, that was wrong. Michael did not lie. His words rushed into her mind. "You sent Beth and the Governor letters. *I* got the horses." There had been fury in his eyes—not lies.

Perplexed, Lucy sat down and hugged her knees. If Michael had not received the letters, who had? She *must* find them—particularly the first. Waves of anxiety swept over her. Was Faith *still* at risk?

Faith emerged from the hut and climbed the slope. "It's too hot to eat, my heart. Let's take Duncan for a swim."

Lucy looked fixedly at the mountains. "I don't want to go to Prospect tomorrow. He will be there with Beth."

All day Faith had sensed it coming and had her argument ready. "Reverend Johnson promised to deliver our letter to Phillip the moment he returned to Sydney, so he is bound to have Phillip's answer."

"You do not need me there for that."

"I don't *need* you there, Lucy, but I want you there. Christenings are supposed to be happy events and, God knows, we've had little enough to celebrate this last year. However, if you really can't bear to see them together, I shall have to manage alone."

Lucy rose and brushed grass from her skirts with a violent motion. "Don't use your wiles on me, minx. I know what you're up to and it won't work. Michael and I are finished."

Faith looked at her desperately. "I am sure he still loves you, Lucy. Tell him about the baby. Talk to him, *please*. Or, at least let me speak. I-I feel so guilty."

In a most uncharacteristic action, Lucy stamped her foot. "You have nothing to feel guilty about. Despite my assurances that I loved him and would return, Michael took Beth to his bed the moment I left the colony. Why should we risk telling him about the child? Let him think what he likes."

Faith's shoulders slumped. "Very well, my heart. Don't upset yourself. I'll attend Sunday service alone."

"No, darling, you are absolutely right. Duncan's christening will be a time of special celebration for our family. I'll come with you, but please, Faith, promise me you won't speak to Michael about the child. Beth resents you so, and if he told her, the situation would pass beyond our control."

The service proved to be a most exciting affair. Immediately devotions concluded, Reverend Johnson announced that the Governor planned to quit the colony in two weeks' time; then he distributed invitations and letters to members of his congregation. Lucy and Faith received a letter from Phillip, accepting with pleasure the post of godparent and requesting that they return to Sydney at their earliest convenience.

In a quandary as to how Chaumilley could be managed during their absence, Lucy scanned the crowd for Michael. I can't very well leave the men unsupervised for two weeks, she thought, catching his eye and beckoning. Although I hate asking Michael for help, logically, he is the best person to advise me . . . "Good morning, Michael," she said after he had shouldered his way through the crowd to her side. "Will you be attending the Governor's farewell?"

He nodded. "Received my invitation a moment ago. You look troubled. Is anything the matter?"

"The Governor has agreed to be Duncan's godparent, and the christening will take place next weekend, so Faith and I will have to leave for Sydney immediately. Could you recommend someone to oversee the Chaumilley laborers?"

Michael thought for a moment. "Richards, an ex-marine from Meredith's company is looking for work. He's got a drinking problem but he'd do in the short term. I'll ride into Parramatta and have a word with him."

She stared at him for a few moments then slowly extended her hand. "Thank you . . . I am most grateful."

Faith, who had viewed the little drama with great interest, smiled like a cat licking cream.

22
End of an Era

Faith listened to the conversation with half an ear while trying to rustle up a breeze with her fan. However, because the thermometer showed ninety-two degrees, it was rather like waving a twig in front of an oven. Last night she and Lucy had been Phillip's hostesses at a dinner for the colony officials; tonight was the turn of the military. She swept her eyes around the table and focused on the most interesting man in the room—the master of the American brigantine, *Philadelphia*. "What brings you to our shores, Captain Patrickson?" she enquired in her most musical lady-of-the-castle voice.

"I ran into your Governor King at the Cape in July of ninety-one, ma'am. He suggested it might be worth my while bringing a speculative cargo to this country."

Patrickson's drawl sent memories of Peter shivering up Faith's spine. "1791! My goodness, Captain Patrickson, what took you so long?"

Patrickson blinked his round fish-eyes and coughed with embarrassment. "Well, I . . . er . . . had to return to Philadelphia first, ma'am."

Faith's heart fluttered as the humorless captain droned out a long-winded justification for his tardiness. Philadelphia was not far from Peter's hometown, Boston. When dinner concluded, she would take Captain Patrickson aside.

An hour later, she slipped her arm through his and, as they strolled the veranda in search of a cool breeze, gave him a brief résumé of her grandfather's American shipping interests. ". . . and I believe that, in recent times, the Devereaux of Boston have become a force to be reckoned with on the east coast of America, Captain. You have heard of them, perchance?"

Patrickson smiled. "The Devereaux family is well known in shipping circles, ma'am."

"Then perhaps we shall see their vessels dropping anchor in Sydney Cove in the near future?"

"I doubt that, ma'am. The Devereaux's interests lie in fishing, not trade. However, at the time of my departure, several shipowners were discussing the possibility of trade in these waters."

How the man waffled! "Do the Devereaux still intend to establish a fishing industry in the Southern Ocean?"

Patrickson's fish-eyes opened so wide they almost popped out of his head. "Indeed, you *are* well informed, Lady Stewart. Yes, as a matter of fact, young Devereaux was outfitting a ship for that purpose."

"Young Devereaux—oh, you must mean Peter." When he nodded, Faith almost swooned with relief. Definite news at last. "What was Peter's specific destination, Captain?"

Patrickson's reply came from a great distance. "I couldn't say, ma'am. He left Rhode Island months before I arrived."

Phillip's last evening in the colony; he dined with the handful of First Fleeters he considered his personal friends.

As the dinner conversation washed over him like waves in the sea, Michael concentrated on Lucy, who sat directly opposite. She was laughing, and the lilting sound of it teased his senses. He remembered other laughter—soft, sleepy, late-night laughter—

laughter that had been just for him. She looked like a luscious rose ready to be plucked. Her hair was piled on top of her head, her body was elegantly draped in pink satin, and around her voluptuous throat hung a single strand of pearls, delicate orbs that glowed soft and lustrous against her skin.

Noticing his look, Lucy quickly lowered her eyes. Earlier, when they had met in the foyer, he had been polite and offhand, but now he was staring at her in a way that made her tremble. She toyed with her food then looked at him from beneath lowered lashes. He was still staring—making no attempt to hide what he was thinking. . . . Her toes curled in her shoes, her palms grew sweaty, and an intense physical excitement swept through her. His eyes were devouring her neck and shoulders. She could feel the pearls burning into her skin. Involuntarily her hand came up and she stroked them, longing to tear them off. He raised his eyes and smiled at her in that slow, tantalizing way, eyes crinkling at the corners, lips curling upward. Their old game—he was playing it here in front of everyone! How *dare* he.

Michael was jubilant. *Should I continue holding back, or go after her relentlessly?* he wondered as she turned away and began concentrating on Phillip's words as if her life depended on it.

"My friends, trade must not be furthered at the expense of land cultivation. Both the remoteness of this colony and the unpredictability of its climate dictate that it will prosper only by becoming self-sufficient. Breed your livestock, don't slaughter them indiscriminately. Yes, at all costs protect your animals . . ."

"Do not concern yourself, sir. We all remember those years of starvation when the ships did not come, and we shall follow your instructions to the letter," said George Johnston.

Phillip smiled and his drawn countenance softened momentarily. "They are not meant to be instructions, George, just a bit of friendly advice. My era is over. Let us hope that those who follow me will be superior builders and farmers."

"Many may follow, but none will surpass you, sir," David Collins said huskily. "Your perseverence has been the main-spring of this colony's survival."

"Nor could your successors hope to match your humanity, sir," said Denis Considen.

"Or your fair-mindedness," said Tom.

"Or your patience," said John.

"Or your kindness," said Faith.

"Or your modesty," said Lucy.

Phillip winked at Michael. "If they keep this up, we'll have to add 'insufferable vanity' to the list."

Michael laughed. "Don't expect me to rescue you, sir. I consider it a great privilege to have served under you these last six years."

Phillip raised his glass. "They were six years I would not have missed for anything, my dear friends. Let us drink to the First Fleeters, bound and free, and to the colony they founded."

As everyone gathered in the foyer to bid Phillip farewell, Michael joined Lucy and Faith. "I cannot imagine what this colony will be like without him. Can you, Lucy?"

"No, I can't," she answered warily. "Still, it's time he concentrated on regaining his health."

He continued staring at her. "You look like a lovely rose—flaming fire within the delicate beauty without. But I prefer your hair loose around your shoulders so I can twist the strands . . . and twine them around my fingers."

Lucy drew her breath in sharply and darted a quick glance around the foyer. "Really? I thought your tastes ran more to *blond* ringlets these days."

He threw back his head and laughed. "My tastes haven't changed, Lucy. May I call on you tomorrow and refresh your memory?"

Lucy's cheeks flamed. "No, you may not."

"The next day, perhaps?"

"No!"

"The next?"

"You may call on *me* whenever you please," Faith interposed brightly, and gave him her hand.

"Thank you, Faith." He bid them good night and joined the group around the Governor.

Monday, December 10, 1792

"Farewell, *Beanah*," Lucy whispered as she and Faith watched Arthur Phillip descend the slope in front of Government House and join Major Grose and the officers of the New South Wales Corps at the Governor's Wharf.

"*Beanah*, my heart?"

"That's what the natives call him. It means father." Lucy glanced at the stricken countenances of the convicts. They had also perceived him as a stern but fatherly figure. *Who will care for them now?* she wondered. To date, Major Grose had displayed no such protective leanings. The perimeter of *his* vision appeared to be the ease and comfort of his troops.

"What will we do without him?" Faith asked tremulously.

Lucy embraced her. "Build on the foundations he has laid for us, beloved. Hold me . . . hold me tight."

23
Laura Taura Revisited

To mark his first day in office, Grose initiated several revolutionary changes. Contrary to the express orders of the English Parliament, he issued land grants to the officers of the corps and provided them with ten convicts apiece to cultivate their new estates; he appointed Macarthur Inspector of Public Works, and ordered him to divert all convict labor to building the barracks in Sydney and Parramatta; he replaced the civil magistrates with officers of the corps; and he increased the weekly food ration of the officers and men of the corps.

"Grose objects to convicts receiving the same rations as the military," George Johnston told those gathered in the hospital mess that evening. "He thinks people who have been sent out here as a punishment should receive less."

"If Phillip had adopted that attitude, the convicts would have starved," Denis Considen said hotly.

George frowned. "I know that, Denis. I don't necessarily agree with what Grose has done, I am just relating his reasons."

"I have no doubt which way the winds of good fortune will blow in future," Tom growled. "Straight into the lap of the damned military."

Michael nodded grimly. "The whole thing reeks of hypocrisy. During Phillip's administration the military refused to take part in the civil direction of this colony, yet the moment he leaves the reverse is the case. The military now controls the judicature, trade, land, and labor. Who, I ask, is to be the watchdog of the military?"

"Grose is Governor now," George reminded them, "and we would be wise to adapt to the changes of the time."

Lucy and Faith had just sat down to breakfast when the maid ushered Michael into the parlor. Lucy flicked her hair back from her shoulders and glared at him but Faith balanced her frost with a sunny smile. "Good morning, Michael. Please join us."

"It seems a little crowded in here," he said, observing that the parlor was stacked to the rafters with boxes.

"They are goods I purchased from the masters of *Royal Admiral* and *Philadelphia*," Faith informed him. "I shall keep them a few months then, when the time is right, sell them at a handsome profit."

Michael sat down opposite Lucy. "Hello, Lucy. It appears that our new Governor sowed some wild oats yesterday."

"Yes," she replied guardedly. He was doing it again, hunting her with his eyes. It confused her and excited her all at once. She did not know whether to slap his face—or throw herself into his arms.

"This hut is only a temporary dwelling," Faith said after a long silence. "Mr. Bloodworth, the builder, has already begun work on our townhouse. The man is an absolute genius, Michael. The storage cellars he has designed will communicate with the house by a staircase and have passageways between the buttery and kitchens."

Michael smiled at her warmly. She was trying so hard and he loved her for it. "You are acquiring quite a reputation in the world of barter, madam. We mere men will need to watch our step."

She reached across the table and clasped his hand. "The opportunities here are limitless."

"I agree, Faith. That's why I've called at such an ungodly hour. The convicts and settlers have been selling the stock Phillip gave them and, what is worse, those they cannot sell they are slaughtering."

"Oh no," Lucy cried. "Phillip said those animals were to be preserved at all costs, Michael."

He leaned closer. "I plan to purchase as many as possible, Lucy, but unfortunately, my money drafts don't have the same buying power as gold or Bengal rum. Therefore, I have a proposition to put to you and Faith. If you will exchange my notes for coin, and match my financial outlay, I shall undertake to purchase the stock and transport it to Worthing where we can divide it evenly.''

"What a splendid idea," cried Faith. "Not only will we be fulfilling Captain Phillip's wishes but we shall be acquiring valuable bloodstock without the additional expense of importing it. Thank you for thinking of us. We will be delighted to join you in the venture, won't we, Lucy?"

Lucy nodded eagerly. "Money is no problem." She walked to the corner of the room and threw back a rug to reveal a trapdoor. "We brought out three thousand ounces of silver dollars. How soon will you begin, Michael?"

He took the key from her and undid the padlocks. "The sooner the better, otherwise the military will beat us to the best.''

That afternoon, Lucy and Faith had an appointment with the fortune-teller.

Laura Taura greeted them politely and invited them inside.

"What do you wish to know?" she asked, as they seated themselves at the table and Lucy introduced her sister.

Faith recited the Guardian's prophecy and asked Laura Taura if she could make sense of it.

"My gift is of 'seeing,' not of 'interpretation,' but I will do my best," Laura Taura replied in the deep, musical voice Lucy remembered so well. She tossed the cube with strange symbols in the air. It landed in the center of the table displaying a circular symbol at the top and a cross at the bottom. "Your number is four," she told Faith and tossed the cube again.

It landed with the same symbol facing up. "Your number is also four," she told Lucy. Then she looked *at* them and *through* them and *beyond* them. "Aah . . . now, I remember. Lucy Gamble of the severed tie. Born the eleventh day of the eleventh month of the sixty-sixth year. Four paired equals eight. Eight is the number of fate.''

Laura Taura turned to Faith. "Let me see your right hand, please." She studied the hand, stared intently at Faith then stroked the crossed scar on her index finger. Despite the intense heat, Faith shivered. "Stewart is wrong for you . . ." said Laura Taura, shaking her head.

"Stewart is my married name," Faith explained, "but I was recently widowed."

For a moment, the fortune-teller's eyes blazed like the sun emerging from behind dark clouds. "No, no, you must put the madness and the blood from your mind. Focus on the prophecy . . . only that." She continued stroking the scar. "The first prophecy of four: 'Truth's word will stem the blood.' Yes, I see . . . an old man died in a bed of lies, yet the truth he spake stemmed the tears of your soul."

Faith nodded. "The scar on my finger has not bled since the night Grandfather died."

Laura Taura continued stroking the scar. "The second prophecy of four: 'Strive then, the tie to bind.' With a *mother's* charisma your sister called. And, *guided* by your need, you came."

Faith nodded. "Now, only by cleaving to her, do I feel whole. Does this do her harm, Laura Taura?"

The fortune-teller smiled. "No, it is meet and right. You are her spiritual staff."

She turned then to Lucy. "Let me see your left hand, please."

Lucy complied.

Laura Taura bent the four fingers of Lucy's hand backward until the palm grew white and the lines on it turned crimson. "Ah . . . there is the join." She pointed to a horizontal line an inch below Lucy's left index finger. Lucy was shocked. With her hand held thus, she saw that the line was indeed a scar. Laura Taura stroked the scar and looked at Lucy intently. "The third prophecy of four concerns you, Lucy Gamble . . ." The hairs on the back of Lucy's neck shot erect.

> "Duty the path to love."
> *Duty* puts love to the test.
> Tested and tried, love is true.
> Running through fields of flames
> He finds the right path to you.

"Not true!" Lucy cried.

Laura Taura stared at her serenely. "His heart is staunch, Lucy Gamble."

"But he has taken another woman."

"I have told you the truth, Lucy Gamble. You may interpret it how you please. Let us turn to the fourth prophecy of four,

508

which concerns you both.'' She smiled at Faith. "May I have your right hand, please?"

She placed Faith's index finger diagonally across the scar on Lucy's palm. The twins jerked convulsively. Laura Taura clasped their hands tighter and stared at them in her strange, penetrating way. "Do exactly as I say. Close your eyes and concentrate on the fourth prophecy."

After a long silence, Laura Taura spoke.

> "Destiny, child, to find."
> I am loved.
> I am protected.
> I am denied.
> I am rejected.
> I lie beside
> The river of blood . . .

Faith's heart grew taut with fear. She had not mentioned the woman, or the river of blood.

The fortune-teller's breathing grew labored. "Concentrate, concentrate . . . there is more . . .

> I see a Great One
> Guarding the entrance to
> The Valley of Death.
> The entrance is narrow—
> Like the entrance of a womb.
> The womb is a grave . . .
> It opens . . .
> And the *unborn* is shed!

With an uncanny cry, Laura Taura let go their hands and slumped forward in her chair, weeping.

"What is wrong?" Faith asked through bloodless lips.

Laura Taura slowly raised her head. "The truth, though sublime, is often melancholy, my child. Soon you will have your heart's desire. But do not seek it at the time of the full moon; that would be folly."

24

Duty the Path to Love

Lucy stood by the window looking out at the cloudless day. She had been profoundly affected by Laura Taura's translation of the four prophecies and, although the fourth still remained a mystery, she no longer doubted that strange forces were at play in their lives.

Faith joined her. "Put it out of your mind, Lucy, it does no good to dwell on it . . . believe me." She saw Michael striding along the path driving two goats before him. "Michael!" she called, and waved.

Lucy half-raised her hand then let it drop. Despite Laura Taura's attestations, Michael *had* been unfaithful. Ben was living proof of that.

"It's time we returned to the hinterland," Michael said, as he entered the hut. "Tomorrow, I'll ship what we have purchased upharbor, acquire what I can at Parramatta then transport them to Worthing. When you have built enclosures, I shall bring your share to Chaumilley."

"Can we assist with anything further?" Lucy asked.

His eyes locked with hers. "Yes, as a matter of fact. In the weeks ahead the people on our respective properties will need to work together closely. I'd appreciate it if you would have a word with Moses. Since that day on the hill, he has treated me like a leper." He sensed her withdrawal, but pressed on. "I condemn myself daily for what I said, Lucy, and you know it."

Lucy believed him but her stubborn heart would not weaken. She walked to the door and yanked it open. "Moses, would you come here?"

As the giant lumbered into the parlor, Faith squeezed Michael's hand and whispered, "Keep trying, dearest."

"Sit down, Moses," Michael invited, taking a sheet of paper from his pocket and spreading it out on the table. "I've drawn up some plans for the Chaumilley enclosures and I'd like you to look at them."

*   *   *

When Michael returned to John's house that evening, Beth met him on the veranda. "You've been with her for two whole days," she accused shrilly. "I've got a right to know what's going on, Michael."

The last thing he wanted was another blazing row. "Let's take a stroll along the beach," he suggested. "We can discuss things there."

"I-I know why you want to take a stroll along the bloomin' beach. It's because Lucy's gone there, she left the hut just after you, I saw her."

He grabbed her elbow and pulled her along the path toward Long Cove. "The situation between us is intolerable, Beth. I want an end to it."

Words gushed from her mouth in a breathless jumble. "It's intolerable because you lied to me, Michael. You swore you had finished with Lucy, but you *lied!*"

"You are right, Beth. I have loved Lucy from the moment I met her and I have no intention of giving her up—not for you, Ben, or anyone. That is the truth."

Beth sagged like a wilting flower and if he had not caught her she would have collapsed on the ground. "I'm sorry, Bethy," he said gently. "I need Lucy like I need air. Life is impossible without her."

Beth clutched his sleeve desperately. "But what about Ben and me, Michael? Are you abandoning us now?"

"I have no intention of abandoning you or our son, Beth. You asked for an explanation and I think it's time you understood my intentions toward Lucy. I am leaving Sydney tomorrow but, before I go, I want to see you and Ben comfortably settled. I spoke to John last night. If you wish, you can live in William Balmain's cottage until I build you something larger."

Beth burst into tears. "But we were going to spend Christmas with Tom and Elizabeth. Now, Ben and me'll be all alone. Oh Michael, how can you be so cruel to your own little boy?"

Michael cursed himself for an insensitive dolt. He had forgotten about Christmas. He took Beth in his arms. "Please don't cry, my dear. Of course we'll spend Christmas with them. But in the new year, when we discuss your future again, will you promise to be more sensible?"

She nodded through her tears. "Yes, Michael—I promise." But in Beth's heart, the fear kept growing. No matter how reassuring the words, in the end, love always deserted her.

Not only was Reverend Johnson's sermon overlong, it was utterly uninspiring, and Faith thought the sound of Christmas carols ringing out over black, smoldering bush land quite absurd. However, at the conclusion of the service, when the Reverend informed the congregation that the American ship *Hope* had arrived in Sydney three days earlier, she instantly forgave him the tedium of the last two hours.

"Dare I hope for news of Peter?" she asked Lucy with shining eyes.

Lucy removed her bonnet ribbons from Duncan's mouth. "Laura Taura said you would soon have your heart's desire and she has been uncannily accurate—excepting for Michael's fidelity."

"Here comes Michael now." Faith pointed to Michael and Tom who were pushing through the crowd.

Though reluctant, Lucy and Faith felt duty bound to accept Tom's invitation to partake of Christmas dinner with him and Elizabeth at the farm.

The visit began brightly enough. However, after presents were exchanged and toasts drunk, it became acutely uncomfortable for everyone.

"Sorry to hear of your losses in the bushfire," Faith said to Elizabeth Burleigh after a particularly long silence. "I have purchased a number of household items from the ships. You are welcome to any that take your fancy."

Elizabeth did not want Beth to think that she was fraternizing with the enemy. "No thanks, *Lady* Stewart. Beth and my friends have stood by me through this trouble."

"Faith was only trying to help," Lucy snapped. Elizabeth turned scarlet and looked down at her feet.

"A large body of natives attacked some settlers at Prospect last week," Tom advanced with a note of desperation in his voice.

The silence grew until Lucy said, "Natives often visit Chaumilley, but they don't cause any trouble. They just kill a few ducks then go on their way."

Beth sniffed. "They might only kill ducks at Chaumilley, Lucy, but they hacked William Robe and his son to death at Prospect."

Michael attempted to rescue the situation. "If you trace such stories to their source, Beth, you'll find that the settler involved either fired upon the natives or detained their children. We have had no trouble at Worthing.''

"That's not to say we won't," Bethy hurled back.

Lucy rose. "Thank you for inviting us, Tom and Elizabeth. We must be leaving now."

"Stay, Lucy, please." Michael's voice was raw with emotion. "It's been three years since we spent Christmas together."

Their eyes locked and for a few moments they looked at each other with perfect understanding, then Lucy shook her head. "No, Michael, it's pointless."

Sighing in a defeated way, he scooped Duncan into his arms. "I shall see you and Faith to the cart."

"Beth never misses an opportunity to disparage me," Faith said, as Moses steered the cart along the track toward Prospect Hill. "She spent most of the time staring daggers at me, and she seems to have drawn others into the hostility."

Lucy sighed dejectedly. "She is deeply disturbed about something . . ."

Faith raised knowing eyebrows. "If I was her, I'd be deeply disturbed, too, Michael has no interest in her. In fact, he—" She broke off, noticing the tears in Lucy's eyes. "What is it, my heart?"

"I owe my life to Beth. Many times she used her body to protect mine . . ." Lucy's voice trailed away, and she shook her head. "Now we can barely speak to each other."

Faith placed a comforting arm around Lucy's shoulders. "Sorry, Lucy. In the future I will be more tolerant of her and curb my sharp tongue."

Michael awoke on Friday determined to see Lucy, and by mid-morning he and his men were herding stock into her new enclosures. He found her on the far side of the lake looking for onion weeds. "Where is everyone? The place looked deserted when I rode in."

Lucy rose and smoothed out her skirts, "Moses has driven Faith down to Sydney. She wants to see what the *Hope* has for sale."

Michael raised a quizzical eyebrow. "Faith seems uncommonly interested in American ships these days. Would it have anything to do with Peter?"

Lucy smiled. "Possibly."

He looked her slowly up and down. "Care to see your new stock? I brought you eight shapely sheep, two gorgeous goats . . . and one sensual sow."

Lucy threw back her head and laughed until her eyes grew misty. "They must be a fascinating collection. I'll just deliver these onions to Cook then we'll inspect them. After that, perhaps you'd like to see the cleared ground?"

"Only if it looks as succulent as you."

She laughed again, this time a little uncertainly. "Really, Michael, you make me feel like a piece of fruit."

Gathering up her skirts in one hand and her basket of onion weeds in the other, she set off toward the homestead. He retrieved his horse and followed, enjoying the sway of her hips and the bouncing movement of her buttocks as she picked her way through the wilting grass.

"Why are you dawdling?" she asked, stopping and glancing over her shoulder.

"I've been trying to think which piece of fruit you remind me of," he said with mock seriousness. "I have decided that you look like a ripe golden peach. I love peaches—but I haven't had one for two years, five months . . . and three days." He knew he was moving too fast but it was like trying to stop an avalanche. "Lucy," he groaned, reaching out and stroking her cheek, "Lucy, Lucy . . . love me." His fingers slid down her neck to the soft warm flesh between her breasts.

She stepped back from him, eyes spitting green fire. "Don't touch me, Michael."

He caught her around the waist and pulled her against him. "Darling, let's stop this. I forgive you for the child—I forgive you for everything, Lucy."

As he bent to kiss her, Lucy struck him across the mouth.

"What the hell was that for?"

"For thinking I would deliberately endanger our child's life . . . and for ruining *my* life, you damned scaramouch!"

He grabbed her fists. "Now that we have established I am to blame for everything, can we please stop torturing each other and put our life back together?"

She wrenched free of him. "No, you tallowy cur. I lie awake every night thinking of you and Beth in your big brass bed."

"Beth and I aren't lovers, Lucy. Nor have we ever been."

Lucy's eyes narrowed dangerously. "What about Ben?"

"If you'll calm down, I'll explain about Ben. The day I

514

returned to Sydney and discovered you gone, I almost went mad. I got rotten drunk, so drunk that when Beth came to the hut that night, in my stupor, I thought she was you. I wanted you so badly, darling. I know it doesn't excuse what I did, but—"

"How *very* convenient. A case of mistaken identity while in the grip of drunken derangement. You're right, Michael, it doesn't excuse anything. You did what you did, now we must live with the consequences."

Michael swung himself into the saddle. "I have no intention of leaving you alone, Lucy. I love you and will pursue you relentlessly until you give in. See you at Prospect on Sunday."

Lucy stood on top of the slope staring at the retreating farm carts. The morning sun seered the eastern horizon and a hot wind gusted in from the northeast. It was going to be a scorcher. No Sunday service for her today, just Chaumilley's peace and tranquility.

She wandered through the field of dead grass to the lake, shed her shift and waded into the water. Although the level of the lake had dropped alarmingly, there was still a deep hole in the middle. When she reached it, she closed her eyes and floated on her back, pleased that she had won her inner struggle and resisted the temptation of Prospect. Pleasant memories of Michael crisscrossed her mind—traces of impressions, sensations of emotions—until that one irreconcilable thought dropped like a stone into her consciousness: Michael and Beth in their big brass bed. And that thought hung there and clung there and kept weighing her down.

With a sense of heightened expectancy, Michael watched the Chaumilley farm carts approach. Since Friday, he had been puzzling over something Lucy had said about the child, and last night he had finally figured it out. The solution was so simple he wondered why he had never considered it before. It was just the sort of thing Lucy would do . . .

Handing Ben to Beth, he jumped out of the cart and pushed his way through the congregation toward the Chaumilley carts. But as he drew closer his elated mood took a sudden downturn. The hell with it. The stubborn madam had stayed at home.

"Is Mistress Gamble alone at Chaumilley?" he asked the cook.

The woman removed her bonnet and mopped perspiration from her face. "Yes, sir. I offered to stay, you know, but Miss Lucy wouldn't hear of it. 'No, Cook,' she says, 'I am quite looking forward to being by myself.' "

"Is anything the matter?" Beth asked, when he returned to their cart.

"Lucy is at Chaumilley alone. Of all the damned fool things. What can she be thinking of?"

"She'll be all right, Michael. You said yourself, the natives aren't dangerous."

"I don't like it, Beth. I don't like it at all."

Five minutes later his feelings of disquiet turned to alarm when the cinders began falling from the sky and clouds of smoke came billowing over the treetops. "That's it," he said, signaling to John Best who was standing some distance away.

Best left his companions and hurried to the cart. "Something wrong, Lieutenant?"

"Get our people together, John, we've leaving for home immediately. I don't like the look of that smoke, and the wind feels like it's blowing straight out of hell."

"Right you are, Lieutenant." Ignoring the protests of the more pious members of the congregation, Best let out several piercing whistles to alert his men.

Soon afterward they were on their way, but had proceeded only half a mile along the track when they were stopped by a foot patrol. "You'll have to turn back, sir," said the corporal in charge. "We've orders to evacuate everyone to Parramatta. The whole country's ablaze."

"But I *must* get through," Michael said desperately.

"Not this way, sir. Fire's burning out of control right along the ridges." The corporal swept the horizon in a wide arc.

Michael jumped down and started unhitching the horse. "Everyone out! John, over here, quickly. Take the Worthing and Chaumilley people to Tom Arndell's farm. He's already been burned out, they'll be safe there. I'm going in after Lucy."

"I'll come with you," Best offered, helping him to unbuckle the straps.

Michael shook his head. "No, John, I'm relying on you to look after things at this end. Take everyone to Tom's—and stay put." Seeing the terror in Beth's eyes, he took her in his arms. "You and Ben will be quite safe, my dear. Be strong and do exactly what John Best says." He embraced his son and handed him into her care. "Look after our little boy, Bethy."

516

His words cut through Beth's panic. "I-I will, Michael. Oh, poor Lucy. You'd better go—go quickly."

Michael climbed on the horse, gripped its mane to steady himself then sped away through the undergrowth in a northwesterly direction, taking the old route, the route of the seven streams. He rode recklessly, trying to put as much distance as possible between him and the fire but, by the time he reached the sixth stream, the wall of flames was only mile behind, running north to south across the horizon like an arrowhead pointing at Chaumilley.

He skirted the precipitous ravine of *Yowi Yowi* and found a level place to cross some distance upstream. Although the banks were twenty feet apart and the water was flowing steadily despite the drought, he doubted it would check the inferno behind him. He plunged across the shallows to the other side, galloped through the withered grass to the seventh stream, and crossed it into open country. The horse was laboring now but he dared not ease up. "Come on, boy," he urged, spying the familiar slope ahead. "Stay with me, stay with me."

Hearing a deep, whooshing roar, he glanced over his shoulder and tasted the gall of fear. The bush, once crowned in vibrant green, had been swallowed by a fiery monster that rushed toward him at incredible speed, devouring everything in its path. "Come on, boy, faster, *faster*."

A sharp crack rang out. The horse squealed, and the earth came rushing up to meet him.

Lucy walked to the door and looked out. It was as if the dry, wilting earth was waiting for something—something frighteningly near. A red ring encircled the sun and the Blue Mountains shimmered and blurred. In the enclosures, the stock were lowing and bleating pitifully. Lucy longed to set them free but she knew that, if she did, they would join the wild bush animals and all Michael's work would be lost.

She climbed the slope and looked out over the empty land. The eastern sky was dark as midnight and the wind was so hot it sucked the moisture from her eyes and burned her nostrils. She studied the horizon, focusing with all her might. A moment later, a hundred-foot wall of flame jumped the ridge. Like a fire-breathing dragon it rushed toward her, setting the world alight.

She stumbled down the slope to the enclosures, freed the poor things trapped inside, then ran to the hut and scooped up anything she could lay her hands on.

When a semblance of sanity returned, she dropped everything and ran outside into the maelstrom of smoke and wind. *Go to the lake while there's still time,* she told herself. *Go! Go!* She ran a few yards, stopped, and gazed about her distractedly. Where *was* the lake? She turned in a slow circle, trying to take a bearing from the wind but it gusted from every direction. "Which way? Which way?"

His voice floated on the wind. "Lucy! Where are you?"

Sobbing with joy, she ran toward the sound. "Michael, I'm here!"

A moment later, he materialized out of the smoke and caught her in a wild embrace. "Lucy, thank God! Come on, darling. The river. Run, *run!*" He grabbed her hand and pulled her along as flaming meteors dropped from the sky and ignited the grass all around them.

Lucy screamed with terror.

His eyes bore into her. "We must go through it, Lucy. Are you with me, darling?"

"Yes," she sobbed. "To the end."

Looking neither right nor left, they sped through the field of flames toward the cleared section of ground; and all the time they ran, Lucy knew they would make it. *Knew* it. Ignoring the seering heat, oblivious of the flames lapping at her legs, she matched Michael stride for stride, until she tripped over a branch and dropped to her knees, mouth agape, battling to draw air into her suffocating lungs.

He yanked her up, willing her on with his eyes. "Not much farther. Hold on . . . hold on." Supporting her around the waist, he stumbled through the dense smoke to the riverbank. But the fire had encircled the cleared section and the rushes were a wall of flames."

"Michael, what will—" Lucy broke off and screamed in agony as her dress ignited and flames ran up her back.

Roaring like a bull, Michael charged down the bank, through the flaming rushes, plunged into the shallows and rolled her over and over until the flames went out. She came up gasping and spluttering and screamed again as fiery cinders dropped from the sky and hit the water hissing smoke. He tore off her shoes and shoved her ahead of him into deeper water. "Swim!"

The river here was a hundred-feet wide and by the time they reached the other side, Lucy was utterly spent. With the last of his strength, Michael dragged her up the steep bank. They collapsed and lay on their backs gasping and choking.

When Michael recovered he took her in his arms. "Are you all right, darling?" Lucy tried to speak but had no strength left in her. He smoothed the singed hair away from her forehead with gentle motions.

Tears ran out the corners of Lucy's eyes.

He brushed them away. "Don't cry, darling."

"Michael . . . I love you."

"I know," he whispered, and kissed her.

For the first time in two long years Lucy felt his lips. She raised her head, trying to strengthen the contact but was too weak and fell back. "*Faith* was pregnant. I wrote you a dozen letters, Michael . . ."

"It doesn't matter any more, darling. Say you will forgive me so we can make a new start."

The tears rolled down Lucy's cheeks. How absurd of her to think he had been unfaithful. His heart was staunch; he had run through fields of flames to reach her. "There is nothing to forgive. But I was so jealous, Michael."

He caressed her neck. "Foolish Lucy. You are the only one for me."

Then he touched her and the sweet, long remembered warmth spread into every cell of Lucy's body. "Michael, oh my darling, my darling. It's been agony without you."

He lowered her gently onto the sand and, in a little while they transcended the flaming holocaust.

PART FOUR

Dog Days of the Setting Moon

25
Return of "the Guide"

Peter Devereaux climbed the companionway to the deck and joined the mate at the rail. "Anything yet, Mr. Jefferson?"

"No, Capt'n. Weather's still thick as chowder. Hey! What's that?" Jefferson's voice was suddenly hoarse with excitement as the haze lifted and two dim cliffs came into sight.

Peter studied them closely. "That's Port Jackson, Mr. Jefferson. Set the ship toward the northern headland."

The helmsman ran the ship round almost at right angles to the wind and it raced toward the entrance like an eager bride entering a church. As it swept past North Head, Peter stared at the tall, jutting edifice with a mixture of bitterness and regret. Two and a half years ago, he had stood on that windswept bluff watching her sail away . . .

"We made it!" Jefferson's voice broke into Peter's dark thoughts. "Jesus, Capt'n, there were times when I thought we never would."

"When you've finished congratulating yourself, Mr. Jefferson, would you check the aft pumps and send the bos'n up here on the double? I'll need a detailed damage report to give the Port Authorities."

"Yes, sir," replied Jefferson and quickly disappeared below. When the skipper had *that* set of jaw he was best left alone.

The bustling township that greeted Peter as *Iliad* eased into Sydney Cove was a far cry from the dilapidated village he had left in 1790. Nor did the robust inhabitants crowding the foreshores bear any resemblance to the emaciated skeletons of the Second Fleet. He glanced over his shoulder at the hut on the western shore and saw her.

She stood in the doorway as bright and as clear as a summer's day. With an exclamation of disbelief, he raised his spyglass. Dark, luxuriant hair, an ankle-length shift glowing white against her body . . . had he really been away, or merely slumbering in her suspended oblivion? She mouthed his name and he knew beyond doubt it was she. The scar around his heart pricked painfully and white heat seered his insides. He did not want to see her. He had won his freedom in an agony of empty days and sleepless nights . . .

A feeling of unutterable joy swept through Faith when she saw him. She trembled, remembering the bitterness of their goodbye, then she thought of the days of unrestrained love on Ice Island and her spirits soared. She *would* thwart the Guardian and reverse her destiny. Peter, the Guide, *would* love her again. She saw him glance in her direction and raise the spyglass to his eye. Almost suffocated by the wild beating of her heart, she whispered his name. "Peter . . ."

He stared at her for a few moments longer then turned away.

At first Faith was dismayed, but as she stood before the mirror in Lucy's room her confidence returned. Naturally, he would react that way. He thought she was still married to Hugh. However, a few questions would establish her widowed state, then he would call on her. She tried to gather her scattered thoughts. How should she behave when they met? Cool? Warm? Prim? Proper? "I shall behave quite naturally," she decided. "And it will help my confidence if I am looking my best."

Her excitement mounting, she searched the clothes racks until she found a lovely lime and white lace with a matching parasol. "No jewelery," she decided. "Definitely no jewelery— nothing to detract from the gown." Its low off-the-shoulder neckline was a little unseemly for Sunday but because she was Lady Stewart, she would get away with it. Her hair she would wear loose around her shoulders, the way he liked it. As she raked the comb through the wild tangles, she smiled. The only use he had for hairpins was as fishhooks. She stared at her flushed face and laughed nervously. "I'm behaving like a girl who is just about to step out with her first suitor."

Faith paced the parlor like a caged cat. Why hadn't Peter called?

Hester, whom she had posted by the window, had seen him go ashore an hour ago.

"Captain Hill's here." Hester curtsied shyly to the tall, impeccably dressed officer, as she ushered him into the parlor.

Hill stopped in his tracks and surveyed Faith in stunned admiration. "What a vision you are. I'll have to use my saber on the competition today."

Faith pressed her lips to Duncan's pudgy cheeks, snatched up her parasol and swept out the door. "Don't dillydally, William, we shall be late for church."

Despite the earliness of the hour, the heat was intense and by the time they reached Church Hill Faith's face and shoulders were shiny with perspiration. Hawklike, she scanned the congregation as she made her way toward the front. Double damn! No sign of him. Well, before the day was much older, she was determined they would meet.

"How can you look so divinely beautiful while everyone around you is perishing from the heat?" William asked as he helped Faith alight from the carriage outside the hut.

Although she twirled her parasol and fluttered her eyelashes at him, her heart was not in the game. "Thank you for your gallant compliment, sir, but I assure you I, too, am perishing. Let's stroll over to the Governor's Wharf."

"Seems as though everyone in Sydney's turned out to see the *Iliad*." Hill said.

Faith turned in a slow circle, a glazed look in her eyes. "Which way? Which way?"

He guided her past the new storehouse. "This way. Say! Isn't that Peter Devereaux?"

Joy, confusion, fear, and relief flooded Faith's mind. Peter was standing at the end of the wharf, chatting to Governor Grose and the ladies and gentlemen of the corps.

Hill began towing her after him along the wharf. "Well, I'll be bound! Your savior has returned, my dear."

Fountains of orange and red exploded in Faith's head and Hill's hollow, distorted voice seemed to roll in from a great distance. "We *will* make it. Run! Run!" She tried to match his stride but the wharf boards burned her feet.

"Ah, here is Lady Stewart, now," Grose said to Peter as Faith and Hill approached. "Tragic to be widowed so young, eh? Apparently, the child is one consolation. Image of his father, they say."

She was even more beautiful than Peter remembered—taller, and fuller somehow. Motherhood became her.

"Good Lord, it *is* you, Devereaux." William Hill pumped his hand. "How are you, old chap?"

"Fine, thanks." Peter returned the handshake with a pressure that made Hill grimace, then nodded briefly to Faith. "Hello, Lady Stewart."

Faith pressed her hands to her ribcage, panting and gasping, trying to drag air into her lungs. "H-hello . . ."

Peter stared fixedly at Faith. Something was wrong. Her eyes were glazed and she was flushed and out of breath.

Faith dropped to her knees, mouth gaping, battling to draw air into her suffocating lungs.

"What is it? What's wrong?" Peter asked, grabbing her around the waist and hoisting her to her feet.

She screamed in agony as her dress ignited and flames ran up her back. "No! Lucy! No! No!"

"Miss Faith!" The voice penetrated Faith's consciousness like the crack of a whip. She turned in the direction of the sound and saw Moses running along the wharf through clouds of smoke. Breaking free of Peter, she stumbled toward him.

Tears of anguish spilled from the giant's eyes. "Doc Arndell sent word that the country's burning up round Chaumilley. Miss Lucy's trapped in there—and the Lieutenant's gone after her. We've got to go!"

Faith clasped his hand and they started to run.

26

The Search

Peter left the tent and climbed the hill behind the Prospect settlement. Faith was sitting on a long, flat rock facing west, her finery of the previous day replaced by borrowed clothes and her features barely recognizable beneath a mask of soot.

"Drink this," he said, squatting beside her and holding out a mug of steaming soup.

"Any news?" Her voice was vague and remote.

"The wind has shifted to a more favorable quarter," he said gently. "If it continues, the fires will burn themselves out in a few hours." He proferred the mug again. "Drink. You won't be much use if you are fainting from hunger."

She took the mug and dutifully drew the hot liquid into her mouth. "Lucy is alive. I feel it here." She held a hand over her heart.

He sat down beside her and, in the following silence, studied her intently. She had an awesome passiveness—an almost death-like stillness—about her, as if she was caught in an enchantment. He felt the urge to shake her out of it, to shock her back to life. "So," he said at length, "you are a widow."

"Yes." She made no attempt to explain and he did not press her. He remembered a day long ago on Ice Island when she had sat on the crag above the cave staring out to sea and running her fingers through her hair. The memory of those long strands twirling in the wind sent a shaft of pain through his heart. He had scaled the pinnacles of heaven with her when she had loved him, and been dashed to the depths of hell when she had left him. He thought of his voyage to Boston—the endless days setting sails and the sleepless nights in stinking fo'c'sles. He thought of the months he'd spent outfitting *Iliad*, and of the hard, frozen year just past, when he had battled the elements around Kerguelen Island and finally come to terms with his life. Had all that soul-searching been for nothing? His mouth set in a hard line. No, he would never let her hurt him again. He'd stand by her through this but that was all. He did not want to love her any more.

He gripped her shoulders. "Come down soon, the search party is leaving at first light."

Faith watched his retreating shadow until it blended into the darker blackness of the hill, then she placed her hands over her heart and, comforted by its steady beat, turned toward the fires glowing in the west.

Peter sat with one leg hooked over the saddle looking at the charred, smoldering desert. Although the sun still hung low on the horizon, a white heat haze already shimmered over the land. It would be hell out there today. He glanced at Faith. She wore a wide-brimmed hat pulled low over her eyes and a scarf around her face to aid breathing. His decision to leave the horses behind meant she must walk like the others. However, with flaming patches ahead that could only be traversed on foot, he had no choice.

"The wind is still blowing from a favorable quarter, men," he told the twenty-five searchers gathered around the stone cairn marking the turnoff to Chaumilley, "but if it shifts suddenly we'll have to run for it, so keep your neighbor in sight at all times." He paused and swept them with a penetrating gaze. "The horses stay here. It's too dangerous to take them farther." He dismounted and the others followed suit.

Leaving two men behind with the horses, the searchers set out across the ruins of the land. It was a hard, desperate trek and by the time they reached the sixth stream close by the ravine of *Yowi Yowi,* most were staggering with exhaustion. Not her. She drank from the stream then stood like a statue, facing west. The men watched her with a mixture of perplexity and awe, unable to reconcile this remote Amazon with the flamboyant social goddess Lady Stewart.

Shortly afterward, they set off again. As they trod the scorched earth Peter looked up at the red-tinged sky and the carrions hovering overhead like chattering devils, and was reminded of a troupe of mythical sinners tramping the ramparts of hell. Every so often, a leaf would flutter to the ground, catch fire and run helter-skelter in a line of dancing flames until halted by a blackened rock or piece of bleeding bark. Aware that an easterly wind would set the whole country alight, he urged the searchers to greater effort. Although most muttered and blasphemed, Faith trudged beside him silent and uncomplaining—her streaming, smoke-filled eyes fixed on the distant slope. His eyes glistened and his heart swelled with pride, but he forced the feeling down. Life was not just grand heroic moments; its mundane days had to be lived through also.

They reached more open ground and waded through clouds of soot and cinders until John White cried, "Jesus, what's that?" and pointed to a black, bloated object with four projectories reaching to the sky like supplicating arms.

They stumbled toward it, waving their arms to disperse the feasting crows. It was a horse, its right front fetlock snapped clean through. As they crowded around its roasted remains, John turned in a circle and raked the landscape with haunted eyes. "It's probably Michael's. Where is he?" They fanned out, examining every tree trunk, peering behind every bush, turning over every rock but found nothing. They continued westward until they reached the foot of the long slope leading to Chaumilley.

Faith broke away from the group and scrambled up the incline. No lush green valley greeted her, just a blackened scarecrow desert, like all the rest. She pressed her fists to her mouth and moaned, a small, forlorn sound that touched the men who had gathered protectively around her.

"The hut." Moses pointed to the smoldering ruins.

"I'll come with you," offered John Best.

The others waited on the slope until the two men completed the search.

"Nothing?" asked Peter.

Moses wiped streaming eyes and shook his head.

"Lucy is at the river," said Faith.

Ignoring the hordes of screeching crows diving and swooping overhead, she led them in a roundabout route to the river.

"Lucy!" she cried. "Lucy! Where are you, my heart?"

A moment later, Lucy and Michael appeared at the top of the bank on the other side.

As Faith careered down the slope into the water, Tom gasped incredulously. "I don't believe it! She led us to the exact spot."

The old wooden clock on the mantelpiece had just struck six and the day was mellowing into dusk when the search party reached Tom's farm. Beth, who had been keeping vigil on the veranda, sighed with relief when she saw Lucy and Michael in the lead cart. They were safe. But her relief turned to dismay when she saw the expression on Michael's face as he lifted Lucy down from the cart. Obviously, there would be no place in his life for her and Ben any more. She passed her son to Susannah and rose. "Look after Ben. I'm not staying here to be humiliated."

Michael saw Beth rush away and he frowned. Although he had no intention of abandoning her, he was determined there would be no more guilty capitulations on his part. Lucy and he belonged together and Beth had to accept that. "After we have rested, darling, let's find Beth and discuss the plans we made at the river."

They found Beth sitting on the riverbank in front of Parramatta hospital.

With narrowed eyes and a sense of dread she watched them approach. Why couldn't they leave her alone? She didn't want to see them, she didn't want to talk to them, and she didn't want to listen to their accusations about the letters.

"Hello, Beth. We'd like to discuss the future with you," said Michael, squatting beside her. Lucy sat down on the other side of Beth, her heart full of hope. Surely Beth would come around.

Beth looked up at the stars in the twilight sky. "I hope it rains soon. The garden at Worthing must be dry as an old shoe."

"I am sorry, my dear," said Michael, "Worthing was destroyed by the fire."

She stared at him disbelievingly. "Worthing gone?" She raised shaking hands to her cheeks. "I-I never once thought that Worthing . . ." Michael and Lucy were gone. Worthing was gone. All Ben's little treasures were gone. This was God's punishment for stealing Lucy's letters. "Then we're finished," she said in a small, flat voice.

Michael smiled widely. "Of course not. We shall start again. We'll buy the thirty acres dividing Chaumilley and Worthing, and build the new house on the site Lucy and I chose originally."

Beth looked at him uncomprehendingly. "You mean, start all over again as if the last two and a half years never happened?"

He nodded. "We'll begin clearing Chaumilley tomorrow and start building the house at the end of the week, won't we darling?" He turned to Lucy and smiled.

Beth scrambled to her feet. "I've got to go. It's Benjamin's feed time."

Lucy rose and laid a hand on Beth's arm. "Don't go yet, Beth. Mistakes have been made, I know, but it's time for forgiveness and healing. Let's put the past behind us." She stared apprehensively at the woman before her. This Beth bore no resemblance to the friend who had protected her at Newgate and worked beside her at Sydney hospital. "Most of what happened was my fault. I should not have left the colony without speaking to Michael, but everything happened so fast, I didn't have time to think. I wanted to explain everything to Moses when I reached Norfolk, but—"

"Don't blame yourself, darling," Michael intervened. "You had no choice. I should have trusted you. How I could have assumed that the baby—" He stopped, seeing Lucy's warning look.

"I sent Michael several letters, but every one went astray," Lucy went on quickly. "I cannot understand it."

Beth pulled out of Lucy's grasp. "I don't care about your bloomin' letters, Lucy, and I don't care about you either. You think you can walk out of people's lives, then just walk back in when *you* feel like it. Well, Michael might be fool enough to welcome you back, but not me."

"Don't do this, Beth. You're making it difficult for everyone, especially yourself," said Michael.

Beth put her hands on his chest and pushed with all her might. "You can have your precious Lucy and your precious Chaumilley, Michael, but Ben stays with me. He's part of the last two years that can't be so conveniently forgot."

"You had better go after her," Lucy sighed.

"I want her and Ben with us, Lucy."

She wound her arms around his neck and kissed him. "We'll keep trying, darling. I know you and Ben will be together again."

He crushed her to him and buried his face in her hair. "God knows how much I love you, Lucy. I love you, I love you."

"I love you, too," she whispered and thought herself the most fortunate woman in the world.

"You look tired," Lucy said to Faith when they returned to Tom's parlor after farewelling the people for Sydney. "Moses has pitched your tent. Why don't you retire?"

Faith massaged her neck and moved her head up and down, trying to ease the tightness in her muscles. "I shall soon. What will we do now, my heart?"

Michael grinned. "How are you at arranging weddings? It's about time, don't you think?"

Faith embraced him wildly. "Oh, thank heavens for that."

"If I begin work the moment I return to Sydney, I should have everything organized by February."

"The wedding will take place next week.

"But Michael, a wedding of this scale cannot be arranged in a *week*, said Faith."

He folded his arms. "I don't mind Lucy returning to Sydney with you while I clear a few things at Chaumilley, but I won't be separated from her for more than a week."

"I won't wait longer than a week for Michael either," Lucy added emphatically.

Faith capitulated with a theatrical sigh. "Oh, very well. I will just have to do my best."

Peter watched her departure expressionlessly. Faith the indomitable heroine had been packed away and good old "trouble with a capital *T*" Lady Stewart had reappeared. *To hell with her anyway,* he told himself, doing his best to ignore the turmoil she evoked in him. *In two months' time I'll be on my way to the Southern Ocean to hunt whales.*

27

The Camp Fire

Peter lit the thin Virginian cigar with a twig and contemplated the camp fire. The army of workers had departed at sunset, but he and Michael had decided to spend the night at Chaumilley and leave the first thing in the morning.

"Will Faith live at Chaumilley with you?"

The question surprised Michael for Peter had not mentioned Faith all week. "Despite her devotion to Lucy, I think she will spend most of her time in Sydney when the townhouse is completed."

He told Peter about Faith's plan to establish a merchant empire in the colony.

"I thought trade was controlled by the military."

"Faith has managed to wangle her way into the cartel as William Hill's not so silent partner."

Peter studied the glowing tip of his cigar. "Anything between her and Hill?"

Michael smiled. So, the enigmatic and aloof Peter Devereaux was more interested in Faith than he made out. "Hill is madly in love with her."

Peter stretched his legs in front of him and surveyed his boots. "How does she feel about Hill?"

"I couldn't really say. She treats every officer of the corps with the same charming indifference. It drives 'em crazy."

Peter tossed a log into the center of the fire and stared at the flames. "What happened to her husband?"

Michael told him the story. Peter continued gazing at the fire. "So, when it did not work out for them in Scotland, they returned here."

Michael shook his head. "No, Lucy always intended to return. If I had trusted her instead of going on a rampage of self-pity the situation with Beth and the misunderstanding about the baby would never have occurred." Realizing his indiscretion, Michael looked at Peter with consternation. Of course, Peter was unaware of Faith's previous pregnancy. "Well . . . er . . . Lucy did not understand about Ben." It was time to change the subject he decided. "What about you and Faith?"

Peter shrugged. "As soon as the *Iliad* is repaired, I'll go whaling, then home to Boston to outfit more ships."

"Faith loves you, Peter."

"Faith loves Lucy. *Men,* she uses."

"You're being too hard on her. Faith left you because she had a duty to her husband and family, not because she had fallen out of love with you. Since returning to New South Whales she has lived in hope of seeing you again."

Peter leaned on his knees and rested his head in his hands. "God knows, I've never loved anyone the way I loved Faith. But she is incapable of being honest and I cannot spend the rest of my life with a woman I don't trust." He raised his head and looked at Michael with glistening eyes. "I'm just trying to protect myself. I couldn't go through that hell again." He picked up the brandy bottle and refilled their glasses. "Let's have one more drink, then turn in. You've got a wedding to go to, remember?"

Two days later, Lucy, resplendent in white muslin, married Michael beneath her giant fig tree on the hill. The military formed an honor guard; Tom gave the bride away; John dropped the ring; Faith wept; Duncan behaved delightfully; Governor and Mrs. Grose attended, as did George Barrington, Prince of Pickpockets; and although everyone wore their finest, Moses, bizarre in Stewart kilt and top hat, surpassed them all.

At the conclusion of the ceremony the hundred guests repaired to the hospital clearing for the wedding breakfast. The day was cloudless, the food was delicious and everyone cheered when John, well fortified, rose from his seat at the bridal table. "Governor and Mrs. Grose, the bride and groom, honored guests, ladies and gentlemen, others."

Lucy sought Michael's hand as the toasts rolled effortlessly off John's tongue. "How soon can we leave?"

He smiled. "As soon as the dancing begins."

530

"Ladies and gentlemen—the bride and groom."

"The bride and groom!" echoed the guests fervently.

But he was not finished with them yet. Grinning, he yanked Tom to his feet. "Will you say a few words on behalf of the bride's family, Thomas?"

Tom's speech was as short as John's was long. "On behalf of the bride's beautiful family . . ." He paused and beamed at Faith. "I thank you for attending. Now, let the dancing begin!"

When Peter did not come forward to claim her, Faith turned away from the group of petitioners and accepted William Hill's arm.

"When can I come home to Chaumilley?" she asked, as she and Hill caught up.

"Not long," Lucy said as Michael lifted her into the cart. "Go back to the celebrations and enjoy yourself, darling."

Now the moment of parting had arrived, Faith felt lost. "Oh, I shall miss you both," she wept, embracing Michael.

"Hey, what's this?" he laughed. "Go back to the party like a good girl. We'll see you in ten days."

"Oh, Michael, must it be that long?"

"Ten days," he said firmly, leaping up beside Lucy and taking the reins.

Faith returned to the festivities and played the usual games with the officers but her heart was not in it. She smiled encouragingly whenever she caught Peter's eye but he kept his distance so that, in the end, she crossed to the other side of the clearing and extended her hand. "Would you dance with me, Peter?"

For a heart-stopping moment he sat there staring at her unsmilingly, then he set down his glass and escorted her onto the dance floor. She knew her impulsive action would incite gossip but it was worth it to feel his arms around her; and when he drew her close and told her how beautiful she was, the sad years faded and she felt young and carefree again.

"This is the first time we have danced," she said breathlessly as he whirled her around.

He raised an eyebrow. "Didn't that jig on the shingles after killing the old beachmaster count?"

"Everything we did on Ice Island counted—only then, I didn't realize what we had."

"What a pretty speech, Lady Stewart." His voice had a hard edge to it and there was not the slightest warmth in his smile.

Faith's heart sank. "You were right about the years ahead

being empty, Peter. I missed you. I missed . . . *you*." She searched his eyes, looking for love but saw only lust, and when his body hardened against her, she blushed.

"Why are you blushing?"

Unable to answer, she shook her head and was relieved when the music ended and he led her back to the bridal table.

28

Folly Under the Full Moon

It was midnight in the Valley and the carrions were circling the full moon.

The Guardian pointed to the bloated body of the woman lying beside the river of blood.

> Seed of fallacy,
> When you took shape
> And found form
> The Gods erred in Time
> And two generations of
> One seed were born.
> Therefore, seeds of fallacy
> The Gods have conferred and decreed
> That your progeny
> Will revert to
> Your sister,
> As next generation
> Of her seed.
> Go!
> The prophecy must be fulfilled!

Faith's eyes flew open and she sat bolt upright in bed. "No, no, no," she moaned, twisting her head from side to side. "No, I want another chance."

She fled through the hut and opened the door. The world outside was devoid of all movement. Had she awoken in another dimension, in sight of, yet unattached to the earth? She ran to the beach and crept across the sand to the water's edge. The *Iliad* lay slumbering beneath the starry sky, its decks bathed in spangled moonlight. At the stern, a solitary light burned, like a beacon of hope. "Peter, the Guide," she whispered. "Peter, the Guide."

Peter sat at the desk in his cabin perusing the latest work estimates. If he was to quit New South Wales by mid-March, he'd need to employ more workers. He leaned back in the chair and stretched his arms over his head to ease the tightness across his shoulders. He'd been awake since before dawn supervising the work and he was tired. A slight click came from the other side of the cabin and the boards near the door creaked. "Who's there?" he asked, half rising in his chair.

The lamp above him oscillated with the movement of the ship and he saw her, standing on the edge of darkness, soaked to the skin, her breasts rising and falling beneath the thin nightgown. She looked so lovely and defenseless the aching need for her twisted like a knife inside him. He left the desk and walked to her. "What are you doing here?"

"I had to come . . . Peter, the Guide."

Her voice had a breathless quality that excited him even more than her appearance. "Foolish. The cove is full of sharks." He stopped, seeing the glaze of terror in her eyes. "Faith, what's wrong?"

She opened and closed her mouth but no sound came.

He gripped her shoulders and shook her, trying to bring her out of it. "Faith, for God's sake tell me what's the matter with you?"

"H-he called me seed of fallacy . . . and said I had no further sanctuary in life. I must deliver the child in nine moons. I don't want to die, I want to stay with you and Lucy."

Peter's bitter resolves melted like snow in the face of her terror. "My poor darling," he murmured scooping her up and carrying her to the bed. But when he kissed her, her lips were icy and her body was as rigid as stone.

"If I had admitted that I loved you more than life itself the night we said good-bye, I could have changed my destiny," she went on in the same faraway voice as he removed her nightgown and slipped a silk shirt over her head. "But now it's too late, Peter, I am doomed."

None of it made sense to Peter but he could see that she truly believed it. "Don't be afraid," he soothed, taking her in his arms and rocking her. "I challenged your tormentor on Ice Island and I shall challenge him again."

Tears rolled down her cheeks. "On Ice Island things were at their beginning. Now they have grown to such proportions no one can stop them."

"I can. I am the Guide."

Her eyes snapped into focus. "You are the only one powerful enough to withstand him. That's why I had to find you, Peter."

"You did right, my darling. Rest now, I have you safe. No one can harm you."

She closed her eyes and he stroked her forehead gently and rhythmically until she slept.

Peter awoke with a start. It hadn't been a dream, she was still beside him, her dark hair tumbled over his arm and her lips tantalizingly close.

He kissed them. They were soft and yielding.

What an enigma she was, with her guides and guardians and haunting, horrible dreams. How reckless of her to swim to him through the night. But that was her way—if she wanted something she went after it with all her strength and never considered the consequences. He moved his hand slowly over the curves of her body and squeezed the rounded flesh of her buttocks.

Her eyes fluttered open. "Hmmm . . . don't stop."

He sighed deeply. "I don't want to love you, Faith. God knows, I've tried to forget you."

"Please give me another chance, Peter. I love you more than life itself."

"Are they the magic words that will heal the hurt?"

She nodded gravely. "Yes. With those words we can turn Time around and change our destiny. I love you, Peter Devereaux, more than Duncan, more than Hugh—more, much more than my own life—"

He stopped her words with his mouth and, as they abandoned themselves to the wild, ravaging ritual of their lovemaking, the full moon shone in through the portholes and bathed their bodies in dazzling white.

When the first streamers of dawn crept tentatively into the cabin, Peter left the bed and rummaged through his sea chest.

"What are you doing?" Faith asked sleepily, coming up on her elbows and kicking away the crumpled sheets.

He tossed a sweater and trousers on the bed. "It's time to go. You can't leave the ship like that, Lady Stewart."

She swung her long legs to the floor and obediently donned the clothes. "Yes, Peter. Then what?"

He helped her with the sweater. "Do you remember how to handle an oar?"

"Oh, Peter, our dear little longboat." She wound her arms around his neck, and sobbed against his chest.

"Damn it, Faith, you're crying again."

"I can't help it; I'm so happy."

He extricated himself and reached for his shirt. "You won't be if that maid of yours alerts the settlement that you are missing from your bed. Come, it's almost daylight."

That evening as Faith paced the parlor waiting for Peter, she reflected on the events that had endowed her life with new purpose. Last night when she and Peter had recaptured the love they had shared on Ice Island, for her there had been an added dimension: in surrendering herself totally to him, she had found fulfillment. She broke off her musing as a loud knock sounded on the door.

"Is Lady Stewart receiving?" Peter asked politely as the maid showed him inside.

Faith ran forward eagerly and clasped his hands. "Good evening, Captain Devereaux. You are most welcome."

"How beautiful you are," he said softly.

They stared into each other's eyes until Duncan tugged at her skirts. "This is my son, Duncan," she said a little uncertainly as she picked him up.

Peter smiled at Duncan. "Hello, young man."

Duncan leaned forward and slurped Peter's chin.

"Lucy is teaching him to kiss," Faith explained. "He isn't very good at it yet . . ."

Peter took Duncan from her and tossed him in the air like a ball. "Kissing can come later. First, we'll teach him how to hunt and fish."

"Can Duncan tell you and Lucy apart?" Peter asked after the maid and Duncan had retired.

"He doesn't bother." Faith moved closer to him on the sofa.

"He calls us both 'Mama.' It's only natural, Lucy has been with him since the moment of his birth."

He caressed her cheek. "I can *always* tell you and Lucy apart. You have a stubborn way of holding your chin. You breathe in deeply just before you ask for something impossible, your bottom lip pouts when you don't get your own way, and your voice takes on a breathless quality when you want—"

"Stop! You make me sound absolutely awful," she laughed.

He hugged her close. "Miss me?"

"Yes!" She sighed closing her eyes and letting the lovely tingling sensations take hold. "Kiss me quickly . . . or I shall pine away."

29

Nemesis

Saturday, January 26, 1793

On the fifth anniversary of the founding of Sydney, Captain William Hill sailed for Norfolk Island with a relief detachment of the corps; Lieutenant John Macarthur took up residence at Parramatta as a supervisor of superintendents, storekeepers, overseers, and convict labor (thus becoming more powerful than any man in the colony, except Governor Grose); and Faith returned to Chaumilley with Peter.

"I think they are ideally matched," Lucy told Michael as they prepared for bed that evening. "Although Hugh tried hard to contain Faith, she had a hundred ways of getting around him. She will find Peter less easy to manipulate."

Michael blew out the candle and joined her in bed. "Has she told him yet about the child she lost?"

"She intends to, Michael, but they are so happy at the moment she is reluctant to spoil things."

Remembering Peter's bitter revelations at the camp fire, Michael understood Faith's reticence. "He's bound to be angry."

"Yes, but Peter is a compassionate person—a man of great warmth. He will forgive her."

Michael chuckled. "I would not have described him so. In my opinion, he's ice cold with the eyes of a hunter."

"Men may see him in that light," Lucy said softly, "but Peter's eyes have amazing depths . . ."

Six weeks later, when Peter and Faith returned to Sydney, Michael and Lucy accompanied them.

"What will you do when the new mizzen is fitted?" Faith asked as she and Peter entered his cabin after inspecting the ship.

He scooped her into his arms and deposited her on top of the desk. "Go hunting for whales in the Southern Ocean. What will you do?"

So deflated was she by the thought of his leaving, she found it difficult to reply. "Oh, I don't know . . ."

Peter swallowed hard to ease the sudden dryness in his throat. "Will you live at Chaumilley with Lucy and Michael . . . or come whaling with me?"

Faith burst into tears.

"Damn it, Faith," he muttered, embracing her, "these days you cry if the wind changes."

"I-I can't help it," she sobbed. "I am so happy, even a sparrow singing in a tree sounds so beautiful, I become unstrung."

This new, vulnerable Faith perplexed Peter. Sometimes she seemed so fragile he was afraid to touch her. "You don't have to decide right now," he said gently. "Take as long as you like. I know how you love Lucy . . ."

She shook her head vigorously. "I don't need to think, Peter. I shall go whaling with you."

He looked deeply into her eyes. "Are you sure, my darling?"

"Yes."

Again, he swallowed. "That being the case, I think we should marry as soon as possible."

"Oh, Peter, do you mean it?"

"Yes, but I warn you, Faith, I won't have it turned into a pageant for jesters."

"Certainly not!"

Peter relaxed. Now the commitment was made, it felt right. "This will be my last long voyage. After we have fished the Southern Ocean, we will continue on to Boston so you and Duncan can meet my family. Then I'll sell my interest in the business and we'll settle in New South Wales."

A flash of the old spirit leapt into her eyes. "Don't change your ways for me. Sail where you will. If that is your life, I'll make it mine."

"Don't make rash statements, Faith. You'd be unhappy separated from Lucy. Besides, I won't be deprived of the sea. These waters offer great prospects for fishing. On my way up the coast I saw sperm whales blowing all around the horizon." He lifted her down and took his spyglass from the shelf. "Let's go up on deck and I'll show you a cove on the north side of the harbor that I'm interested in purchasing."

As Faith listened to his plans to build tryworks for boiling blubber and ramps for hauling slabs, she wondered if this was the right moment to tell him her last, lingering secret. But he looked so happy, she put it off one more time.

Faith remained in Sydney with Peter, who was supervising the installation of his new mizzen but although she spent her days happily decorating the new townhouse and planning her wedding, two niggling worries prevented total peace of mind. She had not told Peter about the child, and she had not made peace with Beth. Knowing how sad Lucy was about Beth, and believing herself largely responsible for the rift, Faith called on her sister's former friend several times but Beth refused to speak to her. Then, one evening, while waiting at the Governor's Wharf for Peter to come ashore, Faith saw Beth walking along the beach on the west side of the cove. *What luck,* she thought. *I'll catch up to her and settle our differences once and for all.*

Peter, who was about to board *Iliad*'s longboat, swore under his breath when he saw her dash along the beach after Beth. "Why doesn't she stay out of it?" he muttered. "It's Lucy's and Michael's business, not hers."

Faith caught up to Beth at the bend where the shore swung round to Dawes Point. "Please wait a minute, Beth. I want a word with you."

"Well, I don't want a word with you, *Lady* Stewart."

As Beth turned away, Faith grabbed her arm. "I know you don't like me much, my dear, and you probably have good cause but will you at least listen to me for a moment?"

Incensed at being accosted by this person whom she perceived to be the cause of her unhappiness, Beth lashed out. "No, I don't like you much, Faith. In fact, I hate you. Go away and leave me alone." She wrenched free and ran farther along the water's edge toward the mangroves.

Faith sped after her and caught her again. "Look, Beth, I shall be leaving the colony at the end of March and before I go I'd like to settle things with you. Captain Devereaux and I are in love and plan to marry.''

Beth laughed scornfully. ''*You,* in love? You couldn't be faithful to one man if you tried. You're not happy unless you've got the whole bunch mooning over you like sick cows.''

''Let's forget me,'' Faith said quickly. ''It's Lucy I am concerned about. She and Michael want to help you. Please let them. You cannot take proper care of your son if you are working day and night in a brothel.''

''Oh, you rotten, rotten hypocrite!'' Beth cried. ''How much did you *care* about Captain Devereaux when you left him? How much did you care about the baby you were carrying? How much did you care about Lucy when you let everyone in the colony think she was the one pregnant? How much did you care about Michael when you made Lucy leave him?''

Faith stiffened. ''W-who told you?''

''Never mind who told me. Lucky Captain Devereaux's baby died, wasn't it? Saved you a lot of explaining when you got back to Scotland. Or, were you planning to dump it in a workhouse for abandoned orphans?'' Beth broke off, her eyes widening with horror. ''No . . . not *you!*''

The vital lifeforces slowly drained out of Faith and she turned. He stood a few yards away, a dark silhouette in the light of the rising moon.

''So, you manipulated us all,'' he said slowly.

''No, it wasn't like that. Not like that . . .'' Her voice was old and tired—a parchment crumbling to dust.

''Were you carrying my child when you left the colony?''

''Yes, but I swear I didn't manipulate anyone, Peter. Lucy decided we should return to Scotland, not I.''

''I don't believe you,'' he said contemptuously. ''Lucy is openhearted and honest, you are the lying schemer.''

''Peter, please,'' she wept. ''I have been dishonest with you in the past but I have changed. I-I love you more than my life, Peter. You are the Guide of my destiny, the Guardian of my soul, the only one powerful enough to reverse the prophecy.''

His eyes glittered in the moonlight. ''Twice you have swayed me with your guides and guardians, Faith, but this is the end.''

Sensing it coming—that final parting—she sank to her knees. ''Peter, don't go, my darling, my dearest. If you leave me, I shall die.''

''Good-bye, Faith,'' he said softly and retraced his steps along the beach.

30

Reconciliation of Sorts

Michael deposited an armful of wood chips in the barrel beside the fire and glanced over Lucy's shoulder at the ducks turning on the spit. "Hmmm, they smell delicious."

She smiled. "Hungry?"

"As ravenous as a lion," he growled, grabbing her around the waist and gnawing at her ear until she pulled away.

"Then fetch Moses. These are ready."

After Michael left, Lucy slid two extra plates into the warming racks and went to the dining-room to lay the table for dinner. Although she did not expect Faith and Peter until the end of next week, she had had an uneasy premonition all day. *You are being silly,* she told herself as she lit the lamps. *What could possibly be wrong?*

They had finished eating and were discussing crops over cups of sarsaparilla tea when they heard rumbling in the distance.

"Someone coming," said Michael, taking up a lamp.

Her uneasiness growing, Lucy followed the men outside to the veranda just as a cumbersome farm cart bearing Faith, Duncan, Beth, and Ben rolled down the slope into the yard. Why was Beth here? Lucy wondered. And where was Peter?

Lucy sent for a maid to help with the children, then led the way to the dining room.

"Is something the matter with Peter?" she asked, sitting beside Faith and clasping her hands.

"He has gone," Faith answered in a remote voice.

When she made no attempt to enlarge on the statement, Lucy turned to Beth, who sat opposite with her head bowed, nervously twisting a handkerchief round her fingers. "What happened, Beth?"

Haltingly, Beth related what had taken place the previous evening.

"Who told *you* about Faith's baby?" Lucy asked, looking accusingly at Michael.

"*I* didn't tell her," said Michael.

"Nor I," muttered Moses.

Beth wound the handkerchief more tightly around her fingers.

540

"No one told me, Lucy. I-I read about it in the letters you sent Michael."

Michael half rose in his chair. "You *what*?"

Beth's pallor increased, but she pressed on. "Please hear me out before you start telling me how ridiculous I am, Michael. You were at Worthing when Lucy's first letter arrived . . ." In a faltering voice she told them what she had done. "Now, because of my meddling, Faith's life is ruined." She hung her head. "Sorry, Faith. So sorry . . ."

"Don't blame yourself," Faith said vaguely. "I had ample opportunity to tell Peter about the child. I believed I could thwart the Guardian but in the world of the Fixed there is no free choice."

Beth looked at Lucy with frightened eyes. "She has been talking strange since Captain Devereaux left. I stayed with her last night and when the *Iliad* was gone from the cove this morning, I decided to bring her home to Chaumilley." Her voice faltered. "I'm sorry, Lucy, I didn't mean to harm Faith; I just got angry when she said I was neglecting Benjamin."

She looked so wretched, Lucy did not have the heart to hate her for the trouble her meddling had caused. "Faith is right, you aren't entirely to blame for the adversities which have befallen us. We all had a hand in bringing them to pass . . ."

Michael nodded grimly. "I agree. Not that I condone what you did with the letters, Beth—I suffered immensely during those two years, thinking Lucy hadn't written—but if I had treated you more considerately, perhaps you would not have gone to such extremes." He glanced at Faith with concern. "But I think it's time we stopped feeling guilty and remorseful about the past and start concentrating on the future."

"Michael's right," said Lucy. "I am tired of conflicts and heartbreak. Let's start afresh, Beth."

Beth's lips trembled. "Would you really forgive me for the terrible things I did, Lucy?"

Lucy remembered a long time ago when Beth had covered her with a shawl and sat shivering beside her in the darkness of the upper gallery at Newgate. "I will forgive you," she said, reaching across the table and squeezing Beth's arm, "if you'll forgive me for being so bemused with my new sister that I neglected my dearest friend."

Beth's eyes swam with tears. "You didn't neglect me, Lucy. I took a set against Faith from the beginning."

"My imperious attitude didn't help matters," said Faith. "How-

541

ever, in seven more moons *He* will rectify the errors I have committed."

Icicles crept up Lucy's spine. "Who are you talking about, Faith?"

"The Guardian."

Silently, Lucy cursed Peter Devereaux for reawakening Faith's morbid fears. "Don't let this estrangement with Peter defeat you, darling. He had every right to be furious about the baby, but you did not deserve the harsh treatment he meted out. What he has done is unforgiveable."

"Why unforgiveable, Lucy? You thought I was perfectly justified in doing the same thing to him . . ."

"There is no similarity between now and 1790, Faith. You had to leave the colony then—you were married to Hugh and carrying Peter's child."

"The circumstances are not so different, Lucy. I am no longer married to Hugh but I am certainly carrying Peter's child."

Lucy turned pale. "Oh, no! How could he leave you, knowing that?"

Faith sighed deeply. "Peter has no idea. I cannot be more than four weeks gone . . ."

"Then . . . then there is some doubt?"

Faith looked at her sister fixedly. "Have you forgotten Laura Taura's warning? I sought Peter on the night of the full moon."

"Oh Lord! What can we do?"

"Nothing," Faith answered hollowly.

Beth twisted her handkerchief with agitated violence. "But Faith, you can't stay in New South Wales. The bloomin' gossips would tear you to shreds."

"Faith is not going anywhere," Michael said firmly. "If we keep our heads instead of panicking and throwing our lives into chaos, what worked once will work again. As far as anyone will know, Lucy will be the one expecting the child."

"It's a lovely notion," Lucy sighed, "but sooner or later our friends would notice something, or the servants would overhear a chance remark."

Michael smiled. "We won't leave *anything* to chance." He turned to Beth. "Can you and Lucy manage this house without servants?"

She nodded solemnly. "Of course we can."

"There are still the farm laborers," Lucy broke in.

Michael shrugged. "In two months I shall move them to Worthing, which is more or less what I planned to do, anyway. Moses, can you erect a new mess and living quarters in eight weeks?"

"I'll do it in six," Moses muttered.

Michael rose and walked to Faith's side. "No need to fret, dearest. You will be perfectly safe here at home with your family."

Faith rested her head on his shoulder. "My reckless behavior has caused you great unhappiness, Michael. Yet you have never judged me. I thank you for that."

He stroked the top of her head. "If you had been honest with Peter, dearest, you could have spared yourself and him this latest heartbreak. Nevertheless, now it is done, you must go on with your life until he returns."

Faith looked at him with such sadness, his heart ached. "Maybe Peter will return one day, but it will be too late for me. Only seven moons remain, then the Guardian—"

Michael gripped her shoulders hard. "Listen to me, Faith. I accept that you have an uncanny spiritual empathy with Lucy, but I don't believe any of this garbage about a 'guardian.' You are a young healthy woman with a family who loves you and intends to support you through this pregnancy. Besides, there is no Valley of Abaddon within ten thousand miles of Chaumilley."

31

Revelation at Sea

For greater safety, the frail cedarwood craft approached the whale head-on and slightly to the lee. Peter signaled the harpooner, an African with arms as thick as oak beams. "Okay, Turk."

Turk threaded thick rope through the barbed head of his harpoon as Peter motioned the four longboats standing two hundred feet off their stern to fan out around the whale. In the last few weeks several good chances had gone begging, but at daybreak this huge sperma-caste had been sighted and after a three-hour chase, excitement was running high.

The oarsmen paddled closer until they were only twenty feet from the quarry. Peter's eyes bored into the back of Turk's head. "Now," he said softly, pointing to a dark scar on the whale's flank. "Aim at that." Turk rose, balanced on the balls of his feet, drew back the harpoon and thrust it at the whale with tremendous force. The whale gave a hollow, plaintive cry and dived.

Like a crazed serpent, the rope uncoiled from the barrel, whirring, whining, hissing, and humming. Seconds lengthened. Still, the line played out. "Come on, come on." Peter muttered. "You can't hold your breath much longer."

Suddenly, the line stopped.

Laughing raucously, the men hauled it in. The whale surfaced a hundred years to port, towed the boat a short distance, then dived. Faster the men hauled, their eyes feverish with excitement. "Come on mates!" they called to those in the other boats. "Closer, closer—fin's away!"

The whale stayed down. Peter fingered the ax resting across his knees, the old uneasiness gnawing at his gut. Something was wrong, the line was almost in, yet it was slack. "Let go!" he screamed.

The haulers dropped the line like a hot poker. Peter chopped at it frenziedly. The world lurched. The boat rose as if held in a giant hand, hung suspended for a moment, then slid down the mountain of black and gray flesh into the water. Peter dodged as the whale's great fluted tail cut the boat in two.

Better get a move on, Peter thought as he sank into icy depths. *Water's too cold for anyone to last long—but the other boats are close.* As he let go of the ax and tugged at his sea boots, something moved in the water beneath him, something dark, rising fast. The bloody whale!

The right side of Peter's body connected with bulk. He shot out the water at breakneck speed, caught a glimpse of sky, experienced a moment of weightlessness, then plummeted toward the sea. As he fell, he saw a spike jutting out at right angles from the whale's flank. Instinctively, his arm shot out. He grasped wood slippery with blood and the world jolted to a halt. Turk's aim had been true. The harpoon had punctured the whale's lung. From his vantage point Peter saw the other boats two hundred yards to windward.

The whale dived. He let go and dropped into the sea beside four of his men.

"Keep still," Peter ordered as the whale surfaced and dashed toward them diving in short bursts. The men trod water, their faces gray with fear.

She wouldn't be afraid, Peter thought, remembering how she had slid calmly across the ice bridge with the rays of the evening sun bathing her in a golden glow. The muscles of his groin clenched, and he laughed.

"You okay, Capt'n?" Jefferson, the mate, asked through chattering teeth.

"Never better," Peter chuckled as the whale surfaced twenty yards away, snapping its great jaws like a rabid dog and spraying blood and viscera from its spiracle. "Hang on men, I think this bastard's about ready to call it a day."

"Capt'n the whale's becoming waterlogged," Jefferson said as he joined Peter at the helm of *Iliad*.

Peter gazed at the red-tipped sea thoughtfully. *She was right not to tell me about the child,* he decided. It would only have complicated matters. The fact that she had lost it saddened him; but how could he realistically mourn an unborn baby three years after its demise?

No, what had saddened him, consumed him with bitterness, and plunged him to the depths of despair was the fact that she had chosen Hugh Stewart instead of him. *That* had been her crime.

"What about the flensers, sir?" Jefferson pointed to a group of men armed with twelve-foot knives, standing on the quarterdeck.

Peter frowned at the sunset. When they had reconciled he had imposed several conditions: no more games, total faithfulness, total honesty, absolute trustworthiness. In other words she was to grow wings and become an angel. "How bloody absurd," he muttered. "How could I expect *her* to be angel? She's willful, spoiled, reckless, and damned impossible at times."

"Capt'n, the flensers!" the mate repeated in agitated tones.

Peter turned to him and grinned. "Cut the tow and bring this ship about, Mr. Jefferson. We're returning to New South Wales."

32

Destiny, Child, to Find

Wednesday, October 16, 1793

Lucy glanced up from her garden and frowned when she saw Faith ascending the slope on the gelding. Even though Michael had brought a sidesaddle to make riding easier, Lucy disapproved of her sister's daily jaunts into the hinterland. *This is the last time,* she decided as she returned to her planting. *In the future, Faith must content herself with walking.*

It was a beautiful golden afternoon and when Faith reached the seventh stream, she struck out to the east in search of sarsaparilla plants for Lucy. She thoroughly enjoyed herself fording streams and trotting through leafy bowers, but her pleasant meanderings came to a sudden halt when a party of natives emerged from the trees and moved threateningly toward her.

Damn, she thought, cocking Michael's pistol and waving it aloft, *I don't dare turn my back on their spears and I can hardly turn tail and gallop away on this silly sidesaddle.*

As she began easing the horse backward at an awkward shuffling gait, a pain knifed through her abdomen. She slumped forward across the horse's neck. The pistol discharged. The animal reared, came down with a bone-jarring jolt and galloped past the natives into the underbrush.

Faith hung on for dear life until the horse checked its gait and plunged up a steep hill. "No," she gasped as they approached a cliff at breakneck speed. "Whoa!"

She yanked the terrified animal's mane with all her might trying to turn its head but her efforts were in vain. They went over the edge at full gallop and dropped into black nothingness.

Lucy was washing at the well when a horseman appeared at the top of the rise and rode down the slope into the yard. Lucy stared at him with amazement. "Peter," she cried, dropping the bucket and running toward him. "Peter Devereaux!"

Grinning, he leapt from the horse and embraced her warmly.

"Peter, how wonderful. Faith will be overjoyed. And you have arrived just in time for the birth of your child."

Now it was Peter's time to look amazed. "A child, Lucy? Do you mean it?"

Lucy's eyes filled with tears. "Indeed I do. Oh, Peter, she has been so lost without you . . ."

Peter glanced around. "Where is she?"

"Out riding, and late as usual." Lucy took his hand and led him toward the house. "Come, we have much to discuss before she returns. To begin with, Faith told you the truth that evening on the beach. I was the one who decided we should leave the colony—" She broke off as an agonizing pain sliced through her abdomen.

"What's wrong?" he asked as she cried out and slumped into his arms.

Lucy broke free of him and stumbled to the top of the slope.

"Where are you, beloved?" she called, scanning the countryside frantically.

"Which way did she go?" Peter asked.

She turned to the west where the day was dying and listened with her inner ear. Nothing. She turned to the east where the full moon was rising. From the furthermost reaches of her consciousness came the faint, unmistakable cry of a baby. "Oh, God," she moaned, "fetch your horse, Peter."

Faith rose like a bubble toward the dazzling circle of light and opened her eyes. She lay on a riverbank at the bottom of a narrow moonlit valley beside the carcass of her horse. "Abaddon," she whispered, lips stiffening with fear.

The nightmare world of her visions had finally come to pass. Carrions swooped down on the horse and tore at its flesh until blood ran in rivulets into the water. Then they rose to the upper ridges of the valley and perched there, yellow eyes glittering.

Faith tried to move. Pain. Pain. Pain. Pain.

She called to her sister. "Lucy, my heart, hear me." She called to the Guide. "Peter, my love, save me." Tentacles of darkness crept from the caverns and enveloped her and, longing for release, she gave herself up to their cloying sweetness.

"Faith!"

The voice was familiar but the darkness invited.

"Faith!"

With a supreme effort, Faith rallied. "Here . . ."

Lucy and Peter ran to the edge of *Yowi Yowi* and saw Faith lying at the bottom. They descended over jagged rocks to the riverbank, dragged the horse clear and while Peter cradled Faith in his arms, Lucy tried to ascertain her injuries.

"Peter . . . you came," Faith said faintly, then tensed as another pain swept through her. "Lucy, quickly . . . the baby."

Desperately Lucy worked, hands sliding, fingers probing, until the baby's head appeared. "A bit more, beloved. Together we can do it. Push, Faith . . . push."

Faith bore down. The baby came with a rush and lay on the banks of the river of blood. Lucy severed the cord and the baby cried—a small sound that touched her soul and sent shivers of ecstasy through her.

"It's a girl, Faith—a lovely healthy little girl."

Peter gently smoothed Faith's tangled locks from her face and kissed her. "I'm sorry, my darling. I will spend the rest of my life making it up to you."

Tears rolled down Faith's cheeks. "I want to say with you, Peter but now I have delivered the child, further sanctuary in life is denied me . . ."

"You will be fine," Lucy said quickly. "The horse took most of the impact."

Faith shook her head. "You don't understand," she said hopelessly. "When the ninth moon sets on the valley, He will take me."

Peter's arm tightened around her. "I have spent my life searching for you, Faith, and I will not give you up. Say the magic words—*say* you love me."

"I love you more than life itself, Peter, but things have gone beyond our sway."

"Nothing is impossible, my darling. Repeat the words of the prophecy so I can reverse it and take you safely from this place."

Her eyes locked with his.

> Truth's word will stem the blood.
> Strive then the tie to bind.
> Duty the path to love.
> Destiny, child, to find.

As Lucy gazed at the baby in her arms, the words of the prophecy echoed like a discordant bell through her mind. "Mother of Destiny," the Ninefold Goddess had whispered from behind the north wind. "Mother of Destiny," Laura Taura had called her that day in Sydney. Lucy finally grasped the significance of the words. Peter could not reverse the prophecy, only she had the power to do that.

With a sense of loss, she placed the baby next to Faith's heart. "Take the child, beloved. You are the Mother of Destiny, not I."

She helped Peter lift Faith then linked arms with him. "Come, Peter, let's take them out of here."

But as they moved off, the wind bore down on them like a maelstrom.

"Prophecy!" cried a voice.

Lucy turned slowly but, even then she turned before Time and there, in the space between one second and the next, stood an old man. A thick mane of hair flew behind him in the wind, snakelike vines writhed around his body, and his face, illuminated in the light of the ninth full moon, was as white and as waxy as leprosy.

"Oh God," she whispered. "I can see him, Faith."

Faith struggled in Peter's arms. "Look away, Lucy, before he brings down the broadsword."

"Time to move on," said Peter.

"I am afraid," Lucy murmured.

Peter smiled at her from the depths of his eyes. "Don't be afraid, Lucy. I shall see you and Faith safely through this."

Slowly and surely, he guided them past the river of blood, between the craters and pitfalls, beyond the Valley of Abaddon toward Chaumilley, the place of peace and tranquility.

ABOUT THE AUTHOR

Patricia Goldie was born in Sydney, Australia and held a variety of jobs there before retiring to Tweed Heads, where she researched and wrote *Under Southern Stars,* with the support of her son Andrew. Now living on the outskirts of Sydney, she is working on her second novel, and prefers the society of her characters to most other diversions.

FIVE UNFORGETTABLE NOVELS
by
CELESTE DE BLASIS

☐ **THE NIGHT CHILD** (27744, $3.95)
The story of a proud, passionate woman and two very special kinds of love.

☐ **THE PROUD BREED** (27196, $4.95)
THE PROUD BREED vividly recreates California's exciting past, from the wild country to the pirated coast, from gambling dens to lavish ballrooms. Here is Celeste De Blasis' beloved bestselling novel: a world you will not want to leave, and will never forget.

☐ **WILD SWAN** (27260, $4.95)
Sweeping from England's West Country in the years of the Napoleonic wars, to the beauty of Maryland horse country, here is a novel richly spun of authentically detailed history and sumptuous romance.

☐ **SWAN'S CHANCE** (25692, $4.50)
SWAN'S CHANCE continues the magnificent saga begun in WILD SWAN: an unforgettable chronicle of a great dynasty.

☐ **SUFFER A SEA CHANGE** (27750, $3.95)
Her love, world and very future change under the light of an island sun as Jessica Banbridge comes to grips with the past and opens herself up to life.

Available wherever Bantam Books are sold or use this page to order.

- -